The Sheep Look Up

Environmentalist Austin Train is on the run. The Trainites, environmental activists – and sometime terrorists – want him to lead their movement. The government wants him in jail or, preferably, executed. The media wants a circus. Everyone has a plan for him – but Austin Train has a plan of his own …

The Shockwave Rider

Nickie Haflinger had lived a score of lifetimes … but technically he didn't exist. He was a fugitive from Tarnover, the high-powered government think tank that had educated him. Having escaped he now had to find a way to restore sanity and personal freedom to the computerised masses – and to save a world tottering on the brink of disaster. He didn't care how he did it … but the government did. That's when his Tarnover teachers got him back in their labs … and Nickie Haflinger was set up for a whole new education!

The Traveller in Black

At a time in the unguessably remote past – or perhaps the distant future – Chaos ruled throughout the universe. Scientific laws of cause and effect held no force; men could not know from one day to the next what to expect from their labours. There was one man to whom had been entrusted the task of bringing reason and order out of Chaos – a quiet man dressed in black who carried a staff made of light, and wherever he went the powers of Chaos swirled around him, buffeting and testing him. He fought them, and little by little he drove them back. But as a creature of Chaos himself, could he survive his own victory …?

Also by John Brunner

John Brunner

SF GATEWAY OMNIBUS

THE SHEEP LOOK UP
THE SHOCKWAVE RIDER
THE TRAVELLER IN BLACK

GOLLANCZ
LONDON

First published in Great Britain in 2014 by
Gollancz
An imprint of the Orion Publishing Group
Orion House, 5 Upper St Martin's Lane,
London WC2H 9EA

An Hachette UK Company

A CIP catalogue record for this book
is available from the British Library

ISBN 978 0 575 10188 3

1 3 5 7 9 10 8 6 4 2

Typeset by Jouve (UK), Milton Keynes
Printed and bounded by CPI Group (UK) Ltd, Croydon, CR0 4YY

The Orion Publishing Group's policy is to use papers
that are natural, renewable and recyclable products and
made from wood grown in sustainable forests. The logging
and manufacturing processes are expected to conform to
the environmental regulations of the country of origin.

www.orionbooks.co.uk
www.gollancz.co.uk

CONTENTS

ENTER THE SF GATEWAY...

Towards the end of 2011, in conjunction with the celebration of fifty years of coherent, continuous science fiction and fantasy publishing, Gollancz launched the SF Gateway.

Over a decade after launching the landmark SF Masterworks series, we realised that the realities of commercial publishing are such that even the Masterworks could only ever scratch the surface of an author's career. Vast troves of classic SF and fantasy were almost certainly destined never again to see print. Until very recently, this meant that anyone interested in reading any of those books would have been confined to scouring second-hand bookshops. The advent of digital publishing changed that paradigm for ever.

Embracing the future even as we honour the past, Gollancz launched the SF Gateway with a view to utilising the technology that now exists to make available, for the first time, the entire backlists of an incredibly wide range of classic and modern SF and fantasy authors. Our plan, at its simplest, was – and still is! – to use this technology to build on the success of the SF and Fantasy Masterworks series and to go even further.

The SF Gateway was designed to be the new home of classic science fiction and fantasy – the most comprehensive electronic library of classic SFF titles ever assembled. The programme has been extremely well received and we've been very happy with the results. So happy, in fact, that we've decided to complete the circle and return a selection of our titles to print, in these omnibus editions.

We hope you enjoy this selection. And we hope that you'll want to explore more of the classic SF and fantasy we have available. These are wonderful books you're holding in your hand, but you'll find much, much more ... through the SF Gateway.

www.sfgateway.com

INTRODUCTION

from The Encyclopedia of Science Fiction

John Brunner (1934–1995) was a UK author, mostly of SF, though he published several thrillers, contemporary novels and volumes of poetry. He began very early to submit SF stories to periodicals – several appeared under the working name K. Houston Brunner, based on his own middle names – and when he was 17 published his first novel, *Galactic Storm* (1951) under the House Name Gill Hunt. Even in a field noted for its early starters, his precocity was remarkable. His first US sale, 'Thou Good and Faithful' as by John Loxmith, was featured in *Astounding* in March 1953, and in the same year he published in another American magazine, as 'The Wanton of Argus' by K. Houston Brunner, the first novel he would later choose to acknowledge, and which eventually appeared as *The Space-Time Juggler* (1963). With its sequel, *The Altar on Asconel* (1965), plus an article on Space Opera and 'The Man from the Big Dark' (1958), it was much later assembled as *Interstellar Empire* (1976). This Interstellar Empire sequence takes place in the twilight of a Galactic Empire – a time rather favoured by Brunner in his Space Operas, and often referred to as the Long Night – when barbarism is general, though the Rimworlds along the Galactic Lens hold some hope for adventurers and mutants, who may eventually rebuild civilization. But the series terminates abruptly, before its various protagonists are able to begin their renaissance, almost certainly reflecting Brunner's ultimate lack of interest in such stories, which he registered in print – though certainly he subsequently revised many of them, not necessarily to their betterment as 'naive' adventures.

In any case, this lessening of interest evinced itself only after very extensive publication of stories and novels describable as literate Space Opera. Initially, from 1953 to about 1957 Brunner's activity was intermittent, mainly through the difficulty of making a living from full-time writing, a problem about which he was always bitterly articulate. In the mid-1950s he was working full-time with a publishing house and elsewhere, writing only occasionally. In 1955 he published one story under the pseudonym Trevor Staines. A little later he sold two novels, again first to magazines: *Threshold of Eternity* (1959) and *The 100th Millennium* (1959); they soon became two of the first novels he placed with Ace Books. With the signing of the contract for the first, Brunner took up full-time freelancing once again.

Over the next six years he published under his own name and as Keith

Woodcott a total of 27 novels with Ace, in addition to work with other publishers. For some readers, this spate of Hard-SF adventure stories still represents Brunner's most relaxed and fluent work as a writer. Two from 1960 are typical of the storytelling enjoyment he was able to create by applying to 'modest' goals the formidable craft he had developed. *The Atlantic Abomination* (1960) is a genuinely terrifying story about a monstrous Alien, long buried beneath the Atlantic, who survives by mentally enslaving 'inferior' species via Psi Power, rather like the thrint in Larry Niven's *World of Ptavvs* (1966). *Sanctuary in the Sky* (1960) is a short and simple Sense-of-Wonder tale, set in the Far Future in a star cluster, very distant from half-forgotten Earth; the cluster teems with various conflicting planetary cultures (all human) that can meet in peace only on the mysterious Waystation, seemingly a synthetic space Habitat. A ship full of squabbling passengers docks at the Station; with them is a mild-mannered stranger, who immediately disappears. It is soon revealed that he's an Earthman, that Waystation is a colony ship owned by Earth, and that he's come to retrieve it. Mankind needs the ship: though this Galaxy is full, 'there are other galaxies'. Decades later, Brunner would rework the thematic concerns of this short novel at much greater length in *A Maze of Stars* (1991).

The mass of Ace novels contains a second series, also truncated, though its structure is more open-ended than that of the Interstellar Empire tales. The Zarathustra Refugee Planets sequence, made up of *Castaways' World* (1963), *Secret Agent of Terra* (1962) and *The Repairmen of Cyclops* (1965), all later assembled in revised versions as *Victims of the Nova* (1989), deals over a long timescale with the survivors of human-colonized Zarathustra; when the planet's sun goes nova, 3000 spaceships carry a few million survivors into exile on a variety of uninhabited worlds. 700 years later, the Corps Galactic has the job of maintaining the isolation of these various cultures, so that, having reverted to barbarism, they can develop naturally; their separate histories constitute a series of experiments in cultural evolution.

Despite these two series, and in contrast to some of his older peers, Brunner only rarely attempted to link or retrofit individual items into series or fixups. Both his space operas and his later, more ambitious works are generally initially conceived in the versions which the reader sees on book publication. Further Ace titles of interest include *The Rites of Ohe* (1963), *To Conquer Chaos* (1964) and *The Day of the Star Cities* (1965).

As the 1960s progressed, more space operas appeared as well as several story collections, including *Out of My Mind* (1967) and *Not Before Time* (1968), which include outstanding items like 'The Last Lonely Man' (1964) and 'The Totally Rich' (1963). Brunner's stories are generally free in form, sometimes experimental. By 1965, with the publication of *The Whole Man* (1964; retitled *Telepathist* for UK publication) and *The Squares of the City*

(1965), it was evident that he would not be content to go on indefinitely writing the SF entertainments of which he had become master, even interesting explorations of tropes like Matter Transmission in novels like *The Dreaming Earth* (1963), material intriguing enough to inspire two of his later attempts to continue publishing works of wide appeal, *Web of Everywhere* (1974) and *The Infinitive of Go* (1980). But tales like this did not attempt to transform his SF habitat. More ambitiously, *The Whole Man*, comprising fundamentally rewritten magazine stories and much new material, and generally considered to be one of Brunner's most successful novels, is an attempt to draw a psychological portrait of a deformed human with Telepathic powers who gradually learns how to use these powers in psychiatrically curative ways: for to communicate is to be human. *The Squares of the City* is a respectable try at a Chess novel in which a chosen venue (in this case a city) serves as the board and two of the characters are players while others are the various pieces. The stiffness of the resulting story may have been inevitable, especially since Brunner was playing out in his fiction a well-known master game. *The Long Result* (1965), more conventionally plotted as a detective/political thriller set on a near-Utopian future Earth on the cusp of being outstripped by a more rapidly developing colony world, posits that racial prejudice, now eliminated from human culture, will resurge as irrational hatred (by a few) of even benign Aliens.

Brunner's *magnum opus* of the 1960s, *Stand on Zanzibar* (1968), perhaps the longest Genre-SF single story to that date, came as the climax of the decade. The Dystopian vision of this complex novel, much of which is set in an exemplary New York, rests on the assumption that Earth's population will continue to expand uncontrollably – the title represents the area soon to be required if the whole population of the planet is to stand in one place. The intersecting stories of two New Yorkers – Norman House, a black executive on a mission to the Third World to facilitate further economic penetration, and Donald Hogan, a White 'synthesist' and government agent, whose mission involves gaining control of a Eugenics discovery – provide dominant strands in an assemblage of narratives whose Infodump function, providing an amplitude of social and cultural contexts, points up their resemblance to similar Modernist techniques used by John Dos Passos (1896–1970) in *USA* (1930–1936), but which fail to conceal the underlying storytelling orthodoxy of the tale. It is perhaps for this reason that the resulting vision has a cumulative, sometimes overpowering effect, while at the same time the meliorist logic of its pulp plotting urgently conveys a sense that answers will be forthcoming, and that the protagonists will win through the story they are living. Through its density of reference, and through Brunner's admirable (though sometimes insecure) grasp of US idiom, the book's anti-Americanism has a satisfyingly American ring to it, so that its tirades do not seem smug; it won the 1968 Hugo and the 1970 BSFA Award, and its French translation won the Prix Apollo in 1973.

Three further novels, all with the same pace and intensity, make together a kind of thematic series of Dystopias. *The Jagged Orbit* (1969) conflates medical and military industrial complexes with the Mafia in a rather too tightly plotted, though occasionally powerful, narrative which also addresses issues of race. *The Sheep Look Up* (1972) (see below) and *The Shockwave Rider* (1975) (see below) were even more successful. Unsurprisingly, given their challenging content, these novels received considerable critical attention, but (also unsurprisingly) they in no way made Brunner's fortune. He was always extremely open about his finances and his hopes for the future, and made no secret of the let-down he felt on discovering that, after these culminating efforts, he was still in the position of being forced to produce commercially to survive. This naiveté was humanly touching, but fatal to his career.

For some years before his death his health was uncertain, which (coinciding with his disillusion) caused a severe slowing down of his once formidable writing speed. In his decreasingly frequent publications after 1972, Brunner tended to return to a somewhat more flamboyant, ironized version of the space-opera idiom he had used earlier, but the relative lack of fluency and enthusiasm of novels like *Total Eclipse* (1974) and *Children of the Thunder* (1989) cannot easily be denied. There is a sense in these novels that skill warred with convictions, and that, as a consequence, Brunner could not any longer *allow* himself the orthodox delights of pure storytelling. He died before the renaissance in Space Opera began to shape British publishing in the 1990s, though the first novels of Iain M. Banks had already proclaimed that something new was in the offing; but there are few signs he would have felt comfortable with the free-flowing exuberance of the reinvented mode, which he may have thought ultimately irresponsible. All the same *A Maze of Stars* (see above), which expanded the Generation Starship which featured in the original *Sanctuary in the Sky* into a full-fledged sentient World Ship, gave some evidence of an intention to try. But even *The Great Steamboat Race* (1983), an associational novel set on the Mississippi River, which he devoted years to writing, shows some signs of a nagging dis-ease. At the point of his sudden death – of a stroke while attending the 1995 WorldCon in Glasgow – it cannot be denied that Brunner's commercial career had stalled, despite a steady output of reliable short fiction.

In the end, his name depends on two strands of his output: on his significant contributions to the space-opera redoubt; and the immensely formidable tract-novels about the state of the world he published between 1968 and 1975. The opinions extractable from these latter works are closer to left-wing than usual with American SF writers of his generation (these opinions, which he articulated publicly many times, may be in part responsible for his failure to acquire a secure US marketing niche, as well as contributing to his loss of belief in the naive victories endemic to generic fiction), and their essentially Dystopian take on humanity's chances of adapting to the demands of species maturity makes him seem more contemporary now than he did in the decade of his death. Over and above the pleasures and challenges he offered us, his life and works deserve full-length study for his role as a significant monitory voice in the West's increasingly urgent debate about humanity's condition as the twentieth century drew to a close.

The first two novels presented here combine intense readability and urgent thinking: it is not a combination always to be found. *The Sheep Look Up* (1972) is perhaps the most unrelenting and convincing dystopia of the four he wrote, and is uncompromisingly well documented. It deals scarifyingly with Pollution in a plot whose relative looseness allows for an almost essayist exposition of the horrors in store for us; forty years on, it is as vigorous and relevant as it was the day it was published. Its portrait of the trivialization of the media and of government, and its prediction that international corporations will manipulate the levers of power in order to maintain the highly-polluting profit margins, all seems uncannily prescient. *The Shockwave Rider* (1975), which is marginally less savage, employs similar reportage techniques in a story about a world enmeshed in a Communications explosion, and has become famous for its prediction of the Computer/Internet virus (here called a worm) and its anticipation of several concerns of Cyberpunk. It is also an exciting read.

The third text reprinted in this omnibus may come as something of a relief. *The Traveller in Black* (1971) is a collection of linked stories featuring the eponymous traveller, whose journeys traverse the world as he seeks out magic in order to destroy it. This may sound heartless, but it soon come clear that by magic Brunner means chaos, superstition, the suppression of reason, orthodoxy, injustice. The traveller's mode of operation is deliciously indirect; each story is a gem and a revelation; for many readers it is the best work Brunner ever wrote. There is no better way to end an omnibus than this.

For a more detailed version of the above, see John Brunner's author entry in *The Encyclopedia of Science Fiction*: http://sf-encyclopedia.com/entry/brunner_john

Some terms above are capitalised when they would not normally be so rendered; this indicates that the terms represent discrete entries in *The Encyclopedia of Science Fiction*.

THE SHEEP LOOK UP

to
ISOBEL GRACE SAUER (née ROSAMOND)
1887–1970
in memoriam

PLEASE HELP
KEEP PIER CLEAN
THROW REFUSE OVERSIDE

– Sign pictured in *God's Own Junkyard,*
edited by Peter Blake

DECEMBER

PROSPECTUS

The day shall dawn when never child but may
Go forth upon the sward secure to play.
No cruel wolves shall trespass in their nooks,
Their lore of lions shall come from picture-books.
No aging tree a falling branch shall shed
To strike an unsuspecting infant's head.
From forests shall be tidy copses born
And every desert shall become a lawn.
Lisping their stories with competing zest,
One shall declare, 'I come from out the West,
Where Grandpa toiled the fearful sea to take
And pen it tamely to a harmless lake!'
Another shall reply, 'My home's the East,
Where, Mama says, dwelt once a savage beast
Whose fangs he oft would bare in horrid rage
Indeed, I've seen one, safely in a cage!'
Likewise the North, where once was only snow,
The rule of halls and cottages shall know,
The lovely music of a baby's laugh,
The road, the railway and the telegraph,
And eke the South; the oceans round the Pole
Shall be domestic. What a noble goal!
Such dreams unfailingly the brain inspire
And to exploring Englishmen do fire …

– 'Christmas in the New Rome', 1862

CARNAGE

Hunted?
By wild animals?
In broad daylight on the Santa Monica freeway? Mad! Mad!

It was the archetype of nightmare: trapped, incapable of moving, with monstrous menacing beasts edging closer. Backed up for better than a mile, three lanes trying to cram into an exit meant for two, reeking and stalking and roaring. For the time being, though, he was more afraid of running than of staying where he was.

Bright fangs repeating the gray gleam of the clouds, a cougar.

Claws innocent of any sheath, a jaguar.

Winding up to strike, a cobra.

Hovering, a falcon. Hungry, a barracuda.

However, when his nerve finally broke and he tried running, it wasn't any of these that got him, but a stingray.

SIGNS OF THE TIMES

THIS BEACH NOT SAFE FOR SWIMMING

NOT DRINKING WATER

UNFIT FOR HUMAN CONSUMPTION

Now Wash Your Hands
(Penalty for noncompliance $50)

FILTERMASK DISPENSER
Use product once only – maximum 1 hour

OXYGEN
25 cents

NOT IN OUR STARS

The radio said, 'You deserve security, Stronghold-style!' Blocking access to the company parking lot on the left of the street was a bus, huge, German, articulated, electric, discharging passengers. Waiting impatiently for it to move on, Philip Mason pricked up his ears. A commercial for a rival corporation?

The unctuous voice went on, backed by non-music from cellos and violas. 'You deserve to sleep undisturbed. To go on vacations as long as you can afford, free from worry about the home you've left behind. Don't they say a man's home is his castle – and shouldn't that be true for you?'

No. Not insurance. Some dirty property developer. What the hell was this bus stopped here for, anyhow? It belonged to the City of Los Angeles okay – right color, name painted on the side – but in place of a destination board it just had a stock sign, ON HIRE, and he couldn't see details of its occupants through its grimy windows. But that was hardly surprising since his own windshield was grimy, too. He had been going to hit the horn; instead, he hit the wash-and-wipe stud, and a moment later was glad of the choice he'd made. Now he could discern half a dozen dull-faced kids, three black, two yellow, one white, and the head of a crutch. Oh.

The speech from the radio continued. 'What we've done for you is build that castle. Nightly, armed men stand guard at all our gates, the only points of access through our spike-topped walls. Stronghold Estates employ the best-trained staff. Our watchmen are drawn from the police, our sharpshooters are all ex-Marines.'

Of whom there's no shortage since they kicked us out of Asia. Ah, the bus signaling a move. Easing forward past its tail and noting from the corner of his eye a placard in its rear window which identified the hiring organization as Earth Community Chest Inc., he flashed his lights at the car next behind, asking permission to cut in front. It was granted, he accelerated – and an instant later had to jam the brakes on again. A cripple was crossing the entrance to the lot, an Asiatic boy in his early teens, most likely Vietnamese, one leg shrunk and doubled up under the hip, his arms widespread to help him keep his balance on a sort of open aluminum cage with numerous straps. Harold, thank God, isn't *that* bad.

All the armed gate-guards black. A prickling of sweat at the idea he might have run the boy down under the muzzles of their guns. Yellow means honorary black. It is sweet to have companions in adversity. And, thinking of companions – Oh, *shut up!*

'There's never any need to fear for your children,' mused the radio. 'Daily, armored buses collect them at your door, take them to the school of your choice. Never for a second are they out of sight of responsible, affectionate adults.'

7

The boy completed his hirpling journey to where the sidewalk resumed, and Philip was finally able to ease his car forward. A guard recognized the company sticker on his windshield and hit the lift for the red-and-white pole that closed the lot. Sweating worse than ever, because he was horribly late and even though that wasn't his fault he was perfused with abstract guilt which made him feel vaguely that *everything* today was his fault, from the Baltimore bombings to the communist takeover in Bali, he stared around. Oh, shit. Packed solid. There wasn't one gap he could squeeze into without guidance unless he wasted more precious time in sawing back and forth with inches to spare.

'They will play in air-conditioned recreation halls,' the radio promised. 'And whatever medical attention they may need is on hand twenty-four hours per day – at low, low contract rates!'

All right for someone earning a hundred thousand a year. For most of us even contract rates are crippling; I should know. Aren't any of those guards going to help me park? Hell, no, all going back to their posts.

Furious, he wound down his window and made violent beckoning gestures. At once the air made him cough and his eyes started to water. He simply wasn't used to these conditions.

'And now a police flash,' said the radio.

Maskless, his expression revealing a trace of – what? Surprise? Contempt? – something, anyway, which was a comment on this charley who couldn't even breathe straight air without choking, the nearest guard moved toward him, sighing.

'Rumors that the sun is out at Santa Ynez are without foundation,' the radio said. 'I'll repeat that.' And did, barely audible against the drone of an aircraft invisible over cloud. Philip piled out, clawing a five-dollar bill from his pocket.

'Take care of this thing for me, will you? I'm Mason, Denver area manager. I'm late for a conference with Mr Chalmers.'

He got that much said before he doubled over in another fit of coughing. The acrid air ate at the back of his throat; he could imagine the tissues becoming horny, dense, impermeable. If this job's likely to involve me in frequent trips to LA I'm going to have to buy a filtermask. And the hell with looking sissy. Saw on the way here it isn't only girls who wear them any more.

The radio mumbled on about extreme congestion affecting all roads northbound.

'Yeah,' the guard said, taking the bill and rolling it neatly one-handed into a cylinder, like a joint. 'Go right on in. They been expecting you.'

He pointed across the lot to where an illuminated sign above a revolving door wished the world a merry Christmas from Angel City Interstate Mutual.

Been expecting? I sure hope that doesn't mean they gave up and went ahead without me!

Feet planted on signs of Libra, Scorpio, Sagittarius, as the revolving door hush-hushed. It turned stiffly; the air-tight seals around it must recently have been renewed. Beyond, a cool marble-walled foyer, also ornamented with zodiacal emblems. Angel City's publicity was geared to the idea of escaping the destiny you'd been born to, and both those who took astrology seriously and those who were sceptical appreciated the semi-poetical quality of the ad copy which resulted.

Here the air was not only purified but delicately perfumed. Waiting on a bench and looking bored, a very pretty light-brown girl in a tight green dress, demurely sleeved, the skirt touching the neat Cuban – correction: Miranda – heels of her black shoes.

But slit to the waist in front. Moreover she was wearing pubic panties, with a tuft of fur at the crotch to suggest hair.

Last night in Vegas. Christ, I must have been out of my mind, knowing I had to sleep well, be in top form for today. But it didn't feel that way at the time. Just … Oh, God, I wish I knew. Bravado? Craving for variety? Dennie, I swear I love you, I'm not going to throw my precious job away, won't even look at this girl! Chalmers's floor is three, isn't it? Where's the directory? Oh, behind those filtermask dispensers.

(Yet, intermixed, pride in working for this firm whose progressive image was carried clear through to ensuring that its secretaries wore the trendiest of clothes. That dress wasn't orlon or nylon, either; it was wool.)

However, it was impossible not to look. She rose and greeted him with a broad smile.

'You're Philip Mason!' Her voice a trifle hoarse. Comforting to know that other people were affected by the air in LA. If only the huskiness didn't lend such a sexy quality … 'We met last time you were here, though probably you wouldn't remember. I'm Bill Chalmers's aide, Felice.'

'Yes, I do remember you.' The cough conquered, though a faint itchy sensation remained on his eyelids. The statement wasn't mere politeness, either – he did now recall her, but his last visit had been in summer and she'd been wearing a short dress and a different hairstyle.

'Is there somewhere I could wash up?' he added, displaying his palms to prove he meant *wash*. They were almost slimy with the airborne nastiness that had eluded the precipitator on his car. It wasn't designed to cope with California.

'Surely! Just along the hallway to the right. I'll wait for you.'

The men's room bore the sign of Aquarius, as the women's did the sign of Virgo. Once when he first joined the company he'd raised a laugh clear around a group of his colleagues by suggesting that in the interests of true equality there should be only one door, marked Gemini. Today he wasn't in a joking mood.

Under the locked door of one of the cubicles: feet. Wary because of the incidence of men's-room muggings these days, he relieved himself with one eye fixed on that door. A faint sucking sound reached his ears, then a chink-ing. Christ, a syringe being filled! Not an addict with an expensive habit who's sneaked in there for privacy? Should I get out my gas gun?

That way lay paranoia. The shoes were elegantly shined, hardly those of an addict who neglected his appearance. Besides, it was over two years since he'd last been mugged. Things were improving. He moved toward the line of washbasins, though he took care to select one whose mirror reflected the occupied cubicle.

Not wanting to leave greasy marks on the light fabric of his pants, he felt cautiously in his pocket for a coin to drop in the water-dispenser. Damna-tion. The dirty thing had been altered since his last visit. He had nickels and quarters, but the sign said only dimes. Wasn't there even one free one? No.

He was on the point of going back to ask Felice for change when the cubicle door swung open. A dark-clad man emerged, shrugging back into a jacket whose right-hand side pocket hung heavy. His features struck a vague chord of memory. Philip relaxed. Neither an addict nor a stranger! Just a diabetic, maybe, or a hepatic. Looking well on it, either way, from his plump cheeks and ruddy complexion. But who …?

'Ah! You must be here for this conference of Chalmers's!' Striding forward, the not-stranger made to extend his hand, then canceled the gesture with a chuckle.

'Sorry, better wash up before shaking with you. Halkin out of San Diego, by the way.'

Tactful with it, too. 'I'm Mason out of Denver. Ah – you don't have a spare dime, do you?'

'Sure! Be my guest.'

'Thank you,' Philip muttered, and carefully stoppered the drain hole before letting the water run. He had no idea how much a dime bought you but if it was the same amount that had cost a nickel a year and a half ago it was barely enough to soap and rinse with. He was thirty-two, yet today he felt like a gan-gling teenager, insecure, confused. His skin itched as though it were dusty. The mirror told him it didn't show, and his swept-back brown hair was still tidy, so that was all right, but Halkin was wearing practical clothes, almost black, whereas he himself had put on his newest and smartest gear – by Colo-rado standards, much influenced of course by the annual influx of the winter-sports jet set – and it was pale blue because Denise said it matched his eyes, and while it could never be crumpled it was already showing grime at collar and cuffs. Memo to self: next time I come to LA …

The water was terrible, not worth the dime. The soap – at least the com-pany kept cakes of it on the basins, instead of demanding another dime for an impregnated tissue – barely lathered between his palms. When he rinsed his face a trickle ran into his mouth and he tasted sea-salt and chlorine.

'You got held up like me, I guess,' Halkin said, turning to dry his hands in the hot-air blower. That was free. 'What was it – those filthy Trainites occu-pying Wilshire?'

Washing his face had been a mistake. There were no towels, paper or otherwise. Philip hadn't thought to check beforehand. There's this big thing about cellulose fibers in the water of the Pacific. I read about it and failed to make the connection. His sense of awkward teenageness worse than ever, he had to twist his head into the stream of warm air, meantime wondering: what do they do for toilet paper – round pebbles, Moslem-style?

Keep up the facade at all costs. 'No, my delay was on the Santa Monica freeway.'

'Oh, yes. I heard traffic was very heavy today. Some rumor about the sun coming out?'

'It wasn't that. Some' – repressing the ridiculous impulse to make sure no one black was in earshot such as Felice or the guards around the parking lot – 'crazy spade jumped out of his car in the middle of a jam and tried to run across the other half of the road.'

'You don't say. Stoned, was he?'

'I guess he must have been. Oh, thanks' – Halkin courteously holding the door. 'Naturally the cars that were still moving in the fast lanes had to brake and swerve and *bang*, must have been forty of them bumped each other. Missed him by a miracle, not that it did him any good. The traffic coming away from the city was doing fifty-sixty at that point, and when he got across the divide he fell in front of a sports car.'

'Good lord.' This had brought them level with Felice, who was keeping an elevator for them, so they ushered her inside and Halkin hovered his hand over the floor-selection buttons. 'Three, isn't it?'

'No, we're not in Bill's office. We're in the conference room on the seventh.'

'Was your car damaged?' Halkin went on.

'No, luckily mine wasn't included in the shunt. But we had to sit there for more than half an hour before they got the road clear … You said you were held up by Trainites?'

'Yes, on Wilshire.' Halkin's professional smile gave way to a scowl. 'Lousy dodgers, most of them, I bet! If I'd known I was sweating out my time for their sake …! You did yours, of course?'

'Yes, of course, in Manila.'

'My stint was in 'Nam and Laos.'

The car was slowing and they all glanced at the lighted numbers. But this wasn't seven, it was five. The doors parted to reveal a woman with a spotty face who said under her breath, 'Ah, shit!' And stepped into the car anyway.

'I'll ride up with you and down again,' she added more loudly. 'You could wait until doomsday in this filthy building.'

*

The windows of the conference room were bright yellow-gray. The proceedings had started without waiting for the last two arrivals; Philip was thankful that he wasn't entering alone. Eight or nine men were present in comfortable chairs with foldaway flaps bearing books, notepads, personal recorders. Facing them across a table shaped like an undernourished boomerang: William Chalmers, vice-president in charge of interstate operations, a black-haired man in his late forties who had developed too much of a paunch to get away with the fashionable figure-hugging gear he was wearing. Standing, interrupted by the intrusion: Thomas Grey, the company's senior actuary, a bald lean man of fifty with such thick spectacles one could imagine their weight accounting for the habitual forward stoop of his shoulders. He looked put out; scratching absently under his left arm, he accorded no more than a curt nod by way of greeting.

Chalmers, however, welcomed the latecomers cordially enough, brushed aside their apologies, waved them to the remaining vacant places – right in the front row, of course. The wall-clock showed two minutes of eleven instead of the scheduled ten-thirty. Trying to ignore it, Philip picked up a folder of papers from his assigned chair and distributed mechanical smiles to those of his colleagues with whom he could claim casual acquaintance.

Casual …

Don't think about Laura. Dennie, I love you! I love Josie, I love Harold, I love my family! But if only you hadn't insisted on my—

Oh, shut up. Talk about mountains out of molehills!

But his situation was precarious, after all. Notoriously, he was by nearly seven years the youngest of Angel City's area managers: LA, Bay, SoCal, Oregon, Utah, Arizona, NM, Texas, Colorado. Texas due for subdivision next year, the grapevine said, but as yet it hadn't happened. That meant that his footsteps were being hounded by hordes of skilled, degree-equipped unemployed. He had six salesmen with Ph.D.'s. Running to stay in the same place …

'If we can continue?' Grey said. Philip composed himself. The first time he had met the actuary he had assumed him to be a dry extension of his computers, lost in a world where only numbers possessed reality. Since then, however, he had learned that it had been Grey who hit on the notion of adopting astrological symbolism for the firm's promotional material, and thereby endowed Angel City with its unique status as the only major insurance company whose business among clients under thirty was expanding as fast as the proportion of the population they represented. Anyone with that much insight was worth listening to.

'Thank you. I was just explaining why you've come.'

*

Eyes rolling back to the limits of their sockets, mouth ajar, breath hissing in her throat! Useless denying it to myself. No woman ever made me feel more like a man!

Philip touched the inside of his cheek with the tip of his tongue. She had slapped him back-handed and marched out of the motel cabin with blazing eyes because he had offered her money. There was a cut. It had bled for five minutes. It was next to his right upper canine, all his life the sharpest of his teeth.

'It's because,' Grey continued, 'of the hike in life insurance premiums we're going to impose from January first. Of course we've always predicated our quotations on the assumption that life expectancy in the United States would continue to rise. But during the past three years it has in fact started to go down.'

A ROOST FOR CHICKENS

Sharp on nine the Trainites had scattered caltraps in the roadway and created a monumental snarl-up twelve blocks by seven. The fuzz, as usual, was elsewhere – there were always plenty of sympathizers willing to cause a diversion. It was impossible to guess how many allies the movement had; at a rough guess, though, one could say that in New York City, Chicago, Detroit, LA or San Francisco people were apt to cheer, while in the surrounding suburbs or the Midwest people were apt to go fetch guns. In other words, they had least support in the areas which had voted for Prexy.

Next the stalled cars had their windows opaqued with a cheap commercial compound used for etching glass, and slogans were painted on their doors. Some were long: THIS VEHICLE IS A DANGER TO LIFE AND LIMB. Many were short: IT STINNKS! But the commonest of all was the universally known catchphrase: STOP, YOU'RE KILLING ME!

And in every case the inscription was concluded with a rough egg-shape above a saltire – the simplified ideogrammatic version of the invariable Trainite symbol, a skull and crossbones reduced to ⚰.

Then, consulting printed data-sheets, many of which were flapping along the gutter hours later in the wind of passing cars, they turned to the nearby store-windows and obscured the goods on offer with similarly appropriate slogans. Unprejudiced, they found something apt for every single store.

It wasn't too hard.

Delighted, kids on the afternoon school shift joined in the job of keeping at bay angry drivers, store-clerks and other meddlers. Some of them weren't smart enough to get lost when the fuzz arrived – by helicopter after frantic radio messages – and made their first trip to Juvenile Hall. But what the hell?

They were of an age to realize a conviction was a keen thing to have. Might stop you being drafted. Might save your life.

Most of the drivers, however, had the sense to stay put, fuming behind their blank windshields as they calculated the cost of repairs and repainting. Practically all of them were armed, but not one was stupid enough to pull a gun. It had been tried during a Trainite demonstration in San Francisco last month. A girl had been shot dead. Others, anonymous in whole-head masks and drab mock-homespun clothing, had dragged the killer from his car and used the same violent acid they applied to glass to write MURDERER on his flesh.

In any case, there was little future in rolling down a window to curse the demonstrators. Throats didn't last long in the raw air.

ENTRAINED

'It's easy enough to make people understand that cars and guns are inherently dangerous. Statistically, almost everyone in the country now has experience of a relative being shot dead either at home or abroad, while the association between cars and traffic fatalities opens the public mind to the concept of other, subtler threats.'

```
MASTER MOTOR MART
New & Used Cars
```

Lead: causes subnormality in children and other disorders. Exceeds 12 mg. per M^3. in surface water off California. Probable contributory factor in decline of Roman Empire whose upper class ate food cooked in lead pans and drank wine fermented in lead-lined vats. Common sources are paint, antiknock gas where still in use, and wildfowl from marshes etc. contaminated over generations by lead shot in the water.

'On the other hand it's far harder to make it clear to people that such a superficially innocuous firm as a beauty parlor is dangerous. And I don't mean because some women are allergic to regular cosmetics.'

```
NANETTE'S BEAUTY CENTER
Cosmetics, Perfumery & Wigs
```

Polychlorinated biphenyls waste products of the plastics, labriation cosmetics industries. Universal distribution at levels similar to DDT, less toxic but having more marked effect on steroid hormones. Found in museum specimens collected as early as 1944. Known to kill birds.

'Similarly it's a short mental step from the notion of killing plants or insects to the notion of killing animals and people. It didn't take the Vietnam disaster to spell that out – it was foreshadowed in everybody's mind.'

FARM & GARDEN INC.
Landscaping & Pest Control Experts

Pelican, brown: failed to breed California where formerly common, 1969 onward, owing to estrogenic effect of DDT on shell secretion. Eggs collapsed when hen birds tried to brood them.

'By contrast, now that we scarcely make use of the substances which used to constitute the bulk of the pharmacopoeia and which were clearly recognizable as poisonous because of their names – arsenic, strychnine, mercury and so on – people seem to assume that any medical drug is good, period. I wasted more of my life than I care to recall going around farms trying to discourage pig and chicken breeders from buying feeds that contained antibiotics, and they simply wouldn't listen. They held that the more of the stuff you scattered around the better. So developing new drugs to replace those wasted in cake for cattle, pap for pigs and pellets for pullets has become like the race between guns and armor!'

Stacy & Sohwerts Inc.
IMPORTED GOURMET FOODS

Train, Austin (proudfoot): b. Los Angeles 1938; e UCLA (B.Sc. 1957), Univ. Coll. London (Ph.D. 1961.); m. 1960 Clara Alice nee Shoolman, div. 1963, n.c; a. c/o publishers. Pub: thesis, 'Metabolic Degradation of Complex Organophosphates' (Univ. of London Press 1962); 'The Great Epidemics' (Potter & Vasarely 1965, rep. as 'Death In the Wind,' Common Sense Books 1972); 'Studies in Refractive Ecology' (P&V 1968, rep. as 'The Resistance Movement in Nature,' CSB 1972); 'Preservatives and Additives in the American Diet' (P&V 1971, rep. as 'You Are What You Have To Eat,' CSB 1972); 'Guide to the Survival of Mankind' (International Information Inc., boards 1972, paper 1973); 'A Handbook for 3000 A.D.' (III, boards 1973, paper 1975); crt. J. Biol. Sci., J. Ecol., J. Biosph., Intl. Ecol. Rev., Nature, Sci. Am., Proc. Acad. Life Sci., Sat. Rev., New Ykr., New Sci. (London), Envrmt. (London), Paris Match, Der Spiegel (Bonn), Blitz (India), Manchete (Rio) etc.

IT'S A GAS

Leaving behind half his lonely brunch (not that the coffee shop where he'd eaten regularly now for almost a year wasn't crowded with lunchers, but sitting next to the fuzz is prickly), Pete Goddard waited for change to be made for him. Across the street, on the big billboards enclosing the site of Harrigan's Harness and Feed Store – it had kept the name although for years before it was demolished it had sold snowmobiles, motorcycle parts and dude Western gear – which now was scheduled to become forty-two desirable apartments and the Towerhill home of American Express and Colorado Chemical Bank, someone had painted about a dozen black skulls and crossbones.

Well, he was feeling a little that way himself. Last night had been a party: first wedding anniversary. His mouth tasted foul and his head ached and moreover Jeannie had had to get up at the ordinary time because she worked too, at the Bamberley hydroponics plant, and he'd broken his promise to clear away the mess so she wouldn't be faced with it this evening. Besides, that patch on her leg, even if it didn't hurt ... But they had good doctors at the plant. Had to have.

New, not disposed to like him, the girl cashier dropped his due coins in his palm and turned back to conversation with a friend.

The wall-clock agreed with his watch that he had eight minutes to make the four-minute drive to the station house. Moreover, it was bitterly cold outside, down to around twenty with a strong wind. Fine for the tourists on the slopes of Mount Hawes, not good for the police who measured temperature on a graph of smashed cars, frostbite cases and petty thefts committed by men thrown out of seasonal work. And women, come to that.

So maybe before going ... By the door, a large red object with a mirror on the upper part of its front. Installed last fall. Japanese. On a plate at the side: *Mitsuyama Corp., Osaka*. Shaped like a weighing machine. Stand here and insert 25¢. Do not smoke while using. Place mouth and nose to soft black flexible mask. Like an obscene animal's kiss.

Usually he laughed at it because up here in the mountains the air was never so bad you needed to tank up on oxygen to make the next block. On the other hand some people did say it was a hell of a good cure for a hangover ...

More detail penetrated his mind. Noticing detail was something he prided himself on; when his probationary period was through, he was going to shoot for detective. Having a good wife could spawn ambition in any man's mind.

The mirror cut in a curve to fit around the mouthpiece: cracked. Slot for quarters. Below it a line defining the coin-hopper. Around that line, scratches. As though someone had tried to pry the box out with a knife.

Pete thought of bus-drivers murdered for the contents of a change machine.

Turning back to the counter he said, 'Miss!'

'What?'

'That oxygen machine of yours—'

'Ah, shit!' the girl said, hitting 'No Sale' on the register. 'Don't tell me the stinking thing is on the fritz *again*! Here's your quarter back. Go try the drugstore on Tremont – they have three.'

THE OPPOSITE OF OVENS

White tile, white enamel, stainless steel … One spoke here in hushed tones, as though in a church. But that was because of the echoes from the hard walls, hard floor, hard ceiling, not out of respect for what was hidden behind the oblong doors, one above another from ankle-level to the height of a tall man's head, one next to another almost as far as the eye could see. Like an endless series of ovens, except that they weren't to cool, but to chill.

The man walking ahead of her was white, too – coat, pants, surgical mask at present dangling below his chin, tight ugly cap around his hair. Even plastic overshoes also white. Apart from what she had brought in with her, dull brown, there was effectively only one other color in here.

Blood-red.

A man going the other way wheeling a trolley laden with waxed-paper containers (white) labeled (in red) for delivery to the labs attached to this morgue. While he and her companion exchanged helloes, Peg Mankiewicz read some of the directions: 108562 SPLEEN SUSP TYPH CULT, 108563 LIVER VERIFY DEGEN CHGES, 108565 MARSH TEST.

'What's a Marsh test?' she said.

'Presence of arsenic,' Dr Stanway answered, sidling past the trolley and continuing down the long line of corpse closets. He was a pale man, as though his environment had bleached every strong tint out of him; his cheeks had the shade and texture of the organ containers, his visible hair was ash-blond, and his eyes were the dilute blue of shallow water. Peg found him more tolerable than the rest of the morgue staff. He was devoid of emotion – either that, or absolutely homosexual – and never plagued her with the jocular passes most of his colleagues indulged in.

Shit. Maybe I should take a wash in vitriol!

She was beautiful: slim, five-six, with satin skin, huge dark eyes, a mouth juicier than peaches. Especially modern peaches. But she hated it because it meant she was forever being hounded by men collecting pubic scalps. Coming on butch was no help; it was that much more of a challenge to men and started the ki-ki types after her as well. Without makeup, perfume or jewelry, in a deliberately unflattering brown coat and drab shoes, she still felt like a pot of honey surrounded by noisy flies.

Poised to unzip if she so much as smiled.

To distract herself she said, 'A murder case?'

'No, that suit someone filed in Orange County. Accused a fruit grower of using an illegal spray.' Eyes roaming the numbered doors. 'Ah, here we are.'

But he didn't open the compartment at once.

'He isn't pretty, you know,' he said after a pause. 'The car splattered his brains all over everywhere.'

Peg buried her hands in the pockets of her coat so that he couldn't see how pale her knuckles were. It might just conceivably might be a thief who'd stolen his ID ...

'Go ahead,' she said.

And it wasn't a thief.

The whole right-hand side of the dark head was – well, *soft*. Also the lower eyelid had been torn away and only roughly laid back where it belonged, so the underside of the eyeball was exposed. A graze clotted with blood rasped from the level of the mouth down and out of sight beneath the chin. And the crown was so badly smashed, they'd put a kind of Saran sack around it, to hold it together.

But it was pointless to pretend this wasn't Decimus.

'Well?' Stanway said at length.

'Yes, put him away.'

He complied. Turning to lead her to the entrance again, he said, 'How did you hear about this? And what makes the guy so important?'

'Oh ... People call the paper, you know. Like ambulance-drivers. We give them a few bucks for tipping us off.'

As though floating ahead of her like a horrible sick-joke balloon on a string: the softened face. She swallowed hard against nausea.

'And he's – I mean he was – one of Austin Train's top men.'

Stanway turned his head sharply. 'No wonder you're interested, then! Local guy, was he? I heard Trainites were out in force again today.'

'No, from Colorado. Runs – ran – a wat near Denver.'

They had come to the end of the corridor between the anti-ovens. With the formal politeness due to her sex, which she ordinarily detested but could accept from this man on a host-and-guest basis, Stanway held the door for her to pass through ahead of him and noticed her properly for the first time since her arrival.

'Say! Would you like to – uh …?' A poor communicator, this Stanway, at least where women were concerned. 'Would you like to sit down? You're kind of green.'

'No thanks!' Over-forcefully. Peg hated to display any sign of weakness for fear it might be interpreted as 'feminine'. She relented fractionally a second later. Of all the men she knew she suspected this one least of hoping to exploit chinks in her guard.

'You see,' she admitted, 'I knew him.'

'Ah.' Satisfied. 'A close friend?'

There was another corridor here, floored with soft green resilient composition and wallpapered with drifts of monotonous Muzak. A girl came out of a gilt-lettered door bearing a tray of coffee-cups. Peg scented fragrant steam.

'Yes … Have the police sent anyone to check on him?'

'Not yet. I hear they're kind of overloaded. The demonstration, I guess.'

'Did they take his belongings from the car?'

'I guess they must have. We didn't even get his ID – just one of those forms they fill out at the scene of the accident.' Dealing with Christ knew how many such per day, Stanway displayed no particular interest. 'Way I read it, though, they'd be concerned. Must have been stoned to do what he did. And if he was one of Train's top men they're bound to show up soon, aren't they?'

They hadn't yet reached the door to the outside, but Peg hastily put on her filtermask.

It covered so much of her traitorous face.

It was a long walk to where she had left her car: a Hailey, of course, on principle. Her vision was so blurred by the time she reached it – not merely because the air stung her eyes – that she twice tried to put the key in the lock upside-down. When she finally realized, she was so annoyed she broke a nail dragging open the door.

And thrust the finger into her mouth and instead of nibbling away the broken bit, tore it. Her finger bled.

But at least the pain offered an anchor to reality. Calming, she wrapped around the injury a tissue from the glove-compartment and thought about calling in her story. It was a story. It would make the TV news services as well as the paper. Killed on the freeway: Decimus Jones, age thirty, busted twice for pot and once for assault, smeared with an average quantity of the grime a young black nowadays expected to acquire. But suddenly reformed (it says here) by the precepts of Austin Train at twenty-six, mastermind of Trainite operations when they spread to Colorado … not that he would have acknowledged the name 'Trainite' any more than Austin did. Austin said the proper term was 'commie', for 'commensalist', meaning that you and your dog, and the flea on the dog's back, and the cow and the horse and the jackrabbit and the gopher and the nematode and the paramecium and the spirochete all sit down to the same table in the end. But that had been just a debating point, when he got sick of people screaming at him that he was a traitor.

Ought to make sure Decimus gets returned to the biosphere right away. Forgot to mention that. Should I go back? Hell, I guess he put it in his will. If they take any notice of a black man's will …

Somebody's going to have to tell Austin. It would be terrible if he first learned the news in print or from TV.

Me?

Oh, shit. Yes. I'm the first to latch on. So it has to be me.

Her mind was abruptly a chaos of muddled images, as though three people had taken simultaneous possession of her head. Stanway by chance had asked precisely that question she felt constrained to answer honestly: 'A close friend?'

Close? More like only! Why? Because he was black and happily married and not interested any more in the exoticism of white girls? (Who'll tell Zena and the kids?) Partly, maybe. But what mattered was that Decimus Jones, healthy, male and hetero, had treated luscious tempting Peg Mankiewicz … as a friend.

It had better be Austin who tells Zena. I *couldn't*. And a merry Christmas to you all.

After that the confusion became total. She could foresee events fanning out from this death as though she were reading a crystal ball. Everyone would automatically echo Stanway: 'Jumping out of his car that way he must have been stoned – or maybe crazy!'

Yet she'd known him as a very sane man, and being stoned belonged too far back in his past. So it could never have been of his own volition. So somebody must have slipped him a cap of something fierce. And there was only one motive she could think of for doing that. To discredit him at any cost.

She suddenly realized she had been staring, without seeing, at proof of a Trainite's passage through this parking lot, a skull and crossbones on the door of a car parked slantwise to hers. Her own, naturally, would be unmarked.

Yes. It must have been done to discredit Decimus. Must have. These stereotyped interchangeable plastic people with dollar signs in their eyes couldn't bear to share their half-ruined planet with anyone who climbed out of his ordained grooves. A black JD dropout was meant to die in a street brawl, or better yet in jail partway through a spell of ninety-nine. For him to be loved and looked up to like a doctor or a priest, by white as well as black – that turned their stomachs!

Turned stomach. Oh, Christ. She fumbled in her purse for a pill she should have taken over an hour ago. And forced it down despite its size without water.
    Usually, nowadays, one had to.

Finally she decided she was getting maudlin and twisted the key in the dashboard lock. There was steam stored from the trip to get here and the car moved silently and instantly away.
    And cleanly. No lead alkyls, hardly any CO, nothing worse than CO_2 and water. Praise be, if Anyone is listening, for those who struggle to save us from the consequences of our own mad cleverness.
    At the exit from the lot, if she had been going to the office she would have turned right. Instead she turned left. There were probably not more than a hundred people in the country who could rely on locating Austin Train when they wanted to. If her editor had known that among them was one of his own reporters who had never used the information for professional purposes, he would have come after her with a gun.

THE BLEEDING HEART IS A RUNNING SORE

… veteran of campaigns in Indochina and the Philippines today became the latest of many distinguished ex-officers to join the Double-V adoption plan, taking into his family an orphaned girl aged eight with severe scars allegedly due to napalm burns. Commenting on his decision the general said, quote, I was not at war with children, only with those seeking the destruction of our way of life. End quote. Questioned concerning his reaction to the growth of the Double-V scheme prior to leaving the White House for his main engagement of the day, a luncheon organized by former members of his official fan club at which he is slated to deliver a major speech on foreign affairs, Prexy said, quote, I guess if they can't break down the front door they have to sneak around the back. End quote. The Congressional inquiry into alleged bribe-taking by officials of the Federal Land Use Commission …

THE ROOT OF THE TROUBLE

'Te-goosey-goosey-galpa—' The rain was pelting down so hard the wipers of the Land Rover could barely cope, and the road was terrible. Despite four-wheel drive they were continually sliding and skidding, and every now and then they met a pothole which made Leonard Ross wince.

21

'Knock 'er down and scalp 'er—'

Dr Williams's singing was barely audible above the roar of the engine and the hammering of the rain, but it was just possible to discern that the tune belonged to a nursery rhyme: Goosey Gander. 'Up hers! LP and your ass—'

Another pothole. Leonard reflexively glanced back to see if his equipment was okay, and wished he hadn't. The rear seat was also occupied by the policeman assigned to escort him, who had a repulsive weeping skin condition, and Leonard's stomach was queasy enough anyhow.

'Nobody will *halp* 'er!' concluded Williams triumphantly, and added without drawing a fresh breath, 'How long have you been with Globe Relief?'

'Oh …' For an instant Leonard didn't realize the question was a question. 'About four years now.'

'And you've never been to this part of the world before?'

'I'm afraid not.'

'Bloody typical!' With a snort. 'At least I hope they gave you all the gen?'

Leonard nodded. They had submerged him with masses of data, and his head was still ringing. But this country was so full of paradoxes! To start with, when he'd seen that the name of his contact at Guanagua was Williams, he'd assumed an American. He hadn't been prepared for a manic Briton who wore a Harris tweed jacket in this stinking subtropical humidity. Yet it seemed of a piece with a nation whose first capital, for 357 years, had been demoted because the citizens objected to the governor keeping a mistress; whose current capital was so relatively unimportant it had never had a railroad, and the international airlines had given up servicing it …

'Every time someone tries to haul this country up by its bootstraps,' Williams said, 'something goes wrong. Act of God! Though if that's really how He likes to amuse Himself, no wonder the Tupamaros are making so much headway! Not around here, of course, but in the cities. Look at this road! By local standards it's a ruddy highway. It's so damned difficult to get goods to market, most people haven't the currency to buy manufactured goods, even proper tools. But now and then someone whips up enthusiasm for cash crops instead of subsistence crops – cotton, coffee, that sort of thing – and it swings along for a while and then all of a sudden, crash. Their hard work goes for nothing. Like this time. Come and see for yourself.'

Unexpectedly he braked the Land Rover at a spot where rocks as high as a man's knee flanked the track. Peering through the rain-smeared windshield, Leonard made out that they had arrived within sight of a shabby village surrounded on two sides by lines of coffee plants, on the others by maize and beans. The layout suggested competent husbandry, but every single plant was wilted.

Jumping out, Williams added, 'Bring your gear!'

'Ah—'

'Look, the rain isn't going to stop for bloody weeks, you know, so you might as well get used to it!'

Reluctantly Leonard picked up his field kit and ducked into the downpour. His glasses blurred instantly, but his sight was too bad for him to discard them. Water trickling down his collar, he followed the line Williams had marked across the sodden ground.

'Doesn't matter where you look,' Williams said, stopping level with the nearest coffee plant. 'You'll find the buggers anywhere.'

Compliantly Leonard began to trowel in the mud. He said after a pause, 'You're English, aren't you, doctor?'

'Welsh, actually.' In a frigid tone.

'Do you mind if I ask what brought you here?'

'A girl, if you really want to know.'

'I'm sorry, I didn't mean to—'

'Pry? Of course not. But I'll tell you anyway. She was the daughter of one of the embassy staff in London. Very beautiful. I was twenty-four, she was nineteen. But her people were Catholics from Comayagua, where they're strict, and naturally they didn't want her marrying a Methodist. So they shipped her home. I finished my studies, saving like mad to buy a passage here, thinking that if I could convince them I was serious ... Hell, I'd have converted if I'd had to!'

Down there close to the scrawny root of the coffee plant: something wriggling. 'And what happened?'

'I got here and discovered she was dead.'

'*What?*'

'Typhus. It's endemic. And this was 1949.'

There seemed to be nothing else anyone could possibly say. Leonard dragged up a clod of dirt and broke it in his hands. Exposed, a frantic creature two inches long, at first glance not unlike an earthworm, but of a bluish-red color, with a slight thickening at one end and a few minute bristles, and writhing with more energy than any earthworm ever had.

'Yet, you know, I've never regretted staying here. There has to be someone on the spot to help these people – it's no use trying to do it all by remote control ... Ah, you got one of them, did you?' His tone reverted to normal. 'Recognize it, by any chance? I can't find a technical name for it in the literature. Of course my reference-books aren't up to much. In Spanish it's *sotojuela*, but around here they say *jigra*.'

One-handed, leaving fingermarks of mud, Leonard extracted a test-tube from his kit and dropped the pest into it. He tried to examine it with his folding glass, but the rain splashed down too heavily.

'If I could get a look at it under cover,' he muttered.

'There may be a roof in the village that isn't leaking. May be ... And this is what the buggers do to the plants, see?' Williams pulled a coffee bush casually out of the ground. It offered no resistance. The stem was spongy with bore-holes and the foliage limp and sickly.

'They attack corn and beans as well?' Leonard asked.

'Haven't found anything they won't eat yet!'

In the hole left by the uprooted plant, five or six of them squirming to hide.

'And how long have they been a nuisance?'

'They've always been a nuisance,' Williams said. 'But until – oh, about the time they cleared this patch for coffee, you only found them in the forest, living off the underbrush. I didn't see more than half a dozen the first ten years I spent at Guanagua. Then about two and a half years ago, boom!'

Leonard straightened, his legs grateful to be released from stooping.

'Well, there's no doubt that this is an emergency, as you claimed. So I'll apply for authorization to use high-strength insecticides, and then when we've—'

'*How* long did you say you'd been with Globe Relief?'

Leonard blinked at him. Suddenly he was unaccountably angry.

'Who do you think this ground belongs to, anyway? We're on the private estate of some high government muckamuck who can bend the law as much as he likes! This area's been sprayed and soaked and *saturated* with insecticides!'

From the direction of the village, walking very slowly, a straggling line of men, women and children had emerged. All were thin, all were ragged and barefoot, and several of the children had the belly-bloat characteristic of pellagra.

'The idiot's made the *jigras* resistant to DDT, heptachlor, dieldrin, pyrethrum, the bloody lot! Think I was such a fool the idea hadn't crossed my mind to check? Those people don't need chemicals, they need *food*!'

DEFICIT

Petronella Page: Hi, world!

Studio audience: Hi!

Page: Well, this time as ever we have for you all kinds of people making news. Among others we're to welcome Big Mama Prescott whose hit 'The Man with the Forty-Five' is currently the center of a fierce debate about the proper – or improper – material for pop songs. (*Audience laughter.*) And then we'll be talking to a whole group of the ex-officers who've given so many children from Southeast Asia the best of all Christmas presents, a new home and a new family. But first off let's welcome someone who's been making headlines in a different area. He's a scientist, and you've been hearing about him because – well, because if his calculations are right they bode not too well for the future of this nation. Here he is, Professor Lucas Quarrey of Columbia. *(Applause.)*

Quarrey: Good eve— I mean, hello, everyone.

Page: Lucas, because not as much attention is paid to scientific matters these days as perhaps ought to be, maybe you'd refresh the viewers' memories concerning the subject that put you in the news.

Quarrey: Gladly, and if there's someone watching who hasn't heard about this it'll come as – uh – as much of a surprise as it did to me when I first saw the print-out from the university computers. Asked to guess what's the largest single item imported by the United States, people might nominate lots of things – iron, aluminum, copper, many raw materials we no longer possess in economic quantities.

Page: And they'd be wrong?

Quarrey: Very wrong indeed. And they'd be just as wrong if they were asked to name our largest single export, too.

Page: So what is our largest import?

Quarrey: Ton for ton – oxygen. We produce less than sixty per cent of the amount we consume.

Page: And our biggest export?

Quarrey: Ton for ton again, it's noxious gases.

Page: Ah, now this is where the controversy has arisen, isn't it? A lot of people have been wondering how you can claim to trace – oh, smoke from New Jersey clear across the Atlantic. Particularly since you're not a meteorologist or weather scientist. What is your specialty in fact?

Quarrey: Particle precipitation. I'm currently heading a research project designing more compact and efficient filters.

Page: For what – cars?

Quarrey: Oh yes. And buses, and factories too. But mainly for aircraft cabins. We have a commission from a major airline to try and improve cabin air at high altitude. On the most traveled routes the air is so full of exhaust fumes from other planes, passengers get airsick even on a dead calm day – *especially* on a dead calm day, because it takes longer for the fumes to disperse.

Page: So you had to start by analyzing what you needed to filter out, right?

Quarrey: Precisely. I designed a gadget to be mounted on the wing of a plane and catch the contaminants on little sticky plates – I have one here, I don't know if your viewers can see it clearly … Yes? Fine. Well, each unit has fifty of these plates, time-switched to collect samples at various stages of a journey. And by plotting the results on a map I've been able to pin down – like you said – factory-smoke from New Jersey over nearly two thousand miles.

Page: Lots of people argue that can't be done with the accuracy you claim.

Quarrey: I wish the people who say that would take the trouble to find out what my equipment is capable of.

Page: Now this is all very disturbing, isn't it? Most people have the impression that since the passage of the Environment Acts things have taken a turn for the better.

Quarrey: I'm afraid this seems to be – uh – an optical illusion, so to speak. For one thing, the Acts don't have enough teeth. One can apply for all kinds of postponements, exemptions, stays of execution, and of course companies which would have their profits shaved by complying with the new regulations use every possible means to evade them. And the other point is that we aren't being as watchful as we used to be. There was a brief flurry of anxiety a few years ago, and the Environment Acts were introduced, as you said, and ever since then we've been sitting back assuming the situation was being taken care of, although in fact it isn't.

Page: I see. Now what do you say to people who maintain that publicizing these allegations of yours is – well, not in the best interests of this country?

Quarrey: You don't serve your country by sweeping unpleasant facts under the carpet. We're not exactly the most popular nation in the world right now, and my view is that we ought to put a stop right away to anything that's apt to make us even less well liked.

Page: I guess there could be something in that. Well, thanks for coming and talking to us, Lucas. Now, right after this next break for station identification …

IN SPITE OF HAVING CHARITY
A MAN LIKE SOUNDING BRASS

'I guess the nearest analogy would be with cheese,' said Mr Bamberley. To show he was paying attention Hugh Pettingill gave a nod. He was twenty, dark-haired, brown-eyed, with a permanently bad-tempered set to his face – pouting mouth, narrowed eyes, prematurely creased forehead. That had been stamped on him during the bad years from fourteen to nineteen. Allegedly this was the first of many good years he was currently living through, and he was fair-minded enough to expose himself to the possibility of being convinced.

This had started with an argument concerning his future. During it he had said something to the effect that the rich industrial countries were ruining the planet, and he was determined never to have anything to do with commerce, or technology, or the armed forces for which Mr Bamberley retained an archaic admiration. Whereupon: this instruction, too firmly phrased to be termed an invitation, to go on a guided tour of the hydroponics plant and find out how constructively technology might be applied.

'I don't see why we shouldn't improve on nature!' Mr Bamberley had chuckled.

Hugh had kept his counter to himself: 'So what has to happen before you realize you haven't?'

Portly, but muscular, Mr Bamberley strode along the steel walkway that spined the roof of the factory, his arms shooting to left and right as he indicated the various stages through which the hydroponically-grown cassava they started with had to pass before it emerged as the end product, 'Nutripon'. There was a vaguely yeasty smell under the huge semi-transparent dome, as though a baker's shop had been taken over by oil technicians.

And in some senses that was an apt comparison. The Bamberley fortune had been made in oil, though that was two generations back, and neither this Mr Bamberley – whose Christian name was Jacob but who preferred to be called Jack – nor his younger brother Roland had ever stumped around in the slush below a derrick. The fortune had long ago grown to the point where it was not only self-supporting but capable of fission, like an amoeba. Roland's portion was his own, greedily clung to, and destined to descend to his only son Hector (whom Hugh regarded on the strength of their sole meeting as a cotton-wool-wrapped snob ... but that couldn't be his fault at fifteen, must be his father's); Jacob had vested his in the Bamberley Trust Corporation twenty years ago, since when it had multiplied cancerously.

Hugh had no idea how many people were involved in cultivating the funds of the Trust, since he had never been to the New York office where its tenders hung out, but he pictured a blurred group of several hundred pruning, manuring, watering. The horticultural images came readily to hand because his adopted father had turned the former family ranch, here in Colorado, into one of the finest botanical gardens in the country. All that had taken on reality in his mind, however, as far as the Trust was concerned, was the central fact that the sum was now so vast, Jacob Bamberley could afford to run this, the world's largest hydroponics factory, as a charitable undertaking. Employing six hundred people, it sold its product at cost and sometimes below, and every last ounce of what was made here was shipped abroad.

Lord Bountiful. Well, it was a better way to use inherited money than the one Roland had chosen, lavishing it all on yourself and your son so that he would never have to face the harsh real world ...

'Cheese,' Mr Bamberley said again. They were overlooking a number of perfectly round vats in which something that distantly resembled spaghetti was being churned in a clear steaming liquid. A masked man in a sterile coverall was taking samples from the vats with a long ladle.

'You give it some kind of chemical treatment here?' Hugh ventured. He hoped this wasn't going to drag on too long; he'd had diarrhea this morning and his stomach was grumbling again.

'Minor correction,' Mr Bamberley said, eyes twinkling. ' "Chemical" is full of wrong associations. Cassava is tricky to handle, though, because its rind contains some highly poisonous compounds. Still, there's nothing extraordinary about a plant some bits of which are safe to eat and other bits of which are not. Probably you can think of other examples?'

Hugh repressed a sigh. He had never said so outright, being far too conscious of the obligations he owed to Jack (orphaned at fourteen in an urban insurrection, dumped in an adolescents' hostel, picked apparently at random to be added to this plump smiling man's growing family of adopted sons: so far, eight), but there were times when he found his habit of asking this kind of question irritating. It was the mannerism of a poor teacher who had grasped the point about making children find out for themselves but not the technique of making them want to ask suitable questions.

He said tiredly, 'Potato tops.'

'Very good!' Mr Bamberley clapped him on the shoulder and turned once more to point at the factory floor.

'Considering the complexity of the treatment which is required before cassava yields an edible product –'

Ah, shit. He's off on another of his lousy lectures.

'– and the unlikelihood of anyone stumbling on it by accident, it's always struck me as one of the clearest proofs of supernal intervention in the affairs of primitive mankind,' Mr Bamberley declaimed. 'Here's no comparative triviality like oxalic acid, but the deadliest of poisons, cyanide! Yet for centuries people have relied on cassava as a staple diet, and survived, and indeed flourished! Isn't it marvelous when you think of it like that?'

Maybe. Except I don't – if I think of it like that, I picture desperate men struggling on the verge of starvation, trying everything that occurs to them in the faint hope that the next person who samples this strange plant won't drop dead.

'Coffee's another case. Who, without prompting, would have thought of drying the berries, husking them, roasting them, then grinding them and *then* infusing them in water?' Mr Bamberley's voice was rising toward sermon pitch. All of a sudden, though, it dropped back to a normal level.

'So calling this a "chemical process" is misleading. What we really do is cook the stuff! But there's one major drawback in relying on cassava as a staple. I may have mentioned …?'

'Shortage of protein,' Hugh said, thinking of himself as one of those question-and-answer toys they give children, with little lights which come on when the proper button is pressed.

'Right in one!' Mr Bamberley beamed. 'Which is why I compare our job to making cheese. Here' – flinging open the door to the next section of the plant, a vast twilit room where spidery metal girders supported shielded ultraviolet lamps – 'we fortify the protein content of the mix. With absolutely natural substances: yeasts, and fungi with especially high nutritive value. If all goes well we turn as much as eight per cent of the cassava into protein, but even six per cent, the average yield, is a vast improvement.'

Walking ahead as he talked toward yet another section where the finished product was draped in huge skeins on drying-racks, like knitting-wool, then chopped into finger-sized lengths.

'And you know something else extraordinary? Cassava's a tropical plant, of course. Yet it grows better here than under so-called "natural" conditions. Do you know why?'

Hugh shook his head.

'Because we draw so much of our water supply from melted snow. That contains less heavy hydrogen – deuterium. A lot of plants simply can't cope with it.'

And now the packing room, where men and women in masks and cover-alls tamped measured quantities into cardboard cartons lined with polyethylene, then loaded the cartons on to humming fork-lift trucks. Some of them waved on noticing Mr Bamberley. He grinned almost from ear to ear as he waved back.

Oh, God. Mine, that is – if any. Not Bamberley's cosy cheery paterfamilias kind, who is certainly tall and handsome and white-skinned behind his long gray beard. I mean, this guy paid for the clothes I'm wearing, the college I attend, the car I drive – even if it is only a sluggish electric. So I'd like to like him. If you can't like the people who are kind to you …

And he makes it so difficult! Always this feeling, just when you think you're there, that something isn't right. Like he gives all the time to Earth Community Chest, and supplies this cheap food to Globe Relief, and out of eight adopted sons not one a crippled Vietnamese …

Hollow. That's the word. Hollow.

But not to start arguments and rows. Another question.

'Where are the cases going that they're filling now?'

'Noshri, I think,' Mr Bamberley said. 'The postwar aid program, you know. But I'll make sure.'

He shouted to a black woman who was stenciling destination names on empty cartons. She tilted the one she'd just finished so it could be read from the gallery.

'Not to Africa!' Mr Bamberley sounded surprised. 'Then someone must have put in a lot of overtime – I'll find out who and make some commendations. They've already started on the new contract with Globe Relief.'

'Which one is that?'

'Oh, for some village in Honduras where the coffee crop failed.'

SPACE FOR THIS INSERTION IS DONATED BY THE PUBLISHERS AS A SERVICE TO THE COMMUNITY

Where a child cries – or is too weak to cry ... Where a mother mourns – for one who will not weep again ...

Where plague and famine and the scourge of war have proved too much for struggling human beings ...

WE BRING HOPE

But we can't do it without your help. Think of us now.

Remember us in your will. Give generously to the world's largest relief organization: GLOBE RELIEF.*

* All donations wholly tax-deductible.

HOUSE TO HOUSE

Gilt-tooled on yard-square panels of green leather – imitation, of course – the zodiacal signs looked down from the walls of the executive lunch-room. The air was full of the chatter of voices and the clink of ice-cubes. Waiting to be attacked when the president of the company joined them (he had promised to show at one sharp) was a table laden with expensive food: hard-boiled eggs, shells intact so that it could be seen they were brown, free-range, rich in carotene; lettuces whose outer leaves had been rasped by slugs; apples and pears wearing their maggot-marks like dueling scars, in this case presumably genuine ones though it had been known for fruit growers to fake them with red-hot wires in areas where insects were no longer found; whole hams, very lean, proud of their immunity from antibiotics and copper sulphate; scrawny chickens; bread as coarse as sandstone, dark as mud and nubbled with wheat grains ...

'Hmm! Looks as though someone bought out the local branch of Puritan!' a voice said within Chalmers's hearing, and he was pleased. He was moving from House to House, measuring a precise three minutes at each stop. Virgo: no women were present apart from Felice with whom he was having an affair and the two girls serving at the bar. In pursuance of its progressive image Angel City had tried appointing female area managers, but of the first two such one had married and quit and the other had suffered a nervous breakdown. Occasionally he had wondered whether Felice slept with him in the hope of climbing that far up the corporation totem-pole.

The policy, however, had been reviewed.

Libra: 'Now me, I'd go straight into scrap-reclamation and sewage-plant construction. They're the growth industries of the eighties. You'll see your investment double in next to no time.'

Scorpio: 'Rats? No, we have a terrier and a tomcat and keep them hungry. But the ants! I spent two thousand on proofing the kitchen and they still got in. So we fell back on – uh – the old reliable. By the way, if you need any, I have a good discreet source of supply.'

Sagittarius: 'Yes, up our way we've established a *modus vivendi* with the Syndicate. Their interest in Puritan, of course. Very strong around our base. Anyone tries to put in a false claim gets a dusty answer straight away.'

No one at Capricorn.

Aquarius: 'No ice, thanks – hey! I said NO ICE! Don't you understand plain English? Doctor's orders. Mustn't touch anything but canned mineral water. I lose more working time thanks to digestive trouble ...'

Pisces: 'Why don't we make acceptance of a life proposal conditional on installing an approved water purifier in the guy's home, like we insist on an approved precipitator in his car? I've sounded out a couple of the big firms, and they show every interest in cooperating.'

No one at Aries.

Taurus: 'If we're going to expand into the cattle states we *must* have solid documentation on the natural incidence of deformed births in domestic animals. I managed to hold his claim down to a refund of the stud fee, but even that came to five thousand, and he insisted the value of this mare that died in foal was twice as much. I had to drop very heavy hints about the cost of litigation before he accepted the settlement.'

Gemini: 'I've had a rash of demands lately for insurance against egg-bundle fetus. Can't help wondering whether there may not be something behind the scare. Maybe a leak from a research lab?'

No one at Cancer ... naturally.

Leo: 'Yes, the reason I was delayed – this crazy spade ...'

Chalmers clucked sympathy when he had heard Philip out, and switched instantly to a less depressing subject. 'By the way! Tania and I will be in Colorado over the holiday. Get in some skiing.'

'Ah-hah? Where you aiming for – Aspen?'

'Oh, Aspen's full of people who read about it in *Playboy*. No, your own stamping ground. Towerhill!'

'Never! Well, call us up! Maybe you could stop by with us and like have lunch?' Sweating slightly from the *Playboy* putdown.

The conclusion of Chalmers's meticulously timed peregrination brought him within arm's reach of Grey at five to one.

'The man from Denver,' Grey said. 'Philip Mason.'

'What about him?' Anticipating what was coming, and relieved to be able to offer an impenetrably defensive answer. Chalmers had a stake in that man; the personnel board had split three to two and his own vote had been in favor.

'There's something wrong. Or else he's not himself today.'

'Not himself. Saw a man killed right before his eyes this morning.' And recounted the story.

Grey pondered a while. Uncomfortable, Chalmers waited. It was disturbing to watch this man think; it made the world seem full of the sound of whizzing wheels.

'Someone will have to keep an eye on him,' Grey said at last.

'But he's one of our best men!' Chalmers felt personally aggrieved. 'He's nearly doubled the business of the Denver office. He was among the first to get wind of the new developments at Towerhill and put us in on the ground floor, and now we cover three-quarters of the place. Besides, this notion of his of sending out proposal forms for short-term injury insurance with hotel booking confirmations is showing a thousand-per-cent profit.'

'I'm not talking about that,' Grey said. 'What I want to know is what he was doing driving his own car into Los Angeles this morning. It's a long pull from Denver. I'd have expected him to fly.'

The door opened to admit the president of the company, and he moved away to greet him. Scowling at his back, Chalmers wondered – not for the first time – when if ever he would dare call Grey 'Mike': short for 'Mycroft', elder brother of Sherlock Holmes. It was only an inner echelon of the top staff who used the nickname to his face.

THE MORAL OF THE TWENTIETH CENTURY

Last valiant sally of a great department store whose customers had quit the city center, six Santa Clauses marched down the road.

'Ho-ho-ho!' Jingle-jangle.

The sidewalks they passed were crowded. Most of the onlookers were black, and many were children whose eyes reflected unfulfillable dreams. The city's heart was dying before its carcass, and these were the poor, trapped in outworn clothes and rat-ridden tenements. If they wanted to escape, like as not they had to steal a car to travel in because the now compulsory clean exhaust systems were expensive. Last time Peg had come down this way it had been to cover the story of a thriving trade in fake filters, home-built out of sheet steel by an enterprising mechanic.

In spite of the few cars, the air stank. She had taken off her mask, not wanting to be conspicuous – at least, no more than was due to being white. In this district people didn't wear them. They seemed inured to the reek. The chests of the children were shallow, as though to discourage over-deep breathing.

She stared at the Santa Clauses. Behind those once-white beards, now grimed from an excursion in the open, she could not make out their features. She did, though, notice that the second man in the line was only moving his lips, not booming out his 'Ho-ho-ho!' His eyes were bulging with the effort of repressing a cough.

Which would be very out of character for Saint Nick.

They broke the line to distribute come-on leaflets, most of which were immediately dropped, and dispersed into a dark alley where notices warned that only 'authorized personnel' might enter. Was one of the six, as she'd been assured, Austin Train? The idea seemed crazy on the surface. Underneath, maybe it wasn't wholly absurd. She hadn't seen Austin since just after he recovered from his breakdown, but when he vanished from the public eye it had been with the promise that he was going to live as the poor were living, even if it meant risking what they risked. That decision had caused trendy Catholic television spokesmen to mention openly the possibility that the Church might recognize a new category of 'secular saints'. She'd watched one such program with Decimus and Zena, and they'd laughed aloud.

But if this was the path Austin had chosen, it was different from Decimus's. His principle, at the Colorado wat, was third-world oriented; his community grew its own food, or tried to – crops had a nasty habit of failing because of wind-borne defoliants or industrial contaminants in the rain – and likewise wove its own cloth, while its chief source of income lay in handicrafts. The underlying concept was to dramatize the predicament of the majority of mankind. Often, prior to a meal, there had been little homilies: 'You're each getting about twice as much at this table as someone in a Bolivian mountain village gets in a day.'

And sometimes there were strange unexciting dishes: glutinous African sauces of fine-chopped okra, tasteless cakes of anonymous grain, samples of relief shipments sympathizers had paid for and mailed to the wat.

'This is what we're giving away,' Decimus would say. 'Not steak or chicken or big fat Idaho potatoes. This is made from' – and it could be algae, or yeast, or grass clippings, or on one occasion, incredibly, sawmill wastes. 'See how *you* like it, and think of those who have only such shit to be grateful for!'

But that had been a long time ago.

Around the back of the store she found a half-empty parking lot. There was a door marked *Employees Only*. She found it barred from inside. Nearby, though, was a reeded-glass window. She could make out blurred images if she leaned close to the panes. Inside, red forms changing to white as the Santa Clauses stripped off their suits and padding.

She listened, hoping to discern Austin's voice.

'In a bad way, aren't you, pal? Ah, leave him be! Well, just don't cough on me, I have kids at home and all the time doctor's bills. Don't we all?'

And so on. Some of them went through a door at the back of the room and noise of running water indicated showers. A man in a dark suit appeared and shouted, 'Easy with that water! There's a shortage!'

'Shortage hell.' Husky, consumptive; the voice might belong to the man who hadn't been able to shout. Louder, he added, 'Is it hot?'

'Shit, of course not!' someone called back. 'Tepid!'

'In that case give me my pay and I'll go. The doc warned me not to get chilled. So I won't be wasting your precious water, okay?'

'Don't blame me.' With a sigh. 'I don't make the rules around here.'

In the dusk none of the men noticed Peg as they headed toward their cars. Five got into three vehicles. The last traced a line of smoke across the lot – liable to be arrested, him. The sixth man didn't make for a car.

'Austin!' Peg said in a low voice.

He didn't break stride and scarcely looked around. 'The girl reporter!' he said. 'Finally decided to throw me to the wolves?'

'What?' She fell in beside him, matching step for step the well-remembered paces that were too long for a man of his height, an average five-ten. Making the muscles do penance came naturally when Austin Train was around.

'You mean you're not here on business?' His tone was tinged with sarcasm.

She prevaricated, pointing to her right beyond the lot; it was going to be hard to hear herself speak the news she had brought. 'My car's that way. Can I give you a lift? It is a Hailey!'

'Ah. The precepts are being kept, hm? Steam is cleaner than gas! No, thanks. I walk. Have you forgotten?'

She caught his hand and forced him to turn and face her. Looking at him, she found little change revealed by the poor light, apart from his having shaved off the beard he'd worn during his period of notoriety. The high cheekbones were the same, the curiously arched eyebrows, almost semicircular, the thin sour lips … Though maybe his sparse brown hair had receded a trifle. It had been nearly three years.

His mouth parodied a smile: a tilt of a few degrees at one corner. Abruptly furious, determined to wipe away his complacency, she burst out, 'I came to tell you Decimus is dead!'

And he said, 'Yes. I know.'

All those hours of searching, without food or rest, aware that every moment increased the likelihood of losing her job – gone to waste? Peg said weakly, 'But it only happened this morning …'

'I'm sorry.' His look of mockery softened. 'You loved him, didn't you? Okay, I'll come to your car.'

Mechanically she walked on; now, for a change, he matched her strides, though it was perceptibly frustrating to his energetic frame. Nothing more was said until they reached the spot where she had left the little Hailey under the harsh beams of a mercury-vapor light.

'I wonder if I did love him,' she said suddenly.

'You were the person who thought she didn't know how, weren't you? But you must have. Coming in search of me like this is proof of it. It can't have been easy.'

'No, it wasn't.' The finger whose nail she had torn was still tender; she had trouble guiding her key into the lock.

'Funny,' Austin said, looking at the car.

'What is?'

'People thinking of steam as being clean. My grandmother lived in a house backing on a railroad. Couldn't hang out laundry for fear of smuts. I grew up thinking of steam as filthy.'

'Sermon time?' Peg snapped, reaching to open the passenger door. 'And you called Train, come to that!'

'A stale joke,' he said, getting in. 'Train as in powder train. A very old name. Originally it meant a trap or snare.'

'Yes, you told me. I'm sorry. Next time I want to try and get one of these Freon-vapor cars … Oh, shit! I'm rambling. Do you – do you mind if I have a cigarette?'

'No.'

'You mean yes.'

'I mean no. You need a tranquilizer, and tobacco isn't the most dangerous kind.' He half turned in the narrow seat. 'Peg, you went to a lot of trouble. I do appreciate it.'

'Then why do I get a welcome about as warm as someone carrying plague?' Fumbling in her purse. 'How did you hear, anyway?'

'He had a meet with me this morning. When he didn't show I made inquiries.'

'Shit, I should have guessed.'

'But he didn't come just to see me. He has a sister working in LA, you know, and there's some family problem he wanted to sort out.'

'No, I don't know. He never told *me* he had a sister!' With a vicious jab at the dashboard lighter.

'They quarreled. Hadn't met for years ... Peg, I really am sorry! It's – well, it's the nature of your job that makes me react badly. I lived in the spotlight for a long time, you know, and I just couldn't stand it any more once I realized what they were doing to me: using me to prove they cared about the world when in fact they didn't give a fart. After me the deluge! So I generated my smokescreen and disappeared. But if things go on the way they've been going lately ...'

He spread his hands. They were the first things that had suggested to Peg she might learn to like him, thorny though he was, because they were fractionally overlarge for his body, the sort of hands nature might have reserved for a sculptor or a pianist, and despite being thick-knuckled they were somehow beautiful. 'Well, if one reporter knows how to find me, another may, and eventually it may be the fuzz.'

'Are you really afraid of being arrested?'

'Do you think I shouldn't be? Don't you know what happened right on Wilshire this morning?'

'Yes, but you don't organize their demonstrations!' The lighter clicked out; her hand shook so much she could barely guide it to the cigarette.

'True. But I wrote their bible and their creed, and if I were put on oath I couldn't deny that I meant every last word.'

'I should hope not,' she muttered, letting go a ragged puff of gray smoke. The taste, though, wasn't soothing but irritating, because she'd stood on that corner for more than half an hour without her filtermask. After a second unpleasant drag she stubbed it.

'How old are you, Austin?'

'What?'

'How old are you is what I said. I'm twenty-eight and it's a matter of public record. The president of the United States is sixty-six. The chairman of the Supreme Court is sixty-two. My editor is fifty-one. Decimus was thirty last September.'

'And he's dead.'

'Yes. Christ, what a waste!' Peg stared blankly through the windshield. Approaching with grunts and snorts was one of the eight-ton crane-trucks used to collect automobiles without legal filters. This one had trapped exotic prey; a Fiat and a Karmann-Ghia were clamped on its chain-hung magnet.

'Nearly forty,' Austin murmured.

'Aries, aren't you?'

'Yes, provided you're asking as a joke.'

'What the hell does that mean?'

'Well, I could say anything. There are over two hundred of me, you know.'

'Joke!' She almost slapped him, wrenching around in her seat. 'Hell, don't you understand? Decimus is filthily horribly disgustingly *dead*.'

'You mean no one saw it coming in his horoscope?'

'Oh, you're inhuman! Why the hell don't you get out? You hate cars!'

And a fraction of a second later: 'No, I didn't mean that! Don't go!' He hadn't moved. Another pause.

'Any idea who did it?' she said at length.

'You're sure it was – ah – *done*?'

'Must have been! Mustn't it?'

'I guess so.' Austin drew his rounded eyebrows together, not looking at her, but she could see sidelong how they formed a child's sketch for a sea gull. (How long before there were kids who didn't know what a gull was?) 'Well, I can imagine a lot of people being glad to see him go. Did you check out the police?'

'I was about to when I decided to find you instead. I thought it ought to be you who broke the news to Zena.'

'It was. Or rather, I called the wat and made sure she'd hear it first from someone she knew.'

'Those poor kids!'

'Better off than some,' Austin reminded her. Which was true, it being dogmatic Trainite policy never to bear your own as long as there were orphans to be fostered.

'I guess so ...' Peg passed a tired hand over her face. 'I wish I'd realized I was wasting my time! Now I don't know if the news has made the papers, or the TV, or anything.' She rolled the car away from the curb at last. 'Where to?' she added.

'Straight ahead about ten blocks. Worried about losing your job, Peg?'

'More thinking why don't I quit right now.'

He hesitated. 'Maybe it would be a good idea if you stuck with it.'

'Why? Because you want someone in the media on your side? Don't give me that. Thanks to Prexy just about everyone is – except the owners.'

'I wasn't thinking of that. More that you might give me – well, the occasional warning.'

'You are afraid, aren't you?' She halted for a red light. 'Okay, if I can. And if the job lasts ... Who's going to take over from Decimus?'

'I don't know. I'm not in charge of anything.'

'Sorry. It's fatally easy to fall into the notion that you are, what with people saying "Trainite" all the time. I do try and remember to say "commensalist", but everyone shortens that to "commie" and it's generally a quick way to start a fist-fight … Does it worry you, having your name taken in vain?'

'What the hell do you think I'm scared of?' He uttered a short harsh laugh. 'It gives me goose-bumps!'

'Obviously not because of the wats. Because of demonstrations like this morning's?'

'Them? No! They annoy people, but they do no real harm. Create a lot of publicity, provide a few object lessons for the bastards who are wrecking the planet for commercial gain … And they allow the demonstrators to feel they're being constructive. No, the kind of thing I have in mind is this. Suppose someone decides a whole city is offending against the biosphere, and pulls the plug on a nuclear bomb?'

'You think they might? That'd be crazy!'

'Isn't the moral of the twentieth century that we *are* crazy?' Austin sighed. 'Worse still, if it did happen, any proof of the insanity of the guy who did it – or guys: the collective bit is becoming more popular, you noticed? – the evidence, anyway, would be burned up. Along with everything else for miles around.'

She didn't know what to say to that.

Two blocks further on, he tapped her arm. 'Here!'

'What?' Peg stared at her surroundings. This was a desolate, down-at-the-heels area, partly razed for redevelopment, the rest struggling along in a vampiric half-life. A few young blacks were passing a furtive joint in the porchway of a bankrupt store; otherwise no one was visible.

'Oh, don't worry about me,' Austin said. 'I told you: there are over two hundred of me.'

'Yes. I didn't understand.'

'People tend not to. But it's literal. You keep seeing references in the underground press. There are at least that many people who decided to call themselves Austin Train after I disappeared – half in California, the rest scattered across the country. I don't know whether to love them or hate them. But I guess they keep the heat off me.'

'Sunshades.'

'Okay, sunshades. But you shouldn't make remarks like that, Peg. It dates you. When did you last see somebody carrying a parasol?' He made to get out of the car. Peg checked him.

'What do you call yourself? No one told me.'

One foot on the road, Austin chuckled. 'Didn't they say you should ask for Fred Smith? Well, thanks for the ride. And by the way!'

'Yes?'

'If anything goes wrong, you can rely on Zena. You know that, don't you? You can always find sanctuary at the wat.'

BADMIXTURE

Certain types of medication, chiefly tranquilizers, must not be taken by someone who has also recently eaten cheese or chocolate.

RELIEF

All of a sudden it felt like a different world. There was an end to the endless succession of round white-rimmed hopeful eyes in dark faces, to the offering of handleless cups and empty cans and greedy dishes and the pale palms of those who were too apathetic even to collect a spent shell-case by way of a container, because everything they had once owned had been snatched from them and they couldn't believe it was worth investing precious energy in acquiring something else. And there was still a whole heap, at least a kilo, in the carton she'd been distributing from, and more cartons were stacked against the wall behind her, and more yet, incredibly many more, were being unloaded down a slide from the dark overshadowing shape of the ancient VC-10 which had somehow been set down on the improvised landing strip.

Disbelieving, Lucy Ramage brushed back a strand of fair hair from her eyes and turned to examine a segment of the peculiar substance she had been measuring out by the flaring acetylene lamp hung from a pole at the end of the trestle table.

It had a name. A trade name, no doubt properly registered. 'Bamberley Nutripon'. The bit she had chosen was about as long as her little finger, cream-colored and of the consistency of stale Cheddar cheese. According to the instructions on every carton it was best to boil it because that made more of the starch digestible, or triturate it in water to make a dough, then fry it in small cakes or bake it on an iron griddle.

That, though, was for later: the elaboration, the cuisine bit. What counted right now was that it could be eaten as it was, and for the first time since she came here four mortal months ago she need not feel guilty about enjoying a balanced meal in her comfortable quarters tonight, because everyone who could be found had been given enough to fill the belly. She had seen them come to the table one by one and gape at the vast quantities they were allotted: ex-soldiers shy of an arm or leg; old men with cataracts filming their eyes; mothers with little children who struggled to make their babies mumble the food because they had starved past the point at which they forgot even how to cry.

And one in particular, there in front of me, when her mother tried to rouse and feed her …

Oh, *God*! No, there can't be a god. At least none that I want to believe in. I won't accept a god who'd let a mother find her baby dead on her hip when there was food in her hand that might have saved it!

Blackness – of sky, ground, human skins – crowded in on her and built an Africa-wide torture chamber in her head.

A helpful grip enfolded her arm as she felt herself sway and a quiet voice spoke in good English.

'You have been overdoing things, I suspect, Miss Ramage!'

She blinked. It was the nice major, Hippolyte Obou, who had been educated at the Sorbonne and was reputedly no older than her own age of twenty-four. He was extremely handsome, if one discounted the tribal scars striping his cheeks, and had always appeared to maintain a detached view of the war.

Which was more than could be said for General Kaika …

But she wasn't here to take sides or criticize. She was here to pick up pieces and patch them together. And although there had been moments when it seemed the job was impossible, everyone had been fed today, food was left over for tomorrow, and another consignment was promised immediately after the new year.

A different world.

'You will come to my office for a pick-you-up,' the major said; he didn't make it a question. 'Then I will ride you back to your accommodation in my jeep.'

'There's no need to—'

But he brushed her words aside, taking her arm again, this time with a touch of gallantry. 'Ah, it is little to do for someone who has brought such a Christmas present! This way, please.'

'The office', a mere hut of planks and clay, had been one of the many head-quarters of the invaders' district commander. Fighting had continued at Noshri a week after the official armistice. Right across one wall was stitched the line of holes left by a salvo of fifty-caliber machine-gun slugs. Opposite, the corresponding line of marks had two gaps in it where the slugs had been stopped before they crossed the little room. Lucy tried not to look in that direction, because she had had to tend the obstacles.

It was terribly hot, even this long after sunset. The air was saturated with moisture. She had thought about going half-naked like the local girls, and come close to that climax. Her formal nurse's uniform had vanished within days of her arrival. Her neat new aprons had been ripped into emergency bandages, then her dresses, her caps, and even the legs of her jeans one desperate day. For weeks now she had gone about in what was left of them, threads dangling above her knees, and shirts lacking so many buttons she had to knot the tails in front. At least, though, they were regularly washed by the girl Maua – not local, some sort of camp-follower – acting as her personal maid. Never having had a servant in her life, she had at first rebelled at being given one, and still was not reconciled to the idea; however, others of the UN team had pointed out that the girl was unskilled and by taking routine tasks off her could free Lucy to make maximum use of her own training. And all this because a sea had died which she had never seen ...

At one of the two rickety tables which, apart from chairs, constituted the entire furniture of the office, a tall thin sergeant was adding up figures on a printed form. Major Obou rapped an order at him, and from a battered olive-green ammunition case he dug out a bottle of good French brandy and a tin cup. Handing Lucy two fingers of the liquor, the major raised the bottle to his broad lips.

'Here's how!' he said. 'And do sit down!'

She complied. The drink was too strong for her; after half a mouthful she set the cup on her knees and held it with both hands to stop herself trembling from fatigue. She thought of asking for water to dilute it, but decided it wouldn't be fair to involve the sergeant in that much trouble. Drinkable water was hard to find in Noshri. Rain, caught in buckets and tanks, was safe if you added a purifying tablet, but the rivers were sour with defoliants from the campaign of last summer and the invaders had filled most of the wells with carrion as they retreated.

'That should put – if you forgive the remark – a little color in your cheeks,' encouraged Major Obou. She forced a smile in reply, and wondered for the latest of many times what she should make of this handsome dark man who took such pains to salt his English with bookish idioms, right or wrong. Her eyes were very tired from the heat and dust of the day, so she closed them. But that was no help. Behind the lids she saw the sights she had encountered wherever she went in this formerly flourishing town: a crossroads where a mortar shell had exploded squarely on a bus, leaving a shallow pit hemmed with smashed metal; charred roof-beams jutting over the ashes of what had been furniture and possibly people; trees curtailed by the wing of a crashing aircraft, shot down by a patrolling fighter because it was suspected of carrying arms, though she had seen for herself it contained only medical supplies ...

She touched the base of her left thumbnail. Salvaging what she could from the wreckage, she had cut herself and had to have three stitches in the wound. A nerve had been severed, and there was a patch a quarter-inch on a side where she would never feel anything again.

At least she'd been inoculated against tetanus.

*

41

In one corner of the office a back-pack radio suddenly said something in the local language of which even yet Lucy had learned only a few words. Major Obou answered it, and rose.

'Drink up, Miss Ramage. There will be a government plane in one hour and I must be on hand. Before that I shall keep my promise to convey you home.'

'There's no need to—'

'But there is.' His face was suddenly stern. 'I know it makes no sense to lay blame at anybody's door, and the causes of our war were very complex. But the people here have understood one thing, that it was the greed and care-lessness of – forgive me – people like you which poisoned the Mediterranean and started the chain of events which led to our neighbors from the north invading us. So long as they were apathetic from hunger they were silent. Now that they have been fed, one fears that they will remember what they have been taught by agitators. I am aware that you come from New Zealand, very far away, with good motives. But a man seething with rage because he lost his home, his wife, his children, would not stop to ask where you come from if he met you in the road.'

'Yes.' Lucy gave a nod and, nearly choking, gulped down her drink.

'Splendid,' the major said, instantly his usual affable self, and ushered her outside. His jeep was waiting near the door. He gestured the driver to get in back with the machine-gunner, and took the wheel himself with Lucy at his side. Starting off with a roar, he crossed the boundary of the airstrip at nearly forty and they went bumping down the shell-pocked road to the town with all lights blazing.

'Ah, one day, Miss Ramage,' he shouted, 'when we have reconstructed the country, I hope I shall have a chance to entertain you more conventionally! Indeed I heard today one may again apply for leave. If you'd care to be shown – uh – more appetizing aspects of my homeland, I'd be delighted. One does not wish strangers to go away thinking this is the country where all the time people shoot each other, hm?'

It dawned on Lucy, belatedly because all that kind of thing seemed to belong in another universe, that he was propositioning her. She felt briefly astonished. At home one simply never came in social contact with black people, and seldom even with Maoris. Then she was annoyed at her own astonishment. She hunted for a polite way to formulate her answer, but before she managed it, when they were crossing what had been the main street of Noshri and was now an avenue of ruins, he braked abruptly.

'Ah, someone else realized it was a Christmas present we have received!'

At the side of the road a parody of a Christmas tree had been erected: branches that must have taken hours to collect because the nearby terrain had been sterilized with herbicides, tied to a pole and lit with three candles.

On a strip of white cloth, probably a bandage, someone had written VIVE LA PAIX JOYEUX NOEL.

'Are you Christian, Miss Ramage?'

Lucy was too tired to discuss theological doubts. She gave a nod. 'I also, of course.' Obou accelerated around a bend in the direction of the relatively undamaged houses that had been assigned to the overseas aid workers, UN observers, and the most senior of the government officials supervising mopping-up operations. 'You know, though, it was a strange thing when I first went to Europe, finding so few people there attend a church. Here it had always been for me and my family the – the *right* thing, the *better* thing. In the provinces, right here for example, it was known the people still made idols, still believed in ghosts and juju. But the educated people you took for granted to be Moslems or Christians. I think, though, it will now be hard for Christians in our country. Knowing it has been the greed of Christian countries which— Ah, look! See already what a change your work has made in this sad place!'

Slowing again, he waved at a group of ten or a dozen people, including a couple of women, who had lit a fire in the open air before what had once been a handsome house and were dancing in a ring, clapping their hands for music. They were all barefoot. Lucy thought one of the women must be drunk; her gaudy wraparound dress had fallen from her bosom and her slack breasts shook as she stamped and swayed.

'Ah, they're good people,' Major Obou said. 'Simple, perhaps, but good-natured. I'm so glad this damned war is over. And' – with a trace of boldness – 'glad that it has brought us friends like you from outside.'

He stopped the jeep. They had reached her quarters, one of a cluster of houses originally built by one of the Paris-based companies operating here for its lower-ranking employees. Then they had enjoyed the privacy of dense greenery. Now the shrubs and trees were gone, victims of defoliants, and the ground was newly scarred with shell-holes. When Lucy had arrived the place had stunk of carrion, mostly human. It still stank, but mainly of the exhaust of trucks and planes.

The major handed her down from the jeep with old-world formality. She almost giggled at the spectacle she must present, dirty and ragged. She was a trifle light-headed from the brandy.

'You will remember what I suggested, won't you?' he murmured, squeezing her hand. Then he let it go, saluted, and jumped back in his seat.

The maid Maua prepared a passable meal: canned beans, reconstituted eggs, canned fruit. Meantime Lucy changed her soiled clothes for a toweling robe and rubbed herself over with impregnated cleansing tissues. Water for washing was almost as scarce as that for drinking. Noises reached her as other occupants of this row of houses returned – Swedish and Czech doctors, a

Mexican agronomist and UN officials attached to the Commission on Refugees were her near neighbors. Further along were some Italian nuns. She had never become used to seeing them in shirts and pants but still with their funny coifs on top. What for? To discourage the attention of men?

Which, as she picked at her food, reminded her. Obou had extended an invitation. She didn't feel inclined to accept. Why not – because he was black? She thought not. She hoped not. Because right now she couldn't think of anything like that with real attention? Very likely. The major, after all, was good-looking, well educated, obviously intelligent if he spoke both French and English as well as his mother tongue …

Mother!

Her stomach suddenly convulsed. It was the worst thing to remember while eating. Blindly she ran for the latrine at the back of the house, and there wasted the food she had forced down. Maybe, she thought as she knelt retching, it wasn't the memory which nauseated me, but too much brandy. It made no difference.

So many of those children: dead at birth, mercifully because they were deformed! You'd think that after Vietnam … But people don't think, most of the time. Riot gases, tear smoke, sleep gas, defoliants, nerve gas, all the armory of chemicals used in modern war, had saturated the tissues of these people as they had the ground. Once she had delivered three malformed babies in succession among a party of refugees who thought they had found safety at last. But along the way they had sustained themselves on leaves and roots.

She stumbled back eventually, not to the room where she had been eating but to the bedroom, and fell into a stuporous slumber.

Thinking, in the dead middle of the night, that the noise she was hearing belonged to nightmare – her dreams were regularly haunted by the fear that fighting might break out anew – she forced herself awake. Found she was awake. The noise was real. Gunfire.

Horrified, she sat up and strained her ears. The room was absolutely dark, the windows curtained. Her instant of panic passed. There were indeed shots to be heard, but there was a random, almost a cheerful quality to the rattling racket, like strings of firecrackers. Also, at the very edge of hearing, she could discern drumming – possibly even singing. She made to inch her way toward the window, and was immediately distracted by the discovery that her thighs were wet. Christ. Her period had begun. Funnily, since coming to Noshri, she had stopped suffering the advance warning pains she had been accustomed to at home, as though her mind were so taken up with matters of life and death she had no attention to spare for the complaints of her own body.

She found tissues to wipe herself and called for Maua. Waiting for the maid to enter, she went to the window overlooking the town and peered past the curtains. Oh, yes. Bonfires. Wasteful, but excusable. Liquor had been concealed somewhere, no doubt – she'd seen that drunken woman dancing – or possibly made from garbage. And with Christmas so close …

Bonfires?

The patterns of light suddenly acquired perspective. The yellow flames were not small and near, but far and huge. In the direction of the airstrip.

A plane burning!

'Maua!' she cried, and ran in search of the flashlight she kept by her bed. Finding it, she hurried to the lean-to room where the girl slept. The pallet there was empty.

'Oh, Christ!' Lucy whispered.

She dashed back to the bedroom, intending to seize clothes, Tampax, the little .22 pistol her father had given her which she'd never used. But a moment later there was a slam from the living-room as the outer door was flung open, and she settled for just the gun. She still had on the toweling robe she had slumped asleep in.

Mouth dry, hands shaking, she switched off the flashlight and crept on silent bare feet to the living room.

'Hands up!' she shouted, switching on the torch again, and was instantly appalled by the way her finger was tightening on the trigger. Across the threshold lay a form which mingled khaki, dark-brown, bright-red. The red was blood. It was Major Obou, sprawled on his belly, his right hand limp beside his automatic, his left shoulder slashed to the bone.

'Major?' she tried to, say, and found her voice wasn't there. She saw his good hand, like a colossal spider, scrabbling for the lost gun.

'Major Obou!'

He heard her and rolled his head on the reed matting of the floor. '*Vaut rien,*' he said thickly, and corrected himself. 'No good. No more bullet.'

'But what's happening?' She put down her own gun and stooped with her flashlight playing on his wound, her mind spinning with thirty different things each as urgent as another: call out her neighbor the Swedish doctor, cleanse the cut, close the outside door, make sure he hadn't been followed by his attacker …

He summoned a supreme effort and seized her by the wrist as she made to rise and shut the door.

'Don't go out, miss! Don't go there! All mad, all crazy! Look, my arm! One of my men did that, my own men! See, I caught him take bowl food from widow with baby, and corporal say it third time tonight, so I order with my gun give back, go find more at airstrip for poor others he rob. Right for officer to say, no? Your food not for soldiers, for poor starve devils in town! So he took that axe and hit me, see? Oh, but it hurts!'

'Let me get bandages!' Lucy cried, but he seemed not to hear. Large, staring, his eyes were fixed on nowhere. He tightened his grip and words poured out frantically, his careful European syntax giving way to the grammar of his own language.

'No, not go! Gone crazy, say! Shout the town is full ghosts, ghosts everywhere, shoot at them, fire guns all time at shadow, anything! Say kill ghosts, kill ghosts, *kill kill ghosts!*'

Outside there were footsteps. Lucy tried again to release her hand so she could close the door, failed, and thought at least of switching off the flashlight so that would not attract a mad prowler. What Obou had said made no sense, but the firing was louder and closer and through the open door she could see that more and still more flames were springing up, as though the town were turning into a volcano.

Footsteps again. Nearer. And her 22 was out of reach and Obou's gun was empty. At first gently, then in growing panic, she fought to make him let go. A new bright light shone in the doorway. The instant before it dazzled her she saw a white man in a white shirt holding a pistol; the instant after, she realized what the torch-beam would show – a white girl in the grip of a black man, her thighs apart and smeared with blood, a case of rape.

She started to shout, 'Don't—!'

And was too late. The gun exploded. The bullet spattered her with bits of Obou.

Later someone kept trying to say to her – it was the Swedish doctor, Bertil – 'But we didn't know you were here! When the trouble started we saw Maua and she swore you weren't in the house. We went down into the town, and all these madmen came at us with guns and hatchets, screaming that we were evil ghosts, kill the ghosts!'

I heard that before. Listless, Lucy rocked back and forth, eyes shut, right hand mechanically rubbing the spot on her left arm where she had been given some sort of injection, the two rhythms crisscrossing the lilt of Bertil's accent.

'Be glad you didn't see what we saw: the whole town gone insane, looting and burning and killing!'

The person I saw killing was you. You shot a nice man. I was going on leave with him. I liked his smile. He had a round dark face with funny stripes on his cheeks. He's dead. You killed him.

She moaned and fell to the floor.

JANUARY

MARCHING ORDERS

Go ye and bring the Light
To savage strands afar.
Take ye the Law of Right
Where'er the unblest are.

* Heathens and stubborn Jews,
Lovers of Juggernaut,
Give them the chance to choose
That which the Saviour taught.

Go where the gentle Lord
Is still as yet unknown,
There where the tribes ignored
Strive in the dark alone.

Arm ye to face the foe,
Carib and cannibal,
Men who must live as low
As any animal.

* Cover the naked limb,
Shoe ye the unshod foot,
Silence the pagan hymn,
Conquer the godless brute.

Tell them the news of Love,
Preach them the Prince of Peace,
Tear down their pagan grove,
Give them divine release.

> *– The Sacred Sower: Being a Collection of Hymns and*
> *Devout Songs Adapted to the Use of Missionary Societies,* 1887;
> verses marked* may be omitted if desired.

ABOVE THE SOUND OF SPEED

RM-1808, out of Phoenix for Seattle, had reported acute catting – clear air turbulence – in the vicinity of Salt Lake City. Hearing of this, the navigator of TW-6036, the Montreal–Los Angeles direct SST, punched the keys of his computer and passed a course-correction to the pilot. Then he leaned back to resume his snooze.

They would be super for over a thousand miles yet.

SNOW JOB

Disregarded, the twenty-nine-inch color TV displayed images of today's violence. The camera lingeringly swept the gutters of far-off Noshri, pausing occasionally at corpses. A dog, miraculous survivor of the period last summer when people had paid a hundred local francs for a rat, fifty for a handful of mealies, was seen snuffling the body of a child, and a tall black soldier broke its back with the butt of his carbine.

'Shit! You see what that black mother did to that poor dog?'

'What?'

But the screen had switched to the wreckage of a plane.

This was Towerhill, latest of the prosperous winter-sports resorts of Colorado, and they were in the Apennine Lodge, smartest and most expensive of its accommodations. Brand-new, the place struggled hard to appear old. Skis hung from plastic beams, a simulated log fire burned in a stone hearth. Beyond a double-glazed window taking up most of one wall powerful arc lights played on a magnificent dark-striped snow-slope running nearly to the crest of Mount Hawes. Until last year, although this town was barely fifty miles from Denver, the road had been bad and only a handful of visitors had chanced on it. The increasing tendency for people to take mountain vacations, however, since the sea had become too filthy to be tolerable, could not be ignored. The road now was excellent and the area had exploded. There were three ultramodern ski-lifts and a branch of Puritan Health Supermarkets. There were facilities for skijoring behind snowmobiles and Colorado Chemical Bank planned to double the size of its operation here. One could go skating and curling and American Express had taken up its option on some offices. Next year they promised a ski-jump of Olympic standard.

On the screen a group of men, women and children were shown shivering outside a cluster of improbably-shaped buildings. They were poorly dressed but on average rather good-looking. Meantime police with dogs conducted a search.

Oh. Trainites. What the hell?

After his second drink Bill Chalmers was feeling better. It had been a filthy day: driving to Denver this morning over roads that had been ploughed and sanded but were still slithery; sweating out that awful lunch at the Masons', aware of 'an atmosphere' but unable to pin down the cause; breaking it up finally when their son Anton, six, had a row with the Mason kids aged five and four and ran away screaming …

But they were back safely, and he liked Towerhill: its air of affluence which was a snook cocked at the prophets of doom, its enclosing mountains, its unbelievably blessedly fresh air. One saw big-city visitors, their first day, going out in filtermasks, not convinced they were okay without them.

The screen showed a map of Central America with an arrow pointing to somewhere, then photographs of two men, both white.

'Tania!'

'Yes, I'd love another,' his wife said, and went right on comparing symptoms with the lawyer's wife from Oakland she'd met yesterday. 'Now me, I had this funny rash, and a prickly feeling all over …'

Christ! Can't anybody talk about anything these days except allergies and neuroses? Once a man could be satisfied to be a breadwinner. Now he has to be a medicine-winner as well. And it never does any good.

'Yes, well!' the lawyer's wife said. 'Now I got this hot-and-cold feeling, and sometimes actual dizziness.'

Abruptly he realized they were talking about pregnancy, and instead of fuming he found himself shivering. Of course he'd taken out abnormality insurance when Anton was on the way, but despite his position with Angel City it hadn't come cheap, and when Anton had been safely delivered Tom Grey had told him just what odds they had been bucking. Words reheard in memory made him tremble: cystic fibrosis, phenylketonuria, hemophilia, hypothyroidism, mongolism, Tetralogy of Fallot, alexia, dichromatism … A list that went on forever, as though it were a miracle anyone at all became a normal adult!

It made one understand why Grey was a bachelor. He himself wouldn't risk a second kid.

The TV went over to sports results. For the first time several people paid it full attention. *'Tania!'*

She finally turned. The lawyer's wife escaped to join her husband on the far side of the room.

'Did you have that heart-to-heart with Denise?'

'Oh, God,' Tania said, leaning back and crossing her arms. 'So that was why you brought us here – to spy on the Masons!'

'It was not!'

'Then what in hell makes it so urgent? You don't have to be back at the office before Monday! And why didn't you ask me in the car instead of snapping my head off every time I spoke?'

All around, their attention caught by voices sharpening toward the pitch of a quarrel, people were turning to look. Hideously embarrassed, Chalmers adopted a conciliatory manner.

'Tania honey, I'm sorry, but it *is* important.'

'Obviously! More important than me or Tony! More important than my first chance in years to relax and make some new friends! Look what you've done – chased Sally away!'

He just sat there.

After a moment, however, she relented. Four years ago they had been through the unemployable stage; she knew what it would mean to lose his job.

'Oh, hell … Yes, I wormed it out of her. She's a crank. Practically a Trainite.'

Chalmers pricked up his ears. 'How do you mean?'

'A crank, like I say. Won't let him fly. Says she wants her grandchildren to see the sun. What difference it makes if a plane flies with one seat empty, *I* don't know! But she thinks Phil's in some kind of trouble because she made him drive to LA, only he won't come out and put the blame squarely on her. And she wants desperately to know what the problem is. In fact she brought the matter up. I didn't have to. Because he was awful over Christmas, apparently. What's more he keeps finding excuses not to screw her. Wouldn't have made it even on New Year's, she said, not unless she'd actually *seduced* him—'

The last word was drowned out by a sudden thudding noise from the sky, as though a giant had clapped hands around a mosquito. Everyone winced. An anonymous voice said, 'Oh, a filthy sonic boom. Don't you hate them?'

But it should have been over in an instant. It continued: after the initial bang, a growling sound, lower-pitched, but enduring, like stones being rubbed by the current of a fast river or a vigorous tide on a pebbly headland. Poised to renew their conversation, people realized that this wasn't right. The noise grew louder, grinding. They turned and looked at the window.

Tania screamed.

With implacable majesty, to the beating of countless drums, half a million tons of snow and ice were marching on the town of Towerhill.

CHARGE ACCOUNT

Reporter: General, it's no exaggeration to say the world has been appalled at your decision to arrest and expel the American relief workers from Noshri—

General Kaika: Do you expect us to let them remain when they have poisoned thousands of our people, killed them or, worse still, driven them mad?

Reporter: There's no proof that—

General Kaika: Yes, there is proof. All the people of the town went mad. They attacked our own troops who had freed them from the occupying forces. They were poisoned by the evil food sent under the pretence of relief supplies.

Reporter: But what conceivable motive could—?

General Kaika: Plenty of motive. For one thing, Americans go to any length to prevent an independent country whose government does not have white skin. Colored governments must bow to Washington. Consider China. Consider Vietnam, Cambodia, Laos, Thailand, Ceylon, Indonesia. If ever we have a strong united country of black people in Africa they will no longer be able to tread down their black countrymen.

Reporter: Are you saying there was a deliberate plot to weaken your forces and win the war for the invaders?

General Kaika: I am making investigations to confirm. But it is white men who made the war to start with.

Reporter: There weren't even any white mercenaries with the—

General Kaika: Was it black men who filled the Mediterranean with poison? No, it was destroyed by the filthy wastes from European factories!

Reporter: Well, the Aswan dam—

General Kaika: Yes, yes, the Aswan dam may have tipped the balance finally, but before that the sea was dying. Because so many had to starve on the African coast there began this war. That is why I say the white countries are responsible. It is the typical white habit to ruin what you have and then go to steal from other people.

Reporter: Oh, General, you're stretching the facts a bit!

General Kaika: Is the fact that it is dangerous to swim in the Mediterranean? Is the fact that the fish have died?

Reporter: Well, yes, but—

General Kaika: I have no more to say.

RATS

Jeannie was already home, of course, her Stephenson electric tucked into a corner of the garage. Pete was on the ten-to-six shift today and her job at Bamberley's stopped at five.

Pete Goddard hated his wife going to work. He wanted her at home, looking after a couple of kids. That, though, would have to wait until after his next promotion. These days nobody in his right mind would start a family before he could afford proper medical care for his children. Up here in the mountains it wasn't so bad as in the cities; even so you couldn't be too careful.

As he scraped his boots before treading on the front step, there was a slamming sound in the sky. He glanced up just in time to meet an eyeful of snow shaken off the overhang of the porch. Ah, shit, a sonic boom. Oughtn't to have been that loud! One grew used to one or two a day, but faint, far away, doing no damage beyond maybe startling you into spilling a cup of coffee. Down at the station house Sergeant Chain could look forward to a rash of complaints. As though there were anything the police here could do. As though there were anything anybody could do.

Jeannie was in the kitchen. Not much of a kitchen, equipped with repossessed appliances. But they usually worked. She was busy at the stove: a pretty girl, much lighter than he and a year older, bound to be plump before thirty but what the hell? He liked plenty of meat. Blowing her a kiss, he collected his evening pill, the one for his allergy, and headed for the sink to draw some water.

But she stopped him with a cry. 'No, Pete! I found a don't-drink notice when I got home. See, on the table?'

Startled, he turned and spotted the bright red paper printed in bold black letters. The familiar phrases leapt out at him: *fault in the purifying plant – must not be drunk without boiling – rectified as soon as possible …*

'Shit!' he exclaimed. 'It's getting to be as bad as Denver!'

'Oh, no, honey! Down in the city they get these all the time, like every week, and that's only our second since the summer. Won't a beer do?'

'A beer? Sure it will!'

'In the icebox. And one for me. I got this complicated recipe going.' She brandished a clipping from the newspaper.

Grinning, he made to comply – and his hand flew to his hip after his not-present gun as he exclaimed in dismay.

'What?' Jeannie spun around. 'Oh, not another rat?'

'Just the biggest I ever saw!' But it was gone now. 'I thought I told you to call the exterminator!' he snapped.

'Well, I did! But he said he has so much business we'll have to wait at least another week.'

'Yeah, I guess so.' Pete sighed. 'Everybody I meet ...' He let the words trail away and opened the icebox. On two shelves, packages with a familiar trade mark: a girl holding an ear of corn between her tits, to make a sort of prick-and-balls pattern of them.

'Hey, you been to Puritan again!'

'Well, I spent my bonus,' Jeannie said defensively. 'And things there aren't that much more expensive! Besides, they do really taste much better.'

'What bonus?'

'Oh, you know! I told you! All us girls in the packing section who worked overtime to get that shipment away before Christmas. Twenty bucks extra from Mr Bamberley!'

'Oh. Oh, yeah.' Taking his beer and hers from the six-pack. What the hell? Twenty bucks today was a spit in the ocean. Though he would rather have put it toward their policy with Angel City, saving against the time when they could afford a baby. All these scare stories about chemicals! Just an excuse to double the prices at Puritan ...

Reminded of the plant, though: 'Say, baby, how's your leg?' That smooth patch of skin, as though part of her thigh had been glazed.

'Oh, they were right first time. It is a fungus. You know we have to wear masks against actino-what's-its-name. I picked up something of the same kind. But the ointment's fixing it.'

Pete repressed a shudder. Catching a fungus! Christ, like something out of a horror movie! It had dragged on for more than a month, and even now he kept finding himself obsessively inspecting his own body. He gulped at his beer.

'Say, honey, I meant to tell you,' Jeannie said suddenly. 'I saw you on TV!'

'What, at the Trainite wat?' He dropped into a chair. 'Yes, I noticed the guy with the camera.'

'What were you there for?'

'Didn't they explain?'

'I only switched on in time to catch the end of it.'

'Ah-hah. Well, we had this call from LA. Remember the cat who used to run the wat was killed down there before Christmas? Seems he was either crazy or stoned. So they said turn the place over for drugs.'

'I thought Trainites didn't hold with them.'

'Well, it's true we didn't find anything ... Weird place, baby! All like fixed up from scrap. Kind of handmade. And the people kind of – I don't know. Odd!'

'I saw some of them at Puritan,' Jeannie said. 'They looked pretty ordinary. And their kids are very well behaved.'

Too soon to talk about the best way to raise kids. Some day, though ...

'They may look harmless,' Pete said. 'But that's because here there aren't enough to cause real trouble. I mean like apart from painting up these dirty skulls and crossbones. Down in LA, though, they block streets, wreck cars, smash up stores!'

'But Carl says everything they do is meant to wake people up to the danger we're in.'

Oh, the hell with Carl! But Pete kept that to himself, knowing how fond Jeannie was of him: her younger brother, nineteen going on twenty, the bright one of their family of five kids who'd dropped out of college after a year complaining of lousy teaching and was currently also working at the Bamberley plant.

'Look, any way they want to live is fine by me,' he grunted. 'But it's my job to stop anybody wrecking or looting or interfering with the way *other* people want to live.'

'Well, Carl's been to the wat several times and according to him— Oh, let's not argue!' Consulting her recipe. 'Well, we have to wait ten minutes now, it says. Let's go into the living room and sit down ...' Her face clouded. 'Know something, honey?'

'What?'

'I do wish I had one of those instant cookers. Microwave. Then it wouldn't matter when you came in, dinner could be ready in a moment.'

The phone rang.

'Go sit down. I'll get it,' she said. He grinned at her and obeyed. But, even before he'd made himself comfortable, she was calling to him in a near-scream.

'Pete! Pete! Get your coat and boots!'

'What? What the hell for?'

'There's been an avalanche! It's buried all those new places the other side of town!'

NO BIGGER THAN A MAN'S HAND

... published today as a United Nations Special Report. The alleged rise of intelligence in so-called backward countries is ascribed by the scientists who conducted the three-year investigation to improved diet and sanitation, while the as-yet unconfirmed decline in advanced nations is attributed to intensified pollution. Asked to comment on the report just prior to leaving for Hollywood, where he is tonight slated to open his annual retrospective, Prexy said, quote, Well, if they're so smart why aren't they clever? End quote. At a press conference in Tegucigalpa the disappearance of Leonard Ross, field agent for Globe Relief, and Dr Isaiah Williams, the British medico who's also unaccounted for, was officially ascribed today to terrorism. Troops are searching the area intensively, but so far have reported no success. Following the shock resignation of the former

president of the 'Save the Med' Fund, Dottore Giovanni Crespinolo, the Italian government has flatly denied his charge that the vast sums donated by corporations and individuals in forty-eight countries in the hope of saving the doomed landlocked sea have been embezzled. Reports from Rome, however ...

MEMENTO LAURAE

Never in his life had Philip Mason felt so miserable. He paced endlessly around the apartment, snapping at the children, telling Denise to leave him alone for God's sake, when all the time what he really wanted to say was that he loved them desperately and always would.

Yet the consequences of New Year's Eve ...

When he felt depressed at the last place, things had been easier to bear: a house, much further from the city center – beyond the river – with its own garden. There he'd been able to hide away and be miserable by himself. But the river fires had been bad last year; more than once he'd been unable to get to work because the bridge was closed, and half the time smoke made it impossible to use the garden or even open the windows.

So they'd moved to this air-conditioned apartment block. Handier for the office. And, of course, for the hospital where Josie's squint was being treated and the short muscles in Harold's leg were being drawn out.

He couldn't explain! Dared not! And now couldn't get out of explaining, either!

But at least he had a few minutes to himself. The kids were asleep, having taken a long time to calm down following their disastrous encounter with Anton Chalmers: pushy, arrogant, greedy, bullying, bad-tempered – but, of course, absolutely healthy. 'Survival of the fittest and all that shit' ... to quote his insufferable father.

And Denise had gone to the Henlowes' apartment on the second floor. That was where you scored in this building. Everyone nowadays seemed to know a means of getting something from somebody. But it was best to stay out on the fringes. It was becoming as bad as what the history books recounted about Prohibition, what with the black gangs fighting on the streets over the right to distribute African khat, and the white gangs blowing up each other's homes for the right to trade in Mexican grass.

So she'd come back in half an hour, having socialized, and show what she'd got, and say, 'Darling, don't worry, whatever's the matter it'll come right in the end, let's turn on and relax, hm?'

Dennie, I love you terribly, and if you're sweet and kind to me one more time tonight I shall scream.

*

Here was the phone. He dialed with shaking fingers, and shortly a woman replied. He said, 'Dr Clayford, please. It's urgent.'

'Dr Clayford will be in his office on Monday as usual,' the woman replied.

'This is Philip Mason. Area manager of—'

'Oh, Mr Mason!' Abruptly cordial. Clayford was one of the physicians Philip sent Angel City's clients to for examination prior to taking out a life policy; it behooved the doctor to be cooperative. 'Just a second, I'll see if my husband's free.'

'Thank you.' Nervous, he fumbled out a cigarette. His smoking had nearly doubled since his trip to LA. He'd been trying to cut it down; instead, here he was getting through two packs a day.

'Yes?' A gruff voice. He started.

'Ah, doctor!' One didn't say 'doc' to Clayford, let alone call him by his first name. He was an old-fashioned family GP, who at sixty still affected the dark suits and white shirts that had marked out sober young men with 'a great future ahead of them' when he was in college. Talking to him was a little like talking to a minister; one felt a sense of distance, an intangible barrier. But right now it had to be breached.

'Look, I need your advice, and – uh – help.'

'Well?'

Philip swallowed hard. 'It's like this. Just before Christmas I was called to LA, to the headquarters of my company, and because my wife doesn't like planes – you know, pollution – I drove, and broke the trip in Vegas. And there I – uh – well, I got involved with a girl. Absolutely without meaning to. Time and opportunity, you know!'

'So?'

'So … Well, I wasn't certain until days later, but now I don't think there's any doubt. She left me with – uh – gonorrhea.'

Stained undershorts floating around him, like mocking bats.

'I see.' Clayford not in the least sympathetic. 'Well, you should go to the clinic on Market, then. I believe they're open Saturday mornings.' Philip had seen it, in a depressed and depressing area: ashamed of its function, persecuted by the righteous majority, always full of young people pretending rebellious defiance.

'But surely, doctor—'

'Mr Mason, that's my professional advice, and there's an end of it.'

'But my wife!'

'Have you had relations with her since this escapade of yours?'

'Well, on New Year's—' Philip began, head full of all the reasons: can't not, this is *the* day of the year, it's kind of symbolic and we've made a tradition of it since we first met …

'Then you'll have to take her with you,' Clayford said, and didn't even add a good night.

*

The bastard! The filthy stuck-up stiff-necked—!

Oh, what's the use?

He set down the phone, thinking of all the suggestions he'd had ready: a white lie, say about hepatitis which everyone knew to be endemic in California, anything that might require a short course of a suitable antibiotic …

My God! All I have is the second commonest infectious disease after measles! It says so in the papers all the time.

Distraction. Anything. Switch on the TV. Maybe the doctor at the clinic will be more helpful and I'll still be able to cover up. If I only had to confess about screwing Laura that'd be okay, Denise wouldn't leave me over that. But telling her she's been given the clap courtesy of a man-hungry stranger …!

Transistorized, the sound came on quicker than the picture, and his ears suddenly stung with the sense of what was being said. It was the late news summary. He felt as though the earth had opened and he was falling, miles deep.

'– still coming in about the extent of tonight's avalanche disaster at Towerhill.'

The picture jelled. Police cars. Searchlights. Helicopters. Fire trucks. Ambulances. Bulldozers. Snowplows.

'The Apennine Lodge, which stood right here, is totally buried,' a voice said in doom-laden tones. A shapeless mass of snow with men digging. 'Other nearby lodges and hotels were carried downhill, some for a quarter of a mile. Damage will certainly be in excess of fifteen million and may well run as high as fifty million dollars—'

'Phil, I'm back!' Denise called, having worked her way through the complex locks of the entrance door. 'Say, I managed to score from Jed and Beryl, and—'

'There's been an avalanche at Towerhill!' he shouted.

'What?' She advanced into the living-room, a slim girl with delicate bones, a graceful walk, an auburn wig that exactly matched her former mop of curls and completely hid her ringworm scars. Sometimes Philip thought she was the most beautiful woman he had ever seen.

'Oh, lord,' she said thinly. On the screen, a body being lifted out of dirty snow. 'That's where Bill and Tania are staying!' She sat down automatically on the arm of his chair. He clutched her fingers and spoke through terror, despair, nausea.

'They said fifteen million bucks' worth of damage, maybe fifty. And you know who carries their insurance? We do!'

She looked at him, shocked. 'Phil, think of the damage when you get back to the office! You should call up, find out if Bill and Tania are okay, and Anton too. Right now you ought to be worrying about people, not money!'

'I am. You and me.'

'Phil—'

'I haven't finished reinsuring that place. I had so much new business to cope with. And not one of my staff has made it through the winter without falling sick. I only had about half the risk reinsured.'

Comprehension dawned, and a look of horror.

'I'm through,' Philip said. 'God, I wish I were dead.'

AHEAD OF THE NEWS

'Globe Relief? Mr Thorne, please,' said the State Department expert in Central American affairs, and then: 'Morning, Gerry – Dirk here. Say, how's your eye? ... That's good ... Me? I'm fine. Touch of mono is all. Well, why I'm calling up, I thought you'd like to be among the first to know they found your boy Ross. Washed up on a rock alongside that river that runs through San Pablo ... No, no sign of the English doctor yet ... Well, they say his head was battered in. It could have been on the rocks of the river, but they're doing an autopsy to confirm ... Yes, with luck. Those stinking Tupas have had it all their own way for far too long. We finally have the excuse to hit back. I'll keep you posted.'

IT FIGURES

The armed guards who patrolled the headquarters of Angel City Interstate Mutual over the dead ten-day period of the holiday were surprised to find one of the corporation's senior executives keeping them company.

But not surprised that the man in question should be Dr Thomas Grey. From him they were used to eccentricity.

'Crazy!' people said, and were happy to assume that because he was so devoted to his profession he had never even married he must necessarily be a crank.

In fact, that was extremely unfair to him. He was probably among the most rational men alive.

'To the editor of *The Christian Science Monitor*: Sir ...'

His typing was, as always, impeccable, the envy of professional secretaries. He sat in the near-silence of the fourth floor, surrounded by the metal carcasses of computers.

'One is dismayed to find a journal with an international reputation echoing the cries of what I have no hesitation in calling scare-mongers – people who apparently would have us revert to the wild state without even the caveman's privilege of wearing furs.'

He glanced around to confirm that no malfunction lamps were shining, and took the opportunity to scratch himself. He had a slight but nagging dermatitis due to washing-powder enzymes.

'Admittedly, we alter the order of things by the way we live. But the same can be said of any organism. How many of those who cry out for vast sums to be spent on preserving coral reefs from starfish realize that the reefs are themselves the result of a living species' impact on the ecology of the planet? Grass completely revolutionized the "balance of nature"; so did the evolution of trees. Every plant, every animal, every fish – one might safely say every humble microorganism, too – has a discernible influence on the world.'

A light winked at him. He broke off, went to change a spool of tape, returned to his chair. Having read once more through the editorial in the *Monitor* which had so offended him – it might, in his view, have been written by that bigot Austin Train himself – he sharpened the next barb of his reply.

'If the extremists had their way, we would sit and mope, resigned to having four out of five children die because the nuts and berries within walking distance had been frosted.'

He was only passing time by writing this letter; he did not expect it to do any good. What he was chiefly here for was to add a few more tiny bricks to the monumental structure of a private undertaking he had been engaged on for years. Having begun as a hobby, it had developed into something approaching an obsession, and constituted the main reason why he was still working for Angel City. The company had a lot of spare computer capacity; right now, there was a nationwide glut of it. Accordingly no one objected when he made use of it on evenings and weekends. He had been well paid for most of his working life, and thanks to having simple tastes he was now rich. But hiring the computer capacity he currently needed would wipe out his fortune in a month.

Of course he scrupulously reimbursed the firm for the materials be used, the tape, the paper and the power.

His project stemmed from the fact that, being a very rational man indeed, he could become nearly as angry as a dedicated Trainite when the most spectacular fruit of some promising new human achievement turned out to be a disaster. Computers, he maintained, had made it possible for virtually every advance to be studied beforehand in enough model situations to allow of sober, constructive exploitation. Of course, renting them was expensive – but so was hiring lawyers to defend you if you were charged with infringing the Environment Acts: so was fighting an FDA ban; so was a suit from some injured nobody with a strong pressure-group at his back. And when you added money spent on vain attempts to shut the stable door by such organizations as Earth Community Chest, Globe Relief or the 'Save the Med' Fund, the total cost became heartbreaking. What a waste!

When, at thirty-three, he had abandoned his former career as a freelance R&D consultant and decided to train as an actuary, he had vaguely hoped that an insurance company, being concerned with the effects of human shortsightedness, might set up a special department to foster his project and pay for proper staff. That hadn't worked out. It had had to remain effectively a one-man show.

So he was a long, long way from his ultimate goal: nothing less than a world-simulation program.

But he was a patient man, and the shock of such catastrophes as the creation of the Mekong Desert had brought more and more people around to the conclusion he had reached long ago. Whether or not it could be done, it absolutely *must* be done.

Of course, he was in the same predicament as weather forecasters had been before computers, continually overwhelmed by fresh data that required slow, piecemeal processing. But he had already worked out many trial-and-error techniques for automatically updating his program, and in another twenty years ... He enjoyed good health, and watched his diet carefully.

Besides, he wasn't after perfect accuracy. Something about as precise as weather forecasting would suit admirably. Just so long as it permitted men who were neither reckless nor cowardly to monitor human progress. (He often used the word in conversation. Many of his acquaintances regarded him as old-fashioned because of it.)

When someone next complains that the use of insecticides has resulted in an orchard-bred pest eating his magnolias, remind him that but for the improved diet made possible when the orchards were cleared of maggots he might not own a garden to plant magnolias in. Verb. sap.

Yours, etc.,
T.M. Grey,
Ph.D., M.Sc.

COME CLEAN

One thing you can tell right away about the owner of a Hailey. He has a healthy respect for other people.
A Hailey takes up no more of the road than is necessary.
The noise a Hailey makes is only a gentle hum.
And it leaves the air far cleaner than gas-driven cars.
Even if they are filter-tipped.
So the driver of a Hailey can get close enough to other people to see their smiles

and hear their murmurs of approval What's your car doing for interpersonal relations?

YOU DIG

The shovel bit in, carried away another cubic foot or so of snow – and there wasn't anywhere to put it except on top of more snow.

Still, at least he hadn't hit a body when he plunged it in.

Pete Goddard ached. Or rather, what he could feel of himself ached. It had started in his soles when he'd been in the snow for half an hour. Then it had crept up to his ankles. Around the time the pain infected his calves he'd lost contact with his feet. He had to take it for granted they were still inside his boots.

Also his hands were tender and assured of blisters despite his gloves. It was down to twenty with a vicious wind; his eyes were sore and if the tears that leaked from them hadn't been salty he believed they would have frozen on his cheeks.

This was a foretaste of hell. Stark lights, harsh as curses, had been dragged up treacherous snow-mounds, coupled to emergency generators whose complaints at overload filled the air with a noise like grinding teeth. All the time there were shouts: 'Here, quick!' And every shout meant another victim, most likely dead, but sometimes with a broken back, broken leg, broken pelvis. The avalanche had operated like a press. It had condensed the buildings closest to Mount Hawes into a state akin to fiberboard: human remains, structural timbers, cars, winter-sports gear, food, liquor, furniture, carpets, more human remains, had been squashed together until they could be crushed no further, and then the whole horrible disgusting mass had been forced downhill to transfer the shock to more distant locations.

Red among the snow here. He burrowed with his fingers for fear his shovel might hurt someone, and discovered a side of beef.

'Hey! Mister policeman!'

A kid's voice. For an instant he was haunted by the fear of standing on a buried child. But the call was from here on the surface, loud to overcome the drone of a helicopter. He glanced up. Facing him, balanced on a broken wall, a light-colored boy of eleven or twelve, wearing dark woolen pants and a parka and offering a tin cup that steamed like a geyser.

'Like some soup?'

Pete's stomach reminded him suddenly that he'd been on the point of eating when he left home. He dropped his shovel.

'Sure would,' he agreed. This was no place for a kid – no telling what horrors he might see – but getting food down him was a good idea. It was bound to be a long job. He took the cup and made to sip, but the soup was hotter even than it looked. The kid was carrying a big vacuum-jug behind him on a strap. Must be efficient.

'You found many dead people?' the boy inquired.

'A few,' Pete muttered.

'I never saw anybody dead before. Now I've seen maybe a dozen.'

His tone was matter-of-fact, but Pete was shocked. After a pause he said, 'Uh – I guess your mom knows you're here?'

'Sure, that's her soup. When she heard about the accident she put on a big pan of it and told us all to wrap up warm and come and help.'

Well, okay; you don't tell other people what's good and what's bad for their kids. And it was kind of a constructive action. Pete tried the soup again, found it had cooled quickly in the bitter wind, and swallowed greedily. It was delicious, with big chunks of vegetables in it and strong-scented herbs.

'I was interested to see the dead people,' the kid said suddenly. 'My father was killed the other day.'

Pete blinked at him.

'Not my real father. I called him that because he adopted me. And my two sisters. It was in the papers, and they even put his picture on TV.'

'What does your mom use for this soup?' Pete said, thinking to change a ghoulish subject. 'It's great.'

'I'll tell her you said so. It's like yeast extract, and any vegetables around, and' – the boy gave a strangely adult shrug – 'water, boiled up with marjoram and stuff … Finished?'

'Not quite.'

'I only have this one cup, you see, so after it's been drunk from I have to clean it in the snow to kill the germs and go find someone else.' The boy's tone was virtuous. 'Did you see my dad's picture on TV?'

'Ah …' Pete's mind raced. 'Well, I don't get to watch it too much, you know. I'm pretty tied up with my job.'

'Yeah, sure! Just thought you might have *seen* him.' A hint of unhappiness tinged the words. 'I miss him a lot … Finished now?'

Pete drained the mug and gave it back. 'You tell your mom she makes great soup, okay?' he said, and clapped the boy's shoulder. At the back of his mind he was thinking about Jeannie; she being so much lighter than he, their kids ought to come out just about the same shade as this boy here. If only they were equally bright, equally healthy …

'Sure will,' the boy said, and added, struck by a thought, 'Say, you need anyone else up here? You're working pretty much on your own, aren't you?'

'Well, we have to spread out because there are so many places to dig,' Pete said. He was never at ease talking to children, having had problems when he

THE SHEEP LOOK UP

was a kid himself. His father hadn't died and made the papers, but simply vanished.

'Well, there's lots of us down by the ambulances.'

'Us?'

'Sure. We're from the Trainite wat my dad used to run before he died. I'll send someone up to help you – Harry, maybe. He's big. What's your name, so he'll know who to come to?'

'Uh … I'm Pete. Pete Goddard.'

'I'm Rick Jones. Okay, someone will be along in a minute!'

'Hey!'

But the kid had gone scrambling and leaping down the trenched mounds of snow. Pete reclaimed his shovel, alarmed. Only this morning at the wat he'd had to guard the occupants as they stood out in the cold while detectives searched for drugs. Having a Trainite partner him …

The hell with it. What mattered was to pull out any more poor bastards who might be buried under this load of white shit.

It was okay. Harry wasn't one of the people he'd met this morning. He wasn't too much bigger than Pete, but he was fresher. He hardly said more than hello before he started shifting snow, and they concentrated on the job until they uncovered their first victim: dead, blue with cyanosis and cold. Stretcher-bearers came, and a young Air Force officer – they'd turned out the Academy, of course – took particulars of the ID in the man's pocket. He was local. Pete had given him a parking ticket once. One of the stretcher-bearers had a transistor radio, and while it was in earshot it said something about Towerhill being declared a disaster zone.

'First of many,' Harry muttered.

'What?'

'I said first of many. You don't think this is the only avalanche they're going to cause with their stinking SST's, do you? The Swiss won't let them overfly the country between October and May – said they'd shoot them down first. So did the Austrians.'

Pete handed Harry his shovel. 'Let's dig,' he sighed.

About ten minutes later it became clear what they'd got into at this spot: a whole collapsed room, if not a building. Uphill, a wall of rough stone had broken the worst impact of the avalanche, but it had shifted on its foundations and twisted into an irregular line of precariously poised fragments. Over that the roof-beams had folded, but not fallen, leaving a small vacant space in which—

'Christ!' Harry said. 'Alive!'

Something moved feebly in darkness. White darkness. The snow had burst in through a window, fanned out on the floor.

'Ay-yah-ahh!' The treble cry of a child.

'Look out, you fucking idiot!' Pete roared as Harry made to drop his shovel and dive straight in under the arching timbers. He grabbed his arm.

'What? That's a kid! Get your hands off—!'

'Look, look, *look*!' And Pete pointed to the huge trembling overhang of snow that had broken against the stone wall like a frozen wave. Because of their digging it loured above the space in which the child – children, he realized, hearing a second cry discord with the first – in which the children were trapped.

'Ah ... Yeah.' Harry regained his self-possession and blinked down into the dark hollow. A bed, overset. A lot of snow. 'See what you mean. We could bring that whole pile down on us. Got a flashlight?'

'Loaned it to someone. Go get another. And lots of help. See, that beam?' Pete didn't dare so much as touch it. Now it was exposed, the single crucial roof-strut that had spared the children looked like a match, and on the slanted broken roof that it supported lay God knew how many tons of snow and rock.

'Sure! Be back right away!' Turning to run.

'Hang on, kids,' Pete called into the cold dark. 'We'll get you out soon's we can.'

One of the half-seen shapes moved. Stood up. Shedding snow.

Moving snow.

Trying to climb to the light!

'Oh, my God! Harry, HARRY! BE QUICK!'

Crying. And the crying drowned by the noise of weight leaning on a fractured beam. *The* beam, the one that held back the incredible mass of snow. He saw it spray tiny white flakes, like dust, that danced in the glow of the distant emergency lights.

Christ ... Jeannie, Jeannie, it could be a kid of ours down there – I don't mean *could*, not at fifty bucks a day, but I mean it's a kid, and we could have kids, and ...

But those thoughts were spin-off, and had nothing to do with him moving. Shovel dropped. The beam yielding. Turning so his shoulders came under it, his numb hands felt for it. The weight, the incredible intolerable unthinkable weight. He looked down and saw his boots had been driven in over ankles in the packed snow.

At least, though, he could still hear the crying.

THE TINIEST TRACE

'Did it go okay, Peg?' Mel Torrance called as she wended her way through the maze of desks, glass partitions, file cabinets. The paper was losing money.

Most papers were losing money. Even Mel had only a cubbyhole for an office, whose door stood permanently open except when he was taking his pills. He was embarrassed about that for some reason.

Ridiculous. Who do you know who doesn't have to take pills of some kind nowadays? Which reminds me, I'm past due for mine.

'Oh, fine,' Peg muttered. She'd been out to cover a sewer explosion. Someone had poured something he shouldn't have down the drain, and it had reacted with something else. Big deal. It happened all the time. Today nobody had even been killed.

'Did Rod get any good pictures?'

'Said he'd have some for you in about two hours.'

'He didn't get Polaroids? Shit, of course not – the pol count is up today, isn't it?' Mel sighed. Days you couldn't get Polaroids were starting to outnumber those when you could; it was something in the air that affected the emulsion. 'Well, a couple of hours should be okay … Message for you, by the way. It's on your desk.'

'Later.'

But the note said she should contact the city morgue, so she put the call in while rolling paper into her typewriter with her other hand, and after five wrong numbers – about par for the course – the phone said, 'Stanway.'

'Peg Mankiewicz.'

'Oh, yes.' Stanway's voice dropped a trifle. 'Look, we finally had the definitive lab report on your friend Jones.'

'Christ! You mean they've been on at him all this time?' Peg heard her voice ragged. Couldn't they even leave his corpse alone? Weren't they content with hurling insults at his memory? 'This self-appointed prophet of a better world who turned out to be just another acid-head.' Quote/unquote.

'Well, it's a slow process looking for these very tiny traces of a drug,' Stanway said, missing the point. 'Paper chromatography work. Long-column separation, even, sometimes.'

'All right, what did they find?'

'A hallucinogen in his system. Not LSD or psilocybin or any of the regular ones, but something with a similar molecular structure. I don't really understand the report myself – I'm an anatomist, not a biochemist. But I thought you'd like to know right away.'

Like! No, it was the thing in all the world she least wanted to hear. But there it was: evidence.

'Any special reason why they went to all that trouble?'

Stanway hesitated. He said at length, 'Well, the fuzz insisted.'

'The lousy mothers! They didn't find drugs in his car!' Not strictly his, but rented. Trainites did their best not to contribute to pollution, and the entire community of sixty-some at the Denver wat owned one vehicle between them, a jeep. Apart from bicycles.

Moreover they didn't hold with drugs, not even pot, though they did tolerate beer and wine.

She slid open a drawer in her desk, where she kept the file she'd compiled about Decimus's death, and reread the list of things that had been found in the car – more or less what you would expect. A traveling-bag with a change of clothes, razor, toothbrush and so on, a folder of papers about chemicals in food, another concerned with the family business which had brought him to LA to see his sister Felice, and a sort of picnic basket. That fitted, too; he'd have brought his own food along, the good wholesome kind the wat community grew themselves.

Stanway coughed in the phone. It started as a polite attention-catching noise; a few seconds, and it developed into a real cough, punctuated with gasps of, 'Sorry!' When he recovered, he said, 'Was there anything else?'

'No.' Absently. 'Thanks very much for letting me know.'

Having hung up she sat for long minutes staring at nothing. Anger burned in her mind like a sullen flame. She was convinced – beyond the possibility of argument – Decimus must have been poisoned.

But how? By whom? They'd backtracked on his route, discovered a couple of truck-drivers who'd noticed him asleep in the park outside a diner when they stopped for a snack, then found him awake when they came out again, shaving in the men's room; also a gas station where he'd filled up – and that was that. No one else seemed to have seen or spoken to him on the way.

And his sister, of course, knew nothing useful. She'd refused to be interviewed directly after his death, claiming with good grounds that since she hadn't met her brother in years she hardly knew him, but then the makeup for their December 23rd issue had been half a column short and Peg had dashed off a moralizing Christmassy bit about Decimus which Mel reluctantly approved with only minor changes, and Felice had seen it and called up and thanked her. But they still hadn't met, and it was clear from the way she spoke that she didn't sympathize with her brother's views.

That food. Had it been analyzed? No, of course not. And it was mainly crumbs anyhow. Probably just thrown out …

Sudden decision. She reached for the phone again and this time by a minor miracle got through to Angel City first go. She asked for Felice.

'I'm afraid she's in conference right now. Shall I take a message?'

Peg hesitated. 'Yes! Yes, tell her Peg Mankiewicz called. Tell her that her brother was definitely poisoned.'

'I'm sorry, I don't quite understand.' And a sneeze, hastily apologized for.

'Oh, shit,' Peg said wearily. 'Never mind.'

She found her eyesight was blurred. Tears? No. Watering. And her forehead tight and starting to throb. Hell and damnation, another lousy bout of sinusitis.

She hurried to the water-cooler to wash down her belated pill.

AND IT GOES ON

… and Dr Isaiah Williams, whose body was recovered from a ravine near San Pablo. Inquiries are being hampered by what an Army spokesman termed the obstinate attitude of the local people. 'They won't admit they know their left hands from their right,' he asserted. Here at home Senator Richard Howell (Rep., Col.) today launched a fierce attack on the quote chlorophyll addicts unquote who, he claims, are hamstringing American business, already stagger- ing under the load of high unemployment and recession, by insisting that our manufacturers comply with regulations ignored by foreign competition. In Southern Italy rioting continues in many small towns formerly dependent on fishing. Meantime, dust storms in the Camargue …

EARTHMOVER

'Hi, Fred!'

'Hi!'

Austin Train/Fred Smith continued up the stairs. It was incredibly noisy here – squalling kids, TV sound, radio, a record, someone practicing drums, and ahead on the top floor his neighbors the Blores quarreling again. Their apartment was like a bombed site. Either there would be murder done one day, or the eventual victor would inherit a mere heap of rubble.

Which was full of lessons for today. But the hell with it. He was tired, and the cut on his leg which he'd sustained a couple of days ago had swollen up and begun to throb. It looked as though it might be infected.

Pausing as he thrust his key into his own door, be noticed there was a new graffito on the landing, the Trainite slogan: YOU'RE KILLING ME.

In purple lipstick. Very fashionable.

He glanced around, not really worried as to whether someone had broken in during his absence and robbed him, apart from the inconvenience of having to buy replacements. This belonged to Fred Smith, not Austin Train. The store-closet and icebox were full of commonplace cheap foods (if any food could be called cheap nowadays): canned, frozen, freeze-dried, irradiated, precooked and even predigested. The walls were chipped and needed paint.

The windows were mostly okay but one pane was blocked with cardboard. There were fleas the exterminator couldn't kill and rats that scrabbled in the walls and mice who left droppings like a cocked snook and roaches that thrived on insecticide, even the illegal kinds. He wouldn't touch those himself – that would have been carrying his 'Fred Smith' role too far – but everyone else in the house knew where to score for DDT and dieldrin and so forth, and it hadn't helped.

He didn't really see his surroundings, though. One could live this way, and he was proving it. It meant something to him to be here. It implied—

Hope? Possibly. Suppose that great heretic St Francis of Assisi had been put (as he, Austin Train, had been) in front of twenty-eight million viewers on the *Petronella Page Show* and told to define his reasons for behaving as he did. We are told that 'the meek shall inherit the earth'. It follows that the meek are chosen of God. I shall try to be meek, not because I want the earth – you can keep it, after the way you've fucked it around it's not worth having – but because I too should like to be chosen of God. QED.

Besides, I like animals better than you bastards.

Of all the vices human beings are capable of, Austin Train detested hypocrisy most. He hadn't realized that until a matter of three years or so ago, following the period of notoriety which had begun a couple of years before with the publication of his *Handbook for 3000 A D*. Prior to that he had enjoyed moderate success; a group of his books had been reissued as matched paperbacks and attracted attention from an increasingly worried public, but it had all been low-key stuff. Suddenly, one might say overnight, he had become a celebrity, in demand for TV interviews, commissioned to write for popular journals, called in as consultant on government committees. And then, equally abruptly, stop.

He had six hundred thousand dollars in the bank and lived in a slum tenement in the heart of a dying city.

Back there – he had come to think of it as another world – lying and fakery were a way of life. Sponsoring the programs on which he appeared as Cassandra: a plastics company, daily pouring half a million gallons of hot and poisoned water into a river that served eleven cities before it reached the ocean. Printing the articles he wrote: a corporation whose paper demanded the felling of half a forest every month. Ruling the country which paraded him as a prime example of the benefits of free speech: madmen who had made a desert and misnamed it peace.

It made him sick.

Literally.

He lay in the hospital for two months, shivering without cease, spat at people who came to wish him well, tore up cables from strangers saying they hoped he'd get better quickly, threw food on the floor because it was poisoned, caught nurses around the neck and lectured them, helplessly pinioned, on egg-bundle fetus, sulphur dioxide, lead alkyls, DDE. Not that they heard much of what he told them. They were screaming too loudly.

When they released him, doped on tranquilizers, he went to live with the people who didn't make a professional habit of omitting to let their left hands know. He settled in the dirtiest back streets of the city he'd been born in. He'd considered alternatives: Barcelona, by the open cesspool of the Mediterranean; the rabbit-warrens of Rome, almost permanently under martial law; Osaka, where they were marketing airlocks to be fitted in place of regular front doors. Still, he wanted to be able to talk to the people around him – so he came home. 'I am a man,' he had said many times during his moment of fame. 'I am as guilty as you, and you are as guilty as me. We can repent together, or we can die together; it must be our joint decision.'

He hadn't expected to leave behind, in that world he'd abandoned, such a surprising legacy: the Trainites, who had no formal organization, not even a newspaper, yet now and then manifested themselves – one might almost believe as the result of some telepathic trigger, some upsurge of the collective unconscious – to put a brand on some company or enterprise that was endangering mankind. Obviously, he had not created them. They must have been there, waiting. Mainly they were the former radical students for whom it had become a matter of principle to say, 'Yes, I'm a commie!' That habit had followed the Vietnam disaster, when the tons upon thousands of tons of herbicides, defoliants, riot gases, toxic agents, had finally broken the land down into desert. All of a sudden, in a single summer, dead plants, dead animals, dead rivers.

Dead people.

And when he popularized the term 'commensalist' a little later, the reference was rapidly transferred. But didn't stick. Instead the news media invented the name 'Trainite', and now it was universal.

He was half pleased by the flattery this implied, half frightened for complex reasons of which he had cited one to Peg. He dreamed occasionally of meeting the men who had taken his name in place of their own, and would wake sweating and moaning, because that led to visions of endless millions of identical people, impossible to tell apart.

Anyway, here he was in half the upper floor of a derelict building in downtown LA, formerly offices, converted to dwellings five years ago, never repaired or painted since. The people around him, though, didn't lie except to protect their egos, and he found that tolerable. What he loathed was a deed such as he would no longer term a crime, but a sin. Unto the third and fourth generation, General Motors, you have visited your greed on the children.

Unto the twentieth, AEC, you have twisted their limbs and closed their eyes. Unto the last dawn of man you have cursed us, O Father. Our Father. Our Father Which art in Washington, give us this day our daily calcium propionate, sodium diacetate monoglyceride, potassium bromate, calcium phosphate, monobasic chloramine T, aluminum potassium sulphate, sodium benzoate, butylated hydroxyanisole, mono-iso-propyl citrate, axerophthol and calciferol. Include with it a little flour and salt.

Amen.

Something had infected his hair-roots and eyebrows, that made the skin flake away in dry crusty yellow scurf and left little raw patches of exposed flesh. He rubbed in a lotion Mrs Blore had recommended; she and her husband suffered from the same complaint, and so did the kids on the lower floor. The lotion certainly helped – his scalp wasn't nearly as sore as it had been last week.

Then he ate, absently, not so much food as fuel: tasting of cottonwool or cardboard, the human counterpart of the fertilizers they were continuing to pour on land that daily grew more and more barren, hardened, scoriated, turned to dust. Like his scalp. He was shaping something he sensed to be important. He had given up books, even his favorites: the Bible, the *Bhagavad-Gita*, the *Precepts of Patanjali*, the *I Ching*, the *Popul Vuh*, the *Book of the Dead* …

If I don't know enough now, I shall never know enough. I couldn't stand that.

While he ate, he was thinking. While he worked during the day, he had been thinking. He had a job with the city sanitation department, and garbage was full of morals: sermons in trash-cans, books in running drains. The others on the gang he worked with thought he was odd, maybe touched in the head. Could be. What had touched him, though, felt – significant. Suddenly, in recent weeks, the conviction had come on him: I matter. I count. I have an insight. I think a thing no one else thinks. I believe with the certainty of faith. I must *must* make others hear and understand.

When it is time.

At night, when he lay down to sleep, he felt that his brain was resonating with the heartbeat of the planet.

SHOWDOWN

'Get me a wig – quickly!'

Startled by the shout, Terry Fenton glanced up from inventorying his equipment: paints, powders, dyes, lacquers – all of the finest quality, of course, Peruvian and Mexican, based on herbal essences and vegetable waxes and flower pigments, not a trace of anything synthetic. Nothing but the best for Terry Fenton. He was at the apex of his profession, senior makeup supervisor for the entire New York studio complex of ABS, far more trendily clad and infinitely better groomed than almost all the stars who nightly fed visual pablum to the admass.

'Pet! Christ, what have you done to your *hair*?'

Forty, but glamorous and rigorously dieted slim, Petronella Page stormed to her usual chair. She was wearing a magnificent pants suit in abstract scarlet and yellow and her face was so flawless Terry would as ever need to add only minor touches. But her hair was streaked with irregular muddy marks.

She ran the Monday and Wednesday late-night talk show, and was popular, and expected to take on Friday as well because the trans-Atlantic commuting compere, the Englishman Adrian Sprague, was verging on a nervous breakdown at long-awaited last and moreover had missed three shows in three months owing to bomb scares aboard the planes he was taking.

'I'll sue the mother!' she said between clenched teeth as the full horror of her appearance clanged back from the merciless mirrors.

'But what *happened*?' Terry snapped his fingers and his current assistant, Marlon, a light-brown boy who adored him, absolutely adored him, and thought Petronella was okay – for a woman, you know – came scurrying into the room. So also, a moment later, did Lola Grown, assistant to Ian Farley the producer, with a pile of briefing documents concerning the night's guests. The show was due on camera in about twenty minutes.

'Thank God you finally made it!' Lola cried. 'Ian's been pissing himself!'

'Shut up! Drop dead!' Petronella rasped, and slapped the papers out of Lola's hand as she offered them. 'I don't give a fart who we have on the show, not if it's the stinking King of England! I sure as hell am *not* going out looking like this!'

'You won't have to, baby,' Terry soothed, inspecting the discolored tresses. Lola, on the point of weeping, went down on hands and knees to reclaim the scattered papers. 'Lord, though, why didn't you have it done at Guido's same as usual?'

'This happened at Guido's.'

'What?' Terry was horrified. He insisted on everyone he handled having their hair washed, styled, cut at Guido's, because it was the only place in New York where they guaranteed their shampoos were done with imported rainwater. They shipped it specially from Chile.

'Silver nitrate,' Petronella sighed. 'I contacted Guido at home and blew my stack, and he checked up and called back almost weeping. Seems they've been rainmaking down there – remember I had a rainmaker on the show last year? Guido thinks it reacted with the setting lotion.'

Marlon brought a choice of wigs. Terry seized one, and a brush and comb and aerosol of lacquer. He brutally sabotaged Guido's efforts into a tight layer close to the scalp and set about re-creating the same style on the wig.

'Going to take long?' Petronella demanded.

'Couple of minutes,' Terry said. He forbore to add that anything Guido's best stylist could do, he could copy, only in a tenth of the time. Everyone knew how good he was.

'Thank God. Lola, you bitch, where are my briefings?'

'Here!' the girl snuffled. Petronella flicked through the pages.

'Oh, yes, I remember. Jacob Bamberley—'

'He likes to be called Jack!' Lola cut in.

'Stuff what he likes, *I* run this show. Terry baby, we got the man who sent all that poisoned shit to Africa. Know what I'm going to make him do? I'm going to make him eat a bowlful of it right at the start of the show, then come back to him at the end so people can see what it's done to him.'

Turning to the next briefing, she added thoughtfully, 'and I shall definitely call him Jacob.'

This was a Globe Relief operation on behalf of Globe Relief. When it became clear that Kaika's accusations weren't just propaganda, it had been a matter of panic stations all around. It was no use stressing the true fact that Globe was the largest aid organization on the planet and invariably the soonest on the scene of a disaster. Simply because it was American-based and American-funded, it was tarred with the Vietnam brush. There was almost certain to be a UN inquiry shortly.

Accordingly State had made it very clear that unless Globe came up promptly with a full defense the organization would have to be thrown to the wolves. Inestimable trouble had already been caused by black militants instantly prepared to believe in chemical genocide.

The obvious steps had naturally been taken. Samples of the Nutripon still in store had been analyzed and given a clean bill. Now suspicion had turned on the yeasts and fungi in the hydroponics plant: could a rogue, akin say to the ergot mold of rye, have infected one batch of the stuff with a natural psychedelic poison? It would have helped if they'd had a sample from Noshri to study, but apparently it had all been consumed or burned during the riots. So it was going to be a slow job.

Casting around for some form of distraction, the directors of Globe had realized that Jacob Bamberley was due in New York for his monthly visit to the headquarters of the Bamberley Trust, and seen a heaven-sent chance to pass the buck one stage further. They pulled a lot of strings extremely hard. The *Petronella Page Show* had a nightly audience of around thirty million;

sometimes on a Monday when people stayed home after the heavy spending of a weekend, it approached forty. To be exposed on it, moreover, meant a lot of spin-off in newspaper and magazine publicity. They wanted that exposure now, today. 'Thrice armed is he whose cause is just, but four times he who gets a blow in fust.'

Besides, if war is hell, so is peace.

So here he was under the bright studio lights, flanked on one side by Gerry Thorne from Globe, small and tense and with a tic in his left check, and on the other by Moses Greenbriar, senior treasurer of the Bamberley Trust, a fat and jolly man who could answer any questions about the financing of the hydroponics plant.

Terry and his wig had worked a miracle. Nonetheless Petronella was still in a foul mood when she took her place. She cheered up slightly as the first commercials were run, because they had wonderful sponsors on this show and inasmuch as she was proud of anything she was proud of these: Puritan Health Supermarkets, Hailey Cars – or rather the agency which imported them from Britain, where they cost too much to be common – and Johnson & Johnson's filtermasks. Even so the smile she bestowed on the audience was forced.

'Hi, world!' And, mindful of their status as a representative cross-section of the species Man, they echoed her.

'Now this time we got for you people who are very much making news, and people we predict will make the news tomorrow. And not only here but half around the world, such as for instance in Africa.'

Ah, good. She didn't have to tell Ian Farley more than once about anything. As arranged, the cameras had picked up on Mr Bamberley, ignoring the men at his left and right, and were closing like the gun-muzzles of a firing squad.

'We've all been shocked and horrified by the outbreak of – well, mass insanity that occurred at Noshri before Christmas. Just as we thought that terrible war was finally over, we've seen the pictures and heard the stories of people literally running amok. We've even heard accusations of' – hushed – 'cannibalism among the starving survivors.

'Now it's been charged that poison in relief supplies caused these people to go out of their minds. Specifically, a consignment of Nutripon from the Bamberley hydroponics plant near Denver, Colorado ...'

Bless you, Ian baby!

Farley had kept one camera practically squinting up Mr Bamberley's nostrils throughout the intro. Of course that wasn't what stayed on the monitor all the time; the audience and Petronella had been intercut. But Bamberley wasn't to know that. He was visibly afraid to twist around and get a sight of the monitor, in case he *was* on it.

Oh, Ian baby, I don't have to tell you, do I?

'Jacob! You don't mind if I call you Jacob?' With a dazzling smile.

'Well, people usually—'

'I'm sure they do. No one with such a reputation for good works could be other than on the best of terms with everyone.' The voice syrupy, the tiniest fraction too far in the direction of sentimentality. 'So now, Jacob, this stuff Nutripon that's been called in question – what exactly does it consist of?'

'Well, it's cassava, processed in a way not unlike making cheese—'

'Cassava. I see.' Time to let the smile make way for a slight frown. 'Now I'm no expert on this' – though the briefings had been thorough as always and she was a quick study – 'but I seem to remember cassava is kind of a dangerous plant to meddle with. Eye disease, isn't that right?'

'Well, I guess you must be referring to cassava amblyopia, which is—'

'An eye condition?' She noticed, though the admass didn't because the camera wasn't on the guy, that Gerry Thorne reflexively touched one of his own eyes at that. Right; he'd had conjunctivitis recently. And now here he was pulling out a pair of shades against the brilliant lights. Splendid. He looked positively sinister in them. Prompt to his unspoken cue, Ian pulled back his camera.

'Yes, but you see Nutripon is fortified—'

'Just a second!' The word was on the teleprompter, but she hadn't needed the reminder; it was too full of possibilities. 'I hadn't quite covered my point. Isn't there cyanide in cassava?'

'In the raw rind, yes, but not after it's been processed!' Mr Bamberley was sweating. Petronella looked forward to the moment when he would begin to squirm. His companions had reached it already.

'You claim your treatment makes it quite safe?'

'Oh, yes!'

'Are the details of the treatment a trade secret, or can anybody hear them?'

'Goodness, not in the least secret! Though I'm afraid if you want the technical details you'd have to—'

'Yes, we appreciate that you're not a hydroponics expert. You do grow the stuff hydroponically, right?'

'Quite correct, we do.'

'That means you grow it artificially, in sand or cellulite, in controlled conditions with a solution of nutrient chemicals. That's what "hydroponics" means, isn't it?' Barb after barb stabbing into the audience's ears, fresh from their exposure to the Puritan commercial with its emphasis on food grown in the open air, in natural soil.

'Yes. Uh – yes!' Mr Bamberley was becoming confused. Beside him Green-briar, the fat man, was signaling with his eyebrows: *Call on me, I can cope!*

Ho no, baby. *Ho* no! We aren't here to help Globe Relief justify itself to all those blacks who already believe your charley outfit has been genociding their African cousins. No more are we here to help you elude the stockhold-ers in the Bamberley Trust who resent seeing what might have been profit in their pockets squandered on ungrateful bastards overseas. No, baby! That ain't what we're here for at all!

Like to know what we are here for? Then stick around.

She smiled again, sweetly. 'There are no doubt reasons for growing your cas-sava in this way. Does it have anything to do with reducing the amount of cyanide in it?'

'No, no, no! The most important reason is that we need something that's widely acceptable in those areas where famine is likeliest to strike, and cas-sava is—'

'Yes, you ship everything you make abroad, don't you?' Petronella inserted, with the precision of a surgeon's scalpel. The breath he was taking to launch into the next segment of his prepared exposition had to be diverted to a dif-ferent purpose.

'Well, yes, everything we make does go for aid projects.'

'And this is a non-profit operation?' Petronella said, knowing the official answer. 'You are, after all, one of the richest men in the world; according to its last annual report the Bamberley Trust disposes of assets in excess of half a billion dollars. Don't you take any profit on your relief contracts?'

'Definitely not! At most we aim to cover our costs. The hydroponics plant is absolutely *not* required to make a profit.'

'Why not?'

The phrase stuck there, as though a thrown knife had found a lodging in mid-air. Mr Bamberley blinked.

'I beg your pardon?'

'I asked why not. All your other business interests have to, or you get rid of them. During the past year, for instance, you disposed of a chain of super-markets in Tennessee, which hadn't shown a profit in two years, and shed all your airline holdings. Well?'

'Uh – well!' Mr Bamberley did exactly what she had hoped he would, and Thorne and Greenbriar had been praying he would *not* do: tugged a hand-kerchief from his pocket and wiped his face. It was very hot under the lights – designedly so. 'Well, I regard this as a … well, a charitable undertak-ing, you see. A practical way of helping people with my – uh – my good fortune.'

'Not the only expression of your charitable impulses, I gather,' Petronella murmured.

'No, of course not. I believe – I mean, I'm a Christian and all Christians should believe – that we're the children of the Lord, made in His image, and no man is an island, heh-heh!' Terribly embarrassed, like so many professing a religion when faced with admitting the fact before anonymous millions. But sincere. Oh, *painfully* sincere.

'Yes, I'm told you've surrounded yourself with boys who've been orphaned. Eight of them right now.'

'Ah, you mean my adopted sons. Well, yes. It's one thing, isn't it, to send aid to some faraway country? And something else again to bring deserving cases into your own home.' Blinking on every word, flicker-flicker.

In the goldfish bowl Ian making fierce gestures: don't lean on the queer bit too hard. But the hell with him. The Bible Belt goes to bed early, this may be the last chance to catch them.

'We've talked a lot about adoption on this show recently – because of the success of the Double-V scheme, of course. Are you a patron of Double-V?'

'Ah … As a matter of fact, no, because there are after all a great many orphans right here in this country. Worse still, children abandoned by their parents!'

'Yes, that is an alarming problem, isn't it? We had a social worker on the show last month who mentioned just that point, in connection with these gangs of black kids who have taken to terrorizing city centers. She said thousands of them have suffered just as badly as the Asian children who are being adopted in. But none of your – ah – sons are black, are they?'

Dead silence. Just long enough to let the point fester. And then resuming in a let's-get-on-with-it tone, 'Well, I guess that's by the way, Jacob.' Your private life is your concern and presumably a white Protestant is entitled to prefer white Protestant boys.' Fester, fester! 'So let's get back to the main line of the discussion.'

That was one of her favorite words. Sharp-tongued guests on the show sometimes managed to sneak in the more accurate term, 'interrogation,' but tonight she was in top form, and even though Thorne was pale and shaking and Greenbriar almost bouncing up and down with fury, neither had contrived to interrupt her. Maybe she wouldn't sue Guido after all. Blessings in disguise, and all that shit.

'So anyhow: what have you to say to the charge that the food you sent to Noshri was poisoned?'

'As God is my witness, Nutripon is wholesome and delicious!' Mr Bamberley sat up very straight and jutted his jaw forward as though trying to look like Winston Churchill.

'I'm glad to hear it. But have you yourself been to Noshri to investigate, or any of your associates?' Naturally not; Kaika had booted the American relief workers out of the country and broken off diplomatic relations.

'Ah …' Mr Bamberley was trembling now, enough for the cameras to pick it up. 'It simply hasn't been possible – but our quality controls are of the highest standard, we test the product at every stage of manufacture!'

'So the consignment in question must have been poisoned after it left the factory?'

'I'm not admitting it was poisoned at all!'

Got him. He'd actually used the word. And it was clear how dreadful an effect that had had on Thorne and Greenbriar. The admass would have seen, too; Ian had pulled back his cameras. The man being pilloried between two thieves. Everyone but *everyone* knew about those two – mansion homes, luxury cars, private planes …

'Never mind! *We'd*' – identifying emphasis, you out there for whom I speak – 'like to conduct a small experiment of our own, which won't of course be scientifically rigorous but may indicate *something* …' Camera 1 pulled in on her and she spoke confidingly to it.

'This afternoon we sent one of our staff to Kennedy International Airport where a consignment of this processed cassava was being loaded on a chartered aircraft. We bought a carton of it.' Not *case*. Overtones of breakfast cereal. 'We paid the price on the loading manifest, which was eighty-three dollars – oh, don't worry that we deprived anybody! We substituted food of equivalent value, such as powdered milk and dried egg and bags of flour, and put that into the shipment to replace what we'd taken.

'Then we brought the stuff back here, and followed the instructions on the packet precisely, and – well, here's the result. Lola?'

Recovered from her pre-show fit of sniveling, Lola came smiling on to the stage carrying a tray on which reposed a large bowl, steaming slightly, a spoon and fork, and a cruet. A glass of water was already in front of Mr Bamberley.

'Jacob, a random sample of your relief supplies. May we see you eat it?'

'Well, yes!' Running a finger around his collar – but what else could he say? 'I did have …'

'Yes?'

He had been going to add: a very rich dinner. But one couldn't admit that, not when the subject was the feeding of starving millions. (And all across the country one could almost hear people saying, 'Eighty-three dollars? For that muck?') He compromised. 'I did have dinner before I came to the studio, so I may not have much of an appetite, but I'll be glad to prove that this is safe to eat!'

Thorne and Greenbriar looked frightened – the latter especially, wishing he hadn't fed his employer so well. Suppose he were taken ill, not because of the Nutripon but because of that dish of eggplants in oil, or the lobster! Seafood was such a gamble nowadays, even with an FDA certificate …

'That's a good boy, Jacob!' Petronella approved ironically. 'Well, world, here's a sight to remember: one of this rich country's richest men eating a sample of the diet we ship to poverty-stricken, famine-ridden lands overseas. Later on, at the end of the show, we'll call Jacob back and ask how he liked his unexpected snack.'

Under the table, out of camera view, she couldn't resist the temptation to rub her hands.

But …

'What the hell?' She spoke very softly to the mike in the right-hand wing of her throne-like chair, the one which was reserved for outright emergencies. Ian was signaling frantically from the goldfish bowl, and suddenly his voice rang out from the speaker under its window.

'Ladies and gentlemen, I'm afraid we shall have to discontinue the show. Please proceed calmly to the exits. We've been warned that there is a bomb in the building. We're sure this is a hoax, but—'

They screamed.

Panicked.

Fought like maddened animals, charging the doors. One of the doors broke off its hinges and a girl was cut across the face by its fall and the rest pushed her out of the way and she tripped and they walked on her, stamped on her, broke her ribs and her nose and crushed her left hand into blue pulp.

But they got out, which was all they cared about.

'The bomb is for you, Mr Bamberley,' Ian Farley said as he, Petronella, others of the staff took their backstage route to the street.

'What?' He was whiter than his own Nutripon: pasty, like raw dough.

'Yes. Someone called up and said he was black and a cousin of the people you've been poisoning in Africa, and he was going to take revenge on their behalf.'

FEBRUARY

IN PRAISE OF BIOCIDE

Than fund he ther fisceras:
The makede hyrn mickel welcom:
Craft was in hir kilyng:
Than hyede hym to hontyng:
Fowlis and faunis:
Sauf that his sotil shaft:
Ol that war on lyve:
Togh it ben to tel:

    Ferce fukkis:
    Dove and dawe:
    Faible falwe:
    Deth draggede:

Wantede the water:
Scars war to se:
Than cam the croude:
Ful war the festers:
So fal the Saxon:
So befal foemen:

and weltoghte fugeleras,
as maistre of londes.
with hem the cyning
hartis and brockis.
fain had the fled hym,
strock hem on ronyng.
overcarn he of bestis.
talye of targetis.
For that
    felte smerte,
    darte to herte,
    fel aperte,
    divers sterte.
welvers ne froggis,
sluggis ne snakis.
to cyninges hal again.
fourten daies fed the.
so be hir sloghter,
wold frighten hys relm …

– 'The Chronicle of That Great Progress Made by our Lord the King through his Eastern Lands This Summer Past', 938 (text corrupt, a late copy by a post-Conquest scribe).

THIS HURTS ME MORE

Yesterday Phelan Murphy had stood by, sick at heart, while the government man argued about the cattle with Dr Advowson. It was very cold; it was the coldest and longest winter in ten years. The pastures were in terrible condition. Some were still under snow from the November falls, and those which were snow-free were naturally overgrazed. To keep his stock alive he had had to buy bales of hay and dump them around the fields. It had been expensive, because the land had been in a poor state last summer, too. Some said – it had even been in *The Independent* – that it had to do with smoke from the factories near Shannon Airport.

But the government man had said he didn't know anything about that.

Now, today, he was back, with soldiers. The market at Balpenny was not to be held. They had brought big signs saying LIMISTÉAR CORAINTIN and set them up on the roadside. More cows had died in the night, bellies bloated, blood leaking from their mouths and nostrils, frozen smears of blood under their tails. Before the children were allowed to go to school they had to dip their rubber boots in pans of milky disinfectant. The same had been sprayed on the tires of the bus.

The soldiers took spades and picks and dug holes in the frozen ground, and brought bags of quicklime. Cows too weak to try and move away allowed the humane killer to be put to their heads: thud. Again, a minute later: thud. And again.

Bridie had wept most of the night, and the children – not knowing why – had copied her.

'Damned fools!' Dr Advowson kept repeating and repeating under his breath, chewing his pipe at Phelan's side. 'I did my best to stop them, but – oh, the damned *idiots*!'

'There'll be compensation,' the government man said, listing on a long printed form the details of the animals that were being killed.

Then the soldiers dragged the carcasses to the pits.

THE CONTINUING DEBATE

… left for Honduras this morning. Questioned concerning his decision just prior to his annual birthday banquet and family reunion at which he is slated to deliver a major speech on overseas aid, Prexy said, quote, Those Tupas got to understand that if you bite the hand that feeds you, you're apt to get a mouthful of fist. End quote. Pressure for a UN inquiry into the Noshri tragedy continues to grow. Trainites and black militant groups are threatening to attack planes carrying further relief consignments if this is not done immediately, according to various anonymous letters and phone calls received recently at our studios. Hopes are high that the matter may however be settled without such an inquiry. In Paris this morning famed scientist Dr Louis-Marie Duval, who has been examining a group of the survivors …

FIRE WHEN READY

'No, Peg, it won't do,' Mel Torrance said, and exploded into a sneeze.

She looked at him with hurt in her eyes: knowing it showed, hating herself for letting it show, unable to prevent it. He held out to her the draft of the story she'd given him; when she made no move to accept it he let it go, and it sideslipped over the desk edge, settling to the floor like a tired untidy bird.

'I'm sick of your obsession with this lousy bastard Jones! He's been dead since December. It's been proved he was stoned when he died. I am *not* about to give houseroom to your crazy fantasies about him being poisoned!'

'But—'

He rushed on. 'Listen, will you? Now Jones was a Trainite, right? And these Trainites are getting to be a filthy nuisance! They block traffic, they foul up business, they commit sabotage, they've even gone as far as murder—'

'Nonsense!'

'That man in San Francisco last fall?'

'He'd shot a girl, an unarmed girl!' Peg was trembling from head to foot.

'He died of his acid burns, didn't he? Are you saying these mothers have the right to take the law into their own hands? Are they vigilantes? Are they a lynch-mob?'

'I—'

'Yes, yes, *yes*!' Mel stormed. 'Every last bunch of Trainites is a potential lynch-mob! I don't give a fart what they claim their motives are – I judge by results, and what I see is that they wreck, they destroy, and when it comes to the crunch, they kill.'

'The killers are the people who are ruining the world to line their pockets, poisoning us, burying us under garbage!'

'Are you a Trainite, Peg?'

Drawing back, she passed her hand over her face. 'I – I guess I sympathize,' she said at length. 'I mean in LA you have to. Beaches fouled with oil and sewage, air so bad you can't go out without a mask, the water at your sink reeking of chlorine …' Her forehead was pounding again; her sinus trouble was dragging endlessly on.

'Sure, there's some truth in all that. Like up at our place in Sherman Oaks we lost half the flowers in our garden last summer – bad wind from somewhere, had defoliants in it so we couldn't even make compost out of what was left. Sure, things aren't exactly like paradise. But that's no reason for making them like hell, is it? That's what these Trainites are doing. They don't offer something better than what we already have, or if they did I'd sign on like a shot and so would just about everybody. But they simply spoil it and leave rubble in its place.'

He sneezed again, cursed and grabbed an inhaler from the corner of his desk. Peg said, feeling helpless, 'You don't understand what they're trying to do. If you'd known Decimus you might—'

'I've heard all I ever want to hear about your Decimus,' Mel snapped. 'Last chance, Peg. Get down off this hobby-horse of yours, start doing the same kind of good work you used to, or quit.'

'I quit.'

'Good. Goodbye. I'll make sure the accounts department issues your month's salary in lieu of notice. Now take that litter off my floor and pack your gear. I'm busy.'

Outside, rising from a chair, a pretty colored girl who said, 'Ah, you must be Peg Mankiewicz. I'm Felice Jones – Why, what's wrong?'

'I've been fired,' Peg said bitterly.

'No, you haven't!' A shout from Mel's office. 'I heard that! You resigned!'

THE NATURAL LOOK

Did you ever study the small Print on a cosmetics package? Ever try to pronounce the jaw-breaking words? Ever find you were below your best at a party – or on a date with a very special man – because you were wondering what all those complicated chemicals might be?

You can always pronounce what we put in MAYA PURA.

Try it right now. Say 'natural'. Say 'flower petals'. Say 'herbal essence'. See?

Yes, of course. And because you see, other people will notice.

POSSESSION IS NINE POINTS

'*Retro me, Sathanas!*' the priest roared: haggard, unshaven, his cassock filthy with mud and dried blood. He held up his crucifix before the advancing jeep. Behind him the people of the village stood their ground, fearful but determined, many armed with ancient guns and the rest with whatever came to hand – axes, machetes, knives.

From the jeep two men got down on opposite sides. One was called Irving S. Hannigan; he'd come from Washington to investigate the death of Leonard Ross. He wasn't enjoying the assignment. It was like trying to catch a handful of smoke, because everyone you talked to who might know anything helpful seemed to lose touch with reality without warning and go off rambling about angels and the Queen of Heaven.

The other was Major José Concepción Madariaga de Crizo Garcia, youngest son of one of the country's largest landowners, raised from the cradle to command instant obedience from the rabble.

'Make way, you old fool!' he rasped. 'Hurry up!'

The priest stood his ground, fixing him with wild bloodshot eyes. Sensing something he hadn't expected, the major glanced at the American for advice. This Hannigan was apparently some kind of detective, or spy, or government agent at any rate, and might have the 'common touch' inaccessible to an officer and an aristocrat.

'These people don't look like a Tupa resistance group to me,' Hannigan murmured. 'Try telling them we've brought food.'

That was as might be, the major thought. The problem with Tupamaros was that they always looked like just anybody – a valet, a cook, a clerk in a store – until the crunch came. However, the idea was a sound one; the rabble were always much concerned with their bellies.

He said in a soothing tone, 'Father, we have come to help your people. The government has sent us with food and medicine.'

'We have had this kind of help before,' the priest rumbled. He looked and sounded as though he had been without proper sleep for a month. 'But do you bring holy water from the Vatican?'

'What?'

'Do you bring sacred relics that will frighten devils?'

The major shook his head, bewildered.

'They're agents of the devil themselves!' shouted a burly man who had been standing at the back of the crowd with a shotgun. Now he battered his way to the front, taking station beside the priest.

'The town is full of wicked spirits!' he cried. 'Men, women, even children are possessed! We've seen the demons walk through walls, enter our homes, even trespass in the church!'

'True!' the priest said, and clutched his crucifix very tightly.

'Ah, they're out of their minds,' the major muttered. 'Or pretending to be! Let's see how they like a volley over their heads!'

Hannigan scowled. 'If they are crazy, it won't do any good. If they aren't, we'll learn more by playing along with them. Try again.'

Sighing, but aware of who was in charge, the major turned back to the priest, who suddenly spat in the dirt at his feet.

'We want nothing to do with you,' he said. 'Or your foreign masters. Go to the bishop, if he can spare a moment from his mistresses. Go to the cardinal, if he isn't too busy stuffing his belly. Tell them our poor hamlet of San Pablo is infested with devils. Bring us the kind of help that will exorcise them. Meantime we know our duty. We shall fast and pray.'

'Aye!' chorused the villagers.

'Yes, but while you're fasting,' Hannigan cut in in fair Spanish, 'your children are likely to starve, aren't they?'

'Better to starve and go to heaven than live possessed by imps of Satan,' rasped the burly man. 'Holy water from Rome, that's what we need! Use your airplanes to bring us that!'

'You could bless the food we've brought,' Hannigan insisted. 'Sprinkle it with water from your church font—'

'We're accursed!' the priest burst out. 'Holy water here has no effect! It's the time of the coming of Antichrist!'

A gun went off. Hannigan and the major dropped reflexively on their bellies. Over their heads the soldiers in the jeeps returned a withering fire, and the priest and his congregation fell like wheat before the scythe.

Obviously they must have been Tupas after all.

THE OFFER OF RESISTANCE

It was the third time Philip Mason had come to the cheerless waiting room of the Market Street clinic, decorated solely with warning posters. But it was the first time he'd found the place so empty. Before, he'd found it crowded with youngsters. Today only one other patient was present, and instead of being teenaged or in his twenties, he was in his late thirties, well-dressed, growing comfortably plump, and in general assignable to Philip's own social bracket

Before Philip could take refuge as usual behind some shabby back issue of *Scientific American* or *The National Geographic*, the stranger had caught his eye and grinned at him. He was dark-haired, brown-eyed, clean-shaven, in general unremarkable bar two things: his obvious atypical prosperity and a small round scar on the back of his left hand. A bullet mark?

'Morning!' he said in precisely that matter-of-fact tone Philip would have liked to be able to command but couldn't. The whole world was leaning on him. Denise was permanently hurt by his behavior. The Towerhill avalanche was still spawning so many claims he hadn't dared punch for the total for over a week. And ...

Oh, that mother Clayford! But it was a Pyrrhic victory to know he was going to lose his fees for insurance examinations.

He dived into the shelter of a magazine he'd already read.

In a little while they called his number and he went for the regular humiliating treatment – massage with a sterile-gloved finger up his anus, a drip of prostatic secretion smeared on a slide. Things had been better the past few days and then this morning they'd been worse again, and Dennie—

Stop, stop. He was in the office of Dr McNeil, and the doctor was youthful, casual, unprejudiced. Philip liked this man a few years his junior, who kept a silly doll of a Highland bagpiper on the corner of his desk. He'd come here the first time almost incapable of talking, and McNeil had drawn him out in minutes, making him feel – just so long as he was in the office – that this really was a complaint anyone might suffer from, not to be ashamed of, easily put right. Though not, of course, under any circumstances to be neglected.

'How are you getting on?' McNeil said, taking the folder Philip had brought with him and extracting the morning's test report to add to the file of Mason Philip A. #605-193.

Philip told him.

'I see.' McNeil plucked his lower lip. 'Well, I guess that's not too surprising. The strain of G you have' – he always said 'G,' not gonorrhea – 'seems to be resistant.'

'Oh my God. You mean I'm not cured?'

'No, not yet. Says this report.' McNeil shut the file with a slap, memorializing another stage in the development of the disaster. 'Still, there's definitely no indication of syph, which is a comfort – sometimes those spirochetes can be right buggers. Say! Don't look as if the world's about to end!'

He chuckled, leaning back in his chair. 'I'm afraid your problem's getting commoner and commoner. You're not a health-food addict, are you?'

'Uh … Not seriously,' Philip muttered. 'Though we buy from Puritan pretty often.' Wondering what on earth this had to do with VD.

'Thought not. You might have got off lighter if you had been. You see, what happens is, you pick up some sub-clinical infection – I don't mean only social diseases, but anything from a whitlow to a sore throat – and at the same time you're getting traces of antibiotic in your diet: what's left in the chicken particularly, but also pork and even steak that you've been eating. And there's just enough of the stuff to select for the resistant strains among the millions of organisms in your body, and when we come along and try to tackle them they thumb their noses at us. Are you with me?'

Philip gave a distracted nod, his mind on Denise and the kids.

'Still, not to worry,' McNeil resumed, opening the file again. 'We're ahead of the game so far, still got two or three tricks up our sleeves.'

'My wife,' Philip whispered.

'Judging by this, though,' McNeil said, not seeming to have heard, 'we'd better do a bit of sifting first. Look, can you come back tomorrow? I'd like to check out your cultures. There's a risk we might have to go over to injections. But we'll get the better of the blighters, never fear.'

At which point he appeared to recall being interrupted.

'Oh, yes, your wife. She – uh – still doesn't know?'

'No,' Philip confessed miserably. 'I made sure she took the penicillin, of course, but I said it was hepatitis I'd caught. She did want to know why I hadn't got medicine for the kids as well, but I managed to evade that. Now, though, Josie – my daughter – she was sick in the night, and …'

'And, to be blunt, you don't have a hope in hell of keeping the truth from her,' McNeil said briskly. 'I did warn you it would cause – ah – rifts in the lute. Look, why don't we cut our losses? I'll send the diagnosis and lab reports to your own doctor, and—'

'Clayford,' Philip said raggedly.

'Hell.' McNeil bit his lip. 'I was forgetting. Yes, that toffy-nosed devil. A good God-fearing type, isn't he? Won't touch a VD case, as though he were a parson refusing to visit someone in jail for witchcraft!' He shuddered elaborately.

'Well, in that case … It's probably unethical, but I don't regard it as wrong to save people embarrassment. If you like, I'll take on you and your wife as private patients. I only do this clinic part-time, you know. Sort of on principle. Conditioning, I suppose. I trained in England.'

Philip nodded. He had noticed many English turns of phrase in McNeil's speech, though his accent was purely American. 'What brought you here, then?'

'Not the shortcomings of their state health service, as most people instantly assume.' McNeil chuckled. 'Hell, it may be a mess, but half the doctors I've met over here – Clayford, for one – get offended if people fall ill out of office hours. Try refusing house calls in Britain and you get struck off the medical register … No, my mother was born right here, and when my father died she decided to retire to her home town. So when I passed twenty-six I came to join her.'

Why—? Oh, of course. The draft limit.

McNeil slapped the desk and rose. 'Think it over. I'd make it as easy on your wife as possible, of course. But I'm afraid I must insist on your bringing the matter into the open. Good afternoon.'

'Bad news,' a voice said at Philip's elbow as he descended the stairs. The clinic was over a store selling sports equipment and kinky leather goods.

'What?' Philip glanced around. The speaker was the man who'd been in the waiting room.

'I said bad news. I could read it in the stoop of your shoulders.'

'It's none of your fucking business,' Philip snapped.

'Well put. I'm feeling pretty low myself. Come and have a drink.'

'Ah, go to hell!'

'I'm there,' the stranger said, suddenly serious. 'Aren't you? Shit, I'm thirty-seven and I never caught a dose before, thought it was something you could laugh off nowadays, like a head cold.' He had one, by the sound of him; his n's were more like d's, as though he were holding his nose. 'Turns out the stinking bug's resistant. So far it's been four months.'

'Four months!' Philip was appalled, envisaging how endless such a sentence would be for himself.

'Now they're giving me six million units a day of some new miracle drug. In the ass. It hurts like fire, but at least it's started to cure me. What about that drink?'

Philip hesitated.

'Name's Alan Prosser,' the stranger said. 'Prosser Enterprises. Plumbing equipment, sewage pipes, garbage-disposal systems, that kind of shit.'

'Christ.' Philip blinked at him. 'We had your stuff put in at our last place. I remember. But I never met you.' He frowned. 'Someone called—'

'Bud Burkhardt?'

'Yes! Your partner?'

'Ex-partner.' With a scowl. 'The mother walked out no me. Went to Towerhill, manage the new branch of Puritan ... Did you say "our" last place?'

'Yes.'

'So you're married, hm? Then maybe I shouldn't talk about my troubles!'

'You not?'

'Was.' Prosser's face suddenly grew strained and lined, as though ten years had passed between words. He raised his left hand to display the palm. There was a round mark on it to match the scar on the back, like a brand.

'What happened?' Philip said uncertainly.

'Shot. The same slug that left this mark on me. We'd wandered into the fringes of a Trainite demonstration, and some trigger-happy National Guardsman ... Oh, shit, it's ancient history. And luckily Belle couldn't have kids. What about that drink?'

'Yes. Okay. Only one, though. It's supposed to be – uh – bad for the condition.'

'Ah, shit. Not having it is far worse for the mind.'

THE INDISPENSABLE ASSISTANTS

Grade-A MEXICAN HONEYBEES $165.95/gallon!
Grade-A EUROPEAN BEES only $220/gallon!
Best quality IRISH EARTHWORMS $67.50/quart!
GUARANTEED live on delivery! Plant Fertility Corp., San Clemente,
Calif. (Licensed by California State Board of Agriculture.)

BROKENMINDED

After the terrible collective madness of Christmastide in Noshri, Lucy Ramage somehow managed to keep going for a while alongside those members of the original Globe Relief and UN teams who hadn't been deported. It was as though the work of the preceding four months had been wiped out like chalk writing by a wet cloth. Indeed, things were worse than before. When she first arrived, people used to come out willingly from wherever they had found shelter – tumbledown shacks, smashed cars, wrecked buses, holes in the ground – and asked for food and first aid. Now they skulked and shied away, remained in hiding and stared at the world with mad distrustful faces, eyes wide and white-rimmed. To persuade someone to take food, you first had to swallow a mouthful yourself; to bandage a wound was often possible, but they wouldn't allow you to apply ointment or administer oral drugs. They were all agreed on what had happened to them: they were victims of a terrifying magic.

Some, it seemed, had been driven totally insane. For the rest of their lives they would limp around moaning, or break into causeless tears, or scream until their throats were raw at the sight of a harmless insect.

There were insects in Noshri again now. During the war they had completely disappeared.

Directly after the worst time, Lucy had been interrogated by hostile government officials concerning the nature of the madness. Fretting to get back to the miserable people who needed her help, she condensed what she had to report into the briefest possible version and delivered it in dry emotionless tones.

'Characteristic symptoms? They included violent perspiration, facial tics, occasional spasms of the long muscles in the thighs and calves, and extremely marked pupillary dilation. Vomiting? That was reported in only a minority of cases. But everyone suffered acid diarrhea and occasionally the stools were mixed with fresh blood.

'How long to take effect? Typically, about one to three hours after the onset of the sweating and pupillary dilation, a sensation of floating ensued, and one saw the victims staring at their hands and feet unable to believe they any longer belonged to them. This stage was rapidly succeeded by one of hysterical terror, with visual and auditory hallucinations, and in the great majority of cases total loss of self-control. Outbursts of wild rage, often leading to random wrecking of the immediate surroundings and particularly to arson, and later to assault on anybody and anything that moved – especially crying children, who were frequently kicked and beaten to death by their own parents because their noise proved intolerable – lasted six to thirty-six hours. Most sufferers did not sleep for the longer period. If no other target offered itself their own bodies took the brunt and they gashed or battered themselves. I also saw many run to the river and jump in, crying they were dying of thirst. This probably connects with the extreme dehydration the diarrhea entailed.

'The content of the hallucinations? Remarkably uniform. Voices came first, especially those of parents, senior relatives, and – in the case of ex-soldiers – officers and NCO's. Since the majority of these were dead the conviction that ghosts were walking followed logically. Many of those killed were mistaken for evil spirits. Because personal appearance is radically changed by the condition (e.g., the huge staring eyes, the awkward walk due to muscular cramps) close relatives often did not recognize one another and ran screaming even from a wife or husband.

'After-effects? Melancholia, acute hypnophobia – that's fear of going to sleep because of the high incidence of nightmares – anxiety, unaccountable fits of violence ... A man was murdered the other day for no better reason than that he let his shadow fall on someone else's foot.

'Treatment? Well, we've had some success with doctoring the water supply – you know we're still selling drinking water from carts, and dumping half a pound of tranquilizers into every barrel seems to have helped, a little. But the tranquilizers are running short, so ...'

Shrug.

She, too, was afraid to sleep. She dreamed always of the little bloody bits of human flesh that had spattered her. Either she doped herself with amphetamines, or – when they ceased to have any effect and her eyelids began to sting – she took enough barbiturates to drive her into coma, insulated against dreams. While she was awake she hardly ate, but wandered around coaxing people from hiding, washing gangrened wounds, helping to rig improvised shelters. At first the black soldiers now cleaning up the town were hostile; when they saw how meekly she worked, and how hard, they grew used to her and more than once when she found herself falling down with fatigue strong anonymous black arms carried her bodily home. Often the man was surprised at being called major when he was a mere private.

She learned about the charge that the relief food contained a hallucinogen from Bertil, who believed the suggestion that it had been infected with ergot or something like it; he said that had been responsible for outbreaks of medieval dancing mania. She was told about it again by the army officers investigating the calamity, who believed there had been poison deliberately added.

She herself had no views on the matter.

Reporters naturally came in swarms. Although the news value of the war had more or less died with the armistice, General Kaika was anxious that the whole world should see the extent of the continuing disaster, so he put government planes at the disposal of journalists and TV camera teams. He even relaxed his embargo on Americans for the sake of a team from ABS's Paris office, provided they were led by a Frenchman. When they heard about Lucy they sensed an angle: beautiful blonde caught up in a night of horror. No one apparently knew exactly where she was, so they set off in search of her.

They came on her burrowing in the ruins of a house. She had uncovered a body the soldiers had overlooked, that of a child about ten years old. She was disinterring it with a pocket-knife.

When she realized the interviewer was an American she bared her teeth and attacked him. He had to have eight stitches in a gash that ran from his collarbone to his sternum.

They flew her, under sedation, to England, to a country mental hospital, where she awoke to discover green lawns, the first flowers of spring peering out under the overcast sky, cows grazing in a field the other side of a pleasant valley, and steel bars across an unopenable window.

EAT IT IN GOOD HEALTH

Special this week at your Puritan Health Supermarket!
Okinawa squash, reg. $0.89 – $0.75!
Penguin eggs (low on DDT, PCB) reg $6.35 doz. – $6.05!
Pacific potatoes (unwashed), reg. $o.8g lb. – $0.69!
Butter from sunny New Zealand, reg. $1.35 qrt. – $1.15!
YOU TOO CAN AFFORD GOOD HEALTH AT PURITAN!

THE STRONG CAME FORTH

His haunted dreams had finally faded and Pete Goddard was sleeping okay again. His first wakening after the collapse, though, had been appalling: terror, paralysis, pain.

Except that he wasn't paralyzed. They had merely put his legs into traction, cased the whole lower part of his trunk in tight plastic wraps, *stretched* him with weights hung from ceiling-mounted pulleys. As soon as he was alert enough to understand, they explained what they were doing to him, and why, and he very nearly couldn't believe the why.

They said that all by himself he had held up three-quarters of a ton.

Oh, it wasn't any kind of a record. The physiotherapist who attended him daily had mentioned a woman, hysterical with fear for the life of her child, who had lifted a car weighing a ton and a half; also a professional strongman who had demonstrated a lift of two full tons, slung from a harness around his waist. It had something to do with the engineering properties of the femur. She showed him diagrams that he fought to comprehend.

But it was strange how the nurses seemed to be frightened of him, and kept asking whether he had trained as a weight-lifter. Well, he had, though not for over a year, not since he met Jeannie. He said wearily he had kept in shape.

Obviously one couldn't do this kind of thing and not be very badly damaged. All the musculature of his shoulders had suffered subcutaneous hemorrhage, so that he wore a colossal bruise a foot wide, and even supporting the weight of his own arm now tired him within seconds. The cartilaginous discs separating his vertebrae had been crushed when his spine locked into the single solid column that enabled him to stand the weight. All the synovial membranes in his leg joints had been overloaded, so that his knees and ankles had also locked rigid, and the arches of both his feet had collapsed. He had briefly become a pillar of bone, and he didn't remember. He had known only one thing during that terrible time: he couldn't do anything any more except stand straight.

For the first few days he lay there in the hospital he was frightened as much of having to pay for what was being done to him as he was of not being able to walk again. He was doped to kill the pain, of course, and that made his mind fuzzy too, so when they allowed Jeannie to see him he couldn't explain what was troubling him and finally he broke down crying from frustration and they thought it was pain and doped him with a double dose.

But, a day or two after – he wasn't keeping track of time right then – they let him have other visitors, and it all came clear. There were reporters, and photographers, and a man from California, the uncle of the two children he'd saved. Harry had crawled under the beam and brought them back with him, but he'd held up the roof.

Their parents were dead. So their uncle, a successful bee importer, was going to adopt them, and pay for this hospitalization – the best of everything, he said, up to fifty thousand bucks. He insisted he could easily afford it; he'd got right in on the ground floor when the bees of California became extinct in the sixties, and now he ran a million-dollar undertaking.

He also remarked, sounding puzzled, that he'd tried to get Harry to accept a reward, too, but the guy wouldn't take a cent. Said something about ghouls. Some kind of Trainite prejudice.

Then a week or two later a senator called Howard or Howell or something brought him an illuminated scroll, a citation for courage, signed by Prexy himself. They framed it and hung it facing his bed.

'Hi, honey.'

'Hi, doll.'

They brushed lips. Jeannie had come in as usual, regular as clockwork. But there was something odd about her appearance. Lying surrounded by the papers and books he used to pass the time – his arms were moving freely thanks to the physiotherapist's massage and he could turn pages fine – he took a second look. Her left hand was bandaged.

'You cut yourself, baby?' he demanded.

'Uh ...' She made to hide it, changed her mind. 'No, I got bitten.'

'Bitten! What by – a dog?'

'No, a rat. I reached in the cupboard for a bag of flour ... I keep calling the exterminator, but he can't come. Got too many calls – hey, what you doing?' Pete had seized the bellpush by his bed.

'Calling the nurse! You put that dressing on yourself?'

'Well – yes.'

'You have it attended to properly! You know what rats carry? Sometimes plague! Or it might go septic.'

The nurse came, prompt because of his benefactor's money, and led Jeannie protesting away. While she was gone he lay there fuming, thinking: Rats? So many rats the exterminator can't cope? Hell!

And it was just as well he insisted. Jeannie had a sub-clinical fever due to septicemia. When they found out she'd kissed him, they gave him a prophylactic injection as well.

Trying to lighten the mood when she came back with her hand neatly wrapped in white, he said, 'Say, baby, good news. Tomorrow they're going to let me try and walk!'

'Honey, that's really great!' Her eyes shone. But mainly with tears. 'Is it ...?'

'Is it going to be the same?'

She nodded.

'They think it will be. But not for a pretty long time. I'll have to wear a brace for my back, to start with anyway.'

'How long?'

He hesitated, then repeated the physiotherapist's estimate. 'Two years.'

'Oh, *Pete*!'

'But everything else is okay!' He brought out the worst terror, the most fearful fear. 'There's nothing wrong with ... I mean, I'm still a *man*.'

Thank God. Thank God. He'd prayed, really prayed, when that point occurred to him. And one of the doctors, whom he was going to remember every time he prayed again, had told him well, as far as can be judged that ought to be okay, as soon as you've got the strength back in your arms try it for yourself. I'll send you some deep-dirt books in case they help.

Jeannie clutched his hand and began to cry.

*

Eventually she was able to ask about the future. Obviously a cripple couldn't go back on the force. Could he?

He shook his head. He could do that now without a twinge of pain. They'd been wonderful, the care they'd taken.

'No. But I got the offer of a job already. Man called by this morning who'd heard I can't get back in the police. Friend of one of the doctors, cat called Prosser. Says to let him know as soon as I'm fit and he'll give me a desk job I can handle.'

'Back in Towerhill, you mean?'

'No, here in Denver. Of course we'd have to move house, but he said the pay would be good … Ah, don't worry, baby. Everything's going to be all right.'

MY FINGERS ARE GREEN AND SOMETIMES DROP OFF

Dear Sir: Thank you for your letter of 18th and enclosures. The sample of dirt contains an exceptionally high proportion of lead and mercury, trace quantities of molybdenum and selenium, and a small amount of salts of silver. There is no detectable cadmium. The water sample is contaminated with lead, arsenic, selenium and compounds of sodium and potassium, particularly sodium nitrite. We suspect that the garden of the house you have bought is sited on infill derived from mine tailings, and suggest you raise the matter with the former owners. You do not mention whether you have children, but if you do we would draw your attention to the dangers they face from lead and sodium nitrite in such quantities. Early settlement of your account would be appreciated.

Yours faithfully.

THE REARING OF THE UGLY HEAD

Having dropped Harold, Josie and the Henlowes' boy at their play-school – social behavior should be encouraged at an early age and the hell with the risk of infection that caused parents like Bill and Tania Chalmers (RIP, victims along with Anton of the Towerhill avalanche) to keep their kids at home as late as was legal: what a nasty personality poor Anton had developed! – Denise Mason continued to Dr Clayford's office.

The room was a perfect frame for his personality. He sat at a mahogany desk, an antique, with a gilt-tooled leather top, in a leather armchair with a swivel base. He was gruff, bluff and tough. He was proud of belonging to what, in a rare moment of jocularity, Denise had once heard him term 'the sulfa generation'. She had been on his list for years, since long before her marriage, even though she didn't much like him because he was distant and difficult to talk to. All the same there was something reassuring in his old-fashioned manner.

He reminded her more than a little of her father.

For the first time ever he didn't stand up as she entered, merely waved her to the chair facing him. Puzzled, she sat down.

'Well, what's the trouble?'

'Well – uh …' Absurdly, she felt herself flushing bright scarlet. 'Well, I've been pretty run down lately. But now I've developed – well, a discharge. And irritation.'

'Vaginal, you mean? Oh, that's the gonorrhea your husband gave you.'

'*What?*'

'I told him to go to the clinic on Market. They specialize in that sort of thing. He didn't tell you?'

She could only shake her head wordlessly. So many things had suddenly become clear.

'Typical,' Clayford said with contempt. 'Absolutely typical. These products of the so-called permissive generation. Dishonest. Greedy, lazy, self-indulgent, ready at the drop of a hat to tell any lie that will protect them from the consequences of their actions. They're the cause of all the troubles in the world today!'

He leaned suddenly across his desk, shaking a pen at her.

'You should see what I have to see, daily in my practice. Children from good homes, sub-normal from lead poisoning! Blind from congenital syphilis, too! Choking with asthma! Bone cancer, leukemia, God knows what!' He was beginning to spray little drops of spittle from his thin lips.

Denise stared at him as though seeing him for the first time.

'You've been treating Philip for a social disease?' she said at last.

'Of course not. I told him where he could get treatment, for you as well as himself. *I'm* not going to help him cover up his tracks. It's that kind of refusal to admit responsibility that's put the world in the mess it's in!'

'He asked you for help, and you refused?'

'I told you,' Clayford grunted. 'I recommended him to the proper clinic.'

Suddenly she couldn't see him any longer. There were stinging tears in her eyes. She stood up in a single jerk that snapped her spine straight like a bowstring when the arrow is released.

'You bastard,' she said. 'You smug pompous devil. You liar. You filthy dishonest old man. You put the poison in the world, you and your generation. You crippled my children. You made sure they'd never eat clean food, drink pure water, breathe sweet air. And when someone comes to you for help you turn your back.'

Suddenly she was crying and hurling things – a big glass inkwell, full of lovely pitch-black ink, a huge beautiful mess all over his white shirt. A book, a tray of papers. Anything.

'Philip isn't – what you called him! He's not, he's not! He's my husband, and I love him!'

She spun around. There was a tall glass-fronted cabinet full of medical texts. She caught at one of the doors, which stood ajar, and leaned her full weight on it, and toppled it in a crashing smashing marvelous miracle of noise.

And marched out.

It was all insured by Angel City, anyway.

DISGRACE

'O Lord!' Mr Bamberley said, head bowed at the head of his fine long table of seasoned oak, 'enter our hearts, we pray, and as this food nourishes our bodies so may our souls be nourished by Thy word, amen!'

Amen, said a ragged chorus, cut short by the rattle of porcelain and silver. The silent black girl who worked as the Bamberleys' maid – her name was Christy and she was fat – offered Hugh a basket of rolls and breadsticks. He took a roll. There was as usual too much vinegar on the salad. It made his tongue curl.

He was home for the weekend from college, and this was the ritual of Sunday lunch after church. Apparently servants, in Mr Bamberley's cosmos, didn't have to be allowed time off for worship, although both Christy and Ethel, the cook, were devout. They could be heard singing gospel songs in the kitchen most of the day.

But Sunday mornings they worked like slaves from six AM to get this family meal ready.

Opposite her husband, plump, with a smile on her face as fixed as a wax doll's, sat Mrs Bamberley – Maud. She was ten years younger than her husband and twenty points lower on the IQ scale. She thought he was wonderful and sometimes gave talks to local women's groups about how wonderful he was. Also she judged flower-arranging competitions and was regularly interviewed by the local press and TV when some vet with a bad conscience joined the Double-V adoption scheme. She was, by courtesy of her husband, a great adopter herself, and when they asked needling questions about race and religion she was prompt with the proper replies: a child of a different color from the rest of the family feels so pitifully self-conscious, and surely all parents want their children to be brought up in their own faith?

Behind her chair, from a wall covered in a very expensive velvet-flock paper, a portrait of her grandfather looked down. He had been an Episcopalian

bishop, but the picture showed him in the costume of a New England gentleman keeping up the Old English custom of riding to hounds: red coat, brown
boots, distinguished with a white dog-collar and black silk front.

Hugh referred to him as being dressed to kill.

The salad was replaced – though Hugh had sampled only a mouthful of
his – by a dish of cold fish with mayonnaise. He didn't even touch this course.
He was suddenly afraid of it because it had come from the sea.

It was the first time he had been here since the disastrous interview Mr Bamberley had given on the *Petronella Page Show*, and the consequent closing
down of the hydroponics plant. Everyone had been prepared to believe, as
soon as that expert in Paris had published his verdict about the victims, that
there was indeed poison in the Nutripon. He'd arrived – home – on Friday
evening. So far there hadn't been a single reference to this event.

Petronella Page was notoriously merciless with any kind of fake. Hugh had
been interested to learn that she agreed with his opinion: Mr Bamberley was
a phony on the grand scale.

Correspondingly, behind Mr Bamberley's own chair, another portrait looked
down, of his grandfather. It showed him – a burly man with his legs planted
a yard apart, fists on his hips – committing rape. At least that was Hugh's
description. People who didn't know the story might be content to recognize
the oil gusher in the background.

The fish was replaced by platters of roast meat, dishes of baked and boiled
potatoes, carrots, cabbage, peas. Also there were sauce-boats of gravy and
imported English horseradish cream. Silent as ever, Christy brought a pitcher
of beer of a brand Hugh didn't like, a weekly treat for the older boys, and
another of lemonade for Maud and 'the kids'.

So far nothing of any consequence had been said.

The remainder of the company at table consisted of Mr Bamberley's adopted
sons, with omissions. Cyril, who as well as being the oldest was also the long-
est-established, was in Manila. He'd graduated with distinction from West
Point and was now personal aide, at twenty-four, to one of the generals setting up what Prexy kept terming 'the Pacific bastion' – in other words, a
white alliance including Australia, New Zealand and what few Latin American countries were still right-wing dictatorships, designed to contain the
pro-Chinese, neo-Marxist tidal wave surging around the planet.

Hugh had met Cyril only once, just after his own recruitment to the family, and taken an instant loathing to him. But at the time he'd been too
overwhelmed with his new prospects to say anything.

The second omission was Jared. Jared, who was twenty-one, was in jail.

One didn't speak of him in Mr Bamberley's presence. He'd been convicted of helping to organize a pro-Tupamaro movement among the Chicanos of New Mexico. Hugh hadn't met him; he was serving a five-year term.

But he thought he'd probably like him a lot.

And Noel, five, was in bed with a fever, but the rest were here. Down at Maud's end there sat Ronald, who was sixteen and rather dull; Cornelius, dutiful and bright but the victim of occasional fits since his twelfth birthday – not epilepsy, something to do with enzymes that fouled up the interchange of energy between one nerve-cell and the next, kept under control by a special diet; then Norman, eight, with the facial tic, and Claude, ten, with the bad teeth that sometimes cracked edge to edge and fell out of his mouth. A fairly typical family in its way, despite having been assembled from so many different sources: those in their teens physically healthy, those younger, not. Hugh had a girlfriend in college with a younger brother who vomited back anything cooked in corn-oil.

And still those mothers won't admit how they've fucked up the world.

'Hugh,' Mr Bamberley said, 'did you speak?'

He hadn't meant to. But he recalled the echo of his words. Not looking to his right, he reached for his beer.

'I'm sorry, Jack. Did you ask me a question?'

'Yes, I did!' Mr Bamberley laid down his knife and fork next to massive slices of beef partly sectioned. 'It was my distinct impression that you – ah – murmured a word I disapprove of.'

Hugh drained his glass and leaned back with a sigh. 'So what if I did?'

Mr Bamberley slowly turned pink all the way to his receding hairline. 'What reason had you for employing such a word?'

'The reason's all around you,' Hugh snapped, and made a gesture that embraced the luxuriously furnished dining-room, the food piled on the table, the maid waiting in the corner like a store-window dummy.

'Explain further!' Mr Bamberley was about to choke with the effort of controlling his fury.

'Okay, I will!' Suddenly Hugh could stand the pressure no longer. He leapt to his feet, his chair crashing over backwards. 'Here you sit, stuffing your fat paunch with food from all over the stinking world, when you've poisoned thousands of poor black buggers in Africa – haven't you? Are you out sharing their suffering, helping them pick up the bits? The hell you are! You're fighting tooth and nail the one thing that might help to get to the bottom of the disaster, screaming that a UN inquiry would "serve no useful purpose" – I saw that quote in the papers! Here you are at your beautiful table, gobbling and guzzling and saying *grace* for Chrissake, as though you expect God to thank you for all the people you've killed and driven out of their minds!'

Mr Bamberley extended toward the door a shaking hand from which his napkin depended like a crumpled flag.

'Leave this room!' he roared. 'Leave this *house*! And don't come back until you're willing to apologize!'

'Exactly what I'd have expected you to say,' Hugh said in a dead voice. He felt suddenly very grown-up indeed, very mature, almost old. 'Right square in the tradition: you kick people in the balls and expect them to do the apologizing. Because of you and people like you we sit here in the richest country in the world surrounded by sick kids—'

'You have a foul mouth and a foul mind!'

'You trying to tell me you adopted Norman because of his tic? Don't give me that shit. I heard from Maud: you found out when the papers had been signed. Look at Claude's teeth, like punk from a rotten stump! Look at Corny envying us because we can eat regular food! You—'

But the tension overcame Corny at that point. It was always stress that brought on his attacks. He collapsed into his plate, face down, shattering it and spattering his special mush all over everywhere. As Maud and Christy rushed to attend him, Hugh delivered his parting shot.

'You and your ancestors treated the world like a fucking great toilet bowl. You shat in it and boasted about the mess you'd made. And now it's full and overflowing, and you're fat and happy and black kids are going crazy to keep you rich. *Goodbye!*'

He slammed the door as hard as he could when storming out, hoping the crash might shake down the portrait of Jacob Holmes Bamberley I.

But the nail was too solidly imbedded in the wall.

NOT MAKING HEADLINES

… guilty of using brominated vegetable oil, an illegal emulsifying agent. Despite defense submissions that no harm had been proved to anyone who ate the food in question, the company was fined one hundred dollars. Now the weather. SO_2, ozone and lead alkyl counts all remain high …

A CALL TO ALMS

Outside the gray stone house that Michael Advowson called home, on the gray road, a green official car was standing, the dirty rain smearing its smart paint. He ignored it. He ignored, equally, the man in the fawn raincoat who rose to meet him in the hallway – or would have done so, but that the stranger blocked the door to his surgery, and Advowson was carrying a bleeding child in his arms, crying at the top of her lungs.

'Get out of my *way!*' he snapped, and shouldered the man bodily aside.

'But, doctor, this is—' The voice of his housekeeper, MrsByrne.

'I know Mr Clark! He was here last month! There, there, darling, it'll stop hurting soon. You be calm!' Laying the little girl on his examination couch. At once the white disposable cover turned bright red around her foot.

'Come inside and make yourself useful or get the hell out,' he added to the man in the raincoat. 'Better make yourself useful. Wash your hands, quick!' Meantime he was seizing from the cabinets around the room bandages, powders, a syringe, scissors to cut away the shoe and sock.

Taking an uncertain step into the room, Clark said, 'What – ah – what happened?'

'Glass. Use that soap, the dark red one. It's antiseptic.'

'I don't quite—'

'I said glass!' Michael soothed the little girl with a pat on the cheek. She was so terrified she had wet herself, but that could be cleaned up in a moment. Continuing as he drove the needle of the syringe through the rubber seal of a phial: 'She was playing up by the Donovan farm, where for years they used to dump rubbish. She trod on a broken bottle, and ...'

With sudden perfectly-controlled strength he grasped the child's leg and held it still by force while he sank the needle home. Almost at once her eyelids closed.

'And she's likely to lose her great toe. Blood-poisoning too, unless we're quick. Is that your car outside, a government car?'

'Well – yes.'

'Then maybe we shan't have to wait on an ambulance. My own car is in to be mended. Now come and help me. Do as I tell you, that's all.'

Clark came: too young to be a father, perhaps, and live day and night with fear of what might happen to his or any child. The great toe had been wholly severed. Michael gave it to him to hold while he staunched the blood.

He was valiant, and at least managed to set the toe on a table before running from the room, and in a moment was heard vomiting on the lawn.

Yet he came back, which also was valiant, and held the toe while Michael secured it with rough rapid stitches – all according to principles enunciated in a medical journal from China (make sure you maintain the blood supply at all costs until there's time to match the nerves and muscles) – and then an ambulance arrived and Michael didn't need to requisition the government car after all.

*

'When a child can't even play safely in a field ...' Michael said. He had called Clark into the sitting-room and the offer of a tot had been approved. Two fingers for each of them. It was sometimes necessary to give the healers medicine too. '*Slainte!*'

'*Slainte!*'

'Now, what was it you came for?' Michael inquired, dropping into his favorite chair. 'Did they send you to apologize for that scandal at Murphy's farm?'

The government man had the grace to look uncomfortable. 'No. But I was told that you were right all along.'

'Kind of them to admit it!' Michael snorted. 'I'm not even a vet, just a boy raised on a farm, but I recognize dicoumarin poisoning from spoiled hay when I see it. But you didn't believe me, did you? No more did they – probably never heard of dicoumarin! Oh, they're such fools, they make me see red. You know if they'd had their way I might not have saved young Eileen's toe?'

Clark blinked at him. He found this aggressive redhead with the green eyes too close together curiously disturbing.

'It's a fact. I learned the right way of it out of a Chinese medical journal, which they tried to stop me subscribing to because it would mean giving the Chinese Western currency!' Scowling, he drained his glass.

'Well, I wouldn't know about that,' the other said, reaching to the inside pocket of his smart blue suit, likely English. 'I was told to give you this.' He proffered an envelope bearing a green wax official seal.

'Ah, perhaps they sent the apology in writing!' Michael grunted, tearing it open. A long pause. Eventually he looked up with a bitter smile.

'Well, that'll teach me not to try and beat the government. Even if you win they find a way of doing you down. Did you know I spent five years as a medical officer in the army? No? Well, I did. So now they're recalling me from the reserve to go with a UN team to investigate the matter of this poisoned food at Noshri. Well, I suppose it's one means of putting me out of the way!'

He threw the letter angrily to the floor.

'But who's going to tend the next child like Eileen Murphy?'

MARCH

LONG MULTIPLICATION

Behold! th' industrious *Hind*, who daily walks
His narrow fields, and with a miser's care
(Tho' with a nobler motive, for to spare
Foul waste, and weeds) inspects the sep'rate stalks,

Who roots out all that are infect with blight
(For plants, like men, fall ill) and, mouthing ire,
Sets the sere stalks upon a smoky fire,
Then chooses from the seed that grew aright

Such as will, after golden harvest-time,
Repeat their kind, but bettered, sweet and sound,
Their chaff stript off by thrashers as of yore:

Him do I sing, as worthy of my rime,
Him whose devotion to the pregnant ground
Makes two ears grow where one ear grew before.

– 'The Agricultural Muse', 1710

A GIFT OF INSECTS

This high up there was still a lot of snow. Peg drove cautiously along the steep and winding road. She had seen scarcely any other cars for several miles. Still, there was always the chance of encountering some idiot who believed he had the road to himself.

Idiot …

Am I one?

She hadn't intended to utter the rhetorical question aloud; however, Felice – shivering because the driver's window was open despite being wrapped to the ears in fur, and real fur at that, Peg suspected, though she'd not been so impolite as to ask outright – said wryly, 'I've been wondering the same about myself. But I should have taken over from Bill Chalmers when he was killed, and finding that bastard Halkin slotted in over my head …'

Peg gave a nod. She knew exactly how Felice felt. She herself was sorry to have lost her job, but underlying her decision had been a fierce pride which was still sustaining her.

'I wasn't thinking about that,' she said. 'I mean, here we are, going to arrive after dark, without even having phoned ahead ...'

'You can phone the wat?' Felice sounded surprised.

'Sure. They even have a listed number, just the one for the whole fifty-sixty of them.' In the name of Jones. Perhaps that was why she hadn't called ahead. She was trying not to think too much about Decimus being dead, even though his sister was right here in the car with her, even though they were retracing his last journey the opposite way.

As though at the end of the trip I expect to find him alive and well.

'Somehow I didn't think of them as having a phone at all,' Felice said.

Well, that was natural, knowing their distrust of modern technology. Moreover, they didn't have too much truck with the outside world. And the outside world disapproved of them, which was a reason. A brief moment of approbation had followed the Towerhill avalanche, when even the governor had commended their rescue work. But that was over.

It being so late, she'd suggested to Felice when they came to the turning signposted for Towerhill that they spend the night there. Since the avalanche it was no secret that the tourists had vanished, phfft. There would be plenty of vacant rooms. No one but ghouls now cared to make for the town.

But Felice had said she preferred not to be a ghoul.

Suddenly, at the very edge of her headlight beams, Peg spotted another car drawn up by the roadside: a little Stephenson electric not meant for long distances, with only a hundred-mile range between rechargings. A young man was inspecting its works. Hearing the soft cat-hiss of the Hailey, he turned and waved.

'Think I should stop?' she muttered to Felice. Normally the idea wouldn't have occurred to her; she'd have carried straight on, and the hell with whether the guy was found frozen in the morning. But since reaching the thousand-foot line, 'way back, she'd been able to drive with the ventilator off and the window down, and crisp fresh mountain air had made her lightheaded. Even the cold was refreshing; she hadn't been this cold in years, living in LA where the only chance of staving off her sinusitis lay in wearing a filtermask and changing the air-purifier on the car every thousand miles and spending as much time as possible indoors.

Apparently Felice had been affected the same way. Instead of uttering sensible warnings about being mugged and left in the snow while thieves drove off in the car, she said, 'Oh, he looks pretty harmless. And I wouldn't like to be stuck here in this cold.'

So Peg pulled up alongside him.

'Say, are you going to the Trainite wat?' he demanded, leaning to her window and brushing back lank hair.

'Yes.'

'Me too. Only my car quit on me – the stinking charge-level gauge stuck at high. Can I ride in with you?'

Peg gave a doubtful glance at the tiny back seat of the Hailey, a mere shelf intended to save a couple with a kid from having to change to a bigger car. It was already almost covered with Felice's traveling-bag and a big canister with a label in bold red and black saying LIVE WITH CARE.

'I just have the one small bag,' the young man pleaded.

'Oh ... Okay.'

'Great, thanks!'

So she got out – the Hailey had only two doors – and watched him closely and noted that he locked the electric car. Then it was presumably his own; she'd half imagined it might be stolen. She relaxed and held the door for him as he returned, carrying an airline-size bag.

'You'll have to move that canister,' she said. 'Mind, it's heavy.'

He complied. 'What is it?' he asked as he read the label.

'Gallon of imported worms,' Felice told him. 'Thought it would make a useful present for the wat.'

'Yeah, good idea.' He settled himself awkwardly, his long legs folded almost double. 'By the way, I'm Hugh, Hugh Pettingill.'

The name sounded as though it ought to mean something. It declined to.

'I'm Peg. This is Felice.' She slammed the door and drove off.

'You live at the wat?'

'No. You?'

'Thinking maybe I ought to.' In the windshield, by the faint glow of the instruments, she caught a glimpse of his face set in a frown, like a Pepper's ghost against the black road and white-gray soiled snow-banks. 'I just been drifting around the past few weeks. Trying to figure things out.'

Me too.

Peg thought of the long hours she'd wasted in her apartment, staring at the TV as though it were some kind of crystal ball and would suggest a right course of action, until that unexpected phone-call from Felice, who wanted to meet her for dinner, wanted to talk about the way she had regarded her late brother, wanted to find out if she'd been wrong in quarreling with him when he committed himself to Trainite ideals.

She said she'd been wondering ever since the day she was told that life expectancy in the United States was going down.

The calmly spoken statement had shaken Peg to the core; the dinner had lasted past midnight, conversation turning to argument and back again, until eventually this plan had come from it: to visit the Denver wat, talk to Decimus's widow Zena, forget the official view of Trainites ('Their founder went crazy and his chief disciple died stoned!') and try to make up their own minds for a change.

Peg had fallen in with the proposal with a sense of fatalism. The prospect of seeing the wat again, Zena and Rick and the other kids, without Decimus – that frightened her. But it had to be done, she recognized that. After all the world hadn't ended with that one man's death.

Not quite.

She grew aware that the boy in the back – youth, young man, whatever – was talking as though he'd spoken to no one for days and desperately needed the chance to disburden his mind.

'I mean, I couldn't go on taking things from him after that, could I? I mean could I?'

She fished back into memory, and abruptly recognized the name. Pettingill. Click. One of Jacob Bamberley's adopted sons vanishing from college. But apparently Felice had been listening with more attention, because she said now, 'Seen any of this food of his, this stuff they claimed was poisoned and killed all those people at Noshri?'

'Seen, sure, but not on his table.' There was venom in Hugh's tone. 'Oh no. Prime beef for him! Smug self-important do-gooding bastard. Expects you to lick his boots for every favor he does, whether you asked for it or not. Wants to be surrounded by billions of people all saying, "Yes, Mr Bamberley! No, Mr Bamberley! Anything you say, Mr Bamberley!" Makes me sick to my stomach.'

He fished inside his heavy parka and produced something in a limp plastic envelope. 'Say, I got some khat. Either of you want a chaw?'

'Sure,' Felice said, reaching back. Peg repressed a shudder. Putting something in your mouth that had been soaked in a stranger's saliva ... Even if they did say the stuff contained a natural bactericide and the risk of infection was less than from kissing.

She didn't go too much for the kissing bit, either.

She said in a harsh voice, 'Better make the most of it. Those must be the lights of the wat, across the valley there. And you know how they feel about drugs.'

'Peg, baby! Oh, Peg, how wonderful! And this must be Felice, yes?' Tall, very dark, with a stately presence Peg had always envied because it might have helped to put down pestiferous men, Zena embraced her and hurried them all away from the cold, into the curious abstract cave that was her home:

marvelously warm from only a few light-bulbs because it was so efficiently insulated, full of a delicious aroma of beans and herbs.

'How's Rick? How are the girls?'

'Oh, they're fine! Just gone to bed a minute ago. I won't disturb them right now, but they'll be so pleased to see you in the morning. Felice dear, I'm so glad to meet you at last – Decimus talked about you a lot, you know, and he was always so sorry you'd fallen out.' And kissed her too.

Meantime Hugh waited by the door with a look on his face that struck Peg as somehow *hungry*. As though there were no place on earth he could go and find a welcome this effusive. She did her best to make amends by presenting him to other members of the wat community as they appeared: burly Harry Molton, bearded Paul Prince and his pretty wife Sue, Ralph Henderson who had gone bald since she last met him, and half a dozen more who were new. Yes, of course they'd offer hospitality. It was part of the thing. They made it literal and brought bread and salt.

Later, showing her to a bed that was going spare tonight, Zena mentioned how badly they were being plagued with people who claimed to be Trainites and weren't: wanted to wreck and burn and kill and went away in a week or two when they didn't find any support here for their violent plans.

A STRAW TO A DROWNING MAN

... positively identified as Uruguayan. Following this disclosure the Honduran government called on one million dollars of standby credit which will be applied to the purchase of arms and other urgently-needed supplies, and appealed to Washington for assistance in combating the Tupamaro threat. The Pentagon announced an hour ago that the aircraft carrier Wounded Knee *has been diverted from routine patrols in the Atlantic and is already flying survey missions over the rebel-held area. Commenting just prior to leaving for a vacation in Honolulu, Prexy said, quote, They can pull just so many feathers out of the eagle's tail before it pecks. End quote. Contacted at his West Virginia home, the president of the Audubon Society, Dr Ike Mostyn, stated that the last reported sighting of a nesting pair of baldheaded eagles three years ago had proved to be a hoax. New York: Professor Lucas Quarrey of Columbia University, under attack for his allegedly anti-American statements recently in the press and on TV, said at a press conference this morning that his contract to research into improved airplane ventilators had been terminated without warning. Asked whether political motivations underlay the decision, the professor said ...*

RIPOSTE

About forty miles out of Medano, almost exactly due west of the border between California and Baja California, the boat hove to, drifting very slowly on the vast circulation of the Pacific.

Even this far from shore, the night stank. The sea moved lazily, its embryo waves aborted before cresting by the layer of oily residues surrounding the hull, impermeable as sheet plastic: a mixture of detergents, sewage, industrial chemicals and the microscopic cellulose fibers due to toilet paper and newsprint. There was no sound of fish breaking surface. There were no fish.

The boat's skipper was blind in one eye and had been so from birth. He was the illegitimate son of a woman who had gone to California to pick grapes and inhaled something they sprayed on the vines to kill insects, and died. Befriended by a helpful priest, he had survived and gone to school and won a government scholarship. Now he knew about physics and chemistry and meteorology and combustion and the action of poisons.

He was also a Tupa, but that went without saying.

The calendar said there should be a full moon tonight. Perhaps there was. One couldn't see it; one almost never could – or the sun, either. On the after-deck twenty-four big balloons were laid out like the empty skins of fish, slightly glistening as a flashlight played across them. There were cylinders of compressed hydrogen. And twenty-four precisely calculated payloads. Carrying them, the balloons could be relied on to rise to about two hundred meters and float shorewards at nine or ten kilometers an hour. They would cross the coast above or near the city of San Diego.

Roger Halkin was exhausted. Strain, like that of the past few days, always aggravated his diabetes. Still, everything was ready for the morning now; all the fragile stuff had been packed, all the records and books, and the house was littered with full cardboard cartons waiting for the moving men.

'Brandy, darling?' asked his wife Belinda.

'I guess I could risk a small one,' he muttered. 'I surely need it.'

He didn't look or sound like a man who had just been promoted vice-president of his company. There were good reasons. As he'd said with gallows humor to Belinda, he was going to vice-preside over a wake. Today had brought bad news, worse than anyone had expected. Except, presumably, for Tom Grey; that cold fish with his almost symbiotic comprehension of computed trends would have known or at least suspected long ago.

It had never been a secret that Angel City had been hit hard by the Tower-hill affair, but the load, one assumed, must have been spread – they regularly reinsured as far afield as Lloyd's of London – and in any event there was a clear case for a claim against the airline whose SST had triggered the avalanche.

Only this morning he'd heard that the airline was going to fight, maintaining that it hadn't been the boom which caused the disaster, but an earthquake; they'd started occurring around Denver in 1962 and were now common. And the suit might take a year and cost a million. So when he stepped into Bill Chalmers's shoes his first task would be to shed half the section he was supposed to be in charge of, Angel City's out-of-state operations.

'If I could get my hands on that stinking idiot from Denver, that Philip Mason,' he said between clenched teeth, 'I'd tear him limb from limb. And I'm not the only one. I—'

He was interrupted by a cry from the back of the house where their boy Teddy was supposed to be asleep. He was eight, and among the lucky ones; he had nothing worse than occasional asthma. Ever since news of their impending move to LA broke, it had been touch and go whether he'd collapse with another bout, but so far they'd escaped that.

'Dad! Mom! Hey, look – there's fireworks!'

'Christ, isn't that kid asleep yet?' Halkin jumped to his feet. 'I'll give him fireworks!'

'Rodge, don't be angry with him!' Belinda cried, and came running after him.

And the kid wasn't in his bed, or even in his room. He was out on the back patio, staring at the sky. Over the city there was nothing to be seen except the usual yellowish reflection of its lights on the low haze that had blotted out the stars since last October.

'Now you come right back indoors!' Belinda snapped, diving past her husband and sweeping the boy off his feet. 'How often do I have to tell you? You *never* go outside without your mask!'

'But I saw fireworks!' the boy howled. 'Right from my window! I wanna watch the rest of the show!'

'I don't see any fireworks,' Halkin muttered, gazing around. 'Maybe you dreamed it. Let's get back inside.' Already the night air was making his eyelids tingle. He could foresee another stint of watching by Teddy's bed with the oxygen mask poised, and that was the last thing he wanted right now. Tomorrow he'd have to have all his wits about him.

'Right up there!' Teddy shouted, and began to gasp and wheeze and choke as well as cry.

They looked up automatically. Yes, overhead! Something very bright, a flower of flame!

And, on the slant roof of the house, a crash, and a wave of fire that splashed, and soaked their clothes, and clung to their skins, and killed them screaming. It was very good napalm, the best American brand, made by Bamberley Oil.

THE PRECAUTIONARY MEASURE

Twice in the past week a man had followed him home. It was the same one who, for the first time about ten days ago, had shown up at the garbage terminal of the SCRR where the wagons were loaded for disposal inland. He was there ostensibly because he was curious about this notion of reclaiming desert by using metal-free and plastic-free household refuse to impregnate the dusty ground with humus, but he'd shown more interest in the men themselves than in the job they were doing.

If he wasn't a policeman, he was probably a reporter. He tried to reach Peg Mankiewicz, but at the office of her former paper all they could tell him was that she had quit the city. Before the third time could arrive, therefore, Austin Train left his rent for the balance of the month where the landlord would find it first and took a bus north to San Francisco. There was plenty of garbage there too.

And there was something going on inside his head he didn't want screwed up by a glare of renewed publicity.

PICK YOURSELF UP AND START OVER

Weary, Philip Mason let himself into the apartment and hung up his coat and filtermask. As soon as she heard the door Denise appeared to kiss him hello, and instead of making it a casual embrace threw her arms tight around him and drove her tongue violently into his mouth.

'How can you bear to after what I've done to you?' he muttered when their lips finally separated.

'You silly fool!' She sounded as though she was crying, but her face was against his cheek where he couldn't see it.

'But it's definite now. I've been fired, and they're selling the office complete to some other company—'

'Idiot! I married *you* because I love you, not to put a ball and chain on you, and I married you and not your job! "In sickness, in health" – and all that shit.'

'I don't deserve you,' he said. 'I swear I don't ... Say!' Struck by a sudden thought. 'Did you remember to call Douglas?' They had taken to calling Dr McNeil by his first name.

Her face clouded. 'Yes.'

'What did he say?'

'Improving, but still not fixed. Another month. Still, that's better news than we've had before ...' She took his arm. 'Come in the living-room, honey. Alan's here, and I was just fixing him a drink.'

'Alan Prosser? What does he want?'

'To talk to you, he said. Come on.'

'Where are the kids? Aren't they here?'

'No, down with the Henlowes. It's Lydia's birthday. They'll be back in about an hour.'

And after greetings Alan leaned back in the big chair he'd been allotted and accepted the drink Denise poured. 'You lucky devil,' he said to Philip.

'Am I?' Philip said sourly, dropping into his own chair.

'Sure! Having a beautiful wife' – Denise was within arm's reach so he patted her bottom and provoked a wan smile – 'a beautiful home that's properly looked after ... Christ, my place is a shambles!'

'Don't you have – well, a housekeeper or something?' Denise asked. She had only met Alan a couple of times, and on neither occasion had he talked much about himself.

'I tried that.' Alan looked lugubrious. 'Got me one of those girls from Dominica.'

'Oh, the island where they cut down all those trees?' Philip said, more to make polite chitchat than because he was interested.

'That's the one. Now dust storms blow off it all the time, reach as far away as Trinidad, so I was told. Sounds like hell. But anyway, this chick: she didn't work out. Pretty, sure, and likable enough, but – well, I practically had to show her how to use the can, you dig? So when she had to go home, nurse her mother who'd taken sick, I wasn't sorry ... Still, I guess you aren't thinking so much about your luck as your troubles right now. You are in trouble, aren't you?'

'Did Denise tell you or did you guess?'

'Neither. I just have good financial contacts coast to coast. And the rumors about Angel City are so loud now you can't ignore them. I had stock in your firm – like insurance companies, they cut the meat close to the bone – but I shed my holding weeks ago. Are they going bankrupt, or are they just going to sell their out-of-state operations and retrench on California?'

'Sell off the fringes, of course.' But Philip was looking at Alan with new respect. The company had sweated blood to conceal the fact that their total loss was in a fair way to breaking them, and their shares had fallen by only twenty or thirty per cent instead of the probable ninety. 'Which includes me,' he continued. 'I've been given the copper handshake and the business here is being traded as a going concern to a New York company who'll put their own people in. So as of now I'm unemployed.'

'No, you're not!'

'What?'

'Got any money? Or can you raise some?'

'Ah … I don't think I'm with you.'

'Plain English, isn't it?' Alan waved his glass in the air. 'Do you have any money? A life policy you can borrow against? Second mortgage? Bank loan? Savings?'

'Well, we've never touched what Dennie's father left her— Say! What's all this about?'

'I'm telling you you're not out of work. Not unless you insist. Remember I told you my partner quit me, Bud Burkhardt that you said you'd met?'

'Sure. What about him?'

'Well, I think he was a damned fool to start with, taking that post at Puritan, so I wasn't sorry to be shot of him—'

'He's with Puritan now?' Denise interrupted. 'The man we met when we had the plumbing done over at our last home?'

'That's right.' Alan nodded. 'He's managing their Towerhill branch!'

'Oh, I see what you mean,' she said, and bit her lip. 'The place is – well, not quite a ghost town now, but …' A wave of her elegantly manicured hand.

'I didn't mean that,' Alan said. 'The profits Puritan take on everything they sell – hell, he's probably already made twice what he could have made if he'd stayed with me. But the Trainites are gunning for Puritan. Didn't you know?'

'No, I didn't!' Philip sat forward in his chair. 'I got some Puritan stock. Always understood it was rock-solid. They do say it's a Syndicate company, don't they?'

'Well, it is. But the Trainites are a force to be reckoned with now, and quite pigheaded enough to take on anybody. Besides, what the hell could the Syndicate do against them?'

'So tell me the rest of it!' Philip said impatiently. 'I'm far enough down on my luck not to want to lose what I have left.'

'Well, I got a lot of Trainites working for me, you know – it's the kind of job they approve of, like providing clean water and getting sewage where it can be useful, and all that stuff. Me, I don't hold with their alarmist ideas, but they're conscientious, reliable, turn up for work on time …' His glass was empty; when he tilted it against his mouth Denise rose to refill it. 'Thanks. Well, most of the ones work for me come from this wat over by Towerhill, and I heard the other day they're involved in this countrywide project, buying stuff at Puritan and analyzing it.'

'Can they?' Denise said.

'I guess so. They're not ignorant, you know – half of them are college dropouts, but they learned plenty before they quit formal study, and apparently every wat has at least one chemist who keeps a check on their food, makes sure it's safe.'

'That sounds sensible,' Philip approved. 'Especially for the sake of the children.'

'Oh, don't think I'm putting down all their ideas. Thanks' – as Denise handed his glass back. 'Just the extremist ones. Must admit, if I had kids, I'd like routine food analysis for them.'

'So would we!' Denise said forcefully. 'Only we made inquiries – and the cost!'

'You don't have to tell *me*.' Alan scowled terribly. 'You know I bought that house when Belle and I got married, and sold it off when she – uh – when she got shot.' Absently curling his fingers around to touch the scar on his palm. 'Well, the other day I got this letter from the guy who bought it, saying he's had the dirt in the garden analyzed and it's full of poison because it was laid out on a heap of old mine tailings, and he's going to sue me.'

'That's not fair,' Denise exclaimed.

'I guess I might have done the same if … But the hell!' Gulping at his fresh drink. 'The lawyers tell me it's caveat emptor stuff, so it's no skin off my nose. But when I think what could have become of *my* kids …!' He shuddered.

'You were talking about your ex-partner,' Philip ventured. The prospect of becoming not just unemployed but unemployable, like so many thousands of others, had been haunting him; that tempting half-promise of Alan's was intriguing, and he wanted to hear more.

'Ah, yes! I was going to say, you know I'm having hell's own job since he quit, coping with the business on my own. I'm not a salesman! I'm the practical type. It's my boast that I never hired anyone to do anything I couldn't do myself. I started off laying pipe and digging drains, and I can still drive some of those lazy bastards on my payroll into the ground. But – well, my head's ringing with projects I don't have time for! Come to that, one day I'd like to get married again, and I can't find time to go look for a girl!'

'Yes, you should remarry,' Denise said. 'You'd make a good husband.'

Alan pulled a face. 'Sure, a great husband! Home at midnight, out again at seven … Hell, that's not the point. The point *is*' – and his new drink emptied at the second swig – 'Phil, I need help. I need someone who understands the administrative side of a business. If you want to buy in, ten thousand bucks' worth, even five, I'd like you for my new partner. I've got my eye on something I know I can't handle on my own.'

He hunched forward and continued before Philip could speak.

'You think of what's going on all over the country – all over the world, come to that. You've been to LA recently, for example. How's the water?'

'Makes you want to puke,' Philip said.

'Did you go down to the beach?'

'Who'd want to?'

'Exactly. Who'd want to? Masochists with a yen for pharyngitis and bowel upsets! Who goes swimming any more except in a private pool? It isn't safe.

Hell, I know girls who won't wash their faces except with bottled water, in case it runs into their mouths.'

Philip glanced at Denise, who gave a firm nod. 'I use it for the kids,' she said. 'To be on the safe side.'

'Well, then, look at this – shit, I thought I brought my bag in with me!' Alan stared around him.

'Under your chair,' Denise said, pointing.

'Ah, thanks.' He drew out a black portfolio and from it produced a pack of brightly-colored brochures.

'There, that's the latest of Mitsuyama's gadgets. A home water-purifier. Rechargeable cartridge system. Cheap – I figure a hundred sixty bucks installed. Cartridges five bucks, last the average family a month, sell 'em in packs of six, lots of repeat business. Recondition them by boiling in a solution that costs fifteen cents a gallon – though naturally you don't tell the clients that. Hell, given the right promotion we could have 'em in every home in Denver inside the year, go on and cover the state!'

'A hundred sixty bucks?' Philip frowned, turning the shiny bright pages of the brochure. 'Doesn't sound like it leaves much margin for profit, what with labor costs.'

'Hell, I could install one of those things in thirty minutes from the moment I came in the front door!'

'Ah. You're after the city franchise.' Philip felt his heart suddenly hammering on his ribs. Alan was right; something like this did have immense commercial potential.

'I'll take the state franchise if I can,' Alan grunted. 'And what's more I think I have it sewn up. My ex-partner Bud – well, I persuaded him he owes me a favor, and he's not so stupid he's forgetting that he may need a favor himself one of these days. He has good contacts at Colorado Chemical. I've been to see them, they like the idea, and if I can convince them I can handle the volume of business they'll back me to a bid five per cent higher than anyone else.'

He sat back with a satisfied grin.

'Well, I don't know they'd approve of me,' Philip said after a pause. 'I mean, Angel City aren't going to give me the best references in the world, are they?'

'Oh, shit on Angel City!' Alan waved his hand airily. 'I explained my publicity gimmick to them, and they like it so much I could hire Fidel Castro for all they'd care.'

'What is it?'

'Remember that black cat who made like a hero because of the Towerhill thing? The policeman – what's his name? Oh, yes: Peter Goddard.'

'But isn't he paralyzed?' Denise demanded.

'Right now, he's on the mend. Walking already, like from one side of the room to the other. Well, more hobbling, I guess. So naturally they won't take him back on the force. But I was down at the hospital a while back, talking to a doctor I know, and I met the uncle of those kids he saved. Stinking rich bastard, rolling in it! Bee importer. And he was going on about this poor bastard who can't go back to his old job, and getting his hospital care paid for but you can't like have permanent pensioners on your roster for the one favor, and I thought Christ, a hero *and* a black man, what more do you want? And now this comes up, and bang, inspiration! We shame those fat white cats – like you and me for example – into buying our filters, and we get everyone else trailing right along.' Alan rubbed his hands gleefully.

'*Oh*, yes! Doesn't it all go click-click into pretty patterns?'

LAB REPORT

SUMMARY: In the presence of Dr Michael Advowson, the observer appointed by the UN, samples were taken from the batch of 'Bamberley Nutripon' allegedly reclaimed from the collapsed cellar in Noshri. These were not from a sealed container and therefore the possibility of later contamination cannot be excluded. Portions were triturated in a variety of solvents and the solution in each case was assayed by standard paper chromatography techniques (Hansen's Analytical Paper Type III). Traces were found in all samples of the same complex alkaloid as had previously been isolated from the urine and blood-serum of human beings from Noshri, resembling certain hydrolyzed derivatives of ergot. Administration of this substance to laboratory animals engendered muscular spasms, aberrant behavior, irrational panic and bloodstained stools. It appears in the highest degree probable that this substance was the causative agent of the Noshri disaster; however, it has not been possible to determine at what point it was introduced into the foodstuff.

– Paris, at the *Institut Pasteur:*
L.-M. DUVAL (*D. Méd., D. Chim.*)

THE MARVELS OF MODERN CIVILIZATION

The small neat secretary, a girl in the smartest of advanced fashionable styles including a skirt slit up to the waist to display at her crotch a tuft of shiny steel wool attached to her panties, listened to the ultramodern intercom on her highly-polished desk. The sound was directionalized, of course. It was cool and quiet in here because instead of windows there were cosmoramic projections, latest of late devices to prevent the intrusion of untasteful exterior reality. Nearby the chimneys reeked a twenty-four-hour day yet the view was of clean white clouds, blue sky, yellow sun not so bright that it dazzled. Superior to the natural article, yes.

Also birds flew or perched between two layers of glass on real branches in air-conditioned environment. It was not ordinary to see birds. Very yes.

'Mr Hideki Katsamura,' the girl said. Mr Hideki Katsamura rose from the plastic seat, faultless imitation of natural fur without risk of disease or perhaps pejorative associations owing to demise of so many regretted species. Solid family man, well-established, excellent command of English, correctly clad with sober fabric. Unflighty. Not excessively anxious to please and bowing to secretaries as some.

The wait had been long but one understood: the pressure of urgent business.

Very modern, the girl opened the door to Dr Hirasaku's office by pushing a hidden button.

Later, when Dr Hirasaku and his co-directors had clearly given instructions for the visit to America allotting the franchises for new water-purifier, also many lists of competing products to be explained inferior and amounts of bids recorded so far and further details to be studied with care, Mr Katsamura went home to new house in suburb of Osaka where the honey-carts called promptly and the center of the street received replenishment of other household waters in landscaped rivulets arched at one-block intervals with highly artistic ancient Chinese-pattern bridges, typical of supermodern pedestrian-precinct city planning must not be jammed uptight with cars. All excellent. All nylon.

RAVELED SLEEVE

The flight they put Michael Advowson on from Paris to New York was routed via London. Subsonic; he insisted. A minor but regular feature of his practice at home had been dressing the scalds of people who had been startled by a sonic boom when picking up the kettle from the fire.

The plane was scheduled to depart Orly at 2129. It was ninety minutes late. There was a bomb scare and they had to search the baggage.

He was in first class, since he wasn't paying the fare himself. When he came aboard he was the only passenger ahead of the dividing curtain. First class kept getting smaller and smaller, harder and harder to fill, and the airlines were always pleased when some large international organization, or a major corporation, lashed out with the higher rate by way of compensating somebody for sending him or her to a place they didn't want to go.

But then there weren't many people in second class, either. People didn't fly the Atlantic any more if they could help it, except from bravado. Even if your plane wasn't sabotaged or hijacked, it was certain to be behind schedule.

Not that there was much to be said for ocean travel either, since the sinking of the *Paolo Rizzi* last summer and the drowning of thirteen hundred passengers in a sea made foul by a hundred and eighty thousand tons of oil from the tanker she'd collided with.

Moral, definitely: stay home.

When they shut off the appalling Muzak, he tried to doze, and nearly made it, but was awoken by the order to fasten his seat belt for the landing at London, which effectively put paid to his chances of sleeping for the moment.

Here, two new passengers took the seats across the aisle from him. In the nearer there was a pretty blonde girl with a drawn, sad expression, and in the window seat a dark-haired man some years her senior who was snoring almost before the plane took off again.

In the vast dim insulated cabin, feeling like Jonah in the belly of the great fish, Michael sat railing against fate.

Why me? Why pick *me* from the quiet fields of Ireland and pitch me into the horrible battlegrounds of the world?

Oh, intellectually he knew very well the reasons for his being selected. Irishmen had often been the mainstay of a UN peace-keeping force; as ex-MO, still on the reserve, who had recently come to the attention of a wide public because he had kicked up a noisy fuss over the slaughtering of cattle which were not in fact suffering an infectious disease ... Everywhere there had been the gantlets of reporters to run, incompetently aided by minor officials of WHO and/or the Commission on Refugees. He detested public life, which was why he had opted for a quiet country practice instead of the posts he could have had his pick of in major city hospitals, advancing to consultant rank before forty, but condemned to involvement in hospital politics, subservient to committees of civil servants – *no thanks*, he had said, very firmly.

But this he hadn't been able to turn down.

Now when he closed his eyes he saw that poor child Eileen who had nearly lost her toe, multiplied over and over and turned black. He'd never before understood, in the guts where it counts, the misery a modern war could cause.

They had shown him the state people still were in at Noshri, victims of mindless terror, dazed, incapable of concentrating on the simplest tasks, often unable to work out how to feed themselves. Then they had flown him back to Paris, to meet the handful of other victims being cared for in good hospital conditions because Professor Duval was studying them. He had taken with him, in a portfolio chained to his wrist, a sample of Nutripon which, during his stay at Noshri, had been discovered in a cellar – a hole in the ground, really – half-filling a shell-case, a hoard perhaps put away by someone who did not believe there would be more food tomorrow, and who had gone insane or died before returning to eat the rest of what he had been given. He had taken part in the examination of it, watched the analysis, supervised the administration of minute doses to laboratory rats and monkeys … There could be no doubt any longer; the food was poisoned. But it remained to be determined how, when, where.

So now to New York, to the UN. When he had never been further from Ireland before than on visits to relatives in Glasgow, Liverpool and London. Often, during the army service which entitled him to his rank of captain and the uniform he was currently compelled to wear since he was traveling on official business, he'd talked to people who had served with peace-keeping forces, sensed the vague pride they felt at being recruited to a cause that had as yet barely been invented, that larger and wealthier countries seemed to despise.

He had tried to encourage that pride in himself. He hadn't had much success.

'What's the uniform?'

An unexpected question from the girl across the aisle as the plane settled to its cruising altitude.

'Ah … Irish Army, miss.'

'Do they approve of foreign soldiers invading America?' There was a hard bright sneer on her face, a hard bright edge of sarcasm on her voice.

He sighed, and turned his jacket – hanging from a hook at the side of his seat – to display the green-and-white UN brassard on its arm. The world-map symbol was becoming better known as the people of the planet became more frightened of themselves.

'Are you going to the UN, then?'

'Yes.'

'Me too. What for?'

'I'm testifying before the inquiry into the Noshri disaster.'

'So am I.'

He blinked at her in surprise.

'You don't believe me?' Her tone was mocking. 'Then you don't know who I am. I'm Lucy Ramage. I'm a nurse. I was working at Noshri. *I* saw what those devils did.' The words had an eerie quality in the thrumming twilit cylinder of the plane. 'I'm going to tell the world about it, too. You know they

locked me up to try and stop me? Said I was crazy and dumped me in a mental home. Well, maybe it's true. What I went through would drive anybody
insane. This is the guy who got me out, snoring beside me. Without him I'd
still be behind bars. Señor Arriegas, that's his name, but he lets me call him
Fernando. He's from the Uruguayan Embassy in London.'

The mention of her name had struck a chord in Michael's memory; he'd
heard about this girl from one of the doctors at Noshri, a big Swede called
Bertil or something. But the reference to Uruguay altered the whole perspective. What in the world could have interested the Tupamaros in a nurse
from – wasn't it New Zealand? – who had been working in Africa? Purely
because they didn't want to miss another chance to foment anti-American
feeling? They were, everyone knew, embittered; when they seized power in
the midst of the chaos their sabotage and Robin Hood-style attacks had created, the United States had kicked Uruguay out of the OAS, like Cuba, and
then attempted to banish them from the UN as well. Thanks to a brilliant
coup by the Secretary-General, who whistled up the support not only of both
communist blocs but of all but a handful of the nominally neutralist nations,
the motion had been overwhelmingly defeated.

So, fuming, Washington had had to choose between expelling the entire
UN from its soil – a move that had a lot of backing, of course – and permit-
ting these avowed Marxist-Maoists to enter the States. The compromise had
been to let them in, but only on UN passports, not those of their own country. A fiction, and everyone knew it, but at least it had saved the rest of the
world from ganging up on America.

Lucy had gone on while he was reviewing all this. He heard her say, 'You
know, back home in New Zealand I never thought much about politics. I
never voted. If I had, I suppose I might have been a Liberal. I only went to
work for Globe Relief because it was a chance to travel, see the world before
I got married and settled down. It's a good place for kids, New Zealand. I
mean I have three nieces and a nephew and they're all okay. But then I saw
all those horrors at Noshri and I realized. What they say about the Americans isn't just propaganda, it's all true. Have you been to Noshri?'

'Yes.' Michael's voice felt like gravel in his throat. It was becoming clearer
by the minute that this girl was mentally disoriented, to put it kindly. She had
all the signs: wandering gaze, high-pitched nonstop talking, irrelevance of
affect, the lot. How to break off this unwished-for conversation without being
downright insulting? Which would certainly lead to a big fuss.

'Yes, I saw in Noshri what the imperialists are doing,' Lucy went on, staring
straight ahead now. 'The rich countries have ruined what they own, so they're
out to steal from the people who have a little left. They want the copper, the
zinc, the tin, the oil. And of course there's the timber, which is getting scarce.'

She sounded as though she was reciting a memorized list. Probably was. 'Now they've thought of a new way to get it – drive everybody crazy so they can't set up a strong stable independent government. It nearly worked at Noshri, would have done but for General Kaika, so now they're trying it in Honduras.'

Michael started. He knew, of course, that there had been some sort of rebellion there, and that the government had called on American aid, but this was the first he'd heard of this particular accusation.

'Ah, you don't want to talk about it, do you?' the girl said. 'Your mind's made up and you don't want to be confused with any more facts!' She crowed with laughter and turned her back, curling up on her seat, knees doubled up and her hands interlocked around them.

The plane droned on through the black sky, above the clouds masking the Atlantic. It suddenly occurred to Michael that he ought to look at the moon. He hadn't seen it all the time he was in Paris, nor the stars.

He slid up the blind of his window and peered out There was no moon visible. When he consulted his diary he discovered that it had set, a tiny sliver, at exactly the time the plane had taken off from London.

Turn right and go home. (He realized he was in his home time zone.)

Wish I could.

APRIL

HERO FIDDLING

Hey, man with the big muscles!
Yes, you!
Steam-powered, gas-powered, electrically-powered,
You with the big concrete and cement footprints!
Globe-girdler, continent-tamer, putting the planet through
      hoops, You I hail!
Packer and preserver of food in incorruptible cans,
Blocker-out of winter-blast with bricks and mortar,
Wheeled, shod, tracked with rails of shining iron,
Multiplier of goods and chattels, chewer-up of forests,
Furrow-maker across the unpopulous plains,
Flier higher than eagles, swimmer swifter than sharks,
Trafficker in the world's wealth, miracle-worker,
I salute you, I sing your praises ...

– 'Song of the States Unborn', 1924

A VICTIM OF THE FIRST WORLD WAR

'I've done *my* best,' Gerry Thorne said, sounding aggrieved, and well he might be. Both he and Moses Greenbriar had been doing nicely out of the aid shipments from the Bamberley hydroponics plant – half a cent per person fed had added up to a considerable sum over the years. Moreover, several of the left and center group in Congress, small though that might nowadays be, had been advocating purchase of Nutripon by organizations like Earth Community Chest to maintain the welfare allotments in major cities where right-wing mayors were axing their welfare budgets on grounds of economy. There had been fairly widespread starvation during the past winter.

'I can't work miracles,' he added.

Well ... maybe only conjuring tricks. Like this second home in the Virgins, splendid with its high stone-and-timber walls and this verandah on which you could pretty often sit right outdoors, provided the wind was from the south, not from the fetid puddle of the Gulf of Mexico or the colossal revolving sewer of the Sargasso. Never mind that the venom of the Trainites had reached this far and there was a fading line of skull-and-crossbones symbols facing the sea. Nobody really begrudged such luxury to a man who'd made his money in a Good Cause. He might have gone to work for DuPont.

The most remarkable thing of all was that you could still swim from here; although the Canary Current did sometimes sweep the ordure of Europe this far over, the Antilles Current came from the relatively clean coast of under-developed South America. This morning's Coast Guard bulletin had said the water was okay, so Elly Greenbriar and Nancy Thorne were proving it.

'But where the hell did the stuff come from? The drug, the whatever!' Thorne's question was rhetorical; the UN inquiry had been set up to determine exactly that.

'Well, it wasn't the factory,' Greenbriar said, and took another sip of his gin. 'We asked the Federal Narcotics Bureau for one of their top forensic chemists, and he tested fifty random samples from the warehouse. All clean. We're set to give his report to the inquiry next week, but it won't be much help.'

'I guess not. We've got everybody against us now, from the stinking isolationists who "don't see why we should give away our precious food to ungrateful bastards", clear to the ungrateful bastards themselves. Anyway, a denial never catches up with a rumor. Did you hear about the raid on San Diego, for example? Some crazy Mex-Tup kid – say, you heard that one? Petronella Page used it on her show the other night. Mex-Tup kid! I thought it was kind of neat.'

'What do you mean, raid?' grunted Greenbriar. 'Raids, plural. Three so far, according to my cousin Sophie.'

'How many?'

'Three. Sophie's lived out there for twenty years, but when she called me the other day she said she's thinking of moving back east. After the first raid they had another – they don't think it was the same gang, because the payload was thermite instead of napalm – and then there was a third that burned out a block of black tenements.'

'Bastards,' Thorne said. 'Burning people in their homes, hell!' His eyes were following a ship that had emerged into blurred view from the haze to the north: new and smart, one of the latest deep-trawling fish factories designed to bring up squid from the relatively safe bottom water. Surface fish nowadays were either so rare as to be prohibitively expensive, like cod and herring, or hopelessly high in dangerous substances such as organic mercury. But so far squid were generally okay.

'Is that the second or third we've seen today?' Greenbriar asked.

'Third. Must be a good season for fishing … I imagine you told your cousin she ought to move?'

'Oh, I've been telling her since the LA quake of '71, but of course she'd have taken such a loss on her home ... Still, I guess she's finally made up her mind.'

'Speaking of losses,' Thorne murmured, 'did you have stock in Angel City?'

Greenbriar gave a rueful smile.

'Me too. And they went through the floor. I switched into Puritan, but I lost a packet even so.'

'You take my advice,' Greenbriar said, 'you switch right back *out* of Puritan.'

'Why in the world? They're a Syndicate operation, aren't they? Which makes them just about the solidest stock in the market.'

'Oh, sure, anything the Syndicate is backing turns to gold. But' – Greenbriar dropped his voice – 'I hear gossip. Maybe only scuttlebutt, of course. Even so ...'

'Such as what?'

'The Trainites are after them.'

'Impossible!' Thorne jolted upright in his chair. 'But the Trainites are on their side, always have been!'

'Then why are they conducting massive analyses of Puritan products?'

'Who says they are? Or even if they are, what does it signify? You know how paranoid they are about what they eat.'

'Paranoid enough to enlist Lucas Quarrey of Columbia?'

Thorne stared.

'It's a fact,' Greenbriar said. 'I know someone who knows him; in fact he's done some minor contract work for the Trust now and then. Apparently he was discreetly approached the other day and asked if he would coordinate this project the Trainites' own chemists have already launched.'

Thorne rounded his mouth into an O. 'That's a change of gear for them, isn't it? But what can they hope to gain by attacking the only company that devotes itself exclusively to pure foods? Let alone bucking the Syndicate, of course.'

'My guess is that they want to try and drive their prices down. Maybe collect data on as many slip-ups as possible – in an operation that size, some stuff must leak through now and then which isn't as good as the advertising claims – and use these as a pistol to hold to the company's head.'

Thorne rubbed his chin. 'Yes, that fits. I remember an article by Train in which he was very scathing about people profiteering from public concern about diet. Who's behind this, though – it couldn't be Train himself, could it?'

'Hardly. Train's dead. Killed himself. I had it on very good authority. Never really recovered from his breakdown, you know. But I guess it could be one of these people who took over his name.' Greenbriar cocked his head and sniffed loudly, 'Hey, spring must be really here!'

'What?' Bewildered, both at the irrelevance and also because here in the Virgins there was always luxuriant vegetation the year around.

Greenbriar chuckled. 'Try a noseful. Violets!'

Thorne complied: hmff, hmff! 'You're right,' he said in surprise. 'But if it's that strong it's not likely to be flowers, is it?'

'I guess not. Hmm! Very odd! Which way's the wind now? Oh yes, it's still off the water.' He stared down toward the beach where Elly and Nancy were splashing about in the shallows, obviously on their way back to the house.

Well, the world was full of mysteries. Thorne shrugged. 'Looks as though they're coming in for lunch,' he said. 'I'll just go tell—'

He was interrupted by a scream.

Both he and Greenbriar leapt from their chairs. Down there in the water Nancy was thrashing wildly about, and Elly, who had wandered some distance from her, had spun around to rush and help her.

'Quick!' Thorne snapped, dumped his glass on the handiest table and ran down the steps to the shore. He continued straight into the water as Elly tried to raise Nancy to her feet.

The stink of violets was incredibly strong.

'Look – out!' Nancy choked, and with one arm around Elly's shoulders pointed to an object just barely showing above the water. Shapeless, encrusted, it could have been mistaken for a rock. But something yellowish was dispersing from it through a narrow crack in its end.

Thorne stared at his wife in horror. Her eyes were swelling, puffing out almost literally as he watched, turning the whole upper part of her face into a hideous bloated mass. Also her lips were dotted with pustules, her shoulders, her breasts.

'Moses! Phone a doctor!' he screamed. 'Helicopter ambulance service!'

The fat man turned and stumbled back indoors, and in the same moment Nancy doubled over, vomiting, then slumped in a faint.

Helped by one of their local manservants who appeared in answer to Greenbriar's frantic shouting, Thorne and Elly carried her awkwardly into the house, laid her down on a couch, sent the cook for clean water, soothing ointment, the first-aid kit.

'They're sending the ambulance right away, with a doctor,' Greenbriar panted, hurrying back from the phone. 'But what can have happened to her? A jellyfish?'

'Damn it, no!' But of course he hadn't been down on the beach, seen the drum, or barrel, or whatever, half-sunk in the sand. 'Did they say what we should do in the meantime?' Thorne demanded.

'I—' Greenbriar put his hand to his mouth in absurdly childlike fashion. 'I didn't ask.'

'Idiot!' Thorne was beside himself with panic. 'Get right back and—'

But Greenbriar was already on his way.

'What the hell *can* it be?' Elly moaned.

'Lewisite,' the doctor said when he'd finished administering emergency oxygen. Not only the doctor, but a nurse and a sergeant of police had turned up in the helicopter.

'What's that?' Thorne asked, bewildered.

'A poison gas.'

'*What?*'

'Yes, the smell of violets is unmistakable. I've seen two or three cases like this – not here, in Florida where I used to live. It's an arsenical compound they invented in the First World War. Didn't get around to using it, so they dumped it in the ocean. What happened in Florida was that they'd dropped a batch into the Hatteras Canyon, and one of these new deep-trawling fishing boats hauled a lot of it up. They had no idea what they'd got – after sixty years they were all crusted with barnacles and things, of course – so they cracked one of the drums open, thinking it might be valuable. When they found it was dangerous, they just pitched the lot overside again, but by then they were in shallow water and some of the drums smashed on the bottom rocks. A hell of a lot washed up on shore.'

'I never heard about that,' Thorne whispered.

'Would you expect to? It would have ruined the winter vacation trade – not that there's much left of it anyway. I got out because I wanted clean beaches for my kids, not because Florida was so healthy I didn't have enough patients!' With an ironical chuckle he turned to examine Nancy again; the oxygen had had its effect and she was breathing easier.

'I guess we can move her now,' he said. 'Don't worry too much. There may not be permanent scars. Though of course if she inhaled or swallowed the stuff ... Well, we'll see.'

'This time,' Thorne said as though he hadn't been listening, 'the news is going to get around. I'll see to that.'

DON'T TOUCH

... alleging, quote, intelligence with a proscribed country. End quote. It's claimed that he attempted to obtain air-pollution data from Cuban sources. Protesting the arrest, some two hundred students from Columbia were joined by approximately a thousand Trainites in a demonstration which the police dispersed with tear smoke. Eighty-eight hospitalizations were reported, but no deaths. Asked to comment just prior to his departure for Hollywood, where he will again preside at the Oscar ceremonies, Prexy said, quote, If that's the guy who

claims we're running short of oxygen, tell him I don't find any difficulty in breathing. End quote. Heavy fighting again today in Guanagua province as Honduran government forces supported by American air cover …

REHEARSAL

Exactly what Hugh Pettingill had expected to find at the wat, he couldn't have said. After only a short while, though, he was certain it wasn't there. Day in, day out, he drifted through it and around it, watching the snows melt and spring come hesitantly to the surrounding high valleys. He didn't click. He didn't fit in. He felt excluded. And despite not being sure whether he wanted to fit in or not, be resented being denied the choice.

Physically, the environment was comfortable: shabby, pieced together from scrap, but practical and in many respects attractive. What jarred on him, though, was the way in which everyone at the wat took it for granted that this was a rehearsal: not for the aftermath of an all-over war, just a dry run for the ordinary life of the twenty-first century. He couldn't see it. For him it was more like escapism, running to hide from the real world.

Granted, they had some things going for them: the food, for example, though plain was delicious, better even than what he'd had at the Bamberleys', and he ate voraciously of the savory soups, the home-baked bread, the vegetables and salads grown under glass. That interested him, a little. He hadn't watched things grow before, except some pot seeds he'd planted at college, and for a while he joined in with some of the routine spring tasks out of doors. When he had to distribute the gallon of worms Felice had brought, though, he found the job so distasteful – tipping all those anonymous wrigglers out in doses of ten or a dozen and watching them dive among what was going to become food that he might eat – he moved on to other things. There was a handicrafts shop, and he helped in the making of some rough stools and tables, because last year for the first time ever more Americans had taken vacations inland than by the sea, and the idea was to run a restaurant for tourists during the coming summer, get some wholesome natural-grown food down them in the hope of showing them what they were missing. But turning out one stool exactly like another grew monotonous. He moved on again.

All the time, though: this feeling that the world was *bound* to go to hell! Okay, so it's true these mothers have turned prairies into dust-bowls and used the sea for a giant sewer and laid concrete where there used to be forests. So stop them! Don't just let them walk over you, crush you face-down into the dirt!

Crush them first!

*

That strange cold Peg: she must, he concluded, be queer, because she didn't – not only not with him, not with anybody. (Not even with Felice whom he'd naturally assumed to be her girl, who did, though also not with him. Shit!) Yet she seemed somehow happy.

Found something here. What? Resignation? Could a former crusading reporter and campaigner for Women's Lib be satisfied with such a drab existence?

Well, the fact stood. Even though Felice had left after a week or so, uttering some kind of weird apology to everyone and saying she'd had a fantastic vacation – hell, *vacation*, in a place where work literally never stopped! – Peg had stayed, and seemed content, inasmuch as you could figure out what she was thinking behind that lovely but stone-cold face …

If he'd been asked before he came here, 'Are you a Trainite?', Hugh would have answered that he was without hesitation, on the strength of having taken part in Trainite demonstrations at college. Recruiters for the big corporations came around all the time nowadays, not just in spring and summer, because the number of students taking up science and engineering had fallen by around 60 per cent and those taking business management by 30 per cent and those who couldn't get into something constructive like agriculture or forestry (which generally meant emigrating, of course) preferred to drop out. So these frantic recruiters were a nuisance and now and then one of them gave particular offense and it was necessary to dump him in a dirty river or strip him and paint the skull and crossbones on his belly.

The people here, though, weren't in the least like the Trainites he'd known outside. And obviously this was more what Austin Train himself had had in mind. This cat Jones had been a personal friend of Train's, and he'd had the guy to stay several times before he vanished. (He wasn't dead; Hugh had learned that much for certain. Nobody, though, would admit to knowing where he was.)

He struggled and struggled to make sense of what was going on around him, and bits of it fitted fine. Only whenever he thought he had the pattern straight in his head, something turned up which completely screwed him.

The simple life bit, the natural foods – so far, so good. Also the clothing woven from natural fibers which would rot: cotton, linen, wool. Fine. The composting of vegetable peelings and such, the sorting and cleaning of the inescapable cans, the return of plastics to the nearest reclamation company, which called for a once-monthly trip by the communal jeep. Great. But if it was the simple life they were after, how come they used electricity? It was all very well to say it was clean power and could be generated from waterfalls and tides. The fact stood: it hadn't been. And their insistence that tomorrow it would have to be and (here it came again, the same dirty argument) they were rehearsing for tomorrow, devising a viable life-style by trial and error – that didn't convince him. Sixty-some people in this wat, and this the largest out of only about four or five hundred in the whole of the States and Canada: how many of the human race were going to learn about this life-style before the crunch came? Every day in the news some fresh warning sign!

Of course it was as well they did have electricity, or his car would still be stranded where Peg and Felice had found him. Instead they'd brought the batteries in and recharged them, and now it was here and any time he wanted to get the hell out, he could. He was becoming daily more tempted. The whole scene here struck him as play-acting.

They listened to radio news a lot and talked a lot about things he was sure they didn't properly understand, like the Honduras war and the starvation in Europe since the Med stagnated. And didn't give. Somehow. Even the kids. There was this Rick in particular that made his skin crawl, Zena's adopted son (and formerly Decimus's; the cat being dead you'd think they might stop talking about him, but they never seemed to, especially Rick who claimed that when he grew up he was going to find the person who'd poisoned his dad. Christ!) – this Rick, anyway, kept hanging around him all day maybe because other people were busy, and asking crazy questions he couldn't answer, like why isn't the sun always square overhead when it's noon on the clock and if you can't tell me what book do I look in for the answer, huh? He wanted to be an astronomer when he grew up, he said. Fat chance. They were closing down observatories all over.

What the hell did all this have to do with being a Trainite? Out there those stinking bastards raping and murdering and poisoning ... Christ. Where's a pistol? Where's a bomb?

He tried to read Austin Train's works. They had a complete set. It was dull.

The only person he met during his stay at the wat whom he took to was an outsider, laid off from the Bamberley hydroponics plant: a light-colored cat about his own age, named Carl Travers. He had a vague feeling he might have seen the guy before, but he wasn't sure.

Carl looked in pretty frequently, and talked friendly, but didn't show any inclination to stay – wouldn't have come so often but for being out of work. He had good khat, which right now Hugh didn't dig too well because it intensified his feeling of having too much energy all pent up inside and no way to let it out, and also pot. So now and then they went out together for a smoke. It had to be out. The Trainites didn't approve.

'You got family?' Hugh said one day when they were pretty high, parked in Carl's second-hand Ford on a curving mountain road watching the sun sink red toward the haze along the coast.

'Like brothers and sisters,' Carl said.

'Older, younger?'

'Younger except Jeannie. I don't see her too often. She married into the fuzz. This cat who got made like a hero in the avalanche.'

'Ah-hah?'

Time passed. Impossible to tell how long. It was the high.

'You?'

'No.' Don't count the Bamberley gang as family. Never mentioned that bunch of creeps to Carl.

'That why you're at the wat?'

'Hell, *I* don't know why I'm at the wat.'

'You don't like it?'

'Nope. You live with your folks?'

'Shit, no. Furnished room, other side of town from them. Self-supporting, me. Working man. I mean, I was.'

More silence. To roll another joint.

'Thinking of moving away. Wait till hell freezes over before they reopen the plant. Never liked the work anyhow.'

'Where to?'

'Maybe Berkeley.'

'Ah, shit, California you don't see the sun one year's end to the next! Whole state stinks!'

'Maybe so, but they gon' have that big quake one day soon, and I'd kinda like to be on hand and laugh … Got friends in Berkeley, though. Was in college a year.'

'Me too.'

'Dropped out?'

'Dropped out.'

More silence. To burn up the joint.

'Make the scene together?'

'Yeah.'

'Man, I'm *high*. Want to screw?'

'Yeah.'

BEFORE WE ARE SO RUDELY INTERRUPTED

'I have an appointment with Mr Bamberley,' Michael said, and glanced at the wall clock. 'I see I'm a few minutes early, though.'

'Oh, you must be Captain Advowson!' the girl at the reception desk said brightly – but not very clearly; there was something in her mouth and her voice was hoarse. On the corner of her desk, an open package of throat pastilles. They scented the vicinity strongly with menthol. 'Do sit down and I'll tell Mr Bamberley you're here. Would you like me to take your filtermask?'

'Thank you.' He undid the strap and gave it to her, and she added it to a rack where there were already eight or ten dangling.

Moving to a chair on the other side of this spacious anteroom, he glanced back at her, and she noticed and smiled, thinking it was because she was pretty. In fact it was because she reminded him of the nurse from Noshri – the same shade of fair hair, the same general cast of features. Though much plumper and lacking the dark undereye pouches that marred Lucy Ramage's good looks.

He'd seen her twice again since their meeting on the plane, once in the flesh at the UN building and once late at night on TV, on a talk show run by a woman called Petronella Page. She'd sat dead still, impervious to even the most subtly vicious verbal jabs, and recited a low-voiced account of incredible suffering which the compère had tried to interrupt, and tried again, and each time failed. Cold as falling snow, setting ultimately into a dead weight of horror, huge, massive, stifling, the words followed one another until when they turned the cameras on the audience they weren't quite quick enough to avoid the sight of a girl in the second row fainting and falling from her chair.

When she started on accusations of deliberate genocide they brought the next commercials in early.

Who the hell *had* poisoned that relief food? Someone out to discredit Western aid programs must have got at the affected consignment, opened the cartons, sprayed the contents, resealed them. Even though Duval insisted that this was inconsistent with the uniform distribution of the drug throughout the interior of the pieces he'd examined ...

How much longer was that damned inquiry going to drag on? He wanted more than anything to go home, but he was under orders to remain until the distinguished international jurists now sifting the evidence issued their final report. If he survived that long.

Gingerly he touched a bruise at the corner of his jaw. About a week ago he'd been to a party, six blocks from his hotel, and he'd been incautious enough to walk home after midnight. Someone had jumped him with a blackjack. Luckily the bruise was the worst effect.

Also he'd developed conjunctivitis two days after his arrival, and as a result was still wearing a piratical black patch over his left eye. Then he'd been warned to get rid of his beard, because the police didn't like them, and a minor shaving cut – on the side opposite his bruise – had become infected, and he'd been assured it was because he'd been stupid enough to shave with regular tap-water. No one he'd met at the UN used anything but an electric shaver, and in fact the drugstore clerk from whom he'd bought his razor and shaving cream had looked puzzled and tried to insist on his buying a bactericidal after-shave lotion as well. But he'd thought the man was just trying to squeeze out a drop of extra profit.

Now the cut had festered into a miniature boil, with an ugly white head on it. It was protected by a bandaid, but sooner or later he feared it would have to be lanced.

Incredible. But he'd been told repeatedly that every stranger to New York suffered the same way. The natives, of course, were resistant, but anyone from more than say a hundred miles distant lacked the immunities the residents had acquired.

And even the residents weren't too happy ... At one of the many parties around the diplomatic circuit which he'd been obliged to attend he'd met a girl in her middle twenties, pretty with dark hair and a good figure, very drunk although the party had only been under way for an hour. She was looking for an ear to bend, and out of politeness – or perhaps boredom – Michael lent her his. She was working at the UN as a secretary, because, she said, she'd wanted to do something to improve the world. And found it simply wasn't possible. She claimed that she'd hoped to marry a man she knew from college, who turned her down when he learned she wanted to work for those stinking commie-front bastards; that he was so far from unique that she'd lost friend after friend until now her only social life was on this level, these endless formal cocktail parties where people of a dozen different nationalities misunderstood one another at the tops of their voices.

'But we're all stuck on this same ball of mud, aren't we?' He heard her voice again in memory, nearly breaking into a sob. 'And the only people who seem to care are the wrong ones, I mean the ones you're not supposed to be friends with. I met this Uruguayan the other day, Fernando Arri – something, I forget. But did you hear what happened to him?'

Michael shook his head.

'He was going home to the place where all the Uruguayans live – they're not allowed off Manhattan, you know, and they have to live in this block near the UN Plaza – and it was raining, and four men who'd been pretending to shelter under an awning jumped him. Kicked him in the balls and knocked out four of his teeth.'

'Good lord,' Michael said. 'Did the police—?'

'Police!' A hard brittle laugh, like a scream. 'They were the police! They found the sole-marks of a police boot on his face!'

At which point she sobered, almost like magic, because it was time for the party to break up, and said, 'Thank you for listening to my drunken babbling. Unless I get someone to take me seriously now and then I think it must really all be a dream. Can I buy you dinner? You deserve it.'

And, when he hesitated, she added, 'I know a marvelous restaurant where they still have real food.'

Which was the bait he couldn't resist. Everything he'd eaten here tasted to him of plastic and chewed paper.

Over the meal – which was good, despite his astonished discovery that what he thought of as everyday basics at home, such as ham and herring, appeared here in the 'gourmet' section of the menu and were charged extra – she talked calmly and reasonably of fearful things. About her elder sister who had borne two children in New York, and they were both sub-normal: not moronic, just slow, the older beginning to read at last after his ninth birthday; about flowers she had tried to grow in a window-box at her apartment that wilted and dropped their leaves after a week; about the cost of hospitalization insurance; about the panhandler she had found wheezing against a wall, begging a quarter for oxygen; about the rain that melted stockings and panty-hose into holes. Michael had experienced New York rain. It had ruined one of his uniforms. But at least he was able to revert to mufti now.

And then, when he escorted her home – by taxi, of course – she said on the threshold, 'I'd like to ask you up and make love. But it'll have to be next time. I have another week to go before it's safe.'

He'd thought: rhythm method? But she'd disabused him.

The commonest disease after measles …

'Captain Advowson!'

He rose and went through the door smilingly held for him.

Bamberley's office was like every other room he had been in since arriving here: armored against exterior reality. Windows that must not be opened. Air processed and scented. Pictures, originals, expensive but bad. Much modern gadgetry. A built-in bar with its door ajar. And not one book.

How long, Michael wondered, before he went mad for lack of an Atlantic breeze blowing across the butter-yellow miles of flowering furze?

Mr Bamberley, affably extending his hand, was not alone. With him was the thin man Gerry Thorne whom Michael had met at the UN inquiry which he'd attended on behalf of Globe Relief, and Moses Greenbriar, the trust's senior treasurer. Thorne appeared distracted. Dutifully Michael shook hands, refused a cigar, accepted a drop of Irish whiskey from a full bottle probably specially obtained in his honor.

'Well, now!' The preliminaries over, Mr Bamberley didn't seem quite in control of the situation, and looked beseechingly at Greenbriar, who coughed discreetly. Which was a mistake, because a second later he coughed for real, and wheezed, and had to stifle it with a tissue and sniff some kind of a cure from a white plastic tube. Michael waited. Eventually he recovered and apologized.

'Well, captain, I imagine you can guess why we've asked you to spare us a little of your valuable time. We're in an impossible position. Our Colorado plant is shut down, as you know, the staff has had to be laid off—'

'And starving people are being deprived of what could make the difference between life and death!' Mr Bamberley burst out.

'I'm sorry to have to say this,' Michael sighed. 'But at Noshri I saw people who would literally be better off dead.'

There was an awkward pause.

'Perhaps,' Greenbriar said at length. 'But the fact stands: Bamberley relief foods have saved thousands, one might even say millions, of lives on previous occasions, and the sabotaging of one consignment must not be allowed to put a full stop to our work. And if these damned Tupas manage to make their accusations stick, regardless of what the official inquiry reports, that's what will happen.'

'You have heard what they're saying, have you?' Mr Bamberley said. 'Lies, of course – damnable lies! They'll stick at nothing to malign this country.'

Outside the UN building itself, this was the first time Michael had heard reference here to the charge that relief food sent to Honduras had been poisoned the same way as that in Noshri. The Uruguayans had made a formal deposition to the inquiry and demanded that a neutral team of doctors be sent to investigate, but no action had been taken. He'd watched for comment on TV or in the few surviving New York newspapers, expecting at least an indignant rebuttal, but to his amazement the matter was being ignored. He'd been told at home, a year or so ago, by someone returned from visiting an American cousin, that the news media were complying with the president's celebrated dictum, 'If the papers know what's good for them they'll print what's good for America!' He hadn't believed it. He was still trying not to. But it was getting harder by the day.

'According to what I learned at the inquiry,' he ventured, 'the Nutripon sent to Honduras was manufactured and dispatched at just about the same time as the African supplies—'

'Yes, and no doubt the Tupas' next step,' Greenbriar broke in, 'will be to fake up some poisoned Nutripon and claim it was found at San Pablo! But if this werc true, why did we hear nothing about it until last month? Why haven't Honduran government doctors reported mass psychosis similar to that at Noshri? Why did the forensic people give the stored Nutripon a clean bill of health, although our stocks went right back to the end of the Christmas–New Year holiday and must have been the very next batch off the production line?'

'Well, of course that's what the inquiry's trying to find out,' Michael said. 'But one assumes that either someone got at your vats and deliberately added the drug – and you insist that's impossible – or some natural ergot-like fungus contaminated your regular yeasts.'

'That seems to be the only acceptable explanation,' Mr Bamberley said with a shrug. 'And it's not something we can be blamed for. We can only take steps to prevent a recurrence, and of course offer compensation for what it's worth.'

'And in pursuit of that goal,' Greenbriar said, 'we're having the air-purifying system of the plant redesigned by a firm specializing in germ-free operation theaters. I think you'll concede they must work to pretty demanding standards?'

'One would hope so,' Michael said dryly. 'But standards are only as good as the people who comply with them. I once saw a small boy given gangrene in a modern hospital because a surgeon who should have known better lifted a dressing to inspect an incision without putting on a mask. He breathed resistant staph all over the wound. The boy died.'

There was another pause, this time a very uncomfortable one. During it, Michael decided he didn't much like Moses Greenbriar. He had already concluded he didn't like Gerry Thome.

Why not? He was getting a glimmering of the reason. It had something to do with the fact that these incredibly rich people had grown fat on charitable undertakings. For Michael – raised as a Catholic, although no longer a believer – the image they evoked was that of the Borgia popes.

'Naturally we'd go to any length to avoid that kind of oversight,' Greenbriar said at last. 'But the main point is this, captain. Clearly, before we can put the plant back into operation, we shall need to have our new arrangements approved by some disinterested party. We can hardly ask for a UN team, as such – as you know, any hint of "UN meddling" in the domestic affairs of this country provokes a tremendous outcry. On the other hand there's a great traditional sympathy, one might almost say a great love, for Ireland, so it occurred to us that we should invite you to—'

He got that far, when there was a sudden vast *thump*, as though the building had been kicked by a passing giant a thousand feet tall, and the not-supposed-to-be-opened windows fell in big brilliant splinters and the ceiling slammed down on them and the stomach-turning street air of New York came rolling in.

Minutes before, a car painted with a skull and crossbones had been illegally parked in front of the building, on 42nd Street. The driver – masked, of course, like everyone on the sidewalks – jumped out and ran toward a nearby drugstore. A patrolman across the street noticed, and thought little of it; Trainites were forever drawing skull-and-crossbones signs on cars, and not everyone could spare the time or money to clean them off straight away. Besides, if the guy had run into a drugstore he was likely in need of urgent medicine.

So he just made a mental note to tell him off when he came back.

Only he didn't come back. He continued out the other door of the drugstore and doubled into the bowels of Grand Central Station, and was well out

of reach when the fuse in the back of the car reached what they later esti-
mated to be over fifty sticks of dynamite.

BLEST ARE THE PURE IN BOWEL

It turned out that Doug McNeil had actually been to Japan. Denise was
gossiping in his office after he'd treated Josie for a minor bout of worms –
probably picked up off a dog, and how could you stop a kid fondling a puppy
or a kitten? – and he happened to mention that he'd attended a medical conference in Tokyo.

So naturally when the question came up of how to entertain this Mr Hideki
Katsamura who was in the States letting the franchises for the new water-
purifier, they consulted him. Katsamura was making a grand tour, starting in
California – where the franchise was obviously going to Roland Bamberley
and thank goodness he'd confined himself to bidding for a single state because
no one else stood a chance – and continuing via Texas and the Atlantic
seaboard to New York and New England, and finally doubling back to Chicago and Denver. Afraid of being outdone because a big Chicago-based
corporation was bidding for exclusive rights covering six states, Alan had
instantly let his reflexes be triggered: the Denver Hilton, a restaurant in Lar-
imer Square, the best nightclub in town, where can I get a girl because of
geishas—?

But Doug said hold it just a moment: not the Hilton but the Brown Palace,
and the old part at that provided they've fixed the earthquake damage. These
Japanese are nuts about other countries' traditions. And don't take him to a
restaurant, either; lots of Japanese are envious of the freedom with which
Europeans and Americans invite guests into their own homes, instead of
entertaining them in restaurants which is Japanese SOP.

Plainly, though, Alan couldn't invite the guy for dinner in his small bachelor pad, and at first it looked as though Philip couldn't either because Denise
went straight into a tizzy. She'd never minded being hostess to Philip's superiors from Angel City, but a Japanese was a different matter. She kept
talking about not knowing how to make tempura or sukiyaki.

'Come off' it!' Doug chided her. 'If you went to Tokyo would you want to
be greeted with hamburgers and French fries? I admit you probably would,
because even when I was there four years ago they'd had to give up most of
their traditional dishes like raw fish. I tried some that was supposed to be
okay, and it tasted great, but I went down with dysentery the next day – did I
have cramps! But anyway that's not the point. You fix steaks, with lots of fried
onions, and maybe start with some New Zealand clam chowder, which is

pretty much like the New England stuff and a sight safer, and get lots of salad from Puritan, and ...'

'It's going to cost the earth!' Denise worried, making up her shopping list.

'It's on the firm,' Alan said. 'Just get the stuff!'

So of course because he'd been such a help they invited Doug, and his pretty English wife Angela, and inevitably, his mother, a spry, bright-eyed woman of sixty-five called Millicent by everybody including her son and daughter-in-law with whom she appeared to have a marvelous relationship. And Alan, of course, and the man from Colorado Chemical who was sponsoring the Prosser Enterprises bid, Sandy Bollinger with his wife Mabel, and to make up the even number because Katsamura was traveling alone without a secretary Alan's right-hand woman, Dorothy Black, thirty-five, plain, single, but a good talker with a fund of jokes.

All planes of course were always late, but they hadn't expected Katsamura's to be quite so far behind schedule. When Philip, tired by an hour's waiting at the airport, made inquiries, he learned that among the baggage being loaded at Chicago O'Hare had been a case marked with a skull and cross-bones, which naturally they opened. When it proved to contain nothing but a printed data sheet repeating Professor Quarrey's findings on high-altitude exhaust residues they concluded it must be meant to distract attention from something else, maybe a bomb. So they searched everything and everybody and instead of arriving at 1650 Mr Katsamura landed at 1912.

During the wait Alan had said, 'By the way, how are you?'

'Doug says another week at most.'

'Isn't it hell, sweating out the time? This is my longest stretch without since I was sixteen.'

At least it was a relief to be able to talk casually about it. With it so common, it was absurd to pretend it didn't exist.

The flight number went up on the arrivals board and they headed for the barrier, looking. Philip was vaguely expecting someone small and yellow with horn-rimmed glasses and a habit of continual stooping, half-formed bows. But there wasn't anyone like that. There was only a man of about forty, wearing a black coat, roughly as tall as himself, slightly sallow and with the skin around his eyes drawn tight on the bone.

'Mr Katsamura?' Alan said, offering his hand.

'Yes, sir!' said Mr Katsamura, who had learned a great deal very quickly during his so far two and a half weeks in the States, chiefly concerning proper social conduct and right use of jargon – correction, *slang*. He shook, smiled, was introduced to Philip too, and apologized for making them wait yet one moment longer.

It was face-losing. But utterly unavoidable. Had been also on the plane. Troublesome and problematic. Moreover, of excessive longstanding: since the first day of the tour! Medicine bought in Texas was used up and had not cured the distressing malfunction. It would be constructive to investigate a doctor here.

Behind him the door swung to which was marked MEN.

Nervous in a gown bought specially for the occasion and a brand-new wig, Denise served cocktails and appetizers when they brought him on from the hotel where he'd dumped his bags – and made further use of excellent American apparatus. Her nervousness faded within minutes. He talked freely and fluently with everyone: to Doug about their respective reactions to the foreignness of each other's countries; to Sandy Bollinger about the impact of the European depression on international finance; to Denise about the ailments of children because his own were continually suffering minor allergies, fevers, similar disorders. Behind his back Millicent caught Philip's eye and ringed her thumb and forefinger: okay! Philip grinned back, thinking what a stroke of luck it had been to meet Doug.

And Katsamura faded to the bathroom again.

'Something's wrong with that guy,' Alan said in a low tone. 'He went at the airport too, and the hotel.'

'*Turismo?*' offered Angela McNeil.

'But he's been in the country over two weeks,' Mabel Bollinger objected. 'Even in Brazil I never had it longer than three or four days.'

'Well, we have a doctor right here,' Dorothy Black said practically.

Doug bit his lip. 'I'll see if I can help,' he said, but sounded doubtful. 'Phil, do you keep any specifics for diarrhea? Chlorhydroxyquinoline, say?'

'Well – uh – no. I generally use khat, and we could hardly offer him that. I mean it's not legal. Honey, you got anything for the kids?'

'Not right now,' Denise said. 'I used up the last lot. Meant to get some more but in all this rush I forgot.'

'Khat, did you say?' Dorothy inquired. 'What does that have to do with it?'

'Entrains constipation as a side effect,' Doug answered. And snapped his fingers. 'Side effect! Yes, I think I have something in my bag.'

'If it's not impolite of me,' he murmured a minute later, 'you do know I'm a doctor, don't you?'

Katsamura flushed sallow rose.

'Swallow two of these – not with tap-water, I got you some bottled water from the kitchen. Here. Tomorrow I'll arrange for Phil Mason to deliver you something better, but this will help for a few hours.' Slipping a little white packet into the other's hand.

Alone again, Katsamura reflected that this was most sound, most sensible, calculated to reduce the risk of later and worse embarrassments. It was known there were substantial funds behind the Prosser bid, if not as great as those at Chicago. This had led to acceptance of the dinner invitation in a private home and other unstrictly protocolic gestures.

He decided suddenly: I will recommend the Colorado franchise go to these people. I should like it to go to them. Most uncommercial. Antibusinesslike. Not allow personal bias to interfere with better judgment. Even so.

How long for the tablets to work? It was to be hoped another two minutes would not spoil the dinner. Hastily he lifted the toilet lid again.

THE TRIAL RUNS

Latro, California: 'Terrible diarrhea, doctor, and I feel so weak!' /
'Take these pills and come back in three days if you're not better.'
Parkington, Texas: 'Terrible diarrhea ...' / 'Take these pills ...'
Hainesport, Louisiana: 'Terrible ...' / 'Take ...'
Baker Bay, Florida ...
Washington, DC ...
Philadelphia, Pennsylvania ...
New York, New York ...
Boston, Massachusetts ...
Chicago, Illinois: 'Doctor, I know it's Sunday, but the kid's in such a terrible state – you've got to help me!' / 'Give him some junior aspirin and bring him to my office tomorrow. Goodbye.'

EVERYWHERE, USA: a sudden upswing in orders for very small coffins, the right size to take a baby dead from acute infantile enteritis.

MAY

GRAB WHILE THE GRABBING'S GOOD

When I came here there was nothing to be seen
But the forest drear and the prairie green.
Coyotes howled in the vale below
With the deer and the bear and the buffalo,
To my whack-fol-the-day, whack-fol-the-do,
Whack-fol-the-day-fol-the-didy-o!

So I took my axe and I cut the trees
And I made me a shack for to lie at ease,
With the walls of log and the roof of sod
And I gave my thanks at night to God,
To my whack …

And I took my gun and my powder-horn
And I killed the varmints that stole my corn.
With meat and bread I had a good life,
So I looked for a woman who would be my wife,
To my whack …

When he was a boy I taught my son
To use the plow and the hoe and the gun.
The fields spread out as the trees came down –
There was room at last for a little town,
To my whack …

There's a church of clapboard with a steeple,
And Sunday morning it's full of people.
There's a bank, a saloon and a general store
And a hundred houses weren't there before,
To my whack …

And now that I'm old and prepared to go
There are cattle instead of the buffalo.
They'll carry my coffin to my grave

Down roads they say they're going to pave,
To my whack …

So I'm happy to know I made my mark
On the land which once was drear and dark,
And I'm happy to know my funeral prayer
Will be heard in the land that was stark and bare,
To my whack …

– 'Boelker's Camp Fire Songster', 1873

BLANKET

'Where are they?' Gerry Thorne kept muttering all through Nancy's funeral in the small Pennsylvania town where she had been born and her parents still resided. 'Where are the mothers? It's a fucking conspiracy!'

Everyone understood he was overwrought; however, this language did not seem fitting while the substitute minister droned through the service. (The regular minister had enteritis.) So they pretended not to hear.

It was not the guests he meant. There were a great many of those, some of them important and/or famous. Jacob Bamberley had flown east specially to attend, with Maud but without the children. (They had enteritis.) Minor officials from the embassies or UN delegations of countries which had been helped by Globe Relief were likewise in the chapel. Moses Greenbriar had intended to come but he and Elly were unwell. (Enteritis.) Old friends of the family who were prominent in the community, such as the mayor, and the principal of the school Nancy had attended (free today because it was closed through enteritis), were also on hand. But he didn't mean them.

'Christ, not even one reporter!' he muttered. 'Let alone a TV team. And I kicked ABS in the ass over and over!'

He was wrong. There was one reporter. A girl had been sent by a local weekly with a circulation of nearly twenty thousand.

There was a slightly embarrassing incident just before the cremation, when a lady trying to slip away to the toilets fell in the aisle and – well, they did their collective best to ignore that, too. But eventually the coffin was consigned to the flames and they emerged under the yellow-gray sky.

Gerry had been against cremation at first, because of the smoke. He'd changed his mind when he saw how she was scarred.

The sun showed as a bright diffuse blur today; the weather had been exceptionally fine all week. Casting no shadow, face as white as paper, the muscles of his jaw standing out, Thorne kept on saying, 'Where are the bastards? I'll murder them for this!'

'There is an epidemic, you know,' said Mr Cowper, his father-in-law, who was very much one to maintain the proprieties and had been shuddering under his black suit throughout the service. 'I'm told it's very bad in New York.'

His wife, who had also annoyed him by snuffling at his side loud enough to be heard by everyone in the chapel, not from grief but a head cold, excused herself for a moment. Usual trouble.

'Epidemic, hell!' Thorne snapped. 'It's official pressure! They don't like the stink I've been kicking up!'

That was true enough, not just a boast. He had taken a savage pride in exploiting his status as a senior executive of Globe Relief to publicize Nancy's death and the cause of it. In consequence resorts all down the Atlantic coast, and throughout the Caribbean, and as far into the ocean as Bermuda, were suffering tens of thousands of canceled bookings. Officials insisted that the quantity of Lewisite dumped in 1919 could not possibly affect so vast an area, and it was mere chance that trawling had brought up two separate batches, and in any case weathering rendered the stuff harmless in a day or two. It made no difference. Thorne had publicized at least one other death from the gas, previously concealed – he had traced relatives of eight other victims, but someone was leaning on them and they wouldn't talk – and that was good enough for the public, having been lied to once before. This year we take our vacation somewhere else. Where is there where Americans aren't likely to be stoned by a howling mob? Spain, Greece? No, got to be out of range of the stench from the Med.

Looks like we might as well stay home.

The substitute minister, Reverend Horace Kirk, came to join them. 'A very touching ceremony, reverend,' said Mr Cowper.

'Thank you.'

'I'll sue the bastards, then,' Thorne said suddenly. 'If that's the way they want it!'

Mr Cowper touched his arm solicitously. 'Gerry, you're overwrought. Come home with us and try to relax!'

'No, I'm going straight to my lawyers. If it takes every cent I have I'll get back at the mothers who dumped that gas!'

'One understands how affected you've been by this tragedy,' Mr Bamberley said, matching Mr Cowper's soothing tone. 'But surely you must realize—'

'Jack!'

To everyone's astonishment, the interruption came from Maud, who was stuffing into her sleeve the handkerchief she had soaked with tears during the service.

'Gerry's right!' she exclaimed. 'It's disgraceful! It's disgusting! I don't care how long ago they say they threw that stuff in the sea – it belongs to the government, and it's killing people, and the government is responsible!'

'Now, Maud dear—'

'Jack, it's all right for you! The worst thing that ever goes wrong for you is when some bug eats your precious what-you-call-ium thingum-bobii! *You* don't spend every hour of every day wondering which of the boys is going to fall sick next! That's all I ever do, from one year's end to the next – if it isn't fits it's fever, if it isn't nausea it's diarrhea! How long can we go on like this? It's like living in hell!'

She broke off, choked with sobs, and leaned blindly on the minister for support, which he awkwardly provided, while her husband stared at her as though he had never seen her before.

Mr Kirk coughed gently, which was a mistake. It was invariably a mistake nowadays, apparently, even in a small town, and Mr Cowper had to take over Maud from him. But be recovered without losing his aplomb, and said, 'Well, Mr Thorne, though I'm not fully acquainted with the details of your sad loss—'

'Aren't you?' Thorne broke in. 'That's not my fault! I got it on TV, I put it in the papers and magazines!'

'As I was about to say …' Frigidly; we are still in the presence of a death and it's not seemly to shout. 'I do feel you'd be ill-advised to sue an organ of the government. The chance of securing compensation is bound to be small, and—'

'The hell with compensation!' Thorne blasted. 'What I want is justice! You can't tell me that when they dumped that gas they didn't know people would want to fish the ocean, bathe in it, build houses fronting on the beach! You can't tell me the bastards didn't know what they were doing – they just relied on not being around when the trouble started! So I'm going to make trouble! Before I'm through I'll have those stinking generals fishing it up with their bare hands!'

He spun on his heel and headed at a run toward his car.

After a long pause Mr Kirk said uncertainly, 'I think it may rain, don't you? Perhaps we should make a move.'

'Ah – yes,' Mr Cowper agreed. 'One wouldn't want to be caught in a shower, would one?'

THUS FAR: NO FATHER

Later, when they were alone, Mr Bamberley snapped at Maud, 'Well, what would you have me do with the boys lock 'em up like Roland does with Hector, so he wouldn't know what dirt looks like if he saw it?'

THE ILL WIND

Like most modern high-priced apartment blocks, the building where the Masons lived was protected by a sliding steel portcullis, bullet-proof glass, and a man with a gun on duty night and day. Doug McNeil presented his ID to the suspicious black who sat in the gas-proof booth today. It was a Saturday, which probably accounted for his not having seen this guard before. What with the soaring cost of living, especially food, a lot of people moonlighted jobs like this for evenings or weekends only.

'You making a house call on a Saturday?' the guard said, disbelieving.

'Why not?' Doug snapped. 'There's a sick kid up there!'

'Well, hell,' the guard said, shaking his heavy head with its fringe of grizzled beard. He opened the grille. Doug was halfway to the elevators when the man called after him.

'Say, doc!'

He glanced around.

'Doc, do you take – uh – colored patients?'

'Sure, why not?'

'Well, doc …' Emerging shyly from his booth, as though afraid of being reprimanded. He was much older than he had looked at first sight, Doug realized; well preserved, but probably in his upper sixties. 'It's my wife. Nothing you can like put a finger on, if you see what I mean, but all the time she gets these like fits of weakness, so if it don't cost too much …?'

Ending on a rising, hopeful note.

Doug tried not to sigh. Without seeing the woman he could make his diagnosis: poor food leading to sub-clinical malnutrition, poor water leading to recurrent minor bowel upsets, general debility and the rest. But he said, 'Well, I'm in the phone book. Douglas McNeil.'

'Thanks, sir! Thanks a million!'

He was still upset by the encounter when he entered the Masons' apartment. Denise was so eager to greet him, she had all the locks open ready, the door on a mere security chain, and didn't bar it as she rushed him inside.

'Doug, thank God you're here! I've had to change Harold's bed twice since I called you!'

Resignedly he followed her, and it was what he'd expected. Three minutes, and he'd written out a prescription the duplicate of – how many? – maybe ninety in the past week. Washing his hands, he recited the usual advice concerning diet and not worrying about minor stomach cramps.

At which point Philip showed up demanding the verdict.

'Not serious,' Doug said, throwing his towel at a hook.

'Not serious! Doug, they've had to close schools all over the city, and every kid in this building seems to have it, and most of the adults, and—'

'And babies sometimes don't recover,' Doug snapped. 'I know!'

He caught himself. 'Sorry,' he added, passing a tired hand over his eyes. 'This is my sixth call today for the same thing, you know. I'm worn out.'

'Yes, of course.' Philip looked apologetic. 'It's just that when it's your own kids …'

'Yours aren't babies any more,' Doug pointed out. 'They should be fine in another few days.'

'Yes, but … Oh, I'm being stupid. Say, can you spare the time for a drink? There are some people here you might like to meet.'

'I guess I need it,' Doug said wryly, and followed him.

In the living-room: a plump, pretty, light-colored girl, perched shyly on the edge of a chair, and next to her a man several shades darker who sat with the characteristic stiffness that Doug instantly assigned to a back-brace. His face was vaguely familiar, and the moment Philip made the introductions he remembered where he'd seen it.

'Mr Goddard! Very glad to meet you, very glad indeed!' And to Denise as she handed him his regular vodka rickey, 'Oh, thanks.'

'Are your children okay, Mrs Mason?' the girl asked.

'Doug says they will be in a few days.'

'What is it, this – this epidemic?' Pete inquired. 'I had a touch of it myself last week. Which made for – uh – problems.' A self-conscious grin. 'I don't get around too fast right now, you see.'

Doug smiled, but it was forced. Dropping into an armchair, he said, 'Oh … Basically it's an abnormal strain of *E. coli*. A bug that ordinarily lives in the bowel quite happily. But the strains vary from place to place, and some get altered by exposure to antibiotics and so forth, and that's why you get diarrhea. It's the same really as *turismo*, or as they call it in England "Delhi belly". You always adjust to the new strain, though. Sooner or later.'

'But don't babies …?' That was Jeannie, hesitant.

'Well, yes, they are vulnerable. They get dehydrated, you see, and of course their food squirts through the system so fast they – well, you get the picture.'

Pete nodded. 'But why is there so much of it right now? It's all over the country, according to the news this morning.'

'Somebody told me it was being spread deliberately,' Jeannie ventured.

'Oh, really!' Doug snorted and sipped his drink. 'You don't have to invent enemy agents to explain it, for heaven's sake! I'm no public health expert, but I imagine it's a simple vicious circle process. You know we're at the limit of our water resources, don't you?'

142

'No need to tell me,' Denise sighed. 'We have a don't-drink notice in force right now. Matter of fact, I suspect that's why the kids caught this bug. They're so proud of being able to go to the sink and help themselves to a glass of water … Sorry, go on.'

'Well, figure it yourself. With eight or ten million people—'

'Eight or ten *million*?' Philip burst out.

'So they say, and we can't have hit the peak yet. Well, obviously, with that many people flushing the pan ten, fifteen, twenty times a day, we're using far more water than usual, and at least half this country is supplied with water that's already been used.'

He spread his hands. 'So there you are. Vicious circle. It'll probably drag on all summer.'

'Christ almighty,' Philip said.

'What are you worrying about?' Doug said sourly. 'You and Alan got your water-purifier franchise, didn't you?'

Philip scowled. 'That's a sick joke if ever I heard one. Still, I guess you're right – look on the bright side. And it's nice to be one of the few who have a bright side to look on … By the way, Pete!'

'Yes?'

'Didn't Alan say he was going to recommend you to Doug?'

'You're a friend of Alan's too?' Doug put in.

'Sure.' Pete nodded. 'Going to work for him.'

'Oh, he's been just great!' Jeannie exclaimed. 'Found us an apartment, and everything. That's why we came to Denver today, to look it over, and it's fine.'

'Not like having a house,' Pete said. 'But.' He contrived a sketch for a shrug despite his back-brace.

Jeannie frowned at him. After a moment she added, 'One thing I didn't ask, though. Mrs Mason—'

'Denise, please!'

'Uh – sure, Denise. Do you have much trouble with rats?'

'No, why?'

'They're bad right now in Towerhill. I been bitten myself. And the other day …' Her voice trailed away.

'What?' Philip prompted.

'They killed a baby,' Pete grunted. 'Just chewed it to death.'

There was a pause. At length Doug drained his glass and rose. 'Well, I don't know of any plague of rats in Denver,' he said. 'But I guess you may have a little trouble with fleas and lice. Around half the houses I go to on my rounds have them now. Resistant, of course.'

'Even to the – uh – strong ones?' Philip said, using the common euphemism for 'banned'.

'Oh, especially those,' Doug said, smiling without humor. 'These are the survivors. They've taken the worst we could offer and come back jeering. The only thing they care about now is a direct hit with a brick, and I'm not too sure about that ... Well, thanks for the drink. I'd better be on my way.'

He was amused to notice, as he took his leave, that all of them were trying not to scratch themselves.

But he didn't find it so funny when a psychosomatic itch overtook him too in the elevator going down.

SIDE EFFECTS

... officially attributed to the debilitating effects of enteritis among troops newly arrived from this country. This marks the greatest single territorial gain for the Tupamaros since the uprising began. No comment on the battle was available from the president this morning owing to his indisposition. The epidemic continues to gather momentum in all states except Alaska and Hawaii, and many major corporations are working with a skeleton staff. Public services have been heavily hit, especially garbagemen and sewage workers. Bus and subway schedules in New York have been cut back, on certain routes to as few as one per hour, while the chief of police in New Orleans has forecast an unprecedented crimewave owing to the sickness of more than half his men. Trainite demonstrations this morning ...

OVERCAST

'These potatoes look as limp as I feel,' said Peg, attempting a joke as she set down the bucket of compost she'd brought to hoe in among the sickly plants. It was her first day back at work after her recent bout of enteritis, and she was still weak and a trifle lightheaded, but she couldn't stand any more sitting around.

'Yes, I guess what they mainly need is some sun,' Zena said absently. Rolling up her sleeves, she frowned at the high faint gray cloud that masked the entire sky.

Peg heard the words and experienced a sudden moment of enlightenment: a sort of rapid astral projection. She seemed, for a flash, to be looking down at herself, not only seeing herself in space but in time also.

It was over, and she was staring at the by now familiar mountains that surrounded the wat, and the curious irregular roofs of the buildings, which themselves were like mountains, dome next to pyramid next to cube. One of the community's architects had studied in England under Albarn.

'Peg, honey, you all right?' Zena demanded.

'Oh, sure,' Peg insisted. She had swayed a little without realizing.

'Well, don't you overdo it, hear? Take as much rest as you need.'

'Yes, of course,' Peg muttered, and picked up her hoe and began to do as she'd been shown: make a little pit next to each of the sickly plants, scoop in an ounce of compost, cover it over. Later they'd water the fertilizer in.

Before she had finished the first hole, however, she heard a sharp exclamation from Zena and glanced around to discover – with a tremor of nausea – that she was holding up something thin and wriggly.

'Hey, look at this!' she cried.

Peg complied, reluctantly, and after a moment could think of nothing better to say than, 'It's an odd color for a worm. Aren't they usually pink?' This thing was a livid color, somewhat bluish, as though it were engorged with venous blood.

'Yes,' Zena muttered. 'I wonder if it's been affected by some sort of poison, same as the potatoes, or if …' One-handed, she used her hoe to expose the roots of the nearest plant.

'Well, there's our answer,' she said grimly. The tubers, which by now should have been a fair size, were only an inch or two in diameter and riddled with holes. And each hole was surrounded by a patch of blackish rot.

'If that's what's ruining this whole field …' Zena turned slowly, surveying the acreage they'd put down to potatoes last fall. 'We been taking it for granted it was – well, something in the rain, or the ground. It usually is.'

Yes. It usually is.

And then, staring at the wriggling thing, Peg was struck by a horrible suspicion.

'Zena! That— Oh, no. They were a different color.'

'What?'

'That gallon of worms Felice brought. I thought for a moment …' Peg shook her head. 'But we looked at them in the store, and they were pink.'

'And they came from Plant Fertility,' Zena said. 'We've had their insects before. Got our bees from them, in fact.' There were a dozen hives around the wat. 'So … Well, we sure as hell don't have enough garlic juice to treat an area this size. So I guess all we can do is call the State Agriculture Board and find out if there's something we can plant between the rows to attract the little buggers. Come on, let's go back inside. No future in this.'

'Zena!' Peg said abruptly.

'Yes?'

'I think I'm going to move on.' How to explain that fit of insight a moment ago? She'd viewed herself as it were in the role of a passenger on the stream of time. She'd been content for weeks to let the wat insulate her, because life here was so undemanding and harmonious. Meanwhile, though, Out There,

145

bad things were happening. Like the bad thing which had drawn her here. Like death and destruction. Like poison in the rain which killed your crops.

'I was expecting that,' Zena said. 'It isn't your kind of life, is it? You need competition, and we don't have it here.'

'No, not exactly.' Peg hunted for the right words, leaning on her hoe. 'More – more making a mark. More wanting to do *one* thing to change the course of the world, instead of preparing to survive while the world does its worst.'

'That was why you became a reporter, I guess.'

'I guess so.' Peg pulled a face. She was more relaxed here, more able to reveal her feelings in her expression or with her body. The wat made its own herb wines, to traditional European recipes, and sold them not only to summer tourists but by mail, and the other night there had been a party to try out an especially successful brew. She'd danced for hours and felt great – just before she went down with enteritis. And no man had plagued her to get in the sack with him, except that poor disorganized boy Hugh whom you couldn't really count as a man yet, and perhaps because of that she'd recently found herself wondering whether she might not try it again and enjoy it this time. On the few previous occasions she'd been as locked up as a bank vault.

That was the point at which young Rick turned up, and they showed him the wriggling insect and he took authoritative charge of it, promising to compare it with all the pictures of pests he could find in the library. On impulse, she added, 'Rick, I'm thinking of moving on.'

'Go back to work on a paper?' he asked absently, examining the insect with concentration.

'I don't know. Maybe.'

'Ah-hah. Come back and see us often, won't you?' He folded a handkerchief carefully around the creature and made off. A moment before going out of sight, he called back, 'And see if you can find out how my dad was poisoned, please!'

It was like being doused in ice water. She stood frozen for long seconds before she was able to say, '*I* didn't tell him Decimus was poisoned, Zena!'

'Of course not.'

'Though ...' She had to swallow. 'Though I'm certain he must have been.'

'I think so, too,' Zena said. 'But we all are.'

That snapped together in Peg's mind with lack of sunlight and rain that didn't nourish plants but killed them, and all of a sudden she let fall her hoe and was crying with her face in her palms. Part of her was standing back in amazement and thinking: Peg Mankiewicz crying? It can't be true!

But it was a catharsis and a cleansing.

'I can't stand it!' she said after a while, feeling Zena's arm comforting around her shoulders. She blinked her tears away and looked at the dying potatoes: stock selected on the assumption that every plant would be doused with artificial fertilizers, systemic insecticides, plastic leaf-sprays to minimize water loss, and the hell with how they tasted so long as they looked good and weighed heavy. Cast back on the resources of nature, they wilted because the resources had been stolen.

'What kind of future do we have, Zena? A few thousand of us living underground in air-conditioned caves, fed from hydroponics plants like Bamberley's? While the rest of our descendants grub around on the poisoned surface, their kids sickly and crippled, worse off than Bushmen after centuries of proud civilization?'

She felt Zena wince. The younger of her adopted daughters suffered from allergies, and half the time went around wheezing and choking and gasping.

'We've got to make them listen!' Peg declared. 'Isn't that the message of all Austin's books? You can't blame the people who can't hear the warnings; you *have* to blame the ones who can, and who ignore them. I have one talent, and that's for stringing words together. Austin's vanished, Decimus is dead, but someone's got to go on shouting!'

On the point of striding away, she checked. 'Give the kids my love,' she said. And added, to her own surprise, in a husky whisper, 'And remember I love you too, won't you?'

FROM THE BOWELS OF THE EARTH

Duplicate at home the famous SPA WATERS OF THE WORLD!

Laugh at that 'Don't-Drink' notice! We supply the salts from every major spa in packet form – VICHY! PERRIER! FONTELLA! APOLLINARIS! MALVERN! ALL $9.95/oz!

Gallon cans of PURE water: $1.50!

SYPHOON BRAND and other famous makes of MIXER IN STOCK!

Guard the health of your family! DON'T TAKE RISKS WITH WATER!

THE DOG DAYS

Christ! Flies!

Austin Train stopped dead in his tracks, listening to the buzz of wings around the heaped-up garbage. There hadn't been a clearance here in five weeks. The epidemic meant the removal gangs were working at under half strength, and there had been an order from high up that the prosperous areas should get the benefit before the poor ones.

'Hell, they chuck their trash straight out the window anyway,' someone had said.

And it looked as though he'd been right. Every can in sight along the narrow alley, which angled back between two buildings four and five stories high, was overflowing, and huge sodden cartons bulged and leaked beside them and on top of that mess was yet one more layer which certainly must have been tossed from windows. The lot stank.

But there were flies. Incredible. Last summer down in LA he hadn't seen one, that he could remember.

His back ached and his feet were sore and that condition on his scalp had killed off most of his hair and the whole of his head itched abominably, but all of a sudden he was cheerful, and he was whistling when he forced the nose of his trolley under the first of the cans to be wheeled to the truck waiting on the main street.

'Hey! Hey, mister!'

A cry from overhead. A small swarthy boy peering from a window on the third floor, most likely a Chicano kid. He waved.

'Wait a minute! Please don't go 'way!'

The kid vanished. Now what was all that about? He shrugged and went on trying to load up the can. It was tricky with so much loose muck in the way. In the end he had to use his boots to expose its base.

A door to the alley swung open and here was the kid, in a torn shirt and faded jeans, a grimy bandage wrapped around his right arm. His eyes were swollen as though from long weeping.

'Mister, would you take away my dog, please? He – he died.' Oh.

Austin sighed and brushed his hands on the side of his pants. 'He upstairs? Too heavy to carry down with your bad arm?'

'No, he's right around the corner in the alley. Not allowed to keep him in the apartment,' the boy said, and snuffled a little. 'I wanted to take him and – well, bury him properly. But mom said not.'

'Your mom's quite right,' Austin approved. Right here in the dense-packed city center you didn't bury carcasses, though the odd dog or cat rotting in the ground wouldn't be half the health hazard of this uncleared garbage. 'Okay, let's see him.'

He followed the kid around the angle of the alley, and there was a kind of kennel nailed together out of scrap wood and plastic. The dog's muzzle protruded over the lip of the entrance. Austin hunkered down to look at the body, and whistled.

'Say! He was a handsome beast, wasn't he?'

The kid sighed. 'Yeah. I called him Rey. Mom said that was "king" in Spanish. He was half German shepherd and half chow … Only he got in this fight, see? And where he was bitten it went all kind of rotten.' He pointed.

148

Austin saw, on the side of the dog's neck, an infected wound. Must have hurt like hell.

'We did everything we could for him. Didn't help. It hurt so much he even bit me.' Waving the bandaged arm. 'Last night he was howling and howling, you could hear him even with the windows shut. So in the end Mom had to take sleeping pills, and said to give him one as well. Wish I hadn't! But the neighbors were kinda angry for the noise ...' An empty shrug.

Austin nodded, estimating the weight of the beast. Not under seventy pounds, maybe eighty. A load. How could a family this poor feed that big an extra mouth? Well, better drag him out. He reached for purchase, and his hand brushed something dangling from the underside of the kennel's roof. What the—?

Oh no!

He unhooked the thing from its nail and drew it out. A fly-killing strip. Spanish brand name. No country of origin, of course.

'Where did you get this?' he demanded.

'Mom bought a box. Flies got so bad when the garbagemen stopped coming. And they were crawling all over Rey's sores, so I put that up.'

'Your mom got more of these in the apartment?'

'Why, sure. In the kitchen, the bedroom, all over. They work fine.'

'You go straight up and tell her she must take them down, They're dangerous.'

'Well ...' Biting his lip. 'Well, okay, I'll tell her you said so. When she wakes up.'

'What?'

'She ain't up yet. Heard her snoring when I got up. And she hates for me to disturb her.'

Austin clenched his fists. 'What kind of sleeping pills does she take – barbiturates, aren't they?'

'*I* don't know!' There was fear and astonishment in the boy's eyes. 'Just pills, I guess!'

Stupid to have asked. He knew already that they had to be. 'Here, take me up to your apartment, quick!'

'Smith!' A roar from the gang-boss, storming up the alley. 'What the hell are you playing at? Hey, where do you think you're going?'

Austin waved the fly-strip under his nose. 'There's a woman sick upstairs! Taken barbiturates in a room with the windows shut and one of these hanging up! Know what they put in these stinking things? Dichlorvos! It's a cholinesterase antagonist! Mix that with barbiturates and—'

'What's all this crazy doubletalk about?' the gang-boss snapped.

'It's about what killed that dog! Come on, hurry!'

*

They saved her life. But of course reporters wanted to talk to this unexpectedly well-informed garbage-man, so he had to move on again before they got the chance.

A PLAN TO MAP THE PLANET

As yet they had undertaken only makeshift repairs to the facade of the Bamberley Trust building. The broken windows had been covered, of course – you couldn't let street air leak in – but the store at ground level had been boarded up. Shortage of labor, Tom Grey deduced.

'Looks like it's been hit by an earthquake!' said his cab-driver cheerfully.

'Well, not really,' Grey contradicted. 'An earthquake produces a highly characteristic type of damage, readily distinguishable from the effect of a bomb.' But he was extremely late for his appointment with Moses Greenbriar, so he was disinclined to pursue the point.

Besides, out here on the street it was most depressing. Garbage was piled high by the curb and against the walls of the buildings. Moreover, the air was unbelievably clammy, from air-conditioning systems no doubt – and people at bus-stops were coughing and wiping their streaming eyes because of the fumes. On the way from the airport he'd seen a fight break out at one stop, between two men in working overalls who – astonishingly – were belaboring each other with umbrellas.

His cab-driver had volunteered the information that this bus-route had been particularly hard hit by the enteritis outbreak, and those people might have been waiting in the open for more than an hour, which was bad for the temper. He'd asked about the umbrellas, and the man had chuckled.

'Ah, that's New York rain!' he said with a sort of perverse pride. 'Got one myself, wouldn't be without it!' He pointed at the shelf under the dash. 'You know, I'm going to quit this job next month. Sick of them Trainites! Saw the skull and crossbones they painted on this cab?' Grey had not; doubtless it was on the other side from the one where he'd entered. 'Had enough, me. Gon' put my savings into a dry-cleaning business. Coining it in that line. Five minutes in the rain, umbrella or no umbrella, and if you don't go to the cleaners right away you need a new suit.'

Many street-lights had broken down and not yet been repaired. National Guardsmen, masked and helmeted but armed only with pistols, were controlling traffic. It had been in the news: the mayor had reserved all policemen who were well enough for duty to cope with essential jobs like night crime patrols.

There had been huge State Health Authority posters at the airport, warning all out-of-town arrivals to purchase a recognized brand of prophylactic stomach tablets, and under no circumstances to drink unpurified water.

'I never had so many drunks to take home in my life,' the cab-driver had said. 'Like they took this warning not to risk the water as orders to fill up on hard liquor.'

'I don't drink,' Tom Grey had said.

He was a little nervous, because he set so much store by his world-simulation program now. Since the financial setbacks suffered by Angel City, first with the Towerhill avalanche, and now because of the enteritis epidemic – they had had enormous success in persuading their youngest clients to take out life insurance policies on their babies at birth, and over ten thousand had so far generated claims – they'd been compelled to find every possible means of improving the situation, even down to renting their computers at cut price to evening and weekend users. Grey therefore needed an alternative sponsor.

Having reviewed every major corporation, he'd decided that Bamberley Trust met all his requirements. It had plenty of capital; it had spare computer capacity, since it was primarily an investment firm and used computers solely for market analysis; and it was desperately in need of something to boost its public image. The UN inquiry into the Noshri disaster had not been able to prove how the dangerous drug was introduced into Nutripon, and the lack of a firm exoneration had allowed suspicion to continue.

He'd forwarded a fully detailed prospectus of his project, with appendices describing sample applications of the completed program. Obviously he had made it persuasive, for they had now invited him to New York to discuss the document.

And, within five minutes of entering Greenbriar's office, he knew – to employ a metaphor that was especially apt on Bamberley territory – he'd struck oil first time.

Of course, with New York in this mess you'd expect people to appreciate the potential advantages.

BURNING YOUR BRIDGES BEFORE YOU COME TO THEM

Chairman: My apologies for the repeated postponements of this meeting, ladies and gentlemen, but – ah – as you know it's been due to the fact that fate wasn't obliging enough to make our various indispositions coincide. For the record, I'm Edward Penwarren, and I'm the president's special representative in this matter. I believe you all know Mr Bamberley, but I guess I should draw attention to the presence of Captain Advowson – sorry, Major Advowson, special delegate from the UN observation team that

151

went to Noshri. Congratulations on your promotion, by the way, major; I believe it's recent. Yes, senator?

Sen. Howell (Rep., Col.): I want to go on record as objecting very strongly to the presence of this foreigner. I've repeatedly stressed both in public and private that this is a purely internal affair and the UN has no business meddling—

Advowson: Senator, I have been trying to get the hell out of your country for the past month. It stinks, and I mean that literally. I've never been so sick in my life. I've never had so many sore throats or so much diarrhea. And I've never before been blown up in a bomb outrage.

Chairman: Gentlemen, if you please—

Howell: Isn't that proof enough that everything this man says and does is prejudiced?

Advowson: Prejudice be damned. Based on the experiences of my first and I devoutly hope only visit to—

Chairman: Order! Major, may I remind you that you are here by invitation? And as for you, senator, I must stress that the president personally approved the composition of this committee as best suited to the requirements of the situation. Thank you. Now the proximate reason for this meeting is a report which has not yet been publicly announced, but which I'm afraid will almost certainly be delivered to UN delegates within the next few days, because a copy of it is unaccounted for. I won't go into the background; the matter is *sub judice*. But what it is, this report, it's a confidential U.S. Medical Corps report on the condition of certain of the survivors from the – uh – the village of San Pablo. I'm sorry, major; did you say something?

Advowson: Only 'Ah-hah!'

Howell: If that's your idea of a constructive contribution to these proceedings—

Advowson: It's just that I've been hearing rumors about—

Chairman: Order! Order! Thank you. Yes, as I was saying, this report. It – ah – it tends to the conclusion that the survivors from San Pablo do display many of the same symptoms as were reported from Noshri. Now I must stress something at once. It's been a long time since Dr Duval in Paris analyzed the Nutripon from Noshri. It is our firm belief that what has happened is this. The Tupas have had a similar substance prepared, to give identical effects, and have deliberately administered it to hapless civilians to discredit the U.S. intervention in Honduras. What was that, major?

Advowson: Never mind. Go on.

Chairman: Supporting this assumption I'd adduce the following point. If – I say if – Nutripon were again at the root of the trouble, the symptoms would have been noticed long ago, back in January maybe at the time when the search was going on for Dr Williams and Leonard Ross. Yet the first mention of recognizable mental disturbance, according to the Medical Corps investigation, was not until March, and was so – uh – so unremarkable in the circumstances, what with the necessity of interrogating suspected Tupas and so forth, that … Well, the point is that a very small proportion of the persons detained for interrogation showed any mental abnormality, and it was not until the beginning of April that any symptoms were recognized which were sufficiently serious to lead to close psychiatric examination and eventual – uh – serum analysis and so forth. I'm not an expert on this, I'm afraid, just quoting the report. Yes, Mr Bamberley?

Bamberley: San Pablo was the first place we were asked to send Nutripon to, I think. Globe Relief asked us before Christmas and we got some off, thanks to my workers putting in a lot of overtime. I never heard that Globe's people out there noticed anything in the way of bad effects.

Chairman: Well, I'm afraid it wouldn't follow. Their local agent was Mr Ross, wasn't it? And he died. Yes, major?

Advowson: Could I ask Mr Bamberley how many people the contract was for? I mean, how many people was he supposed to feed for how long?

Bamberley: I believe I have those data … Yes, here. A hundred adults and eighty children, initially for two days in order to get some kind of relief out on the ground straight away.

Advowson: Well, even at a couple of pounds apiece that doesn't sound like much!

Bamberley: We were closing down for the holiday, remember. It was what we had left from the previous contract, you see – just, like you say, a couple of hundred pounds or so for the worst-hit village. And we sent much greater quantities directly after New Year's, tons and tons of it, and there was no complaint about that lot!

Advowson: If I might ask you something, Mr Chairman? How many survivors have displayed this mental derangement?

Chairman: Only about a dozen or fifteen including children.

Advowson: Is that because only a dozen or fifteen of the villagers are being held for Tupamaro sympathies, or is it because all the rest have been killed?

Howell: Tupa sympathies! Hell, every damn thing he says comes right out of their own lying propaganda! Mr Chairman, I demand his removal from the committee!

Chairman: Senator, kindly do not presume to give me orders! I welcome that question, although I don't approve the way it was phrased, because that's exactly the sort of question we're going to have to answer in the UN. Major, I'm afraid the report doesn't specify, but thank you for drawing my attention to the point and I'll try and find out. Now Mr Bamberley knows the point I'm going to raise next, I believe.

Bamberley: Yes. We seem to have no alternative. We have a great deal of Nutripon still in store, which was prepared before the new filtration system was installed at our plant. It's been suggested that we should have it destroyed with maximum publicity, have its destruction testified to by an unimpeachable witness – the major here, if he's willing, and a scientist of international reputation as well, Lucas Quarrey for example—

Howell: That anti-American bastard! You must be crazy!

Chairman: Senator, you miss the point. The new installation at the factory must be approved by someone whom no one can conceivably call a – a lackey of the imperialists or whatever the phrase is. Professor Quarrey is not noted for his reluctance to speak his mind, as you correctly observe. His opinion will carry that much more weight abroad. Now, if I may continue—

Howell: I haven't finished. Jack, that stockpile must be worth money. How much?

Bamberley: About half a million dollars. And modifications to the plant have cost as much again.

Chairman: Naturally there will be compensation.

Howell: Whose pocket is it going to come out of? The taxpayer's, as usual?

Chairman: Senator, we shall have to think of it as the premium on an insurance policy. Don't you realize what a desperate situation this country is in right now? We've got to get that plant back in operation, *and* wipe out the prejudice against Nutripon, before the fall, because we're almost certainly going to have to distribute the stuff here at home. Over the past few weeks thirty-five million people have been sick for a week or longer. Factories, farms, all kinds of public services have been shut down or cut back. And according to HEW we're going into a second cycle of the epidemic because we've run out of water, we're having to re-release it before it's been completely sterilized. All the don't-drink warnings in the world won't stop people here and there from catching the bug a second time. And you know what it did in Honduras, don't you?

Advowson: Probably not. I doubt that he reads Uruguayan press releases, and you've kept the matter under wraps.

Chairman: Shut up, major. Sorry. In a sense you're right, much as it galls me to admit it. Publicity wouldn't have been very good for morale, would it?

Howell: What the hell are you talking about?

Advowson: The Tenth Counter-Insurgency Corps, I imagine.

Chairman: Damn it, yes of course. Senator, they didn't just fight a rearguard action and withdraw owing to their debilitated condition, which was the story we released to the media. There's been nothing like it since the First World War. They ran away. They were sick. They had fever over a hundred degrees and most of them were delirious. I guess that's an excuse. But it meant that the entire equipment of the Corps was captured intact by the Tupas. As a result Tegucigalpa is having to be supplied by air, and we may have to pull the government out any day now. And of course practically every big-city ghetto is alive with pro-Tupa black militants, and you can imagine what will happen if we can't clear the name of Nutripon before we have to start issuing it as relief allotments. Not content with poisoning innocent Honduran peasants and African blacks, we're starting genocide operations against black Americans too! That'll be the line, and we've got to prevent it at all costs.

THE UNDERGROUND MOVEMENT

Lem Walbridge had built up his holdings from the five hundred acres his father had left, until now he had over three thousand, all under vegetables: potatoes, beans, salads, beets, plus some corn and sunflowers – for oil – and a few gourmet delicacies like zucchini and scorzonera. The man from the State Board of Agriculture knew him well.

'Never seen anything like it!' Lem said for the tenth time, jumping down from his jeep at the edge of a field of sickly-looking beets. He pulled one up at random and displayed it, alive with horrible writhing worms. 'Have you?'

The other nodded. 'Yeah. Few days ago. Right the other side of those hills.'

'But what the hell are these things? Christ, if this goes on I'll be ruined! I'm only going to get half my usual crop to market as it is, and unless I stop these stinking buggers …!' He hurled the rotten beet away with a snort of fury.

'Buy any earthworms this year?'

Lem blinked. 'Well, sure! You have to. Like for soil conditioning.'

'Put any down around here?'

'I guess maybe sixty, seventy quarts, same as usual. But I got a license, they were all approved.'

'You get 'em from Plant Fertility in San Clemente?'

'Sure! Always do! They've been in the business longer'n anyone else. Best quality. And bees, too.'

'Yeah, I was afraid of that. Their stuff goes all over the country, doesn't it? Clear to New England!'

'What in hell does that have to do with it?'

'It's beginning to look as though it has everything to do with it.'

BY THE DEAD SEA

The wind was bad today. Hugh's filtermask was used up, all clogged, and he didn't have the seventy-five cents for another from a roadside dispenser, and anyway the quality of those things was lousy, didn't even last the hour claimed for them.

Lousy ...

Absently he scratched his crotch. He'd more or less got used to lice by now, of course; there just didn't seem to be any way of avoiding them. For every evil under the sun there is a remedy or there's none. If there is one try and find it, if there isn't never mind it.

There must be a hell of a lot of evils in the world nowadays that there weren't any remedies for. Anyway: what sun? He hadn't seen the sun in fucking weeks.

It was hot, though. Leaning on the wall overlooking the Pacific, he wondered what this beach had been like when he was a kid. Scattered with pretty girls, maybe. Strong young men showing off their muscles to impress. Now ...

The water looked more like oil. It was dark gray and barely moved to the breeze. Along the edge of the sand was a rough demarcation line composed of garbage, mainly plastic. Big signs read: THIS BEACH UNSAFE FOR SWIMMING.

Must have been posted last year. This year you wouldn't have needed to put up signs. One whiff of the stench, and *yecch.*

Still, it was great to be out and about again. It had been bad since he hit California. The runs. Everybody had them, but *everybody.* Back in Berkeley, along Telegraph, he'd seen them lying and whimpering, the seats of their jeans stained brown, no one to turn to for help. There had been a free clinic, but it treated V D as well, and the governor had said it encouraged promiscuity and had it closed.

Well, at least you didn't die of the runs, not over about six months of age. Carl had found a part-time job for a couple of weeks after their arrival, nailing together cheap coffins for babies; the cash had been useful.

Though sometimes the runs made you feel you'd *like* to die.

Where in hell was Carl, anyway? The air was hot and harsh, so he'd gone to a soft-drink stand for some Cokes. Taking his time. Bastard. Probably picked someone up.

They were shacking with a girl named Kitty, who'd spread half a dozen mattresses on her floor and didn't really mind who shared them, how many or what sex. She and Carl had been lucky and escaped the runs, and what they brought in, by working, panhandling and hustling, kept the others fed. When Hugh got over the after-effects, he promised himself, he was going to get a decent job. Garbage clearance, maybe. Beach cleaning. Something constructive, anyhow.

Still no sign of Carl returning. But, drifting toward him, a windblown newspaper, almost intact and too heavy for the breeze to move it more than a few inches at each gust. He trod on it and picked it up. Ah, great! A copy of *Tupamaro USA!*

Leaning back against the wall, he shook it around to the front page and at once a name leapt out at him: Bamberley. Not Jacob, Roland. Something about Japanese water-purifiers. Hugh glanced over his shoulder at the befouled ocean and laughed.

But other things of more interest. Trainites in Washington rigged a catapult, Roman-style, bombarded the White House with paper sacks of fleas – hey, crazy, wish I'd been in on that. And a piece about Puritan, saying their food isn't really any better, costs more because of all their advertising …

'Hugh!'

He looked up and here came Carl, and Carl wasn't alone. For an instant he was transfixed by jealousy. He'd never imagined he might drift into this kind of scene. But it had happened, and Carl was a good cat, and … Well, at least Kitty being around allowed him to keep his – uh – hand in.

'Hey, you should meet this guy!' Carl said, beaming as he handed over the straw-stuck Coke bottle he'd brought. 'Hugh Pettingill, Austin Train!'

Austin Train?

Hugh was so shaken he dropped the paper and nearly let go of the Coke as well, but recovered and took the hand proffered by the thickset stranger in shabby red shirt and faded blue pants, who grinned and exposed a row of teeth browned by khat.

'Carl says you met at the Denver wat.'

'Ah … Yeah, we did.'

'What do you think of them up there?'

'Full of gas,' Carl chimed in. 'Right, Hugh baby?'

It didn't seem right to put down a bunch of Trainites to Train himself, but after a moment Hugh nodded. It was true, and what was the good of pretending it wasn't?

'Damned right,' Train said. 'All gab and contemplation. No action. Now down here in Cal the scene isn't the same. You're shacking in Berkeley, right? So you seen Telegraph.'

Hugh nodded again. From end to end, and down most of the cross streets, it was marked with the relics of Trainite demonstrations. Skulls and crossbones stared from every vacant wall.

Like the one on this guy's chest. Not a tattoo but a decal, exposed when he reached up to scratch among the coarse hair inside his shirt.

'Now Carl says you quit the wat because you wanted action,' Train pursued, moving to perch on the sea wall at Hugh's side. Overhead there was a loud droning noise, and they all glanced up, but the plane wasn't visible through the haze.

'Well, something's got to be done,' Hugh muttered. 'And demonstrations aren't enough. They haven't stopped the world getting deeper in shit every day.'

'Too damned true,' the heavy-set man nodded. For the first time Hugh noticed that there was a bulge – not muscle – under the sleeve of his shirt, and without thinking he touched it. The man withdrew with a grimace.

'Easy there! It's still tender.'

'What happened?' He had recognized the softness: an absorbent cotton pad and a bandage.

'Got burned.' With a shrug. 'Making up some napalm out of Vaseline and stuff. Thought we'd take a leaf out of the Tupas' book. You heard they caught that Mexican who staged the raids on San Diego, by the way?'

Hugh felt a stir of excitement. This was the kind of talk he'd been yearning for: practical talk, with a definite end in view. He said, 'Yeah. Some stinking fishery patrol, wasn't it?'

'Right. Claimed he was fishing in illegal waters. Found these balloons all laid out on the foredeck, ready to go.'

'But like I was just saying to Austin,' Carl cut in, 'we're right here in the same country with the mothers. We don't have to strike at random from a distance. We can pick out and identify guilty individuals, right?'

'Only we don't,' Train snapped. 'I mean, like this cat Bamberley.'

'Shit, he's got as much trouble as he deserves,' Hugh said with a shrug. 'They closed his hydroponics factory, and—'

'Not Jacob! Roland!' Train pointed with his toe at the paper Hugh had dropped. 'Going to make a fucking fortune out of these Mitsuyama filters, isn't he? When back before he and his breed got to work on the world, when you felt thirsty you helped yourself at the nearest creek!'

'Right,' Hugh agreed. 'Now they've used the creeks for sewers, and what happens? Millions of people lie around groaning with the runs.'

'That's it,' Train approved. 'We got to stop them. Hell, d'you hear this one? Some pest got at the crops in Idaho – worm of some kind – so they're demanding to be allowed to turn loose all the old poisons, like DDT!'

'Shit, no!' Hugh said, and felt his cheeks pale.

'It's a fact. Aren't there better ways of handling the problem? Sure there are. Like in China they don't have trouble with flies. You see a fly, you swat it, and pretty soon – no more flies.'

'I like the trick they use in Cuba,' Carl said. 'To keep pests off the sugar cane. Plant something between the rows that the bugs make for first, cut it down and turn it into compost.'

'Right! Right! 'Stead of which, over here, they shit in the water until it's dangerous to drink, then make a fucking fortune out of selling us gadgets to purify it again. Why can't they be made to strain out their own shit?'

'Know what I'd like to do?' Carl exclaimed. 'Like to soak those mothers right in their own shit until they turn *brown*!'

'We're all in this together now,' Train said somberly. 'Black, white, red, yellow, we all been screwed up until we got to stick together or go under.'

'Sure, but you know these bastards! Darker you are, more they screw you! Like the atom-bomb. Did they drop it on the Germans? Shit, no – Germans are white same as them. So they dropped it on the little yellow man. And then when they found there were *black* men who were standing up on their hind legs and talking back, they joined forces with the yellow ones because they were kind of pale and pretty damned near as good at messing up the environment. Truth or lies?'

'Trying to make me ashamed of being white, baby?' Hugh snapped.

'Shit, of course not.' Carl put his arm around Hugh's waist. 'But did they send that poisoned food to a white country, baby? Hell, no – they sent it to Africa, and when they found it worked they gave it to the Indians in Honduras, got the excuse they were after to march in with their guns and bombs and napalm and all that shit.'

There was a long pause full of confirmatory nods.

At length Train stirred, feeling in his pocket for a pen. 'Well, right now I got to split – this chica I'm shacked with promised to fix a meal tonight. I get the impression we talk the same language, though, and I'm working on a kind of plan you might like. Let me leave you a number where you can reach me.'

Hugh dived for the abandoned newspaper and tore a strip off its margin for Train to write on.

JUNE

A VIEW STILL EXTREMELY WIDELY ADHERED TO

There's an 'eathen bint out in Malacca
With an 'orrible 'eathenish name.
As for black, they don't come any blacker—
But she answered to 'Jill!'just the same!
Well, a man 'oo's abroad can get lonely,
Missin' friends an' relations an' such.
She wasn't 'me sweet one-an'-only'—
But there's others as done just as much!

I'm not blushin' or makin' excuses,
An' I don't think she'd want that, because
When she stopped blubbin' over 'er bruises
The long an' the short of it was
That I'd bust up 'er 'orrible idol
An' I'd taught 'er respect for a gun—
Yus, I broke 'er to saddle an' bridle
An' I left 'er an Englishman's son!

– 'Lays of the Long Haul', 1905

STEAM ENGINE TIME

Although the sun showed only as a bright patch on pale gray, it was a sunny day in the life of Philip Mason. Against all the odds everything was turning out okay. Talk about blessings in disguise!

They had their franchise. They had the first consignment of a thousand units. Their first spot commercial on the local TV stations – featuring Pete Goddard, who'd done an excellent job considering he had no training as an actor – had brought six hundred inquiries by Monday morning's mail.

Pausing in the task of sorting the inquiries into serious and frivolous – most of the latter abusive, of course, from anonymous Trainites – he glanced at the clothing store catty-corner from Prosser Enterprises. A man in overalls was scrubbing off a slogan which had been painted on its main window over

160

the weekend; it now read ROTTING IS NATU. The accompanying skull and crossbones had gone.

They were having a man-made fiber week. Trainites objected to orlon, nylon, dacron, anything that didn't come from a plant or an animal.

Hah! They don't mind if a sheep catches cold, he thought cynically, so long as they don't – and speaking of colds … He dabbed his watering eyes with a tissue and soaked it with a thorough blast from his nose.

The door of his office opened. It was Alan.

'Hey!' Philip exclaimed. 'I thought you had to stay home today. Dorothy said you—'

Alan grimaced. 'Yeah, I have the runs again okay. But I heard the good news and decided I couldn't miss out.' He stared at the heap of correspondence on Philip's desk.

'Christ, there really are six hundred!'

'And five,' Philip said with a smirk.

'I'd never have believed it.' Shaking his head, Alan dropped into a chair. 'Well, I guess Doug was right, hm?'

'About the enteritis being on our side? I thought that was in kind of bad taste.'

'Don't let that stop you getting the point,' Alan said. 'Know what I like about my job, Phil? They talk all the time about the businessman, the entrepreneur, being an "enemy of mankind" and all that shit, and it *is* shit! I mean, if anyone has a reason to hate society and want to screw it up, it ought to be me, right?' He held up his bullet-scarred hand. 'But I don't. I got my chance to grow fat – least, it looks like that's what's happening – and do I have to be ashamed of how I do it? I do not. Here I am offering a product people really want, really need, and into the bargain creating jobs for people who'd otherwise be on relief. True or false?'

'Well, sure,' Philip said, blinking. 'Especially the point about new jobs. Unemployment throughout the nation was at an all-time high this summer, and on this side of Denver it was particularly bad and would remain so until they finished the modifications to the hydroponics plant and hired back their former six hundred workers.

That too was naturally redounding to the benefit of Prosser Enterprises. Anyone with an ounce of wit could be taught to fit these purifiers in an hour.

'Well, then!' Alan said gruffly, and swiveled his chair to face the window overlooking the street. 'Say, there's another bunch of kids. City's alive with them today. Where they all coming from?'

Across the street a group of about eight or ten youngsters – more boys than girls – had paused to jeer at the man washing the slogan off the clothing store.

'Yes, I saw a whole lot of them getting off a bus at the Trailways terminal,' Philip agreed. 'Must have been – oh – nearly thirty. They asked me the way to the Towerhill road.'

'Looks like this lot is heading the same way,' Alan muttered. 'Wonder what the big attraction is.'

'You could run over and ask them.'

'Thanks, I don't care that much. Say, by the way: how come you're sorting these letters yourself? What became of that girl we hired for you?'

Philip sighed. 'Called in to apologize. Sore throat. She could barely talk on the phone.'

'Ah, hell. Remind me, will you? Top priority on filters for the homes of our staff. See if we can cut the sickness rate a bit, hm? Charity begins at home and all that shit.' He leafed curiously through a few of the letters. 'How many of these are genuine orders and how many are junk?'

'I guess we're running ten to one in favor of genuine ones.'

'That's great. That's terrific!'

The door opened again and Dorothy entered, a sheaf of pages from a memo pad in one hand, a handkerchief in the other with which she was wiping her nose. 'More inquiries all the time,' she said. 'Another thirty this morning already.'

'This is fantastic!' Alan said, taking the papers from her.

From outside there came a rumble of heavy traffic, and Dorothy exclaimed, 'What in the world are those things?'

They glanced up. Pausing at the corner before making a left toward Towerhill, a string of big olive-drab Army trucks, each trailing something on fat deep-cleated tires from which protruded a snub and deadly-looking muzzle. But not guns.

'Hell, I saw those on TV!' Alan said. 'They're the new things they're trying out in Honduras – they're battle-lasers!'

'Christ, I guess they must be!' Philip jumped up and went to the window for a closer look. 'But why are they bringing them up here? Maneuvers or something?'

'I didn't hear they were planning any,' Alan said. 'But of course nowadays you don't. Say! Do you think all these kids coming into town might have got wind of maneuvers and decided to screw them up?'

'Well, it's the kind of damn-fool thing they might do,' Philip agreed.

'Right. In which case they deserve what's coming to them.' Absently Alan rubbed the back of his scarred hand. 'Wicked-looking, aren't they? Wouldn't care to be in the way when they let loose. And speaking of letting loose – excuse me!'

He rushed from the room.

IF IT MOVES, SHOOT IT

... that the Army is using defoliants in Honduras to create free-fire zones. This charge has been strongly denied by the Pentagon. Asked to comment just prior to leaving for Hawaii, where he will convalesce for the next two or three weeks, Prexy said, quote, Well, if you can't see them you can't shoot them. End quote. Support has been growing for a bill which Senator Richard Howell will introduce at the earliest opportunity, forbidding the issue of a passport to any male between sixteen and sixty not in possession of a valid discharge certificate or medical exemption. Welcoming the proposal, a Pentagon spokesman today admitted that of the last class called for the draft more than one in three failed to report. Your steaks are going to cost you more. This warning was today issued by the Department of Agriculture. The price of animal fodder has quote taken off like a rocket unquote, following the mysterious ...

A PLACE TO STAND

'A lady and a gentleman to see you, Miss Mankiewicz,' said the hotel reception-clerk. He was Puerto Rican and adhered to the old-fashioned formalities. 'I don't know if you're expecting them?'

'Who are they?' Peg said. She sounded nervous, knew it, and wasn't surprised. During the previous few weeks she had initiated a very tricky venture, and she was sure that for the past ten days at least someone had been following her. It wasn't beyond the bounds of possibility that she had broken one of the increasingly complex disloyalty laws. The situation was beginning to resemble that in Britain during the eighteenth century: any new law involving a harsher punishment for a vaguer crime was certain of passage through Congress and instant presidential approval.

Granted, Canada wasn't yet a proscribed country. But at this rate it wouldn't be long ...

'A Mr Lopez,' the clerk said. 'And a Miss Ramage. Uh – Ra-*maige*?'

Peg's heart seemed to stop in mid-beat. When she recovered she said, 'Tell them I'll be right down.'

'They say they'd prefer to come up.'

'Whatever they want.'

When she put down the phone her hand was trembling. She'd pulled all kinds of strings recently, but she hadn't expected one of them to draw Lucy Ramage to her. Incredible!

Hastily she gathered up some soiled clothing scattered on her bed and thrust it out of sight. The ashtrays needed emptying, and … Well, it was a ropy hotel anyhow. But she couldn't afford a better one. Thirty bucks a day was her limit.

She'd come to New York because she had a project on her mind. As she'd told Zena, she had only one talent, and right now the logical use to put it to seemed to be muckraking. So she'd asked herself a key question: what was the most important muck? (Actually she had phrased it, subconsciously, in terms of what Decimus had hated most. But it came to the same in the end.)

It almost answered itself: 'Do unto others …'

Very well, the starting point would be that claim of Professor Quarrey's, which had been in the news at the beginning of the year, that the country's greatest export was noxious gas. And who would like to stir up the fuss again? Obviously, the Canadians, cramped into a narrow band to the north of their more powerful neighbors, growing daily angrier about the dirt that drifted to them on the wind, spoiling crops, causing chest diseases and soiling laundry hung out to dry. So she'd called the magazine *Hemisphere* in Toronto, and the editor had immediately offered ten thousand dollars for three articles.

Very conscious that all calls out of the country were apt to be monitored, she'd put the proposition to him in highly general terms: the risk of the Baltic going the same way as the Mediterranean, the danger of further dustbowls like the Mekong Desert, the effects of bringing about climatic change. That was back in the news – the Russians had revived their plan to reverse the Yenisei and Ob. Moreover, there was the Danube problem, worse than the Rhine had ever been, and Welsh nationalists were sabotaging pipelines meant to carry 'their' water into England, and the border war in West Pakistan had been dragging on so long most people seemed to have forgotten that it concerned a river.

And so on.

Almost as soon as she started digging, though, she thought she might never be able to stop. It was out of the question to cover the entire planet. Her pledged total of twelve thousand words would be exhausted by North American material alone.

Among her most useful contacts was Felice, née Jones. Having spent more than two months after her return from the wat in hunting for a new job, she had finally resigned herself to being unemployable and married some guy she'd known for years. He had an unexciting but safe job and she was now able to devote much of her time to acting as Peg's unpaid West Coast correspondent. Despite her former dismissal of her brother's ideals, she was obviously very worried now. What seemed to have revised her opinions was the fact that her new husband was going to insist on children.

Among the questions she had drawn Peg's attention to …

Why had there been a sharp fall in the value of shares in Plant Fertility? In the spring there had been such a demand for their bees and earthworms, they'd been booming; they'd even initiated a market survey to determine if they should add ants and ladybugs. (Felice said there was a Texas firm which had cornered the market in ichneumon wasps, but Peg hadn't got around to finding what they were wanted for.) There had been no official comment about the company's decline, but undoubtedly someone on the inside was selling his stock in huge quantities.

Was there a connection between Plant Fertility's problems and the fact that potatoes were up a dime a pound over spring prices and still rising?

And could animal feed really have been so severely affected as to account for the rise of meat prices from exorbitant to prohibitive? (It had been years since cattle could be grazed on open land anywhere in the country.) Or was there – as rumor claimed – a wave of contagious abortion decimating the herds, which no antibiotic would touch?

Peg thought: likely both.

Another question. Was it true that Angel City had decided to give up life insurance and realize the value of their out-of-state property because the decline in life expectancy was so sharp it threatened to cut through the profit line?

Similarly: Stephenson Electric Transport was the only car maker in the States whose product met with complete approval from the Trainites. They had been due for a colossal takeover bid from Ford. The negotiations were hanging fire; was that really due to a threat from Chrysler that they'd have them hit with an injunction under the Environment Acts for generating excessive ozone? (Which would leave the pure-exhaust field wide open for foreign companies: Hailey, Peugeot who had just unwrapped their first steamer, and the Japanese Freonvapor cars.)

Was it true that the Trainites had turned sour on Puritan and dug up some kind of dirt about their operations?

She didn't know. And she was becoming daily more frightened at her inability to find out.

Of course, there were good reasons why companies in trouble with the Trainites should fight tooth and nail to keep their dirty secrets from the public. The government couldn't go on forever bailing out mismanaged giant corporations, even though it was their own supporters, people who ranted against 'UN meddling' and 'creeping socialism,' who yelled the loudest for federal aid when they got into a mess. With an eye to her next series of articles, she'd compiled a list of companies which were state-owned in all but name and would go broke overnight if the government ever called in its loans. So far it included a chemical company caught by the ban on 'strong' insecticides; an oil company ruined by public revulsion against defoliants; a pharmaceutical company that had nearly become a subsidiary of Maya Pura, the enormously successful Mexican producers of herbal remedies and cosmetics (to be bought out by Dagoes! Oh, the shame!); six major computer manufacturers who had glutted the market for their costly products; and, inevitably, several airlines.

And every day senators and Congressmen who in public were inclined to turn purple at the mere mention of state control wheeled and dealed behind the scenes to secure for their home states the fattest government-financed contracts they could nab, or pleaded that if such-and-such a firm which had been run into the ground by its incompetent directors wasn't helped, the unemployment index would rise another point.

It was as though the entire country had been turned into a pork-barrel, with two hundred million people squabbling over the contents. Talk about taking in each other's laundry – this was more like termites, each eating its predecessor's excrement!

On top of which, in some sense at least, the most crucial point of all was not what had happened but what people were afraid might happen. Consider the calamitous drop in air passengers, down 60 per cent in ten years. Consider that one man, Gerry Thorne of Globe Relief, had ruined the summer tourist trade from Maine to Trinidad, just by securing publicity for the death of his wife.

One man with a bomb could break an airline. One man with a cause could break ten thousand hotel proprietors. One man with enough leverage …

Or one woman. Peg was after leverage of her own. That was why she wanted to talk to Lucy Ramage.

At which point there came a knock at her door. She checked the spyhole before opening; it was a favorite mugger's trick in New York hotels to hang around the desk until someone was invited up to a room, then club the visitor in the elevator and come calling in his place.

But she recognized Lucy Ramage from seeing her on TV.

She admitted her and her companion, a swarthy man with recently healed cuts on his face, lacking teeth from both top and bottom jaws. She took their filtermasks, asked if they'd like a drink – both refused – and got down to business right away, sensing they were impatient.

'I'm glad I finally managed to reach you,' she said. 'It's been a hassle. Like plodding through a swamp.'

'It must have seemed harder than it really was,' the man said with a faint smile. 'I apologize. The delay was on our side. We work under – ah – difficulties here, and we wanted to investigate your credentials before reacting.'

A blinding light broke on Peg. 'Your name isn't Lopez! It's—' She snapped her fingers in frustration. 'You're the Uruguayan who got beaten up and claimed it was by off-duty policemen!'

'Fernando Arriegas,' the man said, nodding.

'Are you – are you recovered?' Peg felt herself flushing, as though from shame for her country.

'I was lucky.' Arriegas curled his lip. 'They destroyed only one of my testicles. I am told I may still hope to be a father – if it is ever safe again to bring a child into this sick world. However, let us not talk about me. You have been trying to contact Lucy. Trying very hard.'

Peg nodded.

'Why?' Lucy said, leaning forward. She was wearing a plastic coat despite the warmth of the weather, and her hands were in its deep pockets out of sight. But there was nothing particularly surprising in that; plastic was the best armor against New York rain. Rubber just rotted.

'I – well.' Peg cleared her throat; she was dreadfully catarrhal at the moment. 'I'm working on a series of articles for *Hemisphere*, in Toronto. The general theme is what the rich countries are doing to the poor ones even without intending to harm them, and of course the tragedy at Noshri ...' She spread her hands.

'Not to mention the tragedy in Honduras,' Arriegas murmured. He glanced at Lucy, and from the big pockets of her coat she handed him a transparent bag full of objects like soft macaroni.

'You recognize?' he asked, showing it to Peg.

'Is that Nutripon?'

'Yes, of course. What is more, it is Nutripon from San Pablo, a sample of the supplies that drove its people mad and caused them to kill an Englishman and an American, believing them to be devils. For which involuntary crime some ten or twelve thousand Hondurans have now been killed.' His voice was as flat as a machine's. 'We recaptured – that is to say, the Honduran Tupas did, but their cause is our cause – recaptured San Pablo and went over it with a fine-toothed comb. Part of the original delivery of this food was found in the ruins of the church, where apparently the people took it in the hope of exorcising the evil from it. They must have been dreadfully hungry. We have sent some for analysis in Havana, but the rest we have reserved for other important applications, such as insuring that any American who writes about the *tragedy*' – he leaned on the word with heavy irony – 'should know what he or she is talking about.'

Peg felt her jaw drop. She forced out, 'You mean you want *me* to eat some?'

'Exactly. Most of your brainwashed reporters have repeated the lie that our accusations are untrue. We wish at least one to be able to say the contrary.'

He tore a strip of cellulose tape from the bag with a tiny crying noise. 'Here! It says on the carton it can be eaten raw – and you need not worry about it being stale. The carton we took this from was completely intact when we found it.'

'Hurry up!' snapped Lucy. Peg glanced at her, and suddenly realized that those big pockets were big enough to conceal a gun. They had concealed one. It was in Lucy's hand now, and the muzzle seemed as wide as a subway tunnel.

It was silenced.

'You're insane!' Peg whispered, 'They must know you're here – they'll catch you in minutes if you use that thing!'

'But we shan't have to,' Arriegas said with a thin sneer. 'You are not so stupid as to resist. We have studied this poison very carefully. We know that this much' – hefting the bag – 'produces the effect of a little trip on acid, no more. Or perhaps I should better say STP, because I'm afraid the trip has not been known to be a good one. Maybe you'll be the lucky first, if your conscience is clear.'

'And you'd rather live until tomorrow than die now,' Lucy said. 'Besides, you won't die. I've eaten more than that. Much more.'

'Wh-when?' Peg stammered, unable to tear her fascinated gaze from the bag.

'I found some in a ruined house,' Lucy said. 'Next to the body of a child. I don't know if it was a boy or a girl, it was so crushed. And I suddenly realized I had to share this thing. It was like a vision. Like licking the sores of a leper. I thought I'd stopped believing in God. Maybe I have. Maybe I did it because now I only believe in Satan.'

She leaned forward with sudden fearful earnestness.

'Look, take some and eat it – *please*! Because you've *got* to! We'll make you eat it if we must, but it would be so much better if you realized what you have to understand! You've got to see, feel, *grasp* what was done to those poor helpless people – coming to my table where I was doling out the relief supplies, thinking they were being given wholesome nourishment after so long without any food but a few poisoned leaves and roots. You can't write about it, you can't even *talk* about it, unless you know what a horrible loathsome disgusting trick was played on them!'

Almost as though they were acting of their own accord, Peg's fingers took hold of a piece of the food. A sense of doom engulfed her. She looked beseechingly at Arriegas, but could read no mercy in his stone-chill eyes.

'Lucy is right,' he said. 'Think to yourself: I am so weak from hunger I can barely stand. Think: they have sent help for me, tonight for the first time in months I will sleep soundly with my belly full, and tomorrow there will be more to eat, and the day after. This living hell has come to an end at last. Think about that while you eat. Then later perhaps you will comprehend the magnitude of this cruelty.'

But why me? It's not my fault! I'm on their side!

And realized in the same instant as the thought was formulated that it was wrong. It had been shaped, over and over, more times than could conceivably be counted, by millions of others before her … and what impact had it had on the world? Had she not spent these past weeks in continual horror at the misjudgment, the incompetence, the outright lunacy of mankind?

These two must be crazy. No doubt about it. But it was even crazier to think that the world as it stood could be called 'sane.'

Perhaps if she ate just one or two bits, enough to satisfy them … Convulsively Peg thrust the piece she held between her lips and started to chew. But her mouth was so dry, her teeth merely balled it into a lump she couldn't swallow.

'Try harder,' Arriegas said clinically. 'I assure you not to worry. Here is only two ounces, what I myself have eaten. Those who went mad at Noshri ate more than half a kilo.'

'Give her water,' Lucy said. Cautiously, so as not to block her aim, Arriegas reached for a pitcher and glass that stood on the bedside table. Peg obediently gulped a mouthful, and the food went down.

'More.'

She took more.

'More!'

She took more. Was it illusion, or was something happening to her already? She felt giddy, careless of the consequences of what she was doing. The food tasted pretty good, savory on the tongue, and her saliva was back so she could get it down very fast. She took half a dozen bits and thrust them all in together.

And the room seemed to rock from side to side, in rhythm with the chomping of her jaw.

'I—' she said in surprise, and they looked at her with eyes like laser-beams.

'I think I'm going to faint,' she said after a pause. She reached for the table to set down the water-glass, and missed. It dropped on the carpet and didn't break, but lashed out a crystalline tongue, the last of its contents. She made to stand up.

'Stay where you are!' Lucy ordered, jerking the gun. 'Fernando, grab hold of her. We'll have to force the rest down her throat.'

Peg tried to say that wouldn't be any use, but the world tilted and she slid to meet the ground. With a distant corner of her mind she assured herself that this wasn't due to a drug in the food. This stemmed from pure terror.

There was a vast rushing noise in her ears.

But her eyes were open, and she could see everything with a weirdly distorted perspective, as though she were a wide-angle lens with very sharp curvature at the sides. What she saw was the door slamming open and someone – a man – striding in. He was horribly out of proportion, his legs as thin as matches, his torso grotesquely bulging toward a head the size of a pumpkin. She didn't want to look at anyone so ugly. She shut her eyes. In the same instant there were two plopping noises and a heavy weight slumped across her legs. Infuriated, she thrust at it with her hands, trying to push it away.

Wet?

She forced her eyes open again and saw this time through a swimming blur like a wind-blown veil. Bright red surrounded by pale gold. Yes, of course. The back of a head. Lucy Ramage's head. With a hole clear through. A shot perfectly targeted. She had dropped sideways across Peg's thighs. Also there was Arriegas, doubled up and spewing pink froth and red trickles. It was on her now, on her clothes. Less gold, more red. All the time more red. It flooded out to the limits of her already hazy vision. There was darkness.

THE GO SIGNAL

'Well, honey, how does it grab you?' Jeannie said proudly as she helped Pete into the living-room. He wouldn't be able to drive himself for a long time, of course, so she had to take him to and from work. But he was getting very clever with his crutches, and this apartment was on the entrance floor, so there weren't too many steps, which he did find hard.

It had been filthy, because it had stood vacant for months – few people wanted ground-floor apartments, they being the easiest for burglars – and as they'd been warned it had been full of fleas. But the exterminator said they were in the best families nowadays, heh-heh!, and they were dealt with, and there was new paint everywhere and today Jeannie must have worked like fury because she had new curtains up and new slipcovers on the old furniture.

'Looks great, baby! Just great.' And blew her a kiss.

'Like a beer?'

'I could use one.'

'Sit down, I'll bring it.' And off to the kitchen. It was still equipped with their old stuff from Towerhill, except they'd had to get a new icebox; the old one had died and the only firm in Denver still making repairs had a two-month waiting list. Through the door she called, 'How was your first day at work?'

'Pretty good. Matter of fact I don't hardly feel tired.'

'What does a stock supervisor do?'

'Kind of like a dispatcher, I guess. Make sure we record everything we send out for installation, keep a check on what's used and what comes back. Easy bread.'

Coming back, she found he wasn't in his chair but heading for the other door.

'Where you going?'

'Bathroom. Back in a minute.'

And, returning, took the beer. In a glass, yet. Moving up the scale!

'I got news for you,' Jeannie said. 'Did you hear they're going to open up the plant again? All the modifications are done, and as soon as they—'

'Baby, you're not going back to the plant.'

'Well, not straight away, honey, of course not. I mean until you can drive again, and like that. But here in Denver it's …' A vague gesture. 'Paying so much rent, and all.'

'No,' Pete said again, and fished with two fingers in the breast pocket of his shirt. The little plastic dispenser of contraceptive pills. New, untouched. The monthly cycle began today.

'And you can forget about these, too,' he said.

'Pete!'

'Cool it, baby. You know what they're going to pay me.'

She gave a hesitant nod.

'Add on what I get for these TV commercials, then.'

Another nod.

'Well, isn't that enough to raise a kid on?'

She didn't say anything.

'Ah, hell, baby, come on!' he exclaimed. 'Now while we got the chance, now's the time! Shit, you know how they're going to lay out the next commercial I make? In the middle like Santa Claus surrounded by kids, telling the mothers all over the state that this here big hero who saved those kids' lives wants them to buy water-filters and save their kids from bellyache!' His tone was abruptly bitter, and just as abruptly reverted to normal.

'Well, it's a good thing to be selling if you have to sell something for a living. I talked to Doc McNeil and he said so. Said it could have helped a lot of babies that died of that enteritis.'

'Yes, honey,' Jeannie said. 'But suppose – ours …'

'Baby, I said I talked to Doc McNeil. That's one of the things I talked about. And he says shoot. He says …'

'What?' She leaned forward on her chair.

'He says if I like fall down stairs, or do something else bad to myself, there may not – uh – be another chance.'

There was a long cold silence. At length Jeannie set her glass aside.

'I get you, honey,' she whispered. 'Sorry, I never thought of that. What about right now?'

'Yeah, and right here. Doc says it's better if I lie on my back on a hard floor.'

RIGHT ABOUT NOW

A DC-10 coming in to land at Tegucigalpa was hit by Tupamaro tracer and crashed on the control tower, which confirmed the decision to pull out. The previous record for the duration of a don't-drink notice was broken in New Orleans (that's a long river and a lot of people use it). The Bamberleys' family doctor called to treat the latest of Cornelius's fits – which was going to earn him a good old-fashioned beating when he recovered, because he knew he was forbidden to eat candy. The enteritis epidemic was declared officially over for the fourth time. And they completed the autopsy on Dr Stanway, conducted at his own morgue; verdict, the extremely common one of degenerative nephritis.

He was, admittedly, only thirty-one. But he had after all spent his whole life in Los Angeles and Orange County.

Not surprising.

COMPANIONS IN ADVERSITY

'Delighted to meet you, Mr Thorne,' Professor Quarrey said. His clothes hung loose on him, as though he had lost ten pounds in the past few weeks. 'Do sit down. Would you like some sherry?'

An aptly academic drink. Thorne smiled and took the nearest chair as the professor's wife – looking even more exhausted than her husband, with large dark rings under her eyes – filled glasses and offered a dish of nuts. She had a plaster on her nape; the shape of the lump underneath suggested a boil.

'Here's to a fellow-sufferer,' Quarrey said. Thorne gave a humorless laugh and drank.

'Congratulations on your acquittal, by the way,' he said. 'I confess I was expecting you to be pilloried.'

'There was some – ah – horse-trading behind the scenes,' Quarrey said. 'You're aware that they plan to resume production at Bamberley Hydroponics?'

'Yes, I saw Moses Greenbriar recently and he told me.'

'Well, they want someone who can't be accused of being a government yes-man to approve their new filtration system. As you know, that's my field, and I was approached, very discreetly, and asked whether I'd co-operate in exchange for a dismissal of that ridiculous charge.' A sigh. 'It may not have been very courageous of me, but I said yes.'

'But they haven't stopped persecuting us!' his wife chimed in, joining her husband on the shabby davenport facing Thorne. 'I'm sure our telephone is being tapped.'

'And they definitely open my mail,' Quarrey grunted. 'Which I wouldn't mind if they had the courtesy to screen out the abusive letters … You get any of those? I imagine you do.'

Thorne nodded.

'There's our prize exhibit,' Quarrey said, pointing to the wall behind his guest. 'I had it framed to remind me just how important it is to keep trying.'

Thorne twisted around. In a smart new frame, a sheet torn from a cheap yellow memo block. He read the semi-literate capitals that almost covered it: 'TO MISTER COMMIE ASS LICKING QUAREY YOU SAY ONE MORE WORD AGANST AMRICA WELL HANG YOU BY YOUR PRICK ON A FAGPOLE GET OUT OR WELL BURN DOWN YOUR HOME AND YOUR NIGGERFUCKING WIFE TOO OUHT TO HAVE A GUN STUFF UP HER CUNT NOW YOU NOW WHAT LOYAL AMRICANS THINK OF TRATORS.'

'The fagpole is an original touch,' Quarrey said with a tired smile, and sipped his sherry.

There was a long silence. Thorne wanted it to end, but he couldn't think of the best words. He had been growing daily more ashamed since Nancy died – ashamed of not having understood before, in the guts where it counts, what suffering really meant. It was a tough job managing the vast sums that the guilty conscience of the Western world siphoned into Globe Relief, and no one denied that, including him; he was dealing with sums that exceeded the turnover of all but the largest European and American corporations. That alone, though, wasn't justification for the income he'd been drawing, even if it did average out to less than half a cent per person helped. So he'd taken refuge behind the additional defense that he had a wife to provide for and might well one day adopt a kid. (By a twenty-two-to-one chance he and Nancy had both been carrying the recessive gene for cystic fibrosis, and a child of their own would be mentally retarded.)

Without Nancy, it was as though cataracts had been taken from his eyes. It had become suddenly clear: there are madmen in charge, and they must be stopped!

He had read feverishly, beginning with Austin Train's famous source-books that had taken one, two, even three years apiece to compile, soberly documenting the course of organochlorides in the biosphere, factory-smoke on the wind, pinning down some – not all, because often the information was denied to the public – of the places where dangerous substances had been dumped. Among the first things he'd come across was a description of the gas-disposal program in 1919. And on top of that radioactive waste, nerve gas, fluorine compounds, cyanide solutions …

It was as though you tore up the floorboards of an apartment you'd just bought and found a corpse grinning at you.

But even more educational were the things be couldn't find out. In the New York Public Library Train's works were on open shelves – there would have been riots if they hadn't been – but of the total of 1130 other books cited in the various bibliographies, 167 were withdrawn or restricted.

He'd asked why, and the answers came back pat – 'Oh, there was a libel case over that. Something about General Motors, I believe.' And – 'Well, someone defaced our only copy, it says here, and it was out of print by then, I'm afraid.'

One book in particular he remembered, a text on accidents with nuclear weapons, which was duly brought to him by a smiling librarian. But when he opened the front cover he found a hole had been carefully cut from first page to last.

'Do you know what's become of Austin Train?' Mrs Quarrey said suddenly.

Thorne blinked. 'As a matter of fact that was one of the questions I came to ask your husband. I understand the Trainites contacted you some while ago and asked for help in a nationwide survey they're doing on Puritan products – is that true?'

Quarrey nodded.

'And I've been hunting high and low in the hope of locating Train, but so far all my leads have taken me to one of these – these Doppelgängers of his.' Thorne hesitated. 'Do you think he's dead?'

'One does keep hearing rumors,' Quarrey sighed. 'He never had any direct connection with the Trainites, of course, but the latest story I've heard did come from a Trainite, for what that's worth. Claimed that he was burned to death in that slum apartment in San Diego.'

'I've heard that too,' Thorne agreed. 'But I think it's another of these mistaken identity cases. Incidentally, do you know where that crazy fisherman got his napalm?'

'I don't think so.'

'It was part of a consignment we supplied to the Mexicans to burn off marijuana fields.'

'Well, that's the chickens coming home to roost with a vengeance,' Quarrey said with a sour chuckle. 'Why have you been hunting so hard for Train, by the way? More sherry?'

'Please, it's very good … Well, I guess because he seems to be about the only person who might lead us out of this mess. I mean so many people respect him and at least give lip-service to his principles. Do you agree?'

'In a way,' the professor said thoughtfully. 'We need something to break us out of this – this isolationism we've drifted into. I don't mean that in the standard sense; I mean more isolationism in *time*, as it were. We're divorced from reality, in the same way as the Romans went on thinking of themselves as invulnerable and unchallengeable long after it ceased to be true. The most awful warnings are staring us in the face – the stagnant Mediterranean above all, dead like the Great Lakes – yet we're so proud of being the richest, the most powerful, the whatever, that we won't face facts. We won't admit that we're short of water, we're short of timber, we're short of—'

'Food,' Thorne said positively. 'Or we shall be next winter. That's why they're so eager to resume production of Nutripon. I met a very interesting guy the other day, used to work for Angel City, an actuary called Tom Grey. He's based in New York now, and I met him through Moses Greenbriar, at the Bamberley Trust. He's been compiling masses of social data for years, for some obsessive project of his own, and Moses asked him to extrapolate the question of this year's crop failures. You know crops are bad everywhere.'

'Bad? Disastrous!' Quarrey snorted. 'Idaho, the Dakotas, Colorado, Wisconsin … Yes, you mentioned this survey the Trainites asked me to coordinate; frankly, I'm of two minds about going through with it.'

'Not surprising!' his wife said with asperity. 'He's had his life threatened, Mr Thorne – no, dear, I will not keep quiet about that! It's disgraceful! We've had at least half a dozen anonymous phone calls threatening to kill Lucas if he carries on, and since as I said I'm sure the police are tapping the phone they must know we're telling the truth, but they won't do anything about it.'

'But that's serious!' Thorne exclaimed. 'They must know – everybody knows – Puritan is a Syndicate operation, and if you're trying to drive their prices down—'

'It's not quite like that,' Quarrey cut in.

Thorne stared at him for a moment. Then he leaned back in his chair. 'I'm sorry. I seem to have been jumping to conclusions. I assumed that you were looking for food being sold by Puritan which doesn't match their claims, so as to – uh – pressurize them into cutting their extravagant profit margins.'

'There's no question of having to look for food which isn't up to their advertised standards,' Quarrey said. 'You stand about an even chance of finding it at random.'

There was dead silence. Eventually Thorne shook his head. 'I don't think I quite understand.'

'It's very simple. It must have struck you that in spite of their exorbitant prices Puritan sells a colossal volume of food?'

'Yes, fantastic. It's an index of how frightened people really are. Especially parents of young children.'

'Well, what some Trainite has discovered – I don't know who, this is all being conducted on an anonymous footing – what he's worked out is this. If you divide the amount of home-grown produce Puritan sells per year into the amount of ground you'd need to grow it on, there literally isn't enough uncontaminated land left in North America. Not after the watershed defoliation program of the sixties. And he's analyzed their stuff, and as I say about half of it is no better than you can get in a regular supermarket. I'm still checking out his calculations, but I'm fairly sure he's proved his point.'

'I'm wondering,' Mrs Quarrey said, 'whether it could be Austin Train himself.'

Thorne glanced at her and back at her husband. 'Well, I don't see why you don't publish straight away!' he exclaimed. 'If you've been threatened, wouldn't publicity be the best protection?'

'I told him that,' Mrs Quarrey said firmly.

'And I was going to,' the professor said. 'Until the Trainites told me what's happening to those crops that are failing. Do you know what we've let into the country?'

'Well, some sort of insect pest, I gather. Or pests, at least, seeing they ruin so many different plants.'

'It's the worm that caused the famine in Honduras, and indirectly led to the war.'

'Oh, no!' Thorne's mouth was suddenly dry. 'But *how?*'

'Imported under federal license,' Quarrey said with gloomy relish, as of a preacher at the graveside of an unreformed drunkard. 'They were discovered at the Trainite wat in Colorado, and someone with Tupamaro contacts managed to identify them. Apparently one of the big insect importers sub-contracted his worm business to a guy who was supposed to supply Argentine worms, but he didn't give a hoot, cheated them right and left, palmed off thousands of gallons of these damned pests, and skipped to Australia with the proceeds.'

'Incredible!' Thorne breathed. 'But didn't they realize they weren't getting regular worms?'

'Oh, they were mixed in with ordinary worms. And apart from being slightly bluish and a bit differently shaped, these *jigras*, as they call them, do look pretty much like real worms.'

'But the experts at the importing company!' Thorne clenched his fists. 'Or the customs! Didn't they worry about them being blue?'

'Of course not. He dyed them pink.'

'Of course,' Thorne said bitterly.

'The Trainites take it for granted that the customs officers and the firm's inspectors were bribed, but I find that hard to believe.' Quarrey shrugged. 'However it happened, though, the damage is done. And the damned things are resistant to just about every known insecticide, banned or legal.'

'So you're afraid of the consequences if you frighten people off Puritan,' Thorne said slowly.

'Yes, precisely. We're headed for a hungry winter. My Trainite contacts feel the same way, because even if half the Puritan food isn't as good as it's claimed to be, we're going to need every scrap that's even remotely edible.'

'Half a loaf,' Mrs Quarrey said.

There was another silence. Eventually Thorne drained his glass. 'I'd better be on my way,' he muttered. 'I'm dining with my lawyer. I guess he'll have another shot at making me drop my suit against the Defense Department. What the hell can you do when even your lawyer doesn't think you can get justice?'

'I understood you were enlisting the support of – well, other support,' Quarrey put in.

'Angel City, you mean? Yes, I had high hopes of them. I mean, it's no secret I had a half-million dollar policy on Nancy's life. But they've paid up and kept their mouths shut. As for the nine cases of Lewisite in Florida—'

'*Nine?*'

'I'm morally certain, plus maybe one more. But everyone I've tackled so far has been well paid not to make a fuss.' Thorne gave a bitter smile. 'They can't reach me, though; I was rich already, and now Angel City has made me richer.' He checked his watch.

'Might I have my umbrella, Mrs Quarrey? And I think you took my mask as well.'

But when she opened the apartment door to let him out, there were three men in dark clothes lounging against the opposite wall. His heart lurched into his shoes.

And stopped.

Like the professor's, and his wife's.

'Fish in a barrel,' said one of the killers scornfully, and led his companions away.

BUILDUP OF FORCES

Doug and Angela McNeil saw the troops encamped near the Towerhill road on their way to dinner at a favorite restaurant in the mountains. They had decided to go out on the spur of the moment. They could do that sort of thing because they had no kids. A lot of doctors nowadays didn't have kids.

All along the way they kept passing groups of the strange young people who had been drifting into Denver during the previous few days. By this time hundreds must have arrived. Most had come by bus, and a few among these had brought folding cycles that fitted in a bus's baggage compartment, but the majority were on foot. They obviously hailed from big cities. They had filtermasks around their necks, like the winter tourists who couldn't accept that Colorado air was safe.

'What are they all doing here?' Angela said as they passed one bunch of a dozen or so who had sat down to rest against a big billboard showing the monstrous silhouette of a worm, captioned: HAVE YOU SEEN ANY OF THESE INSECTS? IF YOU DO INFORM THE POLICE RIGHT AWAY!

'I thought at first they must be some kind of Trainite reunion, on their way to the wat. But they're not. Notice they're wearing synthetics? Trainites won't.'

Angela nodded. Right: all the way from nylon shirts to plastic boots.

'So I guess they're just the mountain counterpart of beach bums.'

Unconsciously, Doug had slowed the car to look more closely at them; realizing they wouldn't take kindly to being stared at, he accelerated again. 'They can hardly go to California this year, can they?'

'I guess not.' Angela shuddered.

'And they can't or won't go to Florida because of the poison-gas scare. So that leaves the mountains. Probably the same is happening back east, in the Poconos for example.'

'I can't see them being very warmly welcomed.' Angela sounded troubled. 'Can you?'

'Well, no. And the forces of lawnorder seem to agree.' Doug pointed ahead. Two patrol cars were drawn up on the hard shoulder at a curve, and a group of stern-faced officers were photographing the kids with a Polaroid. Behind one of the cars others were searching a pale youth of about twenty. They had him down to undershorts. One of the police held his arms, though he was offering no resistance; another was feeling in his crotch with evident enjoyment; a third was searching the knapsack he'd been carrying.

A short distance further on was where they saw the troops: on a fairly level stretch of ground they'd erected tents like orange fungi. Five olive-green trucks were parked by the road.

Doug started. 'Say, those are battle-lasers, aren't they?'

'What are?'

'Those trailer things! Christ, are they expecting a civil war? They can't mean to use them against those kids!'

'I should hope not,' Angela agreed.

And then, around the next bend, a heavy iron gate was set in a concrete wall with spikes around the top. Alongside it was a big illuminated sign, which read: BAMBERLEY HYDROPONICS INC. – SERVING THE NEEDS OF THE NEEDY.

There was another sign hung on the gate itself which stated that parties of visitors were welcome daily at 1000 and 1500, but that was covered with a piece of sodden sacking.

CRITICAL

Well at least you could breathe up here. Even if you couldn't see the stars. Michael Advowson drew what consolation he could from that. Relishing freedom from the tyranny of a filtermask – though still irritated by a faint burning on the back of his tongue, which had haunted him since his arrival from Europe – he strolled uphill away from the hydroponics plant. It was good to go on grass, although it was dry and brittle, and brush between bushes, although their leaves were gray. Above all he was on his own, and that was a relief.

Christ. What wouldn't he give to be home right now?

What hurt him most of all, made him feel like a sick child aware of terrible wrongness and yet incapable of explaining it to anyone who might help, was that in spite of the evidence around them, in spite of what their eyes and ears reported – and sometimes their flesh, from bruises, stab wounds, racking coughs, weeping sores – these people believed their way of life was the best in the world, and were prepared to export it at the point of a gun.

Down in Honduras, for example. Heaven's name! Cromwell had done that sort of thing in Ireland – but that was centuries ago, another and more barbaric age!

He wore his uniform most of the time now. It indicated that he was more than just a foreigner, that he possessed rank in a hierarchy, and these people worshipped power. Recognizing his status, they behaved to him with frigid politeness. No. *Correctness*.

But that wasn't what he'd expected. He had kinfolk, going back to the brother of his great-grandfather, who had come here to escape the oppression of the British. He had expected somehow to be – well, greeted as a cousin. Not as a fellow-conspirator.

Loneliness in New York had driven him more and more into the company of the drunken girl who'd picked him up at that diplomatic cocktail party. Sylvia Young, that was her name. He had found something waif-like and wistful behind her facade of sophistication, as though she were in search of a dream from which she could recall only a mood, no details.

The latest meeting had been the night before last, and she was cured, she said, and wanted him to come to bed. But his subconscious was so disturbed he couldn't do anything, and when she snapped at him in frustration he snapped back, saying he'd never known a girl before who'd been infected, at which she gave a bitter laugh and swore she didn't know one who had not.

And the laughing dissolved into tears, and she fell against his shoulder and clung there like a frightened child, and from her moans emerged the shreds of that unspeakably pathetic dream: wanting to live somewhere clean, wanting to raise a son with a chance of being healthy.

'Everybody's kids I know have something wrong! Everybody has something wrong with one of their kids!'

As a doctor Michael knew that wasn't true; the incidence of congenital abnormality, even in the States, was still only three or four per cent. But everyone did insure against it as a matter of course, and talked as though the least fit of ill-temper, the least bout of any childish ailment, were the end of the world.

'There must be something that can be done! There must, there must!'

It had crossed his mind: I could offer you – well, not *entirely* a clean place to live, because near Balpenny, when the wind blows from the direction of the industrial estate around Shannon Airport, you go out for a deep first-thing-in-the-morning breath and find yourself choking. But they've promised to do something about that.

Also animals are sometimes born deformed. Still, you can kill animals with more or less a clear conscience.

But I could say: let me show you lakes that are not foul with the leavings of man. Let me reap you crops grown on animal dung and pure clean rain. Let me feed you apples from trees that were never sprayed with arsenic. Let me cut you bread from a cob loaf, that greets your hands with the affectionate warmth of the oven. Let me give you children that need fear nothing worse than a bottle dropped by a drunk, straight-limbed, smiling, clear of speech. And would you care if that speech were full of the echoes of a tongue that spoke civilization a thousand years ago?

But he hadn't said it, only thought it. And probably now he never would. After tomorrow's burning of the suspect food he intended to go straight home on an Aer Lingus flight from Chicago.

On the crest of a rise he paused and looked around. There was the hydroponics plant sprawling like a colossal caterpillar along the side of a hill. He could just make out by uncurtained lighted windows the home of the plant's manager, an agreeable man named Steinitz. More than one could say of his host, Jacob Bamberley … Staying in that great mansion, the enlarged ranchhouse of the estate his grandfather had bought, was somehow *wrong*, even though it was surrounded by what were reputed to be marvelous botanical gardens. He had only glimpsed them; they appeared to be drab and ill-doing.

He must drive back there shortly. He had been engaged in a final review of preparations with the American officers in charge, Colonel Saddler, Captain Aarons and Lieutenant Wassermann, and the other UN observer, a

Venezuelan called Captain Robles. Michael didn't like any of them, and following the meeting had needed to unwind. Which was why he was out here at midnight under the sky.

Not the stars. Apparently they hadn't been seen here this summer. Mr Bamberley had said at dinner, 'A bad year.' But would next year be any better?

He shivered despite the warmth of the light breeze, and an instant later had the fright of his life. A voice spoke to him from nowhere.

'Well, shit. Who's this nosy son of a bitch?'

He stared frantically around, and only then saw that a shadowy figure stood less than ten paces away: a black man in black clothes, very tall and lean. And in his right hand something lighter, a knife held in the easy fighting poise of someone who understood the proper way to use it, not stupidly raised to shoulder height but low where it could slash open the soft muscles of the belly.

'What the hell—? Who are you?' Michael demanded.

A moment of dead silence. During it other forms materialized from what had seemed bare empty ground.

'You're not American,' the black man said. Man? Maybe boy; there was a lightness to his voice, all head tones and no chest.

'No, I'm not. I'm Irish!'

A flashlight speared him like a butterfly on a pin. How long before that image would be meaningless? He hadn't seen a butterfly in this country.

A new voice, a girl's, said, 'Uniform!'

'Cool it,' the black boy said. 'He says he's Irish. So what are you doing here, Paddy?'

Michael felt sweat prickly on his skin. He said, 'I'm a United Nations observer.'

'And you're observing us, hm?' With irony.

'I didn't realize there was anyone here. I just came out for a walk.'

'Hey, *man*. You surely are a foreigner.' The black boy sheathed his knife and moved forward into the flashlight beam. 'Thought you must be a pig. But they hunt in gangs.'

'He's a skunk!' the girl snapped. Michael had heard the term; it meant soldier. He felt menaced.

'But he isn't wearing a gun,' the black boy said.

The girl's voice changed suddenly. 'Shit, that's right. Hey, Paddy, what kind of army is it where you don't carry a gun?'

'I'm a medical officer,' Michael forced out of his dry throat. 'Want to see my ID?'

The black boy moved closer, looking him over from head to toe. 'Yes,' he said after a while. 'I guess we do.'

Michael tugged it from his pocket. The boy studied it.

'Well, hell. A major, yet. Welcome to this sick shitpile we live in, Mike. How do you like it?'

'I'd give anything to get the hell out,' Michael blurted. 'And they won't let me.'

'*They*' – heavily stressed – 'won't let you do anything.' He handed the ID back and stepped out of Michael's way. 'I'm Fritz,' he added. 'That's Diana – Hal – Curt – Bernie. Come sit down.'

There seemed to be no alternative. Michael moved forward. The group had camped here, he saw now: sleeping-bags hidden by a ring of bushes, a few dull embers on a hearth of flat rocks.

'Smoke?' Fritz said. 'Chaw?'

'Fritz!' – from the girl Diana.

Fritz chuckled. 'Ain't no skin off Mike's ass how we screw ourselves up. Right, Mike?'

The reference to a chaw had suddenly explained to Michael the light tone – close to shrillness – in Fritz's voice. He was high on khat, popular among the American blacks because it came from Africa: a stimulating leaf to be chewed or smoked or infused, exported from Kenya in enormous quantities by the Meru people, who called it meru-ngi.

'No thanks,' he said after a pause.

'Man, you don't know what you're missing.' That was – Bernie? Yes, Bernie. He giggled. 'One of the great natural medicines. You get the runs lately?'

'Yes, of course.'

'No "of course" about it. They said thirty-five million people caught them. We didn't. Where's the chaw?'

'Here.' Curt, next in line, produced the sodden lump from his mouth and handed it on. Michael repressed a shudder. It was interesting, that point about escaping the universal diarrhea. Because of the constipating effect of the drug, no doubt.

He said, 'What brings you here?'

'Tourists, us,' Fritz answered with a high chuckle. 'Just tourists. And you?'

'Oh, they're going to burn all this suspect food tomorrow. I'm here to see the job's properly carried out.'

Dead pause. Suddenly the one called Hal said, 'Well, you won't.'

The girl Diana gave him a fearful sidelong glance. She was very fair, and pretty with it although plump. 'Hal, you watch your mouth!'

'Fact, ain't it? Nobody going stop us!'

Michael said slowly, incredulously, 'You're here to try and get your hands on that food?'

Hesitation. Then nods. Firm ones.

'But why?' He thought of all the young people he'd seen trudging up from

Denver: hundreds! And Steinitz at the factory had said they'd been arriving for days on end.

'Why not?' That was Curt.

'Yeah, why not?' Hal again. 'It'd be the first time, the very first time the government of this lousy country turned some of its *citizens* on.' He made the word 'citizens' sound obscene.

Diana licked her lips. She had broad full lips and a broad long tongue. There was a sound like 'hlryup'.

'Are you crazy?' Michael gasped before he could stop himself.

'Isn't crazy the only sane way to be in this fucked-up world?' Fritz retorted.

'But there's no drug in the food they have stored! I've seen the analyses.'

'Sure, that's what they say.' Shrugging. 'But they said the same about that place in Africa, now they're saying it about Honduras ... Stinking liars!'

'Oh, you don't know what you're talking about. I've *been* to Noshri! I've *seen*!'

Without warning it took possession of him: the memory of sights and sounds and smells, the clutch of mud underfoot, the sense of despair. He told about the children battered to death by their own parents. He told about the soldiers who fled weeping and screaming into the bush. He told about the women who would never again see such a common household object as a knife and not run away from it in terror. He told about the stench and the sickness and the starvation. He told it all, words flooding from him like water through a breached dam. And it wasn't until he had talked his throat sore that he realized he had been saying all the time, 'The American food did this, did that ...'

Lucy Ramage and her Uruguayan friend would have been pleased. But they were dead.

He broke off abruptly, and for the first time in long minutes looked at his listeners instead of the recollected horrors of Africa. They wore, all of them, identical wistful smiles.

'Ho, *man*!' Diana sighed at last. 'To get that high!'

'Yeah!' Curt said. 'Imagine a high that never stops!'

'They want to stop me getting a piece of that,' Hal said, 'they going to have to burn me before they burn the shit.'

'But you can't want to go insane!' Michael exploded. He groped for the right phrase. 'You can't want a – a bum trip that goes on for life!'

'Can't I, baby? Are you ever wrong!' Fritz, his voice cold, dead serious, *dead*. 'Listen, Mike, because you don't understand and you ought to. Who's going to be sane in this country when you know every breath you draw, every glass you fill with water, every swim you take in the river, every meal you eat, is killing you? And you know why, and you know who's doing it to you, and you can't get back at the mothers.'

He was on his feet without warning, towering over Michael, even when Michael also rose. He was more than six foot three, maybe six foot five. He looked like a medieval figure of death: merciless, gaunt, hungry.

'I don't want to die, baby. But I can't stand having to live. I want to tear those stinking buggers limb from limb. I want to gouge out their eyes. I want to stuff their mouths with their own shit. I want to pull their guts out their ass, inch by inch, and wind 'em around their throats until they choke. I want to be so crazy-mad I can think of the things they deserve to have done to them! *Now* maybe you understand!'

'Yeah,' Diana said very softly, and spat the chaw of khat into the embers of their fire, where it hissed.

'Go 'way, Mike.' Fritz sounded suddenly weary. 'Far's you can. Like go home. Leave us take care of the mothers. One day maybe you could come back – or your grandchildren – and find a fit place for people to live, black or white.'

'Or green,' Diana said with a little hysterical giggle. 'Irish, green.' He stared for a long moment into Fritz's eyes, and what he saw there made him turn and run.

Although the majority of the unskilled and semi-skilled workers from the plant had been sent to swell the crowds of unemployed in Denver, a handful of staff had been kept on standby, and with their assistance he and Robles spent the following morning poring over stock records and making sure that every single carton of the suspect Nutripon was removed from the interior of the factory. Troops with fork-lift trucks carried them out to an empty concrete parking lot and stacked them in a monstrous pile in front of the battle-lasers which had been lined up to calcine them into ash.

The records were good, and exact. The work went quickly. He kept hearing – he was meant to hear – comments from the soldiers: what the hell business have these lousy foreigners telling us what to do? One man in particular, a sergeant named Tatum, thin, gangling, tow-haired, seemed to be encouraging his squad to pass such remarks whenever Michael was around. But he bit back his bitter, angry responses. Soon, soon it would be over, and he could go home.

Every now and then he glanced up at the blank gray-green hillside behind the parking lot, expecting to see it alive with human figures: Fritz and his friends, and all the hundreds of others. But although he fancied he saw movement among the bushes, he never saw a face. Almost he could believe he had dreamed that terrible experience last night.

Wanting to go insane? Hardly more than children!

But finally the echoing dome of the warehouse was empty, and nothing else was left in the rest of the factory where new clean shiny air-purifiers dotted the roof and little certificates from the firm specializing in operating theaters had been pasted under ventilation grilles … and he agreed with Robles that they could safely go and inform Colonel Saddler. Robles had been chafing to do that for half an hour. Michael took a perverse delight in making him wait a while longer.

He had worked out, on the basis of what Fritz had said, that among the reasons for his instant dislike of Robles was that the Venezuelan wore an automatic all the time.

'You took your time,' Colonel Saddler rasped. 'I thought we'd burn this lot before lunch!'

He'd said last night that he was hoping for a posting to Honduras.

Distant on the concrete, gray under the gray sky, reporters waited by their cars and camera trucks, ready to record the act of destruction as proof of good intentions toward the world.

'But now I guess we might as well go to chow first,' the colonel went on ill-temperedly. 'Sergeant!'

It was Tatum, the tow-headed man who so resented Michael.

'Sergeant, tell 'em to break for chow, and make sure the fire-hose squad is back here ten minutes ahead of the – What the *hell*?'

They all swung around, and discovered that what Michael had been expecting all morning had occurred. They must have been watching from the hillside with the skill and patience of trained guerrillas. Now, realizing that the job of bringing out the food from the warehouse was over, they had risen into plain sight and were advancing on the chainlink fence that here defined the grounds of the factory. They looked like a medieval army. Two hundred of them? Three? With motorcycle crash-helmets, rock-climbing boots, and on their arms home-made shields that bore like a coat of arms the Trainite symbol of the crossed bones and grinning skull.

'Get those crazy fools out of here!' the colonel roared. 'Bring me a bull-horn! Sergeant, don't let the men go for chow after all! Tell those idiots that if they're not gone in five minutes—'

'Colonel!' Michael exploded. 'You can't.'

'Can't what?' Saddler rounded on him. 'Are you presuming to give me orders – *major*?'

Michael swallowed hard. 'You can't risk firing the food when those kids are out there!'

'I wouldn't be risking anything,' Saddler said. 'They'd be no loss to this country. I bet half of them are dodgers and the rest lied to the draft board. But I'm going to leave it up to them. Thank you, sergeant' – as he was handed the bullhorn he'd requested. Raising it, he yelled, 'You out there! In five minutes …' He strode toward the fence.

In the background, sensing the unexpected, the reporters were scrambling to their feet, cameras and microphones at the ready.

On the hillside, next to a fair-haired girl, a thin black figure, very tall. In his hand, something gleaming. Knife? No, wire-cutters!

Saddler completed the recital of his warning, and turned, checking his watch. 'We'll play the fire hoses on them first, sergeant,' he muttered. 'Don't want that stinking mick—'

And realized that Michael had kept pace with him and stood in earshot. He flushed, and raised his voice.

'I trust that meets with your approval?' he barked. 'I bet most of them could do with a bath anyhow!'

'Maybe they don't come from homes where it's safe to take a bath,' Michael said. He felt a little lightheaded. He had slept very badly after his encounter with the youngsters on the hill.

'What the hell do you mean by that?'

Michael glanced from the corner of his eye at the strange army descending the slope. All around sergeants were ranking their men to guard the perimeter fence. Hoses were being rolled out, which were here as a precaution in case the battle-lasers fired the dry grass and bushes. Over at the well-head – the plant had its own wells, five of them, because the hydroponic process needed such vast amounts of water – engineers stood by their pumps, prepared to start up on the signal. With a dull roar, a helicopter rose into view from the far side of the factory, a man leaning out of its open door with a movie camera. The letters 'ABS' were painted on its side.

'Let me go talk to these kids, colonel,' Michael said. 'I met some of them last night, I think I can handle this—'

Walking steadily, ignoring cries from the noncoms inside the fence, the first wave of young people had reached the wire. A cry from one of the nearest soldiers, nervously watching.

'Say, that bastard's got a gun!'

'Fix bayonets!' the colonel shouted through the bullhorn. 'Don't let them get to the fence!'

Click-click-click. A line of spikes aimed at the bellies beyond the wire.

'Colonel!' Catching Saddler by the sleeve. 'I have an idea!'

And a shout: 'Colonel! Colonel Saddler! Over here!' Waving from a point near the reporters, it was Captain Wassermann.

'Oh, go to hell,' Saddler snapped at Michael, and strode away.

All right, then … Michael took a deep breath and walked toward the fence, around the low edge of the irregular heap of food cartons. In the middle it was maybe twenty feet high by thirty each way, but around the sides it spread out untidily. Some of the cartons had burst.

'Hey, major!' It was the man who had called out about seeing a gun, a Pfc. 'Don't go any closer – they'll kill you!'

'Shut up, soldier!' From Tatum; it was his squad guarding the wire closest to Fritz. 'Let the major do as he likes. It's his funeral.'

Michael walked on. He passed between the soldiers and confronted Fritz, who was standing a yard back, his mouth in a twisted smile, his wire-cutters dangling lax in his right hand.

'So that's what you look like by daylight, major,' he said, and the girl Diana giggled at his side.

'You want to taste this food,' Michael said.

'That's right. So?'

'Which carton?'

'What?'

'I said which carton.' All around, eyes were turning to him. He raised his voice deliberately, wishing he had a bullhorn. 'Last night I told you this food had been analyzed and given a clean bill. You don't believe it. None of you do. So pick a carton and I'll give you some of it. When nothing happens to you, go away.'

There was a dead silence. Eventually Fritz gave a sketch for a nod.

'Yeah, it figures. I can pick any carton I want?'

'Any one.'

'It's a deal.'

'Good. Soldier, your knife, please,' Michael said, turning to the man at his right.

'Major!' Tatum again. 'You can't do that!'

'Why not? They're here for the drug there's supposed to be in the food. When they find out there isn't any they'll go away. Right, Fritz?'

A hesitation. Then: 'Sure.'

'And you were going to chow anyhow, before burning the pile. Soldier, your knife!'

'Don't give it to him!' the sergeant rapped.

'Here's a knife!' Fritz called. 'I'll take the carton it lands in!'

He produced his own and threw it, high in an arc over the fence. It struck one of the nearest cartons and sank home.

'Right,' Michael muttered, and used it to rip a gash in the polyethylene-reinforced cardboard. By now dozens of the young people were converging on this point of the fence, and the news of what Michael was doing was spreading among them like wildfire. Some of them laughed and gave an ironical cheer, and those who were armed – mostly with pistols and knives, but Michael saw one shotgun – tucked their weapons in their belts or laid them down. Tatum, fuming, watched for a few moments, and then suddenly doubled away and could be heard shouting for Saddler, out of sight behind the pile of cartons.

Carrying a huge double handful of the Nutripon, Michael returned to the fence. Seeing him come, Fritz snip-snipped with his cutters, ignoring an order to stop from the Pfc, so that there was a gap a foot square to pass the food through. It was like feeding animals at the zoo, Michael thought detachedly, and watched the stuff melt into greedy hands and gaping months.

'More!' someone shouted who hadn't been lucky in sampling the first batch.

'Wait and see what it does for that lot,' Michael answered. 'It won't do anything, but telling you that doesn't seem to—'

'More!' It was a threatening growl. Yes, like feeding animals. Dangerous, savage animals …

He gave a shrug and turned away, and found Saddler confronting him, purple with fury.

'Major, what the hell are you doing?'

'Those kids believe this food is poisoned,' Michael said. 'They won't let you burn it until you prove it isn't.'

'I'm damned if—'

'Or do you believe it is poisoned? Do you believe it was used to drive thousands of innocent people mad, in Africa, in Honduras?' Michael roared that at the top of his lungs.

A surprised cry from behind him – Fritz's high tones. 'You tell him, Mike! You tell him! Great work, baby!'

For an instant Saddler didn't react, Then he flipped back the top of his holster and drew his pistol. 'You're under arrest,' he said curtly. 'Sergeant, take this man into custody.'

'Hey, no!' A girl's voice, Diana's maybe. Instantly echoed. A buzz of questions and answers moved away on the hillside, like the blurred complaint of insects, and reached a sudden unexpected climax in a single shrill voice, eerie, almost sexless.

'Kill the skunks!'

Later they listed Michael Advowson #1 of sixty-three. When they tried out the battle-lasers on the food, they worked fine.

JULY

GALLOPING CONSUMPTION

The fourteenth of October is a day to be remembered forever
Because a scion of the Royal Family set in motion the new
      power station by pulling a lever.
It was in the presence of many distinguished nobility and gentry.
There was such a press of interested persons the remainder had to
      be excluded by a sentry,
A tall and handsome private of the county regiment
Who from the barracks at Darlington had been sent
And stood guard with the rest of his military fellows,
Resplendent in scarlet, a much more attractive colour than yellow's.
There was a memorable address from the Lord Lieutenant of
      the county,
Who spoke in literary and poetical terms concerning this new
      fruit of Nature's bounty.
From this day forward there can be power in every humble farm and cot,
Which will inevitably improve the standard of living quite a lot.
When we enjoy the benefits of this let us hope everyone's
      thoughts will centre
On Mr Thomas Alva Edison, the celebrated American inventor.

– 'McGonigal Redivivus', 1936

FUSE

… now known to total fifty-nine in addition to the four U.S. Army personnel previously reported. Commenting on the fate of these latter just prior to leaving for Gettysburg, where he will mark Independence Day by delivering the Gettysburg Address in the character of Abe Lincoln before an audience predicted to exceed one hundred thousand, Prexy said, quote, Let it not be forgotten that they have hallowed American ground with their blood. End quote. Among the first items the inquiry will consider is the allegation that the riot was triggered

189

off by Nutripon containing a hallucinogenic drug. It's known that some of the food was distributed, against the orders of the senior American officer present, by the ill-fated Irish observer from the UN, Major Advowson. Now Europe. The frontier between France and Italy has been closed since midnight to stem the horde of starving refugees from the south, and an outbreak of typhus …

THE CRUNCH

Since the terrible day of the – the *trouble* at the hydroponics factory, Maud had kept mostly to her room, refusing to speak to her husband and to do anything but the minimum for the boys. Mr Bamberley had been compelled to hire the older sister of their maid Christy to help out. She needed the money because her husband was unable to work, having some form of palsy due to a chemical he'd once handled. She was vouched for as very capable.

Just as well that somebody was around here. She was effectively in charge of running the household right now. The sixty-three deaths right on his own land – even if they were at the plant instead of on the estate – had driven him nearly as far into a daze as Maud. He had forgone last month's trip to New York, his occasional visits to a nearby country club, even most of his involvement with his church. He sat every day for long hours staring out of the window of the room he invariably termed 'the den' – not 'my', 'the' – which he had preempted when he inherited the house because of its splendid view.

This summer it wasn't what it should have been. For all the work his gardeners put in, the magnificent flower beds that stretched beyond the terrace eighteen feet below the sill were dusty and ill-doing. The grass was patchy and they'd had to returf several sections, at enormous cost. It wasn't due to lack of water. He'd been meaning to call in an expert soil analyst and find out whether it was lack of sunshine or some deficiency in the ground. But he hadn't got around to that yet.

Also the leaves on some of the most magnificent shrubs were marred by dull dry coin-sized blotches, and the flowers seemed to be dropping almost before they opened, and beyond, over the mountains, hung this permanent veil of pale gray haze.

So far this summer he hadn't seen blue sky except from an airplane.

He felt undermined. He felt battered. He felt exhausted. Until a week ago he had only been to the funerals of a handful of people in his whole long life: his grandmother, his parents, and of course most recently Nancy Thorne. Now all of a sudden sixty-three had been added to the total. That mass burial had been appalling!

But the worst part had been the parade the funeral cortége met at the cemetery gates. The police said later that more than two thousand people had joined it, mostly from Denver and the Air Force Academy. There they had stood at the side of the road and clamored their praise of Jacob Bamberley. They had brought flags with them, and banners that read TO HELL WITH THE UN and HANDS OFF AMERICA.

Later, someone had kindled a flaming cross on the mass grave.

Besides, officers from the Army's legal department, collecting evidence, and the FBI, and a smooth-tongued Republican lawyer acting as the governor's special representative, and the governor himself, whom he'd met at fund-raising dinners, and Senator Howell, who was barely less than a stranger, who'd sat in that chair there and said how glad he was that (obscenity, apology) Advowson had got what was coming to him and of course he must himself have put the drug in the food and probably the Tupas had paid him to do it …

All of them asked after Maud. All of them.

Now, though, most of the fuss had died down. It was bound to drag on for a while, as he'd explained to the boys when they put their diffident questions, but only so that justice might be done. There was a great tradition of justice in this country, he'd explained, founded on English common law that dated back a thousand years. If someone had been guilty of those deaths, he would be punished.

As for Maud …

It was the strain, of course. Dr Halpern had said so. Accordingly he hadn't made an issue of her retirement to her room, her insistence on eating and sleeping alone, her refusal to greet him when they happened to encounter one another.

The time had come, though, to put an end to this farce. Today was after all a special day. There was a tradition about the Fourth of July in the Bamberley household, which he had inherited from his father and grandfather. He had risen at dawn to hoist the flag, and the boys – except Cornelius – had been roused to watch. Later, at breakfast, there had been presents: for the youngest, replicas of the Peacemaker Colt and the Bowie knife, for the others facsimiles on parchment of the Declaration of Independence, the Bill of Rights, the Gettysburg Address. Next there would be a formal luncheon, with a little homily such as his father used to deliver concerning the meaning of this anniversary, and in the afternoon they would watch the president on TV, all together, and finally before bedtime there would be fireworks. A firm of contractors from Denver had set up a fine display ready on the lawn; they tackled the job every year.

So, it being twelve-thirty, the – the ordeal.

Mr Bamberley swallowed an extra capsule from the bottle of tranquilizers Dr Halpern had given him, and headed for the dining-room.

Maud was already in her place: the first time for weeks. Beaming, he kissed her check – she barely flinched – and continued toward his own throne-like chair with a greeting for each of the boys. There was a hint of tension, but no doubt that would fade quickly enough.

Taking his stance, he checked that Christy was in position by the sideboard where bowls of salad were laid out – yes, fine – and bowed his head.

'O Lord—'

'No, Jacob,' Maud interrupted.

Astonished, he found she was gazing fixedly at him.

'No, Jacob,' she said again. It was the first time since before they were married that she had called him 'Jacob' instead of 'Jack' or 'dear'.

'You have blood on your hands. I will say grace.'

'What?'

'You have killed hundreds of innocent people. Maybe thousands. It is not seemly that you should say grace for us.'

A huge bursting pressure developed in Mr Bamberley's head. He thundered, 'Maud, have you taken leave of your senses?'

And remembered belatedly that servants must not witness a quarrel between their employers. He gestured for Christy to leave the room. But before she reached the door Maud spoke again.

'Wrong, Jacob. I have come to them. I know why you have never served the food made in your factory at your own table. I've been reading, shut away by myself. I've found out what you did to those poor black children in Africa, and in Honduras, too. And of course to the people who were buried last week. I've learned that Hugh was telling the truth about you.'

Mr Bamberley couldn't believe it. He stood with his mouth ajar like a new-hooked fish.

'So I will say our grace in future,' Maud concluded. 'My conscience is relatively clean. O Lord, Thou Who—'

'Silence!'

And that was the signal for Cornelius to keel over.

Maud made no move to go help him as he crashed to the floor. Over the sparkling silver and handsome porcelain she locked eyes with her husband.

'I'll call the doctor,' Mr Bamberley said at length. 'Clearly you haven't recovered from your – uh – recent indisposition.'

He turned to the door.

'After this incredible outburst I no longer have an appetite. If anyone wants me, I shall be in the den.'

*

He was shaking from head to foot when he reached it and almost fell back against the door as it swung to.

Dear God! What had taken possession of the woman? Never in all their years of marriage had she uttered such – such foulness!

He groped on his desk – handsome, English, antique, roll-topped – for his bottle of tranquilizers, and took another dose: two capsules. Obviously the ones he'd taken already today weren't enough. He was after all a trifle heavier than average.

Facing the desk, a velvet chair. He lapsed into it, panting a little. To think of Maud saying that in front of the boys! What poison might she not have poured into their innocent ears? Even granting that she was – uh – disturbed, on this day of all days …!

Oh, it was all too much. He abandoned the struggle to think. And was thereupon reminded by his body that he'd told a white lie at the table. He did indeed have an appetite. His belly was growling.

What to do? One could hardly phone to the kitchen, since Christy had heard what he said about not being hungry, and in any case she was probably helping to attend to Cornelius—

Cornelius. Of course. That secret store of candy he'd confiscated from the boy, the stuff that had triggered his last attack. Well, a chocolate bar would at least stave off the worst pangs. Perhaps when Dr Halpern had called, Maud would calm down or be confined to her room and they could eat lunch after all, pretending things were back to normal.

He bit savagely down on slightly stale chocolate.

Giddy?
Air!
Window!

Eighteen feet to the polished stone flags of the terrace.

'But he said he never ate candy,' Dr Halpern muttered, his mind full of visions of malpractice suits. 'I warned him about cheese, but he said he never ate … Didn't he mention that?'

Knuckles locked around a tear-wet handkerchief, Maud whimpered, 'Yes, he said you asked about that. He thought it was because he was – uh – overweight.'

That was all right, then. Thank God. Dr Halpern rose.

'I guess we'd better carry him indoors. Is there someone?'

'Just the maids and the cook.'

'They'll have to do.'

BLOWBACK

'We've duplicated it,' the Cuban chemist said tiredly. It had been a terribly long job, and exhausting. But it was done. 'Here. It's exact, down to the last side chain. There isn't much – we don't have facilities to manufacture nerve gas. So be sure you put it to good use.'

'Thank you. We shall.'

Fifteen minutes out of Mexico City for Tokyo a passenger aboard a 747 screamed that he was being eaten by red-hot ants, and managed to open the emergency door at 23,000 feet. He had been to the washroom and drunk from the faucet there before takeoff.

It was, after all, labeled DRINKING WATER.

'What the hell?' the ex-soldier said. 'She's American, isn't she? And you know what those mothers did at Noshri!'

They found her by the washy light of dawn. According to the forensic experts she had been raped by at least three men and possibly as many as twelve. They couldn't say whether it was before or after she was strangled.

It had taken three days to locate her. Her dark skin was hard to spot among the underbrush.

A car pulled into a filling station in Tucson. Two black men got out and headed for the men's room. But when they reached its door they broke into a run.

The gas station burned for two hours.

Dynamite.

Also in Peoria, Milwaukee, Philadelphia, San Bernardino, Jacksonville, Albany, Evanston, Dallas and Baton Rouge.

The first day.

Under construction, a cloverleaf intersection near Huntsville, Alabama. The concrete was just starting to harden when it was hit. It turned out to be cheaper to scrap the lot than attempt repairs.

Also at eight other places where the roads happened to have arrived, not famous for anything in their own right.

At the big Georgia paper mill the saboteur was obviously a chemist. Some kind of catalyst was substituted for a drum of regular sizing solution and vast billowing waves of corrosive fumes ruined the plant. Anonymous calls to a local TV station claimed it had been done to preserve trees.

The same day, in northern California, signs were posted on a stand of redwoods that the governor had authorized for lumbering: about two hundred of the last six hundred in the state. The signs said: FOR EVERY TREE YOU KILL ONE OF YOU WILL DIE TOO.

The promise was carried out with Schmeisser machine-pistols. The actual score was eighteen people for seventeen trees.

Close enough.

In Little Rock Mrs Mercy Cable, who had found a skull and crossbones painted on her car when she came out of the doctor's office with her sick son, died protesting that she had meant to wash it off.

Well, she was black anyway. The mob went home to lunch.

But the most ingenious single *coup* was later laid at the door of a Chicano working for the California State Board of Education. (Prudently he wasn't behind the door at the time; he'd emigrated via Mexico to Uruguay.) He'd used the computerized student records to organize a free mailing of literally thousands of identical envelopes, every one addressed to somebody receiving public education in the state. They never did find out exactly how many there had been, because although they were all postmarked July 1st the mails were so lousy nowadays they arrived over a period of a week, and by the end of that time parents alert to protect their kids from commie propaganda had been warned to destroy the envelopes before the intended recipients could open them. But they guessed that fifty thousand did get through.

On each envelope was printed: A FREE GIFT FOR YOU ON INDEPENDENCE DAY, COURTESY OF THE 'BE A BETTER AMERICAN LEAGUE'. Inside there was a handsome print, in copperplate engraving style, showing a tall man at a table with several companions handing pieces of cloth to a group of nearly naked Indians of both sexes.

Underneath was the caption: *First in a Series Commemorating Traditional American Values. The Governor of Massachusetts Distributes Smallpox-Infected Blankets to the Indians.*

OUT IN THE OPEN, SHUT UP

It was kind of a fraught scene around the Bay right how – there was this big drive on to catch dodgers. Anyone out on the street (though who'd want to be, when the wind was blowing off the miles-wide garbage pile that blocked the Bay?) who was young and male or a reasonable facsimile thereof, was apt to be dragged into a squad car and left to cool in a cell until he produced a discharge certificate or a valid excuse for not serving. Everyone went around sweating and wishing they'd made it to Canada, or to Mexico before that crazy spic mounted his fire-balloon raids on San Diego. Following that the border had become tighter than a khathead's asshole.

Must have something to do with Honduras, they figured, though there hadn't been much news from down there since the Tupas took Tegucigalpa and drove the legal government to San Pedro Sula. The Pentagon was doing the tar-baby bit.

It eased the problem when Hugh and Carl, together with their friends – or rather Kitty's – Chuck and Tab got in a fight one night with a pair of ex-Marines and acquired their discharge certificates after knocking them out. The man they were still calling Ossie even though they had long ago realized he wasn't the original Austin Train knew where he could get them copied and altered. So now they all had documents to prove they'd done their stint … at least to the local pigs. Trying them on at a state border post would have been dicey, which was why they hadn't headed inland.

Train-as-was hadn't mentioned his real name, but they had discussed the idea of his giving up the alias. He was disgusted with his former idol. Why in hell, he kept asking, didn't the mother come out of hiding and assume leadership of the revolutionary forces awaiting centralized command? It was a fair question. This summer the nation was aboil. People drifted in from out of state occasionally, and they all told the same story, though you wouldn't have known the truth from the regular news. You couldn't walk the streets of any major city without seeing the skull and crossbones. People had taken to painting signs on their own front doors; they were being marketed as skin decals like the one Ossie had been wearing when Hugh and Carl met him, and illuminated plastic models were offered to hang on gateposts. The whole agricultural section of the country was seething because of this pest that was killing crops, and that was new – normally the rural communities were blind-loyal. Moreover, the acts of sabotage tabulated in the underground papers came from literally every state, from sugar in a gas tank to caltraps on a freeway.

Also bombs – though they weren't in the Trainite tradition, strictly speaking.

But for Ossie's fair question Carl had a fair answer, and it sounded only too likely to be true.

'My guess is the guy's been liquidated. Making too much trouble for the bosses. Look at what happened to Lucas Quarrey and Gerry Thome!'

Still, things weren't so bad you couldn't hold a party, and on the Fourth of July they decided to hold one. It was kind of swinging ahead of midnight.

Eighteen people in the pad and lots of noise. All very high on pot or khat. Also there was wine but hardly anyone touched it. They put things on the grapes and the pickers died. Kitty hadn't shown, but what the hell? There were other chicks here. So far Hugh had made it with two he hadn't met before, friends of Tab's, and he was reassured and felt great. Making it with Carl so much of the time led to worry, but Tab had scored for L-dopa, and it worked.

There was a phone. Owing to non-payment of a bill it was good for incoming calls only right now, and was going to be removed altogether some time soon. It rang and went on ringing until finally Hugh picked it up to say drop dead. But after he'd listened for a while he yelled for quiet.

'It's about Kitty,' he explained.

Several friends of friends asked who Kitty was. He shut them up.

'Been to this fireworks party on the campus.'

Someone turned down the tape-player until the group on it sounded as though they were on the phone themselves, long-distance.

'Well?'

'Busted. Not *just* busted. Beaten up.'

'Ah, shit!' Carl frog-hopped toward him. 'Her, or the whole bunch? And who's calling?'

'Chuck. He says the lot. Someone's uptight because they been bombing gas stations all over with like Roman candles.'

'Shit, man, why din' we think of that?' Tab clapped his forehead with his open palm, smack.

'But why bust the campus?' demanded one of the girls Hugh had made it with earlier. Name of Cindy, Hugh believed. A student there. Black.

'Someone hoisted the skull and crossbones on that big flagpole near the dean's—'

'Oh, *fantastic!*' Cindy went sprawling backwards in a fit of laughter, flinging wide the shirt which was all she wore to show off her so to say negative tattoo: a skull whose eyes were her nipples, bared teeth across her midriff, crossed bones intersecting at her pubis, which she shaved. It was done by minor cosmetic surgery and could be reversed. She always assured people it could be reversed.

'Yeah,' Hugh muttered. 'But they got like clubbed and dragged in the wagon.'

There was silence as he put down the phone. Ossie said suddenly, 'We got to get back at them. We *got* to!'

'No use just hitting and running!' Carl snapped. 'Got to hurt the man who gives the orders!'

'Well, who gives the orders?' Ossie rounded on him.

'The rich! Shit, baby, who else?'

'Right. And we got a pipeline to the rich – you didn't notice? I've been thinking about this a lot. Hugh, how much is Roland Bamberley worth?'

Some of the listeners went back to what they'd been doing before, mainly screwing, but a few stayed to listen because they sensed this was strong.

'Christ, millions! Thirty? Fifty? *I* don't know!'

'You ever met him?' Ossie pressed.

'Well, just the one time. At Jack Bamberley's.'

'And this son of his – what's his name?'

'Oh, Hector!' Hugh began to giggle. He was adrift on pot and khat both and maybe the L-dopa was having impact too; all three were fighting inside his head to keep him floating. 'Shit, is that ever a ridiculous scene! He keeps that son of his like wrapped in Saran. Know he wasn't even allowed to eat with us? Special food checked out by this tame chemist. Travels everywhere with a bodyguard, night and day – armed, too. Hell, I swear I hardly saw his face. Made to keep his filtermask on all the time he's outdoors, even in Colorado!'

'And he's how old – fifteen?'

'I guess. Going on sixteen now, maybe.' But Hugh was over his giggles and beginning to be puzzled. 'What's this about?'

'One moment. One itty-bitty moment. You read how he got this franchise for the whole state with these Jap water-purifiers?'

'Yeah, they put one in where we go have breakfast sometimes. Make a thing of it on the wall. Posters.'

'Well, don't you think Hector ought to be a little less protected, the rest of us a little more?' Ossie hunkered forward. 'Like shouldn't we get next to him and – uh – invite him to see how the other half lives?' He waved at the smoky room and implied the entire filthy city beyond.

There was a confused silence. Carl said at length, 'You mean like kidnap him? Hold him for ransom?'

'Ah, shit!' Hugh began, but Ossie cut him short.

'Not money, baby. Not a cash ransom. I'm thinking of' – he groped in the air as though seizing a number from a lucky dip – 'like twenty thousand water-purifiers installed free of charge if he wants to see his boy again.'

'Hey, that's music!' Tab exclaimed. He'd stayed to listen. 'Yeah, that makes a lot of sense. Go 'way!' – to Cindy, who was fumbling in his crotch. At once the argument became general, ideas being thrown out a dozen a minute and most of them absurd.

But meantime Hugh was sitting back against the wall and thinking: Christ, it's crazy and it might work. It just, very just, *might*.

It was in the spirit of the whole national scene, too – would kick off a lot of support especially in the cities – and a hell of a sight closer to the original Trainite ideals than throwing bombs.

*

If it hadn't been for Ossie, of course, it would never have progressed from a pipe-dream to actual execution. Hugh wasn't sure quite how it developed – the moment he realized he was going to be the key to the scheme, he got high, and stayed high, and was still high the day they did it. But Ossie had spent fifteen years on the underground scene, getting busted now and then but never spending long inside because he had an instinct for self-preservation that was halfway to paranoia. Also he had contacts, and he used them.

Roland Bamberley had divorced Hector's mother years ago and kept a succession of respectable mistresses, unwilling to remarry because he wanted total control of his fortune. He and his son lived on a Stronghold Estate (where else?) near Point Reyes, built around an artificial lake with clean fresh water and lots of tall trees nearby to keep the air sweet. It was obviously no good tackling the job right there. Not with ex-Marine sharpshooters on patrol.

But Hector did emerge into the open now and then, even though he was invariably accompanied by his armed bodyguard. A friend of his from the same expensive prep school he attended lived on the hillside overlooking Sausalito, which had become a very sought-after location indeed during the past five years, because the greenery was still lush and some trick of micro-meteorology made the air better than average. Ossie had an acquaintance who worked for a local TV station. Obligingly, the guy established that if he wasn't traveling during summer vacation Hector called on his friend once a week for a morning game of tennis (indoors, naturally), after which he stayed to lunch.

So they scouted the area while Ossie worked on a few of his other contacts, and figured out a route back to Berkeley from the north which avoided the main bridges, and did a couple of dry runs complete in every detail bar one: that for the actual operation they would steal a car and later abandon it.

And all of a sudden the day appointed was upon them.

It was just as well Hugh was living in a dream. If he'd believed what was happening was real, he'd have pissed in his pants with terror. As it was, he felt quite calm.

Just around the corner from the home of Hector's friend, which was screened from the road by dense trees and shrubs, there was a stop sign. At it the dark-blue air-conditioned Cadillac dutifully halted. Hugh stepped into plain view and grinned and waved and knocked on the car's window. He had put on his best – or rather, what had been until a day or two ago someone else's best – clothes, and shaved, and generally made himself presentable.

'Say, aren't you Hector? Hector Bamberley?' he shouted.

At the wheel, the bodyguard twisted around, one hand reaching under his jacket for his gun. Not wearing a mask inside the car, of course – Caddies had the best possible precipitators – Hector looked politely puzzled, a trifle startled.

'I'm Hugh! Hugh Pettingill! At your uncle Jack's!'

Recognition dawned. A word to the bodyguard, who gave a frown, and then also remembered their former meeting. He relaxed, then tensed again as Hector automatically touched the window switch.

'Hey, put your mask on if you're going to open that—'

But by then it was too late. Hugh had pitched the sleep-grenade into the car. It landed fair on the middle of the front seat. He spun and raced for the side of the road.

The grenade held the U.S. Army's latest riot-control compound, PL. It had been mailed home from Honduras. Ossie knew someone who knew someone. And there was always a keen demand for weaponry.

They waited the requisite three minutes. The bodyguard's foot had slipped off the brake, of course, but the car had only rolled forward across the main road and gently bumped the bank opposite. They were prepared to take the risk of his remembering Hugh. In two cases out of three PL induced temporary amnesia, like a blow on the head. It was more likely than not that he'd wake up to find he couldn't recall a thing.

Then the others appeared from the scrawny underbrush, and Ossie drove up in the station wagon they'd stolen, and they piled Hector in the back under a blanket and split.

'He looks pretty green,' Hugh muttered as they dumped him in the room – more, an oversize closet – they'd made ready at Kitty's. She hadn't been back since her bust at the Fourth of July party, and no one seemed to know where she'd gone, except it wasn't jail, but they were sure she'd have approved if she'd known what they were doing.

This was a gloryhole without windows, though very well ventilated – they'd made sure of that – with concrete walls, a good solid lockable door, and a sink in the corner whose tap worked fine. They'd fitted it up with a divan bed, a chamber-pot and a supply of paper, some books and magazines to help him pass the time. He'd hate it. But he wouldn't be getting much worse than some people had to live with all the time.

'He looks sick!' Hugh said, more loudly this time.

'Sure he is,' Ossie grunted, pulling the boy's legs straight on the bed.

'They always are when they wake up from PL. But we have the promise of the Pentagon that it isn't fatal.' Grinning without humor.

'Me, I'll go mail the ransom note,' he added, and turned to leave.

When Hector Bamberley struggled back from the depths of coma, he found Hugh squatting against the wall surrounded by roaches, some alive, and some khat. You could chew it, infuse it, smoke it – come to that you could stick it up your ass, but Hugh hadn't tried that. Of the others, he'd decided he preferred smoking. Hastily he donned his filtermask.

Hector said, 'What ...?' Tried to sit up. Fell back. Tried again. He was big for his age, as tall as Hugh, and in first-rate physical shape. So he ought to be, the way he'd been coddled all his life.

He nearly threw up – they'd left the chamber-pot handy in case – but managed not to. At the third attempt he reached a sitting position and focused his eyes. He was very pale, and there was a whimper in his voice when he said, 'I ... Do I know you? I think I saw ...'

It tailed away.

'Where am I?' With a cry. 'What am I doing here?'

Hugh kept on looking steadily at him.

'I do know you.' Putting both hands to his temples and swaying. 'You're ... No, I don't know you after all.'

There was a silence during which he recuperated from the worst effects and was able to drop his hands and regained a little color in his cheeks.

'Where am I?' he said again.

'Here.'

'What are you going to do with me?'

'Take care of you,' Hugh grunted. 'Very good care. Expensive care. Look!' He reached under the bed, barely missing Hector's feet, and drew out a plastic tray on which they had arranged food: sausage, salad, bread, fruit, cheese, and a water-glass. There was no don't-drink notice in force at present, so they'd agreed to take the fact literally.

'This is all from Puritan. Got that?'

'I don't understand!'

'Simple enough,' Hugh sighed. 'You are not going to be starved, that's the first thing. You're not going to be beaten – nothing like that.'

'But ...' Hector took a firm grip on himself. Among the subjects they taught best at his expensive school was self-control. 'All right, so I'm not here to be starved or beaten. What for, then?'

'Because your father inherited a fortune made by ruining the earth. Now he stands to make another out of his ancestors' shit. So we're going to keep you here, and feed you – all stuff from Puritan, the best kind – until your dad agrees to install twenty thousand of his new water-filters free of charge.'

But Hector wasn't seriously listening. 'I know who you are!' he said suddenly. 'You had a quarrel with Uncle Jack and walked out!'

'Did you understand what I told you?' Hugh scrambled to his feet. So much for wearing a filtermask!

'Ah ... Yes, I guess so.' Hector looked nervous. Small wonder. 'Say, I – uh – I need to go to the can.'

Hugh pointed.

'What? You mean you're not even going to let me go to the bathroom?'

'No. You can wash down at the sink. You'll get a towel.' Hugh curled his lip, not that it showed. 'Don't know why you're so eager for the bathroom anyhow. We don't have one of your dad's water-purifiers here. We have to take the regular supply. Think about that. You'll have lots of time.'

Prompt, Tab opened to him, and Carl was seen in the background poised to block an escape. Both were masked.

Hugh stepped out and the door was slammed and locked.

'All cool?' Carl demanded.

'Shit, no. He recognized me.' Hugh threw aside his mask in disgust.

'Ah, I guess he was bound to. I mean, people wear them so much of the time, you go by the eyes and forehead. Should have known I had to take the risk. Well, never mind.' Saying it made him feel bolder. He added, 'Christ, khat makes me thirsty. Got a Coke or something?'

'Here.' Chuck tossed one from a carton they had going in the corner. 'Say, did he look at the books yet?'

'Hell, of course not. Why?'

Chuck grinned. 'I put a stack of porn in with them. Might be handy for him while he's alone.'

EARTHWAKE

'What the hell?'

Elbow in the ribs. Philip Mason swore at his wife. It was dark. Also hot. But the windows had to be shut because of the smoke from the river fires.

And then he realized: another stinking quake.

He sat up. 'Bad one?' he muttered, driving sleep from his eyes with the palms of his hands.

'No, but Harold's crying.' Denise was climbing out of bed, feet fumbling for slippers. There was another brief rumble and something rattled on her dressing-table: perfume bottles, maybe. A wail. No, a top-of-the-lungs yell.

'Okay, I'll come along, too,' Philip sighed, and swung his legs to the floor.

THIS ISN'T THE END OF THE WORLD, IS IT?

Normally Moses Greenbriar distributed greetings like largesse as he waddled toward his office every morning. Today he distributed snarls. He was soaking with perspiration – the air outside was appallingly hot and wet – and he was more than an hour late. He stormed into his office and slammed the door.

'Dr Grey has been waiting for you for over half an hour,' his secretary said nervously via the intercom.

'Shut up! I know!'

He fumbled the lid off a small bottle of capsules, gulped one down, and in a few minutes felt somewhat better. But it was still horribly hot and humid in here. He buzzed the secretary.

'What the hell's wrong with the air conditioning?'

'Uh … It's overloaded, sir. It's on maximum already. They promised to send someone along and adjust it next week.'

'Next week!'

'Yes, sir. They haven't caught up the backlog they accumulated during the enteritis epidemic.'

'Ah, hell!' Greenbriar wiped his face and peeled off his jacket. Who cared if he showed a wet shirt? So would everybody on a day like this. 'Okay, send Dr Grey in.'

And, by the time Grey appeared in the doorway, he'd composed himself with the help of the pill into something resembling his normal affability.

'Tom, do sit down. I'm sorry to have kept you hanging about – it was those dirty Trainites again.'

'I hadn't heard there was another demonstration today,' Grey said, crossing his legs. Greenbriar stared at him resentfully; the guy hardly showed a wrinkle, let alone a patch of sweat.

He said, 'Not a demonstration. They seem to have given up such harmless stunts, don't they? I imagine you heard Hector Bamberley's been kidnapped?'

Grey nodded. 'Was your trouble something to do with—?'

'Shit, no.' Greenbriar seized a cigar and savagely bit off the end. 'Though I can't say it hasn't caused plenty of trouble for us, that – what with Jack Bamberley dead, and Maud under sedation, we were expecting Roland to step into his shoes and help keep the organization on an even keel, stop this disastrous drop in our share price … But what happened to me, the police had a tip-off that some maniac was going to blow the Queens Midtown Tunnel by driving through it with a bomb in his car. And himself too, I guess. So they're stopping and searching everybody. Bet it's another stinking hoax!'

'Yes, threats are an excellent sabotage technique in themselves,' Grey said with clinical interest. 'Very much akin to the German V-1 flying bombs, you know. They carried warheads too small to do much damage, but everyone within earshot naturally took shelter, so they interfered remarkably efficiently with munitions production and public services.'

Greenbriar blinked at him. After a pause, he said, 'Well, maybe, but it's a stinking nuisance all the same … Say, I guess I should have started by saying I'm glad to see you better. You were indisposed, weren't you?'

'Nothing serious,' Grey said. But he sounded, and was, aggrieved. Neither a drinker nor a smoker, celibate, and eating a balanced diet, he suffered from the subconscious assumption that disease germs would realize he was a hard nut to crack and keep their distance. Instead, he had gone down with brucellosis – he, Tom Grey, who never touched unpasteurized milk and invariably ate margarine instead of butter!

Now, naturally, he was cured; there were excellent and fast-acting specifics. But it irked him that he'd been deprived of three precious weeks he could have devoted to his project. At Angel City he had had a great deal of time to pursue what he regarded as the most important aspects of it. Here, by contrast, precisely because he had been engaged to work on it as a main job instead of a private venture, he had to subordinate his own preferences to the priorities of his employers.

'I believe it was because of Jacob's sad demise that you wanted to see me,' he said.

Greenbriar studied the tip of his cigar with critical concentrated attention. He said, 'Well – yes. It's no secret that this is the latest in a series of body-blows, as you might say. Even such an enormously wealthy organization as the Bamberley Trust has limits to the amount of punishment it can take. First the African business, then the Honduran affair, then the riot at the hydroponics plant, and now this – it's turned public opinion against us and practically wiped out confidence in our stock. So we're desperately in need of something, something dramatic, to improve our image. At our last board meeting, I raised the matter of your – ah – precautionary program, and everyone felt that it had strong potential for this application. Is there any chance of putting the use of it on public offer in the immediate future?'

Grey hesitated. He had been half afraid of this. But …

'Well, actually, that brings to my mind a suggestion Anderson made the other week. That young programmer you assigned as my assistant, you know? I suspect he intended it as a pleasantry, but I've been pondering it during my confinement to bed. In effect he argued that we are less in need of extrapolatory analyses to prevent fresh mistakes being made, than of emergency solutions to problems already in existence. Not that he phrased it quite like that, of course.'

'Then how did he phrase it?'

'What he in fact said,' Grey replied, 'was this.' Not for the first time Greenbriar decided he totally lacked a sense of humor; the question had been put, he felt obligated to answer in detail. 'He said, "Doc, instead of looking for ways to avoid more and bigger messes, why not just look for ways out of the mess we're in right now? The way things are shaping, we may not be around long enough to make any more mistakes!"' Defensively he appended, 'As I told you, I suspected him of being jocular.'

'Joking or not, do you think he was right?'

'Well … You know, I have sometimes been accused of inhabiting an ivory tower, but I do keep up with the news even though my tastes incline toward the quiet life. I can't help believing that the public at large would welcome something similar to what Anderson proposed. I can't accept that our political leaders are correct in maintaining that concern about environmental deterioration was a fad, which now sounds stale if it's mentioned in a campaign speech and bores the listeners. My conclusion is rather that because the politicians appear to be bored with it the public are resorting to more extreme measures. You've noticed how many acts of sabotage have been committed lately?'

'Damn it, of course!' Greenbriar spoke curtly. Many of the Trust's major holdings had suffered, being concentrated in growth industrials.

'Well, there's one thing to be said in defense of the saboteurs, isn't there? They are striking at industries with high pollution ratings. Oil, plastics, glass, concrete, products generally which don't decay. And of course paper, which consumes irreplaceable trees.'

'I had the impression you were on the side of progress,' Greenbriar muttered. 'This morning you sound like an apologist for the Trainites.'

'Oh, hardly.' A thin smile. 'Of course I had to reread Train's work for incorporation in my program data, along with every other thinker who's had a major influence on the modern world – Lenin, Gandhi Mao and the rest. But what I'm driving at is this. We've had centuries of unplanned progress, and the result can justly be called chaotic. Uninformed people, aware only that their lives may be revolutionized without warning, are naturally insecure. And they come to distrust their leaders, too, for reasons which might be exemplified by what happened at your hydroponics plant, when half a million dollars' worth of food, despite the government's insistence that it was perfectly edible, was destroyed against the background of starvation in Asia, Africa even Europe. And, what is more' – he leaned forward intently – 'against the depredations *of these jigras* throughout the agricultural states. A huge advertising campaign is being mounted, asking everyone to watch out for and report new outbreaks. But who's going to take it seriously when the government authorizes the burning of so much food purely to score a political point?'

Greenbriar nodded. Moreover, steaks in his favorite restaurant had gone up from $7.50 to $9.50 this summer.

'I suspect,' Grey plowed on, 'that young people in general want to believe in their leaders' good faith. After all, many of them are proud that the world's largest charitable organization is American. But instead of capitalizing on the fund of goodwill that exists, the government repeatedly tramples on it. Instead of exclaiming in horror at the fate of your friend's wife, Mrs Thorne, they refuse to acknowledge any responsibility, they even try and deny the danger is a real one. And, reverting to the riot at your plant: wasn't it a terrible tactical error to use battle-lasers? There's been a considerable outcry over their employment in Honduras, and one must confess that the reports of their effect don't make for pleasant reading. One could imagine young people being deeply disturbed by descriptions of how a person standing at the fringe of the beam may instantly find that an arm or leg has been amputated and cauterized.'

'You're beginning to remind me of Gerry Thorne,' Greenbriar said slowly. Somewhere during that lengthy speech Grey had touched him on a raw nerve. 'He put it more – more forcefully, of course. He said, "There are madmen in charge and they've got to be stopped!"'

He looked at Grey, and the thin man gave a sober nod.

Yes, damned right. What would happen if someone didn't come up – and very soon – with a rational, scientific, practicable plan to cure this country's ills? You couldn't look to that straw dummy Prexy and his cabinet of mediocrities for anything more useful than pious platitudes. Their attitude seemed to be, 'Well, it didn't work last time but it damned well should have done, so we'll do it again!' Meantime, what had been uncommitted support drifted steadily toward the extremist axis of the Trainites, or the radical right, or the Marxists. It was as though the public was taking the stand which came handiest, just so long as there was a stand to be taken that put an end to bumbling along from day to day.

He said, looking down at his fat hands on the desk and noticing that they glistened with perspiration, 'Do you think your program can be adapted to offer – uh – real-world solutions?'

Grey pondered. He said finally, 'I'll be frank. Right from the beginning of my project I've proceeded on the assumption that what's done is done, and the best we could hope for was to avoid compounding our mistakes. Obviously, though, the data that are already accumulated can be employed for other purposes, though certain necessary and perhaps time-consuming adjustments ...'

'But you'd be willing to let us announce that Bamberley Trust is to finance a computerized study which may reveal some useful new ideas? I'll guarantee to keep it down to "may".' Greenbriar was sweating worse than ever. 'To be honest, Tom, we're throwing ourselves on your mercy. We're in terrible trouble. And next year can only be worse if we don't hit on something which will make the public feel more favorably disposed toward us.'

'I'd need extra funds, extra staff,' Grey said.

'You'll get them. I'll see to that.'

SCRATCHED

'Yes? ... Oh, I'm very sorry to hear that. Please convey him our best wishes for a speedy recovery. But the president did ask me to pass this message informally as soon as possible; I may say he feels very strongly about the matter. Of course, not knowing if the rumor is well founded, we didn't want to handle it on an official level … Yes, I would be obliged if you could make sure the ambassador is told at the earliest opportunity. Tell him, please, that any attempt to nominate Austin Train for the Nobel Peace Prize would be regarded as a grave and – I quote the president's actual word – calculated affront to the United States.'

PRIME TIME OVER TARGET

Petronella Page: … and welcome to our new Friday slot where we break our regular habit and cover the entire planet! Later we shall be going to Honduras for interviews right on the firing line, and by satellite to London for in-person opinions concerning the food riots among Britain's five million unemployed, and finally to Stockholm, where we'll speak direct to the newly appointed secretary of the 'Save the Baltic' fund and find out how this latest attempt to rescue an endangered sea is getting on. But right now we have a very sad episode in focus, the kidnapping of fifteen-year-old Hector Bamberley. Over in our San Francisco studios – ah, I see the picture on the monitor now. Mr Roland Bamberley! Hello!

Bamberley: Hello.

Page: Now everyone who follows the news is aware that your son vanished more than a week ago. We also know that a ransom demand of a very strange kind has been received. Are there any clues yet to the identity of the criminals?

Bamberley: Some things have been obvious from the start. To begin with this is clearly a politically motivated crime. During the kidnapping a sleep gas grenade was employed, and those aren't found on bushes, so it's plain that we have to deal with a well-equipped subversive group. And no ordinary kidnappers would have fixed on such a ridiculous ransom.

Page: Some people would argue that on the contrary such a grenade could have been obtained very easily, and that anybody annoyed with the notoriously poor quality of California water might have—

Bamberley: Bunkum.

Page: Is that your only comment?

Bamberley: Yes.

Page: It's been reported that a first delivery of forty thousand Mitsuyama water-filters destined for your company arrived yesterday. Are you intending to—?

Bamberley: No, I am not reserving any of them for this disgraceful so-called ransom! I am neither going to yield to blackmail, nor am I going to connive at the plans of traitors. I've told the police that this kidnapping is the work of a highly organized subversive movement intent on defaming the United States, and if they're any damned good at their job they ought already to have the culprits on record down to their – their taste in liquor! But I decline to collaborate with them in any way.

Page: How would ransoming your son amount to collaboration?

Bamberley: During the late sixties and early seventies there was a massive smear campaign against the United States. The world was told that this country was hell on earth. We've won back some of our proper pride in ourselves, and we dare not waste the ground we've regained. If I gave in, our enemies would pounce on the act as an admission that we supply our own citizens with unwholesome water. Think of the political capital they could make out of that!

Page: But you've already made that admission by arranging to import these purifiers.

Bamberley: Nonsense. I'm a businessman. When a demand exists I take steps to supply it. There's a demand for these purifiers.

Page: Wouldn't some people claim that the existence of the demand proves that the authorities aren't providing pure water? And that by ransoming your son you'd actually be improving the state of affairs?

Bamberley: Some people will say anything.

Page: With respect, that's no answer to my question.

Bamberley: Look, any reasonable person knows there are occasions when you need ultrapure water – to mix a baby formula, for instance. Usually you boil it. Using these filters I'm importing, you don't have to go to that trouble. That's all.

Page: But when it's your only son who— Hello! Mr Bamberley! Hello, San Francisco! … Sorry, world, we seem temporarily to have lost – just one moment, let's pause for – uh – station identification. (Breach in transcript lasting appx. 38 sec.)

Ian Farley: Pet, you'll have to switch to the next subject. Someone's put out our Frisco transmitters. They think it may have been a mortar bomb.

BACK IN FOCUS

There had been this endless – timeless – period of her life when everything looked flat, like a bad photograph. Nothing connected. Nothing meant anything.

She was aware of facts, like: name, Peg Mankiewicz; sex, female; nationality, American. Beyond that, a void. A terrible vacuum into which, the moment she let down her guard, uncontrolled emotions rushed such as fear and misery.

She looked at a window. It was possible to see a small patch of sky through it. The sky was as gray and flat as the entire world had been for – how long? She didn't know. But it was shedding rain. It must just have started. It was as though someone out of sight were flipping the bowl of a tiny spoon laden with thin mud. Plop on the pane: an irregular elliptical darkish splodge. And another, a bit bigger. And another smaller. And so on. Each dirty drop causing runnels in the dirt already accumulated on the outside of the glass.

She didn't much care for the idea of dirty rain. She looked at the foreground instead, and discovered that certain things had rounded out. There was a desk across which a black man of about forty was facing her. He reminded her of Decimus, but fatter. She said, 'I ought to know who you are, oughtn't I?'

'I'm Dr Prentiss. I've been treating you for a month.'

'Oh. Of course.' She frowned, and passed her hand across her forehead. There seemed to be too much of her hair. 'I don't remember quite how I ...'

Staring around the room, she sought for clues. Vaguely, she remembered this place, as though she'd seen it before on an old-fashioned TV set, in black and white. But the carpet was really green, and the walls were white, and there was a bookcase of natural pine in which there were blue and black and brown and red and multi-colored books, and behind this black desk sat – just a second – Dr Prentiss in a gray suit. Good. It all fitted together.

'Yes, I do remember,' she said. 'In the hotel.'

'Ah.' Prentiss made the single non-word sound like an accolade. He leaned back, putting his long but chubby fingers together. 'And –?'

It was like falling into a fairy tale: not the gentle Andersen kind, but the Grimm type, drawn from the cesspits of the communal subconscious. A magic poison, as it were. She didn't want to think about it, but she was thinking about it, and since she couldn't stop thinking about it, it was marginally more bearable to talk than to keep silence.

'Yes,' she said wearily, 'I remember it all now. They broke in, didn't they? Who were they – FBI?'

Prentiss hesitated. 'Well ... Yes, I guess you'd have worked that out anyway. They'd been following the people who called on you.'

'Arriegas,' Peg said. 'And Lucy Ramage.'

Poor babes in the wood. The jungle of New York was too much. Far away, mindless terror. She felt insulated from it now, as though she were trying to remember by proxy. Perhaps with Lucy Ramage's brain. Had she seen the front of her head after the bullet smashed it, or only invented the picture in her imagination? Either way it was repulsive. To distract herself she looked at the clothes she was wearing: shirt and pants of pale blue. Not her own. She detested blue. 'How do you feel now, Peg?' Prentiss inquired.

She almost bridled by reflex, having all her life hated men who presumed instant familiarity. And then realized: she had lost four weeks. Incredible. Time scissored out of her life like a tape being edited. She forced herself to take stock of her condition, and experienced a pang of surprise.

'Well – pretty good! Sort of weak, like when you get up from bed after being ill, but … rested. Relaxed.'

'That's the catharsis. You know the term?'

'Sure. A discharge of tension. Like lancing a boil.'

'Yes, that's right.'

'Was it the food they made me eat which – uh …?'

'Landed you in this hospital?' Prentiss murmured. 'Yes and no. You can't have had time to ingest a dangerous dose of the stuff they'd put in it, and of course when we worked out what had happened we pumped your stomach. But you must have been under strain for a considerable time. You were cocked like a hair trigger, ready to go bang at the least shock.'

That made sense. Although he said something about 'the stuff they put in it …' Surely it was there already? Still, she didn't feel inclined to argue.

She said, 'You make it sound as though they did me a favor without meaning to.'

'That's a very acute insight. I suspect they did. At any rate a lot of repressed material got purged out of your subconscious. That's why you feel pleasantly relaxed right now.'

'What – kind of material?' With vague alarm, as though she'd suddenly discovered that a spyhole had been bored in her bathroom wall.

'I think you know,' Prentiss murmured. 'That's the benefit of this kind of experience, unpleasant though it may be at the time. You begin to admit all kinds of things you've always concealed from yourself.'

'Yes.' Peg looked at the window. The rain was heavy now, and the panes were almost opaque with dirty water. 'Yes, it was the whole stinking world that had got on top of me, wasn't it? All the water filthy – like that.' She pointed. 'All the ground full of chemicals. The air thick with fumes. And not one friend anywhere that I could trust, who'd tell me how to stay alive.'

There, it was out. And it must be the truth because this dark quiet doctor was nodding. He said now, 'But you did have one friend you trusted. You've been talking about him all the time. You probably know who I'm referring to.'

With a start Peg said, 'Oh! Decimus Jones?' He had seemed to be there, somewhere in the gray flatness of the other world

'Yes.'

'But he's dead.'

'Even so, didn't he have friends? Aren't some of his friends your friends too?'

Peg gave a cautious nod. Now she felt so much more like her normal self, her guard was beginning to go up again. There was something fractionally too casual about this smooth black doctor's tone, as though he were leading up to something.

'You certainly talked about them a lot. Gave the impression you're very fond of them. You talked about Jones, as I said, but also about his sister, his wife, his adopted children, lots of other people who knew him and know you. You even mentioned Austin Train.'

So that was it. Peg gathered herself and said in a cool level voice, 'Did I? How strange. Yes, I used to know him, but only slightly, and many years ago. And of course I've run across some of these people who've adopted his name. Ridiculous, that – don't you think? As though it were some kind of protective magic!'

When she had been taken back to her quarters, the man who had been listening in the adjacent room entered, scowling.

'Well, you botched that!' he snapped.

'I did not!' Prentiss countered. 'I did exactly as I was told. If you overlooked the fact that her references to Austin Train could just as well apply to someone who's adopted the name, that's your problem! And why are you so frantic to find the guy, anyhow?'

'Why do you think?' the other man exploded. 'Isn't this damned country falling to pieces around us? And aren't all these dirty saboteurs doing it in the name of Austin Train? Unless we find him and pillory him in public, make him look like the fool and traitor that he is, he can walk back into the spotlight any time he chooses and take command of an army a million strong!'

AUGUST

FOLLOWED BY THE EXPLOSIVE HARPOON

There she blows, bullies, yes, there she blows now!
There she blows, bullies, abaft of the prow!
Jump to it, bullies, come reef your topsails,
Take to the boats and go hunting for whales!

I'm a Newcastle whaler, I've money at home,
But my pleasure is on the Atlantic to roam,
To brave the rough ocean and add to my store—
I've killed fifty whales and I'll kill fifty more!
There she blows …

The holds are all full, there's an end to our toil,
We're going to be rich from the blubber and oil,
And when we're ashore and I walk down the street,
I'll march to the music of coin chinking sweet!
There she blows …

I'll go to the tavern and buy ale and beer,
And the girls will flock round me and call me my dear.
There's no king or emp'ror lives more gallantly
Than a Newcastle whaler just home from the sea!
There she blows …

– Broadside, about 1860,
to the air of 'An Honest Young Woman'

THE GRASS IS ALWAYS BROWNER

… described as quote disastrous unquote by airlines, travel agencies and tour operators. Hotel bookings are down by an average 40, in some cases 60, per cent. Commenting on the report just prior to departing for Disneyland, where he is slated to deliver a major speech on education, Prexy said, quote, Well, you don't have to go abroad to know our way of life is the best in the world. End

quote. A warning that food hoarding might be made a federal offense was today issued by the Department of Agriculture, after another day of rioting in many major cities over sharp price increases. Hijacking of vegetable trucks …

WATERSHED

The phone on Philip Mason's desk rang yet again; it was about the tenth time in an hour. He picked it up and snapped, 'Yes?'

'Well, that's a hell of a tone to use to your wife,' Denise said.

'Oh.' Philip leaned back and passed his hand across his face. 'Sorry.'

'Is something wrong?'

'Kind of. I've had eight or ten calls today demanding instant servicing. People saying their filters are choked.' Philip tried not to let his voice convey too much gloom. 'Teething troubles, I guess, but of course it means postponing new installations and reassigning the available men … Well, what can I do for you?'

'Angie McNeil just called. She and Doug can't make it to dinner tonight after all.'

'Christ, again? That's the third time they've broken the date! What is it this time?'

Denise hesitated. She said after a pause, her voice strained, 'So many emergency calls she says he'll be lucky to be through by midnight. Sounds as though just about everything is breaking loose at once. Brucellosis is the main one, but they have calls for infectious hepatitis, dysentery, measles, rubella, scarlet fever and something Doug suspects may be typhus.'

'Typhus!' Philip almost dropped the phone.

'That's right,' Denise confirmed soberly. 'He says – or rather Angie says – it's because all these people have come up here for their vacations instead of going to the coast. The sanitation and water supply can't cope.'

'You've told Harold and Josie not to help themselves to water?'

'Of course I have!' And she added, 'Sorry, didn't mean to bite your head off.'

'Well, this all sounds terrible, but what exactly do you want me to do?'

'Oh, I laid in food for six, of course, so I thought maybe you could ask Pete and Jeannie instead.'

'Sure, good idea. Matter of fact I can see Pete right now, heading this way. Hang on.' He covered the phone and shouted to Pete, who was visible through the office door, standing ajar because the conditioning couldn't cope with the heat. He was getting around fine now; he'd discarded his crutches and was using only a cane. Entering with a nod to Philip, he dumped something in a plastic sack on his desk.

'Can you and Jeannie come to dinner with us tonight?' Philip said before Pete could speak.

'Ah … Well, I guess we'd like to very much,' Pete said, taken aback. 'Is that Denise on the line? Would you ask her to call Jeannie at home and say if it's okay with her it's fine with me? Thanks very much.'

He sat down as Philip relayed the message and cradled the phone, and reached to open the sack. Philip stared in disbelief at what it contained.

'What in hell's happened to that thing?' he exclaimed.

It was a filter cylinder from a Mitsuyama water-purifier. It was discolored; instead of being off-white, it was dark purulent yellow with patches of brown, and the close-packed plastic leaves it was composed of had been forced apart, as though very high-pressure air had been blasted through it from the tube down its center.

'That's what all the faulty ones look like,' Pete said. 'Mack's found three like that already today. Thought he'd better check with us before exchanging any more.'

'Christ!' Philip touched it gingerly; it was slimy and loathsome. 'Has Alan seen this?'

'By now I guess he must have. He went down to Doc McNeil's clinic. They have real trouble. Twelve units all blocked solid.'

'Oh, *hell*,' Philip muttered. 'And have these people who are calling in really used up all their spare filters?'

'Mack says the three he's spoken to have. They're getting through a pack of six in that many weeks. But I thought they were meant to last half a year.'

'They are!'

'So what's going wrong?'

The phone rang. Philip snatched at it. 'Yes?'

'Alan for you,' Dorothy told him. 'Alan, go ahead—'

'Phil!' Alan cut in. 'We're in trouble!'

'I know. Pete just brought me a filter to look at. What in the world—?'

'Bacteria!'

'You have to be joking,' Philip said after a pause.

'Like hell I am. I've run across this before, in big purifying plants. And you get 'em in domestic softeners, too. But those mothers at Mitsuyama swore blind their gear was proofed against the problem. Get a service engineer down here to the clinic right away, will you?'

Philip repeated the request to Pete, who shook his head. 'Nobody here but Mack, and he has eight more—'

'I heard that!' From Alan. 'Tell Mack everybody else can wait. He's to come here right away. Phil, put me back to Dorothy, would you? I want to book a call to Osaka!'

'Just little bugs,' Pete said incredulously, turning the filter cylinder over and over. 'Making a pile of shit like this!' He shuddered and let the disgusting object fall. 'Scares the hell out of me,' he added after a moment. 'You know there's a new epidemic building up – brucellosis?'

'I did hear,' Philip agreed.

'They say it brings on abortion,' Pete said, eyes focused on nowhere. 'Jeannie's getting nightmares. She's well along now, nearly two months … Ah, hell, it hasn't happened yet.' He hoisted his stiff body off the chair. 'I'll go see Mack on his way.'

The phone rang. It was a man this time, for a change, but he had the same trouble: a six-pack of filters used up in six weeks, and now a mere trickle of water at his sink.

HAVE YOU SEEN ANY OF THESE INSECTS?

If you do inform the police immediately!

LOW SUMMER

Delegates from the five largest wats sat in conference with Zena and Ralph Henderson, in one of the bubble-shaped rooms leading off the big hall where the whole Denver community met for meals, like a side chapel from the nave of an ovoidal cathedral which had shrunk in the wash.

Hunched forward on clear blue cushions, Drew Henker from Phoenix said, 'So we're agreed. We'll have to blast Puritan regardless.' There was a depressed silence. On the brown hills surrounding the wat there were few of the usual bright patches of summer color. Ever since its inception, the people living here had planted flowering shrubs round about to improve the view. But they'd been replaced by the tents and trailers of visitors who had picked the flowers, chopped down the smaller trees for firewood, created garbage dumps overnight and polluted their one clean stream with raw sewage. There had been a lot of trouble, too, with rowdy drunks who found it amusing to throw rocks at the wat's windows.

At least it was dark now so you couldn't see the mess. Eventually Ralph said, 'The idea scares the hell out of me, but I feel it simply has to be done.' He rose and began to pace restlessly back and forth under the curved dome of the roof, having to stoop a fraction at the end of each pass as he turned. He was tall. 'Those damned fools out there' – a wave at the blank black windows – 'won't react to anything short of a real shock. They've been warned over and over, by Austin, by Nader, by Rattray Taylor, everybody. And do they take any notice? Not even when their own bodies fail them. Christ, we've practically had to turn our jeep into an ambulance!'

That was an exaggeration. But it was true that at least a dozen times since the influx of tourists began, strangers had come shouting to the wat for a doctor, or to have septic wounds bound up, or to ask advice for a sick kid.

'Bet they don't offer anything in return,' Rose Shattock from Taos said morosely.

Once more, silence; it became too long. Zena said almost at random, 'Oh, Ralph, I've been meaning to ask you. Rick's been pestering me to know what's causing the patches on all the broad-leaved plants this summer.'

'Which patches? The brown are from lack of water, I guess. But if he means the yellow ones, that's SO2.'

'That's what I told him. I just wanted to make sure I'd given him the right answer.'

'Wish the pollutants would kill the *jigras*,' said Tony Whitefeather from Spokane. 'But they're resistant to literally everything ... Think there's any truth in this idea that they didn't get in by mistake, that the Tupas shipped them deliberately?'

'Why should they have to bother?' Ralph grunted. 'Just let some stinking commercial concern lower its standards ...'

'We bought from them before,' Zena reminded him.

'Sure, but only because we had to. And anyway: importing earthworms, for God's sake! Bees! Ladybugs! Sometimes I think there's a mad scientist in Washington, controlling Prexy by posthypnotic suggestion, who wants us all to live in a nice sterile factory full of glass and stainless steel and eat little pink and blue pills so we don't have to shit.'

'Then he's getting rid of a lot of us first,' Tony Whitefeather said.

'So when the factory's built it won't have to be too big.'

'Like Lucas Quarrey and Gerry Thorne?' suggested Drew Henker.

'Oh, they didn't need to wipe them out,' Ralph countered with a shrug. 'The Syndicate attended to that chore for them. Still, they're due for a shock shortly. You're all staying over, aren't you? So we can discuss the initial news release in the morning.'

Nods all around the circle. They started to rise.

'Any of you know anything about these new Mitsuyama water-purifiers?' Rose Shattock said. 'We've been thinking of investing in some.'

'Us too,' Ralph nodded. 'But the housekeeping committee agreed to postpone it. This will be the first year we haven't managed to grow enough food to last us through the winter, so our spare cash will have to go on provisions bought outside.'

'It's not so much of a problem for you anyhow, is it?' Drew said. 'Come snow-time you can always rely on natural purification.'

'I'm not so sure,' Ralph grunted. 'With all this high-level haze, Christ knows what the snow's going to be like this year.'

'Grimy,' Zena said, and pulled a face.

At the same moment the distant drone of a light aircraft could he heard, growing louder, and they all glanced toward the window. Ralph exclaimed.

'Say! If those are the lights of that plane, he's low!'

'Sure is,' Zena confirmed, peering past his shoulder. 'Must be in trouble!'

'His engine's firing fine … Hey, what's he playing at? He's heading straight for the wat! Crazy joy-rider!'

'He's high, or drunk!' Drew decided. 'The damned fool!'

'Let's get outside and warn him off with a flashlight,' Zena proposed, and headed for the door.

Swinging around, Ralph shouted after her. 'Hey, no! If he is stoned, he'll think you're playing games with him and fly even lower!'

'But we can't just—'

It was as far as she got. The roar of the engine was almost loud enough to drown out speech, but that wasn't what cut off the rest of the sentence.

A sudden line of splintered holes, like the stabs of a sewing-machine needle, spiked the window, the roof, the floor, and Drew and Ralph.

On the second pass the plane dropped a stick of Molotov cocktails. Then it zoomed away into the night.

UNABLE NOW TO SEE THE MOUNTAINS

Surely from here on an August day you used to be able to see the mountains?

Pete looked around. They'd been detoured by police barriers from the route they'd intended to take – there was a house-to-house going on – and now here they were halted at the high point of Colfax, between Lincoln and Sherman, right next to the state capitol, while a group of young patrolmen went from car to car checking ID's and chaffing the pretty girls. On the mile-high step of the capitol frontage parties of tourists who'd been passed by the guards were taking each other's pictures, as usual. Usual Saturday morning crowds on the sidewalks, too.

But no mountains.

Funny. Made Denver feel kind of like a stage set. The arrow-straight line of Colfax pointing into blurred gray.

Almost one could believe that the world outside of what one could see was dissolving – that what the TV showed, the papers reported, was a fake.

On a notice-board hung to the fence enclosing the capitol grounds was a small version of the poster showing a *jigra* which had appeared throughout the Midwest and West in the past few weeks. Over it someone had scrawled the Trainite symbol in red: [scan this in, page 302]

The patrolmen reached their car, checked their ID's and looked into the trunk, and waved them on. He kept staring at that poster until he almost cricked his neck, which was sort of dangerous with his back condition. Another funny sensation: being a passenger all the time. He enjoyed driving. But it would be a long while before he could do that again.

Those stinking symbols were everywhere. They'd had three painted on the car, for instance, which Jeannie had had to clean off – trying not to damage the cellulose – wasting an hour or more on each occasion. If only, when it came to getting rid of one of the cars, they'd been able to keep the Stephenson ... But it was so much smaller, so much harder for him to get in and out of, and of course the trade-in value of an electric was far higher than that of any gas-driven car nowadays, and since they had to find the money for their new refrigerator ...

Damned silly not being able to get the old one repaired! But none of these kids nowadays would have anything to do with technical matters. Like it was black magic, and just touching it put you in the devil's power. They'd been expecting to recruit kids quitting school this year as trainee fitters at Prosser Enterprises. And hadn't hired half what they needed: maybe nine or ten, when they'd planned on thirty.

And now this trouble with the clogged filters. He was handing out two six-packs of the things as replacements under guarantee for every one sent to a new purchaser. Alan was talking about suing Mitsuyama, but that was talk and nothing more. You couldn't touch a billion-dollar corporation like that one, foreign or domestic. Best would be if the same problem hit, say, Bamberley in California or some other, bigger franchise holder who'd be prepared to make the suit a joint one.

Jeannie wasn't her usual talkative self today, but that was fine by him; he wasn't in a chatty mood himself. Anyway, she needed to concentrate. There was a lot of traffic. They were headed for Towerhill, to have lunch with her family, so they were on the road which led to many things not only tourists but local people out for a ride wanted to see: the site of the avalanche, the scene of the sixty-three deaths at the hydroponics plant, the burned-out remains of the Trainite wat ...

Is it true the Syndicate was responsible, trying to kill these daily louder rumors about the quality of Puritan food? Have to be a real bastard of that kind to do what he did! It's one thing to object to Trainite demonstrations and sabotage and all, something else to kill children asleep in their beds.

'Say, honey, look!' Jeannie exclaimed. 'There's a bird!'

But he was too slow, and missed it.

Half a mile out of the city she said, 'Pete, what's doing it?'

'What?'

She pointed to the sere yellow hillside they were passing. The plants on it were dusty. Shabby. Like untended houseplants in an overheated room.

'Well, pollution, I guess,' Pete said uncomfortably.

'Sure, I know. But what does that really mean?'

He forgot to answer. Around the next bend they came in sight of a high-way patrol car drawn up on the hard shoulder. A couple of officers had got out and were walking up the slope to inspect something new, a monstrous skull and crossbones at least thirty feet overall, etched into the dry grass with some dark viscous liquid, maybe used lubricating oil. The driver still sitting in the car was an old acquaintance, so Pete called and waved, but the guy was yawning and didn't notice.

Further on Jeannie said suddenly, 'Honey!'

'Yes?'

'I … Do you still think we ought to call him Franklin?'

That wasn't what she'd been going to say; he was sure of that. Still, he said, 'I like it. Or Mandy for a girl.'

'Yes, Mandy.'

And then in the same breath, in a rush, 'Pete, I feel so dirty inside!'

'Baby, how do you mean?'

'Like – like all my bones need to be taken out and washed!'

'Now that's foolish talk,' Pete said gently.

'No, I mean it,' she muttered. 'I don't have too much to do all day now, while you're at work. Not having the garden any more, or a whole house to keep clean … I can't help thinking about it, honey, not when there's a baby growing inside me!'

'The baby's going to be okay,' Pete declared. 'You couldn't have a better guy than Doc McNeil to see you through.'

'Oh, sure, and I always do just like he tells me. Eat the right kind of food, drink canned water, never touch milk or butter … But – Pete, what the hell kind of world are we going to bring the kid into?'

She snapped a harsh stare at him, lasting only a second, but long enough for him to recognize the real terror in her eyes.

'The doc says I probably won't be able to feed him myself. Says practically no mothers can. Too much DDT in their milk!'

'Baby, all that shit was banned years ago!'

'So how many times did you book someone peddling it?'

Pete had no answer for that. Even during one year of service in the police he had helped to arrest five or six people home-brewing illegal chemicals: not just insecticides, but defoliants, too.

'And proper food costs so much, too,' Jeannie worried on, signaling right as she slowed for the Towerhill turn. 'A dime here, a quarter there, without knowing it you're spending twice as much as you expected. And it's going to get worse. I was talking to Susie Chain the other day. Ran into her in Denver, shopping.'

'Ah-hah?' She was referring to the wife of his former sergeant at Towerhill.

'She has cousins in Idaho, she said, and they've told her they're only going to bring in about a quarter of the potato crop this year. The rest's been spoiled by *jigras*.'

Pete whistled.

'They eat anything, she said. Corn, beets, squash … Say, you seen the Trainite wat?' She pointed across the valley. Blurred by the haze, but visible in enough detail to be gruesome, the hollow shell of the wat lay like a rotted lobster. Small parties of sightseers were wandering around it, poking at the wreckage in search of souvenirs.

The local fire chief had said on TV how many warnings he'd issued about building in Fiberglas and scrap plastic. Worse than timber. Something about the poisonous fumes given off.

'Is that the way our kid's going to go?' Jeannie said bitterly. 'Burned alive like those three were?'

Pete reached over to pat her comfortingly on the knee. But she rushed on. 'Think of all the things he'll never be able to do, Pete! Swim in a river, or even row a boat on it – pick fruit right off the tree and eat it – take off his shoes to walk in wet grass, all squelchy and thick!'

'Oh, honey, you sound like Carl,' Pete chided.

'Why not?' She sniffed. 'Carl's the bright one in our family, always was. Wish he'd write and let me know how he is … You know, I'd half like to catch this brucellosis that's going around, so there wouldn't have to be a baby.'

'Shit, you mustn't say that!' Pete exclaimed in horror. 'If we miss on this one, we may never—'

But at that point the road gave a shudder. It was as though every one of the hundreds of cars in sight simultaneously ran over a rock. He reached for the radio and switched it on, to find out whether the quake was going to be serious. It wasn't. And in another few minutes they were at Jeannie's mother's home and they had to try and pretend that everything was fine, just fine.

FED UP

… purchases of Nutripon to supplement welfare stocks, currently at their lowest level for years owing to the unforeseen impact of unemployment in resort areas deserted by tourists, where ordinarily casual jobs in hotels and restaurants absorb much surplus labor from June through September. Discounting fears expressed by black and poverty-group spokesmen, Secretary for Welfare Barney K. Deane pointed out that the Bamberley plant has been refitted to an extremely

high standard, close to what you get in an operating theater, quote, unquote. Asked whether the plan would be extended later to relieve the impact of scarcity prices on underprivileged families, he said the question was actively under consideration but no decision had been reached. A call to ban exports of food to the United States was today issued by …

BACK

Not much changed. Garbage-cans fuller than ever and stinking. Buzzing flies. Kitty Walsh was pretty high. She stood for a while looking at the flies and wondering – not very seriously – where they'd come from. Imported, maybe? Last year, or the year before, or something, there hadn't been any at all.

But finally she picked her way among the cans and went indoors, trying to take off her filtermask as she went. It got kind of entangled with her hair. She'd let it grow while she was away.

The air inside was full of fumes, too, but that was pot. The windows were taped to keep the stench out. It was very hot.

'Christ, it's Kitty,' Hugh said, and rolled away from Carl. They were both naked. And she was nearly: just a dress, slit up the front, and sandals.

'Where you been, baby?' Carl demanded.

'Places.' She threw down the canvas airline bag which was all she'd brought with her and reached for the joint they were sharing.

'Met this cat when I got busted at the fireworks party,' she said after a while. 'We went to Oregon. I didn't know it was so good up there. We had like three days of blue sky. Maybe four.'

'No shit!' Carl said.

'No shit. Even found a lake we could swim in. And I got a tan, see?' She skinned her dress up under her armpits, and she was just a trifle brown.

After that there was silence for a while. It was the high. There was radio music coming soft from the back room, the gloryhole. She realized that finally and straightened her head, as far as she could. 'Who's in back?' she inquired, glancing around. 'And – say! You put a padlock on that door!'

Hugh and Carl exchanged glances. But it was after all her apartment.

'Hector Bamberley,' Hugh said.

'What?'

'You didn't hear about that deal?'

'Christ, of course I did. You mean …' She almost rose to her feet, but fell back on the mattress-spread floor in a burst of helpless laughter.

'You mean right here? Like under the snouts of the pigs? Ah, shit! That's fantastic!'

Carl sat up, linking his hands around his knees, and chuckled. Hugh, though, said, 'Not so funny. His stinking father won't play. And it's getting to be a grind, keeping watch all the time. Mustn't leave the pad empty, of course. *And* he's sick.'

'Playing sick,' Carl grunted. 'It was one of the first ideas he hit on, trying to make us bring in a doctor he can talk to. Now he's back at the same game. It's getting me down to throw away so much expensive food.'

'Huh?'

'All from Puritan. Ossie insisted. He's masterminding the deal.' Hugh exclaimed, 'Say, isn't it about time we fed him again?'

'Could be,' Carl nodded. 'Kitty, any idea of the time?'

She shook her head. 'Ossie?' she said. 'You mean Austin? But you know he's not for real, don't you?'

'Oh, sure,' Hugh sighed. 'Been thinking of giving the name up, too. Says he's sick of waiting for the real one to come out of hiding and *do* something.'

'If he did,' Kitty said, 'he'd raise the biggest army in history, just by snapping his fingers. Up in Oregon I saw— Hell, never mind. I'll take the food in. Always wanted to meet a millionaire's son. Where is it – in the icebox?'

'Sure, all ready on a tray. And when you come out, bang the door for us to unlock. One, one-two.' Carl demonstrated. 'So we'll know it's you and not him.'

'Okay,' Kitty said, and took one more drag on the joint before going to the kitchen.

Hector was lying asleep, his back to the door. She made a space for the food tray among a mess of books and magazines, mainly porn – German and Danish, good-quality stuff. Then she went around the bed and found that he had his fly open and his hand clasped around his prick. Half-hidden under the pillow was another porn magazine, a lesbian one. On the floor, a soiled tissue. Wet. She dropped it into the chamber pot.

Well, so that was what a millionaire's son looked like. Kind of ordinary.

But cute with it, she decided after a while. Handsome kid. Silly thin fuzz of beard showing on his cheeks. Hmm. Pussy cat.

Wake him?

Wait him out?

She sat down on the floor with her back to the wall and stared at him, not particularly thinking. She was adrift. She'd been floating already when she arrived, and that last extra charge from the joint Hugh and Carl were using had blown her way *way* up. Somehow it seemed like too much trouble to rouse him.

After a while, though, the sight of that open fly had its effect. She parted her legs and started fingering her crotch. It was good when she was as high as this, very slow, almost getting there and then not quite, but not getting lost either. Like climbing a snow-slope, slipping back a little at each step but never quite as far as where you'd been.

She almost failed to notice when his eyes opened and he realized she was in the room. She didn't stop what she was doing when she did notice.

'Who are you?' he demanded in a thin voice.

She looked at his prick. It was filling out. He realized, and dragged a corner of the sheet over it. The bedding was all tangled.

'Kitty,' she said. 'I guess it's kind of boring for you in here, huh?'

'What?' Shakily, he was trying to sit up.

'I mean like is that all you got to pass the time?' Pointing with her unoccupied hand at the magazine poking out under the pillow.

He blinked at her several times, rapidly. Then he flushed bright pink.

'You're cute,' she said. 'Kind of good-looking, too. Say, I made myself pretty horny by now. You too?'

'What the hell's keeping her?' Hugh said muzzily, a long while later.

'Probably screwing him,' Carl said indifferently. 'Ever know Kitty to miss the chance? But what the hell? The poor kid deserves it. I mean like he's been cooperative. It's only his stinking old man who's holding out.'

CHECK AND BALANCE

Petronella Page: Friday again, world, the night we break the regular rules and go clear around the planet. Later, we'll be talking to a senior officer from the famed Special Branch at Scotland Yard, London, about the new British computerized system for control of subversion, widely praised as among the most modern in the world, and then we're going to Paris to talk about the weird weather they're having there, with snow in August, yet. Right now, though, we're going to tackle a subject closer to home. Waiting in the Chicago studios of ABS is a noted educational psychologist with strong views on a matter that concerns everyone with kids – or who's intending to have kids. He prefers to remain anonymous because his views are controversial, so we're going to bend our own standing orders and allow him to be called Dr Doe. Are you there –?

Doe: Sure am, Miss Page.

Page: Fine. Well, let's start with your explanation for the present nationwide shortage of technicians, high incidence of college dropouts, and so on. Most people assume it's the result of distrust of industry and its effect on our lives, but you say it's not that simple.

Doe: Not too complicated, though, despite the fact that a lot of factors are interacting. The pattern is really pretty clear. It's not so much that kids today are more stupid than their parents. It's that they're more timid. More reluctant to take decisions, to commit themselves. They'd rather drift through life.

Page: Why?

Doe: Well, there have been a lot of studies – on rats, mainly – that demonstrate the crucial importance of prenatal environment. Litters born to harassed mothers, or poorly fed mothers, grow up to be easily frightened, afraid to leave an open cage, and what's more their life expectancy is reduced.

Page: Can experiments with rats prove anything about humans?

Doe: We know a lot nowadays about how to extrapolate from rats to people, but we don't only have to rely on that. In a sense we've made ourselves into experimental animals. There are too many of us, too crowded, in an environment we've poisoned with our own – uh – byproducts. Now when this happens to a wild species, or to rats in a lab, the next generation turns out weaker and slower and more timid. This is a defense mechanism.

Page: I don't believe many people will follow that.

Doe: Well, the weaker ones fall victim to predators more easily. That reduces population. Competition is diminished. And the fouling of the environment, too, of course.

Page: But our population isn't diminishing. Are you saying we're having too many children?

Doe: It wouldn't be too many if we could guarantee adequate relaxation – freedom from anxiety – and plenty of nourishing food. We can't. Our water is fouled, our food is contaminated with artificial substances our bodies can't cope with, and all the time there's this feeling that we're in life-or-death competition with our fellow creatures.

Page: This strikes me as very sweeping. What evidence have you apart from rats and these wild creatures you haven't specified?

Doe: The school records, the employment roster, the panic the big corporations are in this year because there's close to a ninety per cent shortfall in graduate recruiting – isn't there?

Page: I didn't say anything. Go on.

Doe: Also, around the beginning of the year, a United Nations report was published which purported to show that intelligence was rising very markedly in the poor countries of the world, whereas by contrast in the wealthy countries—

Page: But that report was discredited. It was pointed out that you can't apply the same criteria to kids in—

Doe: Wrong. Sorry. I know all about that, and about the argument that owing to our superior medical facilities we're keeping alive sub-normal children who die in the underdeveloped countries instead of surviving to drag down the average. But that's not what I'm talking about. I'm referring specifically to apparently normal children, without obvious physical or mental defects. I'm convinced people are subconsciously aware of what's going on, and becoming alarmed by it. For example, there's an ingrained distrust in our society of highly intelligent, highly trained, highly competent persons. One need only look at the last presidential election for proof of that. The public obviously wanted a figurehead, who'd look good and make comforting noises—

Page: Dr Doe, you're wandering from the point, aren't you?

Doe: If you say so. But I'd claim that this illustrates the fundamental anxiety which is now coloring our social attitudes. I'd say we've subconsciously noticed that our kids are less clever, more timid, and begun to worry that we may be less able than our parents were, and in consequence we're running away from anything that might tend to show that was true. When the politicians claim that the public isn't interested any longer in environmental conservation, they're half right. People are actually afraid to be interested, because they suspect – I think rightly – that we'll find if we dig deep enough that we've gone so far beyond the limits of what the planet will tolerate that only a major catastrophe which cuts back both our population and our ability to interfere with the natural biocycle would offer a chance of survival. And it can't be a war which does it, because that would screw up even more of our farmland.

Page: Thank you for talking to us, Dr Doe, but I must say I feel most people will regard your theory as far-fetched. Now after this break for station identification ...

THE END OF A LONG DARK TUNNEL

Christ, Oakland had been bad. But New York was *awful*. Even indoors, even in the lobby of this hotel with its revolving door and the air-conditioning blasting so hard it almost shook the walls, Austin Train's eyes were smarting and the back of his throat hurt. He thought of losing his voice. Also of losing his mind. He had done that once and sometimes he suspected he'd been happier without it. Like those kids who'd testified before the inquiry into the riot at Bamberley Hydroponics, one after another stating in dull flat tones that they wanted most of all to be insane.

But he was here, anyway.

Many times on the journey he'd feared he might not reach his destination. Naturally, with a faked ID in the name of 'Fred Smith', he dared not risk flying to New York, so it was a matter of taking a roundabout route on buses and by rail. Felice had offered him one of her cars, but that too was out of the question, because cars were the favorite means employed by saboteurs to deliver bombs, and they stole, or rented in a false name, so security was tight.

Not that a car would have been much faster anyway, what with the police posts at state lines, the searches, the restricted zones not merely in cities – one expected that during August – but right out in the country, in agricultural areas. Because of hijackers after food trucks, of course.

Problems like that had been among the many reasons why he had postponed his decision to re-emerge into the open. All summer long he had prevaricated, half made up his mind, changed it again and gone back to toting garbage, driving a dumper truck, loading the endless succession of wagons that carted imperishable plastic up the mountains to be jammed into abandoned mine-shafts, baling kitchen refuse to be sold as compost for the desert-reclamation projects, tramping in huge tough sweat-saturated boots over mounds of glass and piles of squashed cans. In its way the job was fascinating. A thousand years from now these scraps that he was helping to bury might be seen on display in a museum.

If there were any museums.

It had been the attack on the Denver wat which settled the matter. When he learned that Zena had taken refuge at Felice's home, only a few miles from where he was staying, he had had to call up and talk to her. And from that it had just all followed logically. Like a flower opening.

And here she came, after he'd been waiting only an hour. It had started to rain during that time – not that rain in New York cleared the air any longer, merely moistened the dirt – and she pushed through the revolving door in a shapeless bundle: plastic coat, plastic one-piece brooties which combined boots and breeches and were on show in every other clothing-store window, and of course a filtermask. She didn't even glance in his direction, but went directly to the desk to collect her room-key.

He saw the clerk lean over to inform her in hushed tones that a Mr Smith was waiting to see her.

She turned to survey the lobby, and the first time she looked his way failed to recognize him. That was hardly surprising. The infection which had turned his scalp to yellow scurf had killed most of his hair; now he was three-quarters bald and on the bare patches there were irregular smears of granular scar-tissue. It had spread to his eyebrows as well, and he'd lost the outer half of the right one. Since they had constituted his most recognizable feature, he'd shaved the other to match. And his eyes had grown weak, so he had arranged for Felice to take him and get glasses made. Altogether he looked very unlike the Austin Train who had been in the spotlight a few years ago.

Then, all of a sudden, she reacted. Came running to throw her arms around him. Christ, what's happened to Peg Mankiewicz, the Ice Princess?

She's crying!

*

Eventually she regained control of herself and drew back with a gasp.

'Oh, lord, I didn't mean to do that! I am sorry!'

'Do what?'

'Spoil your clothes. Look!' She raised her plastic-swathed arm and pointed here, here, here, to the big dirty wet marks she'd left all over his new suit.

'Oh, forget it,' Austin said, in a tone that brooked no contradiction. Standing back, he looked her over, and added after a moment, 'Peg, baby, I think something's changed.'

'Yes.' She smiled. It was a nice smile; it went deep into her dark eyes. 'The world broke me into little bits. And when I was being put back together, I had a chance to decide which bit would go where this time around. I like myself better than I used to.'

Hastily she peeled off her street gear, shaking it regardless of what might become of the carpet – it was shabby anyhow – then folded it over one arm and took Austin's with the other. A gesture that hadn't been in the repertoire of the old Peg.

'Christ, it's marvelous to see you! Let's go have a—'

And broke off in mid-sentence, her face clouding. 'Shit, I forgot. This time of the afternoon the bar's probably shut. Half the staff has gone sick again. Mono, I think. Well, let's go look anyway; we might be lucky. We can't go up to my room – it's full of bugs.'

'Which kind?'

'Both.' She gave a wry grin, "Also I'm followed on the street pretty often. But they don't generally bother me in the hotel. They have the desk clerks in their pocket, paid to report my movements.'

'Is this the same hotel where—?'

'Where they killed Arriegas and Lucy Ramage? Sure it is.'

'But why did you come back to the same place?'

'Because I'm sick and tired of being cowed all the time, looking for a corner to hide in. I've decided to stand my ground, and the hell with them all.'

'Is that going to get you very far? Think of the people who've tried before. Lucas Quarrey – Gerry Thorne – Decimus!'

'And what are they going to do to you?' Peg said, looking levelly into his eyes.

There was an absolute, dead, *terrifying* pause, during which his face was as impassive as a stone mask, all life drained except from his eyes. And they blazed. She felt her mouth open a little and a chill down her spine made her tremble. In his gaze she could read judgment.

When he spoke, it was like lightning striking.

'Crucify me.'

Then they were installed at a dark table in a corner and a resentful man in a white jacket was bringing them drinks. The air was perfumed with something disgustingly artificial, but one had to endure that everywhere.

She was frightened. It was not until their order had been delivered that she was able to frame words again, and instead of asking about him – she sensed that she had learned too much too quickly a moment ago – she said, 'How did you trace me?'

He explained, in a normal enough tone, seeming relaxed.

'I see. How did Zena take the loss of the kids?'

'Very hard – how else? But Felice is being very kind to her, and so's her husband.'

'Have you spoken to anyone else from the wat? Are they going to make a fresh start somewhere else?'

'No, they're just scattering to the other wats,' Austin sighed. 'I phoned Ralph, and apparently everyone was already so tired, so frustrated … The attack was the last straw. Chances were they couldn't have got through the winter. The *jigras* ruined so many of their crops and what they did have in store was soaked with fire-fighting chemicals. And do you know what the worst blow of all was?'

She shook her head wordlessly.

'They'd just had a conference about their findings on Puritan. Drew Henker was there, Tony Whitefeather, Rose Shattock. And the only complete copy of the report was burned. Of course, they'll try and do it over, but …'

'Oh, Christ!' Peg clenched her fists. 'So it was another Syndicate job, was it? Like Thorne and Quarrey? I'd been wondering.'

Austin hesitated. 'The grapevine says,' he murmured at length, 'that the plane was hired by a guy who works for Roland Bamberley.'

Peg's mouth rounded into an O. 'But it can't be true! He's not that crazy, is he? I mean, I know he's convinced his son was kidnapped by Trainites, but surely if he really believed his son was at the wat—'

'Oh, the grapevine carries a lot of garbage,' Austin cut in. 'It may very well not be true. If it is, he must have meant it as a warning, I guess.'

'On the other hand …' Peg stirred her drink absently; the swizzle stick had a fleur-de-lys on the top. 'Have you ever met that stinking mother? I did once. Interviewed him. I wouldn't be surprised if he'd rather lose his son than give in to the ransom demand. Afterwards he'd excuse it to himself by saying the boy died for the sake of his country.'

'Meaning he'd rather have the profit on the water-purifiers than his son.'

'That's right. He's proud of being a businessman, isn't he?' Peg gave a thin sour smile. 'Still, there's nothing much we can do about that. Say, do you know who does have the kid?'

Austin spread his hands. 'All kinds of crazy rumors in Oakland. I don't believe a one of them.'

*

There was another pause. During it, she plucked up the courage to put a direct question about his own plans. By now, seeing him so much changed yet in some indefinable way so much more like himself than he had been for the past three years – perhaps because his confidence was back – she had almost convinced herself that that fearful instant by the door of the bar had been imaginary.

Still, her voice was unfirm as she said, 'Why have you come here, Austin?'

'I guess I've come to the same decision as you. Or not so much come to it. Been driven to it. I have a mission, Peg. I don't want it. But who the hell else is there?'

'Nobody,' Peg said instantly and positively. 'And there are millions of people all over the country who'd agree.'

He gave a brief bitter chuckle. 'But that's the irony of it, Peg. Remember you once asked me whether it bothered me to have my name taken in vain? Well, it does. My God, it does! It was the thing I finally found I couldn't stand any longer. *I'm* not a Trainite!'

Peg waited for him to continue. She was trembling again, but this time from excitement. She'd hoped and prayed for this for so long. He was looking past her, into infinity.

'But then,' he said, 'Jesus wasn't a Christian, was he?'

She started.

'Think I'm crazy, Peg. I can read it on your face.' He leaned forward earnestly. 'So do I, much of the time. And yet ... I can't be sure. I think perhaps I may really be very sane. If you want me to spell out what's happened to me, I'll have to disappoint you. It can't be described, and if it doesn't show it isn't true. It's just that – well, somewhere under this bald ugly dome of mine there's a sense of certainty. Knowledge. As though this sweaty summer shoveling garbage has taught me something no one else understands.' He drew a deep breath.

'Peg, I think I may be able to save the world. Do you believe me?'

She stared at him for a long while. 'I—' she tried to say, and found the next word wouldn't follow. She went on staring. Calm face. Level mouth. Those odd, unfamiliar halves of eyebrows. The glasses which – where had they been when she saw that lightning in his eyes? They had seemed to melt away, not be there at all, so she was looking direct into his soul.

Voicelessly, at last: 'If anyone can, it must be you.'

'Fine.' He gave a grave smile and leaned back. 'So where do I begin? I came to New York because it seemed logical. I thought maybe the *Petronella Page Show*. If they'll have me.'

'If they'll have you?' Peg almost upset her glass. 'Lord, they'd throw out Prexy himself to make a slot for Austin Train! Give you the whole hour without commercials!'

'Do you think so?' He blinked at her with surprising shyness. 'I've been away so long, and—'

She banged the table with her fist. 'Austin, for heaven's sake! Don't you realize you're the most powerful man in the country right now? Whatever you think about the people who call themselves Trainites, they picked the name because *you exist*. Everyone's on your side who can't afford contract medical care for his kids – black, white, young, old! You've just crossed the States west to east. What do you see everywhere from Watts to Tomkins Square? The skull and crossbones, right? And the slogan, too – "Stop, you're killing me!" They're waiting for you, Austin! Waiting with their tongues hanging out!'

'I know!' His tone was almost a cry. 'But I don't want that!'

'You've got it,' she said ruthlessly. 'What you do with it is up to you. I tell you this, though, and I mean it. I don't know about saving the world, but I'm damned certain if you don't speak up this country won't get through the winter without civil war.'

There was a long cold silence. He punctuated it by uttering a single word: 'Yes.'

And then let it resume.

Eventually, however, he seemed to reassemble himself from many far-distant places, and said in a casual voice, 'You know something odd? I can't remember the name of the guy who hit on that symbol.'

'What, the skull and crossbones? I thought you did.'

'No, it was the designer they assigned to my books at International Information. He had a little logo made of it and put it next to the number on every page. And I've forgotten his name. It isn't fair. He ought to have the credit for it.'

'Maybe he'd rather not,' Peg said.

'In that case I sympathize,' Austin grunted, staring at the backs of his hands on the table. 'I have this terrible feeling sometimes that I've stopped being myself. Do you understand that? I mean, I've been taken over – *made* over – into the patron saint of bombing, sabotage, arson, murder, God knows what. Maybe rape! If the skull and crossbones has a meaning, it's a warning. Like the international radiation sign. Instead of that, it's what everyone scrawls when they break a store-window in a fit of drunken rage, break into a bank vault, steal a car. It's an excuse for anything.'

'So what's new about that? It happened to the Suffragettes in England. Any petty criminal would write "Votes for Women" as he left the scene. And people did it deliberately, too, to discredit the movement. Women's Lib had a dose of the same medicine.'

'I guess you're right.' Absently he was sketching the stylized form of the symbol on the table, using the liquid from the wet rings their glasses had left.

There were no coasters. Trainites had branded them a waste of paper, like disposable towels, and this was one case where they'd made their opinion felt.

'Yes,' he went on, 'but if something could be said to have driven me crazy, it's knowing I've been converted into a person who doesn't exist.'

'But you do exist.'

'I think so.'

'Then get up and prove it.' Peg checked her watch. 'When do you want to be put on the Page show?'

'You really think you can fix it?'

'I keep telling you, honey! You're past the point at which you have to *fix* that kind of thing! You just ask.'

'So let's ask.' He drained his glass. 'Where's a phone?'

DIRECT HIT

Target: Grand Forks Missile Base, North Dakota.

Means: a psychotomimetic drug introduced into supposedly secure groceries delivered to the home of Major Eustace V. Barleyman, one of the officers responsible for the group of eleven Minutemen code-named 'Five West Two'. He ingested it in a portion of stewed prunes while breakfasting alone after his tour of duty.

Effect: he nearly killed his son Henry, aged six, and his daughter Patricia, aged four.

Suspect: any Tupa sympathizer with access to the food.

The implications were serious.

Martial law took off like a forest fire.

THE GENUINE ARTICLE

'Christ, it's going to pull the biggest audience in television history! The Wednesday after Labor Day, when everyone's broke because of the holiday and staying home! We've got to lean on them!'

'Leaning on ABS is out of the question. Damn Prexy's loud mouth! First time we ever had a president with *all* the news media gunning for him!'

'Then we'll have to lean on Train. Ah – it is Train, is it? Not one of these stinking ringers?'

'Hell, yes, it all fits. We had a report from LA months ago that he was working on a garbage gang under the name of Smith, but he skipped and after that we got screwed up by the phonies. We had a check run on the prints he left on his beer-glass, though. He's Train.'

'Any idea why he's chosen now to come out of hiding?'

'Must be big, that's all we know.'

'What would he regard as big enough?'

'Maybe something that would lead to Prexy being impeached?'

'Well, in that case— Ah, shit. You're putting me on.'

'I don't know if I am or not, I swear I don't. But it's definite that when ABS start their spot announcements, twenty or thirty million people will head for their TV sets at a run, wanting to be told what to do. Now I know what Germans must have felt like waiting to see how Hitler did in the elections.'

'I guess so. Well, he'll just have to vanish, won't he? Get on to Special Operations and—'

'He thought of that.'

'What?'

'He's given ABS a tape to be broadcast if he doesn't make the show. We can't get at it; it's in ABS's safety-deposit at Manufacturers Hanover. And if he isn't on the show, you can rely on Page to make maximum capital out of that.'

'He's got us over a barrel, then.'

'Yes.'

INSUSCEPTIBLE OF RIGOROUS ANALYSIS

Justice: The inquiry established that there was no psychotomimetic drug in any sample of Nutripon held at the warehouse. It cannot have been this substance which caused the riot at the plant. That has been proven absolutely, even to the satisfaction of the UN.

Defense: On the other hand, analysis of the groceries at Major Barleyman's home shows that such a drug had been introduced into several items. The characteristics correspond

PORTION OF TRANSCRIPT OMITTED ACCESSIBLE ONLY TO PERSONNEL WITH TRIPLE-A-STAR SECURITY CLEARANCE

found to cause unpredictable mental disturbances and other unacceptable side effects. Consequently no studies of it have been conducted since 1963.

Intelligence: It's relevant here that several informants have advised us of an alleged synthesis of the substance which the Tupas claim to have found in relief food at San Pablo, carried out in Havana on the basis of Duval's work in Paris.

Health: Putting that together with the now definitely established fact that the timing and location of the first outbreaks of that crippling enteritis coincide with a journey made by a foreign national during the preceding couple of weeks, ostensibly for legitimate business purposes …

Agriculture: And nobody can make me believe that these damned *jigras* acquired immunity to such a wide range of pesticides without help. Nor that a responsible and respected firm of importers could simply have overlooked the presence of the wrong kind of worm in so many of their consignments.

State: So it's obvious that we don't have to deal with the work of an isolated fanatic, like those fire-balloon raids on San Diego.

President: Yes, there's only one possible conclusion. I'd appreciate at your earliest convenience your views on whether or not to make the matter public, but there can't be any doubt any longer. The United States is under attack.

SEPTEMBER

MOTHER-RAPERS

… 'Mid fume and reek
That caused unmanly Tears to lave my cheek,
Black-vis'd as *Moors* from soil, and huge of thew,
The Founders led me ever onward through
Th' intolerable Mirk. The furnace Spire
They broach'd, and came a sudden gout of Fire
That leach'd the precious Water from my corse
And strain'd my Vision with such awful force
It seem'd I oped my eyes to tropic Sun
Or lightning riving Midnight's dismal dun,
Or stood amaz'd by mighty *Hekla*'s pit.
I marvel'd how Man, by his GOD-sent wit,
Thus tam'd the salamander Element
And loos'd the Metal in the mountain pent
To make us Saws, and Shears, and useful Plows,
Swords for our hands, and Helmets for our brows,
The surgeon's Scalpel, vehicle of Health,
And all our humble Tools for gaining wealth …

– 'De Arte Munificente', Seventeenth century

STANDSTILL

… *unanimously ascribed to fear of Trainite atrocities by traffic experts across the nation. In many places the car-per-hour count was the lowest for thirty years. Those who did venture out this Labor Day often did not meet with the welcome they expected. In Bar Harbor, Maine, townsfolk formed vigilante patrols to turn away drivers of steam and electric cars, persons carrying health foods, and other suspected Trainites. Two fatalities are reported following clashes between tourists and residents. Two more occurred at Milford, Pennsylvania, when clients at a restaurant, angered at not obtaining items listed on the menu, fired it with gasoline bombs. The owner later claimed that supplies had been interrupted by food-truck hijackers. Commenting on the event by the shore of his private lake in Minnesota, Prexy said, quote, Any man has a right to his steak and potatoes, unquote. California: experts assessing mortar damage to the Bay Bridge ...*

FRAUGHT

'We can't go on,' Hugh said doggedly. 'The scene's too fraught. Christ, I been stopped and searched four times in two days.'

'And your ID didn't stand up?' Ossie snapped.

'Shit, if it hadn't would I be here? But for how much longer? No, Ossie, we have to let the kid go.'

'But his old man hasn't come across!'

'That stinking mother *never* going to come across!' Carl snapped. 'He has the Abraham complex in a big way.'

'And Hector is sick,' Kitty said. She was unusually sober. 'Hardly ate anything for a week. And his shit – ugh! All stinky and wet. And he sweats rivers.'

The other two present were Chuck and Tab, the original co-conspirators. Ossie appealed to them.

'Hugh's right,' Chuck said. He scratched his crotch absently; fleas and crabs were worse than ever around the Bay. Tab nodded agreement.

'We got to scatter if we turn him loose,' Ossie said after a pause. He was frowning, but he sounded as though he'd been expecting this decision for a good while.

'No skin,' Hugh said. 'He's seen us, sure, but he doesn't know who any of us are. Except me, and that's my problem.' Saying that made him feel heroic. He'd been rehearsing. 'Ossie, he only knows you as "Austin Train", doesn't he?'

'Did you see ABS found Train?' Kitty put in.

'Sure!' – in chorus from them all, and Ossie continued. 'And I tell you one thing straight! If that bastard doesn't say what needs to be said, I'm going to walk clear to New York and tear him into little pieces. Unless someone beats me to it.'

'Yeah,' Hugh said, and reverted to the subject. 'Well, the rest of us he knows by first names, but there are thousands of Hughs and Chucks and Tabs. And Kittys. Sorry about the pad, baby.'

She shrugged. 'Nothing here I specially want. I can pack all my gear in the one bag.'

'But we can't just like take him down to the street and let him go,' Tab said, worrying.

'When he's asleep, we simply drift,' Hugh countered. 'We leave the door unlocked. When he wants to, he walks out.'

'If he's too sick?' Kitty said.

'Shit, he's not going to die in twenty-four hours. Give ourselves that much start, then call the pigs to come look for him if he hasn't made it on his own feet … Ossie, what're you doing?'

Ossie had taken a scratch-pad and a pen. Without looking up, he said, 'Drafting the note we should leave behind. Got to make our point. Now we gave the kid the best food, like from Puritan, right? And regular water because there's no don't-drink notice in force. So if he fell sick it's because of the filthy mothers who are screwing up the world, right?'

Nods.

'All because his old man loves money more than his son, right? Wouldn't give water-purifiers to the poor.'

'Maybe he did them a favor,' Carl said.

'What?'

'Up in Colorado they're all getting blocked with bacteria. It's a scandal. Talking about suing the makers.'

'Won't mention that,' Ossie said.

Darkness. But starred with the brilliant horrible images of nightmare. He was sick at his stomach. He was wet with perspiration. His penis hurt, his anus hurt, his belly hurt. He screamed for someone to come to him.

No one answered.

He fell off the bed when he tried to stand up, bruised his hip and his left elbow. Staggering to the door to hammer on it, he knocked against the chamber pot and splashed urine and liquid excrement over his feet.

Banging the door opened it. He was too giddy to realize what had happened and was all set to beat on it again. His fists struck air. He fell forward, crying and moaning. Beyond, a room with soiled mattresses covering the floor. Some light from a street lamp. The sky was dark. It was the first time in eternities that he'd seen the sky.

He shouted again, hoarsely, and the world swam. He had fever, he was sure of that. And ached. And there was a foulness inside his pants, fore and aft. Hell. This was hell. The world ought to be clean, sweet, pure!

Weaker and weaker, he hobbled moaning toward the front door of the apartment and found that open, too, giving on to stairs, and he fell down those two or three at a time. At the foot a filthy hallway where children certainly, adults maybe, had relieved themselves. Like paddling in a sewer. But he made it to the street door. Clawed himself up to reach the catch on it. There was a step beyond. He fell down that also, sprawled on hard sidewalk, screaming.

'I'm Hector Bamberley! Help me! There's a reward! My father will give you a reward!'

But boys stoned or crazy were a common sight, and anyhow everyone knew that Roland Bamberley had downright refused to offer a reward for his son, for fear the kidnappers might receive it. It was more than an hour before any of the rare passers-by took him seriously, and by then he had lapsed into delirium.

Besides, the air had deprived him of his voice within a few minutes, and then it was hard to make out what he was trying to say through the bouts of coughing and vomiting.

'Well, doctor?' Leaner than his older brother Jacob, dedicated to exercise and what outdoor life was nowadays possible because he was proud of his stringy, tough, Western-pioneer good looks, Roland Bamberley addressed the masked man emerging from the hospital ward.

The doctor, removing his mask, passed his hand wearily across his forehead. He said, 'Well ...!'

'Tell me!' Stern, like a patriarch secure in the knowledge that God approved of him.

'It's a long list,' the doctor said, and sat down, taking a notepad from the pocket of his white coat. 'He's had a couple of lucid intervals, but much of the time he's been – uh – rambling. Let's see ... Oh, yes. Says he's been well fed. Says the kidnappers gave him nothing but stuff from Puritan and kept complaining about how expensive it was. He's had regular breakfast, lunch and supper. But he had to drink tap-water. Straight tap-water.'

'And?' No emotion discernible.

'He has hepatitis. Acute. He's running a high fever, about one-oh-one point eight. Also he has violent diarrhea, enteritis or dysentery, I imagine, though I'll have to wait for a stool culture on that. Those are the most important things.'

'What about the rest?'

It was an order. The doctor sighed and licked his lips. 'Well ... A skin complaint. Minor. Impetigo. It's endemic in the slums around here. One of his eyes is a bit inflamed, probably conjunctivitis. That's endemic, too. And his tongue is patched and swollen – looks like moniliasis. Fungus complaint. What they call thrush. And of course he had body-lice and fleas.'

The mask of Roland Bamberley's self-possession cracked like a strained ice-floe. 'Lice?' he rasped. 'Fleas?'

The doctor looked at him with a sour twist of his mouth. 'Sure. It'd have been a miracle if he'd escaped them. About thirty per cent of the buildings in the city center are infested. They're immune to insecticides, even the illegal ones. I imagine the enteritis and hepatitis will turn out to be resistant to antibiotics, too. They usually are nowadays.'

Bamberley's cheeks were gray. 'Anything else?' he said in the tight voice of a man looking for an excuse to pick a fight, wanting to be needled one more time so he can let go his charge of ill-temper.

The doctor hesitated.

'Come on, out with it!' Like a coarse file against hardwood.

'Very well. He also has gonorrhea, very advanced, and if he has that he's virtually bound to have NSU, and if he has those then he most likely has syphilis. Though that'll have to wait for the Wassermann.'

There was a long silence. Finally Bamberley said, 'But they must have been worse than animals. People can't live like that.'

'They have to live like that,' the doctor said. 'They aren't given a choice.'

'Liar! Fleas? Lice? Venereal disease? Of course they have a choice!' Bamberley barked.

The doctor shrugged. It wasn't politic to argue with a man as rich as this. Since his brother Jacob died he was almost unbelievably rich. He'd been next in line for the entailed portion of the fortune. Jacob's adopted children weren't eligible.

Nor was Maud.

'Can I see him?' Bamberley said after a while.

'No, sir. That's medical orders. I've put him to sleep, and he must be allowed to rest for at least twenty-four hours. The combination of drugs we've had to give him might – ah – disturb his reasoning powers anyway.'

'But antibiotics—' Bamberley checked, like a hound dog catching a new scent. He said suspiciously, 'There was more. You didn't tell me everything.'

'Oh, hell!' The doctor finally lost patience. He'd been on the job three hours without a break. 'Yes, Mr Bamberley! Of course there was more! You raised him in that practically gnotobiotic environment – he doesn't have the regular natural immunities! Inflamed tonsils! Pharyngitis! Allergies from the shit Puritan sell in their so-called "pure" foods! Scratches that have gone septic, boils on his ass full of stinking pus! Exactly what *everybody* has who lives the way he's been living the past couple of months, only more so!'

'Everybody?' Steely; dangerous.

'Sure, everybody! I guess that was the point the kidnappers were intending to make.'

The instant the words were out, he knew he'd gone too far. Bamberley jumped to his feet.

'You sympathize with those devils! Don't deny it!'

'I didn't say that—'

'But that's what you meant!' In a roar. 'Well, you can take your filthy Trainite ideas somewhere else!'

The doctor debated only a moment whether to speak his mind and clear his conscience or keep his fee and multiply his income. He opted for the second choice, the sensible one. He was thinking of moving to New Zealand.

'I didn't mean to offend you,' he said in a soothing tone. 'Only to point out that your son isn't suffering from anything – well – extraordinary. He hasn't been beaten, or starved, or tortured. He'll recover.'

Suspecting irony, Bamberley glared at him. He said, 'Has he talked about the kidnappers at all?'

'Not really,' the doctor sighed.

'You're holding something back. I'm used to dealing with people – I can tell.'

'Well ...' The doctor had to lick his lips. 'Well, he's mentioned this girl Kitty, of course. He's not a virgin any more, obviously.'

'Thanks to some whore who gave him the clap!'

'Well, sir, he must have cooperated. I mean, you can't rape a boy, can you?'

'Are you *sure* he wasn't raped?' Bamberley gritted.

'What? Oh!' For an instant the doctor thought he might not prevent himself from smiling. 'No, you can rest assured he wasn't the victim of homo-sexual assault.'

'Wouldn't have put it past the bastards!' Bamberley checked his watch. 'What else has he been talking about since you brought him here? Come on! The police will be back as soon as they're through searching the place where he was locked up, and then you'll damned well have to talk, won't you?'

The doctor said reluctantly, 'Well, one thing ...'

'Out with it, damn you!'

'Well, he has been saying, over and over, that he was kidnapped by Austin Train.' The doctor shook his head. 'I don't get it. I'm sure it must be the delirium.'

A SHIFT OF EMPHASIS

Of course everyone knows what a marvelous aid Lenabix are to a slimmer's diet, with their balanced combination of essential nourishment, health-giving vitamins and specially selected tranquilizer. But has it occurred to you that they're also the perfect answer to the question which is facing more and more housewives without a weight problem? 'What can I keep in the house for the rare occasions when our stocks run low, bearing in mind that I have a limited budget?' Yes, the answer has to be – Lenabix! They offer remarkable value for so much nourishment and so many vitamins, and what's more they can be relied on to calm that child who's woken up in the night asking for food. They'll send your kiddie back to refreshing, restful slumber. And have a Lenabix yourself while you're up, won't you? Lenabix!

MINE ENEMIES ARE DELIVERED INTO MY HAND

Oh, marvelous! Wonderful, terrific, fantastic, great! Petronella Page kept running out of superlatives to fit the situation. And she'd come so close to missing the chance: a phone call she almost hadn't taken because she was so furious at having her apartment searched again – *another* house-to-house, the third in a month. Christ, you'd think they'd go look for Trainites where they hung out, in the slums!

And then she'd changed her mind because the name Peg Mankiewicz rang a faint bell, and *wow!* The real Austin Train! A man the nation – the world – had been crying out to hear from, who had hidden himself away for forty months and chosen *her* show to break his silence on. The research department had come up with that evocative figure, forty, and it was exact, and thanks to its Biblical associations it was pregnant but *pregnant* with overtones. Forty days the waters were upon the face of the earth, forty days in the wilderness tempted of Satan … 'Anyone would think you had Jesus on the show!' Ian Farley had said crossly at one point during the frantic pre-broadcast hassles.

'Yes.'

Which stopped him dead. Well, it was true that the crucifixion teams were ready and rehearsing, wasn't it? Not that she was going to let the guy be crucified the first time out. Ian had expected that she would, and it had taken two days to disabuse him and explain why to the Big Bosses in back of him. The crucifixion is for the *second* show – didn't you ever hear of the Right to Reply?

And are there ever going to be people who demand it!

Never in its history had ABS lavished this much attention on one single performer. Come to that, nor had Petronella. But it was essential that they actually put out the show. They'd asked their audience research unit two questions: how many people would watch the first show because they'd heard Train was on it, and how many would watch a second show because they'd seen the first or because they'd missed it?

The answer in both cases was an unbelievable sixty million.

Naturally, threats had started to flood in within minutes of the first spot announcement. They ranged from routine bomb scares to a warning that the studio would be occupied by armed volunteers and the show converted into a kangaroo court to try Austin Train for treason. So, against emergencies, they alerted every local studio they controlled within five hundred miles of New York, and set up extra landlines and line-of-sight links to their main transmitters, so that within half an hour of their deadline they would still have several options open. Then they scheduled the real show – Train had dismissed the idea of pre-recording – for a location they'd never used before, a derelict theater they'd bought for rehearsal space and were anyway intending to fit up before the fall season. Even the technicians installing mikes and cables didn't realize the place was going to be used for the crucial transmission. They only knew they were getting record wages.

But then there weren't many people in their trade nowadays.

'Sixty million, hm? I'm not surprised,' Train said, and that wasn't vanity. He had reasonable grounds. Sitting with Petronella in the high-security penthouse where the Big Bosses had immediately insisted on putting him – at their expense – when they learned he was staying in the same shoddy hotel as Peg Mankiewicz. She was behind and to one side of him, in almost literally the same place she had occupied ever since Petronella first met them. Like a bodyguard. Not a mistress; ABS had verified through their bugs that she slept alone and so did he. Small wonder, Petronella had thought once or twice. She had been dismayed to find what the man looked like now, bald and with those hideous scars on his scalp. Moreover, she found his statue-like composure repellent. He barely moved even his hands when he was talking like this, and refused to touch tobacco, pot, khat, anything stronger than beer or wine and very little of those.

Peg was extremely attractive. But the ABS researchers said she was straight.

Too bad. Petronella returned her attention to what Train was saying.

'It would have been different a few years ago. That size of audience would only have been available for a major public event such as a moon landing or the funeral of a celebrity who'd been assassinated. But now, of course, people so seldom go out. In the cities, because it's dangerous; in the country, because – well, what is there to go out for? The puritan backlash has closed half the movie theaters and most of the drive-ins, particularly where they were a major social center, and thanks to the fear of shortage people don't make more than one shopping trip a week because they keep enough in the house to see them through a siege. Yes, for most people nowadays television is their only contact with the world beyond their daily work.'

Ah. This could lead him on to lawnorder. Petronella baited her hook and cast it, and was rewarded.

'But the police encourage people to be afraid of them – in some cases, more afraid than they are of criminals. The intelligent ones among our young people catch the habit early and grow up with it. Recently, for example, I've seen a giant roundup of every man under thirty in a twenty-block area of Oakland. Most of them spent the night in a cell. No wonder there are twelve cities under martial law.'

'But if they're looking for draft dodgers, who are by definition criminals—'

'More exactly revolutionaries, whether they know it or not. Our society fosters criminals, as the blood of a sheep nourishes the ticks on its back;

indeed, they often find it more profitable past a certain point to conform rather than resist. The money made from bootlegging now finances Puritan, for instance, just as fortunes made from piracy ennobled many famous English families. But draft dodgers have opted out of this system, which has proved that it both demeans the individual and degrades his environment.'

Yum.

'Still, men who refuse to train in defense of their country—'

'No, that's not what an army trains men to do.'

She let him interrupt. This was one guest who wasn't going through the stock interrogation; let him convict himself out of his own mouth. He was doing a better job than she'd ever dreamed of.

'It's natural for a man to defend what's dear to him: his own life, his home, his family. But in order to make him fight on behalf of his rulers, the rich and powerful who are too cunning to fight their own battles – in short to defend not himself but people whom he's never met and moreover would not care to be in the same room with him – you have to condition him into loving violence not for the benefits it bestows on him but for its own sake. Result: the society has to defend itself from its defenders, because what's admirable in wartime is termed psychopathic in peace. It's easier to wreck a man than to repair him. Ask any psychotherapist. And take a look at the crime figures among veterans.'

Petronella was almost beside herself. So far, if this was a sample of what he planned to say during the actual show, he'd have managed to alienate both major political parties, the armed services, all the ex-service organizations except the bleeding heart Double-V, all big business interests, and the police along with everyone who still trusted them. (And possibly Puritan, one of her sponsors – but most of the Syndicate people she'd met were rather proud of their romantic gangster origins and didn't mind who knew about them.)

Oh, yes! This was going to be a *S*E*N*S*A*T*I*O*N*. She could almost see the big blue-and-red headlines which would appear the following day.

Memo to self: have extra phone lines rigged and hire extra operators to take the calls.

'So' – needling – 'what have you done to the people who call themselves Trainites, who kill and blow things up and generally behave like your description of an army, a horde of madmen?'

'Nothing. I am no more responsible for the actions of the Trainites than Jesus for the behavior of the Christians on whom Paul of Tarsus projected his personal neuroses.'

Add the churches to the list of people offended. Keep rolling, baby!

'So you don't approve of their sabotage and arson?'

'I don't approve of the situation that's driven people to such desperate measures. There is, however, such a thing as righteous anger.'

'You think their anger is righteous, when all that we can foresee beyond it is anarchy, nihilism, a world where every man's hand is turned against his brother?'

'Not against his brother. The man who's being poisoned by the additives Universal Mills put in his food knows who his brother is – a stranger, starving in Africa because a foolish war has destroyed his field of mealies. The brother of the man who has to waste half his income on treatment for a child who was born deformed is the peasant in Laos whose wife died aborting an egg-bundle fetus. No, not against his brother. Against the enemies of his species. That they also happen to be human – well, that's regrettable. Is a cancer cell in your lung or liver any more welcome for being tissue spawned from your own body?'

That, unexpectedly, touched her. She was afraid of cancer. Among the reasons she had never married was that she thought of pregnancy as a kind of malignant growth, an uncontrollable independent organism in her belly. She spoke harshly to drive away such thoughts,

'Then you advocate violence as a surgical operation.'

'The people who have brought it about have no more right to object to it than the long-time smoker has to object to cancer and bronchitis.'

'I'd say they have as much right to object as someone who's been promised surgery and discovers the local butcher doing the job,' Petronella retorted, quite pleased with the image. 'Hacking off an arm, a leg, a breast' – better not say that on the show! – 'and leaving the patient crippled ... Unless someone can offer superior alternatives, he has no right to interfere.'

'But there are superior alternatives,' Austin Train said.

Under those curious abridged brows sharp eyes fixed her. Suddenly the room seemed to recede to a great distance.

She had of course seen him both in person – at a major academic conference where he had been a featured speaker – and repeatedly on television during his spell of previous notoriety. Despite his baldness, she had already been sure he wasn't a fake even before the ABS researchers surreptitiously contrived to check his fingerprints against his FBI dossier – in other words, managed to bribe the right person. She recalled him as a forceful and witty speaker with a ready repartee and a penetrating voice. He had once, for example, put down a spokesman for the pesticide industry with a remark that people still quoted at parties: 'And I presume on the eighth day God called you and said, "I changed my mind about insects!"''

Up to now, he had confirmed this long-standing impression. Thousands of people, though, could be both articulate and outrageous, and if it was going to turn out that she'd allotted an entire show to a man who was no more than that ...

And then, all of a sudden, it was as though through those dark eyes an electrical circuit had been struck. She sat fascinated. Snake-and-bird fascinated. Afterwards she could not recall the details of what he had said. She remembered only that she had been absorbed, rapt, lost, for over ten minutes by the clock. She had perceived images conjured up from the dead past: a hand trailed in clear river water, deliciously cool, while the sun smiled and a shoal of tiny fishes darted between her fingers; the crisp flesh of a ripe apple straight from the tree, so juicy it ran down her chin; grass between her bare toes, the turf like springs so that she seemed not to bear the whole of her weight on her soles but to be floating, dreamlike, in slow motion, instantly transported to the moon; the western sky painted with vast heart-tearing slapdash streaks of red below the bright steel-blue of clouds, and stars coming snap-snap into view against the eastern dark; wind gentle in her hair and on her checks, bearing flower perfumes, dusting her with petals; snow cold to the palm as it was shaped into a ball; laughter echoing from a dark lane where only lovers walked, not thieves and muggers; butter like an ingot of soft gold; ocean spray sharp and clean as the edge of an axe; with the same sense of safe, provided rightly used; round pebbles polychrome beside a pool; rain to which a thirsty mouth could open distilling the taste of a continent of air ... And under, and through, and in, and around all this, a conviction: 'Something can be done to get that back!'

She was crying. Small tears like ants had itched their paths down her cheeks. She said, when she realized he had fallen silent, 'But I never knew that! None of it! I was born and raised right here in New York!'

'But don't you think you should have known it?' Austin Train inquired gently.

Petronella woke the morning of the show – or rather, afternoon, because her day was askew – with the muscles of her checks strained toward cramp; she had smiled so long and hard in her sleep.

Then it all stormed in on her: what they expected her to do tonight.

She sat up, afraid of drifting back to those tempting dreams, to that other impossible world where the ground was clean and the trees were green and the sun beamed down after the pure rain. She reached for a cigarette from the bedside shelf to distract herself, and instead of lighting it turned it over and over between her hands, frowning.

The present-day world was still here: the air on the Manhattan streets you breathed at your peril, the food in the Manhattan stores it was safer not to buy, the rain from the Manhattan sky that smirched a new dress in a moment and kept the dry-cleaners in business on wet days, the noise, the rush, and now and then a bang – an SST overshooting Kennedy, a saboteur taking revenge on a building, a policeman trying to stop a fleeing suspect.

Hell, she'd been conned. That *other* world could never have existed. It was simply a pipe-dream of paradise.

Though if Train's imagination could conjure up that kind of vision, it was small wonder he wouldn't touch drugs.

He didn't need them.

She reached finally for the phone and called Ian Farley, and said, 'Ian baby! I've been thinking. The people we need for the second show, the crucifixion …'

Yet, in spite of everything, the vision haunted her. As the echo of her regular greeting died away – 'Hi, world!' – and the star commercials of her sponsors went up on the monitor, she looked at them without her normal pride. Filtermasks? We evolved on this planet; why should we have to strain its air before we fill our lungs? Steam cars? Why cars at all? Ground is there to be walked on. A man, an athlete from England, had crossed North America on foot to show it could be done – and so, come to that, had relays of people protesting … something. (It had happened years ago and she had forgotten the reason. Likely something to do with a war that got aborted.)

And Puritan. She was worried about that account. Train had said in his simple dogmatic fashion that the Trainites were going to ruin them. It might be politic to dissociate from Puritan … though not until the current contract ran out. The Syndicate could be brutal.

She'd wanted to interview someone from the Denver wat that got burned. Of course, with Puritan as a sponsor she hadn't been able to—

And she should have been able to! Suddenly, in the space of less than a minute, she reversed all her decisions about the handling of the show tonight. He had come to take his place beside her, soberly dressed in green – well, it had to be, didn't it? And she was in sky-blue and white. Overtones, baby. And the backdrop: a panorama of a snowcapped mountain range for the first set, then a vast long palm-fringed beach, then a forest, then a rolling wheat-field …

Right! The hell with the crucifixion team. Their turn can be later. Much later. I want to know if that charisma of his *will* go across.

Because I shall never get another chance to find out.

She felt instantly calm, absolutely in control, whereas moments ago she had been more nervous than the first time she was allotted her own show. She looked up, not at the prompter, but at the audience, wondering how they would respond. Heaven only knew how many distinguished guests they had here tonight: in every row she seemed to recognize a dozen faces, ABS's own stars and several senior executives of the network, the entire group Body

English who were currently number one in the charts and Big Mama Prescott who was number three, a couple of academics, an author, a movie director, a fashion photographer, a psychoanalyst, an Olympic runner, the highest-paid call girl in New York …

She wanted to rub her hands as she thought of the admass out there, drawn to their TV sets by the twin compulsions of thirty spot announcements a day during the past week and the nationwide shortage of cash which always followed Labor Day.

A breath, not too deep, for the simple introduction she'd planned to consist of two words: 'Austin Train!'

And—

Like a physical wound. Like a stab penetrating her back just below her left shoulder-blade and entering her heart. Something not right. Something happening in the studio in full view of *how* many millions? Guards! Where the hell are those guards? Why did they let these three men in, who are tramping down the aisle and attracting everyone's attention? One in black, one in gray, one in blue.

They separated, black turning to right, gray to left, the leader in blue marching stolidly toward her, holding a large sheet of white paper with writing on it.

And spoke, before she could.

'Austin Train?'

'What?' she whispered, dazed by the interruption, incapable even of using the mike in the back of her chair to call Ian Farley.

'I am an agent of the Federal Bureau of Investigation,' the man said. He had a good voice; it carried right to the microphones in front of Petronella and Austin, which were live for the admass to hear them by.

'This is a warrant for your arrest on charges of complicity in the kidnapping of Hector Rufus Bamberley, a minor, and of conspiracy to deprive him of his civil rights, specifically his personal liberty and his good health, in that you connived at his infection with' – drawing himself up a little, conscious that some of the words he had to utter were not common fare on television – 'hepatitis, syphilis, gonorrhea and other dangerous diseases. I apologize for interrupting your show, Miss Page, but I am required to execute this arrest. Miss Page …?'

'I think Miss Page has fainted,' Austin said, rising and offering his wrists for the handcuffs.

Later, when she had been brought round, Ian Farley said furiously, 'Kidnapper! Torturer! Christ knows what else – murderer, maybe! And you were going to make a hero out of him! Don't deny it! I could see it in your eyes!'

TO NAME BUT A FEW

Opaque and pale as tissue paper the sky overlay America.

Everywhere the voices of people saying in a doubtful tone, 'But it didn't use to be like this, did it?'
And others saying with scorn, 'Don't give me that shit about the Good Old Days!'

The mental censors rewriting history, not through rose-colored glasses, but gray ones.

Reading, as you might say, from the top down:

Dead satellites.
Discarded first and second stages of rockets, mainly second.
Fragments of vehicles which exploded in orbit.
Experimental material, e.g. reflective copper needles.

Combustion compounds from rocket exhausts.
Experimental substances intended to react with stratospheric ozone, e.g.
    sodium.
Very light radioactive fallout.

CO_2.
Aircraft exhaust.
Medium fallout.
Rainmaking compounds.

Smoke.
Sulphur dioxide.
Lead alkyls.
Mercaptans and other bad smells.

Car exhausts.
Locomotive exhausts.

More smoke.
Local fallout.
Products accidentally vented from underground nuclear tests.

Oceanic fluorine.
Nitric acid.
Sulphuric acid.

Sewage.
Industrial effluents.
Detergents.

Selenium and cadmium from mine tailings.
Fumes from garbage incinerators burning plastic.
Nitrates, phosphates, fungicidal mercuric compounds from 'compacted soils'.

Oil.
Oil-derived insecticides.
Defoliants and herbicides.
Radioactives from aquifers contaminated by underground explosions, chiefly tritium.

Lead, arsenic, oil-well sludge, fly ash, asbestos.
Polyethylene, polystyrene, polyurethane, glass, cans.
Nylon, dacron, rayon, terylene, stylene, orlon, other artificial fibers.

Scrap.
Garbage.
Concrete and cement.
A great deal of short-wave radiation.
Carcinogens, teratogens and mutagens.
Synergistic poisons.
Hormones, antibiotics, additives, medicaments.
Drugs.

Solanine, oxalic acid, caffeine, cyanide, myristicin, pressor armnes, copper sulphate, dihydrochalcones, naringin, ergot.
Botulinus.

Mustard gas, chlorine, Leuisite, phosgene, prussic acid.
T, Q, GA, GB, CID, GE, GF, VE, VX, CA, CN, CS, DM, PL, BW, BZ.

CO.
– to name but a few.

CONSPECTUS

Philip Mason in his office at Prosser Enterprises: burdened with work that had occupied him clear through the holiday weekend, just about getting on top of it, but bothered since a few days ago with this slight but recurrent ache in the joints, especially the knees and ankles. At the edge of his awareness a scrap of information gathered during his brush with the clap: among the minor symptoms are aches in the joints.

But Doug gave me a clean bill of health. Let it not, please not, be arthritis! At thirty-two? (Well, coming up to thirty-three …)

'Brothers and sisters, we are gathered together in the sight of the Lord and the presence of our friends to mourn the passing of Thich Van Quo, whom so many of you knew as Thad. Though, through no fault of his own, he was so grievously afflicted in body, he endeared himself to us all by his geniality, good nature and long-suffering spirit. We hoped that he might spend long among us, but it was not to be.'

Ah, shit, another gate guard gone sick. Which of 'em this time, and complaining of what? (Not that it made much odds. Most likely a hangover, as usual.)

'You're Mrs Laura Vincent? Sit down, please. Well, as you certainly know, there's an ordinance in the State of Nevada which requires that any person against whom a complaint has been recorded concerning the transmission of a social disease must be compulsorily hospitalized, and in your case I'm sorry to say we have five.'

PRESCRIPTION

Mr/Mrs/Miss/child   *Felice Vaughan*   (patient)

.... (address)

Rx 30 caps. Salveomycin x 250 mg. 4 per diem
                              Squiggle   (doctor)

HALKIN – *In loving memory of Roger, Belinda and Teddy, victims of a cruel and unprovoked attack by a maniac on this our beloved country. RIP.*

In his office at the Bamberley Trust Building (it still had an unmended crack across the ceiling, but that wasn't relevant): Tom Grey, cursing. He was seldom a profane man. But there was a painful whitlow on his right forefinger, and it had just caused him – for the eighth or ninth time today – to mis-hit a crucial key on the computer reading he was using.

*

Dear Mr Chalmers: Enclosed please find our check for $14,075.23 in respect of your claim against this company concerning the regretted demise of your son William. The delay in settlement is regretted but recurrent illness has handicapped our staff in recent months.

'Angie? Denise here. Is Doug—? … Yes, of course, it must be awful for him right now. But if he's going to be in his office this afternoon? … Fine. Nothing serious, no. Just this headache, and nausea with it … Yes, but I never suffered from migraine in my life.'

Rioting at New Fillmore East. Body English didn't show for their scheduled concert. Acute pharyngitis.

'Master Motor Mart, good morning … No, I'm afraid he's in the hospital. He got badly burned when the Trainites bombed us.'

NANETTE'S BEAUTY CENTER:
CLOSED UNTIL FURTHER NOTICE.

In the Prosser warehouse: Pete Goddard with acid indigestion. Doubtless due to worry. He hadn't felt it right to bother Doc McNeil what with the typhus outbreak. So he just kept gulping tablets from the box he'd bought at the drugstore, Anti … something.

'Ah, shit! Okay, here you are – *another* pack of filters!'

Thank you for your recent letter addressed to Mr Stacy. Unfortunately Mr Stacy died in 1974. No doubt our present managing director, Mr Schwartz, will be pleased to deal with your inquiry directly he returns from Mexico. However, we have just learned he is indisposed and will not be well enough for the trip before the end of the month.

INTESTACY: – *Stanway, Brian Alderson, B.Med.* Any person having a claim against the estate of the above-named should at once contact …

In her sleazy hotel room: Peg Mankiewicz, boiling mad and saying so by way of her typewriter. Bare to the waist for the heat and resenting even the panties she had on because it was her period.

Bad this month. Funny. Mostly she got off lightly, but this was the ninth day of bleeding. Some time soon she ought to see a gynecologist. Right now, though, painkillers. She had urgent work.

They were holding Train incommunicado. Of course they denied it – said he himself was refusing to see or talk to anyone, even a lawyer. Dirty liars!

(Though of course if the shock had caused a recurrence of his former trouble, a second and more severe breakdown ...)

No. They were lying. She was convinced, and had to say so loudly to anyone who would listen. Half the country was already of that opinion anyway.

Now and then, when she broke off from the typewriter, she scratched the inflamed spot on her left wrist.

'Zena, honey! Zena! ... Oh, God. How much longer before that stinking doctor gets here?'

IN MEMORIAM ISAIAH JAMES PRICE WILLIAMS, BORN 1924 IN CARDIGANSHIRE, WALES, FOULLY MURDERED IN GUANAGUA, HONDU (Remainder deleted. By a mortar shell.)

... as well as can be expected, according to his personal medical attendants. Unofficially, the president is said to be suffering from ...

Esteemed Señor: While we appreciate that the situation in your country is currently very difficult, we must now INSIST on an answer to our letters of May 2, June 3, July 19 and August 11. It was our son Leonard's special wish that he should be interred in our family vault if anything awful happens to him.

'These cramps are killing me! You've got to give me another shot or I can't make tonight's show.'

'You won't make it if I do give you another shot, Miss Page. You might very well fall asleep on camera.'

Three hundred and sixty thousand fans turned out in Nashville for the funeral of Big Mama Prescott, dead in New York of pneumonia aggravated by extreme obesity.

'Next! ... Ah, hell, you again, Train! A'right, sit down and hit me with some more of your jawbreaking words. Me, I'm just a poor ignorant prison doctor! What's given you the collywobbles this time? Something else about jail your delicate constitution can't—? Hey! Get up! I said GET UP – that's an ORDER!'

'Hey! Nurse! Quick!'

An American Hero: Jacob Bamberley.....................33
  A *Personal Account of his Last Days, by Gaylord T. Elliott*
  (Reprinted from *Colorado Patriot*)

*

In a Howard Johnson's which still bore the scars of a recent price riot: Hugh Pettingill. Even without his mask, which he wished he didn't have to take off to eat because the stench here was pretty bad, the plaster he wore to protect the weeping sores around his mouth disguised his features. Nonetheless he kept glancing anxiously around as he forced down the hotcakes which were the only item available from the menu today.

The coffee was awful. Probably wasn't coffee at all. Since the *jigras*, they said in lots of places it was burnt corn kernels or even acorns.

Another two or three mouthfuls and he'd be on his way. Not too soon. Christ, if only the car held out …

FOLLOWING THE REGRETTED DEMISE OF
THE PRESIDENT OF THE ANGEL CITY INTERSTATE
MUTUAL INSURANCE CORPORATION DEALINGS
IN THE STOCK OF THE COMPANY ARE HEREBY
SUSPENDED UNTIL TUESDAY NEXT.

Name:	BURKHARDT Baird Tolliver
Address:	2202 S. Widburn
Grounds for claiming:	DECEASED (heart failure)
Person receiving benefit:	Widow
(* If not above-named)	

Darling Lucy! It's so long since I heard from you! I know this isn't exactly the best place in the world for postal services, but it's among the few highlights of a two-year tour here when the mail plane comes skidding in. Do please write to me soon. I look forward every day to seeing you when I come back to Auckland, away from this eternal polar whiteness.

IN RE: Dependents of OBOU, Hippolyte (Major), *aet. 24, deceased* Noshri, *verdict* shot.

RULED: Unentitled to pension, death not having occurred on active service.

'What's your name? … Please, I'm trying to help you! Name! Who you? *Name!*'

'Maua! You want screw, soldier man? Twenty-five francs one time, hundred francs all night, baby!'

'Oh, God. She's off her rocker like the rest of them. Here, someone get— Hey, let go, you little bitch! *Hey!*'

THIS IS THE LAST WILL AND TESTAMENT OF ME BERTIL OLAV SVENSSON ordinarily resident at 45 Vasasagatan, Malmö, who, being of

sound mind and not having sampled or tasted or ingested poisoned food at·
Noshri (contrary to rumor) but having diagnosed in myself a strain of tra-
choma resistant to all known therapy which will inevitably make me blind,
do purpose to terminate my life. I DEVISE AND BEQUEATH ...

'Christ,' he said. And repeated, 'Christ! It's as if the world is just ...'

'Crumbling?' she offered, and when he didn't disagree, gave a nod. She
hadn't looked his way. She was watching the tanks and armored cars closing
in on the food rioters. A stray rock had starred the window, but they'd fixed
that with adhesive tape to keep out the street air.

'But I can't go to the House with a – a fucking *tube* stuck up me!' Howell
barked.

'Yes, I know that,' the doctor sighed. 'But would you rather live to be governor or die in two weeks?'

'It's that bad?'

'Senator, you try going without a pee for a day or two, see if you prefer the
catheter or not.'

'What the hell is it due to, anyhow?'

'I don't know. Sorry. I'm waiting for the lab report, but they're taking anything up to ten days.'

*Command of the armed forces was today assumed by Colonel Joku Amnibadu,
following the indisposition of General Kaika. It's understood that Brigadier
Plitso, widely tipped as the heir apparent, is in Switzerland for a medical
examination.*

Washing the windshield of her – their – car: Jeannie Goddard. Taking Pete to
work this morning the wipers hadn't coped with the greasy deposit left by the
last rain. And she wanted to see her way clearly to the prenatal clinic. Find
out whether this constant nausea was to be endured, or needed treatment.

But the size of the bill already ...

Well, it was for the baby's sake, after all, not just her own.

'Oh, nothing to worry about, Mrs Mason. A very common thing these days,
this blepharitis, nothing at all to do with your little girl's strabismus. Why, I
must have seen twenty or thirty similar cases in the past month. Now I'll give
you a note for your own doctor – isn't it Dr McNeil? – and ...'

'The number you have reached is not a working number. Please hang up and—'

...

'The number you have reached is not—'

253

...

'The number you have—'

...

'Operator, can I help you? ... Yes, sir, but you must appreciate we're very short of staff right now ... Well, sir, what is the problem? I have lots of other – Can you spell that? ... H-E-N-L ... Henlowe. Yes, sir, just a moment. Ah, here it is. All calls to that number are being referred to— What was that? ... Well, sir, on the memo I have here it says her sister is looking after their little girl until they come out of the hospital ... I don't know, sir, but the memo is dated – I'm sorry? ... You're welcome.' You son of a bitch!

In his office at his handsome antique desk: Dr Clayford. The phone rang.

'Hello? ... No, I will not accept a call from my wife! Tell her to wait until I'm done with my morning appointments. She knows she mustn't bother me at work.'

He slammed down the phone and looked toward the door, trying to discern who the next patient was. But the features blurred, and there was this discomfort at the corner of his right eye.

Funny.

Seems to be swimming.

And that damned noise. Got to complain to the police about—

'Doctor? Doctor!'

That hurt. Nose and cheekbone. Symptoms consistent with ...

'Nurse, I think the doctor's passed out.'

In his magnificent office, Roland Bamberley signing a letter to his lawyers concerning the faults so far found in the Mitsuyama water-purifiers and requesting advice on the possibility of a suit for breach of contract. He broke off after the Christian name because his arm had developed cramp all of a sudden. He shook it, and continued: Bam—

Again, without warning, the agonizing pain. He looked at his hand grasping the pen and saw with surprise how white the fingers were. Experimentally, he flexed them. The pen fell on the paper and left a long black streak; the letter would now have to be retyped.

But he couldn't feel his fingers, only the cramp.

He raised his left hand and began to massage his right one. A minute passed; so did the pain.

'Leave that ball alone! It's Rick's!'

'What? Ah, shit, I know it *was* Rick's, but like Zena said he's gone away and he won't be coming—'

'He is *so* coming back! Let go that ball – that's right! Now I'll put it back where you found it, so when Rick comes here he'll find all his things waiting nice and neat ... I don't like you!'

Shouldn't have tried washing that foot in sea water, Tab thought. But when you tread on a nail sticking out of a piece of board that runs its rusty spike clear through your shoe, and you can't afford to go to a clinic ...

He forced himself to forget about the pain and the swelling and the nasty wetness of the pus. Another passer-by was turning the corner. He hobbled forward.

'Say, friend, can you spare a—?'

'No!'

THINGS AROUND HERE JUST AREN'T THE SAME WITHOUT YOU. WE ACTUALLY GET SOME WORK DONE!

Only kidding! Best wishes to Mel for a quick recovery from the gang at the office.

Dear Sergeant Tatum:

I'm pleased to advise you that in view of your length of service you are to be granted 48 per cent of your eventual pension. I honestly wish it could have been more, but naturally you'll appreciate there is a necessary distinction between injury in the line of duty which entails premature retirement, and the contraction of a disease, even one as severe as polio.

(On wall after wall after wall, from California to Nova Scotia, painted or scrawled or chalked or even carved, the same slogan accompanied by the same device: STOP, YOU'RE KILLING ME! ♀.)

'In place of the advertised program, regrettably postponed owing to the indisposition of key staff members at our New York studios, we're giving you another chance to see ...'

Terry Fenton? Septicemia. (Something got into a self-inflicted cut while he was razor-styling Petronella's hair. She quit going to Guido's the third time there was something awful in the water.)

Ian Farley? Bronchitis. (He'd left his filtermask at home, all the dispensers in the lobby of the ABS Building were empty, and it was a long time before be found a cab.)

Lola Crown? Earache and swollen parotid glands. (It won't yield to the standard therapy for mononucleosis, so maybe it isn't mono at all. They took her off antibiotics. Sulfa drugs might turn the trick, with luck.)

Marlon? Alternating between Terry's bedside and the can. (Convinced the doctor tending him is useless, because he makes such nasty remarks about his – uh – hemorrhoids. Oughtn't to be allowed to practice medicine if he won't help people in real pain. Wish he could feel that acid diarrhea going out!)

And others, from the Big Bosses right on down.

Same as everywhere.

'Mr Greenbriar, look. Uh – would you have any objection to a *male* secretary? We've tried every agency in town, and – I'm sorry? ...

'An out-of-work actor, sir. Stranded by the cutback in programs at ABS ...

'Oh, highly recommended, sir ... Yes, sir. Which ones are those – the blue pills, or the green ones?'

Name (s):	MURPHY Phelan Augustine
	MURPHY Bridget Ann née O'Toole
Address:	'West Farm', nr. Balpenny,
	Co. Waterford, Eire.

APPLICATION FOR ADMISSION TO UNITED KINGDOM: REFUSED

The priest looked doubtfully at the vast bluish bruises on his forearms. Then he hauled up the skirts of his habit to inspect those on his legs. They were just as bad.

Why wouldn't these Satan-serving Tupas go ahead and hang him, as they'd hanged the American, Hannigan, and the major?

Oh, of course. The Tupas had gone away. He'd forgotten.

Since they left, many people in the prison-camp had talked about going home. Somehow they hadn't done anything about it. Several of them had simply lain down and not moved again. All with these dark marks under the skin, many with bleeding mouths, too.

Something to do with food. The Tupas had said something. But one would not take advice from servants of the devil.

Then he saw a mosquito and weakly made to swat it, and missed, and after that he couldn't quite recall what he'd been thinking about.

Entering his office after a call at the hospital, where they had trouble with blocked filters again: Alan Prosser.

'Dorothy! What in hell's happened to your eye? It's all swollen!'

'Just a sty,' Dorothy said wryly. 'My own fault. I washed at the sink when my filter was out. Got something in the root of an eyelash. Come to that, you're not looking so good yourself.'

'No, I'm a bit bilious. Can't seem to keep any food in my belly these past few days. I'll go see Doug this afternoon. Or maybe tomorrow. Christ, is that my mail? It's six inches high!'

'Dr Farquhar? ... Oh, morning, Alec. This is Angie McNeil. Look, Doug's laid up with a mild bout of' – cough – 'so sorry!' – cough, cough, COUGH – 'oh, *dear!* ... No, no, nothing serious, Doug's given me something already, just the dust, I guess ... But what I was calling about: Doug has all these patients in the hospital and ... Oh, blast!' Cough cough cough, COUGH. 'Sorry! ... What? Mervyn got to you already? Damn. Well, do you know' – cough, cough, cough cough, COUGH – 'Sorry! Do you know a good source of what-you-call-'ems around Denver – locums?' Cough. 'Are you sure? No one at all? Doug thought maybe a medical officer at the Air Force Academy ... They what? Are you putting me on? Mumps? Oh, Christ. How long is the quarantine going to last?'

(As though a bucket of sand had been thrown into a complex machine. This year, so many of the people who matter out of circulation, even if only for a week or two, and so many more – millions more – working far below their peak. On the Stock Exchange, dealings suspended in Angel City, Bamberley Trust Corporation, Plant Fertility, Puritan Health Supermarkets ... and others.)

'Lady, I don't care if they're crawling up your cunt, you understand? I have thirty-five more calls to make before I get around to *your* rats!'

The use of the fine house had been assigned to Maud Bamberley during her lifetime, but Jacob had omitted to provide adequate funds to support it, her, and the remaining children. Querulous on the last morning before departure, she rang her bell for Christy. But it was Ethel the cook who answered, limping a little for the verrucae in her right heel. (She'd come to ask advice about them yesterday, but the sight was too disgusting; Maud had told her to wait for Dr Halpern to call again, forgetting that they were compelled to move from here.)

'Christy's sick, ma'am,' Ethel said. 'It's her lungs, I guess. She wheezing all the time.'

'Where is she?' Maud demanded. 'In bed?'

'No, ma'am. She seeing to Mister Noel. He done wetted himself again.'

Dear Jesus. Dear sweet kind loving Jesus. Maud gathered the silk sheets of her bed into a bundle on her left arm and began to croon to it.

Dr Halpern had to come after all, despite his palpitations (since about two weeks ago), and the moving gang went away without anything; perhaps as well because they were eight men under their scheduled strength of fourteen.

Cornelius went with the empty van – it was deemed advisable to hospitalize him what with his rash, his blocked sinuses and his non-stop trembling. Claude was pretty well okay. His broken wrist, three weeks old, was healing nicely considering his inability to metabolize calcium properly.

But Maud had to be given an injection, and when Ronald came to him all adult, as the oldest male in the house and the father of Christy's baby (not yet known to Maud), demanding information, the doctor did not feel justified in offering a favorable prognosis.

Christy's child was about three months gone when she miscarried it from brucellosis. Just as well. Mongoloid. She was forty.

'Honestly, Mrs Byrne, I don't know how Dr Advowson coped – no, no, don't move your head, just hold still … There! That'll do the trick, though it'll smart for a while. Very nasty, these furuncles, especially to someone like yourself – if you'll forgive my saying so – with a generous growth of facial hair. Put the ointment on night and morning!'

Running water into the sink, reaching for the antiseptic soap.

'Sad about little Eileen, wasn't it? Tetanus is a terrible disease.'

Cause of death: Inhalation of vomitus (while intoxicated)
Name of deceased: CLARK—

'Brian, do you spell that name with or without an E at the end?'

'Without. Was it the drink that did for him, then?'

'It was indeed. Trying to drown his sorrows and somebody taught them to swim.'

Before the shrine of his honorable ancestors: Mr Hideki Katsamura. In his right hand the necessary knife. About his body the correct silk – strictly, dacron – robe. No respectable alternative, following announcement of suit impending from California where Mr R. Bamberley had so much difficulty with water-purifiers. Also in Colorado Illinois, New York and Texas.

Place to aim for would be site of ulcer reputed doctor, friend of family, warned yesterday will perforate and cause marked physiological mishap within short time.

In company of ancestors conceivably not burdened with ulcerable intestines.

Arriegas! That name is one in our minds with those of Guevara, Uñil, and other great heroes of the continuing revolution, struck down by the foul agents of the imperialist conspiracy!

*

OWING TO THE INDISPOSITION OF PROFESSOR DUVAL
THE FOLLOWING CLASSES WILL NOT BE HELD, VIZ ...

'Yes, this is Moses Greenbriar ... Oh, how is she? ... Cystitis? Is that
serious?'

... ascribed to the continuing shortage of manpower. Many local police forces ...

(The sound of creaking, as when a tree grows old and can no longer endure
the thrashing of the gale.)

Of all the damned silly things, Carl thought, lying out on a hillside under
bushes to wait for dark and his chance to elude the Colorado border patrols.
Hiccoughs! And he couldn't stop them. They must have been going on for
hours.

After being angry he had started to be afraid. They were making him so
tired.

Name of Patient:	YOUNG Sylvia June (Miss)
Address:	c/o UN
Ward:	B
Diagnosis:	Alcoholic poisoning

'Doug?'

'Yes, honey?'

'I don't want to worry you, but I've tried to get through to Millicent at least
a dozen times, and there's no reply. Do you think I ought to run over there
and see how she is?'

DURING THE INDISPOSITION OF MR BOLLINGER
THE FOLLOWING TEMPORARY RE-ALLOCATION
OF RESPONSIBILITIES ...

'This will clear it up in a few days, Mr Cowper. It's a very effective vermifuge,
this. I imagine it must have been badly-cured pork that caused the trouble.
I've had a number of cases of trichinosomiasis lately.'

*Owing to the indisposition of the Reverend Horace Kirk, joint services will be
held at ...*

'Where the hell is that black bastard? He should have been here two hours
ago! I can't hang around all night!'

'He called in to say his wife's died.'

'Oh, Christ. Who's going to let people in the building, then? I can't do his tour as well as my own!'

'Mom?' And then, louder: 'Mom!'

The kid advanced slowly on the still dark form in the untidy bed. A fly was buzzing against the shut window, trying to get in, against its own interests because there was a flystrip hanging right over the bed. Also on the seat of the chair that doubled for a bedside table, there were the usual sleeping pills.

The boy said again, 'Mom!' This time the word peaked into a cry.

Who takes advice from a garbage-man?

'Sorry, Mr President, Mr Penwarren isn't in today. His doctor told him to take the rest of the week off ... No, nothing serious, I understand. Something he ate disagreed with him.'

FOR SALE: A substantial holding of 3241 ½ acres down to vegetables between Bockville and Candida, formerly operated by Mr Lem Walbridge, together with the farmhouse (18 rooms, 2 baths, good structural condition), various outbuildings, all necessary plant and equipment including late-model tractors (6), cultivating and spraying machinery ...

In a back room at a friend's pad: Ossie. He was making bombs. Now and then he paused to scratch his crotch. He had urticaria, and so did the friend, and so did everybody around here this month. It was the in disease. But those mothers mustn't be allowed to get away with arresting Austin Train on a false charge in plain sight of sixty million people.

NOTICE OF POSTING: Col. Rollo B. Saddler
From: Wickens Army Base, Col.
To: Active service in Honduras.
WITH IMMEDIATE EFFECT your unit is reassigned to ...

Fritz and his friends were among the Sixty-Three. (One capitalizes the number now. Martyrs.)

'Mr Steinitz? Sorry, he's not in the office. He's unwell. So's his deputy. We had this leak in the ventilating pipes, you know, and some of these here spores got loose and they breathed them in. Kind of nasty!'

To all patients of Dr David Halpern:

Please note that until further notice your physician will be Dr Monty B. Murray, at the Flowerwood Memorial Hospital.

Shivering and coughing, Cindy allowed them to undress her. When they found the skull and crossbones on her body they told her to get out of the clinic before she was thrown out.

'You'll be up and about in a day or two, Hector my boy! And then we'll fix that devil Austin Train for good and all.'

Chuck in prison hospital; his forged ID let him down at last. The male nurses making a lot of jokes about his being yellow.
    Jaundice.

Dear Mrs Barleyman: It is my sad duty to inform you that your husband is unlikely to be well enough to return home in the foreseeable future.

'Kitty Walsh? Sit down. I have bad news, but I'm afraid it's your own fault. You should never have let it go on so long. You have acute salpingitis – that's inflammation of the Fallopian tubes, from the ovaries to the womb. You'll never be able to have a baby.'
    'What you mean, bad news? Who'd want to bring a baby into this filthy world?'

MEMORANDUM
    From: Dr Elijah Prentiss
    To: Hospital director
    Owing to this damned fibrositis, I shall not be able to ...

Drew Henker and Ralph Henderson, like the majority of Trainites, had willed their bodies for medical teaching purposes. But they turned out not to be required by any hospital in the state. All of them had as many gunshot wounds as they needed.

'Harold? Harold, where are you? ... Oh, there.' Painkillers had helped Denise's migraine, a little, and she'd dozed off. Waking in alarm she wondered what had become of the children. But it was okay; Josie was lying down, and Harold was sitting in the corner of his bedroom, quite quiet, his bad leg tucked under him as usual.
    'Harold darling, it's about time you ... Harold?'
    He just sat there, staring at nothing.
    He was the first.

THE IMAGE

is of a house: large, old, once very beautiful, built by someone whose imagination matched his skills. But he squandered his substance and fell on evil times. Sublet and then again sublet, the house became infested as though by vermin with occupants who felt no sense of attachment to its fabric, and were prepared to complain forever without themselves accepting responsibility for its upkeep.

Thus from a distance it may be seen that the roof is swaybacked like a standard whale. Certain of the slates were cracked in a long-ago hurricane and not repaired; under them wood has warped and split. A footstep, be it never so light – as of a toddling child – will cause the boards anywhere on any floor to shift on their joists, uttering creaks.

Also the basement is noisome. It has been flooded more than once. The foundations have settled. A stench permeates the air, testimony to generations of drunks who pissed where the need overtook them. There is much woodworm. Closets and cupboards have been shut for years because inside there are the fruiting bodies of the dry-rot fungus, and they stink. The grand staircase is missing a tread about halfway to the noble gallery encircling the entrance hall. One or two of the ancestral portraits remain, but not many; the majority have been sold off, along with the marble statues that once graced the front steps. The coach-house is dank and affords crowded lodging for a family of mentally sub-normal children, orphaned, half-clad, filthy and incestuous. There are fleas.

The lawn is covered with wind-blown rubbish. The goldfish that used to dart among the lily-pads in the ornamental pond were seen to float, belly-up and bloated, one spring following a winter of hard frosts; now they are gone. The graveled driveway is obscured with dandelions and docks. The gates at the end of it have been adrift from their hinges for far longer than anyone can remember, half rusted through. So too the doors within the house, if they haven't been chopped into firewood.

More than half the windows have been broken, and hardly any have been made good. The rest are blocked with rags, or have had bits of cardboard tacked over them.

In the least damaged wing the owner, in an alcoholic haze, conducts delightful conversations with imaginary ambassadors and dukes. Meantime, those of the other inhabitants who know how to write pen endless letters to the government, demanding that someone come and fix the drains.

SPASM

Later, they mapped the earliest cases on the western side of Denver, around Arvada, Wheat Ridge, Lakewood and other districts which had exploded during the past few years. To meet an almost doubled demand for water, which Denver was already sucking from a vast area of thousands of square miles by a piping system as complex and random-seeming as the taproots of a tree, the lakes and reservoirs were no longer adequate: Ralston, Gross, Granby, Carter, Lonetree, Horsetooth …

So they had drilled, and sunk pipes to deep porous strata, and moreover carved great gashes into the rock of the mountains to expose the edges of those strata. The principle was this: when the snow melts, vast quantities of water run off and go to waste. If we draw on the water-table under the mountains, thus making room for more, we must arrange that every spring melting snow will soak into the porous rock and replenish the supply.

It had been new last year. It had worked fairly well, bar the teething troubles which occurred when one of the newly-tapped aquifers proved to be contaminated with sewage. That led to the issuing of don't-drink notices now and then. There had been a few complaints, too, that Boulder Creek and the Thompson and Bear Creek had been even lower this summer than they should have been – but those came only from people with long memories, not from the wealthy new arrivals who had abandoned the old boom state of California for the new boom state of Colorado.

Now, today …

Black Hawk: Giddy, the owner of a newly-built house with a magnificent view fumbled out a cigarette, felt for his lighter, couldn't find it, used a match instead. It fell from his shaking hand onto the day's newspaper. He watched the flame take to the edge of the paper, fascinated. It spread – beautiful, how beautiful! All yellow and gold and orange, centered with black, like a moving flower!

He started to laugh. It was so lovely. He picked up the paper and threw it at a rug to see if that would burn too, and it did, and so, not long afterwards, did he.

Towerhill: 'Mom,' the little boy said in a serious tone, 'I hate you.' And pushed the butcher-knife he'd brought into her belly.

US 72: 'The more we are together, together, together!' sang the driver of the Thunderbird bowling at ninety toward Denver, to the air of *Ach Du Lieber Augustin*, 'the more we are together the happier we'll be! For your friends are my friends and—'

Caught sight of a pretty girl in the next car ahead and jammed on the brakes as he drew alongside and crowded her off the road so he could say hello and kiss her and share his ecstatic happiness.

There was a culvert. Concrete. Crash.

Golden: Luxuriating in the deep warm bath, she sipped and sipped at the tall julep she'd brought with her, the ice-cubes making a melodious jingle as they melted. She was there about an hour and a half, listening to the radio, humming, and at one point masturbating because she had a very special date this afternoon. Eventually, when the glass was empty, she lay back and let the water close over her face.

Wheat Ridge: He struggled and struggled with the faulty TV, and still the picture wouldn't come right. It was all wavy and the colors bled into one another.

As time passed, though, he realized that in fact this was much prettier than regular TV. He sat down before the set and stared at it sometimes chuckling when one of the faces turned green or bright blue. Unthinking, he put his hand to his mouth, meaning childlike to suck his thumb. He happened to be holding a test lead connected to the power.

Sss ...

Thump.

Arvada: Time to start dinner, damn it, or my stinking husband will – and the kid bawling again, and ...

Absently, her mind on the TV she'd spent the afternoon watching, she bundled up the baby and put him in the oven and set the thermostat, and went back to her chair cradling the chicken.

That stopped his racket. Sure did!

Westminster: 'You stinking white bastard,' the black man said, and swung his wrench at the man behind the counter. After that, he sat down and began to stuff his mouth with odds and ends: candy, aspirin, chocolate bars, indigestion tablets. Sometimes he dipped them in the blood from the clerk's head, to improve the color.

Lakewood: Hey, man, wowowow! I never had pot like this before. This is a high – I mean *H*I*I*I*G*H*!!! Ho-ho! I feel light, like I could fly, I mean like I am flying I mean like I'm not even on the floor already just bobbing around in the draught from that fan there WOW! But these four lousy walls in the way – get in the open, enjoy it more, they keep coming and banging up against me, where's the door? Door. Window closer. Open it. Fall out on the wind and just blow away across the mountains, wow.

Four stories from the street, which was hard.
Denver ...

FIT

'Alan-n-n-n!'

It was Pete's voice, from the warehouse. Philip broke off in mid-sentence and looked at Alan and Dorothy. They were having a kind of council of war to review the firm's financial situation. It wasn't good. Replacements under guarantee had wiped out about a third of their expected income and screwed up most of the regular plumbing business they were still carrying on. The only good news was bad: Bamberley in California had hit the same trouble and they expected to mount a joint suit against Mitsuyama. Outcome, in about eighteen months with luck ...

It was another close, clammy, hot day with dense overcast, so the door was open for what breeze might be around and they'd heard shouts and banging noises from the warehouse, but paid no attention. People's tempers always frayed in weather like this.

'That sounds bad!' Alan snapped, and headed for the door. The others followed. Down the corridor separating the administrative section from the—

'It's Mack!' Pete shouted. 'He's gone crazy!'

They stopped, crowded into the doorway of the warehouse: strutted shelves full of cartoned parts, mostly the filters in green and red boxes with Japanese characters on the end. At the door of his cubbyhole office, wood and glass about ten feet on a side, Pete, his face agonized, clinging to the jamb for support because his cane was out of reach. Lying on the floor a yard away. Philip grabbed it, gave it back, steadied him and felt him shaking. From out of sight behind a barrier of shelving came noises: things being dragged down and flung aside.

'What happened?' Alan rasped.

'He – he came in a few minutes ago without his helper,' Pete forced out, panting so violently he could hardly spare the breath for speech. 'Yelled something to me about black mothers thinking they own this place, and went storming down there and started smashing things!'

'Anybody else around?' Philip demanded.

'Nobody! It's four o'clock, so the fitters are still out, and I sent Gladys home. She's sick – tonsilitis.'

'Dorothy, call the pigs,' Philip said. She nodded and ran back along the passage.

'But we can't just let him go on!' Alan snapped. 'Where is he?'

'Here I am!' Mack shouted. 'Peek-a-boo!'

He forced apart the two top cartons of a pile about six feet tall, at the end of an aisle between the shelving, and leered at them. He was a big man with broad shoulders. His face gleamed with perspiration.

'And jigaboo, too!' he added. 'You get that filthy nigger out of my hair or I'll wreck everything in the place!'

'Mack—!'

Alan took a step forward, but in the same instant Mack pitched the cartons to the floor, crash-crash, and there were little crunching noises as the brittle plastic shells of a dozen purifiers broke. Then he started to stamp on the pile. He weighed a good hundred and sixty, maybe eighty.

'You bastard, stop that!' Alan roared.

Mack curled his lip and seized something from the nearest shelf and threw it. Alan ducked. It smashed the glass of Pete's office. Mack giggled like a three-year-old child and went on pounding the cartons to pulp. After a moment or two he started to sing in rhythm.

'I'm – the king – o' the castle! Go wipe – y'r fucking – asshole!'

'He's really crazy,' Philip whispered, feeling as though all the blood had drained from his head to his legs, making his brain sluggish and his feet lead-heavy.

'Yes.' Alan wiped his face. 'Go get my gun. Know where I keep it?'

'Yes.'

But as Philip turned, he almost bumped into Dorothy running back.

'Phil, the line's dead! And I've seen fires – all over the place! Half the downtown section is ablaze!'

The three of them froze: Pete, Philip, Alan. They recalled suddenly things heard during the past half-hour – fire sirens, police sirens, shots. But one was always hearing those, all day, in any big city!

Mack, meantime, went on happily trampling those cartons flat. Now and then he dragged more down to add to the pile.

'Are we at war?' Alan said slowly. It was the thought in all their minds.

'I got a radio in there,' Pete said, pointing into his office now bright with shards of glass.

Philip rushed to it, spun the dial, hunting for a station broadcasting something other than music. In a moment, a man saying, 'Hey, Morris baby, you piss in this cah-fee or sump'n? Say, I hate that last disc. Gonna break it. Heh-heh! An' fuck Body English, they're a bunch of creeps and queers!'

The station went off the air as though a switch had been turned, and that was the moment Mack chose to get bored with his game and shatter another of the office's windows. They all ducked, except Pete because of his back brace.

'Dorothy, bring my gun,' Alan whispered. 'Pete, could you stand him off with it? I guess they taught you to use a gun when you were a pig, huh?'

'Taught me!' Pete snorted. 'My whole training lasted like six weeks! But yeah, I can shoot pretty well.'

'Dorothy—'

She was already gone.

'What the hell can have happened to him?' Philip muttered to Alan, crouching.

'Come on, everybody!' Mack yelled, jumping up and down. 'This is fun! Whyncha join in?'

'That DJ didn't sound as though he had his head too straight,' Pete said equally softly, keeping a wary eye on Mack. 'And what about these fires?'

'Rioting!' Alan snapped. 'Don't worry about that right now, we got problems of our own – ah, thanks!' To Dorothy as she handed him the .32 he kept in his office against intruders. 'Pete, take this, and Phil and I will try and get in back of him, see? If we can jump him we can maybe knock him out. Phil, come on—'

Which was the point at which Mack noticed the gun, not quite hidden as Alan held it toward Pete. His face instantly deformed into a mask of blind fury.

'You son of a bitch!' he bellowed, and charged them. Philip cried out and drew back, thinking to protect Dorothy, and Alan fired.

'You mother!' Mack looked down at his chest, bare in the opening of his shirt, and saw the round hole beside his breastbone. His expression altered to complete astonishment. 'Why, you ...'

A dark patch spread down his pants leg. 'Hell,' he said mildly. 'I wet myself.'

And slowly collapsed on his knees and laid his face on the floor.

Dorothy started to sob.

There was a long silence. Blood began to mingle with the urine.

'Now we got to contact the pigs somehow,' Alan said at length. 'Phone dead or not dead. But ...' He looked from one to another of his companions, beseechingly. 'I did have to do it, didn't I?'

'Yeah.' Pete licked his lips. 'If ever I saw murder in a man's eyes ... Christ, what could have done that to him? He never even joshed me about being black, like some of the men do. And then all of a sudden – this!'

'Dorothy,' Alan said, not tearing his eyes from the corpse, 'could you drive down to—?'

'No,' Dorothy interrupted. She was pressing her hands together to stop them trembling. 'You haven't seen what it's like out there. I can't drive anywhere by myself right now. Wouldn't dare.'

Philip and Alan exchanged glances.

'I guess we better see what she means,' Philip said, and led the way back to his own office – not Alan's where they had been conferring earlier, from which the view was of a high black wall the other side of the road. The instant he thrust open the door, he exclaimed in horrified amazement.

In the distance, smoke was rising in vast billowing clouds to join the eternal gray overcast. Opening the window let in the stench of burning: rubber, plastic, wood, heaven knew what else. It was infinitely worse than any river fire.

A moment, and a highway patrol car came screaming past and made a frantic left toward the downtown area, siren blasting. They caught a glimpse of a man next to the driver, perfectly white, barking into a microphone.

After that, rumbling, Army trucks, at least eight or nine, each crammed with masked men carrying guns.

'Run out and ask what's happening!' Dorothy cried, and Philip jolted into action. But before he made it to the road they'd driven past. He came back wiping his eyes and coughing.

'Too late!' he forced out. 'But there must be some way to find out what's going on! Do we have another radio?'

Yes, mine,' Dorothy said, and hurried to fetch it. Set to the Conelrad band, it uttered a little girl's voice, chanting. Or was it a little girl? 'Castor was bigger than Pollux! So when they were both at their frolics, Pollux offered his ass to Give pleasure to Castor, Who had a huge prick and three bollocks.'

The voice dropped an octave and a half and added in normal businesslike tones, 'Stand by. Keep your sets tuned to this wavelength for further information.'

Philip, growing frantic, wound the dial again. Pasty-pale, Dorothy tried the phone and confirmed that it was totally useless, not even a hum on the line.

'Wowee, man!' the radio said, and gave a neighing laugh. 'This is a great high, surely is. This is a *fantastic*— Hey, you stinking mother, leave that switch alone! This is *my* show! You cut me off and I'll cut you off.' The sound of a bottle being smashed. 'Get away from there or I'll carve you good, hear?'

Another station was playing the Ode to Joy from Beethoven's Ninth at 45 instead of 33, and someone was finding that so funny he was laughing louder than the music.

There was nothing else on the dial at all, not even on the police band, but that meant nothing. The lie of the land here was bad for short wave, and this set wasn't a very good one.

Alan reached past Philip and switched the set off.

'Phil, you got a wife and kids down there. Get along home.'

'But—'

'You heard me!' Gruffly. 'I'll lock up with Dorothy, then drive her home. I got my gun, I'll be all right. You tell the police about Mack on the way, okay?'

Philip nodded, heart hammering. 'I'll ride Pete home too, then. He can't drive.' He hesitated. 'Thanks.'

THE DESCENT INTO HELL

It was hard for Pete to get into Philip's car. Some impulse – a pang of conscience, maybe – had led him to switch to the next size smaller in the range he patronized when he bought the year's new one back in June. Having made sure Pete was settled okay, he felt in the glove compartment. Filtermasks.

'Here!' he said, offering the one Denise generally used – the kids' would be far too small. Pete took it with a mutter of thanks. Even with the precipitator on the ventilator, this stench would be hard to endure. Already the air was full of greasy black smuts.

'Think it is an attack?' he said, muffled. 'Or just rioting?'

'God knows,' Philip answered, bringing something else out of the glove compartment: Denise's .22. 'Take this as well.'

'Right.' Pete set it on his lap, dark hand loosely around the butt.

'So let's go. Your place first.'

Philip gunned the engine and headed for the exit from the parking lot – and had to stand on the brake as he reached it. Coming from the city center like a bat out of hell, a madman with wide staring eyes at the wheel of a Maserati.

VROOM!

'What the—?'

And behind him a Mustang, and a Camaro, and a big Lincoln, and …

There was a gap. Philip grabbed it. And heading into the city: nothing. Not a car for ten blocks, twelve, fifteen! But coming the other way so many cars they were cramming the whole of their half of the road, overflowing into the other half, ignoring red lights, cutting in on each other, scraping though not in fact colliding … 'I seen that before,' Pete said. 'Panic.'

'Yeah.'

Ahead, an Econoline jumped a red from their right and cut across their bows to try and join the out-from-town traffic. It locked fenders with a Cadillac and both stalled.

'Oh-oh,' Philip murmured, and dodged around the Econoline's tail before the light turned red against him. He felt extraordinarily calm. It was as though he had been subconsciously awaiting this day, the day when the heavens would fall, and had used up his whole reservoir of fear and anxiety. He would get home, and either find Denise and the kids, or not find them. Then he'd either find them later somewhere else, or never find them because they were dead. It was all fixed, all outside his control.

He glanced at Pete. 'Is Jeannie home?' he demanded.

'Likely,' Pete grunted. His hands tensed suddenly on the gun. 'Look out ahead!'

A block in front of them: a gas station afire, huge yellow licking tongues of flame. Someone vainly struggling to rig a hose. Passers-by, delighted, yelling and trying to prevent him by throwing cans and bottles. Philip made a fast right and dodged through some side streets he hadn't known about, which brought them out eventually in the right place. Miraculous. People obeying a red light. He got on to the parallel avenue and rolled.

All the time the scream of sirens.

Now and then the crisp snap of guns.

'Try the radio again,' Pete said, and pressed the on button. Music. Everything quite normal. Roaring Mortimer's crazy version of *Summertime* with the high-speed double talk like an old King Pleasure number.

'Summertime boys and girls and those intermediate and the killing is wheezy laze an' gemmun an' it's a GAS a GAS a KNOCK SEE JIM! Heddle-ah-boh!'

At which point: silence. Pete, surprised, turned the set off and on again, but now there was nothing anywhere.

Here, the windows of five or six stores broken. But so far none of the other regular symptoms of a riot day like barriers closing streets and patrol cars and detour signs and … Wonder what became of the Army trucks and the men in them? And everyone on the sidewalks kind of cheerful. Slowing as traffic became more dense in the road ahead, Philip stared from side to side. They were still nowhere near the main area of the fire which was making the air so dirty. It might be somewhere around 18th and Stout, he guessed, maybe at the big post office. He saw a boy grab a middle-aged woman by the skirt and smack her bottom, and she jumped away and left the skirt in his hand, and she wore no panties and walked on quite unconcerned.

'Everybody's going crazy!' Pete whispered. 'Like Mack!'

'I don't believe it,' Philip snapped. 'Look, there's a squad car ahead. We can ask them …'

Surrounded by a grinning group of young people. Hell! Very slowly, Philip crept past the squad car, drawn up by the curb, and saw incredulously why the crowd had gathered. The driver and the man beside him were locked in each other's arms, kissing passionately.

A girl was drawing a skull and crossbones on the car's trunk with a lipstick. It was a good one, artistic, with the right number of teeth and everything.

But at that point someone shot at them, and there was a sudden hole in the rear left corner of the car's roof and the back window shattered and starred.

Philip was so startled, he almost ran off the road, but recovered before he hit any of the pedestrians. And then there was a proper police barrier. Being familiar, it was a reassurance as well as a stinking nuisance.

'Hell, I know that cat!' Pete said as a black patrolman waved them to a stop. He wound down his window and peeled off his mask, risking a fit of coughing. 'Chappie! Chappie Rice!' he called.

'Who the—? Ah, shit, it's Pete Goddard! Didn't see you in months, man!' The patrolman glanced up to make sure no more cars were approaching, and bent to Pete's window.

'Chappie, meet Phil Mason that I work for now. Say, what the hell is going *on*?'

'Man, I just got here! Didn't ought to be on duty, but they recalled everyone they could reach. All I know is the city's like bent its brain. Back in Arvada and Wheat Ridge they put the Army in, two hundred fifty men from Wickens. Like three or four hundred houses afire, gangs of crazy kids out on the street bare-ass naked, singing this wild song and breaking everything up. Over by the post office they's like four big buildings afire, stores and office blocks, and gas stations being blown up all over, and now right here we got a sniper— Say, you see that hole in your roof?'

'We saw it!' Philip snapped. 'Officer, I'm trying to ride Pete home. What's the likeliest way? He lives at – oh, shit! What's the number?' Pete gave it. Chappie Rice looked grave.

'Like they say, man, if I wanted to get there I wouldn't start from here! But if you back up to that last intersection and go three blocks south and ...'

And they made it.

The area was dead. Everything disturbing the city seemed to be very far away, though in fact it was no more than five blocks distant at its closest. The street Pete lived on had closed up tight like a scared clam. There was literally no one in sight as Philip drew up in front of his apartment building, except that curtains were fluttering at windows.

'Wait,' Philip advised. 'Snipers?'

Thirty tense seconds. Nothing happened. Pete said, 'Oh God. Thank God. I see Jeannie!'

Philip glanced toward the window of their home. There she was, waving wildly.

'Thanks for the mask – and the gun!' Pete said, opened the door, awkwardly struggled to get his legs out of it. Philip set the parking brake, hastened around the car to help him, but here came Jeannie at a run.

'Oh, Pete baby! I been trying to call you, and all the phones are out!' She flung her arms around him and nearly knocked him off balance. 'Are you okay, honey?'

'We – uh – we had a bit of trouble at the warehouse,' Pete said. Philip recalled with a pang of dismay that he'd said nothing to the patrolman about Mack's death; against the scale of what was happening to the city it had seemed negligible.

'But are *you* okay?'

271

'Yeah, fine, thanks to Phil.'

Jeannie rounded on Philip and hugged him and kissed him and left his cheek a trace wet: tears. 'I don't know how to thank you!' she exclaimed. 'If anything bad happened to Pete, I'd go crazy.'

Like everybody else ... 'That's all right,' Philip said gruffly. 'I – uh – I better be getting home myself. Can you make it indoors, Pete?'

'Oh, from here it's easy. I do it all the time. Uh – thanks again.'

Philip turned to get back in the car. Crossing the sidewalk, Pete called out.

'See you tomorrow, if they sort all this out!'

'Yeah!'

In his own home street: a car burning lazily, its nose against a mailbox. On the opposite sidewalk, a dog squatting on its haunches howling. The sound made Philip's spine crawl. Nobody was visible around here, either.

Across the entrance to the underground garage beneath his apartment block, the steel anti-thief grille. He stopped inches from it and blasted his horn.

No one came to let him in.

Somewhere he had a key they'd given him, but he'd never used it because ...

He rustled in the glove compartment, hoping it might be there, and while he was stirring up the contents – used tissues smeared with Denise's lipstick, broken sunglasses belonging to Josie, BankAmericard receipts, a spare spark plug, incredible junk – the car, and the ground, shook, and a monstrous thump hurt his ears. He jumped and stared wildly over his shoulder. Soaring into the air not more than a half a block away, a cloud of smoke shot through with dazzling sparks, like a magnesium flare.

The hell with the car!

He leapt out, not slamming the door, not even shutting off the engine, and ran for the street-level entrance. For this grille he did have a key; he'd demanded one because the guards kept falling sick. He didn't shut it behind him, but raced for the elevators—

And couldn't wait for one to arrive, so made for the stairs. Panting, he reached his own floor, and the door of the apartment was locked against him, and he hammered and banged and pounded on it and there was another explosion outside that shook down dust from a crack in the ceiling he didn't recall seeing before.

Inside the apartment, the sound of movement. He shouted.

Locks being unfastened. The clink of the security chain.

And there was Denise weeping.

'Oh, honey!' He swept her into his arms, frantic, and felt her shake and shake. 'Honey, it's all right now! I'm here, and ...'

And I left my gun in the car, and I left the car door open and the engine running. Christ, am I crazy too? Has the whole fucking world taken leave of its senses in an hour?

'It's not all right,' Denise said. Her tears had ceased, and her voice had the chill of marble. She shut the door and turned to face him.

'I can't contact the police.'

'Honey—'

'It's not all right. It's Josie.'

There was an instant of utter silence. Nothing happened. Inside, outside the building – anywhere, to the ends of the universe. 'I thought she was just asleep. But Harold killed her.'

THE REFERRED PAIN

... *burning out of control. As darkness falls, Denver from the air looks like the pit of a volcano. Gas stations, stores and private homes are going up in smoke. All the time, mingled with the roar of flames, one hears the crackle of shots. Sometimes that's the police fighting a desperate rearguard action against the populace of a city which seems to have turned against them in the blink of an eye. Sometimes it's the Army and National Guard reinforcements which are trying to restore order in the surrounding suburbs. Already two thousand men destined for Honduras have been reassigned and parachuted into the area with full battle equipment. For this is no ordinary riot.*

And the lava of this volcano – well, it's people. Tens of thousands of them, old and young, black and white, overflowing into the surrounding country. All major highways serving the city are blocked by colossal jams, involving an esti-mated eighteen thousand cars. Some collided, some broke down, the drivers of others were killed by snipers ... but the reasons don't matter, only the outcome. Abandoning their cars, often within a block or two of home, the population is on the move, carrying what they can, leaving what they can't to the flames. Observers are comparing this to the aftermath of war to give an idea of the scale of it, but that doesn't tell you much. The catastrophe has struck from nowhere, and no one knows what the hell is going on ...

OUT OF HAND

President: But we need those men! The Tupas are within mortar range of San Pedro Sula!

State: Let the spies do their own dirty work for a change. This isn't just a riot – this is civil war.

Defense: I'm afraid that's broadly true, Mr President. This is not a subversive uprising, though. It's more like what you'd expect if someone were to

PORTION OF TRANSCRIPT OMITTED AVAILABLE
ONLY TO PERSONNEL WITH TRIPLE-A-STAR
SECURITY CLEARANCE

so of course the antidote was never stockpiled. We must try and obtain supplies from a pharmaceutical company at once. In the meantime – well.

Intelligence: In the meantime, there's only one thing to do. Put the area under martial law, the whole state if need be, and cordon it with troops under orders to shoot to kill if anyone refuses to obey them.

Justice: Yes, there's no alternative, sir. This country is simply *not* equipped to cope with four hundred thousand lunatics.

OCTOBER

THE TICK-TOCK MEN

FERNANDO: … Why, he does,
   Nor will contented rest until the world,
   The whole great globe and orb by land and sea,
   Ticks to his pleasure like a parish clock.
   You are a cogwheel, Juan, as am I:
   He's shaped us round, and prettied us with jags,
   And gilded us with gold—

JUAN: Add: gelded us!

FERNANDO: Aye, so he has, my brother. And 'tis all
Part of his clockwork. See you, he's the weight;
We follow from him in an engined train;
Ducats are oil to make our axles turn
Without a squeak.

JUAN: I'll squeak, i'faith! I'll rant
   And call down hurricanoes on his head,
   I'll conjure earthquakes to beset his path!

FERNANDO: You've no escapcment, Juan. You're enchained.
   At your vain wrath he will politely nod
   And say you have come forth to strike the hour,
   He's 'bliged to you …

– 'The Tragedy of Ercole', 1625

STATEMENT OF EMERGENCY

'Thank you. Friends and fellow Americans, no president of the United States has ever had a more melancholy task than I have at this moment. It is my sad duty to inform you that our country is in a state of war. A war that is none of our choosing. And, moreover, not a war with bombs and tanks and missiles, not a war that is fought by soldiers gallant on the field of battle, sailors daring the hostile sea, airmen streaking valiant through the skies – but a war that must be fought by you, the people of the United States.

'We have been attacked with the most cowardly, the most monstrous, the most evil weapons ever devised by wicked men. We are the victims of a combined chemical and biological attack. You are all aware that our crops have failed disastrously last summer. We, the members of my cabinet and I, delayed announcing the truth behind that story in the vain hope that we might contain the threat of the *jigras*. We can no longer do so. It is known that they were deliberately introduced into this country. They are the same pest which ruined the entire agriculture of Central America and led to the sad and unwished-for conflict in Honduras.

'That by itself we could endure. We are resilient, brave, long-suffering people, we Americans. What is necessary, we will do. But alas there are some among us who bear the name 'American' and are traitors, determined to overthrow the legitimate government, freely elected, to make the work of the police impossible, to denigrate and decry the country we love. Some of them adhere to alien creeds, the communism of Marx and Mao; some, detestably, adhere to a creed equally alien yet spawned within our own border – that of the Trainites, whose leader, thank God, is safely in jail awaiting his just punishment for kidnapping an innocent boy and imprisoning him and infecting him with foul diseases that endangered his life.

'We are fighting an enemy already in our midst. He must be recognized by his words as well as his deeds. One of the great cities of our nation today writhes in agony because the water supply, the precious diamond stream that nourishes our lives, has been poisoned. You may say: how can we resist an enemy whose weapon is the very faucet at the sink, the very water-cooler we go to for relief in the factory or the office? And I will say this! It is you, the people of our great land, who must provide the answer!

'It is not going to be easy. It is going to be very hard. Our enemies have succeeded in reducing our stocks of food to the point where we must share and share alike. Following my speech, you will be informed of the emergency arrangements we are putting in hand for equal and fair distribution of the food we have. You will be informed, too, of the plans we have for silencing known traitors and subversives. But the remainder is up to you. You know who the enemy is – you met him at work, you heard him talking treason at a party, you heard about his attendance at a commie-front meeting, you saw the anti-American books in his library, you refused to laugh at his so-called jokes that dragged the name of the United States in the mud, you shut your ears to his anti-American propaganda, you told your kids to keep away from his kids who are being taught to follow in his traitor's footsteps, you saw him at a Trainite demonstration, you know how he lied and slandered the loyal

Americans who have built our country up until it is the richest and most powerful nation in history.

'My friends, you elected me to lead you into the third century of our country's existence. I know you can be trusted to do what is right. You know who the enemy is. Go get him before he gets you!'

THAT'S TELLING 'EM!

'Did you hear what that son of a bitch said about Train?'
'I sure did! And he hasn't even been put on trial yet!'

GETTING STRAIGHT

Knock.

Grimy, unshaven, in clothes he had worn for more than a week, Philip snatched for his gun even before opening his eyes. It was still nearly dark in the living-room of the apartment, which they had decided on as a home base. There had been no power since the start of the emergency. Nor had there been water. Before the battery of their one transistor radio ran down, they had learned it had been the water supply which drove the city mad ... and Harold.

He sat there in the corner, soiled, uncaring, sucking his thumb and staring at infinity. He had not spoken since the moment he killed his sister. He might as well have been autistic.

Josie was in the deep freeze with the lid shut. She was starting to stink. But that was nothing to the reek from the toilet.

Denise, as dirty as himself, without her wig, her ringworm scars like brands across her scalp, sat up and whispered, 'Who can that be?'

'How the shit should I know?' Philip snapped, steadying himself on the corner of a table and rubbing sleep from his eyes with the knuckles of his gun hand. He was feeling very sick this morning, worse than yesterday, but they'd broken their one thermometer when trying to take Harold's temperature, and on his only two expeditions out-of-doors so far he hadn't made it to a drugstore. The first had reclaimed his gun; the second had yielded nothing except the information that all the nearby food stores had been looted. They were living off deep-frozen hamburger and orange juice.

Detour on the way to the spyhole, around their improvised hearth. It was no fun living in a modern apartment with all the utilities out. Gas had been cut off around the same time as the power. They'd been lucky to find a sheet of asbestos on which they could rig cook-stove bars. He peered cautiously out, and tensed.

'Army!' he said under his breath, and at the same time became aware of noises from the apartment next door, which had been dead silent for two days.

'Are you sure?' Denise on her knees, trembling. 'It could be someone pretending—'

But there was something convincing about the man outside the door: a top sergeant, face half-hidden by an issue filtermask, holding a clipboard and a pen, making some kind of register, maybe. Then, behind him, another man came into view, a private with medical corps collar badges. He carried a box of phials and a jar of white pills.

'It's okay,' he muttered, and slipped the locks, although he retained the security chain and made sure his gun was poised where it could be seen.

And—

'Drop the gun or I'll drop you!' As though by magic, the sergeant had a carbine leveled; it must have been slung at his back, muzzle down, where a flick of his arm sufficed to bring it into firing position.

'But I'm not going to do anything,' Philip said weakly. 'I live here. It's my home!'

Filthy. Stinking. Grimy. Foul. Mine.

'Drop the gun!'

He shrugged and tossed it on to a nearby cushion.

'That's better,' the sergeant said. 'Are you Philip A. Mason?'

'Y-yes.'

'ID!'

Philip fumbled in his hip pocket for his billfold and offered his driver's license. Taking it, the sergeant added, 'And open this stinking door, will you?'

'I-uh, sure!' He released the chain. The private entered and glanced around, wrinkling his nose. He'd dropped his filtermask below his chin and looked as though he wished he hadn't. But the air in here was no worse than you got by opening a window; some of the fires in the downtown area had burned five days, and the wind was still bringing in smoke from the suburbs.

'And you're Mrs Mason?' the sergeant said, handing the license back. 'And you got two kids?'

The sound of authority in the sergeant's voice, Philip found, was curiously reassuring. Since Josie's death he had been able to imagine that no one any longer anywhere in the world knew what he was about. He himself had spent hours on end, sometimes half the day, staring out of the window at the wreaths of smoke, incapable of reacting, let alone of making plans.

Denise struggled to her feet, clutching a blanket to her bosom. Since she was fully dressed – neither she nor Philip had had their clothes off in the past week – it made no particular odds.

Now a third man entered the apartment, another private, carrying a gunny sack with something heavy in the bottom. On spotting Philip's gun he snatched at it, stripped the remaining shells out, and dropped it in the bag. 'Hey, that's mine!' Philip objected weakly.

'Ban on firearms in this city,' the sergeant grunted. 'We had like twenty thousand people shot to death so far. That your son?' Pointing at Harold, who was not even following the intruders with his eyes.

'Uh – yes.'

'And the other kid, the girl?'

'Well ...'

'She's dead.' Clearly, from Denise.

The sergeant made a check mark, not in the least surprised. 'Uh-huh. How?'

'Harold killed her. Want to see her body?'

That penetrated the sergeant's matter-of-fact pose. Lowering the clip-board, he stared at her.

'He killed her. I thought she was just asleep, but he'd cut her up and covered her with her favorite blanket.' Denise's voice was quite level, drained of all emotion. It had been a week of hell; there was nothing left.

The sergeant and the medical private exchanged glances.

'I guess I'd better get the doc to check this one out,' the private said after a moment. 'It's beyond me, sarge.'

'Yeah.' The sergeant licked his lips. 'Go see if he's through with the bodies next door.'

'Bodies?' Philip took half a pace forward. They'd never been very friendly with the Friedrichs in the adjacent apartment, but they had been on nodding terms, and the day the crisis broke, when he was still thinking of joining forces and resources, he'd gone to try and talk to them – but they'd refused to open the door.

'Sure, bodies,' the sergeant said curtly. 'We didn't find anyone but you alive in this building yet. You done your military service?' Pen poised to make the next check mark on his form.

'I ...' Philip swallowed hard. 'Yeah, here's my discharge certificate.' Out with the billfold again. One had had to carry that all the time since about the time the Honduran operation turned sour; they were very fierce on dodgers.

'Mm-hm? Manila? I was there too,' the sergeant said, busily writing. 'Why in hell didn't you report like you should have done?'

'I don't understand,' Philip said slowly.

'You were supposed to report to Wickens if you weren't either sick or crazy. Or to the Arsenal. Three days ago.' The sergeant handed the certificate back. 'You gon' be in trouble, Mr Mason.'

Philip shook his head. 'Was it on the radio or something?' he said faintly. 'Because our radio's been out for more than three days – we kept it on all the time at the beginning because we were trying to find out what was going on – and the phone's out, and last time I went down to the street I got shot at.'

The sergeant looked at him thoughtfully. 'Well, I guess they won't be hard on you. We need everyone we can find who's neither sick nor crazy.'

'I am kind of sick,' Philip said. 'Fever, I guess.'

'Ah, that's easy. It's this rabbit thing that's giving us headaches – what's it called, Rocco?'

The medical private said, 'Tularemia. But the typhus is worse, and I keep hearing they got smallpox, too.'

Philip looked at Denise and found she was so overcome she was simply gaping. He felt that way himself.

'Got a bag for the kid?' the sergeant went on, turning to the other private, the one collecting guns. The man nodded and produced a thing like a fat black cigar; shaken, it unrolled into a plastic bag about six feet by eighteen inches. 'Coffins,' the sergeant said with a wry grin. 'Best we can—'

'My God, it's Phil Mason!' A shout from the door, and Doug McNeil thrust his way in. 'And Denise! Thank God you're alive, at least!'

He was haggard, newly bearded, and dressed in khaki fatigues a size too big, but from the way he moved he was well. Philip wondered whether he dared fall on his neck and cry

But before he could react in any such ridiculous fashion, Doug had caught sight of Harold. A single glance, and he rounded on Denise. 'He got at the water!'

Denise gave a dull nod. They'd been over that a hundred times, reconstructing the way in which, while his mother was dozing after taking that massive dose of pain-killers for her migraine, be must have drunk from the deadly supply, then taken a knife to his sister's belly.

'Josie?'

'Here,' Philip said, and led Doug to the kitchen.

He was silent for a long time, then turned away, shaking his head.

'Disposal detail!' he snapped at the man with the plastic bag, and added, 'Sorry, Phil. But we have to get all the bodies out of the city and burned, quick as we can. There'll be a mass cremation, with a service. We're holding three a day. Denise can attend if she likes.'

'But not me?'

Doug hesitated. Then, with rapid professional deftness, he checked Philip's pulse, rolled back one of his eyelids, and asked him to put out his tongue.

'No, not you. You're lucky. You have no idea *at all* how lucky you've been. Rocco, you have treated them, have you?'

'Not yet, sir,' the medical private said awkwardly.

'Hell, get on with it!' Moving out of the way of the man trying to get Josie into the plastic bag. Denise had made no move to help. Presumably she couldn't. And continuing to Philip: 'I'm told we had about one and a half guns to every two people. Those that haven't been shot went insane, those that aren't insane mostly have one of the three or four killer diseases that are rife … We're still picking up the bits.'

Rocco was offering a pill and a phial. Numb, Philip took them.

'The pill is a broad-spectrum antibiotic,' Doug said. 'One of the tailored penicillins, all we could get in sufficient quantity right away. It's better than nothing, I guess, though it does provoke allergy reactions in some people. Which is why it hasn't already been sown broadcast to the point where the bugs don't give a fart about it. And the liquid is a specific antidote to the nerve gas.'

'Nerve gas!' A cry from Denise, accepting her own allotment from Rocco.

'Well, that's what we're calling it for convenience. It's actually a military psychotormimetic. God knows how they got it into the water. Must have been literally a ton of it to do this much damage! I don't know all the details, but experts from the Defense Department came rushing in the day before yesterday with supplies of the antidote.' He sighed. 'Trouble is, in most cases it's too late. People who weren't warned in time did the logical thing, like filled the bathtub and every container they had, and went right on drinking the poisoned water. Forty-eight hours, and they were beyond hope.'

'But who did it?' Philip whispered. 'And is it the whole country, or just us?'

'It's just Denver and the environs,' Doug said with a shrug. 'But it might as well have been the whole country. They've put us under martial law, they've instituted rationing, and it's going on until the government change their minds.'

'Doctor, you watch your tongue!' the sergeant snapped.

'Oh, shut up!' Doug retorted. 'I'm not under military discipline – I'm a civilian volunteer. And what's more, I seem to be one of only about a dozen doctors fit for work in the whole of the city and its suburbs. And all I'm saying is that my job would be a sight easier if they told us the whole truth. I'm working in the dark half the time – and so are you, aren't you?'

The sergeant hesitated. 'Well, doc, when it's a case of thousands of lunatics all of a sudden …' He spread his hands.

'Yes,' Doug said ironically. 'All of a sudden!' Looking past Philip's shoulder to where Rocco and Denise were trying to persuade Harold to take the pill and the antibiotic – with no success; he let himself be handled like a dead rabbit, but would not cooperate.

'Phil.' Dropping his voice suddenly. 'You've got to report for duty now – everyone who was ever in the armed forces has been recalled from the reserve, and you're fitter than most of the serving soldiers I've seen around here. That means it's going to be tough on Denise.'

'How do you mean?' Philip's mind had been full of fog for days. It was obstinately refusing to clear.

'Well … Well, Harold's never going to be any different, you know. We're certain about that, when it comes to kids that young. And if you're going to be whipped away, and— I didn't tell you!'

He had been half turned away; now he swung back to confront Philip directly.

'Alan! He was killed!'

'Oh, my God. How?'

'Burned to death in his warehouse. Along with Dorothy. I was on the detail that checked out the ruins.' Doug licked his lips. 'We think someone who'd had trouble with his filters must have put two and two together when the warning went out about poisoned water. Decided it was the Mitsuyama purifiers that had caused it. He and Dorothy went back to the office the day after the crisis, and someone threw gas bombs in. Burned a cop, too. Hadn't someone been shot?'

'Mack,' Philip said slowly. 'Who told you?'

'Pete Goddard. He's okay – and Jeannie. They're helping with casualty admin.'

So a few people at least were likely to survive. Philip said, 'About Harold?'

'Oh. Oh, yes. He's going to be a – a burden for Denise.'

'I guess so.' That damned mental fog wouldn't lift; it was like trying to think between the anesthetic and the coma. 'But they'll get help, won't they? And I mean we do have some money, and—'

'Oh, shit, *Phil*!' So agitated, he had to grasp Philip's arm to halt his words. Still in a low tone, privately: 'The banks are shut, everything's closed down here, and there's no transport out of the city, nothing, *nothing*! And Harold in his condition …' He waved his hand.

'But I've seen worse than him. Being tended like by Earth Community Chest.' So far back in the past, a boy with a shrunken leg hobbling across the entrance to Angel City's parking lot in LA. 'Or being helped by Double-V. I mean, he's a sick kid.'

'They've been proscribed,' Doug said.

'What?'

'Earth Community Chest and Double-V. They were both on the list of subversive organizations to be closed down when the country went on to a war footing. Along with all the civil rights groups, all the left-wing publishers …' Doug shook his head. 'And they won't tell us who we're fighting.'

'Them!' the sergeant said. Philip hadn't realized he was listening. 'This is

the filthiest attack in history! Kids like yours driven crazy! Women! Everyone! Not even killed clean!' Philip gave a slow nod.

'Okay, I won't make my offer after all,' Doug said, and turned away as
Rocco offered him a pad of printed forms. 'By the way, what was Josie's full
name and date of birth? I have to clip this to her bag.'

Philip supplied the data dully. And went on, 'What – what offer?'

'A bag like this one,' Doug said, not looking around. 'It's that, or starve to
death, or be killed in an accident, or die of typhus … Well, you've made it
clear you'd refuse.'

'You're *killing kids?*' Philip burst out.

'No. Saving them the trouble of dying by themselves.' Doug turned and
faced him again. There was something in his eyes which might have been
pity, but Philip wasn't receptive to pity any more.

His voice softened. 'Look, I'll do you another favor. Right now you can't
think straight. You may even have had a subclinical dose of the nerve gas –
the hallucinogen. I'll give you a note to say you won't be well enough to
report for duty until tomorrow. Think about Harold and Denise while you
have the chance. It's the only one you'll get.' Philip gazed at him without
comprehension.

'One more thing,' the sergeant said. 'You got any food? Because we got to
take away anything more than you need for tomorrow. They promised ration
wagons the day after, with like soup and bread.'

And that was too much. Philip turned away to the kitchen with a gesture
and went to lean his forehead on a wall. It was covered with a film of greasy
dirt, but it was at least cool. In the background he heard Denise saying, 'What
about Angie? And Millicent?'

'My mother's dead,' Doug answered. 'But Angie's okay. She was a nurse.
She's with another detail like this one.'

When the door had closed Philip said, 'If I could get my hands on the bastards responsible for this, I'd – I'd …'

And couldn't think of anything bad enough.

THE ROUGH DRAFT

*… include prima facie but not ipso facto the following: (a) Homosexuality or
gross indecency with another male person; (b) Possession of or trading in an
illegal narcotic or other drug; (c) Living upon the earnings of prostitution; (d)
Membership in the Communist Party or one of its front organizations (see
schedule attached); (e) 'Trainism'; (f) Advocating the violent overthrow of the
government; (g) Slandering the President of the United States; (h) …*

ACID TRIP

Hugh was very sick. Sometimes he thought it must be blood-poisoning because he had these like sores on his face, right up to his mouth so when he licked around he tasted the foul sweetness of pus. Sometimes he thought it was something else he could have caught, a separate fever altogether. But most of the time he thought it was a trip he was taking, only he'd forgotten when he dropped the cap of acid. The world was all rubbery, especially his own limbs.

But he knew where he was going, and he'd got there, despite dodging pigs and skunks and there not being any cars on the road to hitch a ride with. His own had quit on him, or he'd driven it into something, or something. He wasn't thinking too good, what with the fever and the lack of food – he hadn't eaten in days, though he'd found plenty of water.

Water?

A drop of rain on his hand. Shit. But at least he was in sight of home. These were the botanical gardens around the Bamberley house – weren't they? He looked, bewildered, the darkness gathering. Real evening.

Those trees. Too bare for this early in the fall and some of them not the kind to drop their leaves anyhow. Blight of some kind? He touched a trunk, found the bark come away at the brush of his hand.

Shit. Never mind trees. The house in that direction. More rain. It reminded him he was thirsty again, and he tilted his head to let the drops run on his tongue. His sense of taste was poor. Some sort of thick whitish mass had covered the inside of his mouth. Kitty had had it in her cunt, he remembered. Fungus. Thrush, they called it. Fucking stupid name. Everybody knew there were no more birds.

The rain was sour. He stopped dead, not believing what his senses reported. Sour? Must be the stinking thrush or something. Rain isn't sour. Only—

'Christ,' he said aloud, and a shaft of terror went down his spine like an icicle. Battery acid! There was no doubt about it; he'd owned an electric car long enough to be certain.

Raining acid!

He screamed and ran headlong for the house, and under the next tree but two a sentry challenged him with a carbine. He stopped and looked at the man blankly.

'Acid rain,' he said. 'It's impossible.'

'Shut up,' the sentry said. 'Who are you?'

'I live here,' Hugh said. 'It's my home.'

'Your name Bamberley?' The sentry cocked his head.

'No – uh – no. I'm Hugh Pettingill.' There were papers in his pocket … somewhere. He found something that felt right, handed it over.

'You were in the Marines!' the sentry said. 'Ah-hah! You're going to be useful when you're cleaned up.' He scrutinized Hugh's face in the gathering dusk. 'Bad sores on your face. You been laid up sick?'

'Y-yeah.' When was I in the Marines?

'But you're reporting now?'

'Yeah.'

'Fine. Go straight on in and ask for Captain Aarons.' The sentry handed back the discharge certificate.

'Where are the – the family? Maud and the rest?'

'Huh? Oh, Mrs Bamberley? Went crazy, I hear. A bit before the rest of them.' A sour grin. 'So since the place was empty, and big, they put us in. Handy to Denver.'

'What are you doing here?'

The man shrugged. 'Work gangs. Clearing the wreckage in the city. Dodgers, Trainites, people like that. Pacifists. Walk 'em into the city every morning, bring 'em back at night. Get some honest work out of 'em. You better carry on to the house and report. See you later, maybe.'

'Yeah,' Hugh said dully, thinking: acid rain? Hell.

One of the work gangs was being returned for the night as he reached the house. They were in chains.

'This certificate's a forgery,' Captain Aarons said curtly. 'He was never in the Marines. Where is he right now?'

Startled, the sergeant said, 'I think he's seeing the doctor, sir. Got like sores on his face.'

'Get him out of there and put him on a work gang,' Aarons said. 'Unless the doc says he's not even fit to dig rubble.'

WORK IN PROGRESS

'Tom, this is Moses. Do you still not have anything we can use?'

'No, damn it, I don't! When the power went out the other night it was like – like hitting a man on the head with a blackjack! Sorting out the data after that isn't being made any easier, either, by the way you keep pestering me! *Goodbye.*'

HOMECOMING

Gradually, this sense of adjustment to the strange new way of the world ...
They had cleared this area now and officially declared it safe for habitation,
but it was so – so *empty*!

Even though it hadn't been home for long, though, it was great to put her
key in her own door, Jeannie thought. And they'd got off so lucky! The fires
hadn't come within a quarter-mile of here; the building hadn't been shot up,
or bombed, or anything.

Though of course the Army had put them into a motel out of the city for
the time being, and they'd worked at what they could, she tending the sick in
spite of being not so well herself and Pete dealing with casualty registration
forms and death certificates, the kind of thing he'd learned already in the
police, easy.

But it was so weird, so *weird*! Knowing the apartments upstairs were
vacant, a whole building with like thirty homes in ... and the street, with the
cars just standing there, no traffic, not even audible in the distance, except
the rumble of Army trucks ... and the state of the country! Every fit man
drafted, no excuses: loyal, to serve under military command, or disloyal, to
serve in some other way like clearing ruins and carrying corpses to be buried. They were still unearthing corpses all the time.

Home, though. Just to check whether she could bring Pete here tonight.
They didn't have gasoline for the car, but the Army was mounting regular
patrols and so were the police, and Chappie Rice, this old friend of Pete's,
would fix it so they could ride to and from work every day. Until the crisis
was over. Would it ever be over?

She was thinking so hard about that she didn't see him.

'Don't move. Put your hands— Christ, it's Jeannie!'

She cried out and spun around, and there he was looking at her over the
back of their long chesterfield: Carl.

But Carl changed, nearly out of recognition. He was so much older. His
thin face was drawn into the lines of premature maturity; he wore a dirty
black sweater with a bandolier crossing the shoulder, and held a sporting
rifle leveled at her.

He looked at her, then at the gun, and abruptly lost the extra years he'd
acquired. Leaping to his feet, he dropped the gun and rushed to embrace her.

'Oh, Carl! Carl, baby!' She was almost crying; she'd been sure her favorite
brother must be dead. 'What are you doing here?'

'Hiding,' he said, and laughed cynically. 'You? Is Pete with you?'

'No – uh – we been put in this motel, see, but tomorrow ...' She explained
rapidly.

'All empty upstairs? Groovy. Then I can move into one of the other apartments.'

'No, they're going to use them to rehouse people whose homes got burnt.'

'Ah, shit.' His face fell. 'Am I ever a stupid *bastard*!'

'What?'

'See …' His age returned to him; he moved away to sit down beside the rifle, his thin fingers caressing its stock. 'See, I got to hide out, Jeannie. This killed a state border guard.'

'Oh, Carl!' She pressed her hands tight together.

'Had to. Him or me. I wanted to get by. And I don't have this love of skunks anyhow … See, I was out in Berkeley, but I had to split from where I was. And when I heard about this big thing here in Denver, I thought Christ, it's the revolution and not before time and I'm damned if I miss out. See what I mean about being a stupid bastard?'

She nodded, her face drawn.

'So when I found out what the real scene was, I could've kicked myself back to Berkeley. I tried to find you, then. You wrote me, I got the letter, said you'd moved, and I knew the street though I forgot the number, so I just worked along till I found Goddard on the plate. Wasn't hard; so few buildings left standing here.'

He stared at nothing.

'I did think it was the revolution. Really did. Guess I was out of touch.'

'But what are you going to do now?' Jeannie cried.

'God knows.' Suddenly weary. 'I'm a dodger, in possession of a forged ID, killed a border guard … I did have to, Jeannie. He called me a black motherfucker and put up his gun. Would've shot me. Only I got him. I guess I'll have to lie low at least until they lift the martial law here, then try and sneak into Canada or something. They got an underground railway going over the border.'

He hesitated. 'That is, unless Pete gives me away first.'

'He wouldn't do that!'

'No? He joined the pigs, didn't he? Matter of fact, I think I may be crazy talking to you this way – you married him. Only I been so long without anyone to talk to.'

'I – I know!' Inspiration. 'Pete's working in casualty administration. Got all kinds of official forms. I'll sneak one, say you were hit with the nerve gas, still kind of on a trip, antidote hasn't worked properly yet! We got dozens like that every day, people like found wandering.'

'Ah-hah?' Interest woke in Carl's eyes. 'And –?'

'And you pretend to be kind of woozy. Not all there. Act dumb, act stupid. You'll have to get in on some kind of like work gang, but … And hide the gun!'

'I heard. They put a ban on private guns, didn't they? Found a car with a radio that was still working, caught one of the official broadcasts.' He rose and came to embrace her again.

'Jeannie, honey, if you weren't my sister I'd kiss the hell out of you. Ten minutes ago I was thinking I should shoot myself.'

All of a sudden the lights came on. They stared in sheer amazement for long seconds. Then Carl let go a yell of pure joy and did kiss her. She let him. It seemed only fair. Besides, he did it very well.

MAKING A GOOD RECOVERY

'The bastard's faking it to evade retribution!'

'No, Mr Bamberley, I assure you. He's genuinely ill. Suffered a massive kidney collapse. But he's responding well to treatment and we should be able to set the trial for the first week of next month. I'm making the arrangements right now. Such as they are. He won't cooperate, won't nominate a lawyer, nothing. Still, that's his lookout. How's your son?'

'Him? Raring to go. Wants to settle with that bastard – what do you think? By the way!'

'Yes?'

'Don't call me "mister". It's Colonel Bamberley, even if I am only in the reserves. And come to that, why aren't you in uniform?'

EVEN KEEL

... restored this evening, and some areas of the city are due for resettlement tomorrow, though others where the fires were fiercest will have to be razed. Commenting on the speed of this return to more-or-less normal circumstances in Denver, the president said, quote, It will be a source of dismay to our enemies to see how rapidly we can get the ship of state back on an even keel. End quote. Pockets of Trainite and black militant resistance in city centers up and down the nation are collapsing as hunger and cold take their toll, and the illnesses which are everywhere rife. New smallpox warnings have been issued in Little Rock and Charleston, Virginia. Pressure to put Austin Train on trial continues to grow, as the long delay has encouraged his supporters who eluded the mass roundup of subversives to resume their sabotage attacks and propaganda. Jigra infestation has been reported in Canada and Mexico today. Now the weather. Over much of the West and Midwest acid rain has been falling, the result of atmospheric action on smoke containing sulphur, and ...

THE LATE NEWS

'Thanks,' Peg said to the driver of the truck. She'd ridden the last part of the way with one of the teams checking out the purity of the local water, making sure the last trace of poison had been flushed away before the pipes were reconnected. The man didn't answer, but sneezed instead.

She showed her authorization to the gate guards and was passed through toward the former Bamberley mansion. They were allowing a lot of privileges to the press; foreign propagandists were making hay of the use of chained prisoners in and around Denver, and she was supposed to write an objective piece about the situation. It was the usual technique, the same they'd used for Train when he was appearing regularly on TV and advising government committees, the same they'd meant to use in the case of Lucas Quarrey.

But she'd taken the assignment purely for the sake of having a travel permit. After this stopover she was determined to get to California, legally or ilegally. They'd taken Austin there, because Bamberley refused to bring his son to New York.

In any case, that was where he had been held captive.

A gang of prisoners was being marched the opposite way along the drive as she approached the house, and to her astonishment she recognized the last man in the line. Hugh. Hugh Pettingill. Horribly changed – his cheeks and lips covered in scabs, his expression slack as an imbecile's. But it was Hugh all right.

She exclaimed, and he turned, and the light of recognition dawned in his eyes. He stopped, and that pulled the chain taut, and the man ahead cursed, and the guard in charge swung around and for a moment Peg thought in horror Hugh was going to say, 'Didn't I meet you at the wat?'

For the guard to know she had ever remotely sympathized with the Trainites would be fatal. Why she was still at large at all, she hadn't known until a few days ago, and she still hardly credited the reason.

It was thanks to Petronella Page.

That hard-boiled bitch who had pilloried hundreds of better men and women on her show had been touched by Austin's teaching; perhaps she was his only genuine convert up to now, perhaps she would remain unique. But she was using the leverage her show gave her to do Peg favors.

She had called up and asked Peg to visit her office; reluctantly, Peg had complied, and there she had been shown a photostat copy of a detention order in the name of Margaret Mankiewicz.

'I had it suspended,' Petronella said.

'How?' (Peg remembered the way her nails had bitten into her palms as she asked.)

'Who do you think has the tape Austin made in case he was prevented from appearing on my show?'

'*What?*'

A slight smile. 'Yes, that's a point you'd probably overlooked. Before anyone else thought of claiming it from the safety deposit, I got my hands on it.' Turning them over to inspect the neglected state they were in, some nails cracked, all the lacquer growing away from the half-moons. Also she was wearing a sweater and old jeans, but that was instant fashion – we're at war, so put on shabby clothes to prove you care.

'It's terrifying,' she said. 'I've played it a dozen times. Made copies, too. At home. I have a good electronics setup. They're in the proper hands. If anything happens to me, they'll be used. The Trainites aren't beaten, just held in check for the moment. Stunned.'

Peg was almost beside herself. 'But why haven't you released the tapes? Had them broadcast? Published the text?'

'Because Austin is still with us, isn't he? And I guess he has a reason for what he's doing, though I can't for the life of me imagine what it is. Still ...' She hesitated. 'I trust that man. The way you do, I guess.'

When Peg didn't answer, she raised her head sharply.

'Don't you?' she demanded.

'He – he had a breakdown once. I wish he'd let me talk to him! I'm so afraid they could drive him insane! Permanently!'

'You know, after the inquiry into the riot at the Bamberley hydroponics plant, I had some of the kids who gave evidence on the show. All of them said crazy was the only way to be. Maybe they were right.'

But she was loose, at least, and freedom was too precious to be gambled with. By a miracle, Hugh realized. He let his face slump back to sullenness.

'Stubbed my toe,' he told the guard, who drove the gang onward.

'... So, you see,' Peg concluded her explanation to the reluctant Colonel Saddler, who had already mentioned three times how furious he was to be back in the States when he'd been beating the pants off those Tupas in Honduras, 'I thought if I could talk to a few of these – uh – workers ...?'

'Pick any you like,' the colonel grunted, and sneezed, and apologized, and went on. A lot of people were sneezing around here today. Peg hoped she wasn't due for another bout of sinusitis. 'You'll find them blatant – blatant! Doesn't matter which you hit on; I'll guarantee you'll find he's a subversive, or a traitor, or pro-Tupa, or a draft-dodger. It is an absolute *lie* that we've arrested innocent civilians. They are people who in time of need have failed to answer their country's call.' Which was how Peg found herself talking to Hugh in relative safety that evening.

'Sorry,' Hugh said in a low voice. 'I nearly gave you away. My head's kind of funny now and then. I drank some water on the way here and it must have had the stuff in it.' He hesitated. 'It is you, isn't it? I mean, I'm not mixing you up with someone else? It's so hard to keep track!' Almost in a whine. 'You were the friend of that guy – uh – Decimus!'

Peg nodded. There was a great ache in her heart. When she'd known Hugh before she hadn't liked him. But he hadn't been in this pitiable condition, trembling, talking as though to prevent himself from thinking.

'I know someone else who was a friend of his,' Hugh said. His eyes were glazing. 'Carl. You met him. Worked at Bamberley Hydroponics. He knew Decimus. Liked him. Maybe I would have, if I'd met him. Carl gave him a present once, he said. Gave him food. Took some from the plant. He worked at packing it or loading it or something.'

'Did you say he gave Decimus food from the plant?' Peg said slowly.

'You're not listening! I just told you, didn't I? A Christmas present, he said. You remember Carl, huh? Seen him lately? Wish I knew where he was. I love Carl. I hope he's okay ...'

He started drumming on his knee with his fingertips as his voice trailed away.

'Your friend Carl,' Peg said, her throat as tight as though a noose had been drawn around it, 'gave Decimus some of the food from the plant, as a Christmas present?'

'Christ, if you don't listen to what I'm saying I might as well shut up,' Hugh said, and walked away.

'Oh, my God,' Peg whispered. 'Oh, my God.'

NOVEMBER

WHEREWITHAL SHALL IT BE SALTED?

A chemist in an old-established corporation
succeeded after many decades of research
in isolating the active principle from oceans

Hopes were high for its immediate appeal
as a safe additive for preserving food
and miraculous enhancer of natural flavour

Regrettably however it was discovered
that in a solution as weak as three per cent
it caused dehydration and delirium and death

– 'Our Father Which Art in Washington', 1978

ALIAS

He had used the name for so long he had even come to think of himself as
'Ossie', but he didn't want the credit for what he was doing now to go to that
mother who had tamely let himself be arrested – and worse yet was now
meekly going to stand trial! – by the lackeys of the establishment he'd had it
in his power to overthrow.

So he had put in his pocket a piece of paper which said, 'I am Bennett
Crowther.' With his photo.

He didn't expect to last much longer. He'd hoped to go down fighting. Now
he could barely walk, barely see, barely breathe. They said it was a new kind
of influenza; it was killing people in China and Japan and just getting a foot-
hold here on the West Coast. Still, the news from Honduras was good: the
Tupas had taken San Pedro Sula and were spreading north, and their first
edict as *de facto* rulers had been to make all industries generating noxious
effluent or fumes subject to immediate nationalization. Take a while for it to
be implemented, what with the famine, but …

He placed the last of his bombs and coughed and spluttered and wheezed. His temperature was a hundred and three but a revolutionary can't go to the hospital, a revolutionary is solitary, self-reliant, dies alone if need be like a wounded wolf. His fingers shook so much he had trouble setting the timer. Also he could scarcely read the dial.

But it would blow some time tomorrow morning and right now that would have to do.

He left the toilet, left the building, went home and never came out.

THERE IS HOPE YET

Armed guards at the courthouse. Some incredibly foolhardy Trainite had waved a skull-and-crossbones flag earlier, had been arrested and dragged away, but the crowd had mostly been quiet. There were two hundred National Guardsmen in the street and fifty armed police in the corridors and the courtroom. The quietness might be illusory. The sabotage wasn't showing any sign of letting up. Every city in the nation over about two thousand population had had some kind of incident by now, and people were frightened. Hungry, too. The first prosecutions were pending for food-hoarding and evasion of ration laws.

But the Trainites generally – or people who had thought of themselves as such, which meant most of the more intelligent young people and some of their elders – were puzzled and dismayed and didn't know what to do. After that incredible gaffe in the president's state-of-war announcement, they'd expected an instant request for the charges to be dropped, on the grounds that they could now never be tried by an unbiased jury. Like a shout of jubilation another wave of demonstrations and riots had broken out … and been suppressed. Without a clue from Train himself, all these people who'd imagined they had found a leader began to wonder whether he might indeed have been involved in the Bamberley kidnapping. The most optimistic started to murmur that he must be dead, or being starved and brainwashed into confessing regardless of his guilt. Only the most sophisticated looked at the sky, which was overcast as usual, and watched the rain eat into clothing, brickwork, concrete – and despaired.

There were TV lights in the courtroom. They would be transmitting the case live, all over the country. The precedent had been set years ago in Denver, but the Watkins case was recorded and edited for broadcasting. This was being covered like the Army-McCarthy hearings, only more so. It was going to have a colossal audience despite its daytime slot. It didn't seem right for the networks to be putting on old movies and repeats of comedy shows when the nation was on a war footing. (One said carefully: 'war footing'. Because there was no enemy yet to throw the big bombs at.)

Moreover, the networks were glad of the chance to economize. Some of the wealthiest sponsors had had to withdraw support. Who was buying cars at the moment? Who was selling insurance?

The country, so to speak, was idling. Industries were closed down all over, either through sabotage or because they were intrinsically non-productive, like advertising. Men, if fit, had been drafted. But millions upon millions of women were at home, not out shopping or visiting friends, because of rationing and the economy drive. There was gasoline only on a permit. There was a policeman or National Guardsman on the corner with a gun, ready to check the permit. There was TV, though, and 'in the national interest' the major networks were today going to pool their facilities.

So the number of viewers would be fantastic.

Great, Roland Bamberley thought as he steered his son in the wake of the armed guards clearing a way through the pressmen before the courthouse. We'll pillory the bastard the way he deserves. Even the president, we know, will be watching.

He sneezed and apologized to Hector, hoping his mask had trapped the germs.

Great, Peg thought, taking her place among the reporters, rubbing her arm where she had received an obligatory injection. Against the new flu, the medic on the door had said, but not to put too much faith in it because it had been rushed into production.

She'd managed to see Austin. Just for a few minutes. And she wasn't worried any more about him being crazy.

She wasn't sure even yet what bombshell he had up his sleeve. She was convinced, though, that his purpose in refusing to cooperate, to apply for bail, to engage a lawyer, must be a valid one. He had dropped one clue; when she told him what she'd just learned about Decimus's fate, he gave a faint smile and commented that at least in jail he wasn't exposed to that kind of risk. And that was that. But it was enough.

It hadn't occurred to her before, but it had now crossed her mind that maybe things were going the way he wanted, the right way. And that being so he was safer in prison than out.

She'd know soon, anyhow, and so would the world. If only Zena could be here! And Felice! But Felice was too sick and Zena was in jail. Widow of a famous Trainite.

That would be put right when they tore down the jails.

The judge took his place, trying not to scowl at the TV lights because he knew he was the star of the show. He looked out over the court: prosecuting attorney (nod), lawyer appointed by the state to defend Train who hated his client anyway and had learned to detest him even more owing to his obstinate non-cooperation, press, TV commentator murmuring into his mike, prospective jurors ...

'Is everything in order?' he asked the clerk. 'Then let the prisoner be brought in.'

Meekly into the box, amid a rustle and buzz as people half rose to stare at him.

'Who's that?' Hector Bamberley asked his father.

'What do you mean, "Who's that?" '

The prosecuting attorney twisted in his seat. 'What did Hector say? I didn't quite catch it.'

The judge, poised to launch the proceedings, noticed the conversation and frowned his disapproval. TV cameras were closing on Hector and his father, while another remained fixed on Austin. The judge coughed to attract attention back to him, which was foolish; it was a good thirty seconds before he was in a state to talk clearly again, and by then Austin had said in a clear voice, well carried by the microphones, 'Your honor, if that's Hector Bamberley over there, perhaps you'd ask if he's ever seen me before. My name, of course, is Austin Train.'

Someone booed from the back of the court. Gasping, the judge said, 'Be quiet! I must make one thing clear from the very outset – I will not tolerate any disturbances during this trial!'

'But that's not Austin Train!' Hector shouted. He looked as though he was about to cry. 'I never saw him in my life!'

There was a moment of astonished silence. Then Peg, deliberately, gave a giggle. A nice loud one. It was echoed.

'Quiet!' the judge snapped. She received glares from all sides and one of the armed ushers moved menacingly toward her. She subsided.

'Now, young man,' the judge said in an avuncular tone, 'I realize this trial is a great strain for you after all you've been through, but I assure you your chance to speak—'

'I *won't* shut up!' Not to the judge; to his father who was trying to keep him in his seat. Forcing himself to his feet, he went on, 'Sir, that isn't in the least like the man who locked me up. That one was fatter, with lots of hair, brown teeth, no glasses, always dirty—'

'But you said you were kidnapped by Austin Train!' his father roared.

'That's not him!' Hector cried.

It looked as though the judge might be going to faint; a camera zoomed in on him as he briefly shut his eyes. Recovering, to the accompaniment of a hubbub of comment in the court as well as the coughs and snuffles which were so continual now in any public place it would have seemed uncanny for them to stop, he said, 'Am I to understand that this boy has never been confronted with the accused?'

A hasty consultation. Then: 'Your honor, a recess please!'

'Denied!' the judge said without hesitation. 'This is the most extraordinary, I may say the most ridiculous case of confusion I have ever encountered in nearly twenty years. I'm waiting for an answer to my question!'

Everyone looked toward the Bamberleys. Eventually Roland rose, very stiffly, like an old man.

'Well, your honor, in view of the strain on my son – and he's barely recovered even now from all the disgusting diseases he was given ...'

'I see,' the judge said. 'I see. Who is responsible for this incredible piece of incompetence?'

'Well, your honor,' the prosecuting attorney said, looking dazed as though the sky had just fallen on him, 'he did positively identify pictures of Train—'

'I said yes to make you stop badgering me!' Hector flared. 'You were worse than the people who kidnapped me, the way you kept on and on!'

By this time the court was in uproar; the boy's voice could scarcely be heard. Peg was jigging up and down in her seat with sheer delight. Oh, shame to have suspected Austin of being crazy! They built the pillory and here they're in it themselves!

'Order!' the judge shouted, rapping with his gavel, and the noise died away little by little. Obviously everyone present wanted some sort of explanation as much as he did.

'Now!' he continued when he had the chance. 'Am I to understand that you, Hector, identified this man from photographs?'

'Oh, they kept on showing me photographs all right,' was the sullen answer. 'They said he could have been wearing a wig, couldn't he? They said he worked as a garbage-man – wouldn't that make him dirty? So in the end I said, yes, yes, yes, just to make them leave me alone!'

He sat down suddenly and buried his face in his hands. At his side his father stood, frozen and pale as a marble statue.

'Your honor!' Austin said suddenly. The judge turned as though so bewildered he would accept help from any quarter.

'What is it?'

Peg clenched her fists because if she didn't keep control she feared she might scream like a teenager at a Body English concert. There had been a – a *ring* to those last two words. Something of the timbre which had been in his voice when he converted Petronella Page. Was he going to get a chance now to speak to all the millions watching?

*

'Your honor, I gather you'd welcome an explanation of the way this laughable situation has arisen.'

'I do indeed want an explanation!' the judge rasped. 'And certainly it ought to come from you! You've sat in jail with your mouth shut when a single word could have saved us this – this farce!' And he added, 'But be brief!'

'I'll try, your honor. Briefly, then, it's because even though my prosecutors knew there are some two hundred people who've adopted my name, they were so eager to crucify me they ignored the fact and so stupid they didn't bother to show me to Hector.'

'Train!' The judge was on the verge of explosion. 'Silence! This is a court of law, not a forum for your treasonable mouthings!'

'I have kept quiet in face of even a prejudgment by the president!' Austin barked. 'I'll leave it to the American public to decide what justice I'd have received from a judge who accuses me of treason – which I'm not on trial for!'

'Made it!' Peg whooped, discovering to her surprise that she was out of her seat and waving despite the orders of an armed man to sit down. She obeyed, contentedly enough. Now he was over the watershed; if they cut him off at this point, literally millions and millions of people would be demanding why, and prepared to do something about it.

And the judge knew it. His face had gone paper-white, and his mouth was working as though he was about to throw up. Suddenly, without warning, he left his chair and stormed out of the court. There was commotion in his wake.

Austin waited, his hands on the bar of the box. At length he murmured to the microphone nearest him, 'I think most people would like to hear what I have to say, even if the judge is afraid to.'

'Oh, I love you! I love you!' Peg whispered. She felt tears coursing down her checks. It was the most spectacular theatrical gesture she had ever seen: Petronella Page's treatment of the studio audience amplified to the tenth power. She tried to shout, 'Yes, go on!' But her voice was lost somewhere in the depths of her throat.

It didn't matter. There were fifty other shouts to compensate. 'Thank you, my sick friends,' Austin said as the cameras closed on him. 'Poisoned, diseased, and now about to be starved as well ... No, I'm not joking; I wish I were. And above all, I wasn't joking when I spoke of the people who have put me on trial as being stupid.

'That is the worst thing they have done to you: damaged your intelligence. And it's small consolation that now they are doing it to themselves.

'Those charges that the intelligence of people in this country is being undermined by pollution are all true – if they weren't, do you think I'd be here, the wrong man, the man who didn't kidnap Hector Bamberley? Who could have been so *silly*?'

There was laughter. Nervous, drive-away-the-ghosts laughter. 'And because of that' – he drew himself up straight – 'at all costs, to me, to anyone, *at all costs* if the human race is to survive, the forcible exportation of the way of life invented by these stupid men must … be … *stopped.*'

His voice suddenly rose to a roar. 'The planet Earth can't afford it!'

He's got them, Peg thought. I never believed he'd do it. But he's got them. Christ, that cameraman: he's shaking, shaking from head to foot. In a moment he's going to weep like Petronella did!

'Our way of life,' Austin said, resuming a conversational tone. 'Yes … You're aware that we're under martial law? It's been claimed that we're at war, that at Denver we suffered a sneak chemical attack. As a matter of fact, the stuff that caused the Denver Madness is a military psychotomimetic based on the ergot that infects rye, known by the U.S. Army code "BW", manufactured on an experimental basis at Fort Detrick, Maryland, from 1959 to 1963, stored at the Rocky Mountain Arsenal until the latter year, and then disposed of in steel drums in an abandoned silver mine. Are you interested in hearing what happened to it?'

He grinned suddenly; it made his newly bald head resemble the skull of one of the Trainite symbols they had – for a very short time – marketed for people to hang on their gates, three-dimensional in sterile plastic.

'Well, shortly before Christmas last year, one of the now frequent earthquakes in that area ruptured the first of the drums. Its contents leaked into the water-table serving the wells at the Bamberley Hydroponics Plant. As far as I've been able to discover, only one American citizen died from that contamination, my late friend Decimus Jones. Hearing he was about to make a trip to California, an acquaintance of his made him a present of some Nutripon filched from the factory. Part of the same batch that went to Noshri and San Pablo. He went insane, and he died.

'You now know who started the war in Honduras, by the way.'

Quite distinctly, Peg heard several people say, 'So that's what happened!'

'Later there was another earthquake. It must have broken open not one but scores of the drums containing BW. So now you know about Denver and the Madness, too. You know why you're eating scant rations, why you're forbidden to travel freely, why you're at risk of being stopped and searched by any soldier who dislikes your face. The other thing you should know concerns the *jigras*. They weren't made deliberately resistant for use as a weapon against us! They simply learned the technique of biological adaptation. Any of you had trouble lately with fleas? Lice? Roaches? Mosquitoes?'

Roland Bamberley was sitting silent, Peg realized suddenly, when he should by rights have been on his feet screaming. Why? She glanced at him, and saw that his face was perfectly rigid, his eyes were shut, and he was clutching his right arm.

But no one was making any move to help him, though he was obviously in such pain he had almost fainted. What could be wrong?

And then she forgot about that. Austin was talking again.

'I could have said most of this months ago, all in fact except the story of Decimus Jones. Indeed, I was going to. On the Page show, as you'll recall. But then, when I realized what was going to happen to me, I decided I was better advised to wait. One more thing remained to be done.

'When did you last bask in the sun, friends? When did you last dare drink from a creek? When did you last risk picking fruit and eating it straight from the tree? What were your doctor's bills last year? Which of you live in cities where you don't wear a filtermask? Which of you spent this year's vacation in the mountains because the sea is fringed with garbage? Which of you right now is not suffering from a nagging minor complaint – bowel upset, head-ache, catarrh, or like Mr Bamberley there' – he pointed – 'acute claudication of a major artery? Someone should attend to him, please. He needs an imme-diate dose of a good vasodilator.'

Astonished, the medic by the courtroom door who had administered shots to the press selected the right hypodermic from his kit and ran to obey. There was a spontaneous burst of clapping which Austin waved down.

'He'll recover, though I'm afraid he can't expect to live very long. None of us can. I don't mean because we're going to be gunned down, though that's likely, but because our life expectancy is slipping. Ten years ago it was thirty-second in the world – strange, that: the world's richest country having only the thirty-second-best life expectancy – but now it's down to thirty-seventh and still falling … Still, there's hope for man!'

Let there be, Peg said under her breath. Oh, let there be! She remembered: 'I think I can save the world!'

She'd been right about the cameraman. His cheeks were wet.

'In Europe, as you know, they've killed the Mediterranean, just as we killed the Great Lakes. They're in a fair way to killing the Baltic, with help from the Russians who have already killed the Caspian. Well, this living organism we call Mother Earth can't stand that treatment for long – her bowels tormented, her arteries clogged, her lungs choked … But what's happened inevitably as a result? Such a social upheaval that all thoughts of spreading this – this can-cer of ours have had to be forgotten! Yes, there's hope! When starving refugees are besieging frontiers, armies can't be spared to propagate the cancer any further. They have to be called home – like ours!'

Again his voice rose to that pitch that commanded total attention.

'Keep it here! For God's sake if you believe in Him, but in any case for Man's sake, keep it here! Although it's already too late for us, it may not be too late for the rest of the planet! We owe it to those who come after that there never be another Mekong Desert! There must never be another Oklahoma dustbowl! There must never be another dead sea! I beg you, I plead with you to take a solemn oath: though your children will be twisted, and dull-witted, and slow of speech, there will remain somewhere, for long enough, a place where children grow up healthy, bright and sane! Vow it! Swear it! Pledge it for the species we have so nearly— Yes?'

Blinking at the cameraman with tear-wet cheeks, who now sniveled, 'I'm sorry, Mr Train, but it's no good!' He tapped the earphones he was wearing. 'The president has ordered you to be cut off!'

There was total silence. It was as though Austin were an inflated dummy and someone had just located the valve to let the gas out. He seemed inches shorter as he turned aside, and scarcely anyone heard him mutter, 'Well, I did try.'

'But you mustn't stop!' Peg heard herself scream, leaping to her feet. 'You—'

The wall behind him buckled and the ceiling leaned on his head with the full weight of a concrete beam. Then the roof began to cascade down on everybody in a stream of rubble.

Ossie's last bomb had worked well.

ARMED

'There, baby – how does that grab you?' Pete said proudly. Jeannie clapped her hands and gasped. 'Oh, honey! I always wanted one of them! A microwave cooker!' She rounded on him. 'But how did you get hold of it?'

He knew why she was asking. Goods of all kinds had become scarce in the past weeks. Partly it was due to lack of transportation; trucks were being reserved to essentials, mainly food, and convoyed from city to city under Army guard. But also it was because people were dropping out of their jobs, emigrating from cities like a new wave of Okies. One had seen what happened in Denver. If the same fate overtook New York, or Los Angeles, or Chicago …

There were reports of farmers standing off would-be squatters with a gun. Not, of course, in the papers or on TV.

'It was liberated,' Pete said with a grin.

'You mean you stole it?' Carl, from the doorway. 'Tush, tush. And you an ex-pig. Who shall guard the guardians?'

'I did not steal it!' Pete snapped. He found his brother-in-law almost impossible to tolerate. Even after that crazy speech on TV he still seemed to think that Austin Train was God. And the hell of it was, so did far too many other people. It was making Pete nervous. The station house in Towerhill where he'd worked most of last year had been bombed and Sergeant Chain, his former chief, was dead. There had been a rattle of gunfire only a few blocks distant as he came home tonight, most likely a suspected curfew-breaker being stopped from running. The whole city felt like a factory whose owners had gone bankrupt without warning: a shell, emptied of its workers, who now stood at its gate seething with fury.

'Then how did you get it?' Carl pressed. Aware he was being needled, Pete drew a deep breath.

'It came from that big discount warehouse over in Arvada. The owner got killed. His widow's just been telling people to help themselves.'

'Looting with permission, huh?'

'No! The Army's supervising it all, and I got a certificate—'

'Oh, quit wrangling, you two!' Jeannie ordered. 'Don't spoil my treat. This is something I've wanted for ages, Carl. I don't care how we got it, so there.'

Carl sighed and turned away. After a moment Pete said awkwardly, 'Like a beer, Carl? I managed to locate a six-pack. In the icebox.'

'Ah … Yeah, I guess I would; thanks. I'll bring you one in the living-room, shall I?'

It was so hard all the time pretending to be dull from the aftermath of the BW, when at long long last the revolution had arrived! Well – maybe not quite THE REVOLUTION, in capitals, but certainly the chance to make a revolution work. There had never before been so many people so absolutely angry with the system, and striking back against it.

He was stuck here, though, until the opportunity arose to slip through the cordon around the city and go underground. Because of the massive forces which had been poured into Denver to clear up after the Madness, this was almost certainly the most completely controlled city in the nation. What a place to be stranded! He distrusted Pete because he had been in the police, and he was even afraid of Jeannie because he'd confessed to her the killing of that state border guard.

Hell, how could these two be so wilfully *blind*? They conceded that the Madness had been caused by poison gas, but because it was Train who had given chapter and verse about it, they were ready to argue that 'It wasn't the government's fault!' They wanted the clock turned back to where it was before, they wanted the government to regain control even though it had lied to and cheated and even killed its people!

If they were capable of that degree of stupidity and docility, they might all too easily sell him out …

301

'You picked the right day to have it delivered, too,' Jeannie was saying as she patted the cooker's shining side. 'Mom got me a chicken. Don't hang around too long with your beer, will you? Dinner's only going to be a minute with this beauty.'

Carl curled his lip in disgust as he collected the beer cans and headed for the adjacent room in Pete's wake. Sitting down, he said, 'Seen the sun lately, have you?'

'Oh, stop it!' Pete snapped. 'I've heard it all before! But things are getting back to normal, aren't they? We got water on again, morning and evening. We got power though we don't have gas. Yeah, back to normal.'

'You're damned right,' Carl said with earnestness. 'This is going to be "normal" from now on. The situation we're in now, I mean. Martial law. Travel restrictions. Protest banned. Half the country rocking with dynamite explosions. This is the future, unless we prevent it. And what sort of a life is it going to be for my nephew?'

'The kid's going to be okay,' Pete insisted. 'Doc McNeil says he's coming on fine, we got special rations for Jeannie because she's pregnant—'

'And you're happy with that?' Carl exploded. 'You're happy that he's never going to be able to move from one city to another because he wants to, without applying for police permission? That's the kind of freedom we're going to lose for good unless we seize it back for ourselves!'

'I thought you were the one who objected to freedom,' Pete sighed. 'At least the freedom to make what you want, where you want. Where would you let someone build a factory?'

'Any place it wouldn't spoil other people's lives,' Carl retorted. 'But why have so many factories, anyway? Why can't you like have a car that lasts half your lifetime? Why?'

'Now then, you two!' Jeannie shouted from the kitchen, interrupting the cheerful tune she'd been humming. 'I want this to be a nice happy evening, hear?'

'Okay,' Carl called back, and went on in a lower tone. 'But what bugs me is this – and I'm not the only one, thank God. *They're still there.* The people who covered up the sun, the people who jailed Train on a count he wasn't guilty of, the people who made that poison gas: they're still there, and they'll be there until the stink gets so bad they move to New Zealand. They'll be able to afford to. You and I can't. That's what we've got to put right!'

'Even if it's true about the gas,' Pete grunted, 'Train himself said it was an accident. An earthquake.'

'What's accidental about an earthquake in Denver? Mom told me: there weren't any around here when I was a baby. All that poisoned waste they poured down old mine-shafts made the rocks slip under the mountains. Nothing accidental there, man!'

It was the same argument. Tenth time through? Twelfth? 'Here goes nothing!' Jeannie sang out merrily from the kitchen. Sharpen your appetites!'

'Know one of the reasons I got that cooker?' Pete said under his breath. 'To cut short the time I have to listen to your talk before we go to the table.' He chuckled and sipped his beer.

And there was a thump from the kitchen and the sound of a dish breaking, and Carl ran to the door and stared in, and said, 'Oh, Christ. What happened? She get a – a shock, maybe?'

Hobbling frantically in his wake, clutching at tables and chair-backs because his cane was out of reach, Pete stared in horror at Jeannie prostrate on the floor. Carl dived for the socket and unplugged the cooker.

'But it's brand-new!' Pete said foolishly. 'Jeannie! Jeannie!'

There was an hour to wait in the lobby of the hospital, where the breeze drifted in through broken windows and brought with it the scent of smoke. They had passed the fire on the way, and the police escort who was riding with them to vouch for their right to traverse the street-corner checkpoints after curfew – it was Pete's old friend, Chappie Rice – said it was the third he'd heard about tonight, all due to arson. Carl paced up and down, staring at the flames and wishing they might engulf the country. Pete, confined to a chair by his weak back, spent the time in quiet cursing.

At long long last Doug McNeil came down the passage and Carl rushed to meet him.

'Is she—?'

'Jeannie's going to live,' Doug muttered. 'Just. Pete, what make is that cooker of yours? Is it an Instanter?'

'Why …' Staring, Pete gave a nod. 'How did you know?' Doug didn't look at him. He said, 'I thought it might be. We've had trouble with that brand before. I've seen – oh, four cases. Don't know what the hell stopped them from closing down the company.' He drew a deep breath.

'It leaked, Pete. Leaked some of its radiation. Bad shielding. And it literally cooked Jeannie's baby in her womb.'

At two in the morning Carl was roused by the sound of movement in the living-room, and padded barefoot to see what was happening. He found Pete turning the pages of a book and making notes on a memo-pad. 'What are you doing?' he demanded.

Pete didn't raise his head. He said, 'I'm learning how to build a bomb.'

THE SHOCK OF RECOGNITION

Still not used to being in uniform again after ten years in civilian clothes … Philip Mason wriggled his shoulders inside his shirt. The cloth was rough. But discomfort was among the penalties people were going to have to pay to buy back the good life of the past, and it didn't really amount to much, in his view.

There must be a hell of a lot of people refusing to part with even that token, though. He glanced up uneasily as a vast noise came from the sky, and saw a flight of helicopter gunships just disappearing into the overcast, no doubt to mount another strike against the insurrection in Cheyenne. It was incredible how the cities were going off like a string of firecrackers, one after another …

He wondered whether the guy he'd taken over this demolition gang from was up there in one of those gunships. He'd been pulled out, like the majority of the career soldiers originally assigned to reconstruction duty, as the situation worsened. They said that in Harlem and the Bronx the Army was committing tanks …

But best not to worry about other people's problems. Best to concentrate on the way things were coming right for himself, little by little, just as these ruins here were being cleared. It was going to take months to make Denver presentable again; it was already showing signs of the firm central control it enjoyed, though, and there were even a few stores open around noon each day for three hours. For himself life had been fairly easy since he was promoted acting sergeant: a gas ration, use of his car, permission to sleep and eat at home with Dennie except when it was his turn as duty noncom.

And with Harold. But he tried not to think about Harold any more than Harold apparently thought about him.

'Hey!'

He turned to see who was calling. From across the street where another gang was clearing a house which had been burned to a shell like the one his own men were pulling down, a National Guard sergeant. He looked vaguely familiar. Hunting in memory, Philip placed him. One of the fitters he and Alan (poor Alan!) had hired to install the Mitsuyama purifiers.

If only they'd been installed all over the city! If only they hadn't clogged with those filthy bacteria!

But it was no use wishing.

He told his pfc to keep the gang working and strolled over to say hello. He couldn't quite remember the man's name. Chicano, though. Gomez? Perez? Something like that.

'You're Mason, aren't you?' the man said. 'Thought I recognized you. You're the mother that put in those foreign filters and poisoned the water. What the hell are you doing running around loose – and in one of our uniforms, too? Well, if no one else has taken care of you, I will.'

He unslung his rifle and shot Philip at pointblank range.

THE RATIONAL PROPOSAL

Page: Well, I'm sorry about the gunfire on that last segment, which I hope didn't spoil your viewing and listening pleasure, but as you heard the fire in Chicago Old Town is now officially 'under control' and the rioters are being contained. Before we go on to our next guest, I've been asked to say that the guerrilla strikes against Jacksonville, Omaha and San Bernardino, which our on-the-spot reporter mentioned while speculating about the cause of the Chicago fire, are unconfirmed, repeat not confirmed. So! Let me just reassure our audience here in the studio that even if something similar to what we were just hearing about took place in New York, we'd be in no danger – this building was designed in conjunction with Civil Defense experts. Are we ready for …? Yes, fine, I see we are. Well, world, everyone knows by this time that an astonishingly large proportion of our population accepted the precepts of the late Austin Train and still clings to them, despite what the president has said about their being based on an appeal to emotion and a rejection of rationality. Just where that's led us, you all know. One man, however, while all this has been going on, has been quietly and persistency pursuing another path. As you've almost certainly heard, the famous Dr Thomas Grey of the Bamberley Trust has been trying for years to work out, with the aid of computers and all possible modern methods, a solution to the desperate problems facing us. I'm delighted that he's chosen this show to take the wraps off his findings. Tom Grey! (*Audience applause.*)

Grey: Thank you, Miss Page.

Page: Speaking of wraps, I notice you have your arm in a sling, Tom. I hope – Oh, excuse me just a second … I'm sorry, world, but we've been asked to yield a minute of air time for a public service announcement. We'll be back with you in a moment. Go ahead.

Naval commander: This is an emergency announcement from the Department of Defense, Navy. Hear this, hear this, all personnel currently on shore leave in the following states: New York, New Jersey, Pennsylvania, Florida, Texas, California. Report at once to the nearest Army or Air Force base or National Guard headquarters and place yourselves at the disposal of the commanding officer. Your assistance is required in quelling civil disorder. That is all.

Page: I see we have someone right here in the studio who's off to answer that call. We'll just stand by for a moment while he's leaving. (*Audience applause.*) That's okay, then. Tom, I was wondering about your arm.

Grey: It's nothing serious, I'm glad to say. I – uh – I got caught on the fringes of one of those civil disorders they were just talking about. (*Audience laughter.*) But I got off with just a wrenched shoulder.

Page: Fighting back? (*Audience laughter.*)

Grey: No, my car ran over a caltrap and hit a lamppost. (*Audience laughter.*)

Page: Well, I hope you're better soon. Now about this idea of yours— Just a second, is something wrong?

Voice from audience: Smoke! I'm sure I can smell smoke!

Page: I'll check with my producer. Ian? … You're right, friend, but it's nothing to worry about. It's blowing up from Newark, apparently. You know there's a big fire there. Count yourself lucky to be in here – I'm told it's far worse out-of-doors! (*Audience laughter.*) Tom, this undertaking of yours must have been incredibly complex. You've had to analyze literally every major factor affecting our predicament, right?

Grey: Yes, every one.

Page: And you're now in a position to reveal the chief conclusion— Sorry! Hold on. Yes, Ian, what is it this time? … Oh. Yes, of course; that sounds urgent. I'll tell them … Another announcement for you, world – sorry to keep interrupting like this, but of course we can't ignore what's going on. And this is an important and very tragic piece of news. It seems the Niagara Falls Bridge is out – either blown or collapsed, no one yet knows which, but because there are so many people trying to get over the Canadian border there, all TV and radio networks are being asked to tell people to avoid the area so that essential help can get through – the highways are kind of crowded up that way, I'm told … Tom, as I was saying: you can unveil your conclusions now, right?

Grey: Yes, and they're crucially important. Of course, I've been able to take into account only such items as natural resources, oxygen level, food stocks, water reserves, and so on, and – ah – it's curiously ironical in a way because one might say—

Page: Tom, I'm sorry, but the producer is buzzing me again. Yes? … I see. Will do. Tom, they're going to pre-empt us in about two minutes. The president is winding up to a new pitch. Can you keep your main point short, please?

Grey: Well, as I was about to say, it's sort of ironical, because we're already engaged, in a sense, in the course of action my findings dictate.

Page: Don't keep the world on tenterhooks, Tom! Out with it! What's the best thing we can do to ensure a long, happy, healthy future for mankind?

Grey: We can just about restore the balance of the ecology, the biosphere, and so on – in other words we can live within our means instead of on an unrepayable overdraft, as we've been doing for the past half century – if we exterminate the two hundred million most extravagant and wasteful of our species.

Page: Follow that if you can, Mr President. It's your reward for pre-convicting Austin Train. World, what about lighting him a funeral pyre? Doesn't he deserve—?

(*Transcript ends.*)

THE SMOKE OF THAT GREAT BURNING

Opening the door to the visiting doctor, all set to apologize for the flour on her hands – she had been baking – Mrs Byrne sniffed. Smoke! And if she could smell it with her heavy head cold, it must be a tremendous fire!

'We ought to call the brigade!' she exclaimed. 'Is it a hayrick?'

'The brigade would have a long way to go,' the doctor told her curtly. 'It's from America. The wind's blowing that way.'

NEXT YEAR

THE SHOCKWAVE RIDER

ACKNOWLEDGMENT

People like me who are concerned to portray in fictional terms aspects of that foreign country, the future, whither we are all willy-nilly being deported, do not make our guesses in a vacuum. We are frequently – and in this case I am specifically – indebted to those who are analyzing the limitless possibilities of tomorrow with some more practical aim in view … as for instance the slim yet admirable hope that our children may inherit a world more influenced by imagination and foresight than our own.

The 'scenario' (to employ a fashionable cliché) of *The Shockwave Rider* derives in large part from Alvin Toffler's stimulating study *Future Shock*, and in consequence I'm much obliged to him.

J. K. H. B.

BOOK 1

The Basic Straining Manual

A THOUGHT FOR TODAY

Take 'em an inch and they'll give you a hell.

DATA-RETRIVIAL MODE

The man in the bare steel chair was as naked as the room's white walls. They had shaved his head and body completely; only his eyelashes remained. Tiny adhesive pads held sensors in position at a dozen places on his scalp, on his temples close to the corners of his eyes, at each side of his mouth, on his throat, over his heart and over his solar plexus and at every major ganglion down to his ankles.

From each sensor a lead, fine as gossamer, ran to the sole object – apart from the steel chair and two other chairs, both softly padded – that might be said to furnish the room. That was a data-analysis console about two meters broad by a meter and a half high, with display screens and signal lights on its slanted top, convenient to one of the padded chairs.

Additionally, on adjustable rods cantilevered out from the back of the steel chair, there were microphones and a three-vee camera.

The shaven man was not alone. Also present were three other people: a young woman in a slick white coverall engaged in checking the location of the sensors; a gaunt black man wearing a fashionable dark red jerkin suit clipped to the breast of which was a card bearing his picture and the name Paul T. Freeman; and a heavy-set white man of about fifty, dressed in dark blue, whose similar card named him as Ralph C. Hartz.

After long contemplation of the scene, Hartz spoke.

'So that's the dodger who went further and faster for longer than any of the others.'

'Haflinger's career,' Freeman said mildly, '*is* somewhat impressive. You've picked up on his record?'

'Naturally. That's why I'm here. It may be an atavistic impulse, but I did feel inclined to see with my own eyes the man who posted such an amazing score of new personae. One might almost better ask what he hasn't done than what he has. Utopia designer, life-style counselor, Delphi gambler, computer-sabotage consultant, systems rationalizer, and God knows what else besides.'

'Priest, too,' Freeman said. 'We're progressing into that area today. But what's remarkable is not the number of separate occupations he's pursued. It's the contrast between successive versions of himself.'

'Surely you'd expect him to muddle his trail as radically as possible?'

'You miss the point. The fact that he eluded us for so long implies that he's learned to live with and to some extent control his overload reflexes, using the sort of regular commercial tranquilizer you or I would take to cushion the shock of moving to a new house, and in no great quantity, either.'

'Hmm …' Hartz pondered. 'You're right; that is amazing. Are you ready to start today's run? I don't have too much time to spend here at Tarnover, you know.'

Not looking up, the girl in white plastic said, 'Yes, sir, he's status go.'

She headed for the door. Taking a seat at Freeman's gestured invitation, Hartz said doubtfully, 'Don't you have to give him a shot or something? He looks pretty thoroughly sedated.'

Settling comfortably in his own chair adjacent to the data console, Freeman said, 'No, it's not a question of drugs. It's done with induced current in the motor centers. One of our specialties, you know. All I have to do is move this switch and he'll recover consciousness – though not, of course, the power of ambulation. Just enough to let him answer in adequate detail. By the way, before I turn him on, I should fill in what's happening. Yesterday I broke off when I tapped into what seemed to be an exceptionally heavily loaded image, so I'm going to regress him to the appropriate date and key in the same again, and we'll see what develops.'

'What kind of image?'

'A girl of about ten running like hell through the dark.'

FOR PURPOSES OF IDENTIFICATION

At present I am being Arthur Edward Lazarus, profession minister, age forty-six, celibate: founder and proprietor of the Church of Infinite Insight, a converted (and what better way for a church to start than with a successful conversion?) drive-in movie theater near Toledo, Ohio, which stood derelict for years not so much because people gave up going to the movies – they still make them, there's always an audience for wide-screen porn of the type that gets pirate three-vee satellites sanded out of orbit in next to no time – as because it's on land disputed between the Billykings, a Protestant tribe, and the Grailers, Catholic. No one cares to have his property tribaled. However, normally they respect churches, and the territory of the nearest Moslem tribe, the Jihad Babies, lies ten miles to the west.

My code, of course, begins with 4GH, and has done so for the past six years.

Memo to selves: find out whether there's been any change in the status of a 4GH, and particularly whether something better has been introduced ... a complication devoutly to be fished.

MAHER-SHALAL-HASH-BAZ

She ran, blinded by sorrow, under a sky that boasted a thousand extra stars moving more swiftly than a minute hand. The air of the June night rasped her throat with dust, every muscle ached in her legs, her belly, even her arms, but she kept right on as hard as she could pelt. It was so hot, the tears that leaked from her eyes dried as they were shed.

Sometimes she went on more or less level roadway, not repaired for years but still quite sound; sometimes she crossed rough ground, the sites perhaps of factories whose owners had transferred their operations up to orbit, or of homes which had been tribaled in some long-ago riot.

In the blackness ahead loomed lights and illuminated signs bordering a highway. Three of the signs advertised a church and offered free Delphi counseling to registered members of its congregation.

Wildly glancing around, blinking her eyes to clear perception, she saw a monstrous multi-colored dome, as though a lampshade made from a puffer-fish were to be blown up larger than a whale.

Pacing her at a discreet distance, tracking a tracer concealed in the paper frock which was all she wore except sandals, a man in an electric car fought his yawns and hoped that on this particular Sunday the pursuit would not be too long or too dull.

MINOR PROFIT IN THE BELLY
OF THE GREAT FISH

As well as presiding at the church, Reverend Lazarus lived in it, his home being a trailer parked behind the cosmoramic altar – formerly the projection screen, twenty meters high. How else could a man with a minister's vocation afford so much privacy and so much space?

Surrounded by the nonstop hum of the compressor that kept his poly-chrome plastic dome inflated – three hundred meters by two hundred by ninety high – he sat alone at his desk in the nose compartment of the trailer, his tiny office, comping the take from the day's collections. He was worried. His deal with the coley group who provided music at his services was on a percentage basis, but he had to guarantee a thousand, and attendance was falling off as the church's novelty declined. Today only about seven hundred people had come here; there had not even been a jam as they drove back on to the highway.

Moreover, for the first time in the nine months since the church was launched, today's collections had yielded more scrip than cash. Cash didn't circulate much any more – at least not on this continent – except in the paid-avoidance areas, where people drew a federal grant for going without some of the twenty-first century's more expensive gadgetry, but activating a line to the federal credit computers on a Sunday, their regular down-time day, meant a heavy surcharge, beyond the means of most churches including his. So churchgoers generally remembered to bring coins or bills or one of the little booklets of scrip vouchers issued to them when they joined.

The trouble with all this scrip, though – as he knew from sad experience – was that when he presented it to his bank tomorrow at least half of it would be returned marked VOID: the bigger the sum pledged, the more likely. Some would have been handed in by people already so deep in pointless debt the computers had banned expenditure on nonessentials; any new church inevitably attracted a lot of shock victims. But some would have been canceled overnight as the result of a family row: 'You credded *how* much? My God, what did I do to deserve a twitch like you? Get that scrip deeveed *this minute!*'

Still, some people had been ignorantly generous. There was a stack of over fifty copper dollars, worth three hundred to any electronics firm, asteroid ores being poor in high-conduction metals. It was illegal to sell currency for scrap, but everybody did it, saying they'd found old saucepans in the attic of a secondhand house, or a disused cable while digging over the back yard.

Riding high on the public Delphi boards right now was a prediction that the next dollar issue would be plastic with a one- or two-year life. Well, *plus ça* small change *plus c'est* biodegradable …

He tipped the coins into his smelter without counting them because only the weight of the eventual ingot mattered, and turned to the other task he was obliged to complete before he quit work for the day: analysis of the Delphi forms the congregation had filled out. There were many fewer than there had been back in April; then, he'd expected fourteen or fifteen hundred, whereas this week's input was barely half that. Even seven hundred and some opinions, though, was a far wider spread than most individuals could hope to invoke, particularly while in the grip of acute depression or some other life-style crisis.

By definition, his congregation *all* had life-style crises.

The forms bore a series of bald statements each summarizing a personal problem, followed by blank spaces where any paid-up member of the church was invited to offer a solution. Today there were nine items, a sad contrast with those palmy days in the spring when he'd had to continue on the second side of the form. Now the word must be out on the mouth-to-mouth circuit: 'Last time they only gave us nine things to delph, so next Sunday we're going to …'

What's the opposite of a snowball? A thawball?

Despite the failure of his old high hopes, though, he determined to go through the proper motions. He owed it to himself, to those who regularly attended his services, and above all to those whose heart-cries of agony had been eavesdropped on today.

Item A on the list he disregarded. He had invented it as a juicy lure. There was nothing like a scandal of the kind that might eventually make the media to grab people's attention. The bait was the vague hope that one day soon they might notice a news report and be able to tell each other, 'Say, that bit where the poker got shot for messing with his daughter – remember we comped that one at church?'

A link with yesterday, tenuous, but to be prized.

Wryly he re-read what he had dreamed up: *I am a girl, fourteen. All the time my father is drunk and wants to plug into me but he creds so much for liquor I don't get none to pay my piece when I go out and they repossessed my …*

The responses were drearily predictable. The girl should apply to the courts and have herself declared of age, she should tell her mother at once, she should denounce her father anonymously, she should get a doc-block put on his credit, bail out of home and go live in a teener dorm – and so forth.

'Lord!' he said to the air. 'If I programed a computer to feed my confessional booth, people would get better advice than that!'

Nothing about this project was working out in the least as he had hoped.

Moreover, the next item enshrined a genuine tragedy. But how could one help a woman still young, in her thirties, a trained electronics engineer, who went to orbit on a six-month contract and discovered too late that she was subject to osteochalcolysis – loss of calcium and other minerals from her skeleton in zerogee conditions – and had to abort the job and now was in danger of breaking bones if she so much as tripped? Without chance of appeal her guild had awarded her contract-breaker status. She couldn't sue for reinstatement unless she worked to pay the lawyer, she couldn't work unless the guild allowed it, she … Round and round and round.

There's a lot of brave new misery in our brave new world!

Sighing, he shook the forms together and piled them under the scanner lens of his desk computer for consolidation and a verdict. For so few it wasn't worth renting time on the public net. To the purr of the air compressor was added the hush-hush of the paper-sorter's plastic fingers.

The computer was secondhand and nearly obsolete, but it still worked most of the time. So, provided it didn't have a b-d overnight, when the shy kids and the worried parents and the healthy but inexplicably unhappy middlers and the lost despairing old 'uns came back for their ration of spiritual reassurance, each would depart clutching a paper straw, a certificate redolent of old-fashioned absolute authority: its heading printed in imitation gold leaf declaring that it was an authentic and legal Delphi assessment based on contributions from not fewer than _____* hundred consultees (* *Insert number; document invalid if total fails to exceed* 99) and delivered under oath/deposition in presence of adult witnesses/notary's seal ** (** *Delete as applicable*) on _____ (month) _____ (day) 20 _____ (year).

A shoddy little makeshift memorial to the collapse of his plans about converting the congregation into his own tame CIMA pool and giving himself the place to stand from which he could move the Earth. He knew now he had picked the wrong pitch, but there was still a faint ache when he thought back to his arrival in Ohio.

At least, though, what he had done might have saved a few people from drugs, or suicide, or murder. If it achieved nothing else, a Delphi certificate did convey the subconscious impression: *I matter after all, because it says right here that hundreds of people have worried about my troubles!*

And he had made a couple of coups on the public boards by taking the unintentional advice of the collective.

The day's work was over. But, moving into the trailer's living zone, he found he did not feel at all sleepy. He considered calling up somebody to play a game at fencing, then remembered that the last of the regular local opponents he'd contacted on arrival had just moved out, and at 2300 it was too late to try and trace another player by calling the Ohio State Fencing Committee.

So the fencing screen stayed rolled in its tube along with the light-pencil and the scorer. He resigned himself to an hour of straight three-vee.

In an excess of impulsive generosity, one of the first people to join his church had given him an abominably expensive present, a monitor that could be programed with his tastes and would automatically select a channel with a suitable broadcast on it. He slumped into a chair and switched on. Promptly it lit the screen, and he found himself invited to advise the opposition party in Jamaica what to do about the widespread starvation on the island so as to depose the government at the next election. Currently the weight of opinion was clustering behind the suggestion that they buy a freight dirigible and airlift packages of synthetic food to the worst-hit areas. So far nobody seemed to have pointed out that the cost of a suitable airship would run into seven figures and Jamaica was as usual bankrupt.

Not tonight! I can't face any more stupidity!

But when he rejected that, the screen went dark. Could there really be nothing else on all the multifarious channels of the three-vee which held any interest for the Reverend Lazarus? He cut out the monitor and tried manual switching.

First he found a coley group, all blue-skin makeup and feathers in their hair, not playing instruments but moving among invisible columns of weak microwaves and provoking disturbances which a computer translated into sound ... hopefully, music. They were stiff and awkward and their coordination was lousy. His own amateur group, composed of kids fresh out of high school, was better at keeping the key and homing on the tonic chord.

Changing, he found a scandal bulletin, voicing unprovable and slanderous – but by virtue of computerized editing not actionable – rumors designed to reassure people by convincing them the world really was as bad as they suspected. In El Paso, Texas, the name of the mayor had been mentioned following the arrest of a man running an illegal Delphi pool taking bets on the number of deaths, broken limbs and lost eyes during hockey and football games; it wasn't the pool *per se* that was illegal, but the fact that it had been returning less than the statutory fifty percent of money staked to the winning bettors. Well, doubtless the mayor's name had indeed been mentioned, several times. And over in Britain, the secretary of the Racial Purification Board had invited Princess Shirley and Prince Jim to become joint patrons of it, because it was known they held strong views on immigration to that unhappy island. Given the rate at which poverty was depopulating all but the areas closest to the Continent, one could scarcely foresee Australians or New Zealanders being impressed. And was it true that last week's long-range rocket attack on tourist hotels in the Seychelles had been financed by a rival hotel chain, not by irredentist members of the Seychellois Liberation Party?

The hell with that.

But what he got next was circus – as everybody called it, despite the official title 'experiential reward and punishment complex'. He must have hit on a field-leader – perhaps the most famous of all, which operated out of Quemadura CA taking advantage of some unrepealed local statute or other – because it was using live animals. Half a dozen scared, wide-eyed kids were lining up to walk a plank no more than five centimeters wide spanning a pool where restless alligators gaped and writhed. Their eager parents were cheering them on. A bold red sign in the corner of the screen said that each step each of them managed to take before slipping would be worth $1000. He switched once more, this time with a shudder.

The adjacent channel should have been spare. It wasn't. A Chinese pirate satellite had taken it over to try and reach midwestern American émigrés. There was a Chinese tribe near Cleveland, so he'd heard, or maybe it was Dayton. Not speaking the language, he moved on, and there were commercials. One was for a life-styling consultancy that he knew maintained private wards for those clients whose condition was worsened instead of improved by the expensive suggestions they'd been given; another was for a euphoric claimed not to be addictive but which was – the company marketing it was being sued by the FDA, only according to the mouth-to-mouth circuit they'd reached the judge, he was good and clutched, and they'd have cleared their profit and would be willing to withdraw the product voluntarily before the case actually came to trial, leaving another few hundred thousand addicts to be cared for by the underfunded, overworked Federal Health Service.

Then there was another pirate broadcast, Australian by the accents, and a girl in a costume of six strategic bubbles was saying, 'Y'know, if all the people with life-style crises were laid end to end … Well, I mean, who'd be left to actually *lay* them?'

That prompted him to a faint grin, and since it was rare to pick up an Australian show he had half-decided to stick with this for a while when a loud buzzer shrilled at him.

Someone was in the confessional booth at the main gate. And presumably at this time of night therefore desperate.

Well, being disturbed at all hours was one of the penalties he'd recognized as inescapable when he created the church. He rose, sighing, and shut off his screen.

Memo to selves: going into three-vee for a while might be a good idea. Get back in touch with the media. Or has priesthood used up the limited amount of public exposure the possessor of a 4GH can permit himself in a given span of time? If not, how much left?

Must find out. *Must.*

Composing his features into a benign expression, he activated the three-vee link to the confessional. He was apprehensive. It was no news to the few who kept in circuit that the Billykings and the Grailers had counted seven dead in last week's match, and the latter had come out ahead. As one might expect; they were the more brutal. Where the Billykings were normally content to disable their captives and leave them to struggle home as best they might, the Grailers' habit was to rope and gag them and hide them in some convenient ruin to die of thirst.

So the caller tonight might not be in need of counsel or even medication. It might be someone sussing out the church with a view to razing it. After all, in the eyes of both tribes it was a pagan shame.

But the screen showed him a girl probably too young to be inducted in either tribe: at a glance, no older than ten, her hair tousled, her eyes red-rimmed with weeping, her cheeks stained with dust down which tears had runneled. A child who had over-reached her ability to imitate an adult, presumably, lost and frightened in the dark— Oh! No! Something more, and worse. For he could see she was holding a knife, and on both its blade and her green frock there were smears so red they could well be fresh blood.

'Yes, little sister?' he said in a neutral tone.

'Father, I got to make confession or I'll be damned!' she sobbed. 'I shivved my mom – cut her all to bits! I guess I must have killed her! I'm *sure* I did!'

Time seemed to stop for a long moment. Then, with what calm he could summon, he uttered what had to be said for the benefit of the record ... because, while the booth itself was sacrosanct, this veephone circuit like all such was tied into the city police-net, and thence to the tireless federal monitors at Canaveral. Or wherever. There were so many of them now, they couldn't all be in the same place.

Memo to selves: would be worth knowing where the rest are.

His voice as gritty as a gravel road, he said, 'My child' – aware as ever of the irony in the phrase – 'you're welcome to unburden your conscience by confiding in me. But I must explain that the secrecy of the confessional doesn't apply when you're talking to a microphone.'

She gazed at his image with such intensity he fancied for a moment he could see himself from her point of view: a lean dark man with a broken nose, wearing a black jerkin and a white collar ornamented with little gilt crosses. Eventually she shook her head, as though her mind were too full of recent horror to leave room for any new shocks.

Gently he explained again, and this time she connected.

'You mean,' she forced out, 'you'll call the croakers?'

'Of course not. But they must be looking for you now in any case. And since you've admitted what you did over my mikes ... Do you understand?'

Her face crumpled. She let fall her knife with a tinkling sound that the pickups caught, faint as fairy bells. A few seconds, and she was crying anew.

'Wait there,' he said. 'I'll be with you in a moment.'

RECESS

A sharp wind tasting of winter blew over the hills surrounding Tarnover and broke red and gold leaves off the trees, but the sky was clear and the sun was bright. Waiting his turn in line at the best of the establishment's twenty restaurants, redolent of old-fashioned luxury up to and including portions of ready-heated food on open display, Hartz gazed admiringly at the view.

'Beautiful,' he said at length. 'Just beautiful.'

'Hm?' Freeman had been pressing his skin on both temples toward the back of his head, as though attempting to squeeze out overpowering weariness. Now he glanced at the window and agreed, 'Oh – yes, I guess it is. I don't get too much time to notice it these days.'

'You seem tired,' Hartz said sympathetically. 'And I'm not surprised. You have a tough job on your hands.'

'And a slow one. Nine hours per day, in segments of three hours each. It gets wearing.'

'But it has to be done.'

'Yes, it has to be done.'

HOW TO GROW DELPHINIUMS

It works, approximately, like this.

First you corner a large – if possible, a very large – number of people who, while they've never formally studied the subject you're going to ask them about and hence are unlikely to recall the correct answer, are nonetheless plugged into the culture to which the question relates.

Then you ask them, as it might be, to estimate how many people died in the great influenza epidemic which followed World War I, or how many loaves were condemned by EEC food inspectors as unfit for human consumption during June 1970.

Curiously, when you consolidate their replies they tend to cluster around the actual figure as recorded in almanacs, yearbooks and statistical returns.

It's rather as though this paradox has proved true: that while nobody knows what's going on around here, everybody knows what's going on around here.

Well, if it works for the past, why can't it work for the future? Three hundred million people with access to the integrated North American data-net is a nice big number of potential consultees.

Unfortunately most of them are running scared from the awful specter of tomorrow. How best to corner people who just do not want to know?

Greed works for some, and for others hope. And most of the remainder will never have any impact on the world to speak of.

Good enough, as they say, for folk music …

A MOMENT FOR MILLSTONES

On the point of undogging his trailer's sealed door and disconnecting the alarms, he hesitated.

Sunday. A moderately good collection, if not a record-breaker. (He sniffed. Hot air. From the smelter.)

And she *might* be a precociously good actress …

He pictured a tribe raiding, looting, vanishing before the croakers swooped, leaving behind no one but a minor immune from police interrogation, hysterical with laughter at the success of her 'practical joke'.

Therefore, prior to shutting down the alarms, he activated all the church's electronics except the coley music system and the automated collection trolleys. When he rounded the base of the altar – ex-screen – it was as though fire raged in the whale's-belly of the dome. Lights flashed all colors of the rainbow and a few to spare, while a three-vee remote over his head not only repeated his image monstrous on the face of the altar but also stored it, minutely detailed, in a recorder buried beneath a yard of concrete. If he were attacked, the recording would be evidence.

Moreover, he carried a gun … but he was never without it.

These precautions, slender though they were, constituted the maximum a priest was expected to take. More could easily worry the federal computers into assessing him as a potential paranoid. They'd been sensitive on such matters ever since, last summer, a rabbi in Seattle who had mined the approaches to his shul forgot to turn off the firing-circuit before a bar mitzvah.

Generally the Fedcomps approved of people with strong religious convictions. They were less likely than some to kick up a fuss. But there were limits, not to mention mavericks.

A few years ago his defenses would have been adequate. Now their flimsiness made him tremble as he walked down the wall-less aisle defined by the black rubber streaks car tires had left over decades. Sure, the fence at the base of the dome was electrified except where access had to be left for the confessional, and the booth itself was explosive-resistant and had its own air supply against a gas attack, but even so …!

Memo to selves: next time, a role where I can take more care of life and limb. Privacy is fine, and I needed it when I arrived here. But this place was never meant to be operated by a single individual. I can't scan every shifting shadow, make sure no nimble shivver is using it for cover!

Thinking of which as I stare around: my vision is unaided. At forty-six??? Out of three hundred million there are bound to be some people that age who have never bought corrective lenses, most because they can't afford them. But suppose the Bureau of Health or some pharmo-medical combine decided there were few enough middlers without glasses to organize an exhaustive study of them? Suppose the people at Tarnover decided there must be a genetic effect involved? *Ow.*

Memo to selves, in red italics: stay closer to chronological age!

At that point in his musing he entered the confessional – and found that through its shatterproof three-centimeter window he was *not* looking at a little girl in a dress spattered with blood.

Instead, the exterior section of the booth was occupied by a burly blond man with a streak of blue in his tightly curled hair, wearing a fashionable rose-and-carmine shirt and an apologetic smile.

'So sorry you've been disturbed, Father,' he said. 'Though it's a stroke of luck that little Gaila found her way here … My name's Shad Fluckner, by the way.'

This poker looked too young to be the girl's father: no more than twenty-five, twenty-six. On the other hand, his congregation included women married for the third or fourth time and now to men as much as twenty years younger. Stepfather?

In that case, why the smile? Because he'd used this kid he didn't give a plastic penny for to rid himself of a rich but dragsome older wife? Fouler things had been admitted in this booth.

Foggily he said, 'Are you kin to – ah – Gaila, then?'

'Not in law, but you could say that after what we've been through together I'm closer to her than her legal kinfolk. I work for Anti-Trauma Inc., you see. Very sensibly, the moment Gaila's parents detected signs of deviant behavior in her, they signed her up for a full course of treatment. Last year we cured her sibling rivalry – classic penis-envy directed against her younger brother – and right now she's working into her Electra complex. With luck we'll progress her to Poppaea level this coming fall … Oh, incidentally: she babbled something about you calling in the croakers. You don't need to worry. She's on file with the police computers as a non-act case.'

'She told me' – slowly and with effort – 'she'd stabbed her mother. Killed her.'

'Oh, far as she's concerned, sure she did! Just like she's unconsciously wanted to ever since her mother betrayed her by letting her be born. But it was all a setup, naturally. We dosed her with scotophobin and shut her in a dark room, to negate the womb-retreat impulse, gave her a phallic weapon to degrade residual sexual envy, and turned an anonymous companion loose in there with her. When she struck out, we turned up the lights to show her mother's body lying all bloody on the floor, and then we gave her the chance to run like hell. With me trailing her, of course. Wouldn't have wanted her to come to any harm.'

His slightly bored tone indicated that for him this was just another routine chore. But when he had concluded his exposition, he brightened as though a sudden idea had occurred to him. He produced a recorder from his pocket.

'Say, Father! My publicity department would welcome any favorable comment about our methods you may care to make. Coming from a man of the cloth, it would carry extra weight. Suppose you said something to the effect that enabling kids to act out their. most violent impulses in a controlled situation is preferable to letting them commit such crimes in real life, thereby endangering their immortal—'

'Yes, I do have a comment you can record! If there is anything more disgusting than war, it's what your company is doing. At least in warfare there is passion. What you do is calculated, and more likely by machines than men!'

Fluckner withdrew his head a fraction, as though afraid he might be punched through the intervening glass. He said defensively, 'But what we've done is to enlist science in the service of morality. Surely you see—'

'What I see is the first person I ever felt justified in cursing. You have offended against our little ones, therefore a millstone shall be tied around your neck and you shall be cast into the depths of the sea. Depart from me into eternal darkness!'

Fluckner's face grew mottled-red on the instant, and harsh anger invaded his voice.

'You'll regret saying that, I promise you! You've insulted not just me but thousands of good citizens who rely on my company to save their children from hellfire. You'll pay for that!'

He spun on his heel and marched away.

LIGHT AND POWER CORRUPT

'Yes, of course Gaila's doing fine! What happier discovery could a kid make – what more welcome reinforcement can you offer her – than to find the mother she consciously loves, yet unconsciously hates, has been killed and in spite of that is still alive? We've been over that before!'

He had to wipe his forehead, hoping his mask of perspiration would be ascribed to the summer heat.

'And now may I use your phone? Alone, if you don't mind. It's best for the parents not to know too many details of our methods.'

In a bright room with an underfloor pool reflecting sparkling random lights across an ecumenical array of a crucifix, a Buddha and a six-handed Kali draped with roses, Shad Fluckner composed the code of Continental Power and Light's anonymous-denunciation department.

When he heard the proper tone, he followed it with the code for the Church of Infinite Insight, then a group equating to 'fraudulent misapplication of charitable donations', then another for 'assets sequestered pending legal judgment', which would automatically deevee the minister's credit rating, and lastly one for 'notify all credit-appraisal computers'.

That should do the trick. He dusted his hands in satisfaction and left the room. There was effectively no chance of the call being traced to him. It had been two years since he worked for Power and Light, and their personnel was turning over at sixty-five percent annually, so any of half a million people might have fed in the false data.

By the time Reverend Lazarus fought his way through the maze of interlinked credit-appraisal computers and nailed the tapeworm that had just been hatched, he could well be ragged and starving.

Serve him right.

ON LINE BUT NOT REAL TIME

During a lull in the proceedings, while a nurse was spraying the subject's throat to restore his voice, Hartz glanced at his watch.

'Even if this is a slow job,' he muttered, 'you can't run at this rate very often, obviously – less than a day per day.'

Freeman gave his habitual skull-like smile. 'If so, I'd still be questioning him about his experience as a life-style counselor. But remember: once we knew where to look, we were able to put all data concerning his earlier personae into store. We know what he *did;* now we need to find out how he *felt*. In some cases the connection between a key memory and his unusually strong reaction is fairly plain, and you've been lucky today in that we've hit on such a link.'

'His identifying with the girl who was running in panic? A parallel with his own hunted life?'

'More than that. Much more, I'm afraid. Consider the curse he pronounced on this man Fluckner, and the trigger that provoked it. That was consistent with the attitudes of Reverend Lazarus, certainly. What we have to find out is how deeply it reflected his real self. Nurse, if you've finished, I'd like to carry on.'

MOVING DAY, OVERCAST AND HOT

Must MUST learn to control my temper even in face of an insult to humanity like—

What the hell?

He emerged with a gasp from coma-like sleep. Last night he had lain awake for hours with Fluckner's threat reverberating in memory, and ultimately resorted to a pill. It took a long time for an all-important fact to penetrate his muzzy mind.

The hum of the air compressor had stopped.

Rolling over, he checked the self-powered illuminated clock at the head of his bed. It showed 7:45 A.M. But the windows of his trailer were solidly dark, although by now the sun must be high in the sky, the forecast had been for more fine weather, and when it was stretched taut the plastic membrane of his roof was quite translucent.

Therefore the power had been cut off and the dome had collapsed. All twenty-two and a half tons of it.

Naked, feeling terribly vulnerable, he swung his feet out of bed and fumbled for the switch of the nearest lamp to confirm his deduction. The darkness was oppressive; worse, the air had grown foul already – no doubt from the deposit of dirt, grease and fetid moisture which while the dome was distended had formed an unnoticeable film but now had been condensed into a layer like the muck lining a sewer pipe.

The light duly failed to shine.

A strike? Hardly likely; those key workers who still had the leverage to close down the nation's automated power system always waited for frost and snow before striking. An overload blackout? Scarcely more probable. There hadn't been a summer overload since 1990. People had seemingly been cured of regarding power as free like air.

Admittedly, a whole new generation had grown up since 1990 ... including himself.

A reactor meltdown?

After last year's triple-header of disasters, the Delphi boards currently showed much money riding on a lapse of two full years before the next such. Nonetheless he grabbed his one and only battery radio. By law an all-news monophonic station was still required to broadcast in each conurbation of a million or more people, so that the public could be warned of riots, tribal matches and disasters. The cells were low on power, but by placing the set close to his ear he determined that the duty newscaster was talking about record bets on today's football fatalities. If there had been a meltdown, radiation warnings would have been pouring out nonstop.

So what in the world ...? Oh. Fluckner?

He felt a shiver crawl down his spine, and realized that he was gazing hungrily at the little blurred glow from his clock, as though this darkness were symbolic of the womb (echoes of Gaila and those like her, condemned to grow up not as human beings but as mules, offspring of a bastard mating between Freudian psychoanalysis and behaviorism), and that mysterious glimmer presaged his emergence into a strange new world.

Which, as he admitted to himself with a pang of disappointment, it obviously did.

At least, even though the air stank, it wasn't overfull of CO_2: he had no headache, just a hint of nausea. Somewhat reassured, he felt his way into the living zone, where against emergencies he kept a big battery lamp. Its cells were still powerful, being automatically recharged from the main supply. But when he clicked it on its yellowish gleam made everything around him menacing and unfamiliar. As he moved it, shadows scuttered on the polished metal walls, mimics of those that last night he had imagined offering cover to teeners bent on the work of Baron Samedi, Saint Nicholas or even Kali.

He splashed his face with what should have been ice water from the middle faucet over his washbasin. It didn't help. The power had been off so long, the tank was tepid. Unrefreshed, he opened the trailer door and looked out. Under the graceful curve formed by the plastic as it slumped over the altar a distant glimmer of light suggested he might be able to escape unaided.

But it would be preferable to get his power back.

In his office the smelter was cold and the copper ingot lay ready for removal. The desk computer, with a more demanding task, had been caught before finishing it. The fourth – no, the fifth – of today's Delphi assessments protruded from it like a pale stiff tongue, duly stamped with his automatic notary's seal. That, however, was not important right now. What he had to discover was whether Fluckner (who else could or would have discredited him overnight?) had contrived to isolate his phone as well as his power supply.

The answer was yes. A sweet recorded voice told him his phone credit was in abeyance pending judgment in the lawsuit that was apt to end with all his assets being garnisheed. If he wanted service to be renewed he must furnish proof that the verdict had gone in his favor.

Lawsuit? What lawsuit? Surely you can't take someone to court in this state for wishing a curse on you?

Then the answer dawned on him, and he almost laughed. Fluckner had resorted to one of the oldest tricks in the store and turned loose in the continental net a self-perpetuating tapeworm, probably headed by a denunciation group 'borrowed' from a major corporation, which would shunt itself from one nexus to another every time his credit-code was punched into a keyboard. It could take days to kill a worm like that, and sometimes weeks.

Unless the victim possessed a means to override the original command. This one did. Any 4GH code-holder—

His embryo laughter died. What if, since he last exploited its potential, the validity of a 4GH had been downgraded or even deveed?

There was only one way to find out. Dutiful, the machinery was waiting for him to furnish the asked-for evidence. He punched his full code into the phone, added the standard group for 'input error due to malicious malpractice', and tailed it with an order to give the reference number of the lawsuit he had allegedly been cited in.

The normal dial tone sounded within seconds.

He had been holding his breath, unaware, and let it go with a gasp that sounded terribly loud in the unfamiliar silence. (How many separate soft hums had ended? Computer, water cooler, water heater, air conditioner, alarm monitor … et cetera. It was not customary to recall offhand how many powered devices one owned; therefore he didn't.)

Promptly he sent a retaliatory worm chasing Fluckner's. That should take care of the immediate problem in three to thirty minutes, depending on whether or not he beat the inevitable Monday morning circuit overload. He was fairly sure he wouldn't. According to recent report, there were so many worms and counterworms loose in the data-net now, the machines had been instructed to give them low priority unless they related to a medical emergency.

Well, he'd know as soon as the lights came on.

Now it was time for Reverend Lazarus to commit suicide. Fortified by a glass of lukewarm mock orange juice, sickly-sweet but not actively harmful to his metabolism – he was careful about the brands he patronized – he pondered the details of his next incarnation.

Thirty minutes and the power returned. Sixty, and the dome was inflated. Ninety, and he started on his rebirth.

It was always a bad experience, this computerized parturition. Today, because he had not intended to give up the Lazarus role yet and in consequence had not properly prepared his mind, it was the worst ever. His skin crawled, his heart hammered, sweat made his palms slippery, and his buttocks – bare, since he had not wasted time on getting dressed – itched all over the area in contact with his chair.

Even having found out that his code remained valid, he had to break off twice while priming the Fedcomps with his new lies. His fingers were trembling so badly, he was afraid of mis-hitting the phone buttons, and regular phones like this weren't equipped with a 'display-last-five' facility.

But eventually he punched the final group to activate the phage that would eliminate all trace of Lazarus, the super-tapeworm compared to which Fluckner's was negligible, and he was able to stretch and scratch and do all the other things he had to forgo in order not to interrupt the invention of his new self.

No one below congressional level was entitled to call for a printout of the data stored behind a 4GH. It must have been devised for people with official permission to live other lives than their own. More than once he had been tempted to try to discover just what sort of person his code in theory made him – an FBI operative on undercover assignment, a counter-espionage agent, a White House special representative mopping up the mess his boss had left ... But he had never actually been so foolish. He was like a rat, skulking in the walls of modem society. The moment he showed his nose, the exterminators would be sent for.

He dressed in the wrong clothes and collected what he felt he need not leave behind, a single bagful of oddments like transferable Delphi tickets and his new copper ingot. He also pocketed two inhalers of tranquilizer, which he knew he would require before the day was out.

Finally he set a bomb under his desk and wired it to the phone so that he could trigger it whenever he chose.

The destruction of the church might figure in the media's daily crime list – murders so many, robberies so many, rapes so many – but quite often they didn't get down as far as arson because there wasn't time. That, so long as nobody filed a claim for insurance money, would be that. With ready-made suspects at hand in the shape of the Grailers and the Billykings, the harried local police would be content to treat the case as open and shut.

He gave one final glance around as he prepared to quit the plastic dome for the last time. Traffic hummed on the highway, but there was nobody in sight who might have paid special attention to him. In some ways, he reflected, this was a much less complex century to live in than the twentieth must have been.

If only it were as simple as it looked.

THE NUMBER YOU HAVE REACHED

Back when it was still TV and not three-vee, a famous, crusty, cynical historian named Angus Porter, who had survived long enough to become a Grand Old Man and whose lifelong leftist views were in consequence now tolerated as forgivable eccentricity, had put the matter in a nutshell.

Or, as some would-be wit promptly said, in a nut case.

Invited to comment on the world nuclear disarmament treaty of 1989, he said, 'This is the third stage of human social evolution. First we had the legs race. Then we had the arms race. Now we're going to have the brain race.

'And, if we're lucky, the final stage will be the human race.'

THE PERSONIFICATION OF A TALENT

'So that's how he managed it!' Hartz said, marveling. He stared at the shaven body in the steel chair as though he had never seen this man before. 'I'd never have believed it possible to punch a whole new identity into the net from a domestic phone – certainly not without the help of a computer larger than he owned.'

'It's a talent,' Freeman said, surveying the screens and lights on his console. 'Compare it to the ability of a pianist, if you like. Back before tape, there were soloists who could carry twenty concerti in their heads, note-perfect, *and* could improvise for an hour on a four-note theme. That's disappeared, much as poets no longer recite by the thousand lines the way they apparently could in Homer's day. But it's not especially remarkable.'

Hartz said after a moment, 'Know something? I've seen a good few disturbing things, here at Tarnover, and been told about a great many more. But I don't think anything has …' He had to force himself to utter the next words, but with a valiant effort he made the confession. 'So frightened me as hearing you say that.'

'I'm not sure I follow you.'

'Why, calling this amazing talent "not especially remarkable"!'

'But it isn't.' Freeman leaned back in his padded chair. 'Not by our standards, at any rate.'

'That's just it,' Hartz muttered. '*Your* standards. Sometimes they don't seem altogether …'

'Human?'

Hartz nodded.

'Oh, but I assure you they are. We're a very gifted species. Most of what we're doing here is concerned with the recovery of talents we've neglected. We've been content to remain shockingly ignorant about some of our most precious mental resources. Until we've plugged those gaps in our knowledge, we can't plan our path toward the future.' He glanced at his watch. 'I think we've had enough for today. I'll call the nurse and have him taken away for feeding and cleansing.'

'That worries me, too. Hearing you speak about him in – in such depersonalized terms. While I admire your thoroughness, your dedication, I have reservations about your methods.'

Freeman rose, stretching slightly as he did so to relieve his cramped limbs.

'We use those methods which we've found to work, Mr Hartz. Moreover, please recall we're dealing with a criminal, a deserter who, if he'd had the chance, would willingly have evolved into a traitor. There are other people engaged in projects similar to ours, and some of them are not just single-minded but downright brutal. I'm sure you wouldn't wish people of that stamp to outstrip us.'

'Of course not,' Hartz said uncomfortably, running his finger around his collar as though it had suddenly grown too tight.

Freeman smiled. The effect was that of a black turnip-ghost.

'Shall I have the pleasure of your company tomorrow?'

'No, I have to get back to Washington. But – uh …'

'Yes?'

'What did he do after leaving Toledo in such a hurry?'

'Oh, he took a vacation. Very sensible. In fact, the best thing he could possibly have done.'

FOR PURPOSES OF RE-IDENTIFICATION

At present I am being Sandy (short, as I admit to people when I get stonkered and confidential, not for good old Alexander but for *Lysander*, of all things!)

P. (worse yet, for *Pericles!!!*) Locke, aged thirty-two swingle and in view of my beardless condition probably skew. However, I'm trying to give that up and might even consider getting married one of these years.

I shall remain Sandy Locke for a while at least, even after I finish my vacation at this resort hotel in the Georgia Sea Islands, medium-fashionable, not so boringly up-to-the-second as some even if it does boast an underwater wing for womb-retreat therapy and the manager is a graduate psychologist. At least there's no obligatory experiential R&P.

It's my second vacation this year and I shall take at least one further in late fall. But I'm among people who aren't likely to mistake 'taking another vacation' for 'surpled and unemployable', as some would that I can think of. Many of my fellow guests are taking their third this year already and plan to make the total five. These latter, though, are considerably older, shot of the care and cost of kids. To be a triple-vacationer at thirty-two marks me as a comer … in all three senses. Right now the third kind matters; I need a job.

I've picked a good age, not so difficult as forty-six to put on when you're chronologically twenty-eight (the sudden recollection of spectacles! Ow!) and youthful enough to attract the middlers while being mature enough to impress the teeners. *Memo to selves:* could thirty-two be stretched until I'm actually, say, thirty-six? Keep eyes and ears ajar for data.

WINED AND DENIED

Past forty but not saying by how much, beautiful and apt to stay so for a long while yet, currently looking her best by reason of a bright brown tan, hair bleached by sun instead of shampoo, and an hour more sleep per night than she'd enjoyed for ages, Ina Grierson was also tough. Proof lay in the fact that she was heading the transient-executive recruitment dept at the Kansas City HQ of Ground-to-Space Industries Inc., world's largest builders of orbital factories.

The question was, though: tough *enough*?

She thought of the old saying about being promoted to your level of incompetence – what was it called, the Peter-Pays-Paul Principle, or something like that? – and fumed and fretted. Her daughter kept declining to quit school, just signed up year after year for weirder and wilder courses of study (and all at the same university, for heaven's sake! Wouldn't be so bad if she'd consent to go someplace else). Ina felt tied, wanted to break away, move to the Gulf or Colorado or even the Bay Area, given that the slippage techniques were as efficient as the seismologists claimed and there wasn't going to be another million-victim quake, not ever … or at least for fifty years.

On her own terms, of course – no one else's.

Last year she'd rejected five offers. This year, so far only one. Next year?

Having a daughter out of step like Kate – hell! Why couldn't the stupid slittie act normal like everybody else, dig up her roots and plug them in some other socket, preferably on a different continent?

If Anti-Trauma Inc. had started up soon enough …!

Tactless people sometimes wondered publicly why Ina insisted on remaining in the same city as her daughter, who was, after all, twenty-two and had had her own apt since entering college and was not noticeably clinging or dependent. But Ina hated to be asked about that.

She never like being asked questions she couldn't answer.

One week into her two-week vacation Ina wanted to be cheered up but the man she'd kept company with since arrival had left today. That meant dining alone. Worse and worse. Eventually, with much effort she put on her favorite red-and-gold evening gear and went to the open-air dining terrace where soft music mingled with the hush of waves. She felt a little better after two drinks. To put the regular sparkle back in her world, what about champagne?

And a minute later she was shouting at the waiter (this being an expensive and exclusive establishment instead of the cast-from-a-mold type where you dealt always with machines that kept going wrong … not that human beings were immune from *that*): 'What the hell do you mean, there isn't any?'

Her shrill voice caused heads to turn.

'That gentleman over there' – pointing – 'just ordered the last bottle we have in stock.'

'Call the manager!'

Who came, and explained with regret that was probably unfeigned (who likes to find his pride and joy deeveed by a mere bunch of circuitry?) why there was nothing he could do. The computer in charge of resources utilization at the HQ of the chain controlling this and a hundred other hotels had decided to allot what champagne was available to resorts where it could be sold at twice the price the traffic in the Sea Islands could bear. The decision was today's. Tomorrow the wine list would have been reprinted.

Meanwhile the waiter had faded in response to a signal from another table, and when he returned Ina was struggling not to scream with fury.

He laid a slip of paper in front of her. It bore a message in firm clear handwriting, unusual now that most literate kids were taught to type at seven. She read it at a glance:

The lucky shivver with the champagne has an idea. Share the bottle? – Sandy Locke

She raised her eyes and found grinning at her a man in a fashionable pirate shirt open to the waist, a gaudy headband, gilt wristers, one long lean finger poised at arm's length on the cork.

She felt her anger fade like mist at sunrise.

He was a strange one, this Sandy. He dismissed her complaint about how ridiculous it was never to have any more champagne at this hotel and steered the conversation into other channels. That made her ill-tempered all over again, and she went to bed alone.

But when the breakfast-trolley rolled automatically to her bedside at 0900, there was a bottle of champagne on it tied with a ribbon and accompanied by a posy. When she met Sandy by the pool at eleven, he asked whether she had enjoyed it.

'So it was you who fixed it! Do you work for this hotel chain?'

'This slumpy linkage? I'm insulted. Third-rank operations aren't my framework. Shall we swim?'

The next question died on her lips. She had been going to ask what pull he had, whether it was government or a hypercorp. But another explanation fitted, and if that were the right one, the implications were so enticing she dared not broach the matter without a buildup. She said, 'Sure, let's.' And peeled off her clothes.

The wine list was not reprinted after all, and the manager wore a very puzzled expression. That convinced Ina her guess might be correct. Next morning while they were breakfasting in bed she put it squarely to Sandy.

'Poker, I think you must be a CSC.'

'Only if this bed isn't bugged.'

'Is it?'

'No. I made sure. There are some things I simply don't care to let computers know.'

'How right you are.' She shivered. 'Some of my colleagues at G2S, you know, live at Trianon, where they test new life-styles. And they boast about how their actions are monitored night and day, compare the advantages of various ultramodern bugs … I don't know how they can stand it.'

'Stand?' he echoed sardonically. 'Not a matter of standing, except social standing, I guess. More, it kind of props them up. A few years and they'll forget they have feet of their own.'

All day Ina was near to shaking with excitement. To think that by pure chance she had bumped into a genuine three-vee tactile-true member of that prestigious elite, the tiny secretive tribe of computer-sabotage consultants …! It was a perfectly legal discipline, provided its practitioners didn't tamper with data reserved to a government dept under the McBann-Krutch 'greatest-good-of-the-greatest-number' act, but its experts didn't advertise themselves any more than industrial spies, and it would have been politer to ask whether he was into DDR, 'difficult data retrieval'. Luckily he'd taken no offense.

Delicately she hinted at what was worrying her. How much longer was she still going to be able to move upward, not crosswise, when she changed jobs? At first his response was casual: 'Oh, turn freelance, why not, the way I did? It's not so much different from the regular plug-in life-style. When you get adjusted to it.'

Echoes underlying 'freelance' resounded in her head: the lone knight riding out to champion his lady fair and Christian justice, the King's Messenger, the secret agent, the merchant venturer …

'I've thought about it, naturally. But I'd dearly like to know what G2S has added to my file before I decide.'

'You could try asking me to find out.'

'You mean' – hardly daring to hope – 'you're for rent?'

'Right now?' He put the nip into nipple with sharp well-cared-for teeth. 'No, my jiggle-oh rating is strictly O. This kind of thing I do for free.'

'You know what I mean!'

He laughed. 'Don't slidewise out of control. Of course I know. And it might be kind of fun to poke G2S.'

'Are you serious?'

'I could be, when my vacation's over. Which it isn't.'

Musingly, at two in the morning – her sleeping time was being eroded, but what the hell? – she said, 'It isn't knowing that the machines know things about you which you wouldn't tell your straightener, let alone your spouse or chief. It's not knowing what the things *are* which they know.'

'Sweedack. The number of people I've seen destabled by just that form of uncertainty, clear into paranoia!'

'Sweedack?'

'Ah, you don't follow hockey.'

'Now and then, but I'm not what you'd call a 'fish for it.'

'Nor me, but you have to stay in circuit. It's French. Came south with Canadian hockey players. Short for *je suis d'accord*. Thought everybody had picked up on it.'

Before she could guard her tongue she had said, 'Oh, yes! I've heard Kate say it to her friends.'

'Who?'

'Uh … My daughter.' And she trembled, imagining the inevitable sequence: *I didn't know you had a daughter. She in high school?*
No – uh – at UMKC.

Followed by the brief silence full of subtraction which would all too closely betray her location on the age scale.

But this man, ultimately tactful, merely laughed. 'Quit worrying. I know all about you. Think I'd have generated so much champagne on spec?'

That figured. In seconds she was laughing too. When she recovered, she said, 'Would you really come to KC?'

'If you can afford me.'

'G2S can afford anybody. What do you usually click on as?'

'A systems rationalizer.'

She brightened. 'Fantastic! We lost our head-of-dept in that area. He broke his contract and— Say, you didn't know that too, did you?' Suddenly suspicious.

He shook his head, stifling a yawn. 'Never had any reason to probe G2S until I met you.'

'No. No, of course not. What attracted you to your line of work, Sandy?'

'I guess my daddy was a phone freak and I inherited the gene.'

'I want a proper answer.'

'I don't know. Unless maybe it's a sneaking feeling that people are wrong when they say human beings can't keep track of the world any more, we have to leave it up to the machines. I don't want to be hung out to dry on a dead branch of the evolutionary tree.'

'Nor do I. Right, I'll get you to KC, Sandy. I think your attitude is healthy. And we could do with a blast of fresh air.'

SOLD TO THE MAN AT THE TOP

'I am not bleating you. This shivver is escape-velocity type. And we've been short one systems rash since Kurt bailed out and not wishing to cast nasturtiums at George she hasn't made my job any less of a bed of nails – let alone yours, hm?

'Sure, he asked for a trial period himself. Eight weeks, maybe twelve, see how he meshes with the rest of us.

'Right now he's on vacation. I told you: I met him in the Sea Islands. You can reach him there.

'Great. Here, take down his code. 4GH …'

UNSETTLEMENT PROGRAM

The palisade of thousand-meter towers around Mid-Continental Airport had two gaps in it, memorializing not – for once – buildings that had been riot-blown or tribaled but the crash sites of two veetol airliners, one taking off and one landing, which had slidewised simultaneously off their repulsors last week. Rumor had it the reason might be found in the launch of Ground-to-Space's latest orbital factory from their field westward in the cross-river state of Kansas; allegedly someone had omitted to notify the airlines of the volume and extent of the blast wave. But an inquiry was still in progress, and anyhow G2S was far too much of a Power in the Land hereabouts for any negligence charge to emerge from the hearings.

Nonetheless the outcome was a popular subject for bets on illegal short-term Delphi pools. Legal pools, naturally, were forbidden to pre-guess a court's verdict.

The façades of the remaining towers, whether homes or offices, were as blank as ancient gravestones and as gloomy. They had mostly been erected during the shitabrick phase architecture had suffered through in the early nineties. There was a more flattering term for the style – antideco – but it was too lame to have caught on. Such structures were as dehumanized as the coffins employed to bury the victims of the Great Bay Quake, and stemmed from the same cause. The damage sustained when San Francisco, plus most of Berkeley and Oakland, collapsed overnight had come close to bankrupting the country, so that every-thing but *everything* had to be designed with the fewest possible frills.

In a desperate attempt to make a virtue of necessity, all such buildings had been made 'ecofast' – in other words, they were heavily insulated, they incorporated elaborate garbage-reclamation systems, every apartment was supplied with a flat area outside that caught at least some sunlight, allegedly large enough to be hydroponically planted with sufficient vegetables and fruit to meet the requirements of an average family. The consequence had been to fix in the public mind the impression that any genuinely efficient building must be stark, ugly, undesirable and dull.

It seemed that necessity was too hateful for anybody to enjoy being virtuous.

Thanks to some smart route adjustment by his airline's computers, his plane was a few minutes early. Ina had agreed to meet him on the main concourse, but when he emerged, tingling slightly, from the static-discharge chamber by the plane gate, she wasn't in sight.

It would be out of character for him to waste spare minutes. Rubbing his arms, reflecting that even if electric lift for aircraft was efficient, economical and non-polluting it was damnably hard on the passengers when they had to shed their accumulated volts, he caught sight of a sign pointing the way to the public Delphi boards.

Most of his belongings, bought to fit his new identity, were on their way direct to G2S's recruit-settlement block. But he did have a travel bag weigh-ing nine kaygees. From under the nose of a sour woman who favored him with a string of curses he nabbed an autoporter and – after consulting the illuminated fee table on its flank – credded the minimum: $35 for an hour's service. Rates were higher here than at Toledo, but that was to be expected; the cost of living at Trianon, a hundred kilometers away, was the second highest in the world.

From now until his credit expired the machine would carry his bag in its soft plastic jaws and follow him as faithfully as a well-trained hound, which indeed it resembled, down to the whimper it was programed to utter at the 55-minute mark, and the howl at 58.

At 60 it would drop the bag and slink away.

With it at his heels he stood surveying the high-slung display, tracking the shifting figures with the ease of much practice. He looked first at his favorite sector, social legislation, and was pleased to see he had two won bets due to be collected shortly. Despite all the pressure that had been applied, the president would not after all be able to make jail sentences mandatory for slandering his personal aides – it would cost him his majority if he tried. And Russian math-teaching methods were definitely going to be introduced here, given that money was still piling in when the odds had shortened to five-to-four. Well, if the U.S. team were ever to make a decent showing in the Mathematical Olympiads, there was no alternative.

Odds, though, were poor on that sector of the board, except ten-to-one against the adoption of the proposed new amendment to the Constitution which would redefine electoral zones in terms of professions and age groups rather than geographical location. It might make sense, but people were scarcely ready for it yet. Next generation, maybe.

He turned his attention to social analysis, which was offering many double and a few treble figures. He put a thousand on the chance that the mugging-per-adult rate in New York City would break ten percent this year; it had been hovering around eight for an improbably long time and people were losing their enthusiasm, but there was a new police chief in the Bronx with a get-tough reputation and that ought to sew the matter up.

And the technical breakthrough odds were also nice and fat. For old time's sake he put another thousand on the introduction of an Earth–Moon gravis-lide before 2025. That was a perennial disappointment. The idea was to haul cargo off the Moon on a cable stretching past the neutral point and spill it direct into Earth's gravity-well so it could coast to a landing free of charge. It had failed twice already. But someone in New Zealand was on the track of mile-long single-crystal filaments. Given those …

A couple of hungry-faced old men, one black and the other white, who clearly were not here to travel but merely to pass the time, noticed him placing the wager. They studied his expensive clothes, assessed his air of financial well-being, and after some argument agreed to risk fifty apiece.

'It beats horse racing,' he heard one of them say.

'I used to like the horses!' the other objected, and they moved on, their voices querulous as though both craved the tension discharge of a quarrel but dared not start one for fear of losing an only friend.

Hmm! I wonder whether the Delphi systems in Russia, or East Germany, are patterned on stock markets and totalizators the way ours obviously are. One knows that in China they—

But at that moment he caught sight of odds being quoted which he simply didn't believe. One gets three in favor of genetic optimization becoming a commercial service by 2020, instead of a privilege reserved to government officials, hypercorp execs and billionaires? Last time he saw a board it had been up around 200, regardless of the fact that the public was clearly hungry for it. Such a violent crash in the odds must surely be due to inside information. One of the thousand-and-some staff and 'students' at Tarnover must have yielded to the temptation to go sell his headful of data, and company scientists somewhere must be busily trying to turn a vague hope into a self-fulfilling prophecy.

Unless …

Oh, no! It can't be that they know somebody did get away? After all this time, after these six mortal, hateful years, has the precious secret of my escape leaked out?

There couldn't possibly be a connection! Even so –!

The world swam around him for the space of half a dozen thumping heartbeats. Someone jostled him roughly; he was barely able to perceive that it was an economist, wearing a sewn-on badge in bright green and white saying UNDERPOWER! – one of the people who on principle declined to use up their full power allotment and did their utmost to prevent others from using theirs. There were alleged to be a great many economists at KC.

Then a bright voice was saying, 'Sandy, good to see you – Is something wrong?'

Vast effort pulled him back together, smiling, calm, in a condition to note how changed Ina was from the image she'd presented at the resort. She wore a light but severe coverall in plain black and white, and her long hair was in a snood. She was very much the head-of-dept doing a special favor to this recruit who was slotting into a higher-than-average level of the hierarchy.

Therefore he didn't kiss her, didn't even take her hand, simply said, 'Hello. No, nothing's wrong. Except I just saw what the odds are on my favorite long shot. One of these mornings I'll wake to find my credit well and truly docked.'

As he spoke, he started toward the exit. Ina, and the autoporter, kept pace.

'You have baggage?' she inquired.

'Just this. I sent the rest direct. I hear you have a great settlement block.'

'Oh, yes. It has a fine record. Been in use for ten years and so far not one environmental psychosis. Speaking of accommodation, I should have asked if you plan to bring a house with you. Currently we have room for one on site; we don't start building our next factory until September.'

'No, I've had my house four years so I decided to trade it in. Matter of fact, I might get my next built here. I'm told there are good architects around KC.'

'Well, I wouldn't know. I prefer to plug into an apt, but someone at the party might advise you.'

'I'll ask around. What time is it set for?'

'Eight o'clock. The welcome suite is right on the entrance floor. All your signifying colleagues will be there.'

PARADOX, NEXT STOP AFTER THE BOONDOCKS

'It's not because my mind is made up that I don't want you to confuse me with any more facts.

'It's because my mind isn't made up. I already have more facts than I can cope with.

'So SHUT UP, do you hear me? SHUT UP!'

YOU'RE BEING FRAMED

Although this was strictly transient accommodation, it differed subtly from a hotel suite. He noted with approval the touches that made it more like a smart private apartment. Retractable textured walls could subdivide the main room in half a dozen ways, according to taste. The decor on his arrival was in neutral shades: beige, pale blue and white. He made use at once of the switch by the door to change that to rich dark green, russet and old gold. It was done with lights behind translucent paneling. The conveniences, such as the three-vee, the polarity-reversal clothing cleaner and the electrotoner attached to the bathtub, were not the basic hotel-chain type but the more expensive home-use version. Perhaps most important of all, you could not only draw back the curtains but even open the windows. That was a facility not found in hotels nowadays.

Out of curiosity he did open one, and found he was looking over treetops toward the source of a roaring noise which a moment ago had been inaudible thanks to superefficient soundproofing.

What in the world –?

Followed a moment later by the wry contradiction: *What out of this world –?*

A brilliant light, dazzling as a magnesium flare, rose into sight above the trees and to the roar was added the impact of blast. He just managed to discern the needle-form of a one-man orbital ship before the glare compelled him to shut his eyes and turn away, groping for the window-closure again.

No doubt that would be one of G2S's troubleshooters on his way to orbit. The company was proud of its prompt and efficient after-sales service, and since even now three out of four orbital factories were one-off projects – new industries kept deciding to jump up there every other week – that was an essential element in preserving its field-leader rating.

Which was not, in fact, as stable as the G2S board wished the public to believe. He'd investigated. Among the tasks he expected to be assigned, even though Ina hadn't mentioned it, was penetration of a rival corporation's research into so-called olivers, electronic alter egos designed to save the owner the strain of worrying about all his person-to-person contacts. A sort of twenty-first-century counterpart to the ancient Roman nomenclator, who discreetly whispered data into the ear of the emperor and endowed him with the reputation of a phenomenal memory. G2S was badly in need of diversification, but before picking up the option it had on a small independent company's work in this area, it wanted to make certain nobody else had reached the stage of commercial launching.

It would be a good-sized feather in his cap if he produced the answer within a few days of starting work.

Continuing his tour of inspection he discovered, neatly tucked away under the bed, a tension reliever with a reversible proboscis which a woman could let stand out and a man could simply push inward ... or not, according to taste. Above it was a small but fine-detail screen, the images fed to which were changed – said a little label – on an eight-day rota; there were also headphones and a mask offering twenty odors.

Replacing the instrument in its sanitizing case, he decided he'd have to experiment with it at least once or twice; it was appropriate to the plug-in life-style, after all. But at most two or three times. Corporations like G2S were wary of people who relied excessively on machines in place of person-to-person contact. They would be watching.

He sighed. To think that some people were (had to be?) content with mechanical gratification ... But maybe it was best in certain special cases: for instance, for those who had to establish deep emotional attachments or none at all, who suffered agonies when a change of employment or a posting to another city shattered their connections, who were safest when keeping their chance colleagues at a distance.

Not for the first time he reflected on the good fortune – heavily disguised – which had stunted his own capacity for intense emotional involvement to the point where he was content with mere liking. It was so much superior to the transitory possessiveness he had been exposed to in childhood, the strict impersonality maintained during his teener years at Tarnover.

Best not to think about Tarnover.

Showering down, he relished his new situation. Much would depend on the personalities of the people he was about to meet at the welcome party, but they were bound to be good stable plug-in types, and certainly the nature of the job was ideal for his talents. Most commercial systems were sub-logical and significantly redundant, so he'd have no trouble tidying up a few tangles, saving G2S a couple of million a year, by way of proving he really was a systems rash. They'd regard him within weeks as an invaluable recruit.

Meantime, taking advantage of the corporation's status, he could gain access to data-nets that were ordinarily secure. That was the whole point of coming to KC. He wanted – more, he needed – data that as a priest he'd never have dared to probe for. Six years was about as far ahead as he'd been able to plan when he escaped from Tarnover, so ...

He was stepping out of the shower compartment, dried by blasts of warm air, when he heard the sound of his circulation enormous in his ears: thud, thud, thud-thud-thud-thud, faster with each passing second. Giddy, furious, he clutched at the rim of the hand-basin to steady himself and caught a glimpse of Sandy Locke's face in the mirror above it – haggard, aged by decades on the instant – before he realized he wasn't going to make it to the tranquilizers he'd left in the main room. He was going to have to stay right here and fight back with yoga-style deep breathing.

His mouth was dry, his belly was drum-taut, his teeth wanted to chatter but couldn't because his jaw muscles were so tense, his vision wavered and there was a line of cramp as brutal as a knife-cut all the way up his right calf. And he was *cold*.

But luckily it wasn't a bad attack. In less than ten minutes he was able to reach his inhalers, and he was only three minutes late joining the party.

BETWEEN 500 AND 2000 TIMES A DAY

Somewhere out there, a house or an apartment or a hotel or motel room: beautiful, comfortable, a living hell.

Stonkered or clutched or quite simply going insane, someone reaches for the phone and punches the most famous number on the continent: the ten nines that key you into Hearing Aid.

And talks to a blank though lighted screen. It's a service. Imposing no penances, it's kinder than the confessional. Demanding no fees, it's affordable where psychotherapy is not. Offering no advice, it's better than arguing with that son (or daughter) of a bitch who thinks he/she knows all the answers and goes on and on and on until you want to SCREAM.

In a way it's like using the *I Ching*. It's a means of concentrating attention on reality. Above all, it provides an outlet for all the frustration you've struggled to digest for fear that, learning of it, your friends would brand you *failure*.

It must help some of the unhappy ones. The suicide rate is holding steady.

FLESHBACK SEQUENCE

Today, said the impersonal instruments, it would be advisable to waken the subject fully; too long spent in the trance-like state of recall that he had endured for the past forty-two days might endanger his conscious personality. The recommendation was not unwelcome to Paul Freeman. He was growing more and more intrigued by this man whose past had been mapped along so improbable a course.

On the other hand there was a diktat in force, straight from the Federal Bureau of Data Processing, which instructed him to produce a full report in the shortest possible time. Hence Hartz's flying visit. And that had lasted a whole working day, moreover, when one might have expected the typical 'hello-how-interesting-goodbye' pattern. Someone in Washington must have a hunch ... or at any rate have gone out so far on a limb as to need results regardless of what they were.

He compromised. For a single day he would talk person-to-person instead of merely replaying facts from store in a living memory.

He quite looked forward to the change.

'You know where you are?'

The totally shaven man licked his lips. His gaze flickered around the stark white walls.

'No, but I figure it must be Tarnover. I always pictured rooms like this in that faceless secret block on the east side of the campus.'

'How do you feel about Tarnover?'

'It makes me want to be scared stiff. But I guess you dose me with something so I can't.'

'But that wasn't how you felt when you first came here.'

'Hell, no. In the beginning it seemed wonderful. Should it not to a kid with my background?'

That was documented: father disappeared when he was five, mother stood the strain for a year and vanished into an alcoholic haze. But the boy was resilient. They decided he would make an ideal rent-a-child: obviously bright, rather quiet, tolerably well mannered and cleanly in his habits. So, from six to twelve, he lived in a succession of modern, smart, sometimes luxurious company homes occupied by childless married couples posted in on temporary assignment from other cities. He was generally well liked by these 'parents' and one couple seriously considered adopting him but decided against landing themselves permanently with a boy of another color. Anyhow, they consoled themselves, he was getting a terrific introduction to the plug-in life-style.

He appeared to accept the decision with good grace. But several times after that, when left alone in the house for an evening (which was in fact often, for he was a good boy and to be trusted), he went to the phone – with a sense of dreadful guilt – and punched the ten nines as he dimly recalled seeing his mother do, his real mother, during the last terrible few months before something went wrong inside her head. To the blank screen he would pour out a nonstop volley of filth and curses. And wait, shaking, for the calm anonymous voice to say, 'Only I heard that. I hope it helped.'

Paradoxically: yes, it did.

'What about school, Haflinger?'

'Was it really my name …? Don't bother to answer; that was rhetorical. I just didn't like it. Overtones of "half", as though I was condemned never to become a finished person. And I didn't care for Nick, either.'

'Do you know why not?'

'Sure I do. In spite of anything it may say to the contrary on my record, I have excellent juvenile recall. Infantile too, in fact. I found out early about Auld Nick, the Scottish term for the devil. Also "to nick", meaning to arrest or sometimes to steal. And above all Saint Nick. I never did manage to find out how the same figment could give rise to both Santa Claus and Saint Nicholas, the patron saint of thieves.'

'Maybe it was a matter of giving with one hand and taking away with the other. Did you know that in Holland Sinter Klaas brought gifts to children in the company of a black man who whipped the ones who hadn't behaved well enough to deserve a present?'

'That's news to me, and very interesting, Mr – Mr Freeman, isn't it?'

'You were going to tell me how you remember school.'

'Should have known better than to try and strike up a brotherly chat. Yes, school. Much the same – the teachers turned over even faster than my temporary parents, and every new arrival seemed to have a new theory of education, so we never did learn very much. But of course in most respects it was a hell of a lot worse than – uh – *home*.'

The high walls. The guarded gates. The classrooms where the walls were lined with broken teaching machines, waiting for the engineers who never seemed to come, inevitably vandalized after a couple of days and rendered unrepairable. The stark corridors where so often sand greeted the soles with a gritty kiss, marking a spot where blood had been shed. The blood on the floor was his only once; he was clever, to the point of being considered odd because he kept trying to learn when everybody else knew the right thing to do was sit tight and wait to be eighteen. He contrived to avoid all the shivs, clubs and guns bar one, and his wound was shallow and left no scar.

The one thing he was not clever enough to do was escape. Authoritatively the State Board of Education had laid it down that there must be one major element of stability in the life of a rent-a-child; therefore he must continue at this same school regardless of where he currently happened to reside, and none of his temporary parents remained in the vicinity long enough to fight that ruling to the bitter end.

When he was twelve a teacher arrived named Adele Brixham, who kept on trying same as he did. She noticed him. Before she was ambushed and gang-raped and overloaded, she must have filed some sort of report. At any rate, a week or so later the classroom and the approach corridor were invaded by a government platoon, men and women in uniform carrying guns, webbers and fetters, and for a change the roll was called complete bar one girl who was in the hospital.

And there were tests which for a change could not be ignored, because someone with hard eyes and a holster stood by you to make sure. Nickie Haflinger sank all his frustrated lust for achievement into the six hours they lasted: three before, three after a supervised lunch eaten in the classroom. Even to visit the can you were escorted. It was a new thing for those of the kids who hadn't been arrested yet.

After IQ and EQ – empathic quotient – and perceptual and social tests, like the regular kind only more so, came the kickers: laterality tests, double-take tests, open-dilemma tests, value-judgment tests, wisdom tests … and those were fun! For the final thirty minutes of the session he was purely drunk on the notion that when something happened which had never happened before one human being could make a right decision about the outcome, and that person might be Nickie Haflinger!

The government people had brought a portable computer with them. Little by little he grew aware that each time it printed out, more and more of the gray-garbed strangers looked at him rather than the other children. The rest realized what was going on, too, and that expression came to their faces which he had long ago learned to recognize: *Today, after class, he's the one we'll carve the ass off!*

He was shaking as much from terror as excitement when the six hours ended, but he hadn't been able to stop himself from applying all he knew and all he could guess to the tests.

But there was no attack, no sanding along the streets between here and his current home. The woman in overall charge switched off the computer and jerked her head his way, and three men with guns drawn closed on him and one said in a kindly tone, 'Stay right there, sonny, and don't worry.'

His classmates drifted away, giving puzzled backward glances and kicking the doorposts with fury as they left. Later someone else was sanded – the term came from 'S-and-D', search and destroy – and lost an eye. But by then he had arrived home in a government limo.

It was carefully explained, to him and his 'parents', that he was being requisitioned in the service of his country under special regulation number such-and-such issued by the Secretary of Defense as authorized by clause number whatever of some or other Act of Congress … He didn't take in the details. He was giddy. He'd been promised that for the first time in his life he could stay where he was going as long as he liked.

Next morning he woke at Tarnover, and thought he had been transported halfway to heaven.

'Now I realize I was in hell. Why are you alone? I had the vague impression that when you woke up I'd find there were two of you, even though you were doing all the talking. Is there usually someone else in here?'

Freeman shook his head, his eyes watchful.

'But there has been. I'm sure of it. He said something about the way you regard me. Said he felt scared.'

'Yes, that's so. You had a visitor, who sat in on one day's interrogation, and he did say that. But he doesn't work at Tarnover.'

'The place where you take the improbable for granted.'

'So to speak.'

'I see. I'm reminded of one of my favorite funny stories when I was a kid. I haven't told it in years. With luck it'll have gone far enough out of style not to bore you. Seems that an oil company, back in – oh – the thirties of last century would fit, wanted to impress a sheikh. So they laid on a plane when they were few and far between in that part of the world.'

'And when he was at ten thousand feet, perfectly calm and collected, they said, "Aren't you impressed?" And the sheikh said, "You mean it's not supposed to do this?" Yes, I know the story. I learned it from your dossier.'

There was a short pause full of veiled tension. Eventually Freeman said, 'What convinced you that you were in hell?'

After the legs race, the arms race; after the arms race …

Angus Porter's epigram was not just a slick crack to be over-quoted at parties. But few people realized how literally true the *bon mot* had become.

At Tarnover, at Crediton Hill, at some hole in the Rockies he had never managed to identify beyond the code name 'Electric Skillet', and at other places scattered from Oregon to Louisiana, there were secret centers with a special task. They were dedicated to exploiting genius. Their ancestry could be traced back to the primitive 'think tanks' of the mid-twentieth century, but only in the sense that a solid-state computer was descended from Hollerith's punched-card analyzer.

Every superpower, and a great many second- and third-rank nations, had similar centers. The brain race had been running for decades, and some countries had entered it with a head start. (The pun was popular, and forgivable.)

In Russia, for example, great publicity had long attended the Mathematical Olympiads, and it was a signal honor to be allowed to study at Akadiemgorodok. In China, too, the sheer pressure of population had forced an advance from ad hoc improvisation along predetermined Marxist-Maoist guidelines to a deliberate search for optimal administrative techniques, employing a form of cross-impact matrix analysis for which the Chinese language was peculiarly well adapted. Well before the turn of the century a pattern had been systematized that proved immensely successful. To every commune and small village was sent a deck of cards bearing ideograms relevant to impending changes, whether social or technical. By shuffling and dealing the symbols into fresh combinations, fresh ideas could automatically be generated, and the people at a series of public meetings discussed the implications at length and appointed one of their number to summarize their views and report back to Peking. It was cheap and amazingly efficient.

But it didn't work in any Western language except Esperanto.

The U.S.A. entered the race on the grand scale very late. Not until the nation was reeling under the impact of the Great Bay Quake was the harsh lesson learned that the economy could not absorb disasters of even this magnitude – let alone a nuclear strike which would exterminate millions plural. Even then it took years for the switch from brawn to brain to become definitive in North America.

In some ways the change remained incomplete. At Electric Skillet the primary concern was still with weaponry … but at least the stress was on defense in its literal meaning, not on counterstrike or preemptive strategies. (The name, of course, had been chosen on the frying-pan-and-fire principle.)

Newer concepts, though, were embodied at Crediton Hill. There, top-rank analysts constantly monitored the national Delphi pools to maintain a high social-mollification index. Three times since 1990 agitators had nearly brought about a bloody revolution, but each had been aborted. What the public currently yearned for could be deduced by watching the betting, and steps could be taken to ensure that what was feasible was done, what was not was carefully deeveed. It was a task that taxed the skills of top CIMA experts to ensure that when the government artificially cut Delphi odds to distract attention from something undesirable no other element in the mix was dragged down with it.

And newest of all was the ultra-secret work of Tarnover and those other centers whose existence, but not whose names, one was aware of. The goal?

To pin down before anybody else did the genetic elements of wisdom.

'You make wisdom seem like a dirty word, Haflinger.'

'Maybe I'm ahead of my time again. What you people are doing is bound to debase the term, and soon at that.'

'I won't waste time by saying I disagree. If I didn't I wouldn't be here. But perhaps you'd define what you understand by the term.'

'My definition is the same as yours. The only difference is that I mean what I say, and you manipulate it. What a wise man can do, that can't done by someone who's merely clever, is make a right judgment in an unprecedented situation. A wise man would never be overloaded by the plug-in life-style. He'd never need to go get mended in a mental hospital. He'd adjust to shifts of fashion, the coming-and-going of fad-type phrases, the ultrasonic-blender confusion of twenty-first-century society, as a dolphin rides the bow wave of a ship, out ahead but always making in the right direction. And having a hell of a good time with it.'

'You make it sound eminently desirable. So why are you opposed to our work?'

'Because what's being done here – and elsewhere – isn't motivated by love of wisdom, or the wish to make it available to everyone. It's motivated by terror, suspicion, and greed. You and everybody above and below you from the janitor to – hell, probably to the president himself and beyond that to the people who pull the president's strings! – the *lot* of you are afraid that by taking thought someone else may already have added a cubit to his wisdom while you're still fiddling around on the foolishness level. You're so scared that they may have hit on the answer in Brazil or the Philippines or Ghana, you daren't even go and ask. It makes me sick. If there is a person on the planet who has the answer, if there's even the shadow of a chance he does, then the only sane thing to do is go sit on his doorstep until he has time to talk to you.'

'You believe there is *an* answer – one, and only one?'

'Hell, no. More likely there are thousands. But I do know this: as long as you're determined to be the first to reach the – or a – solution, just so long will you fail to find it. In the meantime, other people with other problems will be humbly pleased because things aren't so bad this year as they were last.'

In China … One always began with China. It was the most populous country on the planet, hence the logical starting point.

Once there had been Mao. Then followed The Consortium, which was more like an interregnum, the Cultural Revolution redoubled in no trumps (except that the stock translation 'Cultural Revolution' was ludicrously wrong and the people involved understood by the term something more like 'agonizing reappraisal'), and then there was Feng Soo Yat … very suddenly, and with so little warning that on foreign-affairs Delphi boards high odds in favor of China crumbling into anarchy and violence swung to three hundred against in three days. He was the epitome of the Oriental wise man: young, reputedly still in his thirties, yet capable of running his goverment with such delicate touches and so keen an insight that he never needed to explain or justify his decisions. They simply worked.

He might have been trained to display such powers of judgment; he might have been specially bred to possess them. One thing was sure: he hadn't lived long enough to grow into them.

Not if he started from where most people had to.

Also in Brazil there had been no religious warfare since Lourenço Pereira seized power – whoever he might be – and that was a welcome contrast to the turn-of-the-century period when Catholics and Macumbans had fought pitched battles in the streets of São Paulo. And in the Philippines the reforms introduced by their first-ever woman president, Sara Castaldo, had slashed their dreadful annual murder rate by half, and in Ghana when Premier Akim Gomba said to clean house they started cleaning house and laughed and cheered, and in Korea since the *coup* by Inn Lim Pak there had been a remarkable fall-off in the crap-and-screw charter flights which formerly had come in from Sydney, Melbourne and Honolulu at the rate of three or four a day, and … and generally speaking in the most unlikely places wisdom appeared to be on the increase.

'So you're impressed by what's been happening in other countries. Why don't you want your own homeland to benefit from – shall we call it a shot in the arm of wisdom?'

'My homeland? I was born here, sure, but … Never mind; that's a stale argument these days, I guess. The point is that what's being peddled here as wisdom isn't.'

'I sense a long debate ahead. Perhaps we should start again tomorrow.'

'Which mode are you going to put me in?'

'The same as today. We're drawing closer to the point at which you ultimately overloaded. I want to compare your conscious and unconscious recollections of the events leading up to the climax.'

'Don't try and bleat me. You mean you're bored with talking to an automaton. I'm more interesting when I'm fully awake.'

'On the contrary. Your past is far more intriguing than either your present or your future. Both of those are completely programed. Good night. There's no point in my saying "Sleep well" – that's programed too.'

KNOWN FACTORS CONTRIBUTING TO
HAFLINGER'S DESERTION

The shy, quiet, reserved boy who came to Tarnover had spent so much of his childhood being traded from one set of 'parents' to the next that he had developed a chameleon-like adaptability. He had liked almost all his 'fathers' and 'mothers' – small wonder, given the computerized care with which child was matched to adult – and he had been, briefly, exposed to an enormous range of interests. If his current 'dad' enjoyed sports, he spent hours with a baseball or a football; if his 'mom' was musical he sang to her accompaniment, or picked his way up and down a keyboard … and so on.

But he had never let himself become deeply engaged in anything. It would have been dangerous, as dangerous as coming to love somebody. At his next home it might not have been possible to continue.

At first, therefore, he was unsure of himself: diffident with his fellow students, among whom he was one of the youngest – most were in their mid-teens – and excessively formal when talking to members of the staff. He had a vague mental picture of government establishments, which was based on three-vee and movie portrayals of cadet schools and army bases. But there was nothing in the least military about Tarnover. There were rules, naturally, and among the students some customary traditions had already grown up although the place had been founded a mere decade earlier, but they were casually observed, and the atmosphere was – not friendly, but comradely. There was a sense of people banded together for a common purpose, undertaking a shared quest; in sum, there was a feeling of solidarity.

It was so novel to Nickie that he took months to realize how much he liked it.

Above all, he relished meeting people, not only adults but kids too, who obviously enjoyed knowing things. Accustomed to keeping his mouth shut in class, to imitating the sullen obstinacy of his fellow pupils because he had seen what happened to those who showed off their knowledge, he was astonished and for a while badly disturbed by this. Nobody tried to push him. He knew he was being watched, but that was all. He was told what was available for him to do, and his instructions stopped there. Provided he did one of the dozen or twenty choices, that was enough. Later he wouldn't even be obliged to choose from a list. He could make his own.

Suddenly he clicked on. His mind buzzed like a hive of bees with new and fascinating concepts: minus one has a square root, there are nearly a billion Chinese, a Shannon tree compresses written English by fifteen percent, so *that's* how a tranquilizer works, the word 'okay' comes from the Wolof *waw-kay* meaning 'by all means' or 'certainly' …

His comfortable private room was equipped with a computer remote;

there were hundreds of them around the campus, more than one for each person living there. He used it voraciously, absorbing encyclopedias of data.

Very quickly he became convinced how necessary it was for his country and no other to be the first to apply wisdom to the running of the world. With change so radical and swift, what else would serve? And if a repressive, unfree culture got there ahead …

Shuddering when he recalled what life under a non-wise system had done to him, Nickie was ripe to be persuaded.

He didn't even mind the twice-yearly sampling of his cerebellar tissue which he and all the students had to undergo. (Only later did he start putting quote marks around 'student' and thinking of himself and the others more as 'inmates'.) It was done with a microprobe and the loss was a negligible fifty cells.

And he was impressed to the point of awe by the single-mindedness of the biologists who worked in the anonymous-looking group of buildings on the east side of the campus. Their detachment was incredible and a little alarming, but their purpose seemed admirable. Organ grafts were routine to them – heart, kidney, lung, they made the transplant as impersonally as a mechanic would fit a spare part. Now they were after more ambitious goals: limb replacement complete with sensor and motor functions, restoration of vision to the blind, external gestation of the embryo … Now and then, without realizing what the slogans implied, Nickie had read advertisements in bold type headed BUY BABY BUNTING and IF YOU ABORT THEN WE'LL SUPPORT! But not until he arrived at Tarnover did he actually see one of the government fetus-trucks making its delivery of unwanted incomplete babies.

That troubled him a little, but it wasn't hard for him to decide that it was better for the not-yet-children to come here and be useful in research than for them to burn in a hospital incinerator.

After that, however, he wasn't quite as interested in genetics as he had begun to be. It could well have been coincidence, of course; most of the time he was hungrily rounding out his incomplete picture of the modern world, concentrating on history, sociology, political geography, comparative religion, linguistics and fiction in every possible form. His instructors were pleased and his fellow students were envious: here was one of the lucky ones, who was certain to go a long, long way.

There were graduates from Tarnover out in the larger world now. Not many. To build the student body up to its present total of seven hundred plus had taken nine years, and a good deal of the early work done here had gone to waste on the error side of the trial-and-error methods inevitable with any system as radically new as this. That was over. Sometimes a graduate returned for a short visit and expressed pleasure at the smoothness with which the establishment now ran, and told half-sad, half-funny stories about mistakes made when he or she was still a student. Most centered on the original assumption that an element of rivalry was indispensable if the people here were to function at maximum efficiency. On the contrary; one of the basic characteristics of a wise person is the ability to see how competition wastes time and effort. Some ludicrous contradictions had arisen before that problem was straightened out.

Existence at Tarnover was isolated. Vacations were naturally permitted – many of the students had living families, unlike Nickie. Pretty often one of his friends would take him home over Christmas or Thanksgiving or Labor Day. But he was well aware of the danger inherent in talking freely. No formal oath was administered, no security clearance issued, but all the kids were conscious, indeed proud, that their country's survival might depend on what they were doing. Besides, being a guest in another person's home reminded him uncomfortably of the old days. So he never accepted an invitation lasting more than a week, and always returned thankfully to what he now regarded as his ideal environment: the place where the air was constantly crackling with new ideas, yet the day-to-day pattern of life was wholly stable.

Naturally there were changes. Sometimes a student, less often an instructor, went away without warning. There was a phrase for that; it was said they had 'bowed out' – bowed in the sense of an overstressed girder, or a tree before a gale. One instructor resigned because he was not allowed to attend a conference in Singapore. No one sympathized. People from Tarnover did not attend foreign congresses. They rarely went to those in North America. There were reasons not to be questioned.

By the time he was seventeen Nickie felt he had made up for most of his childhood. He had learned affection, above all. It wasn't just that he'd had girls – he was a presentable young man now, and a good talker, and according to what he was told an enterprising lover. More important was the fact that the permanence of Tarnover had allowed him to go beyond merely liking adults. There were many instructors to whom he had become genuinely attached. It was almost as though he had been born late into a vast extended family. He had more kinfolk, more dependable, than ninety percent of the population of the continent.

And then the day came when …

Most of the education imparted here was what you taught yourself with the help of computers and teaching machines. Logically enough. Knowledge that you wanted to acquire before you knew where to look for it sticks better than knowledge you never even suspected in advance. But now and then a problem arose where personal guidance was essential. It had been two years since he'd dug into biology at all, and in connection with a project he was planning in the psychology of communication he needed advice on the physiological aspects of sensory input. The computer remote in his room was not the same one he had had when he arrived, but a newer and more efficient model which by way of a private joke he had baptized Roger, after Friar Bacon of the talking head.

It told him within seconds that he should call on Dr Joel Bosch in the biology section tomorrow at 1000. He had not met Dr Bosch, but he knew about him: a South African, an immigrant to the States seven or eight years ago, who had been accepted on the staff of Tarnover after long and thorough loyalty evaluation, and reputedly was doing excellent work.

Nickie felt doubtful. One had heard about South Africans ... but on the other hand he had never met one, so he suspended judgment.

He arrived on time, and Bosch bade him enter and sit down. He obeyed more by feel than sight, for his attention had instantly been riveted by – by a *thing* in one corner of the light and airy office.

It had a face. It had a torso. It had one normal-looking hand set straight in at the shoulder, one withered hand on the end of an arm straw-thin and almost innocent of muscle, and no legs. It rested in a system of supports that held its overlarge head upright, and it looked at him with an expression of indescribable jealousy. It was like a thalidomide parody of a little girl.

Portly, affable, Bosch chuckled at his visitor's reaction. 'That's Miranda,' he explained, dropping into his own chair. 'Go ahead, stare all you like. She's used to it – or if she isn't by now, then she's damned well going to have to get used to it.'

'What ...?' Words failed him.

'Our pride and joy. Our greatest achievement. And you're accidentally privileged to be among the first to know about it. We've kept her very quiet because we didn't know how much input she could stand, and if we'd let even the faintest hint leak out people would have been standing on line from here to the Pacific, demanding a chance to meet her. Which they will, but in due time. We're adjusting her to the world by slow degrees, now we know she really is a conscious being. Matter of fact, she probably has at least an average IQ, but it took us a while to figure out a way of letting her talk.'

Staring, hypnotized, Nickie saw that a sort of bellows mechanism was pumping slowly in and out alongside her shrunken body, and a connection ran from it to her throat.

'Of course even if she hadn't survived this long she would still have been a milestone on the road,' Bosch pursued. 'Hence her name – Miranda, "to be wondered at".' He gave a broad grin. 'We built her! That's to say, we combined the gametes under controlled conditions, we selected the genes we wanted and shoved them to the right side during crossover, we brought her to term in an artificial womb – yes, we literally built her. And we've learned countless lessons from her already. Next time the result should be independently viable instead of relying on all that gadgetry.' An airy wave.

'Right, to business. I'm sure you don't mind her listening in. She won't understand what we're talking about, but she's here, as I said, to accustom her to the idea that there are lots of people in the world instead of just three or four attendants taking care of her. According to the computers you want a fast rundown on …'

Mechanically Nickie explained the reason for his visit, and Bosch obliged him with the titles of a dozen useful recent papers on relevant subjects. He barely heard what was said. When he left the office he stumbled rather than walked back to his room.

Alone that night, and sleepless, he asked himself a question that was not on the program, and agonized his way to its answer.

Consciously he was aware that not everyone would have displayed the same reaction. Most of his friends would have been as delighted as Bosch, stared at Miranda with interest instead of dismay, asked scores of informed questions and complimented the team responsible for her.

But for half his life before the age of twelve, for six of his most formative years, Nickie Haflinger had been more furniture than person and willy-nilly had been forced to like it.

As though he had come upon the problem in a random test of the type that formed a standard element in his education – training people to be taken by surprise and still get it right was an integral part of Tarnover thinking – he saw it, literally saw it, in his mind's eye. It was spelled out on the buff paper they used for 'this section to be answered in terms of the calculus of morality', marking it off from the green used for administration and politics, the pink for social prognostication, and so on.

He could even imagine the style of type it was printed in. And it ran:

Distinguish between (a) the smelting of ore which could have become a tool in order to make a weapon and (b) the modification of germ plasm which might have been a person in order to make a tool. Do not continue your answer below the thick black line.

And the answer, the hateful horrible answer, boiled down to this.

No difference. No distinction. Both are wicked.

He didn't want to believe that conclusion. Taking it at face value implied giving up all that had been most precious in his short life. Tarnover had become his home in a more total sense than he had previously imagined possible.

But he felt insulted, clear down to the marrow of his bones.

I thought I was here to become myself with maximum perfection. I'm no longer sure that I was right. Suppose, just suppose, I'm here to become the person who's regarded as most usable ...

Miranda died; her life supports were less than perfect. But she was re-incarnated in numerous successors, and even when there was none of them around, her image continued to haunt Nickie Haflinger.

Privately, because he was afraid he would fail to explain himself if he talked about this to his friends, he wrestled with the ramifying tentacles of the problem.

The word *wicked* had sprung to his mind unbidden; it had been learned in infancy, most likely from his mother whom he dimly remembered as having been devout, a Pentecostalist or Baptist or the like. His later temporary parents had all been too enlightened to use such loaded terms around a child. Their homes contained computer remotes giving access to all the newest data concerning kids.

So what did the word mean? What in the modern world could be iden-tified as evil, an abomination, *wrong*? He groped his way toward a definition, and found the final clue in his recollection of what Bosch had said. Having discovered that Miranda was a conscious being with an average IQ, they had not given her merciful release. They had not even kept her ignorant of the world, so that she could have had no standard of comparison between her existence and that of mobile, active, free individuals. Instead, they brought her out in public to 'get used to being stared at'. As though their conception of personality began and ended with what could be measured in the labs. As though, capable themselves of suffering, they granted no reality to the suffer-ing of others. 'The subject exhibited a pain response.'

But not, under any circumstances, *we hurt her*.

Outwardly his conduct during his second five years at Tarnover was compat-ible with how he had previously behaved. He took tranquilizers, but they were prescribed for him as for most of his age group. He was sometimes called for counseling sessions after arguing with his instructors, but so were at least half of his peers. Having been jilted by a girl, he teetered on the verge of turning skew, but the typical emotional tempests of adolescence were magnified in this closed environment. All quite within the parameters laid down.

Once – literally once – he found he could stand the pressure no longer, and did something which, had he been found out, would have ensured his expulsion and very likely an operation to blank his memory. (It was rumored ... One could never pin the rumor down.)

From a public veephone at the railcar terminal linking Tarnover to the nearest town he called Hearing Aid, for the first time in years, and for one dark lonely hour poured out the secrets of his heart. It was a catharsis, a purgation. But long before he had regained his room he was shaking, haunted by the fear that Hearing Aid's famous promise ('Only I heard that!') might not be true. How could it be? It was absurd! From Canaveral the tendril-ears of federal computers wove through his society like mycelia. No place could possibly be immune. All night he lay awake in fear, expecting his door to be flung open and stern silent men to take him under arrest. By dawn he was half-minded to kill himself.

Miraculously, there followed no disaster, and a week later that awful impulse had receded in memory, growing vague as a dream. What he recalled all too vividly, though, was his terror.

He resolved it was the last time he'd be such a fool.

Shortly thereafter he began to concentrate on data processing techniques at the expense of his other study subjects, but about one in four of his contemporaries had by then also evinced a preference for some specialty, and this was a valuable talent. (It had been explained to him that in terms of n-value mean-path theory administering the three hundred million people of North America was a determinate problem; however, as with chess or fencing, it was no good to be told that there must be a perfect game if the universe wouldn't last long enough for it to be found by trial and error.)

He had been reserved and self-contained when he arrived. It was not inconsistent that after a gesture in the direction of greater openness he should revert to his old solitary habits. Neither his teachers nor his friends guessed that he had revised himself for a purpose. He wanted out, and there was not supposed to be an out.

The point was never labored, but there were constant reminders that to support one student at Tarnover cost the federal budget approximately three million dollars per year. What had been spent in the last century on missiles, submarines, the maintenance of forward bases overseas, was now lavished on these secret establishments. And it was known in the subtle way such things can be known that a condition of being here was that ultimately one must offer the government a return on its investment. All the graduates who came back to visit were doing so.

But the conviction had gradually grown in Nickie's mind that something was amiss. Were these people dedicated ... or insensitive? Were they patriotic ... or power-hungry? Were they single-minded ... or purblind?

He was determined that somehow, sooner or later, before committing himself to the lifetime repayment they were bound to demand of him, he must break loose long enough to take a detached view and make his mind up about the rights and wrongs of the brain race.

That was what set him on the trail of what he later found to be a 4GH code.

He deduced from first principles that there must be a way of allowing authorized persons to drop an old identity and assume a new one, no questions asked. The nation was tightly webbed in a net of interlocking data-channels, and a time-traveler from a century ago would have been horrified by the degree to which confidential information had been rendered accessible to total strangers capable of adding two plus two. ('The machines that make it more difficult to cheat on income tax can also ensure that blood of the right group is in the ambulance which picks you up from a car crash. *Well?*')

Yet it was known that not merely police informers, FBI agents and counterspies continued to go about their secret business, but also commercial spies – party agents shepherding million-dollar bribes – procurers serving the carnal purposes of the hypercorps. It was still true that if you were rich enough or had the ear of the proper person, you could avoid and evade. Most people were resigned to living wholly on the public level. He was not. He found his code.

A 4GH contained a replicating phage: a group which automatically *and consistently* deleted all record of a previous persona whenever a replacement was keyed in. Possessed of one, an individual could rewrite him- or herself via any terminal connected to the federal data banks. That meant, since 2005, any veephone including a public one.

This was the most precious of all freedoms, the plug-in life-style raised to the *n*th power: freedom to become the person you chose to be instead of the person remembered by the computers. That was what Nickie Haflinger desired so keenly that he spent five years pretending he was still himself. It was the enchanted sword, the invulnerable shield, the winged boots, the cloak of invisibility. It was the ultimate defense.

Or so it seemed.

Therefore, one sunny Saturday morning, he left Tarnover, and on Monday he was a life-style counselor in Little Rock, ostensibly aged thirty-five and – as the data-net certified – licensed to practice anywhere in North America.

THE TANGLED WEB

'Your first career went well for a while,' Freeman said. 'But it came to an abrupt and violent end.'

'Yes.' A harsh chuckle. 'I was nearly shot by a woman I advised to go screw someone of a different color. The massed computers of half a continent were in agreement with me, but she wasn't. I concluded I'd been overoptimistic and rethought myself.'

'Which was when you became an instructor with a three-vee cassette college. I note that for your new post you dropped down to twenty-five, much nearer your real age, even though the bulk of the clientele was forty or over. I wonder why.'

'The answer's simple. Think what lured most of those clients on to the college's reels. It was a sense of losing touch with the world. They were hungry for data supplied by people fifteen or twenty years younger, usually because they'd done what they thought best for their children and been repaid with rejection and insults. They were pathetic. What they wanted was not what they claimed to want. They wanted to be told yes, the world really is pretty much as it was when you were young, there aren't any objective differences, there's some magic charm you can recite and instantly the crazy moiling framework of the modern world will jell into fixed familiar patterns ... The third time a complaint was filed about my tapes I was surpled despite my rigorous proof that I was right. Being right was at a discount in that context, too.'

'So you tried your skill as a full-time Delphi gambler.'

'And made a fortune in next to no time and grew unspeakably bored. I did nothing that anybody else couldn't do, once he realized the government manipulates Delphi odds to keep the social-mollification index high.'

'Provided he had access to as much computer capacity as you did.'

'But in theory everybody does, given a dollar to drop into a pay phone.'

There was a pause. Freeman resumed in a brittle tone, 'Did you have a clearly defined goal in mind which guided you in your choice of roles?'

'You didn't already dig that out of me?'

'Yes, but when you were regressed. I want your contemporary conscious opinion.'

'It's still the same; I never hit on a better way of phrasing it. I was searching for a place to stand so that I could move the Earth.'

'Did you ever consider going overseas?'

'No. The one thing I suspected a 4GH might not be good for was a passport, so if I found the right spot it would have to be in North America.'

'I see. That puts your next career into much clearer perspective. You spent a full year with a utopia-design consultancy.'

'Yes. I was naïve. It took me that long to realize that only the very rich and the very stupid imagine happiness can be bought tailor-made. What's more, I should have discovered right away that it was company policy to maximize variety from one project to the next. I designed three very interesting closed communities, and in fact the last I heard all were still operating. But trying to include in the next utopia what seemed to be most promising in the previous one was what got me redunded again. You know, I sometimes wonder what became of last century's hypothetical life-style labs, where a serious effort was to be made to determine how best human beings can live together.'

'Well, there are the simulation cities, not to mention the paid-avoidance zones.'

'Sure, and there are the places like Trianon where you get a foretaste of tomorrow. But don't bleat me. Trianon couldn't exist if G2S didn't subsidize it with a billion dollars a year. Simulation cities are only for the children of the rich – it costs nearly as much to send the kids back to the past for a year as it does to keep them at Amherst or Bennington. And the paid-avoidance areas were created as a way of economizing on public expenditure after the Great Bay Quake. It was cheaper to pay the refugees to go without up-to-the-minute equipment. Which they couldn't have afforded anyhow.'

'Maybe mankind is more adaptable than they used to believe. Maybe we're coping well enough without such props.'

'In a day and age when they've quit covering individual murders on three-vee, where they just say bluntly, "Today there were so many hundred killings," and change the subject? That's not what I call coping!'

'You don't seem to have coped too well yourself. Each of your personae led to failure, or at any rate it didn't lead to fulfillment of your ambition.'

'Partly true, but only partly. In the enclosed environment of Tarnover I didn't realize how apathetic most people have become, how cut off they feel from the central process of decision-making, how utterly helpless and resigned. But remember: I was doing in my middle twenties what some people have to wait another decade, even two decades, to achieve. You people were hunting for me with all the resources at your command. You still didn't spot me, not even when I changed roles, which was my most vulnerable moment.'

'So you're blaming others for your failure and seeking consolation in your few and shallow successes.'

'I think you're human after all. At any rate that sounded as though you're trying to needle me. But save your breath. I admit my worst mistake.'

'Which was –?'

'To assume that things couldn't possibly be as bad as they were painted. To imagine that I could undertake constructive action on my own. I'll give you an example. A dozen times at least I'd heard the story of how a computer purchased by one of the hyper-corps exclusively – on their own admission – to find means whereby they could make tax-immune payments to government officials for favors received, had been held an allowable business expense. I was convinced it must be folklore. And then I found there really was such a case on record.' A sour chuckle. 'Faced with things like that, I came to accept that I couldn't get anywhere without supporters, sympathizers, colleagues.'

'Which you were hoping to obtain via your church?'

'Two more personae intervened before I hit on that idea. But, broadly speaking, yes.'

'Wasn't it galling to have to rethink yourself so often because of outside circumstances?'

There was another pause, this time a long one.

'Well, to be candid, I sometimes regarded myself as having escaped into the biggest prison on the planet.'

DEAN INGE HE SAY

'There are two kinds of fool. One says, "This is old, and therefore good." And one says, "This is new, and therefore better."'

RECEPTION TODAY IS OF AVERAGE QUALITY

'This is Seymour Schultz, who's one of our orbital troubleshooters.'

A lean dark man wearing blue, smiling and proffering, according to custom, a card bearing his name and code. Projected image: man of action, no-nonsense type.

'Ah, I saw one of your colleagues taking off just now.'

'Yes, that would have been Harry Leaver.'

'And this is Vivienne Ingle, head-of-dept for mental welf.'

Fat in gray and green, never pretty. Projecting: got here on merit, I know more than you do about yourself.

'And Pedro Lopez, and Charlie Verrano, and ...'

Plug-in people as predicted, which meant he could switch off half his attention and still be sure he'd do and say the right conformist things.

'... Rico Posta, veep i/c long-term planning—'

Snap back. Vice-presidents count, often stay put instead of bouncing around. So for this tall bearded man in black and yellow a specially warm handshake and:

'Great to meet you, Rico. Guess you and I will be in circuit quite a lot over this diversification you have in mind.'

'And – oh, yes, my daughter Kate, and over there is Dolores van Bright, asshead of contract law dept, whom you absolutely must meet right away because ...'

But somehow he wasn't at Ina's side any more as she crossed the room to make the introduction. He was smiling at Kate, and that was ridiculous. Because on top of not even being pretty she was bony – damn it, scrawny! Moreover, her face was too sharp: eyes, nose, chin. And her hair: tousled, of no special color, mousy-brown.

But looking at him with a degree of speculative interest he found dreadfully disturbing.

This is crazy. I don't like thin women. I like them cuddly. Ina, for example. And that's true in all versions of myself.

'So you're Sandy Locke.' With a curious husky intonation.

'Mm-hm. Large as life and twice as.'

There was an appraising pause. He was vaguely aware of Ina, who was on the far side of the floor now – and this was a big room, of course – as she glanced around in surprise to relocate him.

'No. Larger, and half,' Kate said unaccountably, and pulled an amusing face that made her nose woffle like a rabbit's. 'Ina's making wild signals at you. Better catch up. I'm not supposed to be here – I just have nothing else to do this evening. But suddenly I'm glad I came. Talk to you later.'

'Hey, Sandy!' Loud over the omnipresent soothing music, bland as the decor warranted to offend nobody. 'This way!'

What the hell happened just now?

The question kept leaping back into his mind even when 'just now' was an hour old, distracting him constantly without warning from the prescribed display of interest in the affairs of these new colleagues of his. It cost him much effort to maintain a veneer of politeness.

'Say, I hear your kid had to go be straightened, poor thing. How's she doing?'

'We collect her Saturday. Good as new or better, so they say.'

'Should have signed her with Anti-Trauma Inc. like us. Don't you agree, Sandy?'

'Hmm? Oh! It's no use asking me. I'm strictly swingle, so for me you're into a no-go zone.'

'Yeah? Shame. Was going to ask your view on fifty-fifty schools – know, where pupils pick half, staff the other half of the curriculum? Fair compromise on the face; in the guts I wonder ...'

'At Trianon?'

'No. Try live the future today, get it all wrong.'

And:

'– wouldn't take on a secondhand home. Too big a clog, reprograming the automatics. Short end to a friendship, inviting someone over and having him webbed solid to the driveway because the moronic machinery misunderstood you.'

'Mine you can update with no more than the poker's code. Tough it isn't at Trianon. Sandy here's a smart shivver – bet he's into the same type thing, right?'

'Presently between houses, friend. Next time maybe I'll move up where you are. Maybe I'll go clear back instead. I'm still sussing the aroma.'

And:

'You were tribed in teentime, Sandy? Hmm? Son of mine wants in the Assegais! Sure their solidarity and morale are great, but – uh ...'

'Fatality rate kind of high? I heard that too. Since they switched from

Baron Samedi to Kali. Me, I'm trying to plug Donna into the Bold Eagles. I mean what's it worth to get custody of a kid from a cross-marriage where she got to take some oath about shivving any white the warlord says?'

'Bold Eagles? Not a hope. Signing up kids at birth now. Go find some nice quiet tribe that follows Saint Nick. The life-assurance rates are lower, to begin with.'

And so on.

But at alarmingly frequent intervals he kept finding that his eyes had strayed past the shoulder of the Important Person he was chatting with and come to rest on the untidy hair or the pointed profile of Ina's daughter.

Why?

Eventually Ina said in a tart tone, 'Kate seems to have you mezzed, Sandy!'

Yes, mesmerized would be a good name for it.

'Takes after you in that respect,' he answered lightly. 'Mainly I'm puzzled to find her here. I thought this was strictly a meet-the-folks deal.'

That was convincing; the girl was one jarring element in an otherwise predictable milieu. Ina softened a little.

'Should have guessed. Should say sorry, too. But she knows quite a lot of the staff, and she called up today to ask if I was doing anything this evening or could she drop by for dinner, so I said there was this party and she could ride my back.'

'So she isn't with the corp. I thought maybe. What's she doing with her life?'

'Nothing.'

'What?'

'Oh, nothing worth mentioning. Going back next fall for *another* course of study. Right here at UMKC, *again*. And she's twenty-two, damn it!' In a lower voice – but Sandy already knew that damaging number, no extra harm involved. 'I could peg it if she wanted to go study in Australia, or even Europe, but … And she blames it all on this cat her father gave her!'

At which point she caught sight of Rico Posta signaling for her to go talk with him and Dolores van Bright, and separated with a mutter of excuses.

A few seconds, and while he was still debating whether to pay another call on the autobar, Kate was at his side. The room was crowded now – fifty-odd guests were present – and last time he saw her she had been the far side of the floor. It followed she had been watching him as keenly as Vivienne. (No, not any more. Hooray. Mental welfare was taking time out.)

What do I do – run?

'How long are you going to be in KC?' Kate demanded.

'The usual. As long as G2S and I agree I should.'

'You're claiming to be the bounce-around type?'

'It's bounce or break,' he said, trying to make the cliché sound like what it was supposed to be: a flip substitute for a proper answer.

'You're the first person I've met who can say that as though he means it,' Kate murmured. Her eyes, dark brown and very piercing, were constantly on his face. 'I knew the moment you came in there was something unusual about you. Where did you bounce in from?'

And, while he was hesitating, she added, 'Oh, I know it's rude to pry into people's pasts. Ina's been telling me since I learned to talk. Like you don't stare, you don't point, you don't make personal remarks. But people do have pasts, and they're on file at Canaveral, so why let machines know what your friends don't?'

'Friends are out of fashion,' he said, more curtly than he had intended ... and how long was it since he had been taken that much off his guard? Even pronouncing that curse on Fluckner – already the encounter felt as though it lay ages behind him – had not been as disturbing as his casual party conversation. Why? Why?

'Which doesn't mean nonexistent,' Kate said. 'You'd be a valuable friend. I can sense it. That makes you rare.'

A sudden possibility struck him. It could be that this plain, thin, unprepossessing girl had found a way to reach men who would not otherwise regard her as attractive. The offer of friendship, deeper than the commonplace acquaintanceships of the plug-in lifestyle, might well appeal to those who hungered for solid emotional fare.

He almost voiced the charge, but he seemed to taste in advance the flavor of the words. They were like ashes on his tongue. Instead, with reluctance, he said, 'Thank you. I take that as a compliment though thousands wouldn't. But right now I'm thinking more of the future than the past. I didn't enjoy my last position too much. What about you? You're studying. What?'

'Everything. If you can be enigmatic, so can I.'

He waited.

'Oh! Last year, water ecology, medieval music and Egyptology. The year before, law, celestial mechanics and handicrafts. Next year, probably— Is something the matter?'

'Not at all. I'm just trying to look impressed.'

'Don't bleat me. I can tell you're not wondering why anybody should waste time on such a mishmosh. I see that look all the time on Ina's face, and her so-called "friends" here at the company.' She paused, pondering. 'Maybe ... Yes, I think so. Envious?'

My God! How did she catch on so quickly? To have the chance without being fettered by the demands of Tarnover, without having it drummed into your mind nonstop that every passing year sees you three million further into the government's debt...

It was 2130. A thudding sound announced the issue from wall vents of a cold buffet supper. Ina returned to ask whether he wanted her to bring him a plateful. He was glad. He could use the distraction to formulate not his but Sandy Locke's proper response.

'Ah, you don't have to know everything. You just have to know where to find it.'

Kate sighed. As she turned away an odd look came into her eyes. He only glimpsed it, but he was quite certain how best to define it.

Disappointment.

AMONG THE MOST HIGHLY PRAISED OF ALL THREE-VEE COMMERCIALS

1. Dead silence, the black of empty space, the harsh bright points of the stars. Slowly into field orbits the wreckage of a factory. Obviously an explosion has opened it like a tin can. Spacesuited figures are seen drifting around it like fetuses attached to the umbilical cords of their regulation life lines. Hold for a beat. Pan to a functioning factory operating at full blast, glistening in the rays of the naked sun and swarming with men and women loading unmanned freight capsules for dispatch to Earth. Voice over: 'On the other hand ... *this* factory was built by G2S.'

2. Without warning we are plunging through the outer atmosphere, at first on a steady course, then vibrating, then wobbling as the ablation cone on the capsule's nose starts to flare. It spins wildly and tumbles end-for-end. Explosion. Cut to half a dozen men in overalls staring furiously at a dying streak of brightness on the night sky. Cut again, this time to a similar group walking across a concrete landing pan toward a smoking capsule that targeted so close to home they don't even need to ride to reach it. Voice over: 'On the other hand ... *this* capsule was engineered by G2S.'

3. Deep space again, this time showing a bulky irregular mass of asteroid rock drifting toward a smelting station, recognizable by its huge mirror of thin mylar. Jets blaze on the asteroid's nearer side, men and women in suits gesticulate frantically. Sound over, faint, of confused yells for help and angry orders to 'Do something!' But the asteroid rock plows its solemn way clear through the mirror and leaves it in shreds that float eerily on nothing. Cut to another smelting station whose mirror is focused on an even larger chunk of ore. Magnetic vapor-guides tidily collect the gas as it boils off, separators – each shining with a different shade of reddish white – deliver valuable pure metals into cooling chambers on the shadow side of the rock. Voice over: 'On the other hand ... *this* orbit was computed at G2S.'

THE KINGDOMS OF THE WORLD

'How did you enjoy working at G2S?' Freeman inquired.

'More than I expected. Being a sort of export agency for frontline technology, it attracts top men and women from every field, and lively minds are always fun to have around. I was most closely in contact with Rico Posta, and in fact it was because of what I did under his instructions that G2S didn't lay an enormous egg by going into olivers at the same time as National Panasonic. Their model would have been twice the price with half the advantages, *and* they wouldn't have wanted to amortize their research over twenty-seven years, either.'

'Something to do with the structure of Japanese society,' Freeman said dryly. 'Nipponside, the things must be invaluable.'

'True!'

Today the atmosphere was comparatively relaxed. There was an element of conversation in the dialogue.

'How about your other colleagues? You began by disliking Vivienne Ingle.'

'Began by being prepared to dislike them all. But though in theory they were standard plug-in types, in practice they were the cream of the category, moving less often than the average exec and prepared to stay where interesting research was going on rather than move from sheer force of habit.'

'You investigated them by tapping the data-net, no doubt.'

'Of course. Remember my excuse for getting hired.'

'Of course. But it can't have taken you long to find out what you originally intended to confirm: your 4GH was still usable. Why did you stay, even to the point of their offering you tenure?'

'That ... That's hard to explain. I guess I hadn't encountered so many people functioning so well before. In my previous personae I chiefly contacted people who were dissatisfied. There's this kind of low-grade paranoia you find all the time and everywhere because people know that people they don't know can find out things about them they'd rather keep quiet. Are you with me?'

'Naturally. But at G2S the staff were different?'

'Mm-hm. Not in the sense of having nothing to hide, not in the sense of being superbly secure – witness Ina, for one. But in general they were enjoying the wave of change. They groused pretty often, but that was a safety valve. Once the pressure blew off, they went back to using the system instead of being used by it.'

'Which is what you find most admirable.'

'Hell, yes. Don't you?'

There was a pause, but no answer.

'Sorry, next time I'll know better. But you exaggerate when you say they were set to offer me tenure. They were prepared to semi-perm me.'

'That would have evolved into tenure.'

'No, I couldn't have let it. I was tempted. But it would have meant slipping into the Sandy Locke role and staying in it for the rest of my life.'

'I see. It sounds as though role-switching can become addictive.'

'What?'

'Never mind. Tell me what you did to make such a good impression.'

'Oh, apart from the oliver bit I sorted out some snarls, saved them a few million a year. Routine stuff. Anybody can be an efficient systems rash if he can mouse around in the federal net.'

'You found that easy?'

'Not quite, but far from difficult. A G2S code heading the inquiry was a key to open many doors. The corp has a max-nat-advantage rating at Canaveral, you know.'

'Did you do as you promised for Ina Grierson?'

'Pecked away at it when I remembered. I lost my enthusiasm when I realized why she hadn't turned freelie already, cut loose and left her daughter to her own devices. So long as she was in reach of her ugly duckling, her confidence was reinforced. Knowing she was far the more conventionally beautiful of the two … She must have hated her ex-husband.'

'You found out who he was, of course.'

'Only when I got tired of her pestering and finally dug deep into her file. Poor shivver. It must have been a horrible way to die.'

'Some people would call it a lesson in nemesis.'

'Not at Tarnover.'

'Maybe not. However, you were saying you enjoyed yourself at G2S.'

'Yes, I was amazingly content. But for one problem. It was spelt K-A-T-E, as if you hadn't guessed.'

STALKED

The university was closed for summer vacation, but instead of taking off for a remote corner of the world or even, like some students, going on a package tour to the Moon, Kate stayed in KC. Next after the welcomefest he met her at a coley club patronized by the more frameworked execs of G2S.

'Sandy, come and dance!' Seizing his arm, almost dragging him away. 'You haven't seen my party trick!'

'Which is –?'

But she was doing it, and he was genuinely startled. The ceiling projectors were invisible; it took fantastic kinaesthetic sensibility to dance one chorus of a simple tune without straying off key, and more still to come back and repeat it. That though was exactly what she did, and the clamorous discord generated by the other dancers was overriden by her strongly-gestured theme, mostly in the bass as though some celestial organ had lost all its treble and alto couplers but none of its volume: the *Ode to Joy* in a stately majestic tempo. From the corner of his eye he noticed that four European visitors sitting at a nearby table were uneasy, wondering whether to stand in honor of their continental anthem.

'How in the—?'

'Don't talk! Harmonize!'

Well, if the last note was from *that* projector and the one adjacent is now delivering *that* note ... He had never taken much interest in coley, but Kate's enthusiasm was infectious; her face was bright, her eyes sparkled. She looked as though some other age might have judged her beautiful.

He tried this movement, that one, another different ... and suddenly there was a chord, a true fifth. Which slipped a little, and had to be corrected, and – *got it*! A whole phrase of the melody in two meticulously harmonizing parts.

'I'll be damned,' she said in a matter-of-fact tone. 'I never met anyone before over about twenty-five and capable of proper coley. We should get together more often!'

And then someone on the far side of the floor who looked no more than fifteen wiped the music of Beethoven and substituted something new, angular, acid – probably Japanese.

After the madrigal concert where he also met her, and the lakeside fish fry where he also met her, and the target-archery meet where he also met her, and the swimming gala where he also met her, and the lecture on advances in the application of topology to business administration where he also met her, he could hold back his challenge no longer.

'Are you following me or something?'

Tonight she was wearing something sexy and diaphanous, and she had had her hair machine-coiffed. But she was still plain, still bony, still disturbing.

'No,' was her answer. 'Pre-guessing you. I don't have you completely pegged yet – I went to the wrong place last night – but I'm closing in fast. You, Sandy Locke, are trying far too hard to adhere to a statistical norm. And I hate to see a good man go to waste.'

With which she spun on her heel and strode – one might almost have said marched – to rejoin her escort, a plump young man who scowled at him as though virulently jealous.

He simply stood there, feeling his stomach draw drumhead-tight and sweat break out on his palms.

To be sought by federal officials: that was one thing. He was accustomed to it after six years, and his precautions had become second nature. But to have his persona as Sandy Locke penetrated with such rapidity by a girl he barely knew ...!

Got to switch her off my circuit! She makes me feel the way I felt when I first quit Tarnover – as though I was certain to be recognized by everyone I passed on the street, as though a web were closing that would trap me for the rest of my life. And I thought that poor kid Gaila had problems ... STOP STOP STOP! I'm being Sandy Locke, and no child ever came sobbing out of the night to beg his help!

SEE ISAIAH 8:1–2

Make speed to the spoil, for the prey hasteneth.

YEARSHIFT

'I thought you'd never show,' Kate said caustically, and stood back from the door of her apartment. He had caught her wearing nothing but shorts, baggy with huge pockets, and a film of dust turning here and there to slime with perspiration. 'Still, you picked a good time. I'm just getting rid of last year's things. You can give me a hand.'

He entered with circumspection, vaguely apprehensive of what he might find inside this home of hers: the upper floor of what at the turn of the century must have been a desirable one-family house. Now it was subdivided, and the area was on the verge of ghettohood. The streets were deep in litter and tribe-signs were plentiful. Bad tribes at that – the Kickapoos and the Bent Minds.

Four rooms here had been interconnected by enlarging doorways into archways; only the bathroom remained isolated. As he glanced around, his attention was immediately caught by a splendidly stuffed mountain lion on a low shelf at the end of the hallway, warmed by a shaft of bright sunlight—

Stuffed?

It came back in memory as clear as though Ina were here to speak the words: 'She blames it all on that cat her father gave her ...'

Regarding him almost as steadily as her unlikely pet, Kate said, 'I wondered how you would react to Bagheera. Congratulations; you get full marks. Most people turn and run. You've just gone a trifle pale around the gills. To answer all your questions in advance – yes, he is entirely tame except when I tell him to be otherwise, and he was a present from my father, who saved him from being used up in a circus. You know who my father was, I presume.'

His mouth very dry, he nodded. 'Henry Lilleberg,' he said in a croaking voice. 'Neurophysiologist. Contracted degenerative myelitis in the course of a research program and died about four years ago.'

'That's right.' She was moving toward the animal, hand outstretched. 'I'll introduce you, and after that you needn't worry.'

Somehow he found himself scratching the beast behind his right ear, and the menace he had originally read in those opal eyes faded away. When he withdrew his hand Bagheera heaved an immense sigh, laid his chin on his paws and went to sleep.

'Good,' Kate said. 'I expected him to like you. Not that that makes you anything special … Had you heard about him from Ina, by the way? Is that why you weren't surprised?'

'You think I wasn't? She said you had a cat, so I assumed— Never mind. It all comes clear now.'

'Such as what?'

'Why you stay on at UMKC instead of sampling other universities. You must be very attached to him.'

'Not especially. Sometimes he's a drag. But when I was sixteen I said I'd accept responsibility for him, and I've kept my word. He's growing old now – won't last more than eighteen months – so … But you're right. Dad had a license to transport protected species interstate, but I wouldn't stand a hope in hell of getting one, let alone a permit to keep him on residential premises anywhere else. I'm not exactly tied hand and foot, though. I can take vacations for a week or two, and the girls downstairs feed and walk him for me, but that's about his limit, and eventually he gets fretful and they have to call me back. Annoys my boyfriends … Come on, this way.'

She led him into the living-room. Meter-high freehand Egyptian hieroglyphs marched around three of its walls; over the fourth, white paint had been slapped.

'I'm losing this,' Kate said. 'It's from the Book of the Dead. Chapter Forty, which I thought was kind of apt.'

'I'm afraid I never read the …' His voice trailed away.

'Wallis Budge titles it "The Chapter of Repulsing the Eater of the Ass". I bleat you not. But I quit repulsing that fiercely.' She gave a mocking grin. 'Anyhow, now you see what you can lend a hand with.'

No wonder she was wearing a layer of dust. The whole apartment was being bayquaked. In the middle of the floor here three piles of objects were growing, separated by chalked lines. One contained charitable items, like clothing not yet past hope; one contained what was scrapworthy, like a last-year's stereo player and a used typewriter and such; one contained stuff that was only garbage, though it was subdivided into disposable and recyclable.

Everywhere shelves were bare, closets were ajar, boxes and cases stood with lids raised. This room had a south aspect and the sun shone through large open windows. The smell of the city blew in on a warm breeze.

Willing to play along he peeled off his shirt and hung it on the nearest chair. 'I do what?' he inquired.

'As I tell you. Mostly help with the heavier junk. Oh, plus one other thing. Talk about yourself while we're at it.'

He reached for his shirt and made to put it back on.

'Point,' she said with an exaggerated sigh, 'taken. So just help.'

Two sweaty hours later the job was finished and he knew a little about her which he hadn't previously guessed. This was the latest of perhaps five, perhaps six, annual demolitions of what was threatening to turn from a present into a past, with all that that implied: a fettering, hampering tail of concern for objects at the expense of memories. Desultorily they chatted as they worked; mostly he asked whether this was to be kept, and she answered yes or no, and from her pattern of choice he was able to paradigm her personality – and was more than a little frightened when he was through.

This girl wasn't at Tarnover. This girl is six years younger than I am, and yet …

The thought stopped there. To continue would have been like holding his finger in a flame to discover how it felt to be burned alive.

'After which we paint walls,' she said, slapping her hands together in satisfaction. 'Though maybe you'd like a beer before we shift modes. I make real beer and there are six bottles in to chill.'

'*Real* beer?' Maintaining Sandy Locke's image at all costs, he made his tone ironical.

'A plastic person like you probably doesn't believe it exists,' she said, and headed for the kitchen before he could devise a comeback.

When she returned with two foam-capped mugs, he had some sort of remark ready, anyway. Pointing at the hieroglyphs, he said, 'It's a shame to paint these over. They're very good.'

'I've had them up since January,' was her curt reply. 'They've furnished my mind, and that's what counts. When you've drunk that, grab a paint-spray.'

He had arrived at around five P.M. A quarter of ten saw them in a freshly whitened framework, cleansed of what Kate no longer felt to be necessary, cleared of what the city scrap-and-garbage team would remove from the stoop come Monday morning and duly mark credit in respect of. There was a sense of space. They sat in the spacefulness eating omelets and drinking the last of the *real* beer, which was good. Through the archway to the kitchen they could see and hear Bagheera gnawing a beefbone with old blunt teeth, uttering an occasional *rrrr* of contentment.

'And now,' Kate said, laying aside her empty plate, 'for the explanations.'

'What do you mean?'

'I'm a virtual stranger. Yet you've spent five hours helping me shift furniture and fill garbage cans and redecorate the walls. What do you want? To plug into me by way of payment?'

370

He sat unspeaking and immobilized.

'If that were it ...' She was gazing at him with a thoughtful air. 'I don't think I'd say no. You'd be good at it, no doubt about that. But it isn't why you came.'

Silence filled the brightly whitened room, dense as the feathers in a pillow.

'I think,' she said eventually, 'you must have come to calibrate me. Well, did you get me all weighed and measured?'

'No,' he said gruffly, and rose and left.

INTERIM REPORT

'Bureau of Data Processing, good afternoon!'

'The Deputy Director, please. Mr Hartz is expecting my call ... Mr Hartz, I thought you should know that I'm approaching a crisis point, and if you care to come back and—'

'Oh. I see. What a pity. Then I'd better just arrange for my tapes to be copied to your office.

'Yes, naturally. By a most-secure circuit.'

IMPERMEABLE

It was a nervous day, very nervous. Today they were boarding him: not just Rico and Dolores and Vivienne and the others he had met but also august remote personages from the intercontinental level. Perhaps he should not have shown a positive reaction when Ina mentioned the corp's willingness to semiperm him, hinted that eventually they might give him tenure.

Stability, for a while at any rate, was tempting. He had no other plans formulated, and out of this context he intended to move when *he* chose, not by order of some counterpart to Shad Fluckner. Yet a sense of risk grew momently more agonizing in his mind. To be focused on by people of such power and influence – what could be more dangerous? Were there not at Tarnover people charged with tracking down and dragging back in chains Nickie Haflinger on whom the government had lavished thirty millions' worth of special training, teaching, conditioning? (By now perhaps there were other fugitives. He dared not try to link up with them. If only ...!)

Still, facing the interview was the least of countless evils. He was preening prior to departure, determined to perfect his conformist image to the last hair on his head, when the buzzer called him to the veephone.

The face showing on the screen belonged to Dolores van Bright, with whom he had got on well during his stay here.

'Hi, Sandy!' was her cordial greeting. 'Just called to wish you luck when you meet the board. We prize you around here, you know. Think you deserve a long-term post.'

'Well, thanks,' he answered, hoping the camera wouldn't catch the gleam of sweat he felt pearling on his skin.

'And I can strew your path with a rose or so.'

'Hm?' Instantly, all his reflexes triggered into fight-or-flight mode.

'I guess I shouldn't, but ... Well, for better or worse. Vivienne dropped a hint, and I checked up, and there's to be an extra member on the selection board. You know Viv thinks you've been overlooked as kind of a major national resource? So some federal twitch is slated to join us. Don't know who, but I believe he's based at Tarnover. Feel honored?'

How he managed to conclude the conversation, he didn't know. But he did, and the phone was dead, and he was ...

On the floor?

He fought himself, and failed to win; he lay sprawled, his legs apart, his mouth dry, his skull ringing like a bell that tolls nine tailors, his guts churning, his fingers clenched and his toes attempting to imitate them. The room swam, the world floated off its mooring, everything EVERYTHING dissolved into mist and he was aware of one sole fact:

Got to get up and go.

Weak-limbed, sour-bellied, half-blind with terror he could no longer resist, he stumbled out of his apartment (*Mine? No! Their apartment!*) and headed for his rendezvous in hell.

THE CONVICTION OF HIS COURAGE

After pressing the appropriate switches Freeman waited patiently for his subject to revert from regressed to present-time mode. Eventually he said, 'It seems that experience remains peculiarly painful. We shall have to work through it again tomorrow.'

The answer came in a weak voice, but strong enough to convey venomous hatred. 'You devil! Who gave you the right to torture me like this?'

'You did.'

'So I committed what you call a crime! But I was never put on trial, never convicted!'

'You're not entitled to a trial.'

'Anybody's entitled to a trial, damn you!'

'That is absolutely true. But you see you are *not* anybody. You are *nobody*. And you chose to be so of your own free will. Legally – officially – you simply don't exist.'

BOOK 2

The Delphi Coracle

SHALLOW MAN IN ALL HIS GORY WAS NOT DISMAYED BY ONE OF THESE

Take no thought for the morrow; that's your privilege. But don't complain if when it gets here you're off guard.

ARARAT

With a distant … Too weak a word. With a *remote* part of his mind he was able to observe himself doing all the wrong things: heading in a direction he hadn't chosen, and running when he should and could have used his company electric car, in sum making a complete fool of himself.

In principle he had made the correct decisions. He would turn up for his appointment with the interview board, he would outface the visitor from Tarnover, he would win the argument because you don't, simply *don't*, haul into custody someone who is being offered permanent employment by a corporation as powerful as G2S. Not without generating a continental stink. And if there's one thing they're afraid of at Tarnover, it's having the media penetrate their guise of feigned subimportance.

The road to hell is paved with good intentions. His were fine. They simply had no effect on his behavior.

'Yes, who is it?' In a curt voice from the speaker under the veephone camera. And then, almost in the same breath, 'Sandy! Hey, you look sick, and I don't mean that as a compliment! Come right on up!'

Sound of antithief locks clicking to neutral.

Sick?

He pondered the word with that strange detached portion of his awareness which was somehow isolated from his body at present, yet continued to function as though it were hung under a balloon trailed behind this fleshly carcass now ascending stairs not by legs alone but by arms clutching at the banister to stop from falling over. Legs race combines with arms race to make brain race and his brain was definitely racing. An invisible tight band had clamped on his head at the level of his temples. Pain made him giddy. He was double-focusing. When the door of Kate's apt opened he saw two of it, two of her in a shabby red wrap-around robe and brown sandals … but that wasn't so bad, because her face was eloquent of sympathy and worry and a double dose of that right now was to be welcomed. He was sweating rivers and imagined that he could have heard his feet squelching in his shoes but for the drumming of his heart, which also drowned out the question she shot at him.

Repeated louder, 'I said, what the hell have you taken?'

He hunted down his voice, an elusive rasp in the caverns of a throat which had dried like a creek bed in a bad summer all the way to his aching lungs.

'No-uh-thing!'

'My God. In that case have you ever got it strong. Come quickly and lie down.'

As swiftly and unreally as in a dream, with as much detachment as though he were viewing these events through the incurious eyes of old Bagheera, he witnessed himself being half-led, half-carried to a couch with a tan cover. In the Early Pleistocene he had sat on it to eat omelets and drink beer. It was a lovely sunny morning. He let his lids fall to exclude it, concentrated on making the best use of the air, which was tinted with a faint lemony fragrance.

She drew drapes against the sun by touching a button, then came in twilight to sit by him and hold his hand. Her fingers sought his pulse as expertly as a trained nurse.

'I knew you were straining too hard,' she said. 'I still can't figure out why – but get the worst of it over and then you can tell me about it. If you like.'

Time passed. The slam of his heart lessened. The sweat streaming from his pores turned from hot to cool, made his smart clothing clammy. He began to shiver and then, with no warning, found he was sobbing. Not weeping – his eyes were dry – but sobbing in huge gusting gasps, as though he were being cruelly and repeatedly punched in the belly by a fist that wasn't there.

At some stage she brought a thick woolen blanket, winterweight, and laid it on him. It had been years since he felt the rough bulk of such a fabric – now, one slept on a pressure bed, insulated by a directed layer of air. It evoked thousands of inchoate childhood memories. His hands clamped like talons to draw it over his head and his knees doubled into the fetal posture and he rolled on his side and miraculously was asleep.

When he awoke he felt curiously relaxed. He felt purged. In the … How long? He checked his watch. In the at-most hour since he dozed off, something more than calm had occupied his mind.

He formed a word silently and liked its taste.

Peace.

But –!

He sat up with a jerk. There was no peace – must be none – *could* be none! It was the wrong world for peace. At the G2S HQ someone from Tarnover must now be adding – correction, must already have added – two plus two.

This person Sandy Locke 'overlooked as kind of a national resource' might have been identified as the lost Nickie Haflinger!

He threw aside the blanket and stood up, belatedly realizing that Kate was nowhere to be seen and perhaps Bagheera had been left on guard and ...

But his complicated thought dissolved under a wave of dizziness. Before he had taken as much as one pace away from the couch, he'd had to lean an outstretched hand against the wall.

Upon which came Kate's voice from the kitchen.

'Good timing, Sandy. Or whatever your real name is. I just fixed some broth for you. Here.'

It approached him in a steaming cup, which he accepted carefully by the less-hot handle. But he didn't look at it. He looked at her. She had changed into a blue and yellow summer shirt and knee-long cultoons also of yellow with the blue repeated in big Chinese ideograms across the seat. And he heard himself say, 'What was that about my name?'

Thinking at the same time: *I was right. There is no room for peace in this modern world. It's illusory. One minute passes, and it's shattered.*

'You were babbling in your sleep,' she said, sitting down on a patched old chair which he had expected her to throw out yet perversely had been retained. 'Oh, please stop twitching your eyes like that! If you're wondering what's become of Bagheera, I took him downstairs; the girls said they'd look after him for a while. And if you're trying to spot a way of escape, it's too soon. Sit down and drink that broth.'

Of the alternatives open, the idea of obeying seemed the most construct-ive. The instant he raised the cup he realized he was ravenous. His blood-sugar level must be terribly debased. Also he was still cold. The warmth of the savory liquid was grateful to him.

At long last he was able to frame a one-word question.

'Babbling ...?'

'I exaggerate. A lot of it made sense. That was why I told G2S you weren't here.'

'*What?*' He almost let go of the cup.

'Don't tell me I did the wrong thing. Because I didn't. Ina got them to call me when you didn't show for your interview. I said no, of course I haven't seen him. He doesn't even like me, I told them. Ina would believe that. She's never realized that men can like me, because I'm all the things she didn't want her daughter to be, such as studious and intelligent and mainly plain. She never dug deeper into any man's personality than the level she dealt with you on: looks good, sounds good, feels good and I can use him.' She gave a harsh laugh, not quite over the brink of bitterness.

He disregarded that comment. 'What did I – uh – let slip?' he demanded. And trembled a little as he awaited the answer.

She hesitated. 'First off … Well, I kind of got the impression you never overloaded before. Can that be true?'

He had been asked often by other people and had always declared, 'No, I guess I'm one of the lucky ones.' And had believed his claim to be truthful. He had seen victims of overload; they hid away, they gibbered when you tried to talk to them, they screamed and struck out and smashed the furniture. These occasional bouts of shaking and cramp and cold, aborted in minutes with one tranquilizer, couldn't be what you'd call overload, not really!

But now he had sensed such violence in his own body, he was aware that from outside his behavior must have paralleled that of a member of his Toledo congregation, and his former chief at the utopia consultancy, and two of his colleagues at the three-vee college, and … others. Countless others. Trapped in fight-or-flight mode when there was no way to attain either solution.

He sighed, setting aside his cup, and drove himself to utter an honest answer.

'Before, drugs have always straightened me in no time. Today – well, somehow I didn't want to think of taking anything … if you see what I mean.'

'You never sweated it out before? Not even once? Small wonder this is such a bad attack.'

Nettled, he snapped back. 'It happens to you all the time, hm? That's why you're so knowledgeable?'

She shook her head, expression neutral. 'No, it never did happen to me. But I've never taken tranquilizers, either. If I feel like crying myself to sleep, I do. Or if I feel like cutting classes because it's such a beautiful day, I do that too. Ina overloaded when I was about five. That was when she and Dad split up. After that she started riding constant herd on my mental state as well as her own. But I got this association fixed in my mind between the pills she took and the way she acted when she broke down – which wasn't pleasant – so I always used to pretend I'd swallowed what she gave me, then spit it out when I was alone. I got very good at hiding tablets and capsules under my tongue. And I guess it was the sensible thing to do. Most of my friends have folded up at least once, some of them two or three times beginning in grade school. And they all seem to be the ones who had – uh – special care taken of them by their folks. Care they'll never recover from.'

Somehow a solitary fly had escaped the defenses of the kitchen. Sated, heavy on its wings, it came buzzing in search of a place to rest and digest. As though a saw blade's teeth were adding an underscore to the words, he felt his next question stressed by the sound.

'Do you mean the sort of thing Anti-Trauma does?'

'The sort of thing parents hire Anti-Trauma to do to their helpless kids!' There was venom in her tone, the first strong feeling he had detected in her. 'But they were far from the first. They're the largest and best-advertised, but they weren't the pioneers. Ina and I were having a fight last year, and she said she wished she'd given me that type of treatment. Once upon a time I quite liked my mother. Now I'm not so sure.'

He said with weariness born of his recent tormented self-reappraisal, 'I guess they think they're doing the right and proper thing. They want their kids to be able to cope, and it's claimed to be a way of adjusting people to the modern world.'

'That,' Kate said, 'is Sandy Locke talking. Whoever you are, I now know for sure that you're not him. He's a role you've put on. In your heart you know what Anti-Trauma does is monstrous ... don't you?'

He hesitated only fractionally before nodding. 'Yes. Beyond any hope of argument, it's evil.'

'Thank you for leveling with me at last. I was sure nobody who's been through what you have could feel otherwise.'

'What am I supposed to have been through?'

'Well, in your sleep you moaned about Tarnover, and since everybody knows what Tarnover is like—'

He jerked as though he had been kicked. 'Wait, wait! That can't be true! Most people don't know Tarnover exists!'

She shrugged. 'Oh, you know what I mean. I've met several of their so-called graduates. People who could have been individuals but instead have been standardized – filed down – straitjacketed!'

'But that's incredible!'

It was her turn to be confused and startled. 'What?'

'That you've met all these people from Tarnover.'

'No, it's not. UMKC is crawling with them. Turn any wet stone. Oh, I exaggerate, but there are five or six.'

The sensations he had been victim of when he arrived threatened to return. His mouth dried completely, as though it had been swabbed with cotton-wool; his heart pounded; he instantly wanted to find a bathroom. But he fought back with all the resources at his command. Steadying his voice was as exhausting as climbing a mountain.

'So where are they in hiding?'

'Nowhere. Stop by the Behavioral Sciences Lab and— Say, Sandy!' She rose anxiously to her feet. 'You'd better lie down again and talk about this later. Obviously it hasn't penetrated that you're suffering from shock, just as surely as if you'd walked away from a veetol crash.'

'I do know!' he barked. 'But there was someone from Tarnover sitting in with the G2S selection board, and if they think to make a physical check of this place ... They thought of calling you up, didn't they?'

She bit her lip, eyes scanning his face in search of clues that were not to be found.

'Why are you so afraid?' she ventured. 'What did they do to you?'

'It's not so much what they did. It's what they will do if they catch me.'

'Because of something you did to them? What?'

'Quit cold after they'd spent thirty million on trying to turn me into the sort of shivver you were just describing.'

During the next few seconds he was asking himself how he could ever have been so stupid as to say that. And with surprise so terrific it was almost worse than what had gone before he then discovered he hadn't been stupid after all.

For she turned and walked to the window to peer out at the street between the not-completely-closed curtains. She said, 'Nobody in sight who *looks* suspicious. What's the first thing they'll do if they figure out who you are – deevee your code? I mean the one you've been using at G2S.'

'I let that out too?' he said in renewed horror.

'You let a lot out. Must have been stacking up in your head for years. Well?'

'Uh – yes, I guess so.'

She checked her watch and compared it with an old-fashioned digital clock that was among the few ornaments she had not disposed of. 'There's a flight to Los Angeles in ninety minutes. I've used it now and then; it's one that you can get on without booking. By tonight we could be at—'

He put his hands to his head, giddy again. 'You're going too fast for me.'

'Fast it's got to be. What can you do apart from being a systems rash? Everything?'

'I ...' He took an enormous grip on himself. 'Yes, or damn nearly.'

'Fine. So come on.'

He remained irresolute. 'Kate, surely you're not going to—'

'Forget about school next year, abandon friends and home and mother, and Bagheera?' Her tone was scathing. 'Shit, no. But how are you going to make out if you don't have a usable code to prop you up while you're building another they don't know about? I guess that must be how you work the trick, hm?'

'Uh – yes, more or less.'

'So move, will you? My code is in good standing, and the girls downstairs will mind Bagheera for a week as willingly as for an evening, and apart from that all I have to do is leave a note for Ina saying I've gone to stay with friends.' She seized the nearest phone and began to compose the code for her mother's mail-store reel.

'But I can't possibly ask you to—'

'You're not asking, I'm offering. You damn well better grab the chance. Because if you don't you'll be as good as dead, won't you?' She waved him silent and spoke the necessary words to mislead Ina.

When she had finished he said, 'Not as good as. Worse than.' And followed her out the door.

IN THE BEGINNING WAS THE HERD

At Tarnover they explained it all so reasonably!

Of course everybody had to be given a personal code! How else could the government do right by its citizens, keep track of the desires, tastes, preferences, purchases, commitments and above all location of a continentful of mobile, free individuals?

Granted, there was an alternative approach. But would you want to see it adopted here? Would you like to find your range of choice restricted to the point where the population became predictable in its collective behavior?

So don't dismiss the computer as a new type of fetters. Think of it rationally, as the most liberating device ever invented, the only tool capable of serving the multifarious needs of modern man.

Think of it, for a change, as *him*. For example, think of the friendly mailman who makes certain your letters reach you no matter how frequently you move or over what vast distances. Think of the loyal secretary who always pays your bills when they come due, regardless of what distractions may be on your mind. Think of the family doctor who's on hand at the hospital when you fall sick, with your entire medical history in focus to guide the unknown specialist. Or if you want to be less personal and more social, think of computers as the cure for the monotony of primitive mass-production methods. As long ago as the sixties of last century it became economic to turn out a hundred items in succession from an assembly line, of which each differed subtly from the others. It cost the salary of an extra programer and – naturally – a computer to handle the task … but everybody was using computers anyhow, and their capacity was so colossal the additional data didn't signify.

(When he pondered the subject, he always found himself flitting back and forth between present and past tense; there was that sensitive a balance between what had been expected, indeed hoped for, and what had eventuated. It seemed that some of the crucial decisions were still being made although generations had elapsed since they were formulated.)

The movement pattern of late twentieth-century America was already the greatest population flow in history. More people moved annually at vacation time than all the armies led by all the world's great conquerors put together, plus the refugees they drove from home. What a relief, then, to do no more than punch your code into a public terminal – or, since 2005, into the nearest veephone, which likely was in the room where you were sitting – and explain *once* that because you'd be in Rome the next two weeks, or surfing at Bondi, or whatever, your house should be watched by the police more keenly than usual, and your mail should be held for so many days unless marked 'urgent', in which case it should be redirected to so-and-so, and the garbage truck needn't come by on its next weekly round, and – and so forth. The muscles of the nation could be felt flexing with joyous new freedom.

Except …

The theory was and always had been: this is the thing the solid citizen has no need to worry about.

Important, later all-important question: what about the hollow citizen?

Because, liberated, the populace took off like so many hot-air balloons.

'Okay, let's!' – move, take that job in another state, go spend all summer by the lake, operate this winter out of a resort in the Rockies, commute by veetol over a thousand miles, see how island living suits us and forget the idea if it's a bust …

Subtler yet more far-reaching: let's trade wives and children on a monthly rota, good for the kids to get used to multiple parents because after all you've been married twice and I've been married three times, and let's quit the city fast before the boss finds out it was me who undercut him on that near-the-knuckle deal, and let's move out of shouting distance of that twitch you were obsessed with so you can cool down, and let's go someplace where the word isn't out on the mouth-to-mouth circuit that you're skew else you'll never have the chance to give up men, and let's see if it's true about those fine dope connections in Topeka and let's – let's – let's …

Plus, all the time and everywhere, the sneaking suspicion: *don't look now, I think we're being followed.*

Two years after they spliced the home-phone service into the continental net the system was screaming in silent agony like the limbs of a marathon runner who knows he can shatter the world's best time provided he can make the final mile.

But, they asked at Tarnover in the same oh-so-reasonable tones, what else could we have done?

LET'S ALL BE DIFFERENT SAME AS ME

'That,' Freeman said thoughtfully, 'sounds like a question you still have found no answer to.'

'Oh, shut up. Put me back in regressed mode, for God's sake. I know you don't call this torture – I know you call it stimulus-response evaluation – but it feels like torture all the same and I'd rather get it over and done with. Since there isn't an alternative.'

Freeman scanned his dials and screens.

'Unfortunately it's not safe to regress you again at the moment. It will take a day or so for the revived effects of your overload at KC to flush out of your system. It was the most violent experience you've undergone as an adult. Extremely traumatizing.'

'I'm infinitely obliged for the data. I suspected so, but it's nice to have it confirmed by your machines.'

'Sweedack. Just as it's good to have what the machines tell us confirmed by your conscious personality.'

'Are you a hockey 'fish?''

'Not in the sense of following one particular team, but the game does offer a microcosm of modern society, doesn't it? Group commitment, chafing against restrictive rules, enactment of display-type aggression more related to status than hate or fear, plus the use of banishment as a means of enforcing conformity. To which you can add the use of the most primitive weapon, the club, albeit stylized.'

'So that's how you view society. I've been wondering. How trivial! How over-simplified! You mention restrictive rules ... but rules only become restrictive when they're obsolescent. We've revised our rules at every stage of our social evolution, ever since we learned to talk, and we're still making new ones that suit us better. We'll carry right on unless fools like you contrive to stop us!'

Leaning forward, Freeman cupped his sharp chin in his right palm.

'We're into an area of fundamental difference of opinion,' he said after a pause. 'I put it to you that no rule consciously invented by mankind since we acquired speech has force equivalent to those inherited from perhaps fifty, perhaps a hundred thousand generations of evolution in the wild state. I fur-ther suggest that the chief reason why modern society is in turmoil is that for too long we claimed that our special human talents could exempt us from the heritage written in our genes.'

'It's because you and those like you think in strict binary terms – "either-or" – as though you've decided machines are our superiors and you want to imitate them, that I have to believe you not only don't have the right answer but can never find it. You treat human beings on the black-box principle. Cue this reflex, that response ensues; cue another and get something different. There's no room in your cosmos for what you call special talents.'

'Come, now.' Freeman gave a faint, gaunt smile. 'You're talking in terms at least two generations old. Have you deleted from your mind all awareness of how sophisticated our methodology has become since the 1960s?'

'And have you suppressed all perception of how it's rigidified, like medi-eval theology, with your collective brilliance concentrated on finding means to abolish any view not in accord with yours? Don't bother to answer that. I'm experiencing the reality of your black-box approach. You're testing me to destruction, not as an individual but as a sample that may or may not match your idealized model of a person. If I don't react as predicted, you'll revise the model and try again. But you won't care about *me*.'

'*Sub specie aeternitatis,*' Freeman said, smiling anew, 'I find no evidence for believing that I matter any more than any other human being who ever existed or who ever will exist. Nor does any of them matter more than I do. We're elements in a process that began in the dim past and will develop through who knows what kind of future.'

'What you say reinforces my favorite image of Tarnover: a rotting carcass, pullulating with indistinguishable maggots, whose sole purpose in life is to grab more of the dead flesh more quickly than their rivals.'

'Ah, yes. The conqueror worm. I find it curious that you should have turned out to be of a religious bent, given the cynicism with which you exploited the trappings of your minister's role at Toledo.'

'But I'm not religious. Chiefly because the end point of religious faith is your type of blind credulity.'

'Excellent. A paradox. Resolve it for me.' Freeman leaned back, crossing his thin legs and setting his thin fingers tip to tip with elbows on the side of his chair.

'You believe that man is comprehensible to himself, or at any rate you act as though you do. Yet you refer constantly to processes that began back then and will continue for ever and ever amen. What you're trying to do is step out of the flow of process, just as superstitious savages did – do! – by invoking divine forces not confined by human limitations. You give lip service to the process, but you won't accept it. On the contrary, you strive to dominate it. And that can't be done unless you stand outside it.'

'Hmm. You're an atavism, aren't you? You have the makings of a school-man! But that doesn't save you from being wrong. We are trying not to want to step out of the flow, because we've recognized the nature of the process and its inevitability. The best that can be hoped for is to direct it into the most tolerable channels. What we're doing at Tarnover is possibly the most valu-able service any small group ever performed for mankind at large. We're diagnosing our social problems and then deliberately setting out to create the person who can solve them.'

'And how many problems have been solved to date?'

'We haven't yet exterminated ourselves.'

'You claim credit for that? I knew you had gall, but this is fantastic! You could just as well argue that in the case of human beings it took the invention of nuclear weapons to trigger the life-saving response most species show when faced with the fangs and claws of a tougher rival.'

'That in fact appears to be true.'

'If you believed that you wouldn't be working so hard to universalize the new conformity.'

'Is that a term you coined yourself?'

'No, I borrowed it from someone whose writings aren't particularly loved at Tarnover: Angus Porter.'

'Well, it's a resounding phrase. But does it mean anything?'

'I wouldn't bother to answer except that it's better to be talking in present time than sitting back inside my head while you interrogate my memory ... because you know damned well what it means. Look at yourself. You're part of it. It's a century old. It began when for the first time people in a wealthy country started tailoring other cultures to their own lowest common denominator: people with money to spend who were afraid of strange food, who told the restaurateur to serve hamburgers instead of enchiladas or fish and chips instead of couscous, who wanted something pretty to hang on the wall at home and not what some local artist had sunk his heart and soul in, who found it too hot in Rio and too cold in Zermatt and insisted on going there anyhow.'

'We're to be blamed because that's how people reacted long before Tarnover was founded?' Freeman shook his head. 'I remain unconvinced.'

'But this is the concept you started with, the one you've clung to! You walked straight into a trap with no way out. You wanted to develop a generalized model of mankind, and this was the handiest to build on: more general than pre-World War I European royalty despite the fact that that was genuinely cosmopolitan, and more homogeneous than the archetypal peasant culture, which is universal but individualized. What you've wound up with is a schema where the people who obey those ancient evolutionary principles you cite so freely – as for example by striking roots in one place that will last a lifetime – are regarded by their fellows as "rather odd". It won't be long before they're persecuted. And then how will you justify your claim that the message in the genes overrides consciously directed modern change?'

'Are you talking about the so-called economists, who won't take advantage of the facilities our technology offers? More fool them; they choose to be stunted.'

'No, I'm talking about the people who are surrounded by such a plethora of opportunity they dither and lapse into anxiety neurosis. Friends and neighbors rally round to help them out, explain the marvels of today and show them how, and go away feeling virtuous. But if tomorrow they have to repeat the process, and the day after, and the day after that ...? No, from the patronizing stage to the persecuting stage has always been a very short step.'

After a brief silence Freeman said, 'But it's easy to reconcile the views I really hold, as distinct from the distorted versions you're offering. Mankind originated as a nomadic species, following game herds and moving from one pasture to another with the seasons. Mobility of similar order has been reintegrated into our culture, at least in the wealthy nations. Yet there are advantages to living in an urban society, like sanitation, easy communications, tolerably cheap transportation … And thanks to our ingenuity with computers, we haven't had to sacrifice these conveniences.'

'One might as well claim that the tide which rubs pebbles smooth on a beach is doing the pebbles a service because being round is prettier than being jagged. It's of no concern to a pebble what shape it is. But it's very important to a person. And every surge of your tide is reducing the variety of shapes a human being can adopt.'

'Your extended metaphors do you credit,' Freeman said. 'But I detect, and so do my monitors, that you're straining after them like a man at a party who's desperately pretending that he's not quite drunk. Today's session is due to end in a few minutes; I'll cut it short and renew the interrogation in the morning.'

THE RIGHT-ON THING FOR THE WRONG-OFF REASON

The experience was exactly like riding in a car when the driver, seeing ahead a patch of bad road with a lot of potholes, tramps hard on the accelerator in preference to slowing down. There was a drumming sound, and certain landmarks beside the route were noticeable, but essentially it was a matter of being *there then* and subsequently *here now*.

Just about enough time was perceived as having elapsed for the passenger to realize *he* wouldn't have traveled so fast on such a lousy bumpy bit of road … and ask himself why not, since it gave excellent results.

Then, very abruptly, it stopped.

'Where the hell have you brought me?'

Looking around a room with rough brown walls, an old-style spring bed, carpet on the floor which wasn't even fitted, a view of sunset through broad shallow windows that distracted him before he could enumerate other objects like chairs and a table and so forth. They registered as belonging in the sort of junk store whose owner would label as ANTIQUE anything older than himself.

'You poor shivver,' Kate said. She was there too. 'You have one hell of a bad case. I asked you, did you think it was a good idea to head for Lap-of-the-Gods? And you said yes.'

He was sitting on a chair which happened to be near him. He closed his hands on its arms until his knuckles were almost white. With much effort he said, 'Then I was crazy. I thought of coming to a town like this long ago and realized it was the first place they'd think of looking.'

Theoretically, for somone trying to mislay a previous identity, no better spot could be found on the continent than this, or some other of the settlements created by refugees from Northern California after the Great Bay Quake. Literally millions of traumatized fugitives had straggled southward. For years they survived in tents and shanties, dependent on federal handouts because they were too mentally disturbed to work for a living and in most cases afraid to enter a building with a solid roof for fear it would crash down and kill them. They were desperate for a sense of stability, and sought it in a thousand irrational cults. Confidence-tricksters and fake evangelists found them easy prey. Soon it was a tourist lure to visit their settlements on Sunday and watch the running battles between adherents of rival – but equally lunatic – beliefs. Insurance extra.

There had been nothing comparable in western civilization since the Lisbon Earthquake shook the foundations of Christianity across half of Europe in 1755.

Now some semblance of regular government was in effect and had been for a quarter-century. But the scars left by the quake were cicatrized into the names of the new cities: Insecurity, Precipice, Protempore, Waystation, Transience … and Lap-of-the-Gods.

Inevitably, because these were new cities in a nation that had lacked a frontier these hundred years, they had attracted the restless, the dissident, sometimes the criminal elements from elsewhere. Up-to-date maps showed them dotted like accidental inkblots from Monterey to San Diego and inland over a belt almost two hundred miles wide. They constituted a nation within a nation. Tourists could still come here. But most often they decided not to. It felt more like home in Istanbul.

'Sandy!' Sitting down in a chair facing him, Kate tapped his knee. 'You're out of it so don't slip back. Talk! And this time make sense. What makes you so terrified of Tarnover?'

'If they catch me they'll do what they meant to do in the first place. What I fled from.'

'That being –?'

'They'll make me over in a version of myself I don't approve.'

'That happens to everybody all the time. The lucky ones win, the others suffer. There's something deeper. Something worse.'

He gave a weary nod. 'Yes, there is. My conviction that if they get the chance to try they'll do it, and I won't have a hope in hell of fighting back.'

There was a dull silence. At last Kate nodded, her face grave.

'I got there. You'd know what was being done to you. And later you'd be fascinated by the tape of your reactions.'

With a humorless laugh he said, 'I think you lie about your age. Nobody could be that cynical so young. Of course you're right.'

Another pause, this time full of gray depression. She broke it by saying, 'I wish you'd been in a fit state to talk before we left KC. You must have been just going through the motions. But never mind. I think we came to a right place. If you've been avoiding towns like Lap-of-the-Gods for – what is it? – six years, then they won't immediately start combing California for you.'

It was amazing how calmly he took that, he thought. To hear his most precious secret mentioned in passing … Above all, it was nearly beyond belief that someone finally was on his side.

Hence the calmness? Very probably.

'Are we in a hotel?' he inquired.

'Sort of. They call it an open lodge. You get a room and then fend for yourself. There's a kitchen through there' – a vague gesture toward the door of the bedroom – 'and there's no limit on how long you can stay. Nor any questions asked when you check in, luckily.'

'You used your code?'

'Did you expect me to use yours? I have lots of credit. I'm not exactly an economist, but I'm blessed with simple tastes.'

'In that case the croakers will come calling any moment.'

'Shit on that. You're thinking in contemporary terms. Check into a hotel, ten seconds later the fact's on file at Canaveral, right? Not here, Sandy. They still process credit by hand. It could be a week before I'm debbed for this room.'

Hope he had almost ceased to believe in burgeoned in his eyes. 'Are you sure?'

'Hell, no. Today could be the day the desk clerk makes up his bills. All I'm saying is it isn't automatic. You know about this town, don't you?'

'I know about so many paid-avoidance areas …' He rubbed his forehead with the heel of his hand. 'Is this one that's settled down to about a 1960 level?'

'I guess that would be fairly close. I haven't been here before, though I have been to Protempore, and I'm told the two are comparable. That's why I hit on it. I didn't want to take you anywhere I might be recognized.'

She leaned toward him. 'Now let's concentrate, shall we? The dobers *aren't* howling at the door, and it's long past time for me to learn the rest of your history. You seem to have spent a long while at Tarnover. Think you're fettered by a posthypnotic?'

He drew a deep breath. 'No. I wondered about that myself and concluded that I can't be. Hypnosis isn't one of their basic tools. And if it were, the command would have been activated long ago, when I first quit the place. Of course, by now they may well use posthypnotics to stop others copying my example … But what I'm hamstrung by is in myself.'

Kate bit her lower lip with small and very white teeth. She said at length,

'Funny. Meeting those grads from Tarnover that I mentioned, I felt sure they'd been treated with some quasi-hypnotic technique. They make my skin crawl, you know. They give the impression that they've learned everything, they could never possibly be wrong. Kind of inhuman. So my assumption has always been that Tarnover is some sort of behavioral-intensive education center for bright deprived kids, where they use extreme forms of stimulation as an inducement to learn. Zero-distraction environments – drugs, maybe – *I* don't know.'

He picked on one key word. 'You said … deprived?'

'Mm-hm.' With a nod. 'I noticed that at once. Either they were orphaned, or they made no bones about hating their parents and family. It gave them a curious solidarity. Almost like White House aides. Or maybe more like the Jesus bit: "Who is my father and my mother?"' She spread her hands.

'When did you first hear about Tarnover?'

'Oh, it was news when I graduated from high school and went to UMKC four years ago. There was no publicity, at least not the drums-and-trumpets type. More kind of, "We got the answer to Akadiemgorodok – we think." Low-key stuff.'

'Shit, but they're clever!' he said savagely. 'If I didn't hate them I'd have to admire them.'

'What?'

'It's the ideal compromise. You just described what they obviously want the world to think about Tarnover; how did you put it? An intensive education center for bright deprived kids? Very admirable!'

'And it isn't?' Her sharp eyes rested on his face like sword points.

'No. It's where they're breeding the elite to run the continent.'

'I wish,' she said, 'I didn't suspect you of being literal.'

'Me too! But … Look, you're in power. Think what's the most dangerous thing about a kid with no parents and a high IQ.'

She stared at him for a long moment, then suggested, 'He won't look at things the way the men in charge do. But he could be more right than they are.'

He slapped his thigh in delight. 'Kate, you impress the hell out of me! You've hit on it. Who are the people recruited to Tarnover and Crediton Hill and the rest of the secret centers? Why, those who might invent sides of their own if the government doesn't enroll them on its side while they're still tractable. Yes, *yes*! But on top of that— Say, did you check this room for bugs?'

The exclamation was overdue; what had become of his customary caution? He was half out of his chair before she said with a trace of scorn, 'Of course I did! And I have a damned good bug detector. One of my boyfriends built it for me. He's a post-grad in the UMKC school of industrial espionage. So relax and keep talking.'

He sank back in relief and mopped his forehead.

'You said these Tarnover trainees you've met are mostly in the Behavioral Sciences Lab. Any of them in biology?'

'I met a couple but not at UMKC Over the state line in Lawrence. Or they were. I loathed them and didn't keep in touch.'

'Did they ever mention the pride and joy of Tarnover – the crippled kids they build with genius IQ?'

'*What?*'

'I met the first of them, who was called Miranda. Of course she was not a genius, so they counted it small loss when she died at four. But techniques have improved. The last example I heard about before I quit still couldn't walk, or even eat, but she could use a computer remote with the best of us and sometimes she was quicker than her teachers. They specialize in girls, naturally. Men, embryonically speaking, are imperfect women, as you know.'

There was never much color in Kate's face. In the next few seconds what little there was drained away, leaving the flesh of her forehead and cheeks as pale as candlewax.

In a tight, thin voice she said, 'Give me the details. There must be a lot more to it than that.'

He complied. When he had recited the full story, she shook her head with an incredulous expression.

'But they must be insane. We need a rest from ultrarapid change, not an extra dose of it. Half the population has given up trying to cope, and the other is punch-drunk without knowing it.'

'Sweedack,' he said dully. 'But of course their defense is that whether or not it's done here, it's bound to be done somewhere by somebody, so …' An empty shrug.

'That's okay. Maybe the people who come along second will profit from our example; maybe they won't repeat all our mistakes. But … Don't the people at Tarnover realize they could reduce our society to hysterics?'

'Apparently not. It's a prime example of Porter's Law, isn't it? They've carried over the attitudes of the arms race into the age of the brain race. They're trying to multiply incommensurables. You must have heard that applying minimax strategy to the question of rearmament invariably results in the conclusion that you must rearm. And their spiritual ancestors kept right on doing so even after H-bombs had written a factor of infinity into the equation of military power. They sought security by piling up more and more *irrelevant* weapons. At Tarnover today they're making the analogous error. They claim to be hunting for the genetic element of wisdom, and I'm sure most of them believe that's what they're really doing. They aren't, of course. What they're on the track of is the 200-plus IQ. And intelligence and wisdom aren't the same.'

He clenched his fists. 'The prospect terrifies me! They must be stopped. Somehow and at any cost. But I've been struggling for six years to think of a way, hoping that the thirty million they lavished on me won't go completely to waste, and I haven't achieved one goddamned thing!'

'Are you held back by fear of being – well, punished?'

He started. 'You're sharp, aren't you? I guess I am!'

'Just for opting out?'

'Oh, I've committed a slew of federal crimes. Used false identities, obtained a notary's seal by fraud, entered forged data in the continental net … Just take it for granted they could find plenty of reasons for me to go to jail.'

'I'm surprised they let you get away in the first place.'

'But they don't compel where they can persuade. They're not stupid. They're aware that one volunteer working his guts out on their behalf is worth a score of reluctant conscripts.'

Gazing past him into nowhere, she said, 'I see. Thinking you were trust-worthy, they gave you too much rope. So when you did escape, what did you do?'

He summarized his careers.

'Hm! If nothing else, you took in a broad cross-section of society. What made you settle for a post at G2S after all that?'

'I needed to gain access to some restricted areas of the net. In particular I had to find out whether my code was still valid. Which it was. But now that they're closing on my identity at KC it's high time I made one last use of it and rewrote myself again. It costs, of course, but I have some won Delphi tickets to collect on, and I'm sure I can adopt a well-paid profession for the time being. Don't they go big for mystical things out here? I can run compu-terized horoscopes, and I can offer gene counseling – I think you can do that in California without a state license – and … Oh, anything that involves use of a computer terminal.'

She gave him a level look.

'But you're in a paid-avoidance area,' she said.

'Hell, so I am!' Suddenly he felt very much alone, unspeakably vulnerable. 'Does the avoidance go deep? I mean even if you can't use any public phone to tap the net, do they forcibly exclude computers?'

'No, but you have to make special application to get time. And there's more cash in circulation than anywhere else on the continent, and veephone ser-vice is restricted: you can't dial out to the rest of the country, you have to cable and ask to be called back. Things like that.'

'But if I can't rewrite myself, what am I going to do?' He was on his feet, shaking.

'Sandy!' She rose also, confronting him with a glare. 'Have you never tried to outface the enemy?'

'What?' He blinked at her.

'I get the impression that every time one of your schemes went wrong, you abandoned it – and the identity that went with it – and switched to something else. Maybe that's why you've always failed. You've relied on this trick talent of yours to bail you out of trouble instead of seeing through what you started. The overload you've suffered today ought to be a warning to you. There's a limit to the number of times you can revise your personality. There's a limit to the load you can pile on your powers of reasoning. Your body just told you, loud and clear, you've gone too far at last.'

'Oh, shit ...' His voice was full of misery. 'In principle I'm certain you're right. But is there any alternative?'

'Sure I have an alternative. One of the best things about a paid-avoidance area is you can still get manual cooking. I don't know what it's like here, but at Protempore it was delicious. We go find a good restaurant and a jug of wine.'

FENCED BUT NOT FOILED

Inter alia the Handbook of the National Association of Players at the Game of Fencing states:

The game may be played manually or electronically.

The field shall consist of 101 parallel equidistant lines coded AA, AB, AC ... BA, BB, BC ... to EA (omitting the letter I), crossed at 90° by 71 parallel equidistant lines 01 to 71.

The object is to enclose with triangles a greater number of coordinate points than the opponent.

The players shall toss or draw for red or blue; red begins.

At each turn each player shall claim two points, one by visibly marking it in the field, the other by entering its coordinates in a list concealed from the opponent (but subject to scrutiny by a referee in match play).

After at least 10 points (5 red, 5 blue) have been visibly claimed, having claimed his visible point for that turn either player may forgo the option of claiming a concealed point and attempt to enclose a triangle by connecting three of his visibly claimed points. Prior to doing so he must require the opponent to enter his concealed points in the field. He may then enclose any triangle that does not include a point claimed by the opponent. A point claimed in a concealed list, which proves on inspection to have been claimed visibly by the opponent, shall be deleted from the concealed list. A triangle may enclose a point claimed by the same color. A point once enclosed may not be claimed. If a player claims such a point in error he shall forfeit both the visible and the concealed point due on that turn.

If a player finds, when the opponent's concealed points are entered in the field, he can enclose no valid triangle, he shall at once enter all his own concealed points, after which play shall proceed normally.

All triangles must have sides at least 2 units long, i.e. two adjacent coordinates cannot serve as apices of the same triangle, though they may serve as apices of two triangles of the same or different colors. No coordinate may serve as the apex of more than one triangle. No triangle may enclose a point enclosed by another triangle. A coordinate claimed by the opponent which lies on a horizontal or vertical line between apices of a proposed triangle shall be deemed included and renders the triangle invalid. A coordinate claimed by the opponent which lies on a true diagonal (45°) between apices of a proposed triangle shall be deemed excluded.

Scores shall be calculated in terms of coordinate points enclosed by valid triangles. An approved device shall be employed such that as each triangle is validly enclosed its apices may be entered into the memory store of the device and upon entry of the third apex the device shall unambiguously display the number of points enclosed. It shall be the responsibility of the player to keep accurate record of his cumulative score, which he shall not conceal from the opponent, except in matches played for stake money or on which there has been wagering or by mutual agreement of the players, when the cumulative score may be kept by a referee or electronically or mechanically, but in such cases there shall be no grounds for appeal by either player against the score shown at the conclusion or at any stage of the game.

It is customary but not obligatory for any game in which one player's score exceeds that of the other by 100 points to be regarded as lost and won.

METONYMIA

According to the instrument display the metabolic level of the subject remained satisfactory; however, his voice was weakening and his reaction times were slowing. It was becoming necessary to update him from regressed mode at ever-shorter intervals. Very probably this was due to the low-stimulus environment, excessively low for someone whose ability to tolerate rapid and extreme change had been graphically documented over the past several weeks. Accordingly Freeman indented for some equipment to ameliorate the situation: a large projection-type three-vee screen, an electrotoner and a personifactor which would give the illusion of one, two or three other people watching.

Waiting for the new machinery to be delivered, though, he perforce had to continue in the former manner, conversing with the subject in present time.

'You're a good fencing player, I believe.'

'Care for a game to break the monotony?' A ghost of old defiance tinted the words.

'I'm a poor player myself; it would be a mismatch. But why did fencing appeal to you rather than, say, go, or even chess?'

'Chess has been automated,' was the prompt reply. 'How long is it since a world champion has done without computer assistance?'

'I see. Yes, I understand nobody has yet written a competent fencing program. Did you try it? You had adequate capacity.'

'Oh, using a program to play chess is work. Games are for fun. I guess I could have spoiled fencing, if I'd spent a year or two on the job. I didn't want to.'

'You wanted to retain it as a nondeterminate analogy of your own predicament, because of its overtones of captivity, enclosure, secure ground and the like – is that it?'

'Think of it in any way you choose. I say the hell with it. One of the worst things wrong with people like you is inability to enjoy themselves. You don't like the idea that there are processes that can't be analyzed. You're the lineal descendant, on the sociological side of the tree, of the researchers who pithed cats and dogs because even their personalities were too complex for comfort. Which is fine for studying synapse formation but no damned good for studying cats.'

'You're a holist.'

'I might have guessed that sooner or later you'd turn that word into an insult.'

'On the contrary. Having studied, as you rightly say, the separate components of the nervous system, we finally feel we're equipped to attack their interaction. We declined to accept personality as a datum. Your attitude resembles that of a man content to gaze at a river without being interested in the springs and the watershed and the seasonal variations in rainfall and the silt it's carrying along.'

'I notice you make no mention of fish in the river. Nor of taking a drink from it.'

'Will watching from the bank inform you why there are no fish this year?'

'Will counting the liters-per-minute tell you why it's beautiful?'

Freeman sighed. 'Always we reach the same sort of deadlock, don't we? I regard your attitude as complementary to mine. You on the other hand deny that mine has any validity. *Impasse.*'

'Wrong. Or at best only half right. Your problem's this: you want to file my attitude as a subcategory of yours, and it doesn't work because the whole can't be included in the part.'

GAME FOR ANYTHING

Venturing out on the streets of Lap-of-the-Gods, he felt a little like someone raised in an inhibited family braving a naturist beach, but the sensation did not last long. This was a surprisingly attractive little town. The architecture was miscellaneous because it had been thrown together in a hurry, yet the urgency had resulted in a basic unity enhanced now by reddish evening sunlight.

The sidewalks were crowded, the roadways not. The only vehicles they saw were bicycles and electric buses. There were many trees, bushes and flowering shrubs. Most of the people seemed to care little about dress; they wore uninspiring garments in blue, buff and tan, and some were shabby. But they smiled a lot and said hello to someone – even to himself and Kate, strangers – every half-dozen paces.

Shortly they came across a restaurant modeled on a Greek taverna, with tables on a terrace under a roof made of vines trained along poles and wires. Three or four games of fencing were in progress, each watched by a group of intent kibitzers.

'That's an idea,' he muttered to Kate, halting. 'Maybe I could pick up a bit of credit if they play for money.'

'Are you a good player? Sorry. Stupid question. But I'm told competition here is stiff.'

'But they're playing manually. Look!'

'Does that have to make them poor players?'

He gazed at her for a long moment. Eventually he said, 'Know something? I think you're good for me.'

'So I should hope,' she answered tartly, and pulled the same face he'd seen at their first meeting, wrinkling her nose and raising her upper lip so her front teeth showed like a rabbit's. 'Moreover I knew you liked me before you knew it, which is kind of rare and to be treasured. Come on, let's add fencing hustler to your list of occupations.'

They found a table where they could watch the play while eating pizza and sipping a rough local wine, and about the time they finished their meal one of the nearest players realized he had just allowed his opponent to notch up the coveted hundred-point margin with a single slender triangle running almost the full width of the field. Swearing at his own incompetence, he resigned and strode away fuming.

The winner, a fat bald once-fair man in a faded pink singlet, complained to anybody who cared to listen, 'But he didn't have to be such a sore loser, did he? I mean did he?' Appealing to Kate, who smiled and shook her head.

'And I can spare at least another hour before I have to go, and— Hey, would either of you care to take over? I noticed you were watching.'

The tone and manner were unmistakable. Here was a full-timer, counterpart of those chess hustlers who used to sit around anonymously pretending to be no good until someone was fool enough to stake money on a game.

Well, it's a way in…

'Sure I'll play you, and be glad to. This is Kate, by the way, and I'm –' He hoped the hesitation would go unremarked; one could convert to Alexander and since Kate was accustomed … 'I'm Sandy.'

'I'm Hank. Sit down. Want to think about odds? I'm kind of competent, as you may have gathered.' The bald man tailed the words with a toothy grin.

'Let's play level, argue about odds when we have grounds for debate.'

'Fine, fine! Would you care to let – uh – a little cash ride on the outcome?' A glint of greed lighted Hank's eyes.

'Cash? Uh … Well, we're fresh into town, so you'd have to take scrip, but if that's okay –? Good. Shall we say a hundred?'

'By all means,' Hank purred, and rubbed his hands under the table. 'And I think we ought to play the first one or two games blitz-tempo.'

The first game aborted almost at once, a not uncommon happening. Attempting on successive turns to triangulate, both found it was impossible, and according to custom rather than rule agreed to try again. The second game was close and Hank lost. The third was even closer and he still lost, and the expiry of his hour gave him an excuse to depart in annoyance, two hundred the poorer. By then many more customers had arrived, some to play – a dozen games were now in progress – and some preferring to kibitz and assess a stranger's form. One of the newcomers, a plump girl carrying a baby, challenged the victor and went down in twelve turns. Two of the other watchers, a thin young black and a thin elderly white, whistled loudly, and the latter promptly took the girl's place.

What is it that feels so weird about this evening …? Got it. I'll be damned. I'm not playing Lazarus's game, or even Sandy Locke's; I'm playing mine, and I'm far better than I ever dreamed!

The sensation was giddying. He seemed to be walking up steps inside his head until he reached a place where there was nothing but pure white light, and it showed him as plainly as though he were telepathic what his opponent was planning. Potential triangles outlined themselves on the board as though their sides were neon bars. The elderly man succumbed in twenty-eight turns, not beaten but content to resign on a margin of fifty points he was unlikely to make up, and ceded his place to the thin young black saying, 'Morris, I think we finally found someone who can give you a hard time.'

Faint warning bells began to sound at that stage, but he was having too much fun to pay attention.

The newcomer was good. He obtained a margin of twenty on the first triangulation and concentrated on preserving it. He did so for another six turns, growing more and more smug. But on the fifteenth turn his smugness vanished. He had tried another triangulation, and when the concealed points were entered there was nothing valid, and he had to post his own concealed list, and on the next turn found himself cut out of an entire corner worth ninety points. His face turned sour and he scowled at the score machine as though suspecting it of lying. Then he gathered his resources in an effort to regain the lost lead.

He failed. The game went to its bitter end and left him fourteen down. Whereupon he thrust his way through the bystanders – by now a couple of dozen strong – and stormed off, slamming fist into palm in impotent fury.

'I'll be damned,' said the elderly man. 'Well, *well*! Look – uh – Sandy, I didn't make too good a showing against you, but believe it or not I'm the area secretary of the Fencing Association, and if you can use a light-pen and screen as well as you use a manual board …!' Beaming, he made an all-embracing gesture. 'I take it you have club qualifications where you come from? If you intend to shift your residential commitment to Lap-of-the-Gods, I can predict who'll win the winter championships. You and Morris together would make an unstoppable—'

'You mean that was *Morris Fagin*?'

All around the group of onlookers there were puzzled reactions: *this poker claims he didn't know?*

'Sandy,' Kate murmured in the nick of time, 'it's getting late. Even later for us than it is for these nice people.'

'I – uh … Yes, you're right. Excuse us, friends; we came a long way today.' He rose, collecting the grimy unfamiliar bills which had accumulated on the corner of the table. It had been years since he handled this much of the generalized scrip known as paper money; at the church in Toledo it had been collected and counted automatically. For most people cash payments stopped at the number of dollar coins you would drop in a pocket without noticing their weight.

'I'm flattered,' he said to the elderly man. 'But you'll have to let me think about it. We may be only passing through. We have no plans to settle here.'

He seized Kate's arm and hurried her away, terribly aware of the sensation he had caused. He could hear his feat being recounted already along the mouth-to-mouth circuit.

As they were undressing he said miserably, 'I sabotaged that one, didn't I?'

Admitting the blunder was novel to him. The experience was just as unpleasant as he had imagined it would be. But in memory echoed Kate's description of the graduates from Tarnover: convinced they were incapable of error.

That's not human. That's mechanical. It's machines whose view of the world is so circumscribed they go right on doing the only thing they can although it's wrong.

'I'm afraid so.' Her tone was matter-of-fact, devoid of criticism. 'Not that you could help it. But to be spotted by an area secretary of the Fencing Association and then to beat the incumbent West Coast champion – yes, that is apt to provoke comment. I'm sorry; I didn't realize you hadn't recognized Fagin.'

'You knew who he was?' In the middle of shedding his pants he stood ridiculous, one leg in and the other out. 'So why the hell didn't you warn me?'

'Do me a favor? Before you pick your first quarrel with me, get a little better acquainted. Then you can do it with justification.'

He had been on the verge of anger. The inclination vanished. He completed undressing, as did she, and then took her in his arms.

'I like you very much as a person,' he said, and bestowed a grave kiss on her forehead. 'I think I'm going to like you just as much as a woman.'

'I hope so,' she answered with equal formality. 'We may have to go a lot of places together.'

He drew back to full stretch, hands on her shoulders.

'Where next? What next?'

As rare in his life as admitting mistakes was asking for advice. It too was disturbing. But it would have to become a habit if he was to stay afloat.

She shook her head. 'Think about that in the morning. It has to be somewhere else, that's definite. But this town is already halfway right … No, too much has happened today. Let's overload it and sleep it out and worry about decisions afterwards.'

With abrupt tigerish violence, as though she had borrowed from Bagheera, she clamped her arms around him and sank her sharp tongue – sharp as her gaze – between his lips.

A LOAD OF CRYSTAL BALLS

In the twentieth century one did not have to be a pontificating pundit to predict that success would breed success and the nations that first were lucky enough to combine massive material resources with advanced knowhow would be those where social change would accelerate until it approximated the limit of what human beings can endure. By 2010, in the wealthiest countries, a classic category of mental patient was composed of boys and girls in their late teens who had come back for a first vacation from college to discover that 'home' was unrecognizable, either because the parents had moved into a new framework, changed jobs and cities, or simply because – as they'd done a dozen times before – they had refurnished and redecorated … without realizing they were opening a door to what came to be termed the 'final straw syndrome'.

It was also not difficult to forecast that no matter how well endowed they were with material resources those countries where the Industrial Revolution arrived late would change proportionately more slowly. After all, the rich get richer and the poor get children. Which is okay so long as lots of them starve in infancy.

What many otherwise well-informed people apparently preferred to overlook was the phenomenon baptized by Angus Porter 'the beetle and wedge', which retained its name long after even the poor nations found it uneconomic to split logs with a hammer and a chunk of steel. Even if your circular saws were pedal-driven, they were much less wasteful. Moreover, you could dictate a neat dividing line.

Beetling forward at full pelt split society. Some did their utmost to head the other way. A great many more decided to go sideways. And some simply dug in their heels and stayed put. The resultant cracks were unpredictable.

One and only one thing preserved even the illusion of national integrity. The gossamer strands of the data-net proved amazingly strong.

Unfortunately nothing came along to reinforce them.

People drew comfort from knowing there were certain objects near at hand, in the U.S.A. or the Soviet Union or Sweden or New Zealand, of which they could boast, 'This is the biggest/longest/fastest frammistan on Earth!' Alas, however, tomorrow it might not be. Paradoxically, therefore, they derived even more emotional sustenance from being able to say, 'This is the most primitive potrzebie, you know, still at work in any industrialized country!'

It was so precious to be able to connect with the calmer, stabler past.

The cracks spread. From national level they reached provincial level, from provincial they reached municipal, and there they met cracks going the other way, which had begun in the privacy of the family.

'We sweated blood to put the son-of-a-bitch through college! He ought to be paying us back, not sunning his ass in New Mexico!'

(For New Mexico read, at will, the Black Sea resort of Varna – or the beaches of Quemoy and Matsu where young Chinese by the thousand were content to pass their time practicing calligraphy, playing fan-tan, and smoking opium – or any of fifty other locations where *la dolce-far-niente vita* had spilled the contents of its seine-net after trawling through a nation, an ethnic grouping, or in the case of India a subcontinent. Sri Lanka had had no government to speak of for a generation.)

As much as anything else, it was the sense of exploitable talent going to waste that prompted the establishment of genius centers like Tarnover, funded on the scale previously reserved to weaponry. It was beyond the comprehension of those raised in traditional patterns of thinking that resources of whatever kind should not be channeled and exploited to dynamize ever-faster growth.

Secret, these centers – like the unseen points claimed in a fencing field – provoked consequences that now and then turned out to be disastrous.

SCENT REFUGE

Even after two solid days in his company Ina Grierson couldn't get over how closely the man from Tarnover resembled Baron Samedi – very dark, very thin, head like a skull overlaid with parchment – so that one constantly expected a black tribe to march in and wreck the place. Some of his time had been devoted to Dolores van Bright, naturally, but she had admitted right away her attempt to help Sandy Locke by warning him there'd be an extra member of the interview board, and after that not even the influence of G2S was going to keep her out of jail.

But it was Ina the man from Tarnover was chiefly concerned to question. Sandy Locke had been hired on her say-so, whence the rest followed logically.

She grew terribly tired of saying over and over to the thin black man (whose name was Paul T. Freeman, but maybe only for the purposes of this assignment), 'Of course I go to bed with men I know nothing about! If I only went to bed with men I *do* know about I'd never get any sex, would I? They all turn out to be bastards in the end.'

Late on the afternoon of the second day of questioning the subject of Kate arose. Ina claimed to be unaware that her daughter had left the city, and the skull-faced man was obliged to believe her, since she had had no chance to go home and check her mail-store reel. Moreover, the girls in the apartment below Kate's, currently looking after Bagheera, insisted she had given no least hint in advance of her intention to travel.

Still, she'd done so. Gone west, and what was more with a companion. Very likely one of her fellow students, of course; many of her friends hailed from California. Besides, she'd talked freely about 'Sandy Locke' to her downstairs neighbors, and called him plastic, artificial, and other derogatory terms. Her mother confirmed that she had said the same on various occasions both public and private.

There being no trace of Haflinger, however, and no other potential clue to his whereabouts, *and* no recent record of Kate's code being used – which meant she must have gone to a paid-avoidance area – Freeman, who was a thorough person, set the wheels in motion, and was rewarded by being able to advise the FBI that lodging for two people had been debbed against Kate Lilleberg in Lap-of-the-Gods.

Very interesting. Very interesting indeed.

TODAY'S SPECIAL

He woke to alarm, recalling his gaffe of yesterday and along with that a great many details he'd have preferred to remain ignorant of concerning the habits of people in paid-avoidance areas. Their federal grants meant that few of them had to work at full-time jobs; they supplemented their frugal allowance by providing services – he thought of the restaurants where there were manual chefs and the food was brought by waiters and waitresses – or making handicrafts. Tourism in towns like this, however, was on the decline, as though people no longer cared to recall that this, the richest nation in history, had been unable to transcend a mere earthquake, so they spent much of their time in gossip. And what right now would offer a more interesting subject than the poker who blew out of nowhere and beat the local fencing champion?

'Sooner or later you're going to have to learn to live with one inescapable fact about yourself,' Kate said over her shoulder as she sat brushing her hair before the room's one lighted mirror. Listening, he curled his fingers. The color of that hair might be nothing out of the ordinary, but its texture was superb. His fingertips remembered it, independently of his mind.

'What?'

'You're a very special person. Why else would they have recruited you to Tarnover? Wherever you go you're bound to attract attention.'

'I daren't!'

'You can't help it.' She laid aside her brush and swiveled to face him; he was sitting glum on the edge of the bed.

'Consider,' she went on. 'Would the people at G2S have offered to perm you if they didn't think you were special even disguised as Sandy Locke? And – and *I* realized you were special, too.'

'You,' he grunted, 'just have more insight than is good for you.'

'You mean: more than is good for you.'

'I guess so.' Now at last he rose to his feet, imagining he could hear his joints creak. To be this frustrated must, he thought, resemble the plight of being old: clearly recalling what it was like to act voluntarily and enjoy life as it came, now trapped in a frame that forbade anything except slow cautious movements and a diet prescribed by doctors.

'I don't want to go through life wearing fetters,' he said abruptly.

'Tarnover talking!' she snapped.

'What?'

'Wear fetters? Wear *fetters*? I never heard such garbage. Has there ever been a time in the whole of history when someone with amazing exceptional gifts could be deluded into thinking they're a handicap?'

'Sure,' he said at once. 'How about conscripts who would rather maim

401

themselves than obey a government order to go fight somebody they never met? Their gifts may have been no more than youth and health, but they were gifts.'

'That's not being deluded. That's being compelled. A recruiting sergeant with a gun on his hip—'

'Same thing! They've merely brought it into finer focus!'

There was a brief electric silence. At length she sighed.

'I give in. I have no right to argue with you about Tarnover – you've been there and I haven't. And in any case it's too early for a row. Go get showered and shaved, and then we'll find some breakfast and talk about where we're going next.'

IS THIS YOU?

Did you have trouble last night in dropping off to sleep?

Even though you were tired in spite of doing nothing to exhaust yourself?

Did you hear your heart? Did it break its normal rhythm?

Do you suffer with digestive upsets? Get a feeling that your gullet has been tied in a knot behind your ribs?

Are you already angry because this advertisement hits the nail on your head?

Then come to Calm Springs before you kill somebody or go insane!

COUNT A BLAST

'You're beginning to be disturbed by me,' the dry hoarse voice announced.

Elbows on chair arms as usual, Freeman set his fingertips together. 'How so?' he parried.

'For one thing, you've taken to talking to me in present-time mode for the last three-hour session every day.'

'You should be grateful for small mercies. Our prognostications show it would be risky to maintain you in regressed mode.'

'Half the truth. The rest can be found in your omission to use that expensive three-vee setup you had installed. You realized that I thrive on high levels of stimulus. But you're groping your way toward my lower threshold. You don't want me to start functioning at peak efficiency. You think that even pinned down like a butterfly on a board I may still be dangerous.'

'I don't think of my fellow men as dangerous. I think of them as capable of occasional dangerous mistakes.'

'You include yourself?'

'I remain constantly alert for the possibility.'

'Being on guard like that itself constitutes aberrant behavior.'

'How can you say that? So long as you were fully on guard we failed to catch you. In terms of your purposes that wasn't aberrant; it was functional. In the end, however … Well, here you are.'

'Yes, here I am. Having learned a lesson you're incapable of learning.'

'Much good may it bring you.' Freeman leaned back. 'You know, last night I was thinking over a new approach – a new argument which may penetrate your obstinacy. Consider this. You speak of us at Tarnover as though we're engaged in a brutal arbitrary attempt to ensure that the best minds of the current generation get inducted into government service. Not at all. We are simply the top end of a series of cultural subgroupings that evolved of their own accord during the second half of last century. Few of us are equipped to cope with the complexity and dazzling variety of twenty-first-century existence. We prefer to identify with small, easily isolable fractions of the total culture. But just as some people can handle only a restricted range of stimuli, and prefer to head for a mountain commune or a paid-avoidance area or even emigrate to an underdeveloped country, so some correspondingly not only cope well but actually require immensely strong stimuli to provoke them into functioning at optimum. We have a wider range of lifestyle choices today than ever before. The question of administration has been rendered infinitely more difficult precisely because we have such breadth of choice. Who's to manage this multiplex society? Must the lot not fall to those who flourish when dealing with complicated situations? Would you rather that people who demonstrably can't organize their own lives were permitted to run those of their fellow citizens?'

'A conventional elitist argument. From you I'd have expected better.'

'Elitist? Nonsense. I'd expected better from you. The word you're looking for is "aesthetic". An oligarchy devoted by simple personal preference to the search for artistic gratification in government – that's what we're after. And it would be rather a good system, don't you think?'

'Provided you were in the top group. Can you visualize yourself in the lower echelons, a person who obeys instead of issuing orders?'

'Oh, yes. That's why I work at Tarnover. I hope that perhaps within my lifetime there will appear people so skilled in dealing with modern society that I and others like me can step out of their way with a clear conscience. In a sense I want to work myself out of a job as fast as possible.'

'Resigning control to crippled kids?'

Freeman sighed. 'Oh, you're obsessed with those laboratory-gestated children! Maybe it will relieve your mind to hear that the latest batch – six of them – are all physically whole and run and jump and feed and dress themselves! If you met them by chance you couldn't tell them from ordinary kids.'

'So why bother to tell me about them? All that's registered in my mind is that they may look like ordinary kids … but they never will be ordinary kids.'

'You have a positive gift for twisting things. No matter what I say to you—'

'I find a means of casting a different light on it. Let me do just that to what you've been saying. You, and the others you mentioned, acknowledge you're imperfect. So you're looking for superior successors. Very well: give me grounds for believing that they won't just be projections on a larger scale of your admittedly imperfect vision.'

'I can't. Only results that speak for themselves can do that.'

'What results do you have to date? You've sunk a lot of time and money in the scheme.'

'Oh, several. One or two may impress even a skeptic.'

'The kids that look like any other kids?'

'No, no. Healthy adults like yourself capable of doing things that have never been done before, such as writing a complete new identity into the data-net over a regular veephone. Bear in mind that before trying to invent new talents we decided to look for those that had been undervalued. The odds there were in our favor. We have records from the past – descriptions of lightning calculators, musicians capable of improvising without a wrong note for hours on end, mnemonists who commited whole books to memory by reading them through once … Oh, there are examples in every field of human endeavor from strategy to scrimshaw. With these for guidelines, we're trying to generate conditions in which corresponding modern talents can flourish.'

He shifted casually in his chair; he sounded more confident by the minute.

'Our commonest current form of mental disorder is personality shock. We have an efficient way to treat it without machinery or drugs. We allow the sufferer to do something he long ago wanted to do and lacked either the courage or the opportunity to fit into his life. Do you deny the claim?'

'Of course not. This continent is littered coast to coast with people who were compelled to study business administration when they should have been painting murals or practicing the fiddle or digging a truck garden, and finally got their chance when it was twenty years too late to lead them anywhere.'

'Except back to a sense of solid identity,' Freeman murmured.

'In the case of the lucky few. But yes, okay.'

'Then let me lay this on you. If you hadn't met Miranda – if you hadn't found out that our suspicions concerning the genetic component of personality were being verified by experiment – would you have deserted from Tarnover?'

'I think sooner or later I'd have quit anyhow. The attitude that can lead to using crippled children as experimental material would have disconnected me.'

'You spin like a weather vane. You've said, or implied, repeatedly that at Tarnover we're conditioning people not to rebel. You can't maintain at the same time that what we're doing would have encouraged you to rebel.'

Freeman gave his skull-like grin and rose, stretching his cramped limbs.

'Our methods are being tested in the only available lab: society at large. So far they show excellent results. Instead of condemning them out of hand you should reflect on how much worse the alternatives are. After what you underwent last summer, you of all people should appreciate what I mean. In the morning we'll rerun the relevant memories and see if they help to straighten you.'

CLIFFHANGER

They had to continue in a paid-avoidance zone. So, to supplement recollection, they bought a four-year-old tourist guide alleged to contain full details of all the post-quake settlements. Most rated four or even six pages of text, plus as many color pictures. Precipice was dismissed in half a page. On the fold-out map included with the booklet only one road – and that a poor one – was shown passing through it, from Quemadura in the south to Pro-tempore thirty miles northwest, plus tracks for an electric railcar service whose schedule was described as irregular. The towns were graded according to what modern facilities could be found there; Precipice came bottom of the list. Among the things Precipicians didn't like might be cited the data-net, veephones, surface vehicles not running on tracks, heavier-than-air craft (though they tolerated helium and hot-air dirigibles), modern merchandising methods and the federal government. This last could be deduced from the datum that they had compounded to pay a flat-rate tax per year instead of income tax, though the sum appeared absurdly high considering there was no industry bar handicrafts (not available to wholesalers).

'It sounds like some sort of Amish setup,' Kate commented, frowning over the brief entry in the guide.

'No, it can't be. They won't allow churches or other religious buildings.' He was gazing into nowhere, focusing on facts casually encountered long ago. 'I borrowed some ideas from the paid-avoidance zones while I was a utopia designer. I needed to figure a way of editing dogmatic religion into a community without the risk of breeding intolerance. I checked out several of these towns, and I distinctly remember ignoring Precipice because in any case I couldn't spare the time to dig right down deep for more data. Almost nothing about the place, bar its location, was in store. Oh, yes: and a population limit of three thousand.'

'Huh? A legally imposed limit, you mean?' On his nod: 'Imposed by whom – the citizens or the state government?'

'The citizens.'

'Compulsory birth control?'

'I don't know. I told you: when I found how little I could fish from the banks, I didn't bother to pursue the matter.'

'Do they ride visitors out again on a rail?'

He gave a half-smile. 'No, that's one other fact I remember. It's an open community, administered by some sort of town meeting, I think, and you may indeed go there to look it over or even to stay indefinitely. They just don't care for advertising, and apparently they regard noising their existence abroad as the same thing in principle.'

'We go there, then,' Kate said decisively, slapping shut the booklet.

'My choice would be the opposite. To be trapped in a backwater … But tell me why.'

'Precisely because there's so little information in the banks. It's beyond belief that the government won't have tried – probably tried extremely hard – to tie Precipice into the net at least to the same extent as Protempore and Lap-of-the-Gods. If the citizens are dogged enough to stand out against such pressure, they might sympathize with your plight the way I do.'

Appalled, he blurted out, 'You mean you want me to march in and announce it?'

'Will you *stop* that?' Kate stamped her foot, eyes flashing. 'Grow out of your megalomania, for pity's sake! Quit thinking in terms of "Sandy Locke versus the world" and start believing that there are other people dissatisfied with the state of things, anxious to set it right. You know' – a level, caustic glare – 'I'm beginning to think you've never sought help from others for fear you might wind up being the one who does the helping. You always like to be in charge, don't you? Particularly of yourself!'

He drew a deep breath and let it out very slowly, forcing his embryonic annoyance to go with it. He said at length, 'I knew what they offered me under the guise of "wisdom" at Tarnover wasn't the genuine article. It was so totally wrong it's taken me until now to realize I finally ran across it. Kate, you're a wise person. The first one I ever met.'

'Don't encourage me to think so. If I ever come to believe it, I shall fall flat on my face.'

OUBLIETTE

By about then the lean black man from Tarnover was through with Ina Grierson and let her go home, stumbling with weariness. Before she fell asleep, however, she had to know one thing that Freeman had declined to tell her:

What the hell was so earthmoving about Sandy Locke?

She was not the most expert of data-mice; however, her position as head-of-dept for transient execs gave her access to the files of G2S employees. Trembling, she punched the code that started with 4GH.

The screen stayed blank.

She tried every route she could think of to gain access to the data, including some that were within the ace of being illegal … though they bent, rather than broke, the regulations laid down by the Bureau of Data Processing, and a blind eye was generally turned.

The result was invariably the same blank screen.

At first she only nibbled her nails; later, she started to gnaw them; finally, she had to cram her fingers into her mouth to stop herself whimpering in mingled terror and exhaustion.

If all her best attempts had failed, there was just one conclusion to be drawn. Sandy Locke, so far as the data-net was concerned, had been deleted from the human race.

For the first time since she broke her heart at seventeen, Ina Grierson cried herself to sleep.

A SHOULDER TO BE WEPT ON BY THE WORLD

So they went to Precipice, where there wasn't one. The town had been founded on the levelest ground for miles, a patch of soft but stable silt due to some long-ago river which still had a few creeks meandering across it. Though hills could be seen on three sides, their slopes were gentle and any earthquake that shifted them in their eon-long slumber would be violent enough to cast loose California entire.

They rode toward it in the electric railcar with the irregular schedule, which they boarded at Transience. Small wonder the car didn't stick to a fixed timetable. As they were informed by the driver – a burly smiling man wearing shorts, sunglasses and sandals – a local ordinance obliged it to give precedence at all crossings to anyone on foot, cycle or horseback, as well as to farm animals and agricultural vehicles. Moreover, when making its final loop around Precipice proper it had to let passengers on or off at any point. Taking full advantage of this facility, local people boarded and descended every few hundred meters. All of them gazed with unashamed curiosity at the strangers.

Who became uncomfortable. Both of them had overlooked one problem involved in traveling around the paid-avoidance zones, being so used to the devices that in theory could eliminate the need for baggage from the plug-in life-style. At all modern hotels could be found ultrasonic clothing cleansers capable of ridding even the bulkiest garment of its accumulated dust and grime in five minutes, and when the cloth began to give way under repeated applications of this violent treatment, there were other machines that would credit you for the fiber, tease it apart, store it for eventual re-use, and issue another garment the same size but a different style and/or color, debbing the customer for the additional fiber and the work involved. Nothing like that was to be found at Lap-of-the-Gods.

Kate had snatched up toilet gear for them before departure, including an old-fashioned reciprocating-head razor left behind by one of her boyfriends, but neither had thought to bring spare clothing. Consequently they were by now looking, and even more feeling, dirty … and those strange eyes constantly scanning them made them fidget.

But things could have been a great deal worse. In many places people would have felt it their duty to put hostile questions to wanderers whose clothes looked as though they had been slept in and who carried almost no other possessions. Luggage might have dwindled; the list of what people felt to be indispensable had long ago reached the stage where both sexes customarily carried bulky purses when bound for any but their most regular destinations.

Yet until they were almost at the end of their journey no one in the railcar, except the informative driver, addressed anything but a greeting to them.

By then they had been able to look over the neighborhood, which they found impressive. The rich alluvial soil was being efficiently farmed; watered by irrigation channels topped up by wind-driven pumps, orchards and corn-fields and half-hectare plots of both leaf and root vegetables shimmered in the sun. That much one could have seen anywhere. Far more remarkable were the buildings. They were virtually invisible. Like partridges hiding among rough grass, some of them eluded the eye altogether until a change of angle revealed a line too straight to be other than artificial, or a flash of sunlight on the black glass of a solar energy collector. The contrast with a typical modern farm, a factory-like place where standard barns and silos prefabricated out of concrete and aluminum were dumped all anyhow, was astonishing.

In a low voice he said to Kate, 'I'd like to know who designed these farms. This isn't junk cobbled together by refugees in panic. This is the sort of landscaping a misanthropic millionaire might crave but not afford! Seen anything as good anywhere else?'

She shook her head. 'Not even at Protempore, much as I liked it. I guess maybe what the refugees originally botched up didn't last. When it fell to bits they were calm enough to get it right on the second try.'

'But this is more than just *right*. This is *magnificent*. The town itself can't possibly live up to the same standard. Are we in sight of it yet, by the way?'

Kate craned to look past the driver. Noticing, a middle-aged woman in blue seated on the opposite side of the car inquired, 'You haven't been to Precipice before?'

'Ah ... No, we haven't.'

'Thought I didn't recognize you. Planning to stay, or just passing through?'

'Can people stay? I thought you had a population limit.'

'Oh, sure, but we're two hundred under at the moment. And in spite of anything you may have heard' – a broad grin accompanied the remark – 'we like to have company drop in. Tolerable company, that is. My name's Polly, by the way.'

'I'm Kate, and—'

Swiftly inserted: 'I'm Alexander – Sandy! Say, I was just wondering who laid out these farms. I never saw buildings that fit so beautifully into a landscape.'

'Ah! Matter of fact, I was about to tell you, go see the man who does almost all our building. That's Ted Horovitz. He's the sheriff, too. You get off at Mean Free Path and walk south until you hit Root Mean Square and then just ask for Ted. If he's not around, talk to the mayor – that's Suzy Dellinger. Got that? Fine. Well, nice to have met you, hope to see you around, this is where I get off.'

She headed for the door.

Involuntarily Kate said, 'Mean Free Path? Root Mean Square? Is that some kind of joke?'

There were four other passengers at this stage of the journey. All of them chuckled. The driver said over his shoulder, 'Sure, the place is littered with jokes. Didn't you know?'

'Kind of rarefied jokes, aren't they?'

'I guess maybe. But they're a monument to how Precipice got started. Of all the people who got drove south by the Bay Quake, the ones who came here were the luckiest. Ever hear mention of Claes College?'

Kate exploded just as he began to say he hadn't.

'You mean *this* was "Disasterville U.S.A."?' She was half out of her seat with excitement, peering eagerly along the curved track toward the town that was now coming into view. Even at first glance, it promised that indeed it did maintain the standard set by the outlying farms; at any rate, there was none of the halfhearted disorganization found at the edge of so many modern communities, but a real sense of border: here, rural; there, urban. No, not after all a sharp division. A – a –

An ancient phrase came to mind: *dissolving view*.

But there was no chance to sort out his confused initial impressions; Kate was saying urgently, 'Sandy, you must have heard of Claes, surely ...? No? Oh, that's terrible!'

She dropped back into her seat and gave him a rapid-fire lecture.

'Claes College was founded about 1981 to revive the medieval sense of the name, a community of scholars sharing knowledge regardless of arbitrary boundaries between disciplines. It didn't last; it faded away after only a few years. But the people involved left one important memorial. When the Bay Quake let go, they dropped everything and moved *en masse* to help with relief work, and someone hit on the idea of undertaking a study of the social forces at work in the post-catastrophe period so that if it ever happened again the worst tragedies could be avoided. The result was a series of monographs under the title "Disasterville U.S.A." I'm amazed you never heard of it.'

She rounded on the driver. 'Practically nobody has heard of it! I must have mentioned it a hundred times and always drawn a blank. But it's not only important – it's unique.'

Dryly the driver said, 'You didn't mention it at Precipice, that's for sure. We grow up on it in school. Ask Brad Compton the librarian to show you our first edition.'

He applied the brakes. 'Coming up to Mean Free now!'

Mean Free Path was indeed a path, winding among shrubs, trees and – houses? They had to be. But they were something else, too. Yes, they had roofs (although the roofs were never four-square) and walls (what one could see of them through masses of creeper) and doubtless doors, none of which happened to be visible from where they had left the railcar ... already out of sight and sound despite its leisurely pace, lost in a tunnel of greenery.

'They are like the farms,' Kate breathed.

'No.' He snapped his fingers. 'There's a difference, and I just figured out what it is. The farms – they're factors in landscape. But these houses *are* landscape.'

'That's right,' Kate said. Her voice was tinged with awe. 'I have the most ridiculous feeling. I'm instantly ready to believe that an architect who could do this ...' The words trailed away.

'An architect who could do this could design a planet,' he said briefly, and took her arm to urge her onward.

Though the path wound, it was level enough to ride a cycle or draw a cart along, paved with slabs of rock conformable to the contour of the land. Shortly they passed a green lawn tinted gold by slanting sunshine. She pointed at it.

'Not a garden,' she said. 'But a glade.'

'Exactly!' He put his hand to his forehead, seeming dizzy. Alarmed, she clutched at him.

'Sandy, is something the matter?'

'No – yes – no … I don't know. But I'm okay.' Dropping his arm, he blinked this way, then that. 'It just hit me. This is *town* – yes? But it doesn't feel like it. I simply know it must be, because …' He swallowed hard. 'Seeing it from the railcar, could you have mistaken this place for anything else?'

'Never in a million years. Hmm!' Her eyes rounded in wonder. 'That's a hell of a trick, isn't it?'

'Yes, and if I didn't realize it was therapeutic I could well be angry. People don't enjoy being fooled, do they?'

'Therapeutic?' She frowned. 'I don't follow you.'

'Set-destruction. We use sets constantly instead of seeing what's there – or feeling or tasting it, come to that. We have a set "town", another "city", another "village" … and we often forget there's a reality the sets were originally based on. We're in too much of a hurry. If this effect is typical of Precipice, I'm not surprised it gets so little space in the guidebook. Tourists would find a massive dose of double-take indigestible. I look forward to meeting this poker Horovitz. As well as being a builder and a sheriff I think he must be a …'

'A what?'

'A something else. Maybe something I don't know a word for.'

The path had been a path. The square proved not to be a square, more a deformed cyclic quadrilateral, but it implied all the necessary elements of a public urban space. It was a great deal bigger than one might have guessed. They found this out by crossing it. Part of it, currently deserted, was paved and ornamented with flower-filled urns; part was park-like, though miniaturized, a severe formal garden; part sloped down to a body of water, less a lake than a pond, some three or four meters below the general level of the land, from whose banks steps rose in elegant curves. Here there were people: old folk on benches in the sun, two games of fencing in progress amid the inevitable cluster of kibitzers, while down by the water – under the indulgent but watchful eyes of a couple of teeners – some naked children were splashing merrily about in pursuit of a huge light ball bigger than any two of their heads.

And enclosing this square were buildings of various heights linked together by slanting roofs and pierced by alleyways but for which they would have composed a solid terrace. As it was, every alley was bridged at first-story level and every bridge was ornamented with delicate carvings in wood or stone.

'My God,' Kate said under her breath. 'It's incredible. Not town. Not here. This is *village*.'

'And yet it's got the city implicit in it – the Grand' Place, the Plaza Mayor, Old London Bridge … Oh, it's fantastic! And look a bit more closely at the houses. They're ecofast, aren't they? Every last one of them! I wouldn't be surprised to find they're running off ground heat!'

She paled a little. 'You're right! I hadn't noticed. One thinks of an ecofast house as being – well, kind of one cell for a honeycomb, factory-made. There are ecofast communities around KC, you know, and they have no more character than an anthill!'

'Let's track down the sheriff at once. I can stand just so many unanswered questions at one go. Excuse me!' He approached the group around the fencing tables. 'Where do we find Ted Horovitz?'

'Through that alley,' one of the watchers said, pointing. 'First door on your right. If he's not there, try the mayor's office. I think he has business with Suzy today.'

Again, as they moved away, they felt many curious eyes on them. As though visitors were a rarity at Precipice. But why weren't there thousands of them, millions? Why wasn't this little town famous the world around?

'Though of course if it were famous—'

'Did you say something?'

'Not exactly. This must be the door. Mr Horovitz?'

'Come right in!'

They entered, and found themselves in an extraordinary room at least ten meters long. Conventionally enough furnished, with chairs and a desk and sundry cases crammed with books and cassettes, it was more like a forest clearing bright with ferns or a cave behind a waterfall hung with strands of glistening vegetation than anybody's office. Greenish light, reflected from wind-wavered panels outside irregular windows, flickered on flock-sprayed surfaces as soft as moss.

Turning to greet them from a carpenter's bench that had seen long service was a stocky man in canvas pants with big pockets full of tools, laying aside a wooden object whose outline was at first elusive, then suddenly familiar: a dulcimer.

In the same moment something moved, emerging from shadow beside the workbench. A dog. A vast, slow-moving graceful dog whose ancestry might have included Great Dane, Irish wolfhound, possibly husky or Chinook … plus something else, something strange, for its skull was improbably high-domed and its eyes, deep-set, looked disturbingly uncanine.

Kate's fingers clamped vise-tight on his arm. He heard her gasp.

'No need to be alarmed,' the man rumbled in a voice half an octave nearer the bass than might have been guessed from his size. 'Never met a dog like this before? You're in for an educational experience. His name is Natty Bumppo. Hold still a moment while he reads you. Sorry, but this is S.O.P. for any visitor. Nat, how do they rate? Any hard drugs – excessive liquor – anything apart from being a bit scared?'

The dog curled his wrinkled upper lip and inhaled a long slow breath, then gave a brisk headshake and a faint growl. Elegantly he lowered his massive hindquarters to the floor, keeping his eyes on the newcomers.

Kate's fingers relaxed, but she was trembling.

'He says you're clear,' Horovitz announced. 'I understand this poker pretty well, you know. Not as well as he understands us humans, maybe, but there it is. Right, sit down!' With a wave toward a nearby lounge; he himself dropped into an armchair facing it and produced an ancient charred pipe from one of his immense pockets. 'What can I do for you?'

They looked at one another. With sudden decision Kate said, 'We found our way here more or less by accident. We were in Lap-of-the-Gods and before that I'd been to Protempore. They can't stand comparison with Precipice. We'd like to visit with you for a while.'

'Mm-hm. Okay ... probably.' Horovitz gestured to the dog. 'Nat, go tell the councilmen we got applicants, please.'

Natty Bumppo rose, snuffed one last time at the strangers, and padded out. The door had a handle which he could open himself; punctiliously, he also closed it.

Following the animal with his eyes, Sandy said, 'Oh, I forgot to tell you our names.'

'Kate and Sandy,' Horovitz murmured. 'I knew to expect you. Polly Ryan said she met you on the railcar.'

'She – uh ...?'

'You heard of phones, I guess. We have 'em. Appearances to the contrary. Maybe you were reading up on us in that bad guidebook.' It was protruding from Kate's side pocket; he leveled an accusing finger at it. 'What we don't have is vee-phone service. The feds have been on at us for years to link into the data-net on the same token basis as the other paid-avoidance communities, but to satisfy their computers you have to have veephone-sized bandpass capacity. They give all kinds of nice persuasive reasons – they keep reminding us of how Transcience was almost taken over by a criminal syndicate, and how nearly everybody in Ararat was fooled by a phony preacher wanted in seven different states for fraud and confidence-trickery ... but we prefer to stay out and solve our own problems. They can't oblige us to tie in so long as our taxes amount to more than our PA grants. So, on principle, no veephones. Don't let that mislead you, though, into imagining we're backward. We're just about the size of a late medieval market town, and we offer almost precisely one hundred times as many facilities.'

'So you've proved it is cheaper to operate on an ecofast basis!' Sandy leaned forward eagerly.

'You noticed? Very interesting! Most people have preconceived ideas about ecofast building; they have to be factory products, they come in one size and one shape and if you want a bigger one you can only stick two together. In fact, as you say, once you really understand the principle you find you've accidentally eliminated most of your concealed overheads. Been to Trianon, either of you?'

'Visiting friends,' Kate said.

'They boast about running at seventy-five percent energy utilization, and they still have to take an annual subsidy from G2S because their pattern is inherently so wasteful. We run at eighty to eighty-five percent. There isn't a community on the planet that's doing better.'

Horovitz appended a half-embarrassed smile to the remark, as though to liberate it from any suspicion of conceit.

'And you're responsible for that?' Sandy demanded. 'The woman we met – Polly – said you do most of the building.'

'Sure, but I can't claim the credit. I didn't figure out the principles, nor how to apply them. That was—'

Kate butted in. 'Oh, yes! The railcar-driver said this is the original Disasterville U.S.A.!'

'You heard about that deal?' Horovitz had been loading his pipe with coarse dark tobacco; he almost dropped the pouch and pipe both. 'Well, *hell!* So they haven't managed to clamp the lid down tight!'

'Ah ... What do you mean?'

A shrug and a grunt. 'The way I hear it, if you punch for data about the Disasterville study, or about anything to do with Claes College, over the regular continental net, you get some kind of discouragement. Like it's entered as "of interest only to specialist students", quote and unquote. Any rate, that's what I heard from Brad. Brad Compton, our librarian.'

'But that's awful!' Kate stared at him. 'I never did actually punch for those data – my father had a full set of Disasterville monographs, and I read them in my early teens. But ... Well, isn't it important that one of the projects they dreamed up at Claes turned into a functional community?'

'Oh, I think so. What sheriff wouldn't, with a crime rate of nearly zero?'

'Are you serious?'

'Mm-hm. We never had a murder yet, and it's two years since we had anybody hospitalized after a fight, and as to robbery – well, stealing just ain't a habit around here.' A faint grin. 'Occasionally it gets imported, but I swear there's no future in it either way.'

Kate said slowly, 'Don't tell me. Let me guess. Is this place the reason why Claes went under? Did the really bright people stay on here instead of going home?'

Horovitz smiled. 'Young lady, you're the first visitor I've met who got that without having to be told. Yup; Precipice skimmed the cream off Claes, and the rump that was left just faded away. As I understand it, that was because only the people who took their own ideas seriously were prepared to face the responsibility entailed. And ridicule, too. After all, at the same time other refugee settlements were at the mercy of crooks and unscrupulous fake evangelists – like we were just talking about – so who was to believe that some crazy mix composed of bits of Ghirardelli and Portmeirion and Valencia and Taliesin and God knows what besides would turn out right when everything else went wrong?'

'I think you must like us,' Sandy said suddenly.

Horovitz blinked at him. 'What?'

'I never saw a façade fall down so fast. The homey-folksy bit, I mean. It didn't suit you anyhow; it's no loss. But on top of being a builder and a sheriff, what are you? I mean, where did you start?'

Horovitz pulled the corners of his mouth down in a lugubrious parody of dismay.

'I plead guilty,' he said after a pause. 'Sure, I regard myself as local, but I have a doctorate in social interaction from Austin, Texas, and a master's in structural technology from Columbia. Which is not something I customarily admit to visitors, even the bright ones – *particularly* not to the bright ones, because they tend to come here for all possible wrong reasons. We're interested in being functional, not in being dissected by in-and-out gangs of cultural anthropologists.'

'How long are you going to wait before becoming famous?'

'Hmm! You *are* a perceptive shivver, aren't you? But a fair question rates a fair answer. We expect half a century will be enough.'

'Are we going to survive that long?'

Horovitz shook his head heavily. 'We don't know. Does anybody?'

The door swung wide. Natty Bumppo returned, giving Horovitz a nudge with his muzzle as he passed. Behind him came a tall stately black woman in a gaudy shirt and tight pants, arm in arm with a fat white man – heavily tanned – in shorts and sandals like the railcar driver.

Horovitz introduced them as Suzy Dellinger, the mayor, and Brad Compton; they were this year's councilmen for the town. He gave a condensed but accurate version of his conversation with Kate and Sandy. The new arrivals listened intently. Having heard him out, Brad Compton made an extraordinary comment.

'Does Nat approve?'

'Seems to,' grunted Horovitz.

'Then I guess we found new tenants for the Thorgrim place. Suzy?' Glancing at the mayor.

'Sure, why not?' She turned to Kate and Sandy. 'Welcome to Precipice! Now, from here you go back to the square, take the second alley on your right, and you're on Drunkard's Walk. Follow it to the intersection with Great Circle Course. The house on the near left of that corner is yours for as long as you care to stay.'

There was a moment of blank incredulity. Then Kate exclaimed, 'Hold it! You're going far too fast! I don't know for certain what Sandy's plans are, but I have to get back to KC in a few days' time. You seem to have decided I'm a permanent settler.'

Sandy chimed in. 'What's more, on the basis of a dog's opinion! Even if he is modded, I don't see how—'

'Modded?' Horovitz broke in. 'No, Nat's not modified. I guess his how-ever-many-great grandfather must have been tinkered with a bit, but he's just the way he grew up. Best of his litter, admittedly.'

'You mean there are a lot of dogs like him around Precipice?' Kate demanded.

'A couple of hundred by now,' Mayor Dellinger replied. 'Descendants of a pack that wandered into town in the summer of 2003. There was a young stud, and two fertile bitches each with four pups, and an old sterile bitch was leading them. She'd been neutered. Doc Squibbs – he's our veterinarian – he's always maintained they must have escaped from some research station and gone looking for a place where they'd be better treated. Which was here. They're great with kids, they can almost literally talk, and if only they lived to a ripe old age there'd be nothing wrong with them at all. Trouble is, they last seven or eight years at most, and that's not fair, is it, Nat?' She reached out to scratch Natty Bumppo behind the ears, and he gave one absent thump with his thick tail. 'But we got friends working on that, and we do our best to breed them for longevity.'

Another pause. Eventually Sandy said with determination, 'Okay, so your dogs can work miracles. But handing us a house, without even asking what we intend to do while we're here—'

Brad Compton gave a hoot of laughter. He broke off in confusion.

'Forgive Brad,' Horovitz said. 'But I thought we'd been over that. Did you miss my point? I told you, we offer a hundred times as many services as a medieval town the same size. You don't just arrive, squat a house, and live on your federal avoidance grant forever and a day, amen. Now and then people try it. They become unhappy and disillusioned and drift away.'

'Well, sure. I mean, I realize you must have all kinds of work to offer us … but that's not what I'm driving at. I want to know what the hell supports this community.'

The three Precipicians smiled at one another. Mayor Dellinger said, 'Shall I tell them?'

'Sure, it's a job for the mayor,' Compton answered.

'Okay.' She turned to face Kate and Sandy. 'We run an operation with no capital, no shareholders and scarcely any plant. Yet we receive a donated income fifteen times as large as our collective avoidance grants.'

'*What?*'

'That's right.' Her tone was sober. 'We provide a service which some people – some very rich people indeed – have found so precious that they've done things like covenant to pay us a tithe of their salary for life. Once we were left the income on an estate of sixty million, and though the family tried like hell to overturn the will in the courts ... I believe you just recognized us, didn't you?'

Shaking, fists clenched, mouth so dry he was almost unable to shape the proper words, Sandy blurted out his guess.

'There's only one thing you could be. But— Oh, my God. Are you really Hearing Aid?'

CROSS TALK

'After which I immediately wanted to ask how they managed to keep that incredible promise of theirs, but—'

'Wait, wait!' Freeman was half out of his chair, peering closely at his data console as though shortening the range could alter what the instrument display was reporting.

'Is something wrong?'

'I ... No, nothing's wrong. I merely observed a rather remarkable event.' Freeman sank back in his chair, and with an air of guilt produced a handkerchief to mop his face. All of a sudden sweat had burst out in rivers on his forehead.

There was a brief silence. Then:

'Damn, you're right. This is the first time you ever transferred me from regressed to present mode and I didn't have to be steered back to the same subject. Ve-ery interesting! Don't bother telling me this indicates how deeply I was affected; I know, and I still am. What I learned from that first conversation at Precipice left me with a weird tip-of-the-tongue sensation, as though I'd realized the people there had the answer to some desperately urgent problem, only I couldn't work out what problem the answer belonged with ... Incidentally, please tell me something. I think I deserve it. After all, I can't prevent you from making me tell you everything, can I?'

Freeman's face was glistening as though he were being roasted on a spit before an immensely hot fire. He mopped away more perspiration before he replied.

'Go ahead and ask.'

'If it had become known that I'd called Hearing Aid and talked for an hour about Miranda and myself and Tarnover … would I have been expelled via an operating theater?'

Freeman hesitated, folding and refolding his handkerchief prior to returning it to his pocket. At long last he did so, and with reluctance spoke.

'Yes. With an IQ of 85 if you were lucky.'

As calmly as before: 'What about Hearing Aid?'

'Nothing would have been done to them.' The admission was almost inaudible. 'You must know why.'

'Oh, sure. Sorry – I admit I only asked to see you squirm with embarrassment. But there's such a David-and-Goliath pattern about Precipice versus the U.S. government. Want me to continue?'

'Do you feel up to it?'

'I think so. Whether or not Precipice will work for everybody, it worked for me. And it's high time I faced the reason why my stay there ended in a disaster, when if I hadn't been a fool it need have been no worse than a minor setback.'

THE MESH OF A RIDDLE

'This is the most incredible place. I never dreamed—'

Walking uphill on the aptly named Drunkard's Walk, Kate interrupted him.

'Sandy, that dog. Natty Bumppo.'

'He gave you quite a fright, didn't he? I'm sorry.'

'No!'

'But you—'

'I know, I know. I was startled. But I wasn't scared. I simply didn't believe it. I thought none of Dad's dogs was left.'

'What?' He almost stumbled, turning to stare at her. 'What on earth could he have to do with your father?'

'Well, I never heard of anybody else who did such marvelous things with animals. Bagheera was one of Dad's too, you know. Almost the last.'

He drew a deep breath. 'Kate dear, would you please begin at the beginning?'

Eyes troubled and full of sadness, she said, 'I guess I ought to. I remember asking if you knew about my father, and you said sure, he was Henry Lilleberg the neurophysiologist, and I left it at that. But it was a prime example of what you said only an hour ago Precipice is designed to cure. Slap a label on and forget about it. Say "neurophysiologist" and you conjure up a stock picture of the sort of person who will dissect out a nervous system, analyze it *in vitro*, publish the findings and go away content, forgetting that the rest of the animal ever existed. That isn't a definition of my father! When I was a little girl he used to bring me amazing pets, which never lasted long because they were already old. But they'd been of service at his labs, and as a result he couldn't bear to throw them down the incinerator chute. He used to say he owed them a bit of fun because he'd cheated them of it when they were young.'

'What kind of animals?'

'Oh, little ones at first, when I was five or six – rats, hamsters, gerbils. Later on there were squirrels and gophers, cats and raccoons. Remember I mentioned he had a license to move protected species interstate? And finally, in the last couple of years before he was taken so ill he had to retire, he was working with some real big ones: dogs like Natty Bumppo and mountain lions like Bagheera.'

'Did he do any research with aquatic mammals … dolphins, porpoises?'

'I don't believe so. At any rate he couldn't have brought those home for me.' A touch of her normal wry humor returned with the words. 'We lived in an apt. We didn't have a pool to keep them in. Why do you ask?'

'I was wondering whether he might have been involved with – hell, I don't know which of several names you might recognize. They kept changing designations as they ran into one dead end after another. But it was a project based in Georgia intended to devise animals capable of defeating an invasion. Originally they thought of small creatures as disease-vectors and saboteurs, like they conditioned rats to gnaw compulsively on tire rubber and electrical insulation. Later there was all this hot air generated about surrogate armies, with animals substituted for infantry. Wars would still be fought, with lots of blood and noise, but no soldiers would be killed – not permanently.'

'I knew the project under the name of Parsimony. But Dad never worked on it. They kept asking him to join, and he kept declining because they'd never tell him all the details of what he'd have to do. It wasn't until he'd contracted his terminal myelitis that he was able to find out how right he'd been.'

'The project was discontinued, wasn't it?'

'Yes, and I know why. They'd been living off Dad's back for years. He was the only man in the country, maybe the world, who was consistently successful in making superintelligent animals breed true.'

'Literally the only one?'

'Oh, even he scarcely believed it. He published his data and always swore he wasn't holding anything back, but other researchers found they couldn't get the same results. In the end it became a joke for him. He used to say, "I just have red fingers." '

'I see. Like a gardener has green ones.'

'Exactly.'

'What were his methods?' The question was more rhetorical than literal. But she answered anyway.

'Don't ask me, go punch a code. All the data are on open reels. Seemingly the government must hope another red-fingered genius will chance on them some day.'

Eyes fixed on nowhere, he said in a musing tone, 'I got disenchanted with biology, but I do recall something about the Lilleberg Hypothesis. An ultra-refined subcategory of natural selection involving hormonal influence not only on the embryo but on the gonads of the parents, which was supposed to determine the crossover points on the chromosomes.'

'Mm-hm. He was ridiculed for proposing it. He was slandered by all his colleagues, accused of trying to show that Lysenko was right after all. Which,' she added hotly, 'was a transparent lie! What he actually did was advance an explanation why in spite of being wrong the Lysenkoists could have fooled themselves. Sandy, why does an establishment always fossilize so quickly? It may be my imagination, but I have this paranoid notion that people in authority today make a policy of seizing on any really original idea and either distorting it or suppressing it. Ted Horovitz was saying something about people being discouraged from digging into the Disasterville studies, for example.'

'Do you really have to ask about government?' he countered grayly. 'I'd have thought the reason was plain. It's the social counterpart of natural selection. Those groups within society that craved power at the expense of everything else – morality, self-respect, honest friendship – they achieved dominance long ago. The mass of the public no longer has any contact with government; all they know is that if they step out of line they'll be trodden on. And the means exist to make the statement literal ... Oh, they must hate Precipice, over there in Washington! A tiny community, and its citizens can thumb their noses at any federal diktat!'

She shuddered visibly. 'But the scientists ...?' she said.

'Their reaction is a different matter. The explosion of human knowledge has accelerated to the point where even the most brilliant can't cope with it any more. Theories have rigidified into dogma just as they did in the Middle Ages. The leading experts feel obligated to protect their creed against the heretics. Right?'

'That certainly fits in Dad's case,' Kate said, nodding and biting her lip. 'But – well, he proved his point! Bagheera's evidence, if nothing else.'

'He wasn't an isolated success, was he?'

'Hell, no. But the only one Dad was able to save from being sold to the big circus at Quemadura. It was just getting started then, and people were invest-ing a lot of money in it and— Say, look there!'

They were passing a patch of level grass where two young children were lying asleep on a blanket. Beside them was a dog the same type and color as Natty Bumppo but smaller, a bitch. She was gazing levelly at the strangers; one corner of her upper lip was curled to show sharp white teeth, and she was uttering a faint – as it were a questioning – growl.

Now she rose, the hair on her spine erect, and approached them. They stopped dead.

'Hello,' Kate said, with a hint of nervousness. 'We're new here. But we've just been to call on Ted, and he and Suzy say we can live in the old Thorgrim house.'

'Kate, you can't seriously expect a dog to understand a complex—'

He broke off, dumbfounded. For the bitch had promptly wagged her tail. Smiling, Kate held out her hand to be smelt. After a moment he copied her.

The dog pondered a while, then nodded in an entirely human fashion, and turned her head to show that on the collar she wore there was a plaque with a few words stamped on it.

'Brynhilde,' Kate read aloud. 'And you belong to some people called Josh and Lorna Treves. Well, how do you do, Brynhilde?'

Solemn, the dog offered each of them her right paw, then returned to her guard duty. They walked on.

'Now do you believe me?' Kate murmured.

'Yes, damn it, I have to. But how on earth could a bunch of your father's dogs have found their way here?'

'Like the mayor said, they probably escaped from a research station and went looking for a good home. Several centers had dogs bred by Dad. Say, I wonder how much further it is to Great Circle Course. Can we have come too far? No street names are marked up anywhere.'

'I noticed. That's of a piece with everything else. Helps to force you back from the abstract set to the reality. Of course it's something that can only work in a small community, but – well, how many thousands of streets have you passed along without registering anything but the name? I think that's one of the forces driving people to distraction. One needs solid perceptual food same as one needs solid nutriment; without it, you die of bulk-hunger. There's an intersection, see?'

They hurried the last few paces, and—

'Oh, *Sandy*!' Kate's voice was a gusty sigh. 'Sandy, can this possibly be right? It's not a house, it's a piece of sculpture! And it's beautiful!'

After a long and astonished silence he said to the air, 'Well, thank *you*!'

And in a fit of exuberance swept her off her feet and carried her over the not-exactly-a-threshold.

THE LOGICALITY OF LIKING

'I wonder what made you like Precipice so much,' Freeman muttered.

'I'd have thought it was obvious. The people there have got right what those at Tarnover got completely wrong.'

'To me it sounds like the regular plug-in life-style. You arrive, you take on a house that's spare and waiting, you—'

'No, no, *no!*' In a crescendo. 'The first thing we found when we walked in was a note from the former occupier, Lars Thorgrim, explaining that he and his family had had to move away because his wife had developed a disease needing regular radiation therapy so they had to live closer to a big hospital. Otherwise they'd never have moved because they'd been so happy in the house, and they hoped that the next people to use it would feel the same. And both their children sent love and kisses. That's not the plug-in life-style, whose basis consists in leaving behind nothing of yourself when you move on.'

'But just as when you joined G2S you were immediately whisked away to a welcome party—'

'For pity's *sake!* At places like G2S you need the excuse of a new arrival to hold a party; it's a business undertaking, designed to let him and his new colleagues snuff around each other's assholes like wary dogs! At Precipice the concept of the party is built into the social structure; those parties were going to be held anyhow, because of a birthday or an anniversary or just because it was a fine warm evening and a batch of homemade wine was shaping well enough to share. I'm disappointed in you. I'd imagined that you would have seen through the government's attempt to deevee Precipice and gone back to the source material.'

For the first time Freeman seemed to be visibly on the defensive. He said in a guarded tone, 'Well, naturally I—'

'Save the excuses. If you had dug deep, I wouldn't be giving you this as news. Oh, think, man, think! The Disasterville U.S.A. study constitutes literally the only first-rank analysis of how the faults inherent in our society are revealed in a post-catastrophe context. Work done at other refugee settlements was trivial and superficial, full of learned clichés. But after saying straight out that the victims of the Bay Quake couldn't cope because they'd quit trying to fend for themselves – having long ago discovered that the reins of power had been gathered into the hands of a corrupt and jealous in-group – the people from Claes College topped it off with what Washington felt to be the ultimate insult. They said, "And this is how to put it right!"'

A dry chuckle.

'Worse still, they proceeded to demonstrate it, and worst of all, they stopped the government from interfering.'

'How long after your arrival were you told about that?'

'I wasn't told. I figured it out myself that same evening. It was a classic example of the kind of thing that's so obvious you ignore it. In my case specifically, after my last contact with Hearing Aid I'd unconsciously blanked off all further consideration of the problem. Otherwise I'd have spotted the solution at once.'

Freeman sighed. 'I thought you were going to defend your obsession with Precipice, not excuse your own shortcomings.'

'I enjoy it when you needle me. It shows that your control is getting ragged. Let me tatter it a bit more. I warn you, I intend to make you lose your temper eventually, and never mind how many tranquilizers you take per day. Excuse me; a joke in poor taste. But – oh, please be candid. Has it never surprised you that so few solid data emerged from the aftermath of the Bay Quake, the greatest single calamity in the country's history?'

Freeman's answer was harsh. 'It was also the most completely documented event in our history!'

'Which implies that a lot of lessons should have been learned, doesn't it? Name a few.'

Freeman sat silent. Once again his face gleamed with sweat. He interlocked his fingers as though to prevent them trembling visibly.

'I think I'm making my point. Fine. Consider. Vast hordes of people had to start from scratch after the quake, and the public at large felt obliged to help them. It was a perfect opportunity to allot priorities: to stand back and assess what was and was not worth having among the countless choices offered by our modern ingenuity. Years, in some cases as much as a decade, elapsed before the economy was strong enough to finance the conversion of the original shantytowns into something permanent. Granted that the refugees themselves were disadvantaged: what about the specialists from outside, the federal planners?'

'They consulted with the settlers, as you well know.'

'But did they help them to make value judgments? Not on your life. They counted the cost in purely financial terms. If it was cheaper to pay this or that community to go without something, that's what the community wound up lacking. Under the confident misapprehension that they were serving the needs of the nation by acting as indispensable guinea pigs. Where was the follow-up? How much money was allocated to finding out whether a community without veephones, or without automatic instant credit-transfer facilities, or without home encyclopedia service, was in any sense better or worse than the rest of the continent? None – *none*! What halfhearted projects were allowed to show their heads were axed in the next session of Congress. Not profitable. The only place where constructive work was done was Precipice, and that was thanks to amateur volunteers.'

'It's easy to prophesy after the event!'

'But Precipice did succeed. The founders knew what they wanted to do, and had valid arguments to support their ideas. The principle of changing one factor and seeing what happens may be fine in the lab. In the larger world, especially when you're dealing with human beings who are badly disturbed following a traumatic experience and have been forcibly returned to basics – hunger, thirst, epidemics – you aren't compelled to be so simplistic. Evidence exists from the historical record that certain social structures are viable and others aren't. The people from Claes recognized that, and did their best to assemble a solid foundation for a new community without bothering to forecast what would evolve from it.'

'Evolution … or devolution?'

'An attempt to backtrack to that fork in our social development where we apparently took a wrong turning.'

'Invoking all kinds of undocumented half-mystical garbage!'

'Such as –?'

'Oh, this ridiculous notion that we're imprinted before birth with the structure of the aboriginal family, the hunter-and-gatherer tribe and the initial version of the village.'

'Have you ever tried to silence a baby?'

'What?'

'You heard me. Humans make mouth noises with the intention of provoking a change in the outside world Nobody denies any longer that even a dumb baby is printed in advance for language. Damn it, enough of our simian cousins have shown they can use a sound-to-symbol relationship! And equally nobody denies that habit patterns involving status, pack leadership— Whoops, hold everything. I just realized I've been manipulated into defending your viewpoint against myself.'

Freeman, relaxing, allowed himself a faint smile.

'And if you continue, you'll expose a basic fallacy in your argument, won't you?' he murmured. 'Precipice may indeed function, after a fashion. But it does so in isolation. Having worked for a utopia consultancy, you must realize that if they're efficiently shielded from the rest of humanity the craziest societies can work … for a while.'

'But Precipice is not isolated. Every day between five hundred and two thousand people punch the ten nines and – well, make confession.'

'Thereby painting a picture of the state of things outside which can be relied on to make Precipicians shudder and feel thankful. True or false, the impression is no doubt comforting.'

Freeman leaned back, conscious of having scored. His voice was almost a purr as he continued, 'You spent time actually listening to some of the calls, I presume?'

'Yes, and at her own insistence so did Kate, though since she wasn't planning to stay she wasn't obliged. They're quite literal about their service. From the central, they route calls to private homes where one adult is always on duty. And someone literally sits and listens.'

'How about the people who can talk for hours nonstop?'

'There aren't many of them, and the computers almost always spot them before they're well under way.'

'For a community so proud of having evaded the data-net, they rely a great deal on computers, don't they?'

'Mm-hm. Must be the only place on Earth where they've made a cottage industry out of the things. It's amazing how useful they are when you don't burden them with irrelevancies, like recording a transaction worth fifty cents.'

'I must find out some time where you draw your dividing line: fifty cents, fifty dollars, fifty thousand dollars … But go on. What were the calls like?'

'I was astonished at how few cranks there were. I was told that cranks get disheartened when they find they can't provoke an argument. Someone who's convinced all human faults are due to wearing shoes, or who just found evidence to impeach the president scrawled on the wall of a public toilet, wants to be met with open disagreement; there's an element of masochism there which isn't satisfied by punching pillows. But people with genuine problems – they're a different matter.'

'Give some examples.'

'Okay. It's a platitude you yourself have used to me to say that the commonest mental disorder now is personality shock. But I never realized before how many people are aware they're lapsing into its sub-clinical penumbra. I recall one poker who confessed he'd tried the White House Trick, and it had worked.'

'What sort of trick?'

'Sometimes it's known as going to the Mexican laundry.'

'Ah. You route a credit allotment – to avoid either tax or recriminations – into and out of a section of the net where nobody can follow it without special permission.'

'That's it. When income-tax time rolls around, you always hear people mentioning it with an envious chuckle, because it's part of modern folklore. That's how politicians and hypercorp execs get away with a tenth of the tax you and I cough up. Well, this shivver I was listening to had vaulted half a million. And he was beside himself with horror. Not terror – he knew he couldn't be caught – but horror. He said it was his first-ever lapse from rectitude, and if his wife hadn't left him for a richer man he'd never have been tempted. Once having done it and found how easy it was, though … how could he ever trust anyone again?'

'But he was trusting Hearing Aid, wasn't he?'

'Yes, and that's one of the miracles performed by the service. While I was a minister I was resigned to having the croakers monitor the link to my confessional, even though what was said face-to-face in the actual booth was adequately private. And there was nothing to stop them noticing that a suspect had called on me, ambushing him as he left, and beating a repeat performance out of him. That type of dishonesty is at the root of our worst problem.'

'I didn't know you acknowledged a "worst" – you seem to find new problems daily. But go on.'

'With pleasure. I'm sure that if I start to foam at the mouth there's a machine standing by to wipe my chin … Oh, hell! It's hypocritical hairsplitting that makes me boil! Theoretically any one of us has access to more information than ever in history, and any phone booth is a gate to it. But suppose you live next door to a poker who's suddenly elected to the state congress, and six weeks later he's had a hundred-thousand-dollar face-lift for his house. Try to find out how he came by the money; you get nowhere. Or try confirming that the company you work for is going to be sold and you're apt to be tossed on the street with no job, three kids and a mortgage. Other people seem to have the information. What about the shivver in the next office who's suddenly laughing when he used to mope? Has he borrowed to buy the firm's stock, knowing he can sell for double and retire?'

'Are you quoting calls to Hearing Aid?'

'Yes, both are actual cases. I bend the rules because I know that if I don't you'll break me.'

'Are you claiming those are typical?'

'Sure they are. Out of all the calls taken, nearly half – I think they say fortyfive percent – are from people who are afraid someone else knows data that they don't and is gaining an unfair advantage by it. For all the claims one hears about the liberating impact of the data-net, the truth is that it's wished on most of us a brand-new reason for paranoia.'

'Considering how short a time you spent at Precipice, your identification with it is amazing.'

'Not at all. It's a phenomenon known as "falling in love" and it happens with places as well as people.'

'Then your first lover's tiff happened rather quickly, too.'

'Needle, needle! Jab away. I'd done something to make amends in advance. A small but genuine consolation, that.'

Freeman tensed. 'So you were the one responsible!'

'For frustrating the latest official assault on Hearing Aid? Yes indeed. I'm proud of it. Apart from marking the first occasion when I used my talent on behalf of other people without being asked and without caring whether I was rewarded – which was a major breakthrough in itself – the job was a pure masterpiece. Working on it, I realized in my guts how an artist or an author can get high on the creative act. The poker who wrote Precipice's original tapeworm was pretty good, but you could theoretically have killed it without shutting down the net – that is, at the cost of losing thirty or forty billion bits of data. Which I gather they were just about prepared to do when I showed up. But mine ... Ho, no! That, I cross my heart, cannot be killed without *dismantling* the net.'

THE BREAKDOWN OF REPRESENTATIVE GOVERNMENT

SUBJECT HAFLINGER NICHOLAS KENTON SELECTED
PROPOSE FACTORS TO ACCOUNT FOR SUBJECTS INFATU-
ATION WITH P A COMMUNITY PRECIPICE CA
(A) FUNCTIONALITY (B) OBJECTIVITY (C) STABILITY
AMPLIFY RESPONSE (A)
(A) IN MOST TOWNS OF SIMILAR SIZE ON THIS CONTINENT
DECISIONS CONCERNING COMMUNAL SERVICES CAN NO
LONGER BE TAKEN BY POPULAR VOTE OWING TO EXTREME
MOBILITY OF POPULATION AND UNWILLINGNESS OF
VOTERS TO PAY FOR FACILITIES THAT WILL BE ENJOYED
ONLY BY THE SUCCEDENT GROUP E G BOND LEVIES TO
FINANCE SCHOOLS SEWAGE SYSTEMS AND HIGHWAY MAIN-
TENANCE HAVE BEEN REPLACED IN 93% OF CASES BY
PATERNALIST LEVIES ON THE DOMINANT EMPLOYER * * *
REFERENCE BARKER PAVLOVSKI & QUAINT THE RESURREC-
TION OF FEUDAL OBLIGATIONS J ANTHROPOL SOC VOL
XXXIX PP 2267–2274
AMPLIFY RESPONSE (B)
(B) INTENSIVE INTERACTION BETWEEN CITIZENS DEEV-
EES INCIDENTAL ATTRIBUTES E G STATUS TYPE OF JOB
RELATIVE WEALTH/POVERTY EMPHASIZES CHARACTER
SOCIABILITY TRUSTWORTHINESS * * * REFERENCE ANON
NEW ROLES FOR OLD AN ANALYSIS OF STATUS CHANGES
AMONG A GROUP OF VICTIMS OF THE GREAT BAY QUAKE
MONOGRAPH #14 DISASTERVILLE USA SERIES

AMPLIFY RESPONSE (C)
(C) POPULATION TURNOVER IN PRECIPICE DESPITE NEAR
AVERAGE VACATION TIME MOBILITY IS LOWEST ON THE
CONTINENT AND HAS NEVER EXCEEDED 1% PER ANNUM * * *
REFERENCE U S CONTINUOUS SAMPLE CENSUS
THANK YOU
YOU ARE WELCOME

– AND THE LIKABILITY OF LODGING

The place took possession of them both so rapidly he could only just believe it. Tongue-tangled, he – and Kate, who was equally affected – strove to identify the reasons.

Perhaps most important, there was more going on here than in other places. There was a sense of time being filled, used, taken advantage of. At G2S, at UMKC, it was more a matter of time being divided up for you; if the ordained segments were too short, you got little done, while if they were too long, you got less done than you could have. Not here. And yet the Precipicians knew how to idle.

Paradox.

There were so many people to meet, not in the way one met them when taking on a new job or joining a new class, but by being passed on, as it were, from one to another. From Josh and Lorna (he, power engineer and sculptor; she, one of Precipice's two medical doctors, organist and notary public) to Doc Squibbs (veterinarian and glass-blower) on to Ferdie Squibbs, his son (electronics maintenance and amateur plant genetics), and his girlfriend Patricia Kallikian (computer programing and anything to do with textiles) on again to …

It was giddying. And the most spectacular possible proof of how genuinely economical it was to run on a maximum-utilization basis. Everyone they met seemed to be pursuing at least two occupations, not moonlighting, not scuffling to make ends meet, but because here they had the chance to indulge more than one preference without worrying about the next hike in utilities charges. Accustomed to a routine five percent increase in the cost of electricity, and ten or twelve in any year when a nuclear reactor melted down – because such installations had long ago ceased to be insurable and the cost of failure could only be recouped from the consumer – the strangers were astonished at the cheapness of energy in this self-reliant community.

Wandering about, they discovered how ingeniously the town had been structured, right from the beginning: its main nucleus at Root Mean Square being echoed by subnuclei that acted as a focus for between three and four hundred people, but neither isolated nor inward-looking, and each with some unique attraction designed to draw occasional visitors from other parts of the town. One had a games area, another a swimming pool, another a constantly changing art exhibition, another a children's zoo with scores of tame, cuddly animals, another a view down a vista flanked by unbelievably gorgeous flowering trees ... and so forth. All, Suzy Dellinger admitted cheerfully, 'of malice aforethought' – the founders of the town had tabulated what was known to help a community run pleasantly, then allotted elements of it to suitable sectors of what had then been a settlement of rickety hovels, battered trailer homes and many tents.

For the first year and a half, they were informed, the builders used nothing but scrap. Plus a great deal of imagination, to compensate for a near-total absence of money.

Additionally, the newcomers were immediately involved. Pausing to chat to a big husky man repairing an electrical connector, they were casually requested to help him lever the covering flagstone back into place; on being introduced to one Eustace Fenelli, who ran a popular bar and restaurant, they found themselves carrying a vast pot of minestrone out of the delectably aromatic kitchen – 'since you happen to be going that way!' Strolling toward the main square with Lorna Treves, and passing a house from which a white-faced man emerged at a run, overjoyed to find Lorna because – as he said – he'd just called and heard she wasn't home, they wound up standing by with sterile dressings and a bowlful of blood while she delicately removed a huge splinter of glass from the leg of a screaming child.

'I never found this before,' Kate whispered later. 'This sense that everybody is ready to help everybody else. I'd heard it was possible. But I thought it was obsolete.'

He nodded thoughtfully. 'On top of that, there's a sense that being helped doesn't demean you. That's what I like most.'

Naturally, among the first places they asked to visit was the actual headquarters of Hearing Aid. With a warning that they might not find it particularly impressive, Brad Compton introduced them to the director, Sweetwater. Just Sweetwater. She was a tall, gaunt woman in her sixties, with long-faded traces on her face and arms of what, she commented, had once been elaborate medicine tattoos. She had believed herself to be a reincarnation of a great Shawnee chief, in touch with the spirit of the beyond, and had operated a clairvoyance and prediction business in Oakland.

'But' – with a wry smile – 'not one of my spirits warned me about the quake. I had a son, and ... Oh, it's ancient history. But before I became a medium I'd been a switchboard operator, so I was one of the first people to volunteer to help with what developed into Hearing Aid. You know how it all started? No? Oh! Well, at all the places where the refugees were forced to settle, most of which were a lot less attractive than our own site – though you should have seen it the day we were stopped at gunpoint by the National Guard and told thus far, no further ... Where was I? Oh, yes: of course everybody, once they'd calmed down, wanted to tell their friends and relatives they'd survived. So the Army spliced in some manual sound-only field telephone trucks, and people were allowed one call apiece not to last more than five minutes, or one other try if the first number didn't answer. I saw people go right back to the end of the line time after time, because their second call had failed and they weren't allowed a third immediately.'

As she talked, she was leading Kate and Sandy away from the library – characteristically, the largest single building in Precipice – down a narrow alley they had not traversed.

'It was a terrible time,' Sweetwater went on. 'But I'm not sorry to have lived through it ... Then, of course, as soon as it was known that there was a phone service, people started jamming every circuit in and into California because they hadn't heard from their friends or kinfolk, and kept at it all night and all day regardless of how many pleas were made over the TV to get off the phone so they wouldn't hold up the rescue work. They had to cut some cities out of circuit altogether, I remember. Just withdraw the phone service completely.'

She shook her head sorrowfully.

'In the end they had to rig facilities for incoming calls because people who got an answer instead of a circuit-overload signal tended not to come back and bother you until tomorrow. Like I say, I volunteered to run a board handling incoming traffic. At first I was kind of sharp with people. You know – brisk, brusque, whatever the hell. "You will be notified if your son/daughter/mother/father has survived but you're holding up essential rescue work and how'd you like it if someone dear to you were dying *right now* because you're using this circuit?"

'And then I made this peculiar discovery. A lot of the calls were from people not trying to trace friends and relatives at all. Just – I don't know – wanting contact with the disaster, I guess. As though their last consolation was to know that other people were even worse off. So sometimes, especially at night, I let them talk. They were pretty good about it – just a few minutes' catharsis and that was that. Round about this time the people from Claes came in, and they found the same thing among the refugees. People simply needing to talk. Not just the older folk, who'd lost fine homes and prized possessions, but the youngsters. They were worse. I recall one kid – well, nineteen, twenty, she must have been – who ought to have become a famous sculptor. She was so good, they'd fixed her a one-man show at a San Francisco gallery. And she had to cling to a tree and watch as the earth gobbled up everything she'd got ready, plus her home, her studio, the lot. She never carved another thing; she went insane. And there were others ... They didn't want counseling, they just wanted to tell people what their lives used to be like. The plans they had for an extension to the house; the way they meant to lay out the garden, only the house headed north and the garden went south; the trip around the world they were going to take next year – lives charted on a course the quake destroyed.'

Pausing now before an unremarkable door, she glanced at them.

'Hence – Hearing Aid. Which gave us a common purpose while we reconstructed, and then simply kept on snowballing.'

'Is that what made Precipice such a success compared to the other paid-avoidance towns?' Sandy demanded. 'Offering a service that other people valued instead of just accepting charity and public money?'

Sweetwater nodded. 'Or at any rate one of the things that helped. Common sense in using our few resources was the other. And here's the central.'

She ushered them into a surprisingly small room, where some dozen comfortable chairs were occupied by people wearing headphones. There was another dozen vacant. The place was as hushed as a cathedral; only the faintest buzz of sound escaped the headphones. Eyes turned, heads nodded, but otherwise there was no break in the concentration.

The newcomers' attention was instantly riveted by the expression of dismay on the face of one listener, a pretty black woman in her thirties. Sweetwater advanced on her, looking a question, but she shook her head, shut her eyes, set her teeth.

'A bad one there,' Sweetwater murmured, returning to the visitors. 'But so long as she thinks she can stand it ...'

'Is the job a great strain?'

'Yes.' Sweetwater's tone was like herself: thin and long-drawn-out. 'When someone vents a lifetime of hate on you and then makes sure you hear the hideous guggle as he cuts his carotid with a kitchen knife – yes, it's a strain. Once I had to listen while a crazy woman threw spoonfuls of vitriol at her baby, tied in a feeding chair. She wanted to get back at its father. The poor kid's screams!'

'But was there nothing you could do?' Kate blurted.

'Yes. Listen. That's the promise that we make. We've always kept it. It may not make a lonely hell less hellish, but it makes it a fraction less lonely.'

They pondered that a while. Then Kate inquired, 'Are these the only people on duty?'

'Oh, no. This central is for people who can't stand their tour at home – interruptions from small children mainly. But most of us prefer to work from home. Granted, the traffic's light right now; you should see our load come

Labor Day, the end of the peak vacation season, when people who hoped against hope the summer would improve their lives realize there really will be another winter.'

'How soon do you want to call on us?' Sandy asked.

'No hurry. And it doesn't have to be both of you. I gather Kate can't stay.'

But it was only the following night that she said suddenly, 'I think I will.'

'What?'

'Stay. Or rather, go away and come back as quickly as I can. Depending on a permit to move Bagheera.'

He started. 'Do you really mean it?'

'Oh, yes. You plan to stay, don't you?'

For a while he didn't answer. At last he said, 'Were you eavesdropping?'

'No, it's nothing I've heard you or anybody else say. It – well, it's the way you've acted today. All of a sudden you're confident. I can literally scent it. I think maybe you've found the confidence to trust people.'

His voice shook a little. 'I hope I have. Because if I can't trust them … But I think I can, and I think you're right to say I've finally learned how. Bless you, Kate. It was you who taught me. Wise woman!'

'*Is* this a safe place? The one from which you can't be dragged back to Tarnover?'

'They promised me it would be.'

'Who did?'

'Ted, and Suzy, and Sweetwater. And Brynhilde.'

'What?'

'It was like this …'

They had been invited for dinner by Josh and Lorna. Josh loved to cook; now and then he took over at Fenelli's for the hell of it, feeding fifty people in an evening. Tonight he'd settled for ten, but when the company was sitting around in the garden afterward other people wandered up, by ones and twos, and accepted a glass of wine or a mug of beer and eventually there was a full-sized party numbering at least forty.

For a long time he stood by himself in a dark corner. Then Ted Horovitz and Suzy came toward him, intending – he gathered – to join Sweetwater, who was just arriving on her own. Catching sight of him, Ted said, 'Sandy, you settling in okay?'

It was a moment of decision. He took that decision. He squared his shoulders and stepped from shadow.

'I'd like a word with you. And I guess it ought to be with Brad, too.'

They exchanged glances. Suzy said, 'Brad won't be here – he's listening. But Sweetwater's the first alternate councilman.'

'Fine.'

His palms sweated. his belly was taut, but in his head there was a great cool calm. The four of them found chairs and sat down a little apart from the rest of the party.

'Well, what is it?' Ted rumbled eventually.

Sandy drew a deep breath. He said, 'I realized a few hours ago that I know something about Precipice that you don't.'

They waited.

'Tell me first, though: am I right in thinking Hearing Aid is defended by a tapeworm?'

After a brief hesitation Sweetwater said with a shrug, 'I'd have thought that was self-evident.'

'The Fedcomps are getting set to kill it.'

That provoked a reaction. All three of his listeners jolted forward on their chairs; Ted had been about to light his favorite pipe, and it was instantly forgotten.

'But they can't without—' Suzy began.

'I don't want the details,' Sandy interrupted. 'I'm just assuming that you have the biggest-ever worm loose in the net, and that it automatically sabotages any attempt to monitor a call to the ten nines. If I'd had to tackle the job, back when they first tied the home-phone service into the net, I'd have written the worm as an explosive scrambler, probably about half a million bits long, with a backup virus facility and a last-ditch infinitely replicating tail. It should just about have been possible to hang that sort of tail on a worm by 2005. I don't know whether yours has one or not and it doesn't matter. What does matter is that while I was a systems rash with G2S recently I moused around the net considerably more than my employers required of me, and I ran across something I only today spotted as significant.'

They were hanging on his every word now.

'For about eighteen months they've been routinely copying Class-A Star data from G2S and every other hypercorporation with a maximum-national-advantage rating and lifting the copies clear of the net for storage. I thought maybe they were tired of hypercorp execs pulling the White House Trick and other similar gimmicks, so they needed a standard reference to appeal to. It didn't occur to me that this might be the preliminary stages of a worm-killing job. I never guessed that big a worm was free and running. Now I see the implications, and I guess you do too, hm?'

Very pale, Ted said, 'Too true! That makes nonsense of the virus facility, let alone the simple scrambler aspect. And in fact our worm doesn't have the kind of tail you mentioned. Later, we were vaguely hoping we could add one … but Washington's tolerance of Hearing Aid was wearing thin, and we didn't want to irritate the authorities.'

'They must hate us,' Sweetwater said. 'Really, they must loathe Precipice.'

'They're scared of us, that's what it is,' Suzy corrected. 'But … Oh, I find it hard to believe they'd be willing to clear up the sort of mess our worm could cause. I've always understood it works in two stages: if someone tries to monitor a call to Hearing Aid it scrambles the nearest major nexus, and if they did try to kill it, they'd find over thirty billion bits of data garbled randomly but not know where the damage had been done. It might be years before the returns all came in. We never found out whether that virus facility actually works, but the front end – the scrambler – that works fine, and the BDP once proved it to their cost.'

Sandy nodded. 'But they're prepared to cope with the virus aspect now. Like I said, they've lifted the max-nat-ad stuff out of the net altogether, ready to be slotted in again afterward.'

He leaned back, reaching for his glass.

'We're obliged to you, Sandy,' Sweetwater said after a brief silence. 'I guess we better put on our thinking caps and see what we can—'

He cut her short. 'No, I'll do it. What you need is a worm with a completely different structure. The type they call a replicating phage. And the first thing you must give it to eat is your original worm.'

'A replicating phage?' Suzy repeated. 'I never heard that term before.'

'Not surprising. They're kind of dangerous. Plenty of them have been used in restricted situations. Like, come election time, you disguise one and slip it into the membership list of the opposition party, hoping they don't have duplicate records. But there are very few in the continental net, and the only big one is inactive until called for. In case you're interested, it was devised at a place called Electric Skillet, and its function is to shut the net down and prevent it being exploited by a conquering army. They think the job would be complete in thirty seconds.'

Ted frowned. 'How come you talk about these phages with authority?' he demanded.

'Well …' Sandy hesitated, then took the plunge. 'Well, I've had mine running behind me for over six years, and it's stood me in good stead. I don't see why one shouldn't do the same for Hearing Aid.'

'So what the hell do you use one for?'

Keeping his voice level with immense effort, he told them. They listened. And then Ted did an extraordinary thing.

He whistled shrilly. From where she kept her watch Brynhilde rose and ambled over.

'Is this poker lying?' Ted inquired.

She snuffed at Sandy's crotch – diffidently as though reluctant to take such liberties – shook her head, and went back the way she had come.

'Okay,' Suzy said. 'What exactly will you need, and how long will it take?'

DOGGED

'Out of the question,' said Dr Joel Bosch. 'He must be lying.'

Acutely aware he was sitting in the same office, perhaps even in the same chair, as Nickie Haflinger the day he encountered the late Miranda, Freeman said patiently, 'But our techniques eliminate all possibility of deliberate falsehood.'

'Clearly that cannot be the case.' Bosch's tone was brisk. 'I'm very well acquainted with Lilleberg's work. It's true he produced some spectacular anomalous results. His explanations of them, however, amounted to no more than doubletalk. We know now what processes must be applied to produce that kind of effect, and Lilleberg never even pretended to use them. They simply didn't exist when he retired.'

'There was considerable controversy over the so-called Lilleberg Hypothesis,' Freeman persisted.

'That controversy was long ago resolved!' Bosch snapped. And added with a strained attempt at greater politeness: 'For reasons which I'm afraid a ... a *nonspecialist* like yourself might find difficult to follow. I'm sorry, but there has to be a flaw in your interrogation methods. I suggest you re-evaluate them. Good afternoon.'

Defeated, Freeman rose. Suddenly a muscle in his left cheek had started to go tic-tic-tic.

HIATUS

Outside, the noise of quiet-humming motors as the tribe assembled. Inside, agonized by indecision, she walked back and forth, back and forth, her nails bitten to the quick.

'... after *that*, of course, I couldn't go on living with him. I mean could I? Flaunting around the neighborhood like that, not caring who knew what he was up to ...'

The sound of the motors faded. There was a phone in the corner of the room. She made no move toward it, even now.

'... just sit there! I mean how can you? I mean here I am all alone and it's the third night in a row and last week was the same and in the name of God come, somebody come and put some weight on these empty dusty stairs and ...'

*

435

If he finds out, he'll kill me. I know he will. But once I called them and in a way I guess it saved my sanity. Any rate it got me here without committing suicide. Tonight someone else – and yet I know Jemmy *would* kill me if he guessed.

'… not so much drinking it as lining it, catch? Jee-*sowss* if I found him cleaning his teeth with it I wouldn't be surprised and if they marketed a bourbon-flavor toothpaste he'd be the first customer not that he brushes his teeth too often and the stink of them rotting is …'

At last, fatalistically, she did approach the phone. It took her two tries to punch the number; first time, she lost count partway through. The screen lit.
'Hey!' In a desperate whisper, as though Jemmy could hear her from kilometers away. 'You got to do something, do it quick! See, my son rides with the Blackass tribe and they just started off for a match with—'
A girl's quiet voice interrupted. 'You have contacted Hearing Aid, which exists exclusively to listen. We do not act, intervene or hold conversations. If you wish assistance, apply to one of the regular emergency services.'
The stinking stupid twitches! Well, hell, what do I owe them anyway? Let 'em find out what fools they are. If they won't take help when it's offered …
But the tribes must be nearly there by now. Burning and wrecking and looting and killing. And I remember my brother Archie with his eyeball hanging loose on his cheek and him only nineteen.
One last try. Then let 'em go to hell if they prefer.

'Now you *listen* this time! I'm calling you to *warn* you! My son Jemmy is riding with the Blackass tribe out of Quemadura and they got this match with the Mariachis out of San Feliciano and it's about how many houses they can fire in Precipice and the warlord has a mortar, hear me, a real army mortar and a case of shells!'
And concluding in a tone close to sobs: 'When he finds out Jemmy's just naturally going to beat me to death. But I couldn't let it happen without I warned you!'

SLACK SHIFT INTO HIGH GEAR

'Call the sheriff!'
At his yell everyone else on this undemanding shift in the headquarters of Hearing Aid – including Kate, who like himself was being trained under supervision before being permitted to take calls at home – looked daggers. Someone said, 'Ssh, I'm listening.'

'Two tribes closing on Precipice for a match, and one of them has an army mortar!'

That worked, galvanizing people into action. But a little too late. Kate said, breaking rules and removing her headphones, 'A while back I had to kill a call that said something about a tribal match. I wonder if—'

He had begun to turn and look at her when the first explosion smashed the evening quiet.

While the others were still jumping with alarm he completed the turn and said, 'You killed a call that tried to warn us?'

To which her answer was drowned out by a sound such as had not been heard before in the history of Precipice, which none who heard it wished to hear again: as though instantly they were trapped inside the largest organ in the world, and its player were striking a full diapason just that teeth-gritting fraction off true pitch. Between a bay and a howl, it was the cry of a hundred and fifty giant dogs answering their leader's call.

Arrgh-OOO …!

Only the pups were left on guard, and the bitches nursing young litters. The rest of Natty Bumppo's forces tore into the night, following the scent of fear, for that first howl alone had been enough to throw the attackers in confusion. There were shots, and one more mortar shell was fired, but it fell wide.

Thirty minutes, and the dogs drove in the tribers, weeping, bleeding and disarmed, to have their bites bound up before being dumped in the town's various lockable sheds and cellars for want of an actual jail. Two dogs were shot, one fatally, and another was stabbed but survived, while thirty-seven tribers – not prepared to encounter an enemy of this stamp – were placed under arrest. The oldest of them proved to be eighteen.

All this, however, was too late to save the house at Great Circle Course and Drunkard's Walk.

GRIEVANCE

There were tears glistening on the cheeks of the subject, and the instruments advised returning him to present-time mode. Following their guidance, Freeman waited patiently until the man regained total consciousness.

He said at last, 'It's remarkable that you were so affected by the destruction of a house to which you barely had a chance to grow attached. Moreover, even if the first warning call had been heeded, there would still not have been enough time to forestall the attack, and it was the very first shell which struck your home.'

'You're soulless. As well as heartless!'

Freeman remained silent.

'Uh-h-h …! Sure, sure, I know. Kate was obeying the regulations; she'd got a grasp of them faster than I had. It is standard practice at Hearing Aid never to accept a call that orders the listener to *do* something, because services exist for that purpose. And even if the woman who called had managed to get the point across about a warning in the first couple of seconds, the reaction would still have been the same. They tell you to try and deevee any call that begins with a hysterical warning, because nine times out of ten it's some religious nut threatening to visit the wrath of God on us. I mean Precipice. And I guess I was aware of that at the time. I know equally well it was pointless to scream and rant at her and I went ahead and did it anyhow, standing there by the burnt-out wreck of the house with the smoke stinging in my eyes and the stench in my nose and a dozen people trying to reason with me. Didn't work. I lost my temper on the grand scale. I think what I did was let go all the potential for rage I'd been bottling up since babyhood. In the end …' He had to swallow and resume.

'I did something I probably last did when I was ten. I hit somebody.'

'Predictably, it was Kate.'

'Yes, of course. And …' He started to laugh, incongruously because tears were still bright on his cheeks. 'And I found myself a second later sprawling in the dirt, with Brynhilde's paw on my chest and that great-toothed jaw looming close and she was shaking her head and – I swear – going "Tsk-tsk, naughty boy!" I could wish she had been a trifle quicker. Because I've never seen Kate since.'

The laughter failed. Misery overspread his face.

'Ah. Losing the house, then, affected you so deeply because it symbolized your relationship with Kate.'

'You don't understand a fraction of the truth. Not a millionth of it. The whole scene, the whole framework, was *composed* of loss. Not just the house, even though it was the first place I'd been to where I felt I could grasp all the overtones of the word "home" – not just Kate, even though with her I'd also started to comprehend for the first time what one can imply by the word "love". No, there was more on top of that, something far closer to me. Loss of the control which had enabled me to change identities at will. That blew away on the wind the moment I realized I'd struck the last person in the world I could want to hurt.'

'Are you certain she would have kept that casual promise about returning from KC? Obtaining a permit to transport her pet mountain lion would have been incredibly difficult. What grounds did you have for believing that she was sincere?'

'Among other things, the fact that she had kept a promise made to that mountain lion. She's not the sort to forget any promise. And by then I'd figured out why else she'd kept on enrolling for course after unrelated course at the same university. Basically it was to provide her with a sense of pattern. She wanted her world-picture to include a little of everything, viewed from the same spot with the same perspective. She'd have been prepared to continue for another decade if necessary.'

'But she met you, and living with you was an education in itself. I see. Well, I can accept the idea. Ten years at Tarnover, at three million per, should indeed have equipped you with data you could pass on.'

'I suspect your sense of humor is limited to irony. Do you ever laugh at a joke?'

'Seldom. I've heard virtually all of them before.'

'No doubt among the components of human personality you're trying to analyze humor is on the list right next to grief.'

'Directly afterward. H follows G.'

There was a pause.

'You know, this is the first time I've not been sure whether you're bleating me.'

'Work it out for yourself.' Freeman rose and stretched. 'It will occupy your mind until our next session.'

STRIKE ONE

After hitting Kate …

That his world had been repainted in shades of bitterness was no defense. Some of these his new neighbors – his new friends – were old enough to have seen not one house but a whole city fall in ruin.

Anyhow, what apology could he offer in a context where even dogs could distinguish force from violence? The tribers who thought it amusing to lob mortar shells at random into a peaceful community had been rounded up. Some were tooth-marked. But the bites had been precisely controlled. That arm had wielded a gun or knife; therefore those fingers had been obliged to open and let the weapon fall. That pair of legs had tried to carry the owner away; therefore that ankle had been nipped just hard enough to make him stumble. All for good reason.

His reason for hitting Kate was not good. They told him why, in quiet patient tones. Deaf to their arguments, he hurled back false justification mixed with insult, until at last they glanced at one another, shrugged and left him.

It was not cold, that night he spent sitting on a stump and staring at the shell of the house. But in his heart there was an arctic chill of such indescribable shame as he had not felt since he became an adult.

In the end he simply walked away, not caring where.

And came many hours later to the place which had vomited over Precipice the Blackass tribe. It was sweaty dust from all-day walking which made his shoes loathsome to his feet, but it seemed to him like the detritus of human cruelty: the materialized version of bloodlust, its ectoplasm.

'I don't know who I am,' he said to an incurious passerby as he entered Quemadura.

'I don't know who the hell you are either,' the stranger snapped, pushing past.

He pondered that.

IGNORANTIA NIHIL EXCUSAT

Ted Horovitz made necessary adjustments to the form-letter program, tapped the print key, and read the result as it emerged from the machine. This, thank goodness, was the last of the thirty-seven.

'Dear Mrs Young, your son Jabez was arrested here last night while in possession of four deadly weapons of which one, a pistol, had been used within the previous few minutes. The hearing has been set for 10:10 tomorrow. You may wish to employ counsel, in which case the enclosed summary of evidence should be furnished to him or her; otherwise you may rest assured that Jabez will be represented by a competent lawyer appointed by the court. He has declared himself unaware of the fact that under our judicial code conviction for this crime entails a mandatory sentence of not less than one year's supervised rehabilitation during which period the convict is forbidden to leave the town limits. (There is no maximum length for such a sentence.) Please note that one of the oldest of all legal principles states: "Ignorance of the law excuses nothing." In other words neither a defense nor an appeal may be founded on the plea, "I didn't know." Yours, &c.'

Turning hopefully to Brad Compton, who among his various other roles acted as their chief legal counselor, he said, 'So that's all until the court assembles, right?'

'Far as I'm concerned,' Brad grunted. 'But don't relax too soon. I was talking to Sweetwater this morning, and it seems she's found something you have to—'

'Ted!' A shrill cry from outside.

'I could half believe that woman's telepathic,' Ted sighed, tapping out his pipe prior to refilling it. 'Yes, Sweetwater, come right in!'

She entered, carrying a folded stack of computer printouts, which she dumped on a table at Ted's side. Dropping into a chair, she slapped the pile of paper with her open palm.

'I knew it. I *knew* what Sandy told us the other night at Josh and Lorna's rang a bell in my memory. A long way back – over eleven years – but it was the kind of call you get once in a lifetime. Once I started digging, I got correlation after correlation. Take a look.'

Ted, frowning, complied; Brad came around behind his chair to read over his shoulder.

There was a long silence, but for the rustle of the concertinaed sheets.

At last Ted said, not looking up, 'Any news of him?'

Sweetwater shook her head. 'Nor Kate either.'

'Kate left town,' Brad said. 'Took the railcar about seven thirty. But nobody knows what's become of Sandy.'

'All of us, though,' Ted muttered, 'know what's apt to become of him … don't we?'

They both nodded.

'Better call Suzy,' Ted said, leaning back with a sigh. 'I got a councilman's motion to submit.'

'Making Sandy a freeman of Precipice?' Sweetwater suggested. 'Making our defenses his defenses?'

'Mm-hm.'

'Well, naturally you have my vote. But …'

'But what?'

'Have you forgotten? We don't know who he is. He told us what. He didn't think to tell us who.'

Ted's jaw dropped. 'His code?' he said after a pause.

'I checked immediately. No such. It's been deleted. And doubtless his protective phage went with it.'

'That makes the job more difficult,' Brad said. 'I still think it ought to be done. And when she reads this information you've uncovered, I'm certain Suzy will agree.'

COLLAPSE OF STOUT PARTY

'Interesting. Very interesting. This might save a lot of trouble. Say, Perce!'

'Yes?'

'Know that hole-in-corner place Precipice CA? Looks like their sheriff went a step too far.'

'Oh, Gerry. Oh, *Gerry*. If you weren't new around here I guess you'd realize nothing at Precipice can go too far. The pokers from Claes who wrote the deal they have with the government were the smartest con men that ever pulled wool over the eyes of a Washington sheep. But for once I'll bite. It would be great to undermine them. What you got?'

'Well, they arrested these here tribers, and—'

'And?'

'Hell, look at the sentences they handed down!'

'Not to leave town for one year minimum, to accept escort by a dog apiece ... So?'

'Goddammit, escort by a dog?'

'They got kind of weird dogs out there. You didn't check, did you?'

'Well, I guess I—'

'Save it, save it. You didn't check. So, not having checked, what did you expect to get out of this?'

'I though maybe – uh – an injunction? Grounds of cruel-and-unusual? Or even kidnaping. I mean one of the tribers is only thirteen.'

'There are four states where they routinely agree applications to be declared competent if the applicant is past his or her thirteenth birthday. California's one. It might be educational for you to find out what the others are. As to cruel-and-unusual, you should also know there's one city where you can still legally be burned alive provided they don't pick a Sunday. They didn't do it much lately, but it's on the books, not repealed. Ask any computer. Oh, get back to work, will you? While you've been gabbing they probably sneaked a brand-new tapeworm past you.'

Pause.

'Perce!'

'What is it this time?'

'Remember what you said about a tapeworm?'

'Oh my God. That was a joke. You mean they spat in our eye again?'

'See for yourself, It's kind of – uh – fierce, isn't it?'

'Fierce is only half of it. Well, I guess it better claim its first victim. You found it. You go tell Mr Hartz to abandon the attack on Hearing Aid.'

'What?'

'You heard me. Carry the good news from Y to X! Tamper with this thing, and – and my God! The data-net would be in chaos in one minute flat or maybe Sooner! *Hurry!*'

BIG TOP

Belly sour with hunger, throat dry with dust, he wandered the darkening streets of Quemadura, scarcely aware that he was part of a trend. There were people and vehicles converging. He went with the crowd. Drained, passive, he ignored reality until suddenly he was spoken to.

'Damn it, shivver, you deaf and dumb or something?'

What?

He emerged from his chrysalis of overload, blinking, and discovered where he was. He'd seen this place before. But only on three-vee, never in reality. Above all he had never smelt it. The air was foul with the stench of frightened animals and eager people.

Many signs, hurtfully bright, flashed on and off to confirm his discovery. Some said CIRCUS BOCCONI: others stated more discreetly that a Roman-style show would start in 11 minutes. The 11 changed to 10 as he watched.

'What kinda seat you want?' rapped the same grumpy voice. 'Ten, twenty, thirty?'

'Uh ...'

He fumbled in his pocket, finding some bills. As part of the ambience, tickets for this show were issued by a live human being, a scar-faced man missing fingers from his right hand. On seeing cash he scowled; however, the machine at the side of his booth decided it was genuine and parted with a ten-dollar ticket.

Wondering what he was doing here, he followed signs saying $10, $10, $10. Shortly he was in a hall: maybe a converted aircraft hangar. There were bleachers and boxes surrounding an arena and a pit. Machines were hanging up phony-looking decor, banners with misspelled Latin slogans, plastic fasces bundled around dull plastic axes.

Making his way with mechanical politeness to a vacant seat in a high row with a poor view, he shamelessly listened to what the earlier arrivals, the keen 'fishes, were saying.

'Wasting those 'gators on kids, *hell*! I mean I hate my kids as much as any- body, but if you can get real live 'gators – well, *hell*!'

'Hope they got some whites on the menu. Sickan-tired of these here blacks, allatime wanna make like grandpa, fight a lion singlehanded and clutched but clutched on *the* heaviest dope!'

'Course it's all faked, like they got radio implants in the animals' brains so they don't get to really hurt anybody 'cause of the insurance being so stiff and—'

A hugely amplified voice rang out. 'Five minutes! In just five short minutes the great spectacle begins! Absolutely and positively no one will be admitted after the start of the show! Remember only Circus Bocconi goes out live live *live* in real time up and down the whole West Coast! And we record as well, retransmit to the unlucky portions of the continent!'

Suddenly he was vaguely frightened, and cast around for a chance to leave again. But the customers were coming thick and fast now, and he was unwilling to push against the flow. Besides, there was a camera coasting his way. It rode a jointed metal arm, like a mantis's foreleg, dangling from a miniature electric trolley on a rail under the roof. Its dual eye, faceted, seemed to be focusing on him. He was even more reluctant to attract attention by leaving than he was to stay and watch the show.

He folded his arms close around his body as though to stop himself from shivering.

– It would only be an hour, he consoled himself.

The introductory acts he was more or less able to disregard though some nausea gathered in a bubble at the base of his gullet during the second item: imported from Iraq, one genuine snake-eater, an ugly man with a bulging forehead hinting at hydrocephalic idiocy who calmly offered his tongue to a snake, let it strike, then drew in his tongue again, bit off its head, chewed and swallowed, then rose shyly grinning to acknowledge the audience's howls of applause.

Then came a stylized match between gladiators, a nod to the ostensible 'Roman' format of the show, which concluded with the retiarius bleeding from a leg wound and the gladiator proper – the man with the sword and shield – strutting around the arena prouder than a turkeycock, having done nothing to speak of.

Dull resentment burgeoned in his mind.

It's disgusting. Butchered to make a Roman holiday. A cheat from start to finish. Filthy. Horrible. This is where parents learn to raise the kids who get their kicks from tribaling a stranger's home. This is where they get taught you should remember how you killed your mother. Cut off your father's balls. Ate the baby to stop mom and dad loving it more than you. Sick. All sick. Crazy sick.

At Tarnover there had been a kind of subcult for circus. Something to do with channeling aggression into socially acceptable paths. The memory was a dim echo. There was a dreadful confusion inside his head. He was hungry and thirsty and above all miserable.

'And now a short break so our sponsors' messages can reach the world,' boomed the master of ceremonies over the monstrously loud PA. 'Time for me to let you know about a unique feature of our Roman shows. Al Jackson, who's our champion gladiator, that you saw a minute back ...'

Pause for a ripple of renewed clapping and shouting.

'Yea-hey! Tough as they come, with family following in his footsteps – y'know his son is warlord of the Blackass tribe?'

Pause. This time not filled. As though the speaker had been waiting for a scream and yell from the tribers, who weren't present.

But he covered the hiatus expertly.

'Al issues a real-time challenge on all these shows – yes, literally a challenge in real time, no fixing, no prearrangement. Want to try your skill against him, take over the net and trident for the final slot? You can, any of you! Just stand up and holler how!'

Without intending, he was on his feet.

'*He* raised the warlord of the Blackass tribe?'

He heard his own voice as though it were coming from light-years' distance.

'Yeah, *man*! A son to be proud of, young Bud Jackson!'

'Then I'm going to take Al to little tiny pieces.' He was leaving his seat, still listening to himself shout at the top of his lungs. 'I'm going to make him weep and beg and plead for mercy. I'm going to teach him all the things his son taught me, and I am going to make him howl, and blubber, and plead and moan. And it's going to go on for a lot longer than this show.'

There was a rattle of applause, and the audience sat up and looked eager. Someone patted him on the shoulder as he passed and wished him luck.

DEFINITION OF TERMS

'A classic instance of the death wish.'

'Garbage. I had no least intention of being dead. I'd watched that fat slob. I knew I could dismantle him even though I was weak and excessively angry. Didn't I prove it? He was seven days in the hospital, you know, and he'll never walk straight again.'

'Agreed. But on the other hand making yourself conspicuous before a three-vee audience …?'

'Yes. Yes, there was that.'

THE MEDIUM IS THE MESS-UP

Traditionally one had defaced or scrawled on posters and billboards, or sometimes – mainly in rural areas – shot at them because the eyes or nipples of a model formed convenient targets.

Later, when a common gadget around the house was a set of transparent screens (like those later used for the electronic version of fencing) to place over the TV set for mock-tennis and similar games, strangely enough the viewers' ratings for commercials went up. Instead of changing channels when advertising began, people took to switching in search of more of the same.

To the content of which they were paying no attention. What they wanted was to memorize the next movement of the actors and actresses and deform their gestures in hilarious fashion with a magnetic pencil. One had to know the timing of the commercials pretty well to become good at the game; some of the images lasted only half a second.

With horror the advertisers and network officials discovered that in nine cases out of ten the most dedicated watchers could not recall what product was being promoted. For them, it wasn't 'that Coke ad' or 'that plug for Drāno' – it was 'the one where you can make her swipe him in the chops'.

Saturation point, and the inception of diminishing returns, was generally dated to the early eighties, when the urban citizen of North America was for the first time hit with an average of over a thousand advertisements *per diem*.

They went right on advertising things, of course. It had become a habit.

SWORD, MASK AND NET

Chuckling, Shad Fluckner laid aside his magnetic pencil. The commercial break was over and the circus program was due to resume. Employees of Anti-Trauma Inc. were more than just encouraged, they were virtually compelled, to watch the broadcasts from Circus Bocconi in Quemadura. Sponsoring circus was one of the best ways the corporation had found to attract new clients. Precisely those parents who spent most time indulging violence on the vicarious level were those most afraid of what would happen if their children's aggression were to be turned on them. In fact, the more circus the parents watched, the sooner they were inclined to sign the kids up for a course of treatment. The relationship could be shown to be linear plus or minus fourteen percent.

It was no sweat for him. He'd always enjoyed circus anyhow. But if they knew, at Anti-Trauma HQ, what one of their employees had figured out to do to their latest commercial, feathers would well and truly fly. Ho-ho! It was a shame he couldn't share his discovery with anyone; his colleagues would interpret it as disloyal except for those who'd decided it was time to move to another job, and … well, he had the same idea in mind himself, and might reach the decision before the lifetime of the commercial expired. Meanwhile it was great fun to fool with.

Still grinning, he composed himself to watch the final segment of the show, the bit where Al Jackson allegedly issued an open challenge to members of the audience. Rigged for sure, this deal, but occasionally …

Hey.

Not so heavily rigged, this one. Not unless they decided to surple Al and—Goddamn, he's screaming! He really is screaming! This is great stuff for once. This is really very sick indeed. This is muchissimo. Hmm … yes!

Eyes bulbing, he leaned closer to the screen. No fake, that blood. Nor the howls of agony, either! Say, who could this poker be who was making mince-meat of Bocconi's star turn –?

'But it's Lazarus,' he said suddenly to the air. 'Beard or no beard, I'd know that shivver anywhere. And he gave me the slip before and this time – oh, *this* time …!'

NEXT IN LINE

'And once he was recognized on three-vee it was only a matter of time,' Hartz said, leaning back behind his desk. It was captioned *Deputy Director*. Thumbing one of many switches, he shut off the rolling replay of the Haflinger tapes.

'Yes, sir,' Freeman said. 'And the FBI was very quick to corner him.'

'Quicker than you to drain him,' Hartz said, and gave a sleepy smile. In the context of this office, his home base, he was a different person from the visitor who had called on Freeman at Tarnover. Perhaps that was why he had declined an invitation to return.

'I beg your pardon,' Freeman said stiffly. 'My brief was to extract all possible data from him. That couldn't be done quickly. Nonetheless, to within a margin of about half a percent, I've achieved it.'

'That may be good enough for you. It's not enough for us.'

'What?'

'I believe I made myself clear. After your long-drawn-out interrogation of this subject we still do not know what we most want to know.'

'That being …?' Freeman's voice grew frostier by the moment.

'The answer, I submit, is self-evident. An intolerable situation exists concerning Precipice vis-à-vis the government. A small dissident group has succeeded in establishing a posture of deterrence in principle no different from that adopted by a crazy terrorist threatening to throw the switch on a nuke. We were ready to eliminate this anomaly. Only Haflinger – Locke – Lazarus – whatever he was calling himself at the time – intervened and sent us back to square one. You have spent weeks interrogating him. In all the mounds of data you've accumulated, in all the kilometers of tape you've totaled, there is no slightest clue to what we want to know.'

'How to deevee the phage he wrote to protect Hearing Aid?'

'Ah, brilliant! You worked it out!' Hartz's tone was laden with excess irony. 'It is, as I said, intolerable that one small community should interfere with the government's right to monitor subversion, disaffection and treason. We have to know how to discontinue that tapeworm!'

'You're crying for the moon,' Freeman said after a pause. 'Haflinger doesn't know how to do that himself. I'd stake my reputation on it.'

'And that's your final word?'

'Yes.'

'I see. Hmm. Regrettable!' Hartz tipped his chair back as far as it would go, twisted it through a few degrees, gazed with concentration into the far corner of the room. 'Well, what about the other contacts he had? What about Kate Lilleberg, for instance? What have you found out about her recent actions?'

'She would appear to have reverted to her former plans,' Freeman sighed. 'She's back in KC, she's filed no application to move her pet mountain lion, and in fact I can think of only one positive decision she has made since her return.'

'That being, I gather, to alter one of her majors for the coming academic year. She now plans to take data processing, doesn't she?'

'Ah ... Yes, I believe she does.'

'A strange coincidence. A very weird coincidence indeed. Don't you think?'

'A connection is possible – in fact it's likely. Calling it coincidence ... no.'

'Good. I'm glad that for once you and I agree on something.' Hartz returned his chair to the upright position and leaned intently toward Freeman. 'Tell me, then: have you formed any opinion concerning the Lilleberg girl? I appreciate you never met her. But you've met people intimately involved with her, such as her mother, her lover and sundry friends.'

'Apparently a person with considerable common sense,' Freeman said after a pause for reflection. 'I can't deny that I'm impressed with what she did to help Haflinger. It's no small achievement to elude ...'

His words faded as though he had suddenly begun to hear what he was saying ahead of time.

'Go on,' Hartz purred.

'I was going to add: such an intensive hunt as has been kept up over six years now. Since Haflinger absconded, I mean. She seemed to – well, to grasp the scale of it at once.'

'And didn't disbelieve what he told her, either. Did she?'

'She didn't behave as though she did. No.'

'Hmm ... Well, I'm pleased to inform you that you'll have adequate opportunity to confirm or deevee your opinion.' Hartz hit another switch; the wall screen in the office lit, showing a vastly enlarged face.

'Computer evaluation here at BDP suggests that your no doubt sophisticated techniques might benefit from reinforcement by – what to call it? – an alternative approach, let's say, which may strike you as old-fashioned yet which has something to be said in its favor. Because we intend to destroy that tapeworm Haflinger gave to Hearing Aid!' With a sudden glare. 'And before the end of this year, what's more! I have the president's personal instructions to that effect.'

Freeman's mouth worked. No sound emerged. He was gazing at the screen.

'Despite any impression I may have given to the contrary,' Hartz continued, 'we here in Washington are most cognizant of your skill, patience and thoroughness. Certainly we don't know anyone who could have done a better job. That's exactly why we're sending you a new subject.'

'But ...' Freeman raised a shaky finger to point. 'But that's Kate Lilleberg!'

'Yes indeed. That is Kate Lilleberg. And we expect her presence at Tarnover to afford the extra leverage you need in order to pry the last most precious secret out of Nickie Haflinger. Now you must excuse me. I can't spare you any more of my time. Good afternoon.'

BOOK 3

Splicing the Brain Race

MAN PROPOSES

'Now the way *I* see it—'

'Who the hell do you think you are?'

THE LONG AND THE SHORT OF IT

This is a basic place, a farm. Listen to it.

Land. House. Barn. Sun. Rain. Snow. Field. Fence. Pond. Corn. Wheat. Hay. Plow. Sow. Reap. Horse. Pig. Cow.

This is an abstract place, a concert hall. Listen to it.

Conductor. Orchestra. Audience. Overture. Concerto. Symphony. Podium. Harmony. Instrument. Oratorio. Variations. Arrangement. Violin. Clarinet. Piccolo. Tympani. Pianoforte. Auditorium.

But consider also:

Harp. Horn. Drum. Song. Pipe.

And similarly:

Alfalfa. Rutabaga. Fertilizer. Combine harvester.

Assign the following (no credit) to one or other of the categories implied by the foregoing parameters:*

Bit. Record. Memory. Switch. Program. Transistor. Tape. Data. Electricity. On-line. Down-time. Printout. Read. Process. Cybernetics.

A CASE OF ARRESTED DEVELOPMENT

For the first time since the arrival on her threshold of the – late? – Sandy Locke, Kate's annunciator sounded when she wasn't expecting anybody.

These days, you simply did *not* go call on somebody without advance warning. It wasn't worth it. For one thing, people were spending less time in their homes, statistics said, than ever before in history – despite the arrival of the world in full color and mock solidity thanks to three-vee in the corner

---

* Do not on any account give the same answer tomorrow as you give today.

of the living-room. And for another, perhaps more important, calling without notice was liable to get you webbed in a net of unbreakable plastic, possibly even gassed, at any home above the poverty level.

So you used the veephone first.

In the middle of her largest room, whose walls she was redecorating with enormous photo-enlargements of microscopic circuit elements – eventually, touched in with metallic paint, they would be quite an efficient private computer – Kate stopped dead and pondered.

Well, no harm in looking at whoever it is.

Sighing, she switched on the camera and found herself staring at a man she didn't know: young, fair, untidy, in casual clothes.

'You're Kate!' he said brightly.

'And you are –?'

'Name of Sid. Sid Fessier. Been spending summer vac in the paid-avoidance zones. Ran into a poker name of Sandy, said to greet you when I bounced off KC, and when it turned out I'd picked a hotel just one block distant … Guess I should have called ahead, but hell – one block on a fine day like today!'

'Well, great. Come on up.'

He whistled as he climbed the stairs: a reel or jig. And when she opened the door, hit her with a webber that tied her into an instant package.

'Bagheera!' she screamed, falling sidelong as the strands of plastic tangled around her legs.

Pop.

Still gathering himself for a pounce which could have carried him the full length of the hallway, straight to the intruder's head, the mountain lion flinched, moaned, made as though to scrabble at an irritation on his chest – and collapsed.

He was good, this man, and very fast. Even as he returned the gun to his pocket he was slapping a patch of adhesive plastic over Kate's mouth to silence her.

'Anesthetic dart,' he murmured. 'No need to worry about him. He'll be taken care of. Right as rain in two or three hours. But I had to give him the maximum dose, you know. Not my favorite pastime, messing with a beast like him.'

Having eased the door softly shut, he now produced a communicator and spoke to it. 'Okay, come and pick her up. But best be quiet. This looks like a neighborhood where folk still take an interest in other people's business.'

'You got the lion?'

'Think I'd be talking to you if I hadn't?'

Tucking the communicator away again, he added over her furious futile grunts and snorts, 'Save your breath, slittie. I don't know what you've done, but it's serious. I have a warrant for your arrest and detention without bail signed by the deputy director of the Federal Bureau of Data Processing, who's kind of high on the Washington totem pole. Anyhow, I'm not the shivver to argue with. Just an errand boy, me.'

DIFFERENTIATED

Things had changed. Not merely on the surface, although his situation was radically altered. Instead of being switched on and off by drugs and cortical stimulation, he had been allowed to sleep naturally last night: moreover, in a real room, hotel-stark but comfortable and well equipped, with actual windows through which he had been able to confirm that he really was at Tarnover. During his interrogation he had been kept in a sort of compartment, a man-sized pigeonhole, where machines maintained his muscle tone for want of walking.

Aside from that, though, something subtler, more significant had occurred. What?

The door of his room opened with a click of locks. A man appeared – commonplace, clad in white, armed. He had expected that if he was taken anywhere away from the room it would be under escort. Rising, he obeyed an order to go into the corridor and turn left.

It was a long walk, and there were many turns. Also there was a descending flight of steps, thirteen of them. Eventually there was a lost corner. Rounding it, he found himself in a passage of which one side was composed of one-way armor glass.

Gazing through it into a dimly lighted room beyond was Freeman.

He accorded the newcomer a nod, then tapped the glass with one soft fingertip.

Beyond, a very thin girl lay naked and unconscious on a padded table while a nurse shaved her head down to the scalp.

There was a long silence. Then, at last:

'Mm-hm. I expected that. But, knowing you as well as I do, I'm prepared to believe it wasn't your idea.'

After which there was another silence, broken this time by Freeman. When he spoke, his voice was full of weariness.

'Take him back to his quarters. Let him think it over for a while.'

YES, MR KELLY! WAS IT ABOUT ANYTHING?

'It should never be forgotten that during all the time we were studying bats, bats had a unique opportunity to study us.'

I AM

What he had said to Freeman was quite true. Ever since, with the conclusion of the intensive phase of his interrogation, he had been able to reason clearly again, he had been expecting to be told that Kate also had been dragged here for 'examination'.

Not that that made any difference, any more than reciting 'nine-eighty-one-see-em-second-squared' makes one better able to survive a fall off a cliff.

He sat in the room assigned to him, which doubtless was monitored the clock around, as though on a stage before a vast audience alert to criticize any departure from the role he was meant to be playing.

The one factor operating in his favor was this: that after years of playing roles, he was finally playing himself instead.

All the data they have, he told himself, relate to others than myself: Reverend Lazarus, Sandy Locke – yes, even Nickie Haflinger. Whoever I am now, and I'm none too sure of my identity at this stage, I definitely am not Nickie Haflinger!

He started to list the ways in which he wasn't the person he was named after, and found the latest was the most important.

I can love.

A chill tremored down his spine as he considered that. There had been little love given or received in Nickie's early life. His father? Resentful of the burden his son imposed, intolerant of the demands of parenthood. His mother? Tried, for a while at least, but lacked an honest basis of affection to support her; hence her collapse into alcoholic psychosis. His temporary surrogate parents? To them one rent-a-boy was like another, so many dollars per week high by so many problems wide.

His friends during his teens, while he was here at Tarnover?

But love was not part of the curriculum. It was parts. It was split up. It was 'intense emotional involvement' and 'excessive interdependence' and 'typical inflated adolescent libido' …

Now, on the other hand, when this new strange person he was evolving into thought of Kate, he clenched his fists and gritted his teeth and shut his eyes and dissolved into pure raw hate, unresisting.

All his life he had had to control his deep reactions: as a pre-teen kid, because if you didn't you could be the one sanded on the way home tonight; as a teener, because every moment of the day and night students here were liable for reassessment to make sure they were worthy of staying, and the first five years he had wanted to stay more than anything else in the world and the second five he had wanted to use Tarnover instead of being used by it;

thereafter because the data-net now ramified into so many areas of private life that his slightest error could bring hunters closing in for the kill.

It followed that yielding to emotion, whether positive or negative, had always seemed dangerous. It was bad to let himself like another person too much; if a child, he or she would run tomorrow with a different gang, mercurial, and whoop and holler after you to your hour of blood and tears; if an adult, he or she would depart for some other job and leave behind merely a memory and a memento. Equally it was bad to let yourself fear or detest somebody too much; it led into areas where you couldn't predict your own behavior or that of others. 'Here be tygers!'

But the capacity for emotion was in his mind, though he'd been unaware of the fact. He recalled with a trace of irony how he had looked over the detensing machine in G2S's transient accommodation block and pitied those with the ability to form strong attachments:

I was pitying myself, I guess. Well, pity was the most that I deserved.

Now he was being forced to recognize just how intensely he could feel, and there was a sound logical reason for encouraging the process.

The data Freeman and those behind him had in store were derived from a coldly calculating person – call him Mister X Minus E. Substitute throughout Mister X Plus E.

And what you're going to wind up with, you sons of bitches, is what you fear above all. A unique solution in irrationals!

A little rain started to smear the west-facing window of his room. He rose and walked over to stare out at the clouds, tinted with red because the sun was setting and the rain was approaching from the east.

I am in approximately the position of someone attempting to filch enough plutonium from a nuclear research plant to build a bomb. I must sneak the stuff out without either causing a noticeable stock-loss, or triggering the perimeter detectors, or incurring radiation burns. Quite a three-pipe problem, Watson. It may take as long as a week, or even ten days.

MIRROR, MIRROR

You are in circular orbit around a planet. You are being overtaken by another object, also in circular orbit, moving several km./sec. faster. You accelerate to try and catch up.

See you later, accelerator.

Much later.

HARTZ AND FLAWS

In the interrogation room the three-vee screen had been replaced by a stretch mirror. Not wanting to seem to look too hard or long at the naked body of the girl stretched out in the steel chair, Hartz glanced at his reflection instead. Catching sight of a smear of perspiration on his forehead, he pulled out a large handkerchief, and inadvertently dislodged his visitor's authorization card, which he was not quick enough to catch before it fluttered to the floor.

Freeman courteously picked it up and handed it back.

Muttering thanks, Hartz replaced it, harrumphed loudly into his handkerchief and then said, 'Your reports have been meager, to say the least.'

'I would naturally have informed you at once had there been any significant developments.'

'Oh, there have been! That's why I'm here!' Hartz snapped, and decided there was no point after all in pretending not to look at the girl. Scrawny as she was, bald, childishly bare-bodied, she scarcely resembled a human being: more, a laboratory animal, some oversize strain of mutant hairless rat.

'What developments?' Freeman stiffened almost imperceptibly, and the tone of his voice hinted at harshness, but only hinted.

'You don't know, hm?' was Hartz's scathing retort. 'But you met her mother, so you should! At least you must realize how much weight she swings thanks to her post with G2S!'

'Her mother,' Freeman returned with strained politeness, 'has been extensively profiled. There's no untoward emotional involvement between the pair of them.'

'Her profile,' Hartz repeated heavily. 'I see. What can you tell me about her from her profile?'

'That Ina Grierson is not unhappy at her daughter's departure from KC. This releases her to accept the kind of post she has been looking for elsewhere.'

'My God. Haven't you gone beyond this profile thing? Didn't you check out the real world lately?'

'I've done precisely as I was instructed!' Freeman flared. 'And what is more, instructed by you!'

'I expect people to use their wits when I give them orders, not leave a continental mess for others to clear away!'

For a long moment the men locked eyes. At last Freeman said placatingly, 'What appears to be the trouble?'

'Appears? Oh, not appears. This is only too real.' Hartz mopped his face again. 'This girl has been here a week now—'

'Five days.'

'It's a full week since her arrest. Don't interrupt.' Hartz thrust his handkerchief back in his pocket. 'If we didn't have a strong ex-Tarnover faction to vote our way on the UMKC board of administration, we'd— Oh, hell, I shouldn't have to tell you this. You should know it already.'

'If there was something you wanted me to know, you could perhaps have taken steps to pipe the data to me,' Freeman said in a tight voice. 'Since you didn't, tell me now.'

Hartz's face reddened, but he bit back the angry reply which clearly had been trembling on his lips. Achieving calm with an effort, he said, 'Outside the P-A zones, hardly anybody goes twenty-four hours without using his or her code for credit purposes. Consequently the location of anybody on the continent can be determined near as dammit at any time. Kate Lilleberg is an adult, sure, but she's also *in statu pupillari* and has never filed a don't-talk order in respect of her mother, her only near relative. So ever since she was whipped out of KC there have been fifty or sixty people with an interest in tracing her, most of whom are on the faculty at UMKC but one of whom, the most troublesome, is a head-of-dept at G2S. How much more do I have to spell out before you realize what a hornets' nest you've wished on me?'

'I've done what?' Freeman said slowly.

'Didn't it cross your mind that if a week passed without her using her code, that would arouse suspicions?'

'What didn't cross my mind,' Freeman retorted, 'was that you'd expect me to make myself responsible for all the fiddling details! Since you insist, I'll take time out and construct some convincing fiction: have her code reported in, for example, from a town in the P-A zones where it can easily take a week for a credit entry to reach the net. The rest, however, I'm afraid I must leave to—'

'Forget it. We already tried that. The moment we realized you hadn't seen to it. Have you forgotten the pose Haflinger adopted at G2S?'

Freeman looked blank. 'How is that relevant?'

'Heaven send me patience. He took a job as a systems rash, didn't he? That position gave him damned near as much access to the net as I can get, cheating on G2S's max-nat-ad rating. In fact he moused around so much it started to interfere with his regular work, so he wrote a program into the *G2S* computers to take care of the routine stuff by itself. You didn't stress that in your interrogation report, did you?'

Freeman's mouth worked. No sound emerged.

'And the program is still functional,' Hartz blasted, 'and Ina Grierson has got to it! And worst of all, it's so simple she knows damned well the entries we filed behind her daughter's code are faked!'

'What? How?'

'How the hell do you think? What did Haflinger want to find out, using stolen G2S codes? Whether his own 4GH was still valid, *right*? And how could he have done that without being able to strip away an ex-post-facto cover label from a federal-authorized implant? Data concerning 4GH codes are not meant to be accessible to the public. They're routinely disguised, aren't they? Well, what Haflinger did was to peel them naked automatically, and in a way our top experts never thought of!'

Clenching his fists, he concluded, 'Now maybe you see what a fix you dumped me in!'

His face like a stone image, Freeman said, 'Oh, I think the credit belongs to Haflinger, not me. And I'm sure he'll be delighted with this news.'

'What the hell do you mean?'

'Among the other data you neglected to supply to me was the fact that you came here to make wild accusations. On the reasonable assumption that you only intended to witness Kate's routine interrogation, I didn't cancel my usual instructions to have Haflinger brought here to watch in the hope it might erode his self-control. Your suggestion, I beg to remind you.'

Checking his watch, he added, 'So for the past four, four and a half minutes Haflinger has been behind that stretch one-way mirror, seeing and hearing everything in this room. As I say, he must be very pleased.'

EXCERPT FROM A NEWS BULLETIN

'... a blow dealt to the hopes of those who were confidently forecasting this academic year would be relatively free of student unrest. Convinced that one of their number, missing since a week ago, has been kidnaped by government agents, a mob of fifteen hundred students today tribaled more than half of the thirty-nine police fireposts on campus at UMKC. As yet no count of casualties came to hand, but ...'

ATAVISM

Facing Rico Posta, Ina felt her cheeks grow pale. But she maintained her voice at normal pitch and volume.

'Rico, whatever you and the rest of the board may say, Kate *is* my daughter. You punch for a double-check on those phony reports about her using her code at Interim.'

'Who says they're phony?'

'Our own computers say so!'

'Uh-uh. A program written by one Sandy Locke says so, and he turned out to be a twitch and—'

'While he was saving us a couple of million a year you didn't think he was a twitch. Otherwise you wouldn't have been among the first to say he should be permed.'

'Well, I …'

She leaned earnestly forward.

'Rico, something muddy's going on. You know it, though you haven't admitted it to yourself. Did you try asking for data about Sandy recently?'

'As a matter of fact – yes.'

'And there aren't any, are there? Not even a report of his death!'

'I guess he could have left the country.'

'Passport?'

There was a silence that crackled like the harbinger of an electrical storm. Ina said at last, 'Ever read a book called *1984*?'

'Sure, in a college literature class.' Rico pursed his lips and gazed into nowhere. 'I get what you mean. You think he's been – uh – declared an unperson.'

'Right. And I think they've done the same to Kate.'

'I …' He had to swallow. 'I guess I wouldn't put it past them, knowing what one does about that gang in Washington. Say, you know something? I get nightmares now and then. About how I punch my code into a board and the signal comes back: deeveed!'

Ina said, 'Me too. And I can't believe we're the only ones.'

STARTING TO GROW AGAIN

Since they quit shaving his scalp daily it had begun to itch. So far he had resisted the temptation to scratch, but he was compelled to rub now and then. To the onlookers, whom he knew to exist though he was not aware of their identity, he imagined that he might perhaps give the impression of being puzzled by the information he was taking in. He was watching a three-vee news broadcast. He'd spent much of his time catching up with the world since he was transferred to these more comfortable quarters.

In fact he was not in the least disoriented by what he learned. There were different items to report – another realignment of alliances in Latin America, a fresh outburst of unauthorized *jehad* in the Yemen, a new product about which the FDA was expressing doubts, something called an A-C Group Granulyser used in upgrading vegetable protein to compete with meat …

But the habit patterns, inevitably, had survived. To the air, with a wry grin, he murmured, 'How long, O Lord? How long?'

In his private estimation: not long now.

And, as though on cue, the lock of the door clicked. He glanced around, expecting one of the usual armed men in white come to take him elsewhere.

To his surprise, however, the visitor was Freeman. And alone.

He carefully closed the door before speaking; when he did so, it was in a perfectly neutral tone.

'You probably noticed that I authorized the delivery of some refreshments to your quarters last night. I need a stiff drink. Make it whisky on the rocks.'

'I take it you're not here?'

'What? Oh!' Freeman gave a hideous grin; his facial skin stretched so tight over his bones that it threatened to tear. 'Quite correct. The monitors are being fed a wholly convincing set of lies.'

'Then – congratulations.'

'What do you mean?'

'This took a lot of courage on your part. Most people lack the guts to disobey an immoral order.'

Slowly, over several seconds, Freeman's grin transformed into a smile.

'Goddamn,' he said. 'Haflinger or whatever you'd rather call yourself. I fought like hell to stay objective, and I didn't make it. Turns out I kind of like you. I can't help it.'

Angrily he kicked around a chair and slumped into it.

A few moments later, over full glasses:

'Tell me something. What reflex got punched by whom to trigger this reaction?'

Freeman bridled. 'No need to gibe at me. You can't take credit for everything that's happened inside my head.'

'At least you say credit, not blame ... I suspect you found out you hate the people who give you your orders.'

'Ah ... Yes. I got loaded with my final straw when they decided to bring Kate here. You were right about it not being my idea. So I did as I was told, neither more nor less.'

'So Hartz blasted you for not being smarter than he is. Galling, isn't it?'

'Worse. Much worse.' Cradling his glass in bony fingers, Freeman leaned forward, staring at nothing. 'All argument aside, I do believe that we need wisdom. Need it desperately. I have a conception of how it would be manifest. Hartz doesn't have it. I think you do. And as to Kate ...' The words trailed away.

'Kate Lilleberg is wise. No question of it.'

'I'm obliged to agree.' With a trace of defiance. 'And because of it – well, you've seen.'

'What else would you expect? I don't mean that sarcastically, by the way. Just as my recruitment to Tarnover was predictable once they learned of my existence, so her arrest was predictable when I led them to her.'

After a fractional hesitation Freeman said, 'I get the idea you stopped classing me as one of *them*.'

'You absconded, didn't you?'

'Hah! I guess I did.' He emptied his glass and waved aside the offer of a refill. 'No, I'll fix it. I know where ... But it isn't right, it can't be right! What the hell did she do to deserve indefinite detention without trial, being interrogated until her soul is as naked as her body? We went off the track somewhere. It shouldn't have turned out this way.'

'You think I may have notions about a different way?'

'Sure.' This response was crisp and instant. 'And I want to hear them. I've lost my bearings. Right now I don't know where in the world I am. You may find it hard to believe, but – well, I've always had an article of faith in my personal universe to the effect that maximizing information flow is objectively good. I mean being frank, and open, and candid, telling the truth as you see it regardless of the consequences.' A harsh laugh. 'A shrink I know keeps insisting it's overcompensation for the way I was taught to hide my body as a kid. I was raised to undress in the dark, sneak in and out the bathroom when nobody was looking, run like hell when I flushed the can for fear someone would notice me and think about what I'd done in there ... Ah, maybe the poker's partly right. Anyhow, I grew up to be a top-rank interrogator, dedicated to extracting information from people without torture and with the least possible amount of suffering. Phrase it that way and it sounds defensible, doesn't it?'

'Of course. But it's a different matter when the data you uncover are earmarked for concealment all over again, this time becoming the private property of those in power.'

'That's it.' Freeman resumed his chair, fresh ice cubes tinkling in his refilled glass. 'I took on the assignment to interrogate you like any other assignment. The list of charges against you was long enough, and there was one in particular that touched me on a sore spot. Feeding false data into the net, naturally. On top of which I'd heard about you. I moved here only three years ago – from Weychopee, incidentally, the place you know as "Electric Skillet" – and even then there was vague gossip among the students about some poker who once faded into the air and never got caught. You've become a sort of legend, did you know?'

'Anybody copying my example?'

Freeman shook his head. 'They made it tougher to bow out. And maybe no one since your day has turned up with the same type of talent.'

'If so, doubtless he or she would have been drawn to your notice. You're a person of considerable standing, aren't you, Dr Freeman? Or is it Mr Freeman? I seem to have your measure pretty accurately. I'll stab for "mister".'

'Correct. My degrees are scholarates, not mere doctorates. I've always been very proud of that. Like surgeons over in Britain, taking offense at being called Dr So-and-so ... But it's irrelevant, it's superfluous, it's silly! Know what hit me hardest when I listened to your account of Precipice?'

'Tell me.'

'The dense texture of people's lives. Filled out instead of being fined down. I'm trained in three disciplines, but I haven't broadened out as a person from that base. I've fined down, focusing all I know along one narrow line.'

'That's what's wrong with Tarnover, isn't it?'

'I – I *half* see what you mean. Amplify, please.'

'Well, you once defended Tarnover with the argument that it's designed to provide an optimal environment for people so well adjusted to the rapid change of modern society that they can be trusted to plan for others as well as for themselves. Or words to that effect. But it's not happening, is it? Why? Because it's still under the overriding control of people who, craving power, achieved it by the same old methods they used in – hell, for all I know, in predynastic Egypt. For them there's only one way to outstrip somebody who's overtaking you. Go faster. But this is the space age, remember. And the other day I hit on a metaphor that neatly sums my point.'

He quoted the case of two bodies each in circular orbit.

Freeman looked faintly surprised. 'But everybody knows—' he began, and then checked. 'Oh. No, not everybody. I wish I'd thought of that. I'd have liked to ask Hartz.'

'I'm sure. But think it through. *Not* everybody knows. In this age of unprecedented information flow, people are haunted by the belief they're actually ignorant. The stock excuse is that this is because there's literally too much to be known.'

Freeman said defensively, 'It's true.' And sipped his whisky.

'Granted. But isn't there another factor that does far more damage? Don't we daily grow more aware that data exist which we're not allowed to get at?'

'You said something about that before.' Freeman's forehead creased with concentration. 'A brand-new reason for paranoia, wasn't that it? But if I'm to accept that you're right, then … Damnation, it sounds as though you're determined to deevee every single course of action we've taken in the past half century.'

'Yes.'

'But that's out of the question!' Freeman straightened in dismay.

'No, that's an illusion. A function of a wrongly chosen viewpoint. Take it by steps. Try the holist approach, which you used to decry. Think of the world as a unit, and the developed – the *over*-developed – nations as analogous to Tarnover, or better yet to Trianon. And think of the most successful of the less-rich countries as akin to those P-A communities which began under such unpromising circumstances yet which are turning out to be more tolerable places to live than most other cities on the continent. In short, what I'm talking about is Project Parsimony writ large: the discontinuation of an experiment that cost far too much to set up and hasn't paid off.'

Freeman pondered for a long while. At last he said, 'If I were to agree that you're right, or even partly right, what would you expect me to do?'

'Well – ah … Well, you could start by letting me and Kate go.'

This silence was full of struggle. Eventually, with abrupt decision, Freeman drained his glass and rose, feeling in the side pocket of his jacket. From it he produced a flat gray plastic case, the size of his palm.

'It's not a regular portable calculator,' he said in a brittle voice. 'It's a vee-phone. Screen's under the lid. Flex and jack inside. There are phone points there, there and there.' Pointing to three corners of the room. 'But don't do anything until you get a code to do it with.'

AT THE DISSOLUTION

What was I saying about overcompensation?

There had been a lot of whisky, of course, and he was unused to drinking.

But am I drunk? I don't feel I am. More, it's that without being partly stonk-ered I couldn't endure the torrent of dreadful truth that's storming through my brain. What Hartz said to me. What Bosch almost said, only he managed to check himself. But I know damn well what he substituted with 'nonspecialist'. Why should I spend the rest of my life knuckling under to liars like Bosch? Claiming the dogs they have at Precipice can't exist! And blockheads like Hartz are even worse. Expecting the people they lord it over to think of things they aren't smart enough to think of themselves, then denying that the fault is theirs!

Carefully Freeman locked his apartment, setting the don't-disturb signs: one on the door, one on each of the veephones.

Now if I can just find my way to the index of reserved codes activated when they surpled 4GH … From Tarnover if from anywhere it should be possible to pull one out and upgrade it to status U-for-unquestionable. That's the best trick of all. If Haflinger had latched on to it he need never have been caught.

Owlishly, but with full command of his not inconsiderable faculties – more important, not obliged to make do with the limited and potentially fallible input of a pocket veephone such as the one with which doubtless Haflinger would shortly be performing his own personal brand of miracle – he sat down to his data console. He wrote, then rewrote, then rewrote, a trial program on tape that could be tidily erased. As he worked he found himself more and more haunted by a tantalizing idea.

I could leech three codes as easily as two…

Eventually the program was status go, but before feeding it he said to the air, 'Why not?' And checked how many codes were currently on reserve. The answer was of the order of a hundred thousand. Only about five depts would have dug into the store since it was ordained, so …

Why the hell not? Here I am pushing forty, and what have I done with my life? I have talents, intelligence, ambition. Going to waste! I hoped I'd be useful to society. I expected to spend my time dragging criminals and traitors into the light of day, exposing them to the contumely of honest citizens. Instead the biggest criminals of all escape scot free and people like Kate who never harmed anybody ... Oh, shit! I stopped being an investigator years ago. What I am now is an inquisitor. And I've lost all faith in the justice of my church.

He gave a sudden harsh laugh, made one final tiny amendment to his tape, and offered it up to the input.

THE INFLUENCE OF AFFLUENCE

'For the convenience of the lazy plebeians, the monthly distributions of corn were converted into a daily allowance of bread ... and when the popular clamor accused the dearness and scarcity of wine ... rigid sobriety was insensibly relaxed; and although the generous design of Aurelian does not appear to have been executed in its full extent, the use of wine was allowed on very easy and liberal terms ... and the meanest Roman could purchase, with a small copper coin, the daily enjoyment of a scene of pomp and luxury which might excite the envy of the kings of Asia ... But the most lively and splendid amusement of the idle multitude depended on the frequent exhibition of public games and spectacles ... the happiness of Rome appeared to hang on the event of a race.'

Always scribble, scribble, scribble! Eh, Mr Gibbon?

LET NOT THY WRONG HEAD KNOW WHAT THY RIGHT HEAD DOETH

Having completed his preparations, he disconnected the phone that had proved so invaluable, folded it, concealed it tidily in the inside pocket of his issue jacket. Then he hung that over a chair back, completed undressing normally, and went to bed at approximately his regular time.

What followed was a miniature – a microcosm – of his life, condensed into a span of no more than thirty-five minutes.

At an unidentifiable time of night one of the silent anonymous white-garbed escorts roused him and instructed him to dress quickly and come along, unperturbed by this departure from routine because for him routine might be expected to consist in unpredictability. It was, had been for centuries, a cheap and simple means of deranging persons under interrogation.

He led the way to a room with two doors, otherwise featureless apart from a bench. That was as far as his orders told him to go; with a curt command to sit down and wait, he departed.

There was a short period of silence. Finally the other door opened and a dumpy woman entered, yawning. She carried clothing in a plastic sack and a clipboard with a form on it. Grumpily she requested him to sign it; he did so, using the name she was expecting, which was not his own. Satisfied, yawning more widely than ever, she went out.

He changed into the garments she had brought: a white jersey shirt, blue-gray pants, blue jacket – well-fitting, unremarkable, unmemorable. Bundling up what he had worn in the sack, he went out the same way she had gone, and was in a corridor with several doors leading off it. After passing three of them, two to right and one to left, he arrived at a waste-reclamation chute and rid himself of his burden. Two doors farther along was an office, not locked. It was equipped with, among other things, a computer terminal. He tapped one key on its input board.

Remotely locked, a drawer slid open in an adjacent file stack. Among the contents of the drawer were temporary ID cards of the type issued to visitors on official business.

Meanwhile the printout station of the computer terminal was humming and a rapid paper tongue was emerging from it.

From the same drawer as the ID cards he extracted a neopolaroid color camera, which he set to self-portrait delay and placed on a handy table. Sitting down to face the camera, he waited the requisite few seconds, retrieved the film, placed his picture on the card and sealed it over with a device which, as the computers had promised, was also kept in the drawer. Finally, he typed in his borrowed name and the rank of major in the U.S. Army Medical Corps.

By then the computer had printed out what it was required to furnish: a requisition, in duplicate, for the custody of Kate Grierson Lilleberg. Having been prepared with a light-writer, which unlike old-fashioned mechanical printers was not limited to any one type style – or indeed to any one alphabet, since every single character was inscribed with a laser beam at minimum power – only examination under a microscope could have revealed that it was not a U.S. Army Form RQH–4479, the standard form of authority to transfer a prisoner from civil to military custody.

Suitably armed now, he replaced everything he had disturbed, tapped the computer board one more time to activate the final part of the program he had left in store, and left the room. Dutifully, the machines remote-locked the cabinet again, and the door of the office, and then undertook such other tasks as deleting their record of either having been unlocked during the night, and making a note of the 'fact' that a temporary ID card had been accidentally spoiled so the stock in hand was one fewer than could be accounted for by recent visitors.

The door at the extreme end of the corridor gave into the open air, at the head of a flight of stairs leading to a dark concrete parking bay where an electric ambulance was standing. Its driver, who wore army uniform with Pfc's badges, gave an uncertain salute, saying, 'Major ...?'

'At ease,' the newcomer said briskly, displaying his ID card and duplicate forms. 'Sorry to have kept you. Any trouble with the girl?'

The driver said with a shrug, 'She's out, sir. Like a busted light-tube oh-you-tee.'

'That's how it should be. They gave you your route card?'

'Sure, they brought it when they delivered the girl. Oh, and this as well. Feels like her code card, I guess.' The soldier proffered a small flat package.

Peeling off the cover proved him half right. Not one code card, but two.

'Thanks. Not that she'll have much use for it where she's going.'

'I guess not.' With a sour grin.

'You already changed your batteries, did you? Fine – let's get under way.'

Dark roads thrummed into the past to the accompaniment of a rattling of numbers, not spoken. He had memorized both codes before starting his vee-phone-mediated sabotage, but there was a lot more to this escape than simply two personal codes. He wanted everything down pat before the ambulance first had to stop for electricity, and the range of this model was only about two hundred miles.

Best if the driver didn't have to get hurt. Though having been fool enough to volunteer for army service, of course, and worse still, having been fool enough to accept orders unquestioningly from a machine ...

But everybody did that. Everybody, all the time. Otherwise none of this would have been possible.

Similarly, none of it would have had to happen.

FOR PURPOSES OF DISORIENTATION

At present and with luck from now on and forever regardless of what code I wear I am being Nicholas Kenton Haflinger. And whoever doesn't like it will have to lump it.

PRESIDING AT AWAKE

'What the –? Who –? Why, Sandy!'

'Quiet. Listen carefully. You're in an army ambulance. We're about two hundred miles east of Tarnover supposedly on the way to Washington. The driver believes I'm a Medical Corps major escorting you. There was no convincing story I could invent to justify clothing fit for you to cross a public street in. All you have is that issue cotton gown. What's more they shaved your head. Do you remember anything about this, or did they keep you all the time in regressed mode?'

She swallowed hard. 'I've had what seem like dreams since they – they kidnaped me. I don't know what's true and what isn't.'

'We'll sort that out later. We're laying over to change batteries. I sent the driver for coffee. He'll be back any moment. I'll find some other excuse to make him hang around, because I've seen an automat where I can buy you a dress, shoes and a wig. At the next stop be ready to put them on and vanish.'

'What – what are we going to do? Even if it comes off?'

Cynically he curled his lip. 'The same as I've been doing all my adult life. Run the net. Only this time in more than one sense. And believe you me, they aren't going to like it.'

Shutting the ambulance's rear door again, he said loudly to the returning driver, 'Damn monitors up front! Showed the sedative control had quit. But she's lying like a log. Say, did you spot a men's room? I guess before we get back on the road I ought to take a leak.'

Over the hum of the many steam and electric vehicles crowding the service area the driver answered, 'Right next to the automat, sir. And – uh – if we're not pulling out at once, I see they got Delphi boards and I'd kinda like to check out a nervous ticket.'

'Sure, go ahead. But keep it down to – let's say five minutes, hm?'

TEMBLOR

'What do you mean, he can't be reached? Listen again and make sure you know who I'm asking for. Paul – T-for-Tommy – Freeman! Want I should spell it?

'His new code? What about his—? Are you certain?

'But they don't have any goddamn right to snatch him out from— Oh, shit. Sometimes I wonder who's in charge around this country, us or the machines. Give me the new code, then.

'I don't *care* what it says in back of its head listing. Just read it over to me. If you can, that is!

'Now you listen to me, you obstructive dimwit. When I give an order I expect it to be obeyed, and I won't be talked back to by a self-appointed shithouse lawyer. You're addressing the Deputy Director of the Federal Bureau of Data Processing Services, and— That's more like it. Come on.

'It begins with *what* group? No, don't bother to repeat it. I heard you. Oh my God. Oh my God.'

SPELLED 'WEEKEND' BUT PRONOUNCED 'WEAKENED'

A highway line drawn from Tarnover to Washington: a line to connect tomorrow with yesterday, via today …

The most mobile population in all of history, the only one so totally addicted to going for the sake of going that it had deeveed excessive cost, energy crises, the disappearance of oil, every kind of obstacle in order to keep up the habit, was as ever on the move, even though half the continent was overlaid by end-of-fall weather, strong winds, low temperatures, rain turning to sleet. It was notoriously the sort of season that urged people to stop looking for and start finding.

He thought about that a lot during the journey.

Why move?

To choose a place right for sinking roots.

Go faster in order to drop back to a lower orbit? Doesn't work. Drop back to a lower orbit; you go faster!

Even Freeman had had to have that pointed out to him. He knew obscurely he wouldn't have to explain it to Kate. And she couldn't be the only person who understood the truth by instinct.

Washington: yesterday. The exercise of personal power; the privileges of office; the individualization of the consensus into a single spokesman's mouth, echo of an age when communities did indeed concur because they weren't assailed with a hundred irreconcilable versions of events. (These days the typical elected representative is returned with fewer than forty percent of the votes cast; not infrequently he's detested by four-fifths of those he purports to speak for, because the population of the state or district has turned over. They'll surple him at the next opportunity, chafe until it arrives. Meanwhile his old supporters have scattered to upset another applecart. Voting registers are maintained by computers nowadays; all it takes to enter you on the roll at your new address is one, count it one, vee-phone call.)

Tarnover: tomorrow, sure. But hopefully the wrong tomorrow. Because it's planned and controlled by people who were born the day before yesterday.

How do you cope with tomorrow when (a) it may not be like the real tomorrow but (b) it's arrived when you weren't ready for it?

One approach is offered by the old all-purpose beatitude: 'Blessed are they who expect the worst ...' Hence reactions like Anti-Trauma Inc. Nothing worse can happen in later life than what was done to you as a child.

(Wrong tomorrow.)

Another is inherent in the concept of the plug-in life-style: no matter where you go, there are people like the ones you left behind, furniture and clothes and food like the ones you left behind, the same drinks available across any bar: 'Say, settle a bet for us, willya? Is this the Paris Hilton or the Istanbul Hilton?'

(Wrong tomorrow. It offers the delusive hope that tomorrow will be pretty much like today, but it got here and it isn't.)

Yet another lies in preparing for it: using public Delphi boards, for example, to monitor what people are ready to adapt to, yearn to adapt to, and won't adapt to at any price.

(Wrong tomorrow. They decided to let traditional market forces flywheel the weight of decision. The favorite who started at odds-on broke his leg at the first fence and the race is far from over.)

Yet another lies in the paid-avoidance areas: you trade in your right to the latest-and-greatest against an allowance of unearned credit, enough to keep body and soul together.

(Wrong tomorrow. It's going to overtake you anyway, and city-smashing quakes are part of it.)

While still another consists in getting good and clutched by some heavy brand of dope, so things that happen can't really hurt.

(Wrong tomorrow. Ash longer, *vita brevis*.)

And so forth.

Religion?

Change cities, by order. Last place it was a Catholic framework; here it's Ecumenical Pentecostal and the minister is kind of into the Tao.

Chemicals?

Almost everybody is high like troops on the way to battle. Shaking! You hear tension sing in the air you breathe. The only way you want awareness shifted is back to normal.

Trust in authority?

But it's your right as a free and equal individual to be as authoritative as anybody else.

Model yourself on a celebrity?

But you were celebrated last week, you had a record-breaking Delphi ticket or your kid was on three-vee defying 'gators or you notched up one full year in the same house and the reporter called in from the local station. For ten whole minutes you've been famous too.

Collapse into overload?

That's already happened, nearly as often as you've been to bed with a head cold.

And patiently, from every single one of these possible pathways, they've turned you back to where you were with a smile of encouragement and a pat on the shoulder and a bright illuminated certificate that reads NO EXIT.

Therefore the world keeps turning, the ads keep changing, there are always programs to watch when you switch on the three-vee, there's always food in the supermarket and power at the socket and water at the sink. Well, not quite always. But near as dammit.

And there's nearly always a friend to answer the phone.

And there's nearly always credit behind your code.

And there's nearly always some other place you can go.

And when the night sky happens to be clear, there are invariably more stars in it, moving faster, than were put there at the Creation. So that's okay.

Pretty well.

More or less.

HELP!

For these and sundry other reasons, at their next battery stop he gave the driver the slip and Kate her dress and shoes and wig and melted into the mass of people boarding a shuttle bus bound for the nearest veetol port. For the driver, who was sure to be puzzled, he left a note saying:

Thanks, soldier. You were very helpful. If you want to know how helpful, punch this code into the nearest phone.

The code, naturally, being his own new acquisition.

PRECEPT DINNED INTO TRAFFIC PATROL OFFICERS DURING TRAINING

Someone is apt to swoop on you from a great height if you ticket a vehicle with a heavy federal code behind the wheel.

MOUSING AROUND UNDER THE FEET OF ELEPHANTS

'Where are we going?' Kate whispered.

'I finally located my place to stand.'

'Precipice?' she suggested, half hopefully, half anxiously. 'Surely that's where they'll head for straight away.'

'Mm-hm. Sorry, I don't mean place. I mean *places*. I should have figured this out long ago. No one place could ever be big enough. I have to be in a hundred of them, all at the same time, and a thousand if I can manage it. It's bound to take a while to put my insight into practice, but – oh, maybe in a couple of months we shall be able to sit back and enjoy the fireworks.'

'I always did like fireworks,' she said with the ghost of a smile, and took his hand.

FOUR-WAY INTERSECTION WITH STOP SIGNS

These days it was easy to lose track of what features belonged with what names. Therefore there were captions under each of the faces on the four-station secure link, names and offices. Hartz gazed at the split-screen array before him, reading from left to right.

From Tarnover, its chancellor: Admiral Bertrand Snyder, ascetic, gray-haired, short-spoken, who had been famous under the sobriquet of 'Singleminded Snyder' during the Hawaiian Insurrection of 2002 … but that was before he entered the Civil Service and a cloud of secrecy.

From the Southern White House, the president's special adviser on security, plump and bespectacled Dr Guglielmo Dorsi, no longer known even to his intimates (though it had not proved possible to eradicate the nickname entirely from his dossiers) as Billy the Shiv.

And from another floor of this same building, his own superior, the Full Director of the Bureau, Mr Aylwin Sullivan, tall, beak-nosed, shock-haired, and deliberately shabby. It had been the style for those working with computers when he launched out on his rocket-like career. Nonetheless it was odd to look at his open-neck shirt, pocketful of old pens, five-o'week shadow, black-rimmed nails.

As though the past had stepped into the present.

All three of the faces on the screen frowned at Hartz: Snyder with annoyance, Dorsi with suspicion, Sullivan with impatience. They let pecking order decide who should speak. Highest in the hierarchy Sullivan said, 'Are you insane? Only a few days ago you insisted we deevee all the 4GH codes assigned to FBI, CIA, Secret Service – and now here you are claiming that the U-group codes must be junked too! You couldn't cause more trouble if you were a paid subversive.'

Dorsi said, 'Let me remind you of this, too. Upon my asking what to use when we replaced the 4GH, you personally advised me that there was no known means of leeching any code from the reserve and assigning it to U-group status without that fact being revealed in your own bureau's computers. No record of such action can be found, can it? I can just see the president's face if I were to go to him with such a crazy story.'

'But when I said that I didn't know—' Hartz began. Snyder cut him short.

'What's more, you've made a direct attack on my integrity and administrative efficiency. You've said in so many words that the person you claim to have carried out this act of sabotage is a graduate of Weychopee who moved to Tarnover at my special request and who was cleared by me in person for essential work here. I wholly agree with Mr Sullivan. You must have taken leave of your senses.'

'Therefore,' Sullivan said, 'I'm requiring you to take leave of absence as well. Preferably indefinite. Are we through with this conference? Good. I have other business to attend to.'

FOR PURPOSES OF OBFUSCATION

I know damn well I am Paul Thomas Freeman, aged thirty-nine, a government employee with scholars' degrees in cybernetics, psychology and political science plus a master's in data processing. Similarly I know that if as a kid I hadn't been recruited much as Haflinger was, I'd probably have wound up as a petty criminal, into smuggling or dope or maybe running an illegal Delphi pool. Maybe I might not have been as smart as I imagine. Maybe I'd be dead.

And I also know I've been brilliantly maneuvered into a corner where I sacrificed everything I've gained in life on a spur-of-the-moment impulse, threw away my career, let myself in – quite possibly – for a treason trial … and with no better excuse than that I like Haflinger better than Hartz and the buggers at his back. A corner? More like a deep dark hole!

So why the hell do I feel so goddamn *happy*?

FULCRUM

When he finished explaining how he had contrived their escape, Kate said incredulously, 'Was that all?'

'Not quite. I also made a call to the ten nines.'

'Ah. I should have guessed.'

A MATTER OF HYSTERICAL RECORD

When the short-lived Allende government was elected to power in Chile and needed a means of balancing that unfortunate country's precarious economy, Allende appealed to the British cybernetics expert Stafford Beer.

Who announced that as few as ten significant quantities, reported from a handful of key locations where adequate communications facilities existed, would enable the state of the economy to be reviewed and adjusted on a day-to-day basis.

Judging by what happened subsequently, his claim infuriated nearly as many people as did the news that there are only four elements in the human genetic code.

LIKE THEY SAY, IT'S BOUNCE OR BREAK

At Ann Arbor, Michigan, research psychologist Dr Zoë Sideropoulos had house guests for a week. She was an expert in hypnosis and had written a well-known study of the regression effect which, in suitable cases, makes possible the recovery of memories ordinarily lost to conscious awareness without such crude physical aids as electrodes planted in the subject's brain.

During the week she made exceptionally intensive use of her home computer terminal. Or rather, that was what the machines believed.

When he was able to take a break from using Dr Sideropoulos's terminal – a new and extremely efficient model – Kate brought him omelets and the nearest surviving commercial equivalent of 'real beer'.

'Eat before it's cold,' she commanded. 'Then talk. In detail and with footnotes.'

'I'm glad you said that. We're going to have a lot of time to fill. I need to scramble some circuitry at Canaveral, or wherever, rather more completely than you scrambled these eggs, and I know for sure I'm going to have to make the computers do things they're specifically forbidden to. But not to worry. When they built their defenses they weren't reckoning on somebody like me.'

He set about demolishing the omelet; it lasted for a dozen hungry bites.

'But I do worry,' Kate muttered. 'Are you *certain* you can trust Paul Freeman?'

He laid aside his empty plate. 'Remember how at Lap-of-the-Gods you upbraided me because I wouldn't believe anyone else was on my side?'

'*Touchée.* But I want my answer.'

'Yes. There's an honest man. And finally he's figured out what constitutes evil in the modern world.'

'So what's your definition?'

'One that I already know you agree with, because we talked about Anti-Trauma Inc. If there is such a phenomenon as absolute evil, it consists in treating another human being as a thing.'

In a dry voice she said, 'I won't argue.'

*

At Boulder, Colorado, Professor Joachim Yent of the School of Economics and Business Administration had house guests for a few days. During that time, it was duly recorded that he made exceptionally frequent use of his home computer terminal.

'Kate, when you take a liking to somebody, do you speed up or slow down?'

'Do I what –? Oh, got it. Slow down, I guess. I mean to get where we can talk to each other I quit skipping for a while.'

'And *vice versa*?'

'Most times, no. In fact you're the only person I ever met who could work it the other way – uh … Sandy? What is your name, damn it? I just realized I still don't know.'

'You decide. Stick with Sandy if you like, or switch to what I started out with: Nicholas, Nickie, Nick. I don't care. I'm myself, not a label.'

She puckered her lips to blow him a kiss. 'I don't care what you're called, either. I only know I'm glad we slowed down to the same speed.'

At Madison, Wisconsin, Dean Prudence McCourtenay of the Faculty of Laws had house guests for a long weekend. It was similarly recorded that during their visit she made more than averagely frequent use of her domestic computer terminal.

It was becoming very cold. Winter had definitely begun.

'Yes, slowing down to the same speed is what everybody needs to do. With a lot of incidental energy to be dissipated. In fact a good many brakes are apt to melt. But the alternative is a head-on flat-out smash.'

'Why?'

'Because everybody isn't like you yet.'

'Sounds like a monotonous world!'

'I mean in the sense of being equally able to cope.'

'But …' She bit her lip. 'It's a fact of existence that some can and some can't. Punishing those who can't is cruel, but holding back those who can for the sake of the rest is—'

He broke in. 'Our present society is cruel both ways. It does punish those who can't cope. We bought our veephones and our data-net and our asteroid ore and the rest of it by spending people who wound up dead or in mental hospitals.' His face darkened briefly. '*And* it holds back those who can cope. I'm an example of that.'

'I find it terribly hard to believe, seeing what you can do now you're working at full stretch!'

'But I *have* been held back, damn it. I didn't know how much I could achieve until I saw you, shaven and limp like a lab specimen due to be carved up and thrown away with no more memorial than an entry in a table of statistics. The sight forced me into – I guess you'd say mental overdrive.'

'What was it like?'

'As inexplicable as orgasm.'

In Shreveport, Louisiana, Dr Chase Richmond Dellinger, a public-health analyst under contract to the city, had house guests during whose stay he had unusually frequent recourse to his home computer terminal. In the south it was still pleasantly warm, of course, but there was a lot of rain this year.

'So I absolutely had to find a way out – not just for you, not just for me, but for everybody. In an eyeblink I had discovered a new urge within myself, and it was as fundamental as hunger, or fear, or sex. I recall one argument I had with Paul Freeman …'

'Yes?'

'The idea came up that it took the advent of the H-bomb to bring about in human beings the response you see in other animals when confronted with bigger claws or teeth.'

'Or a dominant figure in his private cosmos. Like Bagheera rolling over kitten-style to greet me when I get back from school. I do hope they're looking after him properly.'

'We've been promised that.'

'Yes, but … Never mind. I didn't mean to change the subject.'

'On principle I differed with him, but he was quite justified in saying that for all we know maybe that is the case. Well, if it's true that our threshold of survival-prone behavior is so high it takes the prospect of total extermination to activate modes of placation and compromise, may there not be other processes, equally life-preserving, which can similarly be triggered off only at a far higher level of stimulus than you find among our four-legged cousins?'

On his ranch in northern Texas, political historian Rush Compton and his wife Nerice, some years his junior and in occasional practice as a market-research counselor, entertained a couple of house guests. Considerable use was made of their home computer terminal. The weather was fresh and clear, with intermittent gusts of sharp northerly wind.

'Wait a moment. That threshold may be dangerously high. Think of population.'

'Yes indeed. I started with population. Not having a fixed breeding season was among the reasons why mankind achieved dominance; it kept our numbers topped up at an explosive rate. Past a certain stage restrictive processes set in: male libido is reduced or diverted into nonfertile channels, female ovulation is irregularized and sometimes fails completely. But long before we reach that point we find the company of our fellow creatures so unbearable we resort to war, or a tribal match. Kill one another or ourselves.'

'So our evolutionary advantage has turned unnoticed into a handicap.'

'Kate, I love you.'

'I know. I'm glad.'

At his secluded home in Massachusetts, Judge Virgil Horovitz, retired, and his housekeeper Alice Bronson – he was widowed – entertained house guests and used his computer terminal for the first time since his retirement. A gale had stripped most of the trees around his house of their gorgeous red-gold foliage; at night, frost made the fallen leaves crackle and rustle underfoot.

'But what the hell can we do with an insight like yours? We've had insights before, from social theorists and historians and politicians and preachers, and we're in a mess in spite of all. The idea of turning the entire planet into a madhouse in the hope of triggering off some species-saving reflex – no, it's out of the question. Suppose at some early stage of your scheme we hit a level where a billion people go collectively in-insane?'

'That's the best we can look forward to, and I do mean *the best*, if the people at Tarnover are allowed their way.'

'I think you're serious!'

'Oh, maybe it wouldn't be a whole billion. But it could be half the population of North America. And a hundred and some million is enough, isn't it?'

'How would it happen?'

'Theoretically at least, one of the forces operating on us consists in the capacity, which we don't share with other animals, to elect whether or not we shall give way to an ingrained impulse. Our social history is the tale of how we learned to substitute conscious ethical behavior for simple instinct, right? On the other hand, it remains true that few of us are willing to admit how much influence our wild heritage exercises on our behavior. Not directly, because we're not still wild, but indirectly, because society itself is a consequence of our innate predispositions.'

With a rueful chuckle, he added, 'You know, one of the things I most regret about what's happened is that I could have enjoyed my arguments with Paul Freeman. There was so much common ground between us ... But I didn't dare. At all costs I *had* to shake his view of the world. Otherwise he'd never have toppled when Hartz pushed him.'

'Stop digressing, will you?'

'Sorry. Where were we? Oh, I was about to say that at Tarnover they're mistakenly trying to postpone the moment where our reflexes take over. They ought to know that's wrong. Freeman himself cited the best treatment for personality shock, which doesn't use drugs or any other formal therapy, just liberates the victim to do something he's always wanted and never achieved. In spite of evidence like that, though, they go on trying to collect the people most sensitive to our real needs so that they can isolate them from the world. Whereas what they ought to be doing is turning them loose in full knowledge of their own talent, so that when we reach the inevitable overload point our reflexes will work for instead of against our best interests.'

'I recall a point made in one of the Disasterville monographs. I think it was number 6. Stripped of the material belongings which had located them in society, a lot of refugees who formerly held responsible, status-high positions broke down into whining useless parasites. Leadership passed to those with more flexible minds – not only kids who hadn't ossified yet, but adults who previously had been called unpractical, dreamers, even failures. The one thing they had in common seemed to be a free-ranging imagination, regardless of whether it was due to their youth or whether it had lasted into maturity and fettered them with too great a range of possibilities for them to settle to any single course of action.'

'How well I know that feeling. And wouldn't an injection of imagination be good for our society right now? I say we've had an overdose of harsh reality. A bit of fantasy would act as an antidote.'

Near Cincinnati, Ohio, Helga Thorgrim Townes, dramatist, and her husband Nigel Townes, architect, had house guests and were debbed for an exceptional amount of time rented on the data-net. Slight snow was falling in the region, but as yet had not settled to any marked extent.

'I'm not sure that if I hadn't met people from Tarnover I would believe you. If I can judge by them, though …'

'Be assured they're typical. They've been systematically steered away from understanding of the single most important truth about mankind. It's as though you were to comb the continent for the kindest, most generous, most considerate individuals you could find, and then spend years persuading them that because such attitudes are rare, they must be abnormal and should be cured.'

'What most important truth?'

'You tell me. You've known it all your life. You live by its compass.'

'Anything to do with my reason for getting interested in you in the first place? I noticed how hard you were trying to conform to a stock pattern. It seemed like a dreadful waste.'

'That's it. One charge I made against Freeman which I won't retract: I accused him of dealing not in human beings but in approximations to a preordained model of a human being. I really am glad he decided to give it up. Bad habit!'

'Then I know what you're talking about. It's the uncertainty principle.'

'Of course. The opposite of evil. Everything implied by that shopworn term "free will". Ever run across the phrase "the new conformity"?'

'Yes, and it's terrifying. In an age when we have more choice than ever before, more mobility, more information, more opportunity to fulfill ourselves, how is it that people can prefer to be identical? The plug-in life-style makes me puke.'

'But the concept has been sold with such persistence, the majority of people feel afraid not to agree that it's the best way of keeping track in a chaotic world. As it were: "Everybody else says it is – who am I to argue?"'

'I am I.'

'*Tat tvam asi.*'

During the six weeks that the process took, approximately thirteen percent of households owning domestic computer terminals made above-average use of the machines in excess of the normal variation plus-or-minus ten percent. This was up by less than one percent over last year's figures and could be ascribed to the start of the academic year.

SHADOWS BEFORE

'Hey, those odds … they doubled kinda fast, didn't they?'

'What do you mean you can't raise him? He's a five-star priority – his phone can't be out. Try again.'

'Christ, look at this lot, will you? Can't the twitches keep their minds made up two days together?'

'Funny to get this on a weekend, but … Oh, I'm not going to complain about the chance to pick our new location from a list this long. Makes a change, doesn't it, from all the time going where we're told and no option?'

'But – but Mr Sullivan! You did authorize it! Or at any rate it has your code affixed!'

HOMER

'It feels so strange,' Kate said as the cab turned the corner of her home street. Her eyes darted from one familar detail to another.

'I'm not surprised. I've been back to places, of course, but never to resume the same role as when I was there before … nor shall I this time, of course. Any objections?'

'Reservations, maybe.' With a distracted gesture. 'After having been so many different people in such a short time that I can't remember all my names: Carmen, Violet, Chrissie …'

'I liked you specially when you were Lilith.'

She pulled a face at him. 'I'm not joking! Knowing that here if anywhere

I'm bound to be recognized, even though we made sure the croakers pulled their watch – I guess I wasn't quite ready for it.'

'Nor was I. I'd have liked to run longer and do more. But they're no fools, the people who monitor the Fedcomps. Already I'm pretty sure they have an inkling of what's about to crash on them. Before they react, we have to capitalize our last resources. You're still a *cause célèbre* around KC, and judging by how she looked and sounded Ina is boiling with eagerness to put a good heavy G2S code between us and disaster.'

'I'm sure you're right. Your logic is flawless. Even so—'

'You don't have to live by logic. You're wise. And that can transcend logic. No matter how logical your choice may seem in retrospect.'

'I was going to say: even so it'll feel strange to go in and not have Bagheera come to rub against my ankles.'

The apt had been searched by experts. That aside, it was unchanged, though dusty. Kate picked up the paintbrush she had been using when 'Fessier' called and grimaced at its clogged bristles.

'Anything missing?' he inquired, and she made a fast check.

'Nothing much. Some letters, my address-and-code book … Things I can live without. Most are still furnishing my head. But' – she wrinkled her nose – 'the power was off for some time, wasn't it, before you had it restored?'

'Sure, from the day after you were 'naped.'

'In that case, the moment I open the refrigerator the apt will be uninhabitable. I distinctly recall I'd laid in two dozen extra eggs. Come on, we have a lot of garbage cans to fill. There's going to be a party here tonight.'

'A party?'

'Naturally. You never heard of Doubting Thomas? Besides, students are a gabby lot. What you've done is going to be on all strands of the net by this time tomorrow. I want it on the mouth-to-mouth circuit too.'

'But you know damn well I've written in a program that will call a press conference—'

'At noon the day after the balloon goes up,' she cut in. 'Nick, Sandy, whatever the hell, *darling*, the avalanche you plan to start may have swept us into limbo long beforehand. If you're going to hurt them as much as you think, you and I can't safely plan so far ahead.'

He thought about that for a long moment. When he answered his voice shook a little.

'I know. I just haven't faced the idea. Right, leave the clearing-up to me. Get on that phone and contact everybody you can. And you might as well enroll Ina's help, get her to bring some friends from G2S.'

'I already thought of that,' she said with composure, and punched her mother's code.

THE HATCHING OF THE WORM

On her way to visit friends for dinner, Dr Zoë Sideropoulos paused before her home computer terminal long enough to activate a link to the continental net and strike a cluster of three digits on the board. Then she went out to her car.

Returning from an evening seminar, Professor Joachim Yent remembered what day it was and punched three digits into the board of his computer terminal.

Dean Prudence McCourtenay was in bed with a cold; she was a martyr to them every winter. But she had five veephones in her seven-room house, one being at her bedside.

Dr Chase R. Dellinger took five from unexpected work at his lab – something suspect about a batch of newly imported mushroom spawn, perhaps contaminated with a mutant strain – and on his way back paused at a computer remote and tapped three digits into the net.

Nerice Compton misdialed a phone call and swore convincingly; she and Rush had friends in for drinks tonight.

Judge Virgil Horovitz had had a heart attack. At his age, that was not wholly unexpected. Besides, it had happened twice before. On returning from the hospital, his housekeeper remembered to activate the computer terminal and press three digital keys.

At a party with friends, Helga and Nigel Townes demonstrated some amusing tricks one could play with a computer remote. One aborted after three digits. The rest worked perfectly.

In any case, a complete emergency backup program was available which would have done the job by itself. However, many times in the history of Hearing Aid it had been proven that certain key data were better stored externally to the net.

By about 2300 EST the worm needed only fertilization to start laying its unprecedented eggs.

PARTY LINE

'I'll be damned! *Paul!* Well, it's great to see you. Come on in.'

Blinking shyly, Freeman complied. Kate's apartment was alive with guests, mostly young and in brilliant clothes, but with a mix of more soberly clad people from G2S and the UMKC faculty. A portable coley unit had been set up and a trio of dancers were cautiously sticking to the chords of a simple traditional blues prior to launching a collective sequence of variations; as yet, they were still feeling out the unit's tone-color bias.

'How did you know we were here? And what are you doing in KC, anyway? I understood you went to Precipice.'

'In a metaphorical sense.' Freeman gave a grin that made him look oddly boyish, as though he had shed twenty years with his formal working garb. 'But it's an awfully big place when you learn to recognize it … No, in fact I figured out weeks ago that you were sure to be back sooner or later. I asked myself what the least likely place would be for me to find you, and – uh – took away the number I first thought of.'

'It's alarming to think someone found my carefully randomized path so predictable. Ah, here comes Kate.'

Freeman stiffened as though to prepare for a blow, but she greeted him cordially, asked what he wanted to drink, and departed again to bring him beer.

'Isn't that her mother?' Freeman muttered, having scanned the visible area of the apartment. 'Over there in red and green?'

'Yes. You met her, didn't you? And the man she's talking to.'

'Rico Posta, isn't that his name?'

'Right.'

'Hmm … What precisely is going on?'

'We had kind of a big temblor for a while, because of course once the news broke that Kate was back and she actually was kidnaped by a government agent as the students have been claiming, they were set to go tribal the campus. We put that idea into freeze, after a lot of argument, by hinting at all sorts of dire recriminations. And that's what we're discussing at the moment. Come and join us.'

'Such as—'

'Well, we'll start by deeveeing Tarnover.'

Freeman stopped dead in midstride, and a pretty girl banged into him and spilled half a drink and there was a period of apologies. Then: '*What?*'

'It's an obvious first step. A full Congressional inquiry should follow publication in the media of the Tarnover and Crediton Hill budgets. The others are in the pipeline, with Weychopee last because it's hardest to crack open.

And as well as financial revelations, naturally, there will be pictures of Miranda and her successors, and the fatality rates among the experimental children, and so on.'

'That looks like Paul Freeman!' Ina exclaimed, rising. She sounded alarmed.

'Yes indeed. And a bit dazed. I just began to tell him what we're up to.'

Kate arrived with the promised beer, delivered it, sat down on the arm of the chair Ina was using. Rico Posta stood at her side.

'Dazed,' Freeman repeated after a pause. 'Yes, I am. What's the purpose of attacking Tarnover first?'

'To trigger a landslide of emotionalism. I guess you, coming fresh from an environment dedicated to rationality, doubt it's a good policy. But it's exactly what we need, and records from Tarnover are a short means to make it happen. Lots of things make people angry, but political graft and the notion of deliberately maltreating children are among the most powerful. One taps the conscious, the other the subconscious.'

'Oh, both hit the subconscious,' Ina said. 'Rico has the same nightmare I do, about finding someone got to my credit records and deeveed everything I worked for all my life. And I don't stand a prayer of finding out who's responsible.' She turned to face her daughter squarely. 'What's more ... Kate, I never dared tell you this before, but when I was pregnant with you I was so terrified you might not – uh – come out right, I—'

'You overloaded a few years later, and after that you were obsessively worried about me, and when I grew up you still worried because I'm a nonconformist. And I'm plain too. So what? I'm bright and I bounce. I'm a credit to any mother. Ask Nick,' she added with a mischievous grin.

Freeman glanced around. 'Nick? You recovered from your prejudice against the name, then – Old Nick, Saint Nicholas and the rest?'

'As well as being the patron saint of thieves, Saint Nicholas is credited with reviving three murdered children. It's a fair human-type compromise.'

'You've changed,' Freeman said soberly. 'In a lot of ways. And ... and the result is kind of impressive.'

'I owe much of it to you. If I hadn't been derailed from the course I'd followed all my life— You know, that's what's wrong with us on the public level. We fret about how to keep going the same old way when we should be casting around for another way that's better. Our society is hurtling in free fall toward heaven knows where, and as a result we've developed collective osteochalcolysis of the personality.'

'The way to go faster is to slow down,' Kate said with conviction.

Freeman's brow furrowed. 'Yes, perhaps. But how do we choose this better direction?'

'We don't have to. It's programed.'

'How can that possibly be true?'

Rico Posta spoke up in a strained tone. 'I didn't believe it either, not at first. Now I have to. I've seen the evidence.' He took an angry swig of his drink. 'Hell, here I am allegedly vice-president in charge of long-term corporate planning, and *I* didn't know that G2S's social-extrapolation programs automatically mouse into a bunch of federal studies from Crediton Hill! Isn't that crazy? It was set up by my last-but-two predecessor, that system, and he left under a cloud and omitted to advise the poker who took over. Nick got to it with no trouble, and he's taken me on a guided tour of a section of the net I didn't know existed.'

Pointing with a shaking hand, he concluded furiously: 'On that goddamn veephone right over there! I feel sick, just *sick*. If a veep for G2S can't find out what's happening under his nose, what chance do ordinary people have?'

'I wish I'd been here,' Freeman said after a pause. 'What do these Crediton Hill studies indicate?'

'Oh …' Posta took a deep breath. 'More or less this: the cost of staying out front – economically, in terms of prestige, and so forth – has been to invoke the counterpart of the athlete's "second wind", which burns up muscle tissue. You can't keep that up forever. And what we've been burning is people who could have been useful, talented members of society if the pressure had been less intense. As it was, they turned to crime or suicide or went insane.'

Freeman said slowly, 'I remember thinking that I could easily have taken to peddling dope. But I can't see the world the way you do, can I? I owe to the people who recruited me for Weychopee the fact that I didn't wind up in jail or an early grave.'

'Is our society on the right lines when one of its most gifted people can find no better career than crime unless literally millions per year of public money are lavished on him?'

Nick waited for an answer to that question. None came.

Around them the party was in full swing. The coley dancers had the measure of the unit. Their numbers had trebled without causing more than an occasional screech, and their chord pattern had evolved into a full AABA chorus of thirty-two bars, still in the key of the original blues though one of the more adventurous girls was trying to modulate into the minor. Unfortunately someone else was trying to impose triple time. The effect was … interesting.

Watching the dance, Freeman said helplessly, 'Oh, what difference does it make whether I agree or not? I gave you your U-group codes. I knew damn well that was like handing you an H-bomb, and I went right ahead. I only wish I could believe in what you're doing. You sound like an economist – worse, like a nihilist, planning to bring the temple pillars down around our ears.'

'The name for what we're doing wasn't coined by any kind of radical.'

'It has a name?'

'Sure it does,' Kate said firmly. 'Agonizing reappraisal.'

Nick nodded. 'During all my time at Tarnover it was drummed into me that I must search for wisdom. It's the beginning of wisdom when you admit you've gone astray.'

The coley dancers dissolved into discords and laughter. As they scattered in search of fresh drinks they complimented one another on the length of time they had managed to keep dancing. An impatient exhibitionistic youth promptly jumped up and conjured a specialty number from the invisible beams. After the complexities of the nine-part dance it seemed thin and shallow in spite of being technically brilliant.

'Sweedack,' Freeman said eventually, his face glistening with sweat. 'I guess now we hold tight and wait for the tsunami.'

THE RACE BETWEEN GUNS AND ARMOR

On the tree of evolution, last season's flowers die, and often the most beautiful are sterile.

While Triceratops sported his triple horns, while Diplodocus waved his graceful tail, something without a name was stealing their tomorrow.

AN ALARMING ITEM TO FIND ON YOUR OVERNIGHT MAIL-STORE REEL

Origin: Tarnover Bioexperimental Laboratory
Reference: K3/E2/100715 P
Subject: In-vitro genetic modification (project # 38)
Nature: Controlled crossover in gamete union
Surgeons: Dr Jason B. Saville, Dr Maud Crowther
Biologist i/c: Dr Phoebe R. Whymper
Mother: Anon. volunt. GOL ($800 p.w., 1 yr.)
Father: Staff volunt. WVG ($1,000, flat pmt.)
Embryo: Female
Gestation: – 11 days
Survival time: appx. 67 hr.
Description: Typical class G0 and G9 faults, viz. cyclopean eye, cleft palate, open fontanelle, digestive system incomplete, anal-vaginal fusion, pelvic deformities and all toes absent. Cf. project #6.
Conclusion: Programed inducement of crossover only partially successful employing template solution #17K.

Recommendation: Repeat but attempt layering of template on crystalline substrate (in hand) or use of gel version (in hand).

Disposition of remains: Authorized (initialed JBS).

AN ALARMING ITEM TO FIND ON YOUR CREDIT-RATING STATEMENT

Inspection of computerized records has revealed that over half the credit standing to your name derives from nonlegal undertakings, details of which have been forwarded to the Attorney General of the United States. In anticipation of criminal proceedings your permissible credit is limited to the Federal Supportive Norm, viz. $28.50 per day.

The Commission on Poverty has held this insufficient to provide an adequate diet; however, upgrading to the proposed norm of $67.50 per day still awaits presidential approval.

This is a cybernetic datum for the public service.

AN ALARMING ITEM TO FIND ON YOUR DESK COME MONDAY MORNING

To all employees of Marmaduke Smith Metal Products Inc.

The decision taken to commission the building and launching of an orbital factory for your company by Ground-to-Space Industries Inc. (contract noncancelable) was reached as the result of a warning from the chief accountant Mr J. J. Himmelweiss that the corporation faces certain bankruptcy.

At the same meeting of the Board which confirmed the placing of the G2S contract all officers were voted an additional 100 percent of their respective holdings of stock to dispose of at temporarily inflated prices prior to the company's voluntary liquidation which is scheduled for the end of next month.

Thsi is an unauthorized cybernetic announcement.

AN ALARMING ITEM TO FIND ON A COSMETICS PACKAGE

This product contains a known allergen and a known carcinogen. The manufacturers have expended over $650,000 in out-of-court settlements to avoid legal suits by former users. This is a cybernetic datum imprinted on the wrapper without the manufacturers' knowledge or consent.

AN ALARMING ITEM TO FIND ON A PACK OF
'HONEST-TO-GOODNESS'® BEEF STEW

Despite being advertised as domestic, this stew contains 15 to 35 percent imported meat originating in areas where typhus, brucellosis and trichinosomiasis are endemic. Authority to label the contents as domestic produce was obtained following the expenditure of appx. $215,000 in bribes to customs and public-health inspectors. This is a cybernetic datum derived from records not intended for publication.

AN ALARMING ITEM TO FIND ON
A MONTHLY AUTO-DEBIT NOTICE

Advice to clients of Anti-Trauma Inc.

A status check of the first one hundred juveniles treated according to this corporation's methods, all of whom are now at least three years past termination of their courses of therapy, reveals that:

66 are receiving prescribed psychotropic drugs;
62 are classed educationally subaverage;
59 have recently reported nightmares and hallucinations;
43 have been arrested at least once;
37 have run away from home at least once;
19 are in jail or subject to full-time supervision orders;
15 have been convicted of crimes of violence;
15 have been convicted of theft;
13 have been convicted of arson;
8 have been committed to mental hospitals at least once;
6 are dead;
5 have wounded parents, close relatives or guardians;
2 have murdered siblings;
1 awaits trial for molesting a girl aged three.

Totals do not sum to 100 because most are entered under more than one head. This is a cybernetic announcement in the public interest.

AN ALARMING ITEM TO FIND ON YOUR OVERDUE-TAX DEMAND

For the information of the person required to pay this tax
Analysis of last year's federal budget shows that:

* * * 17% of your tax dollar went on	boondoggles
* * * 13%	propaganda, bribes and kickbacks
* * * 11%	federal contracts with companies

which are (a) fronting for criminal activities and/or (b) partly or wholly owned by persons subject to indictment for federal offenses and/or (c) hazardous to health and the environment. Fuller details may be obtained by punching the code number at top left of this form into any veephone. They take about 57 minutes to present.

This is a cybernetic datum appended without Treasury Department authorization.

AN ALARMING ITEM TO HEAR OVER THE VEEPHONE

'No, Mr Sullivan, we can't stop it! There's never been a worm with that tough a head or that long a tail! It's building itself, don't you understand? Already it's passed a billion bits and it's still growing. It's the exact inverse of a phage – whatever it takes in, it adds to itself instead of wiping ... Yes, sir! I'm quite aware that a worm of that type is theoretically impossible! But the fact stands, he's done it, and now it's so goddamn comprehensive that it can't be killed. Not short of demolishing the net!'

THE OUTCOME OF THE BRAIN RACE (COMPUTED)

The first shall be last and the last shall be first.

THE WHOLE CONTINENT ON THE BRINK OF ONE PRECIPICE

The press conference automatically called by Nick's program was to be held in the largest auditorium on the UMKC campus. The students had been delighted to commandeer it. Discreetly, the university authorities declined a request from the state governor to intervene. Among the persons credited with work on Miranda and those like her were two incumbent faculty members, and they were – sensibly – spending today behind locked doors and steel shutters. The students were very unhappy about those deformed babies.

Moreover, for the first time in well over a generation, the mass of public opinion was in agreement with the students. Gratifying. If it didn't heal the split, at least it moved the split to a healthier location.

The hall was packed – it was crammed. If modern technology hadn't shrunk three-vee cameras and sound-recording equipment to a size that the engineers of fifty years ago would have called impossible, the puzzled but dutiful reporters who had arrived to cover a story they were certain must be sensational ... whatever the hell it was, would have been unable to put anything on their tapes. As it was, they were obliged to use poles, electric floaters and their longest-range mikes and lenses because they couldn't get anywhere near the rostrum, and there was a squabble over priority in respect of lines of sight which delayed the start of the conference until well past the scheduled time of noon.

At long last, however, Kate was able to appear on stage, to be greeted by a standing ovation that threatened never to end. It took her a long time to pat down the noise. When she finally did so, the putter-of-cats-among-pigeons made his appearance, and the audience settled to an expectant hush.

'My name is Nicholas Haflinger.' In a loud clear voice, capable of filling the auditorium without the aid of microphones. 'You're wondering why I've called you here. The reason is simple. To answer all your questions. I mean – all. This is the greatest news of our time. As of today, whatever you want to know, provided it's in the data-net, you can now know. In other words, *there are no more secrets.*'

That claim was so sweeping that his listeners sat briefly stunned. Long seconds slid away before there came a diffident call from a woman reporter near the front, one of the lucky ones who had arrived early.

'Rose Jordan, W3BC! What about this story that was on the beams, the bait that pulled us in? This thing where you said G2S will sue officials of the Bureau of Data Processing for kidnaping one of its employees, and also some girlfriend of his?'

'That was me, and the story's absolutely true,' Kate said. 'But you didn't have to come here for the details. Ask any veephone.'

'Yesterday you'd have had to come here,' Nick amplified. 'If there's one thing BDP has brought to a fine art, it's preventing the public from digging unpleasant truths from behind the scenes in government ... right?'

A rattle of agreement: from the students on principle, but from several reporters too, who looked so glum one might presume they'd encountered that kind of trouble.

'Well, that's over. From now on: ask and you shall know.'

'Hey!' In an incredulous tone from a man beside Rose Jordan. 'All kind of weird stuff has been coming off the beams since yesterday, like they've been paying women to bear kids that are sure to be deformed. You mean this is supposed to be true?'

'What makes you doubt it?'

'Well – uh …' The man licked his lips. 'I called my office half an hour back and my chief said it's been authoritatively deeveed. By Aylwin Sullivan personally. Something about a saboteur.'

'That must be me.' Cocking one eyebrow. 'Any word of this sabotage being stopped?'

'Not that I heard.'

'Good. At least they didn't make that ridiculous promise. Because it can't be stopped. I guess you all know about tapeworms …? Good. Well, what I turned loose in the net yesterday was the father and mother – I'll come back to that in a moment – the father and mother of all tapeworms.

'It consists in a comprehensive and irrevocable order to release at any printout station any and all data in store whose publication may conduce to the enhanced well-being, whether physical, psychological or social, of the population of North America.

'Specifically, whether or not anybody has required a printout of it, information concerning gross infringements of Canadian, Mexican and/or United States legal enactments respecting – in order of priority – public health, the protection of the environment, bribery and corruption, fair business and the payment of national taxes, shall be disseminated automatically to all the media. For this purpose "gross" is defined by setting a threshold: no such infringement shall be published unless at least one person made from it an illegal profit of at least ten thousand dollars.'

He had straightened as he spoke. Now he was arrow-rigid, and his voice boomed in huge resounding periods like the tolling of a death bell.

'This is indeed the father and mother of a tapeworm. It's of a type known as parthenogenetic. If you're acquainted with contemporary data-processing jargon, you'll have noticed how much use it makes of terminology derived from the study of living animals. And with reason. Not for nothing is a tapeworm called a tapeworm. It can be made to breed. Most can only do so if they're fertilized; that's to say, if they're interfered with from outside. For example the worm that prevents the Fedcomps from monitoring calls to Hearing Aid, and the similar but larger one that was released at Weychopee – Electric Skillet – to shut down the net in the event of enemy occupation: those are designed to lie dormant until tampered with. That's true of all phage-type worms.

'My newest – my masterpiece – breeds by itself. For a head it wears a max-imum-national-advantage rating, a priority code that I stole from G2S. It was allocated to the corporation because like other hypercorps it's been treated for years as though it were above the law. Imagine how embarrassing it would be to make known all the bribes, all the graft, all the untaxed kickbacks, which don't appear in G2S's annual report to the stockholders ...

'Right behind that, my worm wears a U-group code, which does the same for individuals. The owner of a U-group code will never find himself in court. *Never*. No matter if he rapes the mayor's daughter at midday on Main Street. You don't believe me? Go punch a veephone. Ask for a plain-language print-out of the status label worn by a U-group code. As of about an hour and a half ago it will print out for anybody ... and it's enlightening.'

Two or three people rose in the body of the hall as though bent on con-firming Nick's assertion. He paused to let the disturbance subside.

'In back of that again, there's the key which opens the secure data banks at all secret psychological research establishments, including Tarnover and Crediton Hill. Behind that is one which opens the Treasury files on tax-avoidance suits unpursued by presidential order. Behind that is the one which opens similar files belonging to the Attorney General. Behind that is the one which opens the files of the Food and Drug Authority. And so on. By now I don't know exactly what there is in the worm. More bits are being added automatically as it works its way to places I never dared guess existed. The last I found out about before I came along to talk to you was a key for the CIA's sexual-blackmail file. There's some raunchy material in there, and I predict it will be popular home viewing this winter.

'A couple of final points before someone asks me. First, is this an unforgiv-able invasion of privacy? Invasion of privacy it is; unforgivable ... Well, do you believe that justice shall not only be done but shall be seen to be done? The privacy my worm is designed to invade is that privacy under whose cover justice is not done and injustice is not seen. It doesn't care whether the poker who leeched his tax-free payoff spent it on seducing little girls; it cares only that he was rewarded for committing a crime and wasn't brought to book. It doesn't care if the shivver who bought that congressman was straight or gay; it cares only that a public servant took a bribe. It doesn't care if the judge who misdirected the jury was concerned to keep her lover's identity secret; it cares only that a person was jailed who should have been released.

'And – no, it *can't* be killed. It's indefinitely self-perpetuating so long as the net exists. Even if one segment of it is inactivated, a counterpart of the miss-ing portion will remain in store at some other station and the worm will automatically subdivide and send a duplicate head to collect the spare groups and restore them to their proper place. Incidentally, though, it won't expand to indefinite size and clog the net for other use. It has built-in limits.'

He gave a faint smile.

'Though I say so myself, it's a neat bit of work.'

All of a sudden a man no older than his thirties, but pot-bellied, who had been in a seat near the back of the hall, came yelling down the aisle.

'Traitor!' he howled. 'Goddamned stinking traitor!'

With his right hand he was tugging at something under his jacket; it appeared to have caught. It came free. It was a pistol. He tried to aim it.

But a quick-witted student in a seat on the aisle stuck out his leg. The fat man went sprawling with a yell, and next moment a booted foot tramped on his right wrist and he was disarmed.

From the platform Nick said, 'Ah. That's the first. It won't be the last.'

AND THE TRUTH SHALL MAKE YOU YOU

Q This place Tarnover you keep talking about. I never heard of it.

A It's a government establishment, one of several. All are under the direction of the spiritual successors of the people who deployed nuclear weapons in over-kill quantity. Or maybe I should cite the people who thought nothing of taking a fee to condition little boys out of playing with themselves.

Q What?

A You don't believe there were such people? Punch for data concerning the income of the Behavioral Science Department of the Lawrence campus of the University of Kansas back around 1969, 1970. I swear it's true.

Q Same again, but this time Weychopee.

A Ah, yes. Working for G2S I moused deep into their banks. That's Electric Skillet, the continental defense center. By defense they mean they override the controls on all incoming chunks of asteroid ore and send them crashing down on the eastern hemisphere like a rain of thousand-ton hailstones. I haven't yet checked out how many of the people who bought asteroid drivers from G2S realized that facility was built in.

Q But that's insane!

A Sure it is. The blast wave from the impact would level every structure on this continent taller than fifteen meters. They don't care. They want to turn Ragnarök into rain-of-rocks. Excuse me. Yes?

Q The bottom dropped out of stock in Anti-Trauma. Your doing?

A Mostly theirs. Their failure rate has never fallen below sixty-five percent, but they've kept it such a close secret that last year they doubled their clientele. Never again, I hope.

Q Some weird things happened to Delphi odds lately.

A I'm glad you brought that up. Data from Crediton Hill are in the net by now. Check them out. A lot of you probably have deeveed tickets you can claim against. The legislation authorizing Delphi betting obliged the organizers to make refunds if it could be shown that the pool was manipulated, and there's no reference to the organizers themselves being exempt.

Q But I thought the whole point of Delphi was to tell the government what changes the public was ready for. You mean it's been turned around?

A Go find a veephone and ask for the incidence of federal intervention per annum for the last five years.

Q How the hell were you able to build a tapeworm this complicated?

A It's a talent, like a musician's, or a poet's. I can play a computer read-in literally for hours at a time and never hit a wrong note.

Q Christ almighty. Well, this flood of data you let loose may be okay for people like you. Me, I'm scared shitless.

A I'm sorry you're scared of being free.

Q What?

A The truth shall make you free.

Q You say that as though you believe it.

A Well, hell! If I didn't …! Anybody here get nightmares because you know data exist you can't get at and other people can? Anybody suffering with chronic anxiety, insomnia, digestive trouble, general stress response syndrome? Mm-hm. Turn any wet stone and you find victims. And as to the underlying cause … Any of you play at fencing? Yes? Then you know how frustrating it is to find that your opponent has claimed a point slam in the middle of your best potential triangle. All your cherished schemes go crash because he outsmarted you. Well, that's a game. When it's a matter of real life it's not fun any more, is it? And up to now the data net has been consciously manipulated to prevent us finding out what we most need to know.

Q Come again?

A We know, we feel in our guts, that decisions are constantly being made which are going to wreck our ambitions, our dreams, our personal relationships. But the people making those decisions are keeping them secret, because if they don't they'll lose the leverage they have over their subordinates. It's a marvel we're not all gibbering with terror. A good few of us do wind up gibbering, don't they? Others manage to keep afloat by denying – repressing – awareness of the risk that it's all going to go smash. Others still drive themselves into null passivity, what's been called 'the new conformity', so that even if they are suddenly unplugged from one side of the continent and relocated on the other they'll be able to carry on without noticing the change. Which is sick. Is the purpose of creating the largest information-transmission system in history to present mankind with a brand-new reason for paranoia?

Q And you think what you've done is going to put all this to rights.

A Do I sound that arrogant? I hope not! No, what I've done at best means there's a chance of it coming right that didn't exist before. A chance is better than no chance. The rest ... Well, it's up to all of us, not just to me.

SIEGE PERILOUS

It was quiet at Kate's home: outside, where volunteer students patrolled the streets for three blocks in all directions, proud that here of all places had been chosen to unleash the avalanche of truth; inside also, where Freeman was working at a remote data console donated by G2S on Rico Posta's authority, coupled via regular phone lines to the corporation's own immense computer facilities.

The veephone was quiet too. There had been so many calls, they had recruited a filtration service.

Bringing coffee, Kate said, 'Paul, how's it going?'

'Ask Nick. He can keep more things in his head at one time than I can.'

Working with an ordinary desk calculator and a scratch pad, Nick said, 'Fairly well. There already were a couple of resource-allocation programs in store, and one of them is very damned good. Very flexible. The update facility is particularly elegant.'

'Better than this, then,' Freeman muttered. 'I just found a loophole you could fly an orbital factory through. But I got to one thing that ought to wring some withers.'

'Tell me!' Nick glanced up alertly.

'Proof that all poverty on this continent is artificial except what stems from physical illness, mental incapacity or private choice. Like homesteading a patch of the Canadian northwoods ... or going into a monastery. That's about – oh – a quarter of one percent, max.'

Kate stared at him. 'You make it sound as though we'd be better off, not worse, after some kind of continental disaster. And that's absurd!'

'Not entirely.' Nick went on tapping his calculator as he spoke. 'One case that comes to mind. During and after World War II they cut food rations in Britain to what most of us would think of as starvation level. Two ounces of margarine a week, an egg a month if you were lucky, things like that. But back then they had more sense than they do now. They hired top-rank dietitians to plot their priorities. They raised the tallest, handsomest, healthiest generation in their history. When rickets reappeared again after rationing ended, it made national headlines. We think of abundance and good health as going hand in hand. It doesn't follow. That way lies heart failure, too.'

The phone sounded. Kate gave a start. But Nick had come to a point where he could break off and ponder what he had written. Reaching out absently, he turned the camera so he could be seen by the caller.

And exclaimed, 'Ted Horovitz!'

The others tensed, everything else forgotten.

The sheriff of Precipice exhaled gustily and wiped his face.

'Lord, after fighting my way past your filtration service I was afraid I might be too late! Listen carefully. This is a breach of Hearing Aid rules but I think it's justified. Ever hear of a shivver named Hartz? Claims to be the former Deputy Director of BDP.'

Freeman leaned into camera field. 'I didn't know about the "former" bit,' he said. 'But the rest is solid.'

'Then get the hell away from where you are. Clear the house – the surrounding streets too, for preference. He says a hit job has been authorized against you. Category V, he called it.'

Freeman whistled. 'That means "execute regardless of casualties" – and they generally use a bomb for those!'

'It figures. We got a tip about someone smuggling a bomb into Precipice, too. Sent Natty Bumppo and the rest of the dogs on perimeter patrol— Oh, I'll tell you when you get here.'

'You're able to transport three?' Nick rapped.

Freeman cut him short. 'Not me. I stay close to G2S. I need their facilities. Don't argue!' He smiled; he was more relaxed now, able to do so without looking like a death's head. 'I've done some bad things with my life. If I finish this job I can make up for them all at one go.'

Horovitz glanced at his watch. 'Right. I've arranged for you to be met in about ten minutes. Jake Treves was intending to stop by your place, of course, but I contacted him and warned him there'd be a change of rendezvous. Make a suggestion and I'll pass the word for him to be there.'

NIGHT ERRAND

'You look kind of down,' the driver said.

'Hell, with the continent crumbling around us …!' The passenger in the rear seat of the quiet electric car fumbled with the lock of the briefcase across his knees. 'Everything's gone into a spin. First I get the order to do the job, then they say hold it, we may send in the National Guard instead, then they say back to plan one after all. Jesus, the damage that's been done while they were dithering! Okay, this will be close enough.'

The driver said in astonishment, 'But we're still five blocks away!'

'They got all them students on guard. Could be armed.'

'Yeah, but … Look, I drove this kind of mission before. If you're planning to hit them from here you—'

'Save it. I got what you wouldn't believe.' The passenger clicked open his case and began to assemble something slim and tapered and matt-black. 'Pull over. I got to launch it from a dead stop.'

Obeying, the driver glanced in his mirror. His eyes widened.

'That little-bitty thing brings down a house?'

'Told you you wouldn't believe it,' the passenger answered curtly. He lowered his window and leaned out.

'So what in the—?'

'None of your business!'

Then, relenting with a sigh: 'Ah, what difference does it make? Classified – top secret – doesn't matter since that bugger turned his worm loose. Tomorrow anybody can get at plans for this gadget. It's called a kappa-bird. Ever hear the name?'

The driver frowned. 'Believe I did. You got two other cars around the area, right?'

'Mm-hm. Giving a one-meter fix on the roof of the target.'

'But – hell, a whole *house*?'

'Instant firestorm. Hotter than the surface of the sun.' The passenger gave a wry chuckle. 'Still want to be closer when she blows?'

The driver shook his head emphatically.

'Nor me. Okay, there she goes. Swing around, head south, don't hurry.'

Later there was a bright reflection on the low gray cloud sealing in the city.

WELL DOCUMENTED

Dutifully, at each state border control post, Dr Jake Treves presented a succession of documents to the inspectors: his own ID, his certificate of professional status, his permit as a research biologist to transport protected species interstate, and his manifest for this particular journey.

Upon which the dialogue developed in predictable patterns.

'You really got a mountain lion in this truck?'

'Mm-hm. Safely sedated, of course.'

'Say! I never saw a live mountain lion. Can I …?'

'Sure.'

Invited to slide back the door over a peephole, the inspectors saw an elderly though still sleek male specimen of *Felis concolor*, drowsy but alert enough to curl his lip in annoyance.

Also they smelt a strong feline stench. From an aerosol can. Very useful to induce big cats to breed in captivity.

'Faugh! Sure hope for your sake you got air conditioning in your cab!'

And for getting up the nose of nosyparkers.

COUNCIL OF PERFECTION

For a while Bagheera had padded around Ted Horovitz's moss-green office, searching for Natty Bumppo, whose trace-scent was everywhere, but all the adult dogs were still on perimeter patrol. Now he was lying contentedly at Kate's side while she gently scratched him behind the ears. Occasionally he emitted a purr of satisfaction at having been reunited with her.

The problem of what to do when he discovered he was among more than a hundred dogs built to his own scale would have to wait.

Looking around the company of local people – Josh and Lorna Treves, Suzy Dellinger, Sweetwater, Brad Compton – Ted said briskly, 'Now I know Nick and Kate got a lot of questions for us. Before we get into that area, any of you got questions for them? Keep 'em short, please. Yes, Sweetwater?'

'Nick, how long before they see through your doubletalk about a parthenogenetic worm?'

Nick spread his hands. 'I've no idea. People like Aylwin Sullivan and his top aides probably suspect the truth already. What I'm banking on, though, is … Well, there are two factors. First, I really did write one worm that's too tough for them to tackle. Second, from their point of view, whatever this new gimmick may be it's doing precisely what a parthenogenetic worm would do if such a thing could be written. Now there's a recherché theorem in n-value mean-path analysis which suggests that at some stage in the evolution of a data-net it must become possible to extract from that net functional programs that were never fed into it.'

'Hey, hey!' Brad Compton clapped his plump hands. 'Neat, oh *very* neat! That's what they call the virgin-birth theorem, isn't it? And you've given them a nice subtle signpost to it!' He chuckled and clapped again.

'That's the essence. Not original. I stole the idea. The western powers, back in World War II, pioneered the trick. They set their scientists to building devices which looked as though they absolutely must do *something*, put them in battered metal cases, took them out on a firing range and shot them up with captured enemy ammunition. Then they arranged for the things to be found by the Nazis. One such bit of nonsense could tie up a dozen top research personnel for weeks before they dared decide it wasn't a brand-new secret weapon.'

A ripple of amusement ran around the group.

'In any case,' Nick added, 'it won't make much odds how soon they decide they've been misled. They'd still have to shut down the net to stop what's happening, wouldn't they?'

'No doubt of that,' Mayor Dellinger said crisply. 'At latest count we have ninety-four sets of those Treasury files they changed the lock on, and over sixty of the FBI files, and – well, nothing that I know of has been copied to fewer than forty separate locations. And while the Fedcomps are tracing them we can be sure that people we don't know about will be making copies in their turn.'

'People we'd better not know about,' Lorna Treves muttered. Her husband gave a vigorous nod.

'Yes, it's a fraught situation. Granted, it's what we always said we were preparing for, but ... Oh well; the fact that it took us by surprise is just another example of Toffler's Law, I guess: the future arrives too soon and in the wrong order. Nick, how long before they conclude Kate's home was empty when they bombed it?'

'Again I can't guess. I didn't find time on the way here to stop off at a phone and inquire.'

That provoked another unison smile.

'In any case,' Ted put in, 'I've been taking precautions. Right now, after the media showing of their press conference, Nick and Kate have about the most recognizable faces on the continent. So they're going to be recognized. In one location after another and sometimes simultaneously. Oh, we can keep them hopping for several days.'

'Days,' Josh Treves echoed. 'Well, I guess it's all been computed.'

Brad nodded. 'And, remember, we're dipping the biggest CIMA pool in history.'

There was a pause. Kate stirred when she realized no one else was about to speak.

'Can I put a question, please?'

Ted waved her an invitation.

'It seems kind of silly, but ... Oh, hell! I really want to know. And I think Nick does too.'

'Whatever it is,' Nick said dryly, 'I agree. I'm still operating ninety percent on guesswork.'

'You want the story of Precipice?' Ted grunted. 'Okay, I'll tell it. But the rest of us better get back to work. Among other things the crisis is overextending the resources of Hearing Aid, and if we don't cope ...'

'Brad can stay too,' Sweetwater said, rising. 'He just came off shift, and I won't have him back after the last call he handled.'

'Rough?' Nick said sympathetically. The plump librarian swallowed hard and nodded.

'See you later,' Suzy Dellinger said, and led the way out.

Leaning back with his hands on his ample paunch and gazing at the shimmering green ceiling, Brad said, 'Y'know, we wouldn't be telling you this if you'd done as Polly Ryan suggested the day you arrived.'

'What do you mean?' Kate demanded.

'Come ask for a sight of our first edition of the "Disasterville U.S.A." series. How many of the monographs did your father have?'

'Why, the full set of twenty!'

'Which, of course, looked to him, as to everybody, like a nice round number. Our edition, though, contains a twenty-first. The one that no publisher would handle, no printer would set in type – the one that finally in desperation we printed ourselves and had ready for distribution, only one night a bomb went off in the shed where we'd stored our first ten thousand copies and they burned to ash. Obviously we were fighting a losing battle. So ...' He sighed.

Kate leaned forward tensely. 'What was the twenty-first about?'

'It accounted with names, dates, places, photostats of canceled checks – all the necessary evidence – for half a million of the four million dollars of public money which by then had gone astray and never reached the refugees who were supposed to benefit.'

'You're not telling the whole story,' Ted said in a brittle voice. 'Kate, when you were first here you asked whether Claes College broke up because most of its members stayed at Precipice – remember?'

She nodded, her face strained.

'The answer's yes. After the night when that shed was bombed, they didn't have a choice. Brad and I helped to bury them.'

There was a long empty silence. Eventually Kate said, 'This last monograph – did it have a title?'

'Yes. Prophetically enough, it was to be called *Discovering the Power Base.*'

The next silence stretched so long, the air felt as though it were being drawn out until it threatened to snap. At last Nick uttered a gusting sigh.

'Hell, I never looked at it that way. I must be blind.'

'I won't argue,' the sheriff said, his expression very grave. 'But you were not alone. Yet in retrospect ... Figure it this way. You equip the population of a whole continent with unprecedented techniques: access to information, transportation, so much credit nobody need ever be poor again – assuming, that is, that it's properly shared. Just about at the same time, you admit there's no point in fighting any more major wars because there's too much to lose and not enough to win. In Porter's famous phrase, it's time for the brain race.

'But you're in government. Your continuance in power has always depended on the ultimate sanction: "If you don't obey we'll kill you." Maybe you weren't consciously aware of that basic truth. Maybe it only became clear to you, against your will, when you were obliged to try and work out why things were no longer ticking along as smoothly as they used to. As a result, naturally, of the shift in emphasis from weaponry to individual brilliance as the key national resource.

'But brilliant individuals are cantankerous, unpredictable, fond of having their own way. It seems out of the question to use them as mere tools, mere objects. Almost, you find yourself driven to the conclusion that you're obsolete. Power of your kind isn't going to be viable in the modern world.

'And then it dawns on you. There's another organization exercising immense power which has always been dependent on individuals far more troublesome than those you're being defeated by. In some cases they're outright psychopathic.'

'And this organization is equally determined to maintain its place in the sun,' Brad supplemented. 'It's equally willing to apply the final sanction to those who disobey.'

Kate's jaw dropped.

'I think we got through,' Ted murmured.

'Yes – yes, I'm afraid so.' Kate folded her hands into fists. 'But I can't bring myself to believe it. Nick …?'

'Since your apt was blown up,' Nick said stonily, 'I've been prepared to believe anything about them. It was a miracle we had enough warning to clear the streets. Or did we …? Ted, I've been meaning to ask. Was anybody injured?'

The sheriff gave a sour nod. 'I'm afraid some of the students didn't take the warning literally. Ten were hurt. Two of them have died.'

Kate buried her face in her palms, her shoulders shaking.

'Go ahead, Nick,' Ted invited. 'Spell it out as you see it. You yourself said yesterday: the truth shall make us free. That holds good no matter how abominable the truth.'

'There was exactly one power base available to sustain the old style of government,' Nick grunted. 'Organized crime.'

Ted rose and set to pacing back and forth, back and forth. He said, 'Of course that's not exactly news. It must be fifty or sixty years since the traditional fortunes that used to put this party, then the other, into office either ran dry or came under the control of people who weren't willing to play along. That left a vacuum. Into it criminals looking for ways to convert their huge financial resources into real power flooded like water through a breached dam. They'd always been intimately involved at city and state level; now was their chance to ascend the ladder's final rung. It's true that the Syndicate's first attempt at the presidency was pretty much of a bust. They didn't realize how bright a spotlight could be shone on 1600 Pennsylvania. Moreover, they used tricks that were already well known, like laundering their bribe-money through Mexico and the Virgins. But they learned fast.'

'They did indeed,' Brad said. 'The moral of monograph 21 lies not in the half-million dollars we were able to trace, but in the rest of the money which we couldn't. We know where it went – into political war chests – but we stood no chance of finding the evidence.'

'In the context of the world nuclear disarmament treaty,' Ted muttered, 'we were hoping for something better.'

'I bet you were.' Nick was scowling. 'Oh, I should have figured this out long ago.'

'You weren't so favorably placed,' Brad countered dryly. 'Sharing a tent with ten refugees, without a change of clothing, decent food or even safe water to drink, it was easy to spot the resemblance between the federal agent and the *mafioso*. The fact that they were invariably on the friendliest terms merely underlined what we'd already realized.'

'I should have got there by another route,' Nick said. 'I should have wondered why behavioral science received such colossal government subsidies during the eighties and nineties.'

'An important point,' Ted said with a nod. 'Consistent with the rest of the pattern. The behaviorists reduced the principle of the carrot and the stick to the same kind of "scientific" basis as the Nazis used for their so-called racial science. It's not surprising they became the darlings of the establishment. Governments rely on threat and trauma to survive. The easiest populace to rule is weak, poor, superstitious, preferably terrified of what tomorrow may bring, and constantly being reminded that the man in the street must step into the gutter when his superiors deign to pass him by. Behaviorist techniques offered a means to maintain this situation despite the unprecedented wealth, literacy and ostensible liberty of twenty-first-century North America.'

'If you recognize in Ted's description a resemblance to Sicily,' Brad murmured, 'that's not purely coincidental.'

Kate by now had recovered her self-control and was leaning forward with elbows on knees, listening intently.

'The data-net must have posed a terrible threat to them,' she suggested.

'True, but one they were able to guard against,' Ted answered. 'Until now, I mean. They took every precaution. They built the Delphi system on the base provided by the existing gambling syndicates. They claim it was modeled on the stock market, but there was really very little difference, since by then gambling money was one of the two or three biggest sources of speculative investment. They took to leaving tribes alone when they went on the warpath, and the result was that the most ambitious kids, the ones with both rage and intelligence, wound up dead or crippled. That came naturally. Since time immemorial they'd been carefully isolating gang wars from involvement with the general public. Also they turned over the massive computer capacity designed to get men safely to and from the Moon to tracking a population moving to a new place at the rate of twenty percent a year. And so on. I don't need to recite the whole list.'

'But if they were so careful how did you—?' Kate checked and bit her lip. 'Oh. Stupid of me. Hearing Aid.'

'Mm-hm.' Ted dropped back into his chair. 'Our computer capacity at Precipice has been adequate to dissect out patterns from the calls made to Hearing Aid for about – oh – sixteen or seventeen years. Now and then, moreover, we've had a single call that opened up a whole new area of investigation for us. Yours while you were at Tarnover, for example.' He nodded at Nick. 'We've quietly followed up one lead after another, accumulating things like the keys needed to open federal-secure data banks, convinced that ultimately a crisis must occur that would leave the public dazed and panicky. At which time they would want to be told where they were in the world. To further our design we created the – the underground railroad which we passed you along: friends, colleagues, associates, supporters, sympathizers, in literally hundreds of different professions.'

'Paul Freeman put it neatly,' Nick said. 'According to him, Precipice is a very big place once you learn to recognize it.'

Ted chuckled. 'Oh, yes! If you count in all those people whom we've created freemen, entitled to be defended by our defenses, our population totals five or six times what you find in a census return.'

'We had models to copy,' Brad said. 'The old hippie movement, for one. The eighteenth-century community of science. An organization called Open Door which flourished in the middle of the last century. And so forth.'

'Your foresight was fantastic,' Kate said warmly.

'Pretty fair,' Ted acknowledged. 'Above average, that's for certain. But we never foresaw that the crisis would arrive in the shape of one young man!'

'Not one,' Nick said. 'Several. Tarnover deserter, life-style counselor, preacher, fencing hustler—'

'Person,' Kate said firmly, and laid her hand over his. 'And by the way, Ted!'

'Yes?'

'Thank you for saving Bagheera.'

'Wasn't too hard. Did you talk to Jake Treves on the way here, find out why he was able to help out?'

She shook her head. 'He put us straight into the concealed compartment. We didn't show our heads the whole time.'

'Safer that way, I guess. Well, Jake is one of the people working on the problem of how to get our dogs to live to a ripe old age. It's part of a wide program to find out how stress is linked to aging. When you get the chance you'll enjoy talking to Jake, you know. Your father's hypothesis—'

He was interrupted. Distant in the night there was a sharp bark, followed by another and another.

Brad cocked his head. 'Sounds as though Nat caught the bomber we're expecting.'

Ted rose to his feet. 'If so,' he grunted, 'I wouldn't care to be in his shoes.'

AMONG THE FACTORS THAT CLIMAXED IN A BREAKDOWN OF GOVERNMENT

1: *Thank you for your inquiry concerning the whereabouts of Secret Service Operative Miskin A. Breadloaf. He is under intensive medical care at Precipice, CA recovering from injuries sustained while resisting arrest by Sheriff Theodore Horovitz. He was in possession of six self-seeking catapult bombs, U.S. Army Code QB3, issued to him at 1010 PST yesterday from stocks held in the National Guard Armory at San Feliciano CA in pursuance of Confidential Presidential Directive #919 001 HVW, which states in full:*

'I'm sick of Hearing Aid. Get the buggers who run it and never mind who else you hurt.'

2: *As a result of the failure of Mr Breadloaf's mission a strike has been authorized against Precipice CA at 0130 PST tomorrow by aircraft based at Lowndes Field near San Diego. Since this is to be carried out with junior nukes (USAF Code 19L-12) Mr Breadloaf is not expected to survive.*

(NB: part 2 of the foregoing message is a cybernetic datum published in direct contravention of DoD Regulation #229RR3X3, as being conducive to the physical, psychological and/or social well-being of the population.)

EXTREMELY CROSS SECTION

'Wipe that grin off your face! You knew the company was going broke and I can prove it!'

'Precipice? Where's that?'

'My sister went blind, hear me? Blind! And she never used any eye makeup except your brand!'

'Bomb an American city? Oh, it must be a mistake.'

'It was my money, and I sweated blood to earn it, and it went to feather your stinking nest!'

'Precipice? Seems to me I heard that name before.'

'Christ, what you did to the poor little slittie! She hasn't had a good night's sleep in months, she always wakes up screaming and howling, and I was fool enough to bring her back for more. I could never look her in the face again if I didn't ruin yours.'

'What was that about Precipice?'

'Damn right I voted for him. But if I'd known then what I know now I wouldn't have cast a vote. I'd have cast a brick.'

'A strike? With nukes? My God, I know Hearing Aid isn't exactly popular, but—!'

'Jim, I don't believe you know my lawyer Charles Sweyn. He has something to give you. Charlie? Fine. You'll notice the summons mentions damages of fifty million.'

'I thought we were talking about some town called Precipice.'

'I read what it said on that tax form and I swear to God I'll pay you in buckshot if you show your filthy nose around my place!'

'Really? I always wondered where their base was.'

'Precipice?'

'Hearing Aid?'

'Nukes?'

'My God! Do you think they know about this? Where's a phone? *Quick!*'

TOUCH AND GO

Past one A.M. at the headquarters of Hearing Aid. Ordinarily a dead time of night because most of the continent had orbited into sleep and only a handful of the most lonely, the most dismal, the most despairing were still anxious to talk to an anonymous listener.

Tonight was different. The room was crackling with restrained tension. The goal to which since its foundation Precipice had been dedicated was upon them, and they had never expected it to be so soon.

Solemn expressions were on the faces of the dozen people present. Only half of them were engaged in listening duty; other calls were being relayed to private homes. The remainder were monitoring the progress of their super-tapeworm.

To them generally Nick said, turning away from his board, 'News from Paul Freeman. He got that body-and-soul program on the move, the one he hoped to adapt from the existing federal resources-allocation program. He said it was tough.'

'That was the postwar one?' Sweetwater inquired.

'Right.' Nick stretched his long arms. 'Consequently it was drafted to ensure that only people the government approved of would be allotted food, medicine, clothing and power.'

'You mean,' Kate supplied, 'it was built to make certain that the people fool enough to drag us into a major war would wind up on top again afterwards.'

'So they could screw us up the next time, right. But Paul managed to peel away that factor by substituting a half-like basis for entitlement to credit, and left the rest intact to run the net with even more authority than it had when it was an arm for Weychopee. He was there when it was written. Spotted its weaknesses right away.'

'So what does it do now?' Brad Compton demanded.

'Not a few good things. If people vote for Proposition #1, no greedy shivver will get his wall-to-wall three-vee so long as anybody's homeless. He won't get his round-the-planet airship cruise so long as people are dying from any disease we know how to cure.'

'Smooth enough for starters,' Sweetwater said. 'But has there been any progress on your side, Nick – rationalizing the tax structure? That's what I want to know about. When I think how angry I got paying off the croakers in Oakland because of their local ordinance against mediums …!'

'Oh, yes. Proposition #2 is cooking as nicely as #1,' Nick said, and tapped a quick code into his board. 'It went back to have a couple of loopholes deleted, and if there's no further snag … Ah, good. Coming up in about two minutes.'

Suzy Dellinger said absently, 'You know, I always wondered what democracy might smell like. Finally I detect it in the air.'

'Curious that it should arrive in the form of electronic government,' Sweetwater murmured.

Brad Compton glanced at her. 'Not really, when you think about the history of liberty. It's the story of how principle has gradually been elevated above the whim of tyrants. When the law was defined as more powerful than the king, that was one great breakthrough. Now we've come to another milestone. We're giving power to more people than have ever before enjoyed it, and—'

'And it makes me feel,' Nick interrupted, 'the way they must have felt when they started the first nuclear chain reaction. Will there still be a world in the morning?'

There was a short pause, silent but for the hum of the electrical equipment, as they contemplated the continental pre-empt scheduled for the day after tomorrow. From 0700 local until 1900 every veephone on the continent would display, over and over, two propositions, accompanied by a spoken version for the benefit of the illiterate. Most would be in English, but some would be in Spanish, some in Amerind languages, some in Chinese … the proportions being based on the latest continental census. After each repetition would follow a pause, during which any adult could punch into the phone his or her code, followed by a 'yes' or a 'no'.

And according to the verdict, the computers of the continent would respond.

Proposition #1 concerned the elimination of all but voluntary poverty. Proposition #2—

'Here it comes,' Nick said, scanning the columns of figures and code groups appearing on his screen. 'Seems to be pretty well finalized. Categorizes occupations on three axes. One: necessary special training, or uncommon talent in lieu – that's to cover people with exceptional creative gifts like musicians or artists. Two: drawbacks like unpredictable hours and dirty working conditions. Three: social indispensability.'

Brad slapped his thigh. 'What a monument to Claes College!'

'Mm-hm. There'll be a footnote on every single printout explaining that if we'd paid attention to what the Claes group discovered by working among the Bay Quake refugees this could have been settled a generation back … Hmm! Yes, I think this balances out very nicely. For instance, a doctor will score high on special training and social importance too, but he can only get into the top pay bracket if he accepts responsibility for helping emergency cases, instead of keeping fixed office hours. That puts him high on all three scales. And a garbage collector, though rating low on special training, will do well on scales two and three. All public servants like police and firemen will automatically score high on scale three and most on scale two as well, and – oh, yes. I like the look of it. Particularly since a lot of parasites who were at the top in the old days will now pay tax at ninety percent because they score zero on all three axes.'

'Zero?' someone demanded in disbelief.

'Why not? People in advertising, for example.'

The questioner's eyebrows rose. 'Never thought of that before. But it figures.'

'Think they'll stand for it?' Kate said nervously, patting Bagheera, who lay at her side. Since meeting Natty Bumppo he had refused to be left out of sight of her, although he and the dog had exhibited mutual tolerance, as favorable a reaction as might have been hoped for.

'Their choice is to close down the net,' Nick said, and snapped his fingers. 'Thereby breaking their own necks. Suzy, you look worried.'

The mayor nodded. 'Even if they don't deliberately blow the net when they find they can't interfere with our pre-empt, to make some kind of grand suicidal gesture … there's another and more disturbing question.'

'What?'

'Are people scared into their right minds yet?'

The following silence was broken by the soft buzz of an incoming call. Kate switched it to her board and put on her phones.

Seconds later she uttered a loud gasp, and all heads turned to her.

Peeling off her phones again, she spun her chair, her cheeks as pale as paper and her eyes wide with fear.

'It can't be true! It simply can't be true! My God, it's already twenty past one – the plane must have taken off!'

'What? What?' A chorus of anxious voices.

'That caller claimed to be a cousin of Miskin Breadloaf. The would-be bomber you arrested, Ted. She says Precipice is going to be attacked with nukes at 0130!'

'Ten minutes? We can't possibly evacuate the town in ten minutes!' Suzy whispered, clenching her fists and staring at the wall clock as though willing it to show some earlier time.

'We'll have to try!' Ted snapped, jumping to his feet and heading for the door. 'I'll get Nat to rouse everybody and—' He checked. Nick had suddenly launched into a burst of furious activity, punching his board with fingers that flew faster than a pianist's.

'Nick! Don't waste time – move! We need everybody's help!'

'Shut up!' Nick grated between clenched teeth. 'Go on, wake the town, get everybody away that you can … *but leave me alone!*'

'Nick!' Kate said, taking an uncertain pace toward him.

'You too! Run like hell – because this may not work!'

'If you're going to stay then I—'

'Go, damn it!' Nick hissed. *'Go!'*

'But what are you trying to do?'

'Shut – up – and – go!'

Suddenly Kate found herself out in the chilly dark, and at her side Bagheera was trembling, the hairs on his nape raised and rough under her fingers. There was incredible noise: the dogs barking, Ted shouting through a bull-horn, everybody who could find any means of banging or rattling or clanging using it to create a racket no one could have slept through.

'Leave town! Run like hell! Don't take anything, just run!'

From nowhere a dog appeared in front of her. Kate stopped in alarm, wondering whether she could hold Bagheera back if he was frightened and confused enough to pounce.

The dog wagged its great tail. She abruptly recognized Natty Bumppo.

Head low, neck in a concave bend, in a wholly uncharacteristic puppy-like posture, he approached Bagheera, giving a few more ingratiating strokes with his tail. Bagheera's nape hairs relaxed; he allowed Nat to sniff his muzzle, though his claws were half-unsheathed.

What was the meaning of this pantomime? Should Nat not be on duty, waking people with his barking?

And then Bagheera reached a conclusion. He stretched his neck and rubbed his cheek against Natty Bumppo's nose. His claws disappeared.

'Kate!' someone shouted from behind her. She started. Sweetwater's voice.

'Kate, are you all right?' The tall Indian woman came running to her side. 'Why aren't you—? Oh, of course. You daren't let loose Bagheera!'

Kate took a deep breath. 'I thought I couldn't. Nat just set me right.'

'What?' Sweetwater stared incomprehension.

'If human beings had half the insight of this dog ...!' Kate gave a near-hysterical laugh, releasing her grip on Bagheera's collar. Instantly Natty Bumppo turned around and went bounding into the darkness with Bagheera matching him stride for stride.

'Kate, what the hell are you talking about?' Sweetwater insisted.

'Didn't you see? Nat just made Bagheera a freeman of Precipice!'

'Oh, for—! Kate, come with me! We only have seven minutes left!'

There was no chance to organize the flight; the Precipicians simply scattered, taking the shortest route to the edge of town and continuing into the surrounding farmland. Gasping, her feet cut by sharp grass and stones, Kate was overtaken by a bitch loping easily with a screaming child astride her back; she thought it might have been Brynhilde. Then a branch whipped across her face and she almost fell, but a strong arm caught and steadied her, hurried her another dozen paces, then hurled her to the ground in what shelter was offered by a shallow dip.

'No point in trying to go on,' Ted's gruff voice said out of darkness. 'Better to be closer behind a good solid bank of earth than further away and on your feet in the open.'

Two more people tumbled over the rim of the hollow. One she didn't know; the other was the restaurant keeper, Eustace Fenelli.

'What *is* all the panic?' he demanded with a trace of petulance.

Rapidly Ted explained, and concluded after a glance at his watch, 'The strike is scheduled for 0130, in about a minute and a half.'

For a moment Eustace said nothing. Then, with magnificent simplicity, making the single word into a whole encyclopedia of objurgation: '*Shit!*'

To her astonishment Kate had to giggle.

'I'm glad someone finds it funny!' Eustace grunted. 'Who –? Oh, Kate! Hello. Is Nick here too?'

'He wouldn't come,' she said in the steadiest voice she could achieve.

'He what?'

'He stayed behind.'

'But –! You mean nobody could find and tell him?'

'No. He ... Oh, *Ted!*'

She turned blindly and fell against the sheriff's shoulder, her body racked with dreadful sobs.

Faint in the distance they could now hear the teeth-aching whine of electric lifters, the superpowerful type fitted to low-level short-range strike planes. It grew louder.

Louder.

Louder.

THE LINE OF MOST RESISTANCE

To the President of the United States
URGENT AND MOST SECRET
Sir:
Copied to you herewith is a signal received at Lowndes Field at 0014 hours today, purporting to emanate from yourself as commander in chief and ordering a nuclear strike at coordinates that manifestly are within the continental United States.

In view of the fact that it was superficially convincing, being properly enciphered in a one-time cipher scheduled for use today, it came close to causing a disaster, specifically the death of approx. 3000 civilians in the town of Precipice CA. I regret to have to advise you that the mission was actually initiated, and only by a miracle was it aborted in time (on receipt of DoD signal #376 774 P, which warned all naval, military and air force bases that saboteurs might have gained access to the data net).

I have taken steps to discipline the officer who authorized inception of the mission, and upon my own responsibility have issued a signal summarizing the matter to all West Coast bases. I respectfully suggest that the same be done on a national basis, and at once.

I remain, Sir,
(signed)
Wilbur H. Neugebauer, General

AFTER TOUCH AND GO, GO

They saw the plane as it swooped. They saw it clearly by the eerie blue glow around its repulsors, gulping vast quantities of air into electrical fields so fierce that were a man to put his arm incautiously within their shining ring he would withdraw a stump after mere seconds.

They heard it, too: a howl as of a banshee.

But as it crossed the town … it let fall nothing.

After an hour of waiting, teeth chattering, fists clenched, scarcely daring to raise their heads in case the threatened attack should after all take place, the inhabitants of Precipice rediscovered hope.

And through the dark they stumbled and staggered homeward to an orchestra of wailing children.

*

Somehow – Kate never knew quite how – she found that she was walking with Bagheera at her side again, while next to Ted and a couple of paces ahead was Natty Bumppo.

Bagheera was purring.

It was as though he felt flattered at being declared an honorary dog.

Cautiously Ted opened the door of the Hearing Aid headquarters, while Kate and Sweetwater craned to look past him. Behind, half a dozen other people – Suzy, Eustace, Josh and Lorna, Brad, those who had begun to guess the explanation for their salvation – waited in impatience.

There was Nick, hands on arms, slumped forward fainting over his board. Kate thrust past Ted and ran to his side, calling his name.

He stirred, licking his lips, and sat upright, putting his right hand to his temple. He seemed giddy. But on seeing Kate he forced a smile, and continued it to the others who by now were flooding into the room.

'It worked,' he said in a thin, husky voice. 'I never dared believe it would. I was so scared, so terrified … But I was just in time.'

Ted halted before him, gazing around the room.

'What did you do?'

Nick gave a faint chuckle and pointed to his screen. On it a signal from someone called General Neugebauer to the president was cycling over and over in clear text, there being too much of it to display all at once.

'It was a close call,' he added. 'Damned close. The duty officer at Lowndes must be used to doing as he's told and no questions please … When I realized the plane was already on its way I nearly collapsed.'

Sweetwater, pushing her way through the crowd, stared at the screen.

'Hey,' she said after a moment's thought. '*Was* there a Department of Defense signal number whatever?'

'Of course not.' Nick rose, stretched, stifled a colossal yawn. 'But it seemed like the quickest solution to invent it.'

'Quickest!' Sweetwater withdrew half a pace, eyes large with awe, and started to count off on her fingers. 'Near as I can figure it, you had to write the signal in proper jargon, find a reference number for it, encode it in the proper cipher for today, feed it to Lowndes over the proper circuit—'

'Mark it for automatic decipherment instead of being left over to the morning like most nighttime signals traffic,' Ted butted in. 'Right, Nick?'

'Mh-hm,' he agreed around another and fiercer yawn. 'But that wasn't what took the time. I had to track down General Neugebauer's home code, which is ex-directory at all levels below Class Two Star priority. *And* he wasn't happy at being woken up, either.'

'And you did it in less than ten minutes?' Kate said faintly.

Nick gave a shy grin. 'Oh, looking back on it, I feel I had all the time in the world.'

Drawing herself up to her full height, Suzy Dellinger advanced on him.

'It doesn't often happen,' she said with a trace of awkwardness, 'that a mayor of this town has to undertake the sort of formal ceremony you find in other places. We tend to do it without the trimmings. This is that sort of occasion. I don't have to ask permission of my fellow citizens. Anybody who disagreed wouldn't be a Precipician. Nicholas Kenton Haflinger, in my official capacity, I'm proud to convey the thanks of us all.'

She made to shake hands with him. And was forestalled.

Natty Bumppo had as usual taken station next to his owner. Unexpectedly he rose, shouldered Suzy aside, planted his vast front paws on Nick's chest, and slapped him across both cheeks with his broad red tongue.

Then he resumed his stance beside Ted.

'I – uh ...' Nick had to swallow before he could go on. 'I guess that must be what you call an accolade.'

Suddenly everyone was laughing, except him. And except Kate, whose arms were around him and whose face was wet with tears.

'Nothing like this happened before, did it?' she whispered.

'Not that I know of,' he answered softly.

'And you did the right thing, the only thing ...' She caught him around the neck and drew his ear close to her mouth to utter words no one else was meant to hear.

'*Wise man!*'

Upon which he kissed her, thoroughly and for a long time.

THE CONTENT OF THE PROPOSITIONS

#1: That this is a rich planet. Therefore poverty and hunger are unworthy of it, and since we can abolish them, we must.

#2: That we are a civilized species. Therefore none shall henceforth gain illicit advantage by reason of the fact that we together know more than one of us can know.

THE OUTCOME OF THE PLEBISCITE

Well – how did you vote?

THE TRAVELLER IN BLACK

ONE

Imprint of Chaos

'Ante mare et terras et quod tegit omnia caelum unus erat toto
naturae vultus in orbe, quen dixere Chaos: rudis indigestaque mioles.'

– Ovid: Metamorphoses, 15

1

He had many names, but one nature, and this unique nature made him subject to certain laws not binding upon ordinary persons. In a compensatory fashion, he was also free from certain other laws more commonly in force.

Still, there was nothing to choose as regards rigidity between his particular set of laws and those others. And one rule by which he had very strictly to abide was that at set seasons he should overlook that portion of the All which had been allotted to him as his individual responsibility.

Accordingly, on the day after the conjunction of four significant planets in that vicinity, he set forth on a journey which was to be at once the same as and yet different from those many which had preceded it.

It had been ordained that at this time, unless there were some pressing reason to the contrary, he should tramp commonplace roads, and with good-will enough – it was not a constituent of his nature that he should rail against necessity – he so arranged his route that it wound and turned and curved through all those zones where he might be made answerable for events, and ended within a short distance of where it had begun. It ended, to be precise, at the city called Ryovora: that place of all places in his domains where people had their heads screwed on the right way.

He did this for an excellent reason. It was an assurance to him that when he subsequently reviewed the situation the memory of one spot where he might justly feel pleased with his work would be uppermost in recollection.

Therefore, on a sunny morning when there were birds singing and few clouds in a sky filled with the scent of flowers, he began to trudge along a dusty road towards his first destination.

That was a great black city upreared around a high tower, which was called by its inhabitants Acromel, the place where honey itself was bitter. It was sometimes a cause of mild astonishment – even to him of the many names and the single nature – that this most difficult of cities should be located within a few hours' walking of Ryovora. Nonetheless, it was so.

And to be able to state without fear of contradiction that anything whatsoever *was so* was a gauge and earnest of his achievement.

Before him, the road began to zig-zag on the slope of a hill dotted with grey-leaved bushes. A local wind raised dust-devils among the bushes and erased the footprints of those who passed by. It was under this hill that the traveller had incarcerated Laprivan of the Yellow Eyes, to whom memories of yesterday were hateful; some small power remained to this elemental, and he perforce employed it to wipe yesterday's traces away.

He took his staff in his hand – it was made of light, curdled with a number of interesting forces – and rapped once on an outcrop of bare rock at the side of the pathway.

'Laprivan!' he cried. 'Laprivan of the Yellow Eyes!'

At his call the dust-devils ceased their whirling. Resentfully, they sank back to the earth, so that the dust of which they were composed again covered the bared roots of the grey-leaved bushes. Most folk in the district assumed that the leaves were grey from the dust of passage, or from their nature; it was not so.

Laprivan heaved in his underground prison, and the road shook. Cracks wide enough to have swallowed a farm-cart appeared in its surface. From them, a great voice boomed.

'What do you want with me, today of all days? Have you not had enough even now of tormenting me?'

'I do not torment you,' was the calm reply. 'It is your memory that torments you.'

'Leave me be, then,' said the great voice sullenly. 'Let me go on wiping away that memory.'

'As you wish, so be it,' the traveller answered, and gestured with his staff. The cracks in the road closed click; the dust-devils re-formed; and when he looked back from the crest of the hill his footsteps had already been expunged.

The road wound on, empty, towards Acromel. For some distance before it actually reached the city it ran contiguous with the river called Metamorphia, a fact known to rather few people, because although it seemed that this was the same river which poured in under the high black battlements of the city, It was not the same – for good and sufficient cause. It was the nature of the river Metamorphia to change the nature of things, and consequently it changed its own nature after flowing a prescribed number of leagues.

The traveller paused by a stone wall overlooking the dark stream, and meditatively regarded objects floating past. Some had been fishes, perhaps; others were detritus of the banks – leaves, branches, stones. Those which had been stones continued to float, of course; those which had been of a flotatory nature sank.

He broke a piece of stone from the crumbling parapet of the wall, and cast it down. The alteration it underwent was not altogether pleasant to witness.

He raised his eyes after a while, and descried a girl on the opposite bank, who had come forward out of a clump of trees while he was lost in contemplation. She was extremely beautiful. Moreover she had been at no pains to hide the fact, for she was dressed exclusively in her long, lovely hair.

'You are also aware of the nature of this river,' she said after regarding him for a little.

'I have been advised that the nature of the river is to change the nature of things,' the traveller conceded. 'And consequently it changes its own nature also.'

'Come down with me, then, and bathe in it!'

'Why should you wish your nature changed?' was the reply. 'Are you not beautiful?'

'Beautiful I am!' cried the girl passionately. 'But I am without sense!'

'Then you are Lorega of Acromel, and your fame has spread far.'

'I am Lorega of Acromel, as you say.' She fixed him with her honey-coloured eyes, and shrugged the garb of her hair more closely around her. 'And how do men call you?'

'I have many names, but one nature. You may call me Mazda, or anything you please.'

'Do you not even know your own name, then? Do you not have a name that you prefer?'

'The name matters little if the nature does not change.'

She laughed scornfully. 'You speak in resounding but in empty phrases, Mazda or whoever you may be! If your nature is unchangeable, give demonstration! Let me see you descend into the water of this river!'

'I did not say that,' murmured the traveller peaceably. 'I did not say my nature was unchangeable.'

'Then you are a coward. Nonetheless, come down with me and bathe in this river.'

'I shall not. And it would be well for you to think on this, Lorega of Acromel: that if you are without sense, your intention to bathe in Metamorphia is also without sense.'

'That is too deep for me,' said Lorega unhappily, and a tear stoke down her satiny cheek. 'I cannot reason as wise persons do. Therefore let my nature be changed!'

'As you wish, so be it,' said the traveller in a heavy tone, and motioned with his staff. A great lump of the bank detached itself and fell with a huge splashing into the water. A wave of this water soaked Lorega from head to foot, and she underwent, as did the earth of the bank the moment it broke the surfaces, changes.

Thoughtfully, and a mite sadly, the traveller turned to continue his journey towards Acromel. Behind him, the welkin rang with the miserable cries of what had formerly been Lorega. But he was bound by certain laws. He did not look back.

Before the vast black gate of the city, which was a hundred feet high and a hundred feet wide, two men in shabby clothes were fighting with quarterstaffs. The traveller leaned on his own staff and watched them batter at one another for fully an hour before they both found themselves too weak to continue, and had to stand panting and glaring at each other to recover their breath.

'What is the quarrel between you?' said the traveller then.

'Little man in black, it concerns not you,' grunted the nearer of the two. 'Go your way and leave us be.'

'Wait!' said the other. 'Ask first whether he likewise is bent on the same errand!'

'A good point!' conceded the first, and raised his great cudgel menacingly. 'Speak, you!'

'First I must know what your errand was, before I can say if mine is the same or not,' the traveller pointed out.

'A good point!' admitted the second, who had now also approached to threaten him. 'Know that I am Ripil of the village called Masergon—'

'And I,' interrupted the first, 'am Tolex of the village called Wyve. Last week I set forth from my father's house, he having six other sons older than I—'

'As did I!' Ripil broke in. 'Exactly as did I! You've registered my name, I trust, stranger?' You will have good cause to remember it one day!'

'All men will!' snapped Tolex contemptuously. 'They will remember your name to laugh at it, and when boys scribble it daringly on the wall with charcoal old women will spit on the ground as they hobble past!'

Ripil scowled at him. 'Booby! Possessed of unbelievable effrontery! Go your way before it is too late, and the people of this city hang you in chains before the altar!'

'Your errand, though!' cried the traveller, just in time to forestall a renewal of the fighting.

Tolex gave him a huge but humourless grin. 'Why it's all so simple! This idiot called Ripil came hither thinking to make his fortune, dethrone Duke Vaul, and claim the hand of Lorega of Acromel! As though a dunderheaded village lout could do more than *dream* of such glories!'

'And your own ambition?'

'Why, I have come to make my fortune and be chosen as heir to Duke Vaul, when naturally I shall be assigned Lorega's hand!'

The traveller, not unexpectedly, burst out laughing. In a moment Tolex began to laugh also, thinking that it was Ripil's foolishness alone which had caused the joke, and Ripil, his face black like a storm-cloud, caught up his quarterstaff and began to belabour him anew.

The traveller left them to it, and went forward into the city.

2

In this city called Acromel there was a temple crowning the black tower about which the buildings clustered like a single onyx on a pillar of agate. In this temple, before the red idol of the god Lacrovas-Pellidin-Agshad-Agshad, Duke Vaul yawned behind his hand.

'Take *her*,' he said to the chief priest, nodding his large black-bearded head to his left. The priest bowed to the hard slippery floor and signalled his minions. In a moment the consort who had shared Vaul's life for fifteen years, and until that moment had also shared his throne, was hanging from the gallows in front of the altar, her heart's blood trickling onto Agshad's hands outstretched like a cup to receive it.

And still that was not enough.

Duke Vaul knitted his brows until his forehead was creased like a field trenched to grow vegetables, and drummed with his thick fingers on the arm of his ebony chair. He looked at the idol.

From the vantage-point where he sat, he saw Agshad in the attitude of accepting sacrifice: mouth open, eyes closed, hands outstretched and cupped with blood filling them. On the left Pellidin, who shared Agshad's body but not his head or his limbs, was portrayed in the act of executing justice: to wit, wringing the life from three persons of indeterminate sex – indeterminate, because Pellidin's cruel grasp had compressed their bodies into a gelatinous mess and left only their arms and legs sticking out like the limbs of a beetle. On the right, Lacrovas was portrayed in the mode of obliterating enemies, with a sword in one hand and a morning-star in the other. And finally, facing away from the spot where by preference Duke Vaul had his throne located, there was the second Agshad in the attitude of devotion, with hands clasped together and eyes cast heavenward in a beseeching look. That was the aspect of the Quadruple God with which Duke Vaul had the least concern.

Below the dais on which he presided, priests and acolytes by the hundred – predominantly sacrificers, men expert in every art of human butchery – wove their lines of movement into traditional magical patterns. Their chanting ascended eerily towards the domed roof of the temple, along with the stink of candles made from the fat of those who had hung earlier in the chains before the altar. There was no point in letting their mortal remains waste, was there?

But on the other hand there was no point – so far – in any of this ritual. At least, the desired effect had not been accomplished. If even his own consort had not sufficed to provoke the sought-after reaction, what would? Duke Vaul cast around in his mind.

On impulse, he signalled the deputy chief priest, and pointed a hairy-backed finger at the chief priest himself. 'Take *him*,' he directed.

And that was no good, either.

Accordingly, he sent out the temple guard into the city at half an hour past noon of that day, and the guardsmen set about gathering idle citizens into the yard before the temple. If it wasn't a matter of quality, reasoned Duke Vaul, it might perhaps be a matter of quantity. The second priest – now of course the chief priest by right of succession – had been consulted, and had given it as his considered opinion that a hundred all at once must have the desired effect. Duke Vaul, to be on the safe side, had ordained that a thousand should be brought to the temple, and had set carpenters and metal-smiths to work on the chain-hanging gallows to accommodate them.

The temple guardsmen carried out their assignment with a will, all the better because they feared the lot might fall on them when Duke Vaul had used up his supply of ordinary townsfolk. They brought in everyone they could catch, and among the crowd was a small man in black clothing, who seemed to be consumed with uncontrollable laughter.

His merriment, in fact, was so extreme that it became infectious, and the duke noticed the fact and bellowed across the temple floor in a howl of fury.

'Who is that idiot who laughs in this sacred spot?' his bull voice demanded. 'Does the fellow not realize that these are serious matters and may be disturbed by the least error in our actions? Priests! Drag him forth and make him stand before me!'

In a little while, because the throng was so great, the black-clad traveller was escorted to the foot of the duke's dais. He bowed compliantly enough when the rough hand of a guardsman struck him behind the head, but the cheerful twinkle did not depart from his eyes, and this peculiarity struck Duke Vaul at once.

He began to muse about the consequences of sacrificing one who did not take the Quadruple God seriously, and eventually spoke through the tangle of his beard.

'How do men call you, foolish one?' he boomed.

'I have many names, but one nature.'

'And why are you laughing at these holy matters?'

'But I am not!'

'Then are you laughing at me?' thundered the duke, heaving himself forward on his throne so that the boards of the dais creaked and squealed. His eyes flashed terribly.

'No, I laugh at the foolishness of mankind,' said the black-clad traveller.

'So! In what impressively mirthful manner is this foolishness manifest, pray?'

'Why, thus,' the traveller said, and told the story of Tolex and Ripil, fighting before the gate of the city.

But Duke Vaul did not find the anecdote in the least degree amusing. He commanded that the temple guard should at once go in search of these two, and fumed while they were hunted down. When they arrived, however, it was as corpses they were laid on the temple floor.

'Mighty Duke!' cried the guardsmen respectfully, bowing their heads as one, and then let their captain continue.

'Sire, we found these two clasped dying in each other's arms. Each bore one bloody cudgel; each has a broken skull.'

'Throw them into the river,' said Duke Vaul curtly, and resumed converse with the black-clad traveller.

'You arrogate to yourself the right to laugh at men's foolishness,' he said, and gave a wicked grin. 'Then tell me this: are you yourself entirely wise?'

'Alas, yes,' said the traveller. 'I have but one nature.'

'Then you can succeed where all my so-called wise men have failed. See you this idol?'

'I could hardly avoid seeing it. It is a considerable work of – ah – *art*.'

'It is claimed that a way exists to invest it with life, and when this way is found it will then set forth to lay waste the enemies of this city and execute justice upon them. By every means we have sought to bestow life upon it; we have given it blood, which is life, as you doubtless know, from every class and condition of person. Even my consort, who but a few hours ago sat beside me on this throne' – the duke wiped away an imaginary tear – 'now hangs with her throat gashed on that chain-jangling gibbet before the altar. Still, though, the idol declines to come to life. We need its aid, for our enemies are abroad in every corner of the world; from Ryovora to the ends of the earth they plot our downfall and destruction.'

'Some of what you say is true,' nodded the traveller.

'Some? Only some? What then is false? Tell me! And it had better be correct, or else you shall go to join that stupid chief priest who finally tried my patience! You can see what became of him!'

The traveller glanced up and spread his hands. Indeed, it was perfectly clear – what with the second mouth, the red-oozing one, the priest had lately acquired in his throat.

'Well, first of all,' he said, 'there does exist a way to bring the idol to life. And, second, yes, it will then destroy the enemies of this city. But third, they do not hide in far corners of the land. They are here in Acromel.'

'Say you so?' Duke Vaul frowned. 'You may be right, for, knowing what a powerful weapon we wield against them – or shall wield, when we unknot this riddle – they may well be trying to interfere with our experiments. Good! Go on!'

'How so, short of demonstrating what I mean?'

'You?' The duke jerked forward on his throne, clutching the ebony arms so tightly his knuckles glistened white. 'You can bring the idol to life?'

The traveller gave a weary nod. All the laughter had gone out of him.

'Then do it!' roared Duke Vaul. 'But remember! If you fail, a worse fate awaits you than my chief priest suffered!'

'As you wish, so be it,' sighed the traveller. With his staff he made a single pass in the air before the altar, and the idol moved.

Agshad in the attitude of devotion did not open his clasped hands. But Lacrovas swung his sword, and Duke Vaul's bearded head sprang from his shoulders. Pellidin let fall the three crushed persons from his hand and seized the headless body. That he squeezed instead, and the cupped hands of Agshad in the posture of accepting sacrifice filled with the blood of the duke, expressed like juice from a ripe fruit.

After that the idol stepped down from the altar and began to stamp on the priests.

Thoughtfully, having made his escape unnoticed in the confusion, the traveller took to the road again.

Perhaps there would be nothing worse to behold during this journey than what he had observed in Acromel. Perhaps there would be something a million times as bad. It was to establish such information that he undertook his journeyings.

In Kanish-Kulya they were fighting a war, and each side was breathing threatenings and slaughter against the other.

'Oh that fire would descend from heaven and eat up our enemies!' cried the Kanishmen.

'Oh that the earth would open and swallow up our enemies!' cried the Kulyamen.

'As you wish,' said the traveller, 'so be it.'

He tapped the ground with his staff, and Fegrim who was pent in a volcano answered that tapping and heaved mightily. Afterwards, when the country was beginning to sprout again – for lava makes fertile soil – men dug up bones and skulls as they prepared the ground for planting.

On the shores of Lake Taxhling, men sat around their canoes swapping lies while they waited for a particular favourable star to ascend above the horizon. One lied better than all the rest.

But he lied not as his companion lied – to pass the time, to amuse each other harmlessly. He lied to feed a consuming vanity hungrier than all the bellies of all the people in the villages along the shore of the lake, who waited day in, day out with inexhaustible patience for their menfolk to return with their catch.

Said the braggart, 'If only I could meet with such another fish as I caught single-handed in Lake Moroho when I was a stripling of fifteen! *Then* you would understand the fisherman's art! Alas, though' – with a sigh – 'there are only piddling fish in Lake Taxhling!'

'As you wish, so be it,' said the traveller, who had accepted the offer of food by their fire. And the next dawn the boaster came home screaming with excitement about the huge fish he had caught, as great as the one he had taken in Lake Moroho. His companions crowded around to see it – and the mountains rang with their laughter, because it was smaller than some others they themselves had taken during the night.

'I do not wish him to love me for my beauty or my fortune,' declared the haughty child of a merchant in the city called Barbizond, where there was always a rainbow in the sky owing to the presence of the bright being Sardhin chained inside a thundercloud with fetters of lightning. The girl was beautiful, and rich, and inordinately proud.

'No!' she continually insisted, discarding suitor after suitor. 'I wish to be loved for myself, for what I am!'

'As you wish, so be it,' said the traveller, who had come in the guise of a pilgrim to one of the jousts organized that this lady might view her potential husbands. Twenty-one men had died in the lists that afternoon, and she had thrown her glove in the champion's face and gone to supper.

The next time there were jousts announced, no challenger came, and the girl pulled a face and demanded that more heralds go forth. Her father summoned a hundred heralds. The news went abroad. And personable young men said in every city, 'Fight for a stuck-up shrew like her? Ho-ho! I've better ways to pass my time, and so've my friends!'

At length the truth dawned upon her, and she became miserable. She had never been happy. She had only thought she was happy. Little by little, her pride evaporated. And one day, a young man came by chance to her father's house and found she was a quiet, submissive, pleasant girl, and married her.

Thus the journey approached its end. The traveller felt a natural relief that nothing excessively untoward had occurred as he hastened his footsteps towards the goal and climax of his excursion – towards Ryovora, where men were sensible and clear-sighted, and made no trouble that he had to rectify. After this final visit, he could be assured that his duty was fulfilled.

Not that all was well by any means. There were enchanters still, and ogres, and certain elementals roamed abroad, and of human problems there might be no end. Still, the worst of his afflictions were growing fewer. One by one, the imprints of the original chaos were fading away, like the footmarks of travellers on the road above the hill where Laprivan of the Yellow Eyes was imprisoned.

Then, as the gold and silver towers of Ryovora came to view, he saw that an aura surrounded them as of a brewing storm, and his hope and trust in the people of that city melted away.

3

At the city called Barbizond, where he had been but recently, there was likewise an aura around the tallest towers. There, however, it was a fair thing and pleasant to look upon, imbued with the essence of bright – if cruel, nonetheless lovely – Sardhin chained in his cloud. Ryovora had been immune since time immemorial from such disadvantageous infestations as elementals, principalities and powers; the local folk prided themselves on being creatures of hard plain sense, sober in the making of decisions, practical and rational and causing a minimum of trouble to the world.

That something had happened to alter this state of affairs …! There was a conundrum to make the very universe shiver in chill anticipation!

The traveller turned aside from the track, making no attempt to conceal his frowns, and instead of pursuing a straight course into the city, he diverged across a verdant meadow in the midst of which hovered a mist like the mists of early morning, but more dense. When the grey wisps had closed around him entirely, to the point where they would have incapacitated the vision of any ordinary trespasser, he dissolved one of the forces which curdled the light he employed as a staff, and a clear bright beam penetrated the opacity, It had barely sheared the mist when a quiet voice spoke to him.

'Since you know where you are, I know who you are. Come into the castle, and be welcome.'

The mist lifted, and the traveller went forward into the courtyard of a castle that reared seemingly to heaven, with great towers which almost pierced the sky. Two dragons chained beside the portcullis bowed their heads fawningly to the visitor; four man-like persons whose bodies were of burnished steel came to escort him – one before, one behind, one at each side – through the gateway and across the yard; twenty trumpeters sounded a blast from a gallery as he ascended the steps towards the chief tower and keep, and they also were of polished steel.

There was a scent of magic in this air. Echoes of half-forgotten cantrips resounded, incredibly faint, from the masonry of the walls. Here and there blue light dripped from a projecting cornice; shadows moved with no one to cast them.

Then a door of oak studded with brass swung open on silent hinges, giving access to a room across which slanted a thick bar of sunlight from a window standing wide. The sunlight illumined the shrivelled mummy of a mandrake. In jars covered with black cloth, ranged on an oak shelf, were twenty homunculi. A brazier burned, giving off a thick, very pleasant smell like warm honey.

From behind a table on which heavy books were piled that served also as a perch for a drowsy owl, a person in dark red robes rose to greet the traveller, and spoke, inclining his head.

'It is traditional that no one shall pierce the mist with which I protect my privacy save an invited guest or one who has a single nature. And, the universe being as it is, only one – ah – *individual* has a single nature. I am the enchanter Manuus. Be welcome, sir.'

The black-clad traveller bent his head in reply. A chair was placed for him, not by visible hands; he sat in it, disposing his cloak comfortably over the arm. Manuus took from a cupboard a large flask and two mugs of pottery ornamented with complex symbols in blue enamel. From the flask – which bore symbols in green enamel – he spilled a couple of drops of sparkling liquid, muttering words which made the walls hum faintly. The drops vanished before they reached the floor, and the enchanter gave a nod of satisfaction and filled the mugs.

'What is your business here, sir?' he inquired, resuming his own seat after handing the first mug to his caller.

'There is an aura about Ryovora,' said the traveller. 'Before I enter the city I wish to ascertain what its cause may be.'

Manuus nodded thoughtfully, stroking the wispy grey beard that clung at his chin like a wisp of the mist that guarded his home from casual prying.

'You will forgive me mentioning the fact,' he said in an apologetic tone, 'but it is asserted somewhere in one of these books – in a volume, moreover, in which I have come to place some degree of confidence – that if your nature is single, then it must logically follow that you answer questions as well as asking them.'

'That is so. And I see plainly that you put trust in the tome of which you speak. The faceless drinker to whom you poured libation a moment ago is not elsewhere referred to.'

Silence ensued between them for a space, while each contemplated the other. There was, though, a certain distinction, inasmuch as the enchanter studied the outward guise of the traveller, whereas the traveller examined the totality of his host.

'Ask away, then,' invited the traveller at length. 'And I may say that the more involved your question, the simpler and more difficult to understand will be my answer.'

'And *vice versa*?' suggested Manuus, his old eyes twinkling.

'Exactly.'

'Very well, then. Who are you? Note, please, that I do not ask how you are called. You have an infinity of names.'

The traveller smiled. 'You are a talented man,' he conceded. 'That is a good question, frankly phrased. So I will answer frankly. I am he to whom was entrusted the task of bringing order forth from chaos. Hence the reason why I have but one nature.'

'If your nature were such that you demanded honour in full measure with your worth, all the days of my life would not suffice to do you homage,' said Manuus seriously. 'Ask now what you would know.'

'What's the trouble in Ryovora?'

Maliciously, Manuus made his eyes sparkle. He said, 'I am not bound by your laws, sir. Therefore I will answer in the human style – simply, to simple questions. There is dissatisfaction with the order of things as they are.'

'Fair,' the traveller conceded. 'Ask away.'

Manuus hesitated. 'Who,' he resumed at length, 'imposed—?'

And his tongue locked in his mouth, while the traveller looked on him with an expression blending cynicism and sympathy. When at last the enchanter was able to speak again, he muttered, 'Your pardon. It was of the nature of a test. I had seen it stated that ...'

'That there are certain questions which one literally and physically is forbidden to ask?' The traveller chuckled. 'Why, then, your test has confirmed the fact. I, even I, could not answer the question I suspect you were intending to frame. However, a question that cannot be asked is *ipso facto* no question at all. You may try again.'

Manuus licked his lips. What had transpired within his head during that instant of involuntary paralysis defied comprehension. He was, though, brave and enterprising, and shortly ventured, 'On the other hand I believe I may legitimately ask: what is the purpose of your task?'

'You may.'

'So I do.' Leaning back triumphant in his chair.

'Why! When all things have but one nature, they will be subsumed into the Original All. Time will stop. This conclusion is desirable.'

Manuus looked sourly at the brazier. 'Desirable, perhaps – but appallingly dull. Speak again.'

'In what particular respect are the citizens of Ryovora dissatisfied?'

Manuus turned the question over and over in his brilliant mind, seeking a way to milk from it a further opportunity to interrogate his distinguished visitor. He failed.

'They are displeased that they have no gods,' he replied.

Three bolts of lightning sheared the clear blue sky beyond the window; three claps of thunder in succession made the room re-echo and startled the sleepy owl into giving three little hops across the great book on which he squatted. The black-clad traveller ignored these events, taking a further sip from his mug, but on his face a frown was suddenly engraved.

'Ask a third time,' he invited.

'Why, this is not altogether necessary,' said Manuus in high delight. 'But so I will!' He darted his gaze from place to place within the room as though in quest of inspiration, and finally lit on the proper line of inquiry.

'What was there, before things became as they are now?'

'I will show you,' said the traveller, and dipped one fingertip into his mug. He drew forth a drop of liquid in which was entrapped a sparkling bubble.

'Regard this bubble,' he instructed Manuus, 'And see ...'

In those days, the forces were none of them chained. They raged unchecked through every corner and quarter of the cosmos. Here for instance ruled Laprivan of the Yellow Eyes, capricious, whimsical; when he stared things melted in frightful agony. There a bright being shed radiance, but the radiance was all-consuming, and that which was solid and dull was flashed into fire. At another place, creatures in number one million fought desperately for the possession of a single grain of dust; the fury of their contesting laid waste solar systems.

Once – twice – a third time something burgeoned, which had about it a comforting aura of rationality, predictability, stability; about this nucleus, time was generated from eternity. Time entails memory, memory entails conscience, conscience entails thought for the future, which is itself implied by the existence of time. Twice the forces of chaos raged around this focal point, and swallowed it back into oblivion; then the will of Tuprid and Caschalanva, of Quorril and Lry, and of an infinite number of elemental beings, reigned once more. But none of them was supreme, because in chaos nothing can endure, nothing can be absolute, nothing sure or certain or reliable.

In that age, suns flashed like fires, burning brightly one instant, ashes the next. On planets circling a million suns creatures who could think struggled to reduce the chaos to order, and when they thought they had most nearly achieved it, chance ordained that all their work should go for nothing, absorbed again into the faceless dark.

'But that was before me,' said the traveller, and squashed the bubble so that it burst.

'I have seen,' said Manuus with inexpressible weariness. 'But I have not understood.'

'Man does not comprehend chaos. That is why man is man, and not of another nature.' The traveller smiled at him. 'I wish now to pose my final question; do you grant that I have well and sufficiently answered yours?'

'You have given me another million questions to ask,' sighed Manuus, shaking his grey head. 'But that also, I suppose, stems from the nature of mankind. Ask away.'

'Your supposition is correct. Now my last question: enchanter, what is your opinion of a god?'

'I do not know what a god is,' said Manuus. 'And I doubt that any man knows, though many think they do.'

'Fair enough,' said the black-clad traveller, and rose.

'Have you not even one more question to put to me?' suggested the enchanter with a wan smile.

'No,' said the traveller.

Manuus gave a shrug and rose also. 'Then I can only thank you for having graced my dwelling, sir,' he said formally. 'Few of my colleagues can have enjoyed the honour of receiving you personally.'

The traveller bestowed on him a hard, forthright look.

'I have many names, but one nature,' he said. 'Man has one name, and many more than two natures. But the essential two are these: that he shall strive to impose order on chaos, and that he shall strive to take advantage of chaos. You, sir, are not a better enchanter for having received me here, but a worse one. And, I may say, such people as you are often the greatest allies of the powers who were before me.'

'I resent that, sir,' said Manuus frostily. 'Let it not be said that I oppose one whose task I am aware of.'

'A third element of man's nature,' the traveller murmured, 'is this: that he shall not understand what he is doing. Good day to you, Manuus – though whether it will be is rather up to you than up to me.'

The traveller left Manuus deep in thought, with one elbow on a book in front of him, his chin cupped in his hand, his eyes staring vacantly at his pet owl. The traveller set forward, towards the gold and silver towers of Ryovora, and there went among the populace confirming what he had been told.

That same argument which Manuus had put to him bluntly, he heard indirectly expressed before the houses of the great merchant-enchanters, who conjured this city's goods from the far corners of the world; so too in the market-square, and in private homes, and in taverns and theatres and laboratories and even in the houses of ill-repute. And when as last he came to stand upon the roof of a high silver tower and overlook the sleeping city in the small dead hours, he was convinced.

Yes, truly, the people of Ryovora were dissatisfied, and it was as Manuus had claimed. They had struggled through centuries inquiring of the mute cosmos what its nature and the nature of man might be, and they were left still hungering, to the point of growing weary.

This hunger – so they said – would be assuaged if only they had a god, as did their neighbours in Acromel. News had arrived, of course, that the god of Acromel had caused the death of many citizens, and widespread misery, but they ascribed all that to the stupidity of Duke Vaul. 'We are sensible people!' they insisted. 'We would know how to treat a god!'

The traveller stood gazing out over the placid, sleeping city. Moonlight shone on the roofs of glorious buildings, on the river's ripples, on bridges and mansions and on fine wide roads.

He had asked everywhere. 'What is the nature of a god?' And they had said confidently, 'We have no god, so how can we tell? But if we had one – ah, then we should know!'

The traveller remained rapt in thought until the dawn-flush tinged the east, absorbing and reviewing the desire that inchoately washed against his mind. At last, a breath or two before the sun rose, a quirking smile twisted his mouth upwards, and he put out his staff over the city and said, 'As you wish, so be it.'

Then, his task for the moment being accomplished, he departed.

4

To park a car while one goes for a walk in the woods is not uncommon. To return and find that the car is no longer there is not unprecedented. But to return and find that the road itself, on which the car was parked, has likewise vanished, is a different matter entirely.

Yet for a man who rules himself by the straightforward logic of common sense, there is no need instantly to assume that a problem of this nature is insoluble. Bernard Brown was such a person, and it was to him that this improbable event had just occurred.

'Well!' he said, looking at the indisputably grassy surface of the narrow ride between two high hedges where to the best of his recollection – and his memory was a good one – there had shortly before been a tarmac highway. 'Well!' he said again, and since there was no obvious alternative sat down on a rock and smoked a cigarette in a philosophical manner.

However, no one came by who might enlighten him on the fate either of his car or of the road it had been on so when the cigarette had reduced to a stub, he dropped it in the grass, ground it out with his foot, and began to walk along the lane between the hedges.

By the straightforward logic of common sense, a road which had been here a scant hour ago could not during his absence have removed itself to another location. Therefore it must be he who was misplaced; he had no doubt missed his way in the pleasant summery woodland, and would eventually return if not to the road he had first followed then to some other that intersected with it.

He strode along jauntily enough, not much worried by the turn of affairs, and whistled as he walked. Occasionally the hedges on either side parted after he had gone by, and eyes studied him thoughtfully, but since he did not notice this fact it did not trouble him.

At length the hedges ended, and with them the trees of the wood, and he emerged onto a rutted track between two ploughed fields. On the near side of one of these fields a man with a kerchief tied around his neck and his legs soiled to the knee with dirt was backing up a large and obstreperous horse, harnessed to a cart whose contents were indeterminate but stank incredibly. Politely ignoring the smell, Bernard spoke to the man directly.

'Excuse me! Can you tell me the way to the London road?'

The man considered for a moment. Then he spat in the earth where it was new-turned by his horse's enormous hooves, and said bluntly, 'No.'

Well, that was at least an answer, if not a very helpful one. Bernard Brown shrugged and walked on.

Again the grassy ride passed between hedges, and began to wind so that at any one moment only twenty paces of it before and twenty behind were in clear view. From around a bend ahead a voice could be heard raised in song and growing louder. This voice was of intersexual quality, neither altogether male nor altogether female, and shrilled occasionally on the highest notes with shiver-provoking acidity.

Shortly, the singer came in sight, and Bernard found himself confronted by a young man, with very white hair cut short around his head, riding negligently on a gaily caparisoned horse that moved its head in time with the beat of its master's song. His attire was extraordinary, for he wore a shirt of red and yellow and loose breeches of bright green, the colour of a sour apple, and his horse was if anything more surprising, inasmuch as it was skewbald of purple and pale blue. The rider accompanied his singing on a small plucked instrument, the strings of which chirruped like birds.

When he perceived Bernard, he abandoned his song in mid-phrase, let his instrument fall on a baldric to his side, and halted his horse. Then he leaned one hand on the pommel of his saddle and fixed the pedestrian with bright hard eyes; these were violet.

'Good morrow, stranger,' he said in a light tone. 'And what is your business here?'

'I'm trying to find the London road again,' said Bernard Brown, lifting his eyebrows in astonishment at the spectacle.

'There is no such road near here,' said the young man, and shook his head sorrowfully. 'I know that to be a fact for all the roads in this vicinity belong to me.'

'Now this is all very well,' said Bernard, and gave a smile to show he was party to the joke. 'But while it may amuse you to make such a grandiose assertion, it does not amuse me to be denied essential guidance. I've lost my way somehow, through taking a wrong turning in the woods, and I badly need directions.'

The young man drew himself upright and urged his horse forward – and it could be seen now that this was not a young man riding a horse, nor was there in fact a horse being ridden, but some sort of confusion of the two, in that the man's legs were not separated at all from his mount. They ended in fleshy stalks, uniting with the belly of that part of the composite animal resembling a horse.

'This is extraordinary!' thought Bernard to himself, but being mannerly forbore to remark on the combination.

The young man gave him a hard stare, hand falling to a sharp sword beside his left thigh. 'Who are you?' he demanded. 'And where are you from, that you do not recognize me?'

Nettled, Bernard rejoined, 'Unless you had taken part in a circus, or been exhibited at the Zoo, I would not presume to recognize you!'

The horse-head and the man-head reared together back in amazement, and the bright sword whined through the air. Discreetly, feeling that he had to do with a creature whose mind was as abnormal as its body, Bernard had already stepped out of range when the blade flashed by.

'I am Jorkas!' howled the man-horse creature. 'Now do you still say you do not know me?'

Alarmed at the composite personage's behaviour, Bernard replied in a tone as civil as could be expected after the attack with the sword, 'No, sir, I do not, and I may say that your actions give me little cause to wish we had become acquainted earlier.'

The man-face contorted with unbelievable rage, and the sword swung high for a second blow as the horse-body danced three steps towards Bernard. He was on the point of making an inglorious – and predictably ill-fated – retreat, when a sudden ringing noise indicated that the blade had struck something very resistant in its downward passage. Indeed, the man-creature was shaking its sword-arm as though it had been numbed all the way to the shoulder.

The obstacle the sword had encountered was a glittering staff, upheld in the firm grip of a black-clad man who had somehow contrived to approach the two of them without being noticed. This person was now standing, leaning on the staff, and regarding Jorkas with a wry expression.

Jorkas shrugged, sheathed the sword, and took up his instrument again. His horse-legs bore him cantering away down the lane, and when he was out of sight around the bend his counter-tenor voice was once more heard raised in song.

'Thank you, sir,' Bernard said to his rescuer, wiping his face and not unduly surprised to find he had been perspiring. 'I must confess I was not prepared to meet anything like that in this quiet lane.'

The black-clad one smiled, a faraway look in his eyes. 'I have rendered some small service,' he said matter-of-factly. 'And I would add a smidgin of advice to it, too. If you expect nothing and everything, you will do well.'

Bernard settled his jacket more comfortably around his shoulders and blinked several times in succession 'Well, sir, taken whichever way, I cannot see your advice proving unsound. Particularly if this neighbourhood is populated by more amazing freaks such as Jorkas!'

'Yes, he bears the imprint of chaos, does he not?' said the man in black. 'He is left over, so to speak. He is fairly harmless; things have by-passed him, and his power grows small.'

'The power of that sword, had it reached its target, would have been quite sufficient to dispose of me,' Bernard pointed out. 'Has he escaped from some – some fantastic menagerie?'

'He has rather endured from a period of absolute confusion,' was the reply, which though apparently meaningful served not at all to lessen either Bernard's puzzlement or his alarm. He decided, nonetheless, to forgo further inquiry into the matter, and to revert to his major preoccupation.

'Can you, sir, tell me where lies the London road?'

'I can,' said the other with a chuckle. 'But it would be of small help to you if I did, since you cannot come to it from here. No, listen to me, and I will give you directions which will eventually bring you where you wish to be.'

Since that was the best the black-clad man was willing to offer, Bernard had perforce to nod his acceptance.

'Go forward from here,' said his mentor, 'until you reach three twisted alder-trees standing alone in a meadow. You will recognize them readily enough. Stand before them and bow your head three times, and then take the path around them. In a little while it will bring you to a city. And whatever you do, do *not* speak with a woman in clothing the colour of blood. Otherwise I cannot answer for the consequences.'

'What nonsense!' thought Bernard to himself. But since he had no choice he thanked the other civilly and went on circumspectly down the lane.

The three alder-trees poked up, white and gnarled, from the grass of the promised meadow, like the fingers of a skeleton. Bernard hesitated, looking about him. He felt foolish to be going to do what he had been advised to do. Still, as far as he could tell no one was watching him, and the straightforward logic of common sense had long ago informed him that he was not at present in a location where common sense was greatly prized.

He was troubled, though, that he could see no sign at all of a road beyond this point, so that unless he did what he had been told, and it – ah – worked, he would have to retrace his path, with the concomitant prospect of a second encounter with Jorkas. For that he had no stomach. Accordingly he bowed his head three times, and was amazed to find that he was standing on a clearly-defined path. Which, he likewise noticed, led nowhere except around the alders.

Well, the black-clad man had said he should take the path which led around them. He turned to his left and strode resolutely along the circular path, hopeful of getting somewhere eventually.

At his third turn, when he was feeling truly embarrassed by his own silliness, he looked towards the alder-trees again and saw a very beautiful woman standing among them. She had a face of perfect oval shape, skin like mother-of-pearl and hair blacker than midnight. But she was gowned from shoulders to ankles in a dress that was red as blood.

She spoke to him in a musical voice, sarcastically. 'And where do you think your circumambulations will carry you, my foolish friend? Did no one ever inform you that walking in circles takes you nowhere? Why not go forward? See!'

She raised her right arm, on which golden bracelets jangled, and when Bernard followed her pointing fingers he saw a city clustered around an enormous tower, the top of which resembled an onyx and the shaft of which resembled agate.

A strange sort of city! Yet at least a habitation, not a stretch of deserted countryside. He was half-minded to make hastily towards it, and yet felt a vague foreboding. There was an aura about that city …

He spoke to the air, to himself, not to the woman in red, and said, 'The man who saved me from Jorkas advised me not to speak with a woman in a dress the colour of blood. I assume this advice extends to not following any suggestion she may make to me.' Doggedly he continued his rotatory progress, while the woman's laughter tinkled irritatingly in his ears, and was rewarded on his next circuit to see that she had gone. Somewhere, Somehow.

Moreover, another city was in sight, and this was not so disturbing. Its towers were of gold and silver, and although the sky about it was of an electrical blue shade, that seemed to presage nothing less familiar than the advent of a storm.

'There, perhaps,' reasoned Bernard, 'I may escape this conglomeration of cryptic non-meaningful events, and may trace down someone who can tell me how to get home.'

He struck out across the meadow, and shortly came to a good though dusty road, which led straight towards the city with the gold and silver towers. Determined to reach it in the least possible time, he thrust the road behind him with feet that now began to ache more than a little.

'So!' said the enchanter Manuus, leaning back in his chair with a chuckle. 'So!' he said again, dropping the cover – made of bat's skin as fine and supple as silk – over his scrying-glass. 'Well, well, well, well, *well*!'

5

At the head of the council table – which, because the weather was oppressive, he had caused to be set out under the sycamore trees in the Moth Garden – the Margrave of Ryovora sat, frowning terribly.

Before him, the table stretched almost a hundred feet, in sections that were joined so cleverly the over-arching trees could admire their reflections intact in the polished top. Nothing spoiled the perfection of this table, except the purplish sheen it had acquired from the heavy close air now filling the city.

To right and left of him, ranked in their chairs, sat the nobility of Ryovora, men and women of vast individual distinction: the merchant-enchanters, the persons of inquiring mind, the thinkers, the creators, all those to whom this city owed its fame and reputation.

The Margrave spoke, not looking at those who listened.

'Tell us what has taken place in your quarter of the town, Petrovic.'

Petrovic, a dry little man with a withered face like an old apple, coughed apologetically and said, 'There are omens. I have cast runes to ascertain their meaning. They have no known meaning. Milk has been soured in the pan four mornings running in my demesne.'

'And Ruman?'

Ruman was a man built like an oak tree, whose thick gnarled hands were twisting restlessly in his lap, He said, 'I have slaughtered animals to divine what may be read in their entrails. I agree with Petrovic – these omens have no known significance. But two springs under the wall of the city, which have not failed in more centuries than I can discover, are dry this morning.'

'And Gostala?'

Gostala was a woman with a queenly bosom and a queenly diadem of white hair plaited around her head. She said, 'I have watched the flight of birds each dawn for seven days, and also at sunset. The results are confused. But a two-headed lamb has been born in the village of Dunwray.'

'And Eadwil?'

Eadwil was hardly more than a boy. His chin was innocent of a beard and when he spoke his voice was like a reed pipe; still, one must respect his precocious wisdom. He said, 'I have analyzed the relative situations of the stars and planets, and am driven to the hypotheses that *either* we know nothing at all *or* some unknown heavenly body is influencing events. A comet, perhaps. But yesterday lightning struck three times out of a clear sky, and – and, Margrave, I'm frightened!'

The Margrave nodded and made a comforting gesture in the air. It didn't help much. He said, 'But this cannot be the whole story. I move that we – here, now, in full council – ask Him Who Must Know.'

Eadwil rose to his feet. On his youthful lips trembled a sob, which he stoutly repressed.

'I request your permission to withdraw, then,' he said. 'It is well known how He Who Must Know deals with those in – uh – my condition.'

The Margrave coughed and nodded approval of the discreet reference. Eadwil owed some of his precocity to the postponement of a major upheaval in his physiology, and the elemental they were considering found virgins vulnerable to his powers.

'Agreed,' he said, and Eadwil departed, sighing with relief.

Before they could proceed with the business before them, however, there was a rustling sound from far down the table, and a voice spoke like the sighing of wind in bare winter woods.

'Margrave, I suggest otherwise.'

The Margrave shifted uncomfortably in his chair. That was Tyllwin who spoke, a figure as gaunt as a scarecrow and as thin as a rake, who sat among them by courtesy because no one knew where he had come from or how old he was, but everyone knew he had many and peculiar powers which had never been put to use. Just as well, maybe. Whenever Tyllwin spoke, untoward events followed. The Margrave saw with alarm that several blossoms on nearby trees were withering.

'Speak, Tyllwin,' he muttered, and braced himself.

Tyllwin chuckled, a scratching noise, and the flowers on the whole of one tree turned to fruit and rotted where they hung. His nearest neighbours left their seats hastily and moved towards the Margrave's end of the table.

Tyllwin's huge round head, like a turnip-ghost's, turned to watch them, and a smile curved his dusty lips. He said, 'Is it not certain, masters of Ryovora, that these things foreshadow an important event?'

The rotten fruits fell with a squelching sound, and ants hurried from among the roots of the trees to investigate. The company hardly dared do more than nod.

'Therefore,' said Tyllwin, 'I suggest we investigate the commotion which is shortly to take place at the main gate.'

He fell silent. A few dead leaves blew across the table. Most of them clustered before Tyllwin's place, and he touched them with a bony hand, making them dissolve. The watchers trembled.

Still, the Margrave was relieved to find that nothing more outrageous was going to follow Tyllwin's unexpected loquacity. He said, 'Well, what is the opinion of you all?'

Ruman spoke up, with a glance towards Tyllwin that lasted only half a second after meeting Tyllwin's eyes. He said, 'I have not scried any such commotion.'

'But you have not scried since yesterday,' objected Gostala with feminine practicality.

'True, true. Then I am with Tyllwin.'

'Petrovic?' inquired the Margrave.

'I am aware,' that dried-up individual said in a doubtful tone, 'that the people believe all our troubles would be at an end if we had a god, as other cities do. I hope that in this instance they are wrong; they usually are. Having heard from our neighbours at Acromel how severely they suffer from their deity—'

'This is far from the point,' interrupted Gostala, tapping the table with a thumb-bone which had once been the property of a man fortunate enough – or unfortunate enough – to be her lover. 'I say we do not know. Let us therefore expect nothing and everything.'

'Rational and well-spoken!' approved the Margrave. 'Those in favour …?'

All present laid their right hands on the table, except Tuc, who had left his in the mouth of a dragon beyond an interesting sea of fire far to the north. Even Tyllwin moved with the rest, causing yet more leaves to wither and tremble on the tree that had suffered most since he broke from his impassivity.

'Agreed, then,' said the Margrave. 'Let us go thither.'

The company rose with a bustle and began to adjourn to the main gate. The Margrave, however, remained behind a few moments, contemplating Tyllwin, who had not vacated his place.

When the others were at a distance he judged safe, he addressed the enchanter in a low voice.

'Tyllwin, what is your opinion of a god?'

Tyllwin laughed creakingly. 'I have been asked that before,' he said. 'And I will answer as I did then: I do not know what a god is, and I doubt that many men do, either.'

A branch on the tree overhanging him split with a warning cry, so that the Margrave flung up his hand automatically before his face. When he looked again, Tyllwin was gone.

The commotion at the gates, foreseen by Tyllwin and by no other of the council members, had already begun when the stately procession entered the avenue leading to them. Each enchanter had come after his or her own style: Petrovic walking with his staff called Nitra, from which voices could sometimes be heard when the moon was full; Gostala riding on a creature she had conjured out of the deep water, which was its natural element, that cried aloud in heart-rending agony at every step; Ruman on the shoulders of a giant ape fettered with brass; Eadwil on his own young legs, although his feet shone red-hot when he had gone ten paces – this was to do with a gas about which no one ever inquired closely. The air about them crackled with the struggle between protective conjurations and the tense oppressive aura that enshrouded Ryovora.

In the wide street before the gateway a crowd had gathered, laughing, shouting, exclaiming with wonderment. In the midst of the throng, a man in outlandish attire, his face set in a frown of puzzlement, was vainly trying to contend with a hundred questions simultaneously.

The crowd parted to let the nobility by, and at once closed in again, like water around a slow-moving boat.

The Margrave came up behind the rest, panting somewhat, for he was getting fat, and looked the stranger over curiously, while the people's voices rose to almost a roar and then sank again into a muttering buzz. At last, having cast a beseeching glance at his companions and received no offers of assistance, he was compelled to address the newcomer.

'Sir, who are you and what do you want?'

In the terribly patient tone of one dealing with lunatics, the stranger said, 'My name is Bernard Brown, and all I want is to go home.'

'That is easy enough,' said the Margrave in relief. But if he had paused to reflect that Tyllwin was concerned at this man's arrival, he would not so soon have been optimistic. He rounded on Petrovic. 'Will you oblige?' he said.

Petrovic looked up in the air and down at the ground. He scratched a number of ideograms in the dust with his staff Nitra, then hastily scuffed them over with his foot. He said flatly, 'No.'

'Well if you won't, you won't,' sighed the Margrave. He appealed to Gostala, who merely shook her regal head and went on scrutinizing Bernard Brown.

'Eadwil!' cried the Margrave.

The boy, whose face had gone perfectly pale, stammered a few incomprehensible words and burst into tears.

'See! They can't! What did I tell you?' bellowed a bull-like voice from the crowd, and the Margrave shot a glance at the speaker as sharp as a spear.

'Come forth!' he commanded, and with the aid of a number of bystanders the fellow pushed and shoved until he stood before his ruler. He was an insolent-faced churl with a shock of corn-coloured hair, and wore a leather apron with big pockets in which reposed the tools of his trade. He appeared to be some kind of worker in metal.

'You are –' said the Margrave, and ran through a short formula in his mind. 'You are Brim, a locksmith. What did you mean by what you said?'

'What I said, of course,' the fellow retorted, seeming amused. 'Why, anyone can *see* he's not to be pushed around by ordinary folk!'

'Explain further,' commanded the Margrave.

'Why, 'tes simple as your mind … *sir*.' Brim thrust an errant lock of hair back into place with his blunt thumb. 'I see it plain, and so do all of us. Here we've been saying these years past that what's amiss with Ryovora is we haven't got a god like all those towns around the world every wherever. And now, today, what else do the omens say? Can you tell us *that*?'

He thrust a stubby finger at the Margrave's chest. The Margrave recoiled and looked at him distastefully. But he was by inclination an honest man, so he had to shake his head and admit that although the noble enchanters had speculated long and long about the recent omens they had not been able to arrive at any conclusion.

'There, mates! What did I tell you?' bellowed Brim, whirling to face the crowd. There was an answering yell, and in a moment the situation had turned topsy-turvy. The throng had closed in on Bernard Brown, unmindful that they trod on some of the nobles' toes, and had seized him and gone chairing him down the avenue, while men, women and children ran and skipped behind him, singing a rhythmic song and laughing like hyenas.

'Well!' said the Margrave in vexation. 'This is a most improper and irregular state of affairs!'

6

The Margrave had cause to repeat those words, with still greater emphasis and an even more sombre expression, the following morning. He sat once more at the head of the long table in the Moth Garden, for the air had become if anything more oppressive than yesterday; moreover, reports of omens seemed to have doubled in number.

'This is extremely aggravating!' said the Margrave testily. 'Virtually the entire populace is firmly convinced this stranger is a god, simply because they can't make head or tail of what he says. Accordingly, they have turned me out of my own palace – I spent an uncomfortable night here in the Moth

Garden – and are at work converting it into a temple for this *character* without so much as a by-your-leave!'

Eadwil suppressed an inappropriate smile. 'Moreover,' he supplied, 'all those persons who have voyaged extensively are being interrogated concerning the correct manner in which to pay homage to a new deity. Brim the locksmith, around whom this ferment seems to be most turgid, has travelled to Acromel and is enthusiastic for human sacrifice; there is a group of women who in their youth were captives in Barbizond and wish to hold daily single combats before the altar; a man who formerly fished Lake Taxhling declares that the sole method of adopting the god is to burn down the city twice a year and rebuild it, as the fisherfolk do with their reed-hut villages …'

Petrovic shook his withered head and opinioned, 'No good will come of this.'

'Has anyone knowledge of Tyllwin's whereabouts?' inquired the Margrave, for the gaunt one's place was empty today.

A shudder went down the table, and those in earshot shook their heads, not without expressions of relief.

'Well, then, let us proceed to a decision,' said the Margrave. He shifted in his chair; his night in the open, although the weather was warm, had left him feeling bruised all over.

'The first point to establish,' said Gostala sensibly, 'is whether this Bernard Brown is indeed a god. If not – well!'

'Agreed!' came a chorus in reply.

Ruman snorted and thumped the table with a ham-like fist. 'And how, pray, do we set about that?' he demanded with honey-sweet sarcasm. 'For we have all previously confessed that we do not know what a god is. Was that not the reason why we never had gods in the old days?'

'I fear very much,' said the Margrave heavily, 'that the days of rational procedure in Ryovora may be finished. It would appear that the populace are already treating Bernard Brown as a god; unless, then, we arrive at disproofs adequate to disabuse them, life in Ryovora is doomed to become insufferable.'

'Hah!' said Gostala without mirth.

'I have a suggestion,' ventured Eadwil. 'A god is reputed to have knowledge and power beyond what men may command. Let us therefore interrogate Bernard Brown on the most recondite and esoteric of our arts. If he fails to answer well, let us challenge him before the people, so that it may be seen his talents are small compared to ours.'

'The proposal is rational,' admitted the Margrave. 'As I said, however, the days of rational thought here may be numbered … However, if there is no better idea –?'

None was forthcoming. Accordingly, the company betook themselves to the newly converted temple, which had formerly been the palace of the Margrave.

They found Bernard Brown – much worried, to judge by his expression – seated on a large silver and ebony throne above an enormous improvised altar. Before this throne the townsfolk were coming and going with gifts. Their most prized possessions were heaped about his feet, from their inherited table-plate to their newest garments. On the altar were piled luscious fruits and choice cuts of meat, together with bottles of delicious wine. Bernard Brown was sucking at one of the fruits and attempting to question the people. But they would not answer him; they merely listened respectfully, then went and wrote down what he said, with a view to creating a canon of mystical precepts.

The newcomers paused in the great hall to examine what had been done, and Eadwil spoke privily to the Margrave.

'Has not Tyllwin been here?' he said under his breath.

'You are right!' confirmed the Margrave. 'I can scent his power in the air. Now what snare has that devious personage laid in our path?'

He advanced towards the altar. Taking his stand some ten feet away – because of the heaped-up gifts – he raised his voice and addressed the putative god.

'Sir! We are the nobility of Ryovora, come to determine whether or not you are a god, as the populace maintain!'

Bernard Brown gave a cautious nod. 'I was advised about your intention,' he confided. 'And I have been warned not to deny the possibility. Since meeting with Jorkas on my way here, I have acquired a healthy respect for the advice I am given hereabouts, no matter how lunatic it may seem. Contrariwise, however, being honest, I must state that prior to my arrival in your city the notion that I *might* be a god had never crossed my mind.'

The Margrave exchanged frustrated glances first with Eadwil and then with Ruman, who snorted characteristically and called to Bernard Brown.

'Are we to take it, then, that you believe it possible you're a god?'

'I don't know what to believe,' said Bernard unhappily. 'Until yesterday I had always pictured myself as a perfectly ordinary man. But certainly I am not ordinary in this world, wherever and whatever it may be.'

'Come now!' said Ruman, bridling. 'This is a reputable and well-regarded city! Or was, until you chose to intrude on its traditional sober existence.'

'I chose nothing of the sort, if you will forgive my contradicting you,' sighed Bernard. 'All I want is to be allowed to go home!'

'This does not sound like the utterance of a god,' the Margrave muttered to Eadwil, who nodded.

'Sir,' he said to Bernard, 'we wish to determine your powers. Are you acquainted with the Book of Universal Shame, and can you conjure from it?'

By now, the townspeople had ceased their going and coming before the altar, and were gathering in silence to listen to this discussion. It was plain that a few of them were unconvinced, propitiating Bernard only by way of insurance, as it were.

'I never heard of it,' said Bernard, swallowing.

'Then of the Book of Three Red Elephants? Perhaps of the Casket of Disbelief?'

To each name Bernard shook his head.

Eadwil turned smiling to the Margrave. 'It is most unlikely that he is a god!'

Then, in their turn Petrovic, Gostala and Ruman questioned Bernard about the most esoteric wisdom known to them – which implied the most esoteric wisdom known to anyone. Some few individuals surpassed the enchanters of Ryovora, such as Manuus, but those persons were far beyond the commerce of everyday life and chose to exist alone with their powers, not intruding on mundane affairs.

To each inquiry Bernard was constrained to reply in the negative, and in the watching crowd some began to stare significantly at Brim. The locksmith grew more and more flustered and annoyed, until at last, when Ruman had completed his questioning, he strode forward and faced the altar challengingly, hands on hips.

'Let's have it straight!' he bellowed. 'Are you a god, or is this false pretenses?'

'I – I was advised not to deny it,' said Bernard tentatively, and the Margrave clapped his hand to his forehead.

'Fool that I am!' he exclaimed, and thrust Brim to one side, ignoring the fellow's complaint. 'It was Tyllwin who advised you thus, was it not?'

'I don't suppose it can do much harm to say who it was,' Bernard decided reflectively. 'Uh – whether it was Tyllwin or not, I'm unsure, for he gave me no name. But I can describe him: a very charming elderly gentleman, with a wisp of white beard clinging at his chin.'

'Manuus!' exclaimed several persons together, and the Margrave whirled to face his colleagues.

'How many of you had seen Tyllwin before yesterday?' he demanded.

'Why—' began three or four speakers, and as one fell silent with expressions of amazement.

'You have it!' snapped the Margrave. 'He was there, and some enchantment persuaded us he was seated by right and custom. But I for one now realize that I have no other knowledge of Tyllwin. Well, then! So Manuus is behind all this! We must go to him and tell him that he is not permitted to meddle in Ryovora's affairs. If he chose to live among us as a responsible citizen, that would be a different cauldron of spells. But as things are, we can only respect his privacy so long as he respects ours.'

There was much shuffling of feet. With juvenile dignity Eadwil spoke up.

'Margrave, I regret that I dare not face Manuus in this connection. My powers are inadequate as yet. I hate to shelter behind my youth – but.'

And he took his leave.

One by one, shamefacedly, the others of the council followed his example, until the Margrave was left by himself, and the townsfolk, having garnered from these events only that the nobles had failed to disprove Bernard's divinity, hastily resumed their self-imposed tasks.

'A fine lot we breed in Ryovora!' exclaimed the Margrave scornfully. The scorn was a mask for his own forebodings; he was less of an enchanter than many who served under him, having achieved his eminence on administrative skills. But nonetheless he was a resolute man, and accordingly he summoned his train and set forth to beard Manuus in his castle.

The mists parted in such fashion as to imply that this call was not unexpected, and having left his attendants huddled together in the great yard he ascended to Manuus's sanctum with determined steps. There the enchanter greeted him with warm expressions of respect.

But the Margrave was ill at ease in this place of discomfortable forces, and came to the point as quickly as manners would permit. He said firmly, when he had the chance, 'Sir, since you are Tyllwin's master you know my errand.'

'Correction,' the enchanter parried blandly. 'I *am* Tyllwin. I have certain other natures beside my own – a trait which I share with all persons save one alone.'

The Margrave made an appropriate sign at the mention of him who has many names but one nature, and pressed on with what he had to say.

'We will not tolerate interference, sir,' he declared. 'Since time immemorial we in Ryovora have striven to create a tradition of calm rationality, and to rely upon hard sense. This petty trick of intruding a so-called god like a gaming-piece into our affairs is hardly worthy of a gentleman of your distinction.'

'I agree,' said Manuus. 'And you may therefrom deduce it is not of my choosing.'

'What?'

'In this matter,' the enchanter continued, ignoring the exclamation, 'you and I are on the same side: so to say, the *outside*. It will perhaps interest you to know that he of whom we were speaking a moment ago – whose nature is single – was sitting in that chair only two days ago.'

The Margrave shivered, and wondered what he had stumbled into. He said respectfully, 'Manuus, your powers are beyond imagining!'

'Oh, he did not come at my bidding!' With a thin chuckle. 'Rather the reverse!'

'However that may be, I shall take leave of you,' said the Margrave, rising and bowing. 'For if this matter is *his* concern, I dare do nothing to intervene.'

Manuus shook his head, his eyes twinkling. 'I am afraid you have no choice, Margrave,' he said. 'Like it or not, you and I are both concatenated in this web.'

At which the Margrave departed, his heart so heavy he could barely lift his boots, and when he was gone Manuus fell to ceremonies of a kind that had not been performed in living memory, and strange phenomena attended them. There was a storm on peaceful Lake Taxhling; in Barbizond three madmen ran screaming through the streets; on a hill near Acromel dust-devils ceased their whirling. Last, but not least, several persons in Ryovora itself saw visions of a disturbing nature, and went hastily to the new-designated temple to place yet more offerings at the feet of Bernard Brown and to consult the already sizable record of his sayings.

Studying them, they found no comfort.

7

And thus the matter was to remain for another day. The Margrave, making as was his custom the best of a bad job, called up an obliging spirit and had a pavilion built in the Moth Garden to serve as a temporary surrogate for his palace; there he sat, swearing mightily, far into the night, while he pondered the information Manuus had divulged.

Those other nobles of Ryovora who were best skilled in the art of magic met to discuss in low tones over their wine the riddle of distinguishing divinity from humanity. They remained unswayed by both the clamour of the populace, led by Brim, and the scant evidence furnished by their interrogation of Bernard Brown. It seemed implausible, they allowed, that such a person should be a god; nonetheless, one must respect the powers of Manuus, and perhaps in the mood to make a jest of Ryovora he *could* have conjured up an authentic deity …

The common folk, similarly, found themselves impaled by a dilemma. However, they had been longing for a god of some sort for a considerable while; indisputably someone *strange* had come among them, preceded by complex indecipherable omens, and it was generally deemed advisable to act as though he were a genuine god until some incontestable argument to the contrary should be advanced.

So the night passed; and of those many who spent it restlessly, not the least fervent seeker of repose was Bernard Brown, for all that his couch was a vast stack of gorgeous offerings in velvet and satin.

It had been centuries since another city had marched against Ryovora. The citizens had long ago deduced that their best protection was their reputation; who after all would dare attack that city where pre-eminently the populace enjoyed the gift to plan and reason?

Perennially cautious, nonetheless, they financed the wages of a team of watchmen ... and next day as dawn was breaking the current incumbent of the watchman's post *en route* to his customary breakfast gave a casual glance across the country separating Ryovora from Acromel.

And saw with astonishment – not to mention disbelief – that a red idol a hundred feet high was striding with enormous yells towards him.

Such an idol, the watchman realized, could be none other than the Quadruple God of Acromel.

Around the monstrous crimson feet were fetters of riveted steel; before and behind, men went with blazing torches on poles fifty feet long, prodding and driving it in a desired direction. Sometimes the thing's yelling howled into a ridiculous falsetto when a torch made contact with its blood-coloured limbs, and the drovers had to scatter and flee from the blows of eight gigantic fists. But they returned, and it became plain to see that they now well understood the actions of their idol, and could drive it like a maddened bull because its rage made it unthinking.

The watchman sounded an alarm that spread through the streets of Ryovora like flood-waters through a burst levee, and men, women, even children leapt from sleep to dash hither and thither in confusion.

One by one the nobles were summoned, and assembled on the ramparts in an impressive band; thousand by thousand the common folk acquired makeshift weapons – knives, scythes, axes – and numbered off into centuries to prepare for battle.

So arrayed they waited tensely while the sun cleared the horizon and the Quadruple God with his attendants came to take station before the city walls.

At a sign from one who seemed to be the leader, the torch-wielders compelled the god to halt, and he stood screaming empty threats at the unresponsive sky. Then this same man advanced to stand on a small knoll and gaze insolently at the nobles of Ryovora.

'Greetings!' he called merrily. 'News has come to us in Acromel that you have been fortunate enough to acquire a god in the past few days! Well, as it happens we in Acromel have been fortunate in more ways than one – we have lost Duke Vaul, who had for many years oppressed us, and we have gained power of the Quadruple God.' The man gestured over his shoulder at the misshapen idol.

'It seems to us,' the spokesman went on, 'that our god is very foolish, although extremely strong. It is said that your god is weak, but extremely wise. We have not been able to make head or tail of these cryptic utterances which have been relayed to us! Regardless of that, we wish to try conclusions and thus determine whether brute strength in a god is a quality superior to sageness. I await your answer, sirs and ladies! Failing this trial, we shall of course goad the Quadruple God into Ryovora, and since he overtops all but your highest towers, I suspect that would be a major misfortune for the city.'

He bowed with a flourish of his right hand, and descended from the knoll.

The Margrave, scowling so deeply it seemed a ploughshare must have crossed his brow, called the nobles into conference on the ramparts, and spoke worriedly concerning this challenge. Some were of opinion that if the personage with many names and one nature had taken a hand, there was nothing any of them could do; others poured scorn on this faint-hearted attitude, among them Ruman, whose bull laugh echoed around the walls.

'Never say die!' he boomed. 'Some magic is of an order that will bind even gods, and I have important knowledge of this magic. Go, fetch me a black goat and a white pigeon, and a mirror cracked from edge to edge, and I will discomfit the Quadruple Idiot over there!'

So it was ordained, and Ruman withdrew into a large black cloud with his goat, his pigeon and his mirror, and what he did to them brought about thunderclaps.

But eventually the cloud blew away, and there was no trace of Ruman.

'This is ridiculous!' said Gostala with feminine directness, and Petrovic nodded his old dried-up head.

'I agree,' he rasped. 'Goats, forsooth! Pigeons! Mirrors! Claptrap! Now I came prepared, Margrave – I have here a phial containing the blood of an unborn child. That and my knowledge are all I require.'

Then Petrovic set about his task, and did what he had to do in the sight of all, which was most disturbing. The Margrave, trying not to watch, wished Petrovic had had the decency to conceal himself as Ruman had done.

Yet the business failed, and Petrovic returned to them at last speaking a tongue no one could understand, and burst into tears when he realized what had transpired. The great red idol still fumed and howled and shook his chains.

'Igoroth!' said Gostala in exasperation. 'Dumedinnis! And likewise Algorethon!'

Three odd-looking gentlemen – one in blue, one in white, one in green – walked through a nearby wall and stood before her. None of them was entirely normal in appearance, though it was hard to say in what particular respect.

'Get rid of that – object!' directed Gostala forcefully.

The three peculiar personages looked at her, then at each other, then at her again. Premeditatedly, they shook their heads, and departed, taking her with them.

The Margrave hastily hurled a protective charm about the city, to guard against a re-appearance of the three – for they were notoriously tough to tackle – and bit his lip in frustration. This was a bad business altogether, and the worst fears he had carried away from his interview with Manuus were being overfulfilled.

'These are indeed magics to bind a god,' said Eadwil, his boyish face white and strained because his feet were blazing hot – he had walked from his dwelling when news of the attack was brought. 'But are they magics to bind one such as Manuus? Margrave, I think Tyllwin may be found in the vicinity.'

'You are a true citizen of Ryovora,' the Margrave said with enthusiasm. 'That is clear reasoning.'

He strode forward to the battlements and cupped his hands around his mouth. 'Tyllwin!' he bellowed towards the Acromel party. 'Tyllwin, ha!'

An acre of grass turned brown and died, while songbirds that had been chanting in the trees nearby fell stiffly from their perches. And from the besieging company the gaunt figure of Tyllwin was borne into view on the back of a brawny slave.

'You desire speech with me, Margrave?' said that scarecrow form.

'So this *is* your doing!' exclaimed the Margrave in disgust.

Tyllwin's thin chuckle carried clearly to his ears; also to those of various dogs, causing them to howl.

'Why, Margrave, did I not state that you and I are on the same side in this matter? Admit frankly that the pretended god in your palace is not to your taste! Admit that it is in our common interest to show his fallibility by matching him against this perfectly genuine god from Acromel!'

'It's for this reason that you have destroyed three of the leading enchanters of our city?' bellowed the Margrave. 'Why could you not have left us to deal with the matter ourselves?'

Tyllwin's voice was suddenly as dull as doom. 'Because he whose nature is single has a hand in the affair.'

He fell silent. A horse neighed into the quietness, and the neigh became a scream of agony.

The Margrave looked helplessly at Eadwil, who shook his head. 'Against Manuus, which of us can stand?' he said. 'Moreover, the business is escaping our control. Look down into the street. The Townsfolk have gone to fetch their god, supplicating him for protection.'

Indeed, down the broad avenue leading to the main gate, they saw a pressing throng of men and women, and among them a figure in outlandish attire who was crying out for aid and receiving none. Brim the locksmith could be discerned grasping his elbow, hurrying him willy-nilly along, and occasional voices rang out distinct above the general uproar.

'Save us! Defeat the enemy god! We have no hope except in you!'

'Hah!' said the Margrave in mingled pity and annoyance. 'So nothing will convince them the wretch is not a god, but that he be laid low by the Quad-ruple One. Well, at least we know which way the lot is cast.'

Eadwil mustered the ghost of a smile. 'I wonder!' he said. 'I wonder ...!'

Shortly the leaders of the crowd opened the gates, and poured forth onto an open level space where they could confront the menacing array of troops from Acromel. On seeing those armoured ranks – for the enemy had doubt-less made careful preparations, whereas the folk of Ryovora had been surprised – many felt qualms and tried to draw back, but the press was too great, and at length the mass of them, in number three or four thousand, simmered and seethed but stood still.

Urging his god forward, and sweating, Brim the locksmith made a path to the front of the crowd. 'There!' he bellowed, throwing up his arm to indicate the hideous red idol. 'That's the best they can muster against you! Hark at his howling! Why, already he fears your mere presence!'

'I must go down,' said the Margrave in low tones. 'I have no stomach to stand and watch the poor fools massacred.'

'I will come also,' said Eadwil. And accordingly they descended together to the gate. Among muttered threats from the commoners, saying that if these nobles were going to interfere out of spite they would get short shrift, they elbowed closer and closer to Bernard. The heat of Eadwil's glowing feet helped clear a path.

At last the Margrave was face to face with Bernard Brown, and cast on him a look full of sympathy.

'This is none of our doing,' he said in apologetic tones. 'It seems that the people of Ryovora, so long reputed sensible, have finally taken leave of their senses.'

Bernard Brown blinked unhappily at him. 'I think you are right, sir,' he agreed. 'Especially since this galumphing monstrosity is plainly nothing more than an overgrown child.'

'A *what*?' said the Margrave, and Eadwil was seen to be grinning almost from ear to ear.

'An overgrown child,' repeated Bernard patiently. 'Why, he howls and strikes out and breaks things at random – this is not the behaviour of an intelligent, adult personality! Moreover, one must assume that the folk of Acromel have attempted to establish communication with the idol, must one not?'

'Why – ah ...' The Margrave was bewildered. 'One would imagine so, yes!'

'Yet their preferred mode of communication proves to be torches on sticks.' Bernard spread his hands. 'I deduce that we have here a case of arrested development, and what I would propose ...'

8

Wave upon wave of laughter rang out around the walls of Ryovora, and at once the citizens, led by the Margrave, set about implementing Bernard's plan. Eadwil stood a little apart, his lips set in a smile that bid fair to become permanent.

Meanwhile, the sky grew to full brightness, and the sun hoisted itself towards the meridian. Among the ranks of those from Acromel a certain impatience grew manifest. The long torches which served to goad the idol were withdrawn one by one, soaked in fresh pitch, and re-lit; the chains which tethered his sixteen limbs were anchored firmly to posts hammered in the ground, so that the teams of men afoot and ahorse who weighed him down when he was on the move might relax for a while; but in the comings and goings of the people, there was more restlessness than purpose.

Ultimately, towards mid-day, the spokesman who had previously addressed the nobility of Ryovora again ascended his knoll and called for the Margrave. Sweating from his work, hands filthy, his richly embroidered sleeves turned back above his elbows, the Margrave leaned over the ramparts and gave a wave.

'Margrave! Our god is restive! Time wastes, and we desire to know the outcome of this affair!'

The Margrave glanced down into the avenue below the wall, where work was proceeding apace under Bernard Brown's direction. Far below him, Eadwil raised an arm in signal that all was ready.

'Good!' said the Margrave to himself, and called to the spokesman for Acromel.

'Our city's god is prepared to meet yours!'

The man from Acromel at once spun on his heel and yelled to those charged with loosing the Quadruple God's chains. A moment passed; then, from the front of the crowd before the gate, diffidently yet with unfaltering strides Bernard Brown marched out towards the enemy.

A gust of merriment ascended, and the welkin echoed with scornful gibes. But Bernard kept on marching towards the Quadruple God.

And the Quadruple God paid him no attention.

Behind the approaching man, behind the ramparts of the city, another figure was appearing – a figure so gigantic, so bloated, so huge that the Quadruple God seemed a mere ant by comparison. This apparition had a head with teeth twenty feet long in its gash of a mouth; it had arms like a hundred barrels, it had legs planted either side of a tall building.

This figure was growing. It was rising as though from the depths of the earth, and all four heads of the Quadruple God were striving to fasten their eyes on it at once.

Gracefully, considering its incredible bulk – thanks to an afterthought of Eadwil's – the bloated colossus raised its arms into a menacing posture. From the camp of the men of Acromel, the naked eye could not detect the fine silk cords governing its motions.

And then this construct of inflated wineskins, of paint and cane and waxed fabric supported with hot air, spoke with the massed voice of all the citizens of Ryovora, a voice like the crashing of a waterfall.

'Go away!' said the monster with terrible emphasis. And the Quadruple God burst his chains, stamped on the torch-bearers, and fled.

Only once was his panicky progress interrupted before he gained the familiar sanctuary of his temple at Acromel on the far horizon. That was when a gaunt and scarecrow-like person rushed into his path, crying in a voice which though thin and reedy caused cracks to open in the surface of the land, and strange colours to muddy the clear blue of the sky.

The Quadruple God trampled this nuisance with three of his eight massive feet, and left nothing but a smear like a crushed beetle to mark the spot.

Triumphantly, the people of Ryovora went forward in the wake of the people of Acromel, and with their ad-hoc weapons wrought considerable havoc among the laggards. Not the most tongue-tied of them was Brim the locksmith, who spent more breath on yelling praise of his own perceptiveness than on catching up with the rearguard of the enemy.

But certain of his fellows who had been lukewarm in their acceptance of Bernard Brown as a ready-made god turned aside to surround Brim in a hostile manner. 'Nonsense!' they said emphatically. 'If we had not been lured by fools like you away from our customary trust in common sense, we should have seen what he saw and done what he advised, anyway.'

Then they set about Brim with meticulous thoroughness, and impressed the extent of his stupidity upon him, in such fashion as to ensure he could never again overlook these various mementos. That chore attended to, and the other party in utter disarray, they returned with satisfaction to their homes. By that time the aura of blue depression which had pervaded the atmosphere these many weeks past had dissipated; the cause for rejoicing which this gave them made them forget altogether about Bernard Brown.

The Margrave and his nobles assembled again in the Moth Garden, and the people began to reclaim the offerings they had set before Bernard's altar, to feast on them and deck themselves in gaudy ceremonial attire. To preoccupy the nobles, though, there were still problems, and Eadwil spoke of the most pressing when they were met.

He said, 'I think, sirs and ladies, that the age for enchantments is passing.'

The Margrave nodded. So did several others. Some of them glanced at the place which had been – very briefly – Tyllwin's.

'Regard it this way,' said Eadwil musingly. 'In its nature enchantment, magic, whatever term you give the art, is a survival of the chaos which we know reigned before time. But the imprint of that chaos is fading from the world. The confusion which causes stone idols to walk, elementals to be personified in storm-clouds, humans to blend with animals and spirits to speak from fire and water, is gradually succumbing to that same hard sense on which we in Ryovora traditionally rely.'

'Well spoken!' applauded the Margrave. Eadwil gave him a sidelong glance and concluded thus.

'Manuus is – was – whether as Tyllwin or himself, a master of chaos. So are we all in lesser degree. But the greatest master of all has proved to be a simple stranger lacking all acquaintance with the esoteric arts. Colleagues and friends, magic is of the past. Rationality and logic will rule the future.' He bent his gaze below the table. 'My feet, I may add, have not burned since I arrived at this conclusion. So I think I shall forthwith take steps to set right the other disadvantage consequent upon my command of magic. Excuse me.'

And with a hop and a skip he departed in the wake of a saucy-eyed girl who was bearing fruit from the garden to the feast the people were preparing.

Another who was in the Moth Garden was a black-clad traveller, whose face twitched into a satisfied smile when he heard Eadwil's words. He did not need to wait longer or listen more.

On that same knoll from which the spokesman of Acromel's forces had addressed the Margrave, Bernard Brown sat with his chin in his hands, staring gloomily at nothing. His dismal contemplation was interrupted at length by the presence of one who was not a stranger, who stood before him leaning on a remarkable staff.

'I've seen you before,' said Bernard slowly. 'Well, who are you?'

The black-clad one chuckled. 'He to whom the task was given of bringing order out of chaos in this corner of the universe,' he replied. 'And who are you?'

'I'm not sure I know any longer,' admitted Bernard after a pause. 'I thought I was Bernard Brown until recently, and that I was a rather ordinary kind of person. But these past few days people have been telling me so repeatedly I'm a god that I've almost been convinced of the idea.'

The black-clad man clucked with his tongue. 'I'm afraid that isn't true at all,' he said. 'So – since I was responsible for involving you with all this – I'd better explain.'

He sat down companionably alongside Bernard on the knoll, and gestured in the air with his staff. A short distance away, in a pleasant meadow, some clinging ground-mist cleared to reveal the ruins of a castle, smoking quietly.

'An enchanter called Manuus dwelt there,' he said. 'A person with – so to speak – a vested interest in the chaos which formerly engulfed the entire universe. *This* sort of thing.'

He gestured again, and out of a hill a mile or two this side of Acromel a – a – a ... Well, a pair of yellow eyes peered briefly. What could be seen in those eyes defied description. It made Bernard shudder with amazement and repugnance.

'So where am I?' he demanded. 'Or is it a question of *when* am I?'

'Neither. We are speaking of a borderland between chaos, existing in eternity, and reason, existing in time. At this moment the balance is uncertain, but it is tipping, bit by bit. You have been quite invaluable in tilting it beyond a crucial point.'

'I don't understand!' complained Bernard.

'No matter. If you did understand the nature of chaos, men being what they are, you would certainly be conceited enough to wish to exploit it. This in fact is what those vain enchanters do: turn the forces of chaos to their own advantage. But, logically, to control chaos with reason is to impose lasting order on it. This implies in turn that sooner or later chaos will reign no longer.'

Bernard's face exhibited sudden comprehension. '*I* see!' he exclaimed. 'In other words, these magicians or whatever necessarily destroy what they most desire to preserve, by imposing rational control on it.'

'You get the point exactly,' said the one in black.

'And it's up to you to ensure that things come out right?'

'Alas, yes!'

'Hmm!' Bernard rubbed his chin. 'That sounds like a tough chore! Who landed you with it, if I may ask?'

'You may not. I'm very sorry.' The tone was final; still, the words were succeeded by a chuckle. This black-garbed fellow was really very pleasant, Bernard reflected. Casting around for the other question he had meant to put, he recalled it.

'Well, then! May I at least ask what it was I *did*?'

'That, yes! You see, there was dissatisfaction in Ryovora so long as the people felt they had to have a god. So I gave them one ... of a kind. And after all that, they realized their god had done nothing for them which they could not have achieved by using their heads. My compliments, by the way, on the elegant manner in which you demonstrated that.'

'I was scared silly,' confessed Bernard.

'But you kept your wits about you, and refused to be overawed by mere size. The universe is a big place, and there are many corners of it where chaos on the grand scale still obtains. This, then, is a valuable attitude to inculcate.'

Bernard pondered for a while. At last he shook his head and sighed. 'I guess I'm actually dreaming,' he said. 'I can't believe a word you say.'

'Congragulations, and thank you,' said the black-clad one dryly. 'That you can speak thus is an earnest of my eventual success. Sometimes it seems a very long way away.'

'What will – if this is the right way to put it – what will happen then?'

'*I* don't know,' said his companion. 'Why should I care? I'll have finished my appointed job. And since you have now finished yours …'

When he was alone, the traveller in black stood awhile leaning on his staff of curdled light, gazing at the wreck of Manuus's castle.

Chaos.

He decreed it out of existence. Since Manuus no longer held it tenaciously in being, it disappeared. Across the site the grass grew green and orderly.

The traveller wished that Bernard had not asked his last question. It was discomforting. Now and then he regretted that he must inevitably find out its answer.

Yet it was not in his nature – and his nature was single – to undo anything he had done. Therefore, inexorably, he was approaching that ultimate moment.

He shrugged, and then there was nothing but the knoll and the afternoon sunlight, while people made merry in Ryovora.

TWO

Break the Door of Hell

'I will break the door of hell and smash the bolts; I will bring up the dead to eat food with the living, and the living shall be outnumbered by the host of them.'

– The Epic of Gilgamesh

1

Time had come to Ryovora.

The traveller in black contemplated the fact from the brow of the hill where he had imprisoned Laprivan, more eons ago than it was possible to count. Leaning on his staff made of light, he repressed a shiver. Single though his nature might be, unique though that attribute certainly was, he was not immune from apprehension; his endowments did not include omniscience.

Time had come to that great city: Time, in which could exist order and logic and rational thought. And so it was removed from his domain for ever, vanished from the borderland of chaos situated timeless in eternity.

The task for which his single nature fitted him was the bringing forth of order; accordingly it might have been expected that he should feel the satisfaction of achievement, or even a mildly conceited pleasure. He did not, and for this there were two most cogent reasons and a third which he preferred not to consider.

The first, and most piquing, was that his duty lay on him: this season followed the conjunction of four significant planets hereabout, and he was setting forth to oversee that portion of the All which lay in his charge, as he was constrained to. And he had grown accustomed to terminating his round of inspection at Ryovora. Lapses and backsliding from common sense had occasionally minded him to alter this habit; still, he had never done so, and to discover that Ryovora was elsewhere annoyed him somewhat.

The second reason was not annoying. It was alarming, and dismaying, and unprecedented, and many other distressing epithets.

'In sum,' the traveller in black announced to the air, 'it's unheard-of!'

Another city had arisen in the borderland of chaos, and it was stamped all over with the betraying mark of Time.

How was it possible? Carried in some eddy whose flow ran counter to the universal trend, so that from reason and logic it receded to the random reign of chance? Presumably. Yet the means whereby such an eddy might be created seemed inconceivable. Some great enchantment would be required, and in the grip of Time enchantment was impossible.

'A contradiction in terms!' exclaimed the traveller, speaking aloud again to distract his mind from the third and least palatable reason for regretting the loss of Ryovora. It was known to him that when he had accomplished his task all things would have but one nature; then they would be subsumed into the Original All, and time would have a stop. Beyond which point ...

He glanced around him at the hillside. As ever, among the sparse-leaved grey bushes, dust-devils were sifting their substance, fine as ashes, over the footprints he had left on the path. Raising his staff, he tapped with it on a rock: once, twice, and again.

At the third tap the elemental Laprivan of the Yellow Eyes heaved in his underground prison and cracks appeared in the road. From these his voice boomed, monstrous, making the welkin echo.

'Leave me be!'

'What do you know of the city which stands yonder?' said the traveller in black.

'Nothing,' responded Laprivan with sullenness.

'Nothing? You say so to spare yourself the pain of memory! Shall I send you where Ryovora has gone, into the domain of Time? There memories cannot be expunged by whirling dust!'

The whole hill shuddered, and an avalanche of pale rock rattled on its further side. The sourceless voice moaned, 'What should I know of the city yonder? No man has come from it and passed this way.'

'Bad,' said the traveller thoughtfully. 'Very bad.'

After that he was silent for a long while, until at last the elemental pleaded, 'Leave me be! Leave me to wipe clean the slate of yesterday!'

'As you wish, so be it,' said the traveller absently, and tapped with his staff again. The cracks in the ground closed; the dust-devils resumed their revolutions.

Ignoring all this, the traveller gazed over the green and gracious meadows of the valley. There the strange city lay in noon-tide sunlight like a worn-out toy cast aside by a giant-child. The heedless ruin of Time was everywhere about it, toothmarks of the greatest leveller on brick and stone and metal. It had been fair and rich, that was plain; its gates were of oak and bronze – but the bronze was corroded green; its towers were of silver and orichalcum – but their bright sheen was overlaid with a dull mist like the foul breath of a swamp; its streets were broad and paved with marble – but the flags lifted to the roots of wild plants, and here and there one found holes filled by the rain and noxious with algae and insect-larvae.

Out of Time and into chaos. Almost beyond belief.

At length he stirred himself. There was nothing else for it – so he reasoned – but to set off on his journey of obligation, and come at last not to familiar, welcome Ryovora, but to this enigma wished on him by fate and boding no good whatever.

Anxiety carried him far and fast, and little by little it was mitigated by relief. To learn that Acromel stood where it had, albeit altered; to find that they yet fished Lake Taxhling when the proper stars came out, and that the river Metamorphia fed it with strange unspawned creatures, greedy and unwholesome – this was reassuring, an earnest of balance continued in the cosmos.

And at these places, and many many more, he did what on this as on all his journeys was required of him.

A lonely hut stood on the shelf-edge of a mountain pasture in the land called Eyneran; here when he paused to ask a crust of bread and a sup of ewe's milk from the flock high and distant as clouds on the steep meadow, a woman with a frightened face opened the ill-carpentered door to him, and met his request with a silent shake of the head.

She was wrinkled and worn out beyond her years; yet the hut was sound, a savory smell filled the air, and the clean floor and many copper pots the traveller could see assorted badly with her ragged gown and bare feet. He waited. Shortly a cry – man-deep, yet edged with a child's petulance – rang out.

'Mother, come here! The pot's boiling over! What's keeping you, you lazy slut?'

'Mintra!' whispered the woman, and a patter of feet announced the passage of a girl, some twelve years old, across the floor to tend the pot.

Another cry, still louder: 'Mother, I told you to come here! Mintra can't lift the pot when it's full, you stupid old bag of bones!'

'We can't give you food,' the woman said to the traveller. 'All of it is for my son.'

The traveller nodded, but waited still. Then at last with great heaving and panting the son came into view: gross-bulging in his apparel of velvet worked with gilt wire and stained with slobberings of food, so tall he nearly scraped the roof with his pate, yet so fat he breathed hard for the simple effort of standing upright. His fist, big as a ham, cracked his mother behind the ear.

'Why don't you die, you lazy old cow, and get it over with?' he bellowed.

'It'd be a merciful relief,' the woman whimpered. 'And die I would of my own free will, but that I stand alone between you and Mintra! With me gone you'd take her like a harlot, sister or no!'

'And wouldn't she be a tasty bit for my bed?' chortled the son with an evil grin, his tongue emerging thick as an ox's to stroke his lips lasciviously.

'As you wish,' said the traveller, 'so be it.' And he knocked his staff on the threshold and took his leave.

That night the plague stole silent from the mountain mist, and took the mother as the son had wished; then the girl Mintra fled on light feet down the hill-trails and the fever-giddy glutton went calling her among the heedless sheep until his gross weight dislodged a rock and sent him over a precipice to feed the crows.

In the rich city Gryte a thief spoke to curse the briefness of the summer night, which had cut short his plan to break the wall of a merchant's counting-house.

'Oh that dawn never overtook me!' he cried. 'Oh that I had lasting darkness whereby to ply my trade!'

'As you wish,' said the traveller, 'so be it.' And darkness came: two thick grey cataracts that shut the light away.

Likewise in Medham was another rogue, striving to seduce a lady who feared her charms were passing with the years so that he might win to a coffer of gold secreted in her chamber. 'I love you!' declared this smooth-tongued deceiver. 'I'd wed you had you no more than rags and a shack!'

'As you wish, so be it,' said the traveller, and bailiffs came down the street to advise the lady that her house and treasure were forfeit on another's debt. Upon which the liar turned and ran, not staying to hear a city officer who followed hard on the bailiffs' heels report the honouring of the debt a day past due.

So too in Wocrahin a swaggering bully came down the street on market-day, cuffing aside children with the back of his hand and housewives with the flat of his sword. 'Oh that my way were not cluttered with such riffraff!' he exclaimed, his shoulder butting into the traveller's chest.

'As you wish, so be it,' said the traveller, and when the bully turned the corner the street he walked was empty under a leaden sky – and the buildings on either side, and the taverns, and the shops. Nor did he again in all eternity have to push aside the riffraff he had cursed; he was alone.

This, however, was not the sum total of the traveller's doings as he passed from place to place within his realm. In Kanish-Kulya they had built a wall to keep Kanishmen and Kulyamen apart, and from either side, set into the masonry, grinned down the skulls of those dead in a war for which the reason had long been forgotten. In this strange and dreadful place Fegrim was pent under a volcano; shadowed by its cone the traveller halted and spoke long and seriously with that elemental, and when he was done the country for a mile on every side was dusted with cinders, little and bright as fireflies.

At Gander's Well, branched Yorbeth brooded in the guise of a tall tree whose main root tapped a wonderful subterranean spring and whose boughs, fed with miraculous sap, sprouted leaves and fruit the like of which had not been seen under any sun before. The traveller spent an hour in the shade of that tree, and for the questions he asked was constrained to carry away a red twig and later catch a cat and perform a ceremony with these two items – a price he paid with heavy heart, for he had been told nothing of any great use in his inquiries.

Also he consulted with Farchgrind, and in Leppersley he cast the bones of a girl's foot to read the runes they formed, and after great labour he incarcerated Wolpec in a candle over whose flame he smoked a piece of glass which thereupon showed three truths: one ineluctable, one debatable and one incomprehensible. That was in Teq, when the end of his journey was near.

So presently he came to Barbizond, where there was always a rainbow in the sky because of the bright being Sardhin, chained inside a thundercloud with fetters of lightning. Three courses remained to him: he might free Sardhin and let him speak, and from here to the horizon nothing would be left save himself, the elemental, and that which was of its nature bright, as jewels, or fire, or the edge of a keen-bladed knife; or he might do as once he had done under similar circumstances – address himself to an enchanter and make use of powers that trespassed too far towards naked chaos to be within his own scope – or, finally, he might go forward in ignorance to the strange city and confront the challenge of fate without the armour of foreknowledge.

Some little while remained to him before he needed to take his irreversible decision. Coming to Barbizond, therefore, he made his way down a fine broad avenue where plane and lime trees alternated in the direction of a steel-blue temple. There stood the altar of Hnua-Threl, who was also Sardhin when he chose to be; the people invoked him with daily single combats on the temple floor. They were not a gentle folk, these inhabitants of Barbizond, but they were stately, and died – in tournaments, or by the assassin's knife, or by their own hand – with dignity.

A death had lately occurred, that was plain, for approaching the city gate came a funeral procession: on a high-wheeled cart drawn by apes in brazen harness, the corpse wrapped in sheets of lead, gold and woven leaves; a band of gongmen beating a slow measure to accompany musicians whistling on bird-toned pipes no longer than a finger; eight female slaves naked to the ceaseless warm rain; and last a straggle of mourners, conducting themselves for the most part with appropriate solemnity.

He who passed penultimately of the mourners, however, was a fat and jolly person on each of whose shoulders perched a boy-child, and the two were playing peekaboo around the brim of his enormous leather hat. The traveller stared long at him before stepping out from the shelter of the nearest tree and addressing him courteously.

'Your pardon, sir, but are you not named Eadwil?'

'I am,' the fat one answered, not loath to halt and let the funeral wend its way to the graveyard without his assistance. 'Should I know you, sir?'

'Perhaps not,' said the traveller in black. 'Though I know you. I'd not expected to see you here; you were formerly one of the chief merchant enchanters of Ryovora.'

'A long time ago, sir,' Eadwil answered with a deprecating smile. The two children on his shoulders giggled, and one of them tried to catch hold of the traveller's staff, almost lost his balance, and righted himself with the aid of a pat from Eadwil's broad soft hand.

'May I ask what brought about your change of residence?' the traveller murmured.

'My change of employment,' Eadwil shrugged, again nearly dislodging the more venturesome boy. 'You spoke of me as a merchant enchanter; so I was! But when the decision was taken, many years ago, to let rational thought rule Ryovora and put an end to conjurations there, certain consequences followed. For myself I have no regrets; there was a geas upon me which made my feet glow red-hot when I walked, and now nothing worse attends a long tramp like today's than an occasional blister. And these my grandsons too – hey, you little nuisances? – they'd not be here today if I'd continued to submit to the other main restriction which purchased my powers.' He rubbed the boys' backs affectionately, and they responded by pulling his ears.

This was quite true, as the traveller was aware. Eadwil had postponed the growing of his beard until unusually late in life by making the trade on which his command of magic had been founded.

'So there came an end to my conjuring of fine silks and spices, of rare wines and exotic perfumes!' Eadwil pursed his lips. 'And there were, one must confess, certain persons in Ryovora who felt the lack of these luxuries and accused us retired enchanters of – ha-hm! – betraying them. Therefore I removed to Barbizond. It's a fair city in its way, and even though the local customs are not wholly to my taste, here they do at least have scores of enchanters of their own, so that no one plagues me to be about magical doings ... You have late news of Ryovora, sir? For it comes to my mind that I've heard nothing from my old home in quite a while.'

The traveller shook his head and gave a wry smile. 'It's a fair span since I set foot there. Indeed, I was hoping you might be able to give me certain information which I lack, rather than *vice versa*.'

Eadwil looked politely downcast at being of no help; then one of the boys grew impatient and started to fidget.

'Home?' said his grandfather, and laughed indulgently. 'Very well – old Harpentile is in no state to notice that we failed to attend his burying. Good day to you, sir,' he added to the traveller. 'It's been pleasant to renew our acquaintance, and I greatly hope you find someone who can aid you in these inquiries where I failed you.'

'As you wish, so be it,' said the traveller under his breath, and a great weight seemed to recede from his heart.

2

That accomplished, there was no more to do than sit and wait until the course of fate worked itself out. The traveller took a chair at a curbside tavern; with his elbows on a green table-top, protected from the rain by a pink umbrella, he watched the passers-by and wondered in what guise his helper would come.

The avenue grew crowded as the day wasted. Horsemen in gay jerkins with armour clanking at their saddlebows came by, challengers in some tourney for the hand of an heiress; also there were pedlars, and wonder-workers possessed of a few small tricks – for which they had paid excessively, to judge by their reddened eyes, pocked cheeks, limping gait or even womanly-shrill voices … No wonder, the traveller reflected, Eadwil felt his grandsons were the better bargain.

Women, too, passed: high-wimpled dames attended by maids and dandling curious unnamable pets; harlots in diaphanous cloaks through which it was not quite possible to tell if they were diseased; goodwives with panniers of stinking salted fish and loaves of bread and sealed jars of pollywogs for use in the commonplace home enchantments of this city.

And children likewise: many naked, not necessarily from poverty but because skin was the best raincoat under Barbizond's light continual shower, others in fantastical costumes to match their parents' whims – helmets of huge eggshells, bodices of leaves glued like scales and breeches made to resemble plant-stems in springtime. With spinning windmills, toy lances, tops, hoops and skipping-ropes, they darted among the adults and left a trail of joyful disorder.

There was no joy in the heart of the traveller in black – only a dulled apprehension.

The places at the tables before the tavern filled with customers, until only one was left – the second chair at the table where the traveller waited. Then, to the instant, appeared a curious bewildered figure from the direction of the city gate: a pale-faced, wild-haired man in a russet cape, clinging to a pitiful bag of belongings as though to a baulk of timber in an ocean of insanity. Time had etched his brow with suffering, and the traveller knew him the moment he clapped eyes on him.

Abreast of the tavern the stranger stopped. Enviously his eyes scanned the delicacies placed before the customers: fragrant stoups of wine, mounds of mashed fruit stuck with silver spoons, crisp sheets of the moonbark that only this city's enchanters knew how to conjure across the freezing gulf of space without spoiling. Huddling his bag under his arm, he felt in his script for money and produced one solitary copper coin.

Hesitant, he approached the traveller in black. 'Sir, by your leave,' he muttered, 'will this purchase anything at your tavern here?' And proffered the coin on a trembling palm.

The traveller took it and turned it over, and was at pains to conceal the shock he felt on seeing what name the reverse of the coin bore.

Ys!

A city in Time so great and famous that rumours of it had crossed the tenuous border of chaos, running ahead of those who bore its news until the stories were magnified beyond believing, until there were prophecies caused by the recirculation of those rumours through one corner of eternity and back to Time ahead of reality.

'No?' said the stranger sadly, seeing how long the black-clad one spent staring at his only money.

'Why –!' the latter exclaimed, and rubbed the coin with his fingertips, very lightly. 'I should say so, friend! Is it not good gold that passes anywhere?'

'Gold?' The stranger snatched it back, almost dropping his shabby bag in his agitation, and scrutinized it incredulously. Through the coppery tarnish gleamed the dull warm yellow of precious metal.

Without more ado he slumped into the vacant chair at this table, and a waggle-hipped servant-girl came to his side. 'Food and drink!' he commanded, letting the miraculous coin ring on the table. 'I starve and I'm clemmed with thirst – therefore be quick!'

Eyes twinkling, the traveller regarded his new acquaintance. 'And how are you called, sir?' he demanded.

'Jacques of Ys is my name,' the other sighed. 'Though truth to tell I'm not overmuch inclined to add my origin to my name any longer.'

'Why so?'

'Could you wish to be shamed by connection with a cityful of fools?'

'Considering the matter with due reflection,' said the traveller, 'I think – no.'

'Well, then!' Jacques ran his long bony fingers through his already untidy hair; the water had been trying to slick it down, but half an ocean would have been unequal to the task. He was a gaunt man, neither old nor young, with burning grey eyes and a bush of tawny beard.

'So in what way are the folk of Ys foolish?' probed the traveller.

'Oh, once they were a great people,' grunted Jacques. 'And that's where the trouble started, I suppose. Once we had a fleet – and not on any land-locked lake, either, but on Oceanus itself, mother of storms and gulls. Also we had an army to guard our trade-routes, skilful money-changers, wise counsellors ... Ah, Ys was among the noblest cities of the world!'

'I believe I've heard so,' the traveller agreed.

'Then your news is stale, sir!' Jacques thumped the table. 'Listen! There came changes – in the times, in the weather, in the currents of the sea. To be expected, *I* say, for did not Heraclitus teach us all things flow? But soft living and much ease had stolen the brains out of the people's heads! Faced with the silting-up of our great estuary, did they go to it and build dredgers? They did not! Faced with a landslide that closed our chief silk-road, did they send scouts to locate another way? They did not! Faced with long winters that killed our autumn wheat in the ground, did they sow barley or the hardy northern oat? They did not!'

'Then what did they do?' the traveller inquired. 'If anything.'

'Fell first to moaning and wringing their hands, and lamenting their sad fate; then, when this proved unfruitful and incapable of filling the granaries, turned to a crowning imbecility and invoked the impossible aid of magic. I see you scowl, sir, and well you may, for all the world knows that magic is a vain and ridiculous snare laid by evil demons in the path of mankind.'

This was a stubborn and unobservant fellow, clearly; with his hand closed around a coin that veritable magic – and no petty domestic hearth-spell, either – had turned from copper to gold, he could still make such an assertion. He would not care for this domain in which he now found himself. Still, there was no help for that.

'And to what purposes tended their research in – ah – *magic*?' the traveller asked.

'To bring back the great days of the past, if you please,' said Jacques with majestic scorn, and on the last word crammed his mouth full from a dish the serving-girl placed before him.

While he assuaged his hunger, his companion contemplated these data. Yes, such an event as Jacques had described would account for the paradox of Ys reversing the cosmic trend and exchanging Time for eternity and its attendant confusions. But there must have been a great and terrible lust in the minds of very many people for the change to be brought about; there must have been public foolishness on a scale unparalleled in the All. Thinking on this, the traveller felt his face grow grim.

Reaching for his staff, he made to depart, and Jacques glanced up with his cheeks bulging. Having swallowed frantically, he spoke. 'Sir, did I intrude on your meditations? Your pardon if—'

'No, no! You merely recalled me to some unfinished business. You are correct in your description of the people of Ys. They are fools indeed. So do not – if you will take my advice – go back there.'

'Where else shall I go, then?' Jacques countered, and for a second despair looked out from behind his eyes. 'I set off thinking no place could be worse than my home-town had now become – yet on this brief journey I've seen wonders and marvels that make me question my own good sense. I met a creature on the road that was neither man nor beast, but a blending; I saw a shining sprite washing feet like alabaster in a cloud rimmed with rainbows, and once when I bent to drink from a stream I saw pictures in the water which … No, I dare not say what I thought I saw.'

'That would be the brook called Geirion,' said the traveller, and appended a crooked smile. 'Don't worry – things seen there can never become real. The folk round about go to the brook to rid themselves of baseless fears.'

Jacques glanced over his shoulder at the motley crowd and shivered with dismay. 'Nonetheless, sir, I'm not minded to remain in this peculiar city!'

'It would be more comfortable for you to adapt to the local customs than to go home,' the traveller warned. 'A certain rather spectacular doom is apt to overtake Ys, if things are as you say.'

'Doom!' cried Jacques, and an unholy joy lit his face. 'I told them so – over and again I told them! Would I could witness it, for the satisfaction of seeing how right I was!'

The traveller sighed, but there was no help for it now; his single nature bound him to unique courses of action. He said sourly, 'As you wish, so be it. Go hence towards the city men call Acromel, where honey is bitter, but do not enter it. Go rather around it towards the setting sun, and you will reach a grey hill fledged with grey bushes where there are always dust-devils, which will wipe out your tracks the moment you have passed. From the brow of that hill you may behold Ys at the moment of disaster.'

'Now just a moment!' exclaimed Jacques, rising. 'From my boyhood up I've wandered around Ys, and I know of no such hill, as you describe!'

The traveller shrugged and turned away. Jacques caught his cloak.

'Wait! What's your name, that you say such strange things and send me on such an improbable errand?'

'You may call me Mazda, or anything you choose.' The black-clad traveller shook off the grip with a moue of distaste.

'Hah! That's rich!' Jacques set his hands on his hips and laughed. 'But still … Well, sir, for the sake of wanting to see how Ys goes to its doom, I'll follow your instructions. And my thanks!'

He parodied a bow, flourishing a hat that was not on his head.

'You may not thank me more than this once,' said the traveller sadly, and went his way.

3

Lord Vengis sat in the Hall of State at Ys, and gazed at the nobility assembled in his presence. He tried to ignore the sad condition of the hall. Once this had been a building to marvel at: mirrors higher than a man lined its walls, set between pilasters of marble, gilt and onyx, and the arching roof had been painted by a great master with scenes in eleven bright colours, depicting the birth of Saint Clotilda, the martyrdom of Saint Gaufroy – that one was mostly in red – and the ascension of Saint Eulogos to heaven on the back of a leaping dolphin. Moreover the floor had been carpeted with ermine and bear-pelts.

The pelts had gone. Or, to be more exact, some of them had gone away and returned – but in unusual fashion: they had been cut into coats for the nobles, and now enveloped impressive paunches and bosoms with the assistance of gilt girdles. Moreover, half of the mirrors were fly-specked, and some were cracked, while worst of all some of the slabs of marble forming the floor had been prised up to expose crude foundations of rubble – a rumour having run around as to the effectiveness of marble for sacrificial altars – and on an irregularity due to this cause, in an ill-lit corner, Lord Vengis had twisted his ankle *en route* to his throne.

This place was a condensation of the trouble afflicting the whole of Ys. The harbours that once swallowed the twice-daily ocean tides were blocked with stinking silt; grass grew on the stone moles, as in the wheel-ruts on the fine old roads leading away from the city – at least, according to report; none of the personages present could vouch for the assertion, all having declined to venture out of Ys since things took this turn for the worse. So also in the gardens of the great houses a plant like, but not identical with, mistletoe had spread over the handsome trees, letting fall a horrid sticky fruit on those who walked beneath; in the deep sweet-water wells servants claimed that they heard ominous voices, so that now they refused to let down buckets for fear of drawing up those who spoke; last week's market had reduced to two old men squabbling over a cracked earthen pot and a comb of dirty wild honey.

Lord Vengis glowered at the company, and they fell silent by degrees. Their attendants moved, silent as shadows, to the double doors of entrance, closed them, barred them against all intrusion – for this was no discussion which common people were permitted to overhear.

With the clanging down of the final bar, one leapt to his feet at the end of the front rank of gilded chairs, uttering a groan and cramming his fingers into his mouth. All eyes turned.

'Fool, Bardolus!' Lord Vengis rapped. 'What ails you?'

'In that mirror!' Bardolus gibbered, trying to point and finding his shaky arm disobedient to his will. 'I saw in the mirror—'

'What? What?' chorused a dozen fearful voices.

Bardolus was a small man whose manner was never better than diffident; he was accounted clever, but in a sly fashion that had won him few friends and none who would trust him. He said now, mopping sweat, 'I don't know. I saw something in that mirror that was not also in this hall.'

Time hesitated in its course, until Lord Vengis gave a harsh laugh and slapped the arm of his throne.

'You'll have to grow accustomed to manifestations like that, Bardolus!' he gibed. 'So long as the *things* stay in the mirror, what's to worry you? It's when they emerge into the everyday world that you must look out. Why, only the other day, when I was in my thaumaturgic cabinet testing a certain formula, I— But enough of that.' He coughed, and behind his polite covering hand glanced to see whether his words had had the desired effect. They had, even though the episode to which he referred was an invention. True, he'd spent much time in his cabinet; true, he'd rehearsed many formulae; alas, nothing had so far come of his efforts, not even a harmless spectre in a mirror.

Still, that would change. One could tell by the feel of the very air. There were forces in it that no man could put a name to, and sometimes scalps prickled as they do before a thunderstorm.

'We are here for a reason, you know,' he said after an impressive pause. 'We are agreed on the only course open to us. We admit that modern Ys stands on the shoulders of great men and women. Yet to what has their ambition led us? Unkind fate has burdened us with such difficulties as they never encountered, and we eat stale bread and rancid meat, where they gorged pies running with gravy and soft delicious fruits from the ends of the earth. We drink plain water, none too clean, where they enjoyed wine and mead, and beer like brown crystal!

'We have concluded that for all their – admitted – greatness, *they* are responsible, not us! We did not ask to be born at a time when our trees rot, our crops wither, our harbour is blocked. In every way they are responsible: for siting Ys where it stands, for breeding children to inherit such a miserable legacy!'

'Aye!' came a rumble of assent from around the hall.

'Some faint-hearts, some ignorant fools, have argued with us,' Vengis went on, warming to a speech he had not intended to deliver. 'These, of course, are base-born, lacking the insight which is the birthright of the nobility. Jacques the scrivener, for example, would have had us turn to with hoes and shovels and clear the harbour – and if hoes and shovels were lacking, with our *bare hands*!'

This time the response lay between a shudder and a chuckle. 'What's become of Jacques, by the way?' someone asked audibly.

'Does it matter?' Vengis countered, drawing together his beetling brows. 'We know we are adopting the right course. We have decided that we must employ more potent tools than crude – ah – agricultural implements to cope with so massive a disaster. We must, in short, restore all our fortunes, and the splendour of our city, *and* root out once for all the disaffection among the rabble spread by such as Jacques, by exploiting the mightiest means available to us. Magically, by decree of the will, by harnessing supernatural forces, we shall again make Ys the envy of the world!'

A roar of approval and a barrage of clapping. Unnoticed in the shadows, one listener alone did not applaud; instead, he stood leaning on his staff, shaking his head from side to side.

'Let us have news, then – encouraging news of our progress!' Vengis cried. 'I call first on Dame Seulte, around whose home last time I rode by I could not help noticing an aura pregnant with remarkable phenomena.'

Silence. At length a portly woman near the back of the hall rose – with some difficulty, for her weight – and spoke.

'Dame Seulte, as you know, is my close neighbour, and as she is not here I think perhaps I ought to mention that yesterday she was in high spirits and confident of success in her experiments. She had obtained a free-will gift of a child to offer to – well, to a creature best not named directly. When I met her, she was leading the pretty thing home on a leash of green leather. Such a sweet sight!'

'Dame Rosa!' said a young man from nearer the front, turning in his chair. 'A free-will gift – are you sure?'

And his companion, a pale girl of no more than eighteen in a dress of brown velvet, said doubtfully, 'My maid referred to a fire at Dame Seulte's house this morning ...'

Vengis slapped the arm of his throne again, making a sound as sharp as a gavel's rap. He said sternly, 'No defeatist talk *if* you please, Lady Vivette!'

'But are you sure it was a free-will gift?' persisted the young man at Vivette's side.

Dame Rosa said stiffly, 'Dame Seulte had promised to raise the child as her own, and the parents were poor and hungry; they parted with it willingly.'

'Then there must have been a fire at her home this morning,' said the young man, and shrugged. 'Our copy of the book she conjured from has a leaf that hers lacks, and on it the authorities are cited by dozens. Ingredients obtained by deception are of no avail in that ceremony.'

There was a stunned pause. Dame Seulte, after all, had only been trying to manifest a comparatively straightforward elemental.

'I have more cheerful news,' said a sweet, enticing voice from the opposite side of the assembly. They turned gratefully; this was Lady Meleagra, whose eyes like sapphires, lips like rose-petals and skin like snow had broken hearts for ten of her twenty-one years. As Eadwil had once done in Ryovora – though she was unaware of that precedent – she had purchased her ability upon terms. Herself, she had not yet suffered in consequence; she was, though, constrained to impose a most regrettable proviso on anyone who craved to share the pleasures of her bedchamber. It was an efficacious precaution against undesired supernatural intervention, but it had signally reduced the number of her suitors.

'I sense a change here in Ys,' she mused aloud. 'A great wonder has overtaken this city. So far I do not know its precise nature, but the fact is indisputable. See!'

She extended one graceful arm, swathed in white lace so fine her skin tinted it pink, and in the central aisle dividing the company a *thing* appeared. It was dark, and it writhed; apart from that it had no describable attributes save two glowing eyes alive with hatred. It lasted half a minute before it slowly faded, and at its going the air was permeated by a dank steamy odour against which those foresighted enough to have brought them buried their noses in bouquets of flowers.

By degrees a clamour arose, and on all sides the nobles strove to show they had been equally successful. 'Look!' cried Messer Hautnoix, and between his hands he strung a chain of gleaming bubbles from nowhere, and again, and yet a third time before the glamour faded. And: 'See!' cried Dame Faussein, shaking a drum made of gourd and capped either end with tattooed skin from a drowned sailor; this made the hall pitch-black for as long as it sounded, and all present had the eerie sense that they were adrift in an infinite void. And: 'Watch!' bellowed rough old Messer d'Icque, spreading a scarlet cloth at the full stretch of both arms; on the cloth, a mouth opened and uttered five sonorous words that no one present understood.

Smiles greeted these achievements, and loud approbation gave place to a babble of inquiry as to means. 'Five nights drunk under a gallows!' boasted Messer Hautnoix – 'A day and a night and a day kissing the mouth of the man who bequeathed his skin!' bragged Dame Faussein – 'Doing things to a goat I can't discuss with ladies present,' Messer d'Icque muttered behind his hand.

'But Ub-Shebbab came to me when I did no more than call his name,' said Meleagra, and at these disturbing words those closest to her chair drew as far back as they could without appearing rude.

Vengis on his high throne joined neither in the praising nor in the questioning; his heavy-jowled face remained set as stone. Had he not submitted himself to worse indignities? Had he not made pledges which in retrospect caused him to quail? And what had derived from his struggles? Nothing! Not even a pretty tricksiness like Messer Hautnoix's shining bubbles!

He thumped on his chair-side again, and cut through the chatter with a furious roar.

'Enough! Enough! Are you children early out of school, that you disgrace our meeting with mere gossip? How far do these cantrips advance us to our goal? That's the question!'

A little embarrassed, the company subsided into a period of asking each other with their eyes whether any was bold enough to claim progress in their central problem. At first they avoided looking at Meleagra; then, no other offer being forthcoming, they took that plunge and were rewarded with a sigh and a shake of the head.

'As I thought!' Vengis crowed in scorn. 'You're overwhelmed with bright spectacle, and have forgotten the urgent purpose confronting us. Next time you go to conjure, ask yourselves first this: if I succeed, what comes by way of benefit? Can I eat it? Can I put it on my back, or mend my roof with it? In fine, how will it serve not only me, but the nobility and commonalty of Ys?'

He glared at the now fidgety assembly. 'It's not going to be easy, I know that well. I've had no success to speak of, myself. But at least I haven't been diverted down superfluous by-ways!'

The one standing in shadow shook his head once more. Here truly was a company of fools, and chief of them their chief Vengis: a man of consuming arrogance and vanity, blind to his faults and proud beyond description. This being so ...

He gave a gentle cough, and heads whisked to see from whom the noise issued. Vengis half-rose from his seat in astonishment.

'What are you doing here?' he thundered. 'Who let you in without my leave?'

The traveller in black walked without a sound along the aisle dividing the company until he was face to face with Vengis, and there was that in his eyes which stifled further speech prior to the answering of that double question.

At last he said, 'As to what I am doing here – why, I am listening to and pondering what you've said. As to the leave that was granted me to join you, I go where my presence is required, whether you wish it or no.'

The ranked nobles of the city held their breath. This was the utterance of one holding an authority they dared not challenge.

'What – what do you want of us?' whispered Vengis when he had regained some of his composure.

'Say rather what you want of me,' the traveller riposted with a sardonic cock of his head. 'From the confusion of your meeting I've been unable to make it out. Put it in words for me. That is, if you have any clear idea of your ambitions ...?'

There was a gently insulting turn to that last phrase. Vengis bridled.

'Of course we do!' he blustered. 'Have you not seen the pitiable pass to which our fair city is reduced?'

'I have,' acknowledged the black-garbed intruder. 'And as nearly as I can discern, you hold your ancestors to be to blame.'

'We do so!' Vengis snapped. 'And we crave to make them rectify their crime. We seek to call them back, that they may behold the ruin they've bequeathed us, and compel them to set matters right.'

'Compulsion is no part of my nature,' said the traveller. 'I am acquainted only with free choice. Yet you say you have chosen – what then restrains you from action?'

'What do you think?' That was Bardolus, half-frantic with the tension of the moment. 'We want the power to bring about this aim, and so far all we've managed to achieve is some minor manifestations and a few personal calamities!'

'Like the one which overtook Dame Seulte?'

'Ah … Well, yes, I suppose!'

'And is this the common desire of you all?' asked the traveller with very great sadness, casting his gaze to the furthest corners of the company.

'Aye!' came the chorus of replies.

'As you wish,' said the traveller, 'so be it.' And he departed.

4

Where he went, none of them saw. He passed from among them swiftly as thought, silently as shadows, and they had no more stomach for their consultations since he had spoken.

Yet they felt a lightness, a sense of promise, as they called the servants to unbar the doors and made their several ways towards their homes. The streets by which they passed seemed more crowded than of late, and not a few of them had the impression that they recognised among the throng a familiar face, a known gait, or a garment of distinctive cut. However, such fancies were of a piece with the general mood, and served only to heighten the taut anticipation they had brought away from the Hall of State.

'What think you of Dame Seulte's fate?' said the Lady Vivette to her companion – who was also her brother, but they had judged that an advantage in making their earlier experiments. She spoke as their carriage creaked and jolted into the courtyard of their ancestral home, a short ride only from the Hall of State; behind, the hinges of the gates complained of rust and lack of oil when the retainers forced them to.

'I think she was unwise,' her brother said. His name was Ormond to the world; but recently he had adopted another during a midnight ritual, and Vivette knew what it was and held some power over him in consequence.

'Do you believe we have been gifted by this – this personage?' Vivette inquired. 'I have a feeling myself that perhaps we have.'

Ormond shrugged. 'We can but put it to the test. Shall we now, or wait until after dinner?'

'Now!' Vivette said positively.

So, duly, they made their preparations: putting on fantastical garments which contained unexpected lacunae, and over these various organic items relinquished by their original owners, such as a necklace of children's eyes embedded in glass for Vivette and a mask made from a horse's head for Ormond. Arrayed, they repaired to a room in the highest tower of their mansion, where by custom deceased heads of their family had been laid in state for a day and a night before burial since untold generations ago.

There, in a pentacle bounded by four braziers and a pot of wax boiling over a lamp, they indulged in some not un-pleasurable pastimes, taking care to recite continually turn and turn about a series of impressive cantrips. The room darkened as they went on, and great excitement almost interrupted their concentration, but they stuck at it, and …

'Look!' whispered Vivette, and pointed to the catafalque removed to a corner of the room. Under the black velvet draperies a form was lying – that of a man armed and armoured.

'Why! Just so, in the picture downstairs, did Honorius our great-grandfather lie when he was awaiting burial!' Ormond snapped, and leapt to his feet to pull back the velvet.

Impassive, a steel visor confronted them. Vivette eased it open, and in the dark interior of the helmet eyes gleamed and a rush of foetid breath escaped. Stiffly, with effort, the occupant of the armour arose from the catafalque.

'Come, my descendants, let me kiss you both,' said a rusty voice, and iron arms resistlessly encircled them, though they struggled to get away. 'What, have you no affection to your own kinsman?'

There was a hollow hideous chuckle as the embrace grew tighter; the necklace of eyes cracked, like a handful of cobnuts, the horse-mask went thudding to the floor, and spittle-wet lips clamped first on one mouth, then the other. Both fainted.

When they recovered, the figure in armour was gone, but where it had taken shape on the catafalque lay a manuscript book in bindings of leather and brass, open to the page recording the death of Honorius from a contagious fever against which no medicine was of use, in the three-and-thirtieth year of his age.

Dame Rosa, in her palanquin borne between two white female donkeys, passed the corner on which stood the house formerly owned by Dame Seulte, and drew aside the curtains to peer curiously upward. Sure enough, as her maid had declared, from the window of the room in which Seulte had been accustomed to conduct her experiments, a licking tongue of greasy black smoke had smeared the wall.

She clucked with her tongue. Poor Seulte! Had she but waited another day, she might have enjoyed the fruit of her efforts. That at least was Dame Rosa's belief; she trusted the promise the one in black had made, and looked forward with impatience to the earliest moment she could closet herself with her books and apparatus and rehearse with improvements the most relevant of her formulae.

Her family had in the past been counted among the most lascivious of Ys, and excessive indulgence by its womenfolk in the pleasures of the bed had often threatened to over-populate the resources of their not inconsiderable estates. Accordingly there was a cellar where surplus children had for generations been discreetly disposed of, not by crude and brutal means but by consigning the problem of their nourishment to the fates. She entered this cellar by a bronze door, which she locked with a heavy key, and passed between rows of wooden stalls in each of which a set of rat-gnawed bones lay on foul straw, gyves about one ankle.

She had chosen this place after much thought. Surely, she reasoned, the point of departure to eternity of so many spirits must be imbued with a peculiar potency!

Her method of working involved feathers, four liquids of which the least noxious was fresh blood, and long silent concentration while seated on a stool of unique design with no other covering for her ample frame than her age-sparse hair could afford. Briskly she carried out the introductory rites; then she sat down and closed her eyes, shivering from excitement and not from cold.

She had, the books stated, to keep her eyes shut until she had completed the recital of a cantrip that lasted eight whole pages in minuscule script. There were two pages to go when she heard the first rustlings and clicketings behind her. There was one page to go when the first touch came on her fleshy thigh. Desperately wanting to know what marvels her work had brought about, she raced through the last page, and on the concluding word came the first *bite*.

Thirty starving children mad with hunger, their teeth as keen as any rat's, left gnaw-marks on her bones too.

Bardolus trembled as he piled many curious ingredients high on the charcoal-filled brazier before his mirror. He had chosen the mirror spell out of those known to him because he had, after all, come closest to success with it before – even if he had been taken aback to see a manifestation in the unconstrained mirrors of the Hall of State.

He wished he could find the courage to abandon the entire project, but fear and conceit combined to drive him on. He was beside himself with jealousy to think that a slip of a girl like Meleagra – not to mention that coarse peasant type d'Icque, or stupid complacent Dame Faussein! – had mastered magical powers in such a matter-of-fact fashion, while he still cried out in terror at the consequences of his own thaumaturgy.

He struck a light and ignited the pile. Saturated with the fat of a sow that had devoured her own farrow, it blazed up and gave off a choking smoke that veiled the mirror until it was all consumed.

Then the air cleared, and in the mirror he found a face he knew: that of his mother, who was dead.

'My son Bardolus,' she said with fawning sweetness. 'Look behind you! There is an oaken cupboard which you have known since you were a child. Press the last knob in the carved design, and a secret drawer will open. In the drawer is that which gave me power over your father. Take it as my gift.'

The image faded. A little puzzled, Bardolus hesitated before doing as directed. He remembered his father only dimly; he had been a strange man, alternating between hysterical gaiety and depression so deep he would sit by the hour contemplating a knife or a dish of poison, plucking up the courage to take his own life.

Yet ... *power*.

He pressed the knob and the drawer slid open, revealing a packet made of a strange yellow paper and sealed with green wax. He broke the seal convulsively, and a fine powder spurted at his face, seeming to seek his nostrils of its own accord. He tried to dodge, but that was useless; he inhaled it all, and the packet lay empty on his palm.

Another few seconds, and vast elation filled him. Why, he could do anything! He was ten feet tall, stronger than an ox, more potent than the heroes of legend and so handsome no wench could withstand him if he courted her.

He threw down the packet and raced towards the street.

From the mirror drifted mists that coalesced into the shape of his mother, and ultimately grew strong enough to lift the empty packet in gnarled old fingers and regard it out of blearly eyes.

'You deserve no better fate than the one who got you on my body against my will,' she whispered. 'One hour, Bardolus – one hour of delirium! And afterwards despair. For it will be no use hunting for more of this drug, Bardolus! I never compounded more than one dose at a time, and it was by postponing for a day the next mixing that I held power over your father. There is no one to mix it for you, Bardolus! No one at all!'

5

But these were not all the calamities that overtook Ys, that once-fair city. For those whom the black-clad traveller had challenged truly did not know what would rescue them from their predicament, and out of greed and laziness had demanded the utmost they could conceive. Lost in this plethora of manifestations – somewhere – was precisely and exactly what was needful; that much the traveller was bound to grant. But, as he had warned them, he could not compel anyone to do the right thing. Choice was what he dealt in.

And those who made a wrong choice did so because of what they were.

His friends had generally liked Messer Hautnoix, who was engagingly like a child, what with his delight in such toys as the pretty coloured bubbles he had displayed in the Hall of State. It was characteristic of him that, compelled to spend five nights under a gibbet for the privilege, he passed the entire time drunk to avoid excessive contemplation of his plight.

Yet when he repaired to his chosen ground of the execution dock and chuckled while he cut the throats of a white cock and a black hen, the one who came to him proved to be the first bearer of his line's name, profession-ally the municipal hangman, who had so loved his work that more than once he paid the silence of witnesses who would have saved victims from the rope; this being discovered, they had set him swinging on his own gallows at the last.

Much time having passed since he last performed his office, he seized his chance with alacrity, and sunset found Messer Hautnoix dangling from a noose while his forebear walked back to the city gate, rubbing his bloated hands to think of what he could look forward to.

Dame Faussein, who had paid a drowned sailor so generously for the loan of his skin, made further use of her curious little drum when she came home, regarding tried and tested means as superior to any not yet proven workable. It was regrettable – and she certainly did regret it, though not for long – that this time the darkness to which its beating carried her was the musty interior of her ancestral vault, where the warmth of her living body, while it lasted, gave strange solace to an aunt and two uncles whose relationship, now as in their lifetimes, was more complex than the conventional ties of kinship. Her eyes continued to perceive darkness when the three together had lifted off the enclosing marble lid of their mausoleum and gone forth to see how things now stood with Ys.

Messer d'Icque was indeed of peasant stock – that was no secret in Ys. His inclinations were towards country matters, and it has never been any secret anywhere that events transpire in lonely country districts at which the sophisticates of cities would be nauseated or appalled. The whole of his urban residence had been stunk out for weeks by a dung-pile he had had made in the central courtyard, because it was said to be in the warmth of rotting manure that homunculi came to artificial life. This heap of foulness he ignored today, however; his mind was set on the proper employment of his stock of *animelles*, a springtime by-product on farms where sheep and cattle are bred. His plan, moreover, was not to fry and serve them as a seasonal delicacy.

To him, the ritual completed, came a progenitor who had felt the frustration of an aging wife, racked with childbearing beyond the point at which she was capable of assuaging his desires, and who had violated the daughter of his bailiff; it then also being spring. The bailiff had returned early from the task of which *animelles* were the result, and to avenge the slight on his family's honour had made prompt use of the implement in his hand. For twenty-one generations the sufferer had awaited the chance to afflict on another the operation sustained by himself, and he did so without a by-your-leave. Leaving Messer d'Icque to leak away his life's blood, he thereafter set out to multiply his trophies from all possible male sources.

No word of this had been brought to the beauteous Meleagra when she came home. She had never cared for Messer d'Icque, thinking him rough and ill-bred, and the news that he had involuntarily qualified to share her overnight company would have interested her not at all.

In a boudoir hung with lace draperies, containing a round golden bed and a mirror abstracted from the Hall of State, as being the largest in Ys – which she had mounted cunningly on the ceiling – she caused her maids first to draw curtains at the many high windows, then to light candles which gave off a fragrant, intoxicating aroma. She suffered them to remove her clothing, to prepare her a bath in which she dissolved a handful of polychrome salts, and to sing in harmony while they sponged her from head to toe. Sweetmeats were brought on a white platter and a silver filigree dish, and twenty-four new gowns were displayed before her on the body of a dumb girl who matched the dimensions of her figure.

All the while this was going on, she was musing over a crucial decision: should she, or should she not, act upon the promise the black-clad one had made?

That he had the power to which he laid claim, she never doubted. Two years before anyone else in Ys saw what needed to be done, she had closed a bargain concerning her virginity which she had scrupulously kept – at first partly from fear, but lately out of simple habit.

And what she had purchased by the bargain had enabled her to recognize the single nature of their unaccountable visitor.

A single nature! Surely that must imply its possessor could neither lie nor deceive! In which case she might employ her talents now to produce results compared to which her previous achievements were dross. Her whole life since the age of eleven had been on the edge of a precipice – and there were creatures at the bottom of the chasm which she had eluded only by the most exact pre-planning. Accordingly, the notion of exercising her powers at least once in full foreknowledge of success attracted her. An uncharacteristic yielding to vanity had made her call Ub-Shebbab to the Hall of State; he was the meekest and mildest of the beings she had conjured up, yet her skin prickled when she thought of what might have …

No, that happened only to fools and bunglers. And she was neither. She reached her decision and dismissed her maids. Them gone, she put on a gown which had not been displayed during her bath, worked all over in gold wire with a single sentence in a forgotten language; then she opened a brass chest and took out gifts she had exacted from various suitors before information about her inflexible rule was noised abroad.

There was a twig from Yorbeth, bearing a leaf transparent as glass and a brown, blotched fruit which tinkled like a bell; there was a vial of rainwater caught at the foot of the rainbow overarching Barbizond, which had a trifle of Sardhin's essence in it; there was a block of pumice from the volcano where Fegrim slumbered; there was a jar of grey dust from the hill where Laprivan was shut away; there was a hair from the head of Farchgrind, an inch of candle that had revealed the secret thoughts of Wolpec but had been allowed to burn one instant longer than was safe, and a drawing of two birds and a crocodile made by a possessed child.

Also there was a book.

Following with care the instructions it contained, she danced around her boudoir keening, crawled twice backwards across the floor with a knife between her teeth, and at last cut her forearm and let three drops of her blood fall on the carpet. When she looked for them the stains had vanished.

Nothing else happened in the room. She had expected that; humming, she called her maids back to change her gown for something more conventional and went down to the dining-hall where supper was to be served.

Already as she approached it she could hear the clatter of dishes, the clamour of conversation. That boded a great company. She hurried the last few steps and threw open the door.

Every place at her great table – and there were thirty-six – was taken; the servants had pressed into use benches from the kitchen, too, and the sideboards and the serving-tables were alike packed with a hungry horde. For all the scullions and maids could do, the food, brought on trolleys because there was more of it than a man could lift, disappeared within instants of being set down, and still the howl went up for more. The bread had gone, the meat, the wine; now it was boiled turnips and hedge-greens, broth of bones and barley, and beer much too new to serve by ordinary.

Yet that was not all. Behind, between, among those who ate went others looting. The fine brocade drapes had been torn down to clothe naked bodies, leather-backed chairs stripped to afford protection to sore feet, tapestries turned to cloaks and ponchos. One wild-eyed woman, lacking anything else, had smeared herself with gravy to break up the maggot pallidity of her skin.

Meleagra stood in the doorway for a long heartbeat of time before the chief steward caught sight of her and came running to beg her help.

'Mistress, what shall we do? They are in every room – five hundred of them at the least count! And all, all have claimed the right to what you have, for they say they are your ancestors and this is their home too!'

'My ancestors?' whispered Meleagra. Her eyes, drawn as by a magnet, went to him who had taken her seat at the head of the table, and a silence overcame the entire company.

The one at whom she gazed was a cross-eyed, ill-favoured fellow in a dirty doublet, unshaven and with black around his nails. He gave her a smile that displayed gapped yellow teeth, and spoke in a soft voice with a peasant's accent.

'Ah, Meleagra, sure and you set a fine table! This meal which you account an everyday affair matches the grandest feasts we held in times gone by!'

'Who – who are you?' Meleagra choked out.

'You know me not?' The fellow cocked an eyebrow traversed by a scar. 'Why, Damien, of course, who built the house and founded the family's fortune in the earliest age of Ys. And at my side Cosimo, my first-born here – though I had by-blows aplenty in another town! And Syriax his wife and their children Ruslan, Roland and Igraine; and their children Mark, Valetta, Corin, Ludwig, Matthaus, Letty, Seamus; theirs, Orlando, Hugo, Dianne, twins Nathaniel and Enoch—'

'Stop! Stop!' Meleagra put her hands to her temples; the room seemed to be spinning, and from every side gross faces leered at her, or thin drawn faces gazed with stony regard, or dull faces moped, or …'

'There is no more food!' the steward shouted. 'We have killed all the poultry, the larder's bare, the wine-casks are drained, the last carp is gone from the pond, the beer-barrels are exhausted and even the *well* is dry!'

'You've done this to me?' Meleagra whispered to her remotest ancestor Damien. 'But I gave you breath and life, and this new opportunity – I invited you here!'

'You?' said Damien with contempt. 'Is that the only act of importance you can boast of? Did we your ancestors not build this house, this city, its fair avenues and fine harbours and full stores? Have you done nothing save parasitize upon our leavings? I read in your eyes that that is so! Here we are alive, who died before you saw the light – do you still call yourself the mistress of this house? Hah! You are a thing not worth the thinking of less than dust, for dust can be seen to dance in sunbeams. You are the flame of a candle guttering out. So – *pouf!*'

He blew at the candle closest him upon the great table, and with the extinction of its flame there was no such person as Meleagra – never had been – never could be.

6

Long hours Lord Vengis had paced in the high room above the Hall of State, pondering the day's events and screwing himself to the point where he would again begin his conjurations. The day wasted; shadows lengthened; evening cold began to permeate the building, and he called for fire.

He was afraid.

He had seen in the eyes of the traveller in black a warning which his pride forbade him to heed; he was ashamed because he was afraid, yet shame could not break fear's grip. He wished to do as his colleagues were doing – what if he alone remained untalented in sorcery when blockheads like Bardolus or half-grown wenches like Vivette boasted powers unnamable?

Nonetheless, he dithered and delayed, and had not yet cast a rune nor recited the first line of a single formula when the sergeant of the guard came stiffly to report a disturbance in the town.

'Disturbance?' Vengis rapped. 'Fool, be precise! What do you mean?'

'Why, sir' – and the sergeant rubbed his chin dolefully – 'some hours agone there were complaints of desecration in the graveyard by the cathedral, the curate saying that a vault was open and the bones removed. But seeing as how we've had call for similar extraordinary materials that your lordship required, I decided best not to say anything. Now, though, the affair has ramified. For example, the side wall of the building here is cracked where they entombed alive a woman named Igraine – you've seen the plaque – accused of commerce with a familiar spirit in the guise of a cat ...'

From the street below came a howl as of maddened beasts, and the sergeant flinched visibly. But he continued in his best official manner.

'Then, your lordship, at dusk reports came of strangers in the city, and we called out the patrols for fear of infiltration by some jealous invader. Myself, I've stopped twenty-one persons, and all spoke with the accent of our city and gave names concordant with our nomenclature. But it seems I've seen such names on gravestones before now some, indeed, earlier today when I answered the complaint at the cathedral. And what brings me in to you, begging your indulgence, is the curious business of the man and the two wives.'

'What's that?' whispered Vengis, sweat pearling his face.

'Well, sir, there was this man, one whom I'd challenged, walking with a girl of fifteen-odd. Comes up from nowhere a woman aged as he was – forty, maybe – and says she is his wife and what's this hussy doing with her husband? So then the little girl says they were married legally and then there follows screaming of insults and hair-pulling and at the last we must clap 'em in the jail to cool their heels. Which is – uh – difficult. For every cell, they promise me, is full, and that's more than I can understand. This morning the turnkey's records say there were one hundred and one places vacant for new prisoners.'

Vengis's voice had failed him. He chewed his nails and stared with burning eyes at the sergeant.

'What shall I do, your lordship?' the man finally asked.

'I – I ...' Vengis spun around and strode to a window overlooking the main square. He thrust the casement open and leaned out. By the last dim light of the dying day he could see a myriad people gathering. Some were colourful and substantial, but these were few. Most were grey as the stones they trod, and trailed curious wispy streamers behind them, like cobwebs. But all alike exhibited an air of bewilderment, as though they were lost in the mazes of time and eternity, and could not find a way back to the present moment.

Vengis began to babble incoherently.

There came a thundering knock at the door of the room where they were, and a cavernous groaning voice said, 'Open! Open in the name of the Lord of Ys!'

Shrugging, the sergeant made to obey, but Vengis ran after him, clawing at his arm. 'Don't! Don't let them in!' he wailed.

'But, your lordship,' said the sergeant firmly, 'it *is* in your name that he seeks entry, so it must be a matter of importance. Besides, with your permission, I'm expecting a report from my patrols.'

Vengis searched the room with feverish eyes. In the far corner he spied a closet large as a man; he dashed to it, and slammed the door with him inside.

The sergeant, astonished, went nonetheless to answer the knock, and fell back in dismay before the apparition which confronted him. Gaunt, tall, with a second mouth gaping redly in his throat, here was the figure of legendary Lord Gazemon who had laid the foundation stone of Ys with his own two hands.

Now those hands held a broadsword; now he advanced with slow terrible steps upon the closet in which Vengis thought to secrete himself, and battered down the planks of the door to hale that miserable successor of his into the wan torchlight.

'You know me!' croaked the city's founder.

Gulping, moaning, Vengis contrived a nod, and the huge spectre shook him as a terrier shakes a rat. 'Oh, to what a dwarfish stature have shrunk these weaklings of today!' he bellowed. The sergeant, cowering behind an oaken table, could not tell by which mouth Gazemon spoke – his natural one, or the second which had let out his life.

Again the door rattled to an imperious knock, and he scuttled to answer before Gazemon could address him. With trembling hands he admitted those who stood without: Lorin, who had slain Gazemon by treachery and usurped his throne; Angus, who had reclaimed that throne into the rightful line of descent; then Caed; then Dame Degrance, who passed for a man and ruled like one until the physicians at her deathbed unmasked her sex; then Walter of Meux; then Auberon; then Lams, and the first Vengis, who was a stout and brave leader for the one short year he survived, and others and others to the latest who had sat the chair below prior to the advent of the incumbent lord.

With axes, maces, swords, with pens and scrolls and money-changer's scales according to the form of power by which they had made Ys great, they gathered around the hapless target of their contempt.

'We have walked abroad in the city since we were called from rest,' rumbled Gazemon, his grip still fast on Vengis's shoulder. 'We have seen stagnant puddles in the streets, shutters dangling from one hinge on the cracked walls of once-fine houses; we have been followed by beggars and starving children in Ys which we devoted our lives to, making it a city that the world should envy! You have given our golden towers to tarnish, our iron doors to rust; you have given our splendid harbour to the mud and our fat grain-fields to the weeds; you have squandered our treasury on baubles, forgetful that we paid for it with blood. How say you all, you who listen here? Is it not time that we held an accounting?'

'Aye, time,' they said as one, and hearing the menace in their voices Vengis rolled his eyes upward in their sockets and let go his hold on life.

7

'Oh, there you are!'

Perched on a grey rock atop a grey hill, Jacques the scrivener forwent his gazing at sunset-gilded Ys in favour of a scowl at the traveller in black who had come to join him. There were no footprints to show by what path he had arrived; still, where Laprivan wiped away the past that was no wonder.

'I've sat here long enough, in all conscience,' Jacques complained. 'This wind is cold! And, for all you promised I should witness the doom of Ys, I see nothing but what I've always seen when looking on the city from afar. When will this doom befall, tell me that?'

The traveller sighed. Now the course of events was grinding to its inexorable conclusion, he felt downcast, despite there never having been an alternative. He did not much like Jacques, regarding him as pompous and self-opinionated, but even so ...

'The doom is already in train.'

Jacques leapt from his rock and stamped his foot. 'You mean I've missed it?'

'That, no,' said the traveller. He raised his staff and pointed across the twilight grey of the valley. 'Do you not see, there by the gates, a certain number of persons making in this direction?'

'Why ... Yes, I believe I do.' Jacques peered hard. 'But from this distance I cannot tell who they are.'

'I can,' the traveller murmured. 'They are those who are determined Jacques the scrivener shall not be denied participation in the doom of Ys.'

'What?' Turned sidewise in the gloaming, Jacques's face was ghastly pale. 'Why me? What do they want with me?'

'A reckoning.'

'But ...!' Jacques shifted from foot to foot, as though minded to flee. 'Explain! Pray explain!'

'So I will,' the traveller conceded wearily, and took a comfortable grip to lean on his staff. 'You must understand first that the would-be enchanters of Ys have succeeded beyond their wildest dreams, and – as they desired – have called back those who created the city and maintained it in times past. And they found, as was inevitable, that these ancestors were human beings, with human faults and failings, and not infrequently with remarkable outstanding faults, because this is the way with persons who are remarkable and outstanding in other areas of their lives.'

'But – but I counselled against this foolishness!' stammered Jacques.

'No,' corrected the one in black. 'You did not counsel. You said: you are pig-headed fools not to see that I am absolutely, unalterably right while everybody else is wrong. And when they would not listen to such dogmatic bragging – as who would? – you washed your hands of them and wished them a dreadful doom.'

'Did I wish them any worse than they deserved?' Jacques was trying to keep up a front of bravado, but a whine had crept into his voice and he had to link his fingers to stop his hands from shaking.

'Discuss the matter with those who are coming to find you,' proposed the traveller sardonically. 'Their conviction is different from yours. They hold that by making people disgusted with the views you subscribed to, you prevented rational thought from regaining its mastery of Ys. Where you should have reasoned, you flung insults; where you should have argued soberly and with purpose, you castigated honest men with doubts, calling them purblind idiots. This is what they say. Whether your belief or theirs constitutes the truth, I leave for you and them to riddle out.'

Jacques looked again at the column of people winding out from the city gate, and now could see them in detail. At the head of the line was a black-smith with a hammer on his shoulder; behind him, a ditcher came with a mattock, then a gardener with a sickle and two coopers with heavy barrel-staves. And those behind still bore each their handiest weapon, down to a red-handed goodwife wielding the stick from her butter-churn.

He glanced wildly around for a way of escape, teeth chattering. 'I must run!' he blurted. 'I must hide!'

'It would be of little help,' the traveller said. 'Those people yonder are determined; though you hid in the pit of Fegrim's volcano, they would still track you down.'

'Oh, misery me!' moaned Jacques, burying his head in his hands. 'Would that I had never come to this pass! Would that what I've done could be undone!'

'As you wish, so be it,' said the traveller, and cheered up, for that put a very satisfactory end to this momentary aberration in the smooth progress of the cosmos. He tapped three times on a nearby rock, and under his breath he said, 'Laprivan! Laprivan of the Yellow Eyes!'

Jacques screamed.

Below in the valley, the column of determinedly advancing men and women bound to wreak vengeance on Jacques hesitated, halted, and broke ranks in disorder that grew to panic. For out of the side of the hill Laprivan was peering, and what was behind his eyes belonged to the age when chaos was the All.

Some small power remained to him so long as he survived, and he applied it to this single and unique purpose: to wipe clean the slate of yesterday.

So he looked down on Ys, and saw there what was to him an abomination, the shadow of the past given substance. He reached out one of his arms, and erased – and erased – and erased …

Honorius, sowing contagious fever on the streets, was not.

Thirty sated children, smeared with blood on faces and fingers, were not.

Bardolus's mother, chortling over the fate of her son, was not.

Knotting a noose from every rope in a cord-seller's shop, the first of the line of the Hautnoix was not.

Brandishing his bloody trophies, the adulterous d'Icque was not.

Three who had come forth from a vault were not.

Stripped of its food, its draperies, its gold and silver and precious artworks, the house of Meleagra was silent.

And those who had come to regulate accounts with the decadent lordling Vengis took their leave.

Also many who had come forth from graves and sepulchres, from hollow walls and wayside ditches, from dungeons and the beds of rivers and the bottoms of wells … were not.

'So!' said the traveller in black, when he had restored Laprivan to his captivity. 'You have a reprieve, Jacques – are you glad of that?'

The tawny-bearded man mouthed an affirmative.

'And will you learn a lesson from it?'

'I'll try – as heaven is my witness, I will try!'

'Fairly said,' the traveller declared. 'Go then to join those hiding in the valley. Approach them as a friend, not showing that you're aware why they set forth bearing bludgeons. Say to them that the rule of chaos in Ys is ended, and so is Ys; they must return home for the last time and gather their belongings before they and all the people scatter to the corners of the world.'

'But – but is this our world?' Jacques whimpered. 'On the way to Barbizond I saw – and now here …'

'Ah, you'll have no more of that kind of thing. It belongs to yesterday, and with other traces of yesterday Laprivan has wiped it out.' The traveller allowed himself a smile. 'And do not lament excessively for Ys. For cities, as for men, there comes a Time … Besides, there is a prophecy: a prince shall seek a name for his new capital, and he'll be told of Ys, and out of envy for its greatness he will say, "I name my city Parys, *equal to Ys.*" '

'I have little faith in prophecies as a rule,' said Jacques, staring. 'But in this extraordinary place … Well, no matter. Sir, I take my leave, and – and I thank you. You have held up an honest mirror to me, and I cannot resent it.'

'Go now,' the traveller adjured. 'And be quick.'

He waited long on the brow of the hill while the last daylight dwindled away and the stars wheeled gradually to the conformation marking midnight. It became more and more difficult to see Ys; the towers melted into mist, the walls and gates were shadow-dark among shadows. For a while torches glimmered; then even they failed to be discerned, and when dawn broke there was neither the city, nor the traveller in black, for anybody to behold.

THREE

The Wager Lost by Winning

What Stake will you adventure on this Game? (quoth Arundel).
Why, Sir, though I be naked and penniless, yet stand I in possession of my
Head (saith Amalthea).
That prize I in no wise, quoth Arundel. I had liefer win a Cooking Pot than
such a Numskull. Wager me in place of it that Treasure, which though you
lose it to me shall be yours again when I have done.

– Fortunes and Misfortunes of Amalthea

1

Down the slope of a pleasant vale an army marched in good order: colours at the head fluttering in the warm summer breeze, drummers beating a lively stroke for the men behind perspiring in their brass-plated cuirasses and high-thonged boots. Each of the footmen wore a baldric with an axe and a short-sword in leather frogs, and carried a spear and a wide square shield. Each of the officers rode a horse draped in fine light mail, wore a shirt and breeches of velvet sewn with little steel plates, and carried a long-sword in a decorated sheath. Sunlight glinted on pommels bright with enamel and gilt.

Leaning on his staff, the traveller in black stood in the shade of a chestnut-tree and contemplated them as they filed by. Directly he clapped eyes on them, the banners had told him whence they hailed; no city but Teq employed those three special hues in its flag – gold, and silver, and the red of new-spilled blood. They symbolized the moral of a proverb which the traveller knew well, and held barbarous, to the effect that all treasure must be bought by expending life.

In accordance with that precept, the Lords of Teq, before they inherited their fathers' estates, must kill all challengers, and did so by any means to hand, whether cleanly by the sword or subtly by drugs and venom. Consequently some persons had come to rule in Teq who were less than fit – great only in their commitment to greed.

'That,' said the traveller to the leaves on the chestnut-tree, 'is a highly disturbing spectacle!'

However, he stood as and where he was, neither concealed nor conspicuous, and as ever allowed events to pursue their natural course. Few of the rank-and-file soldiery noticed him as they strode along, being preoccupied with the warmth of the day and the weight of their equipment, but two or three officers favoured him with inquisitive glances. However, they paid no special attention to the sight of this little man in a black cloak, and likely, a mile or two beyond, the recollection of him would be dismissed altogether from their minds.

That was customary, and to be expected. Few folk recognized the traveller in black nowadays, unless they were enchanters of great skill and could detect the uniqueness of one who had many names but a single nature, or perhaps if they were learned in curious arts and aware of the significance of the conjunction of the four planets presently ornamenting the southern sky in a highly specific pattern.

But there had been changes, and those who recognized him now were exceptional.

The journeys the traveller had made had long surpassed the possibility of being counted. Most of them, moreover, were indistinguishable – not because the same events transpired during each or all, but because they were so unalike as to be similar. A little by a little, earnests of his eventual triumph were being borne upon him. Perhaps the loss of Ryovora into time had marked the pivotal moment; however that might be, the fact was incontestable. Soon, as the black-garbed traveller counted soonness, all things would have but one nature. He would be unique no more, and time would have a stop. Whereupon …

Release.

Watching the purposeful progress of the army, the traveller considered that notion with faint surprise. It had never previously crossed his mind. But, clearly, it would be a wise and kindly provision by the One who had assigned him his mission if his single nature should include the capacity of growing weary, so that in his instant of accomplishment he might surrender to oblivion with good grace.

That instant, though, still needed to be worked towards. He waited while the rearguard of the army passed, slow commissary-wagons drawn by mules bumping on the rough track; then, when the drumbeats died in the distance, their last feint reverberation given back by the hills like the failing pulse of a sick giant, he stirred himself to continue on his way.

It was not until he came, somewhat later, to Erminvale that he realized, weary or no, he must yet contend with vastly subtle forces arrayed against him.

For a little while, indeed, he could almost convince himself that this was to be the last of his journeys, and that his next return would find the places he had known tight in the clutch of Time. The borderland between rationality and chaos seemed to be shrinking apace as the harsh constraint of logic settled on this corner of the All. Reason is the step-child of memory, and memory exists in Time, not the arbitrary randomness of eternity.

Thus, beyond Leppersley the folk remembered Farchgrind, and that being's chiefest attribute had been that no one should recall his deceits, but fall prey to them again and again. Yet where once there had been a monstrous pile of follies, each a memento to some new-hatched prank – 'Build thus and worship me and I will give you more wealth than you can carry!', or: 'Build thus and worship me and I will restore you the health and vigour of a man of twenty!' (the wealth of course being tons of ore and the health that of a paralysed cripple) – there were sober families in small neat timber houses, framed with beams pilfered from the ancient temples, who said, 'Yes, we hear Farchgrind if he speaks to us, but we recall what became of grandfather when he believed what he was told, and we carry on about our daily business.'

The traveller talked with Farchgrind almost in sorrow, mentioning this scepticism which had overtaken men, and accepted without contradiction the retort.

'You too,' said the elemental, 'are part of the way things are, and I – I am only part of the way things were!'

Likewise, though there were hoofmarks on the road which Jorkas had patrolled, they were not his; some common carthorse had indented them, and rain tonight or tomorrow would make the mud a palimpsest for another horse to print anew. Moreover, at black Acromel that tall tower like a pillar of onyx crowned with agate where once dukes had made sacrifice to the Quadruple God was broken off short, snapped like a dry stick. In among the ruins fools made ineffectual attempts to revive a dying cult, but their folly was footling compared to the grand insanities of the enchanter Manuus, who once had taken a hand in the affairs of this city, or even of the petty tyrant Vengis, whose laziness and greed brought doom on his fellows and himself.

'Ah, if only I could find the key to this mystery!' said one of them, who had bidden the traveller to share the warmth of a fire fed with leather-bound manuscripts from the ducal library. 'Then should I have men come to me and bow the knee, offer fine robes to bar the cold instead of these shabby rags, savory dishes to grace my palate instead of this spitted rat I'm toasting on a twig, and nubile virgins from the grandest families to pleasure me, instead of that old hag I was stupid enough to take to wife!'

'As you wish, so be it,' said the traveller, and knocked his staff on the altar-slab the fool was using as a hearth.

In the cold dawn that followed, the wife went running to her neighbours to report a miracle: her husband was struck to stone, unmoving yet undead. And, because no other comparable wonder had occurred since the departure of the Quadruple God, all transpired as he had wished. Men set him up on the stump of the great black tower and wrapped their smartest robes about him; they burned expensive delicacies on a brazier, that the scent might waft to his nostrils; and sought beautiful girls that their throats might be cut and their corpses hung before him on gallows stranded with chains – all of this in strict accordance with the ancient custom.

But after a while, when their adulation failed to bring them the favours which they begged, they forgot him and left him helpless to watch the robes fade and the fire die in ashes and the girls' bodies feed the maggots until nothing was left save the bare white bones.

Likewise, a packman met at Gander's Well complained in the shade of brooding Yorbeth whose taproot fed his branches with marvellous sap from that unseen spring, and said, 'Oh, but my lot is cruelly hard! See you, each year when the snows melt, I come hither and with the proper precautions contrive to pluck fruit and leaves from these long boughs. Such growths no sun ever shone on before! See here, a fuzzy ball that cries in a faint voice when your hand closes on it! And here too: a leaf transparent as crystal that shows when you peer through it a scene that no man can swear to identifying! Things of this nature are in great demand by wealthy enchanters.

'But what irks me' – and he leaned forward, grimacing – 'is a matter of simple injustice. Do those enchanters plod the rutted road to Gander's Well? Do they risk death or worse to garner the contents of a heavy pack? Why, no! That's left to me! And what I get I must dispose of for a pittance to strangers who doubtless half the time botch the conjurations they plan to build on what I bring them! Would that I knew beyond a peradventure what marvels can be wrought by using the means I'm making marketable!'

'As you wish,' sighed the traveller, 'so be it.' He knocked with his staff on the coping of the well, and went aside to speak of release to Yorbeth – that release which he himself was coming unexpectedly to envy. For there was one sole way to comprehend the applications of what grew on this tall tree, and that was to take Yorbeth's place within its trunk.

Where, trapped and furious, the packman shortly found himself, possessed of all the secret lore he had suspected, down to the use that might be made of a sheet of the bark when luring Ogram-Vanvit from his lair … and powerless to exploit that for his gain.

Yorbeth of course ceased to be. Heavy-hearted, the traveller went on.

2

In the mountainous land called Eyneran, where folk were above all proud of their sheep and goats, he had once incarcerated the chilly elemental Karth, thanks to whose small remaining power one strange valley stayed frozen beneath a mask of ice when all around the summer flowers grew bright and jangly music drifted from the bell-wethers of the grazing flocks. Here the traveller came upon a fellow who with flint and steel was seeking to ignite the ice, grim-visaged and half-blue with cold.

'Why,' inquired the traveller, 'do you lavish so much effort on this unprofitable pastime?'

'Oh, you're a simpleton like all the rest!' cried the man, frenziedly striking spark after spark. 'Is it not the nature of ice to melt when the hot sun falls on it? Since what is in this valley does not melt, it cannot be ice. Certainly, moreover, it's not stone – it differs in significant respects from rock-crystal, quartz, adament and fluorspar. Therefore it must be of an amberous nature, QED. And amber is congealed resin, and resin burns well, as any drudge knows who has lit a stove with pine-knots. Accordingly this so-called "ice" must burn. Sooner or later,' he concluded in a more dispirited tone, and wiped his brow. The gesture made a little crackling noise, for so bitter was the wind in this peculiar valley that the sweat of his exertion turned at once to a layer of verglas on his skin.

The traveller thought sadly of Jacques of Ys, who also had been persuaded that he alone of all the world was perfectly right, and suppressed his opinion of the would-be ice-burner's logic. Sensing disagreement nonetheless, the fellow gave him a harsh and hostile glare.

'I'm sick of being mocked by everyone!' he exclaimed. 'Would that the true nature of this substance could become clear for you and all to see!'

'As you wish, so be it,' said the traveller, realizing that the time of release had come also to Karth. With the cessation of his dwindled ancient power, sunlight thawed the glacier and warm zephyrs fathered water from its edge.

The man looked, and touched, and tasted, and paddled his hands in it, and cried out in dismay.

'If this is water, that must have been ice – but that was not ice, therefore this is not water!'

Spray lashed him; rivulets formed around his ankles.

'It is not water,' he declared, and stood his ground. But when the pent-up floods broke loose they swept him and his flint and steel far down the hillside and dashed him to death on a rock that was deaf to his entreaties.

Aloof, the black-clad traveller stood on a promontory and watched the whirling waters, thinking that he, so aged that there was not means to measure his duration, knew now what it meant to say, 'I am old.'

So too in Gryte, a fair city and a rich one, there was a lady who could have had her choice of fifty husbands, but kept her heart whole, as she claimed, for one man who would not look at her, though he had wooed and conquered maidens for leagues around.

'Why does he scorn me?' she cried. 'He must be hunting for a wife who will give him surcease from this endless philandering! Can he not come to me, who hungers for him?'

'As you wish, so be it,' said the traveller, and next day the man she dreamed of came a-courting her. She pictured all her hopes fulfilled and made him free of her household and her body. And the day after, he treated her as he had treated the rest: rose from her couch where he had taken his pleasure, not sparing a kind look or a kiss, and left her to wring her hands and moan that she was undone.

Likewise there stood a gravestone in the cemetery at Barbizond, under the arch of rainbow signalling the presence of the bright being Sardhin. Grass by it flourished in the gentle never-ceasing rain. The traveller visited it because he owed a particular debt to the man beneath, who full of years and honour had gone to his repose.

Turning away, the traveller was addressed by a person in a cape of leaves who might have passed at a glance for seven years of age, either boy or girl.

'Good morrow, sir!' this person chirruped in a tremble voice. 'Think you to brace yourself for death by contemplating all these tombs – or have you cause to wish it might overtake some other before yourself?'

'In the latter case, what?' the traveller said.

'Why, then, I could be of service,' the person said slyly. 'I have been for thirty-one years as you see me – dwarfed, sexless and agile. What better end could I turn such a gift to, than to become the finest assassin ever known in Barbizond? You stand surrounded by testimonials to my skill: here a miserly old ruffian whose daughter paid me half his coffer-load, there an eldest son who blocked his brother's way to an inheritance—'

'You speak openly of this foul trade?'

'Why, sir, no one is around to hear me save yourself, and would folk not think you deranged were you to claim a child had boasted of such matters to you?'

'In truth, your childish form is a deep disguise,' the traveller conceded. 'But tell me: do you speak to me merely to solicit new custom, or because that disguise grows oppressively efficient?'

The person scowled. 'Why, I must confess that from time to time the very secrecy which benefits my calling does gall my self-esteem. I gain my living in a unique manner, but no one knows I'm the ultimate expert at my trade save those whom I have served, who dare not admit that they know it. Would that I might be famed far and wide as the past-master of my profession!'

'As you wish, so be it,' said the traveller, and struck his staff against the nearest tomb. That very evening rumours took their rise in Barbizond, and everyone who had lost a relative in suspicious circumstances, to a poison subtler than the enchanters could detect, or a silent noose, or a knife hissing out of shadow, nodded their heads and remarked how marvellously well the appearance of a child of tender years might mask a killer.

The traveller passed the body next morning, sprawled on a dung-heap by the road to Teq.

Will it be now? The question haunted the traveller as he went. With half his being he was apprehensive, for all he had ever known throughout innumerable eons was the task allotted him; with the balance he yearned for it. Karth gone, Yorbeth gone, Jorkas gone – would there shortly also be an end for

Tuprid, and Caschalanva, for Quorril and Lry and Laprivan of the Yellow Eyes?

On impulse, when he came to the grove of ash-trees at Segrimond which was one of the places where such things were possible, he constrained Wolpec to enter the customary candle, but when he tried to smoke a piece of glass over its flame and read the three truths therefrom, the glass cracked. With resignation he concluded that this was not for him to learn, and went his way.

In Kanish-Kulya the wall that had once divided Kanishmen from Kulya-men, decked along its top with skulls, had crumbled until it was barely more than a bank enshrouded with ivy and convolvulus, and roads pierced it along which went the gay carts of pedlars and the tall horses of adventure-seeking knights. Yet in the minds of certain men it was as though the old barrier still stood.

'Not only,' groused a certain Kanish merchant to the traveller, 'does my eldest daughter decline to accept her proper fate, and be sacrificed in trad-itional manner to Fegrim! She adds insult in injury, and proposes to wed a Kulyan brave!'

The traveller, who knew much about the elemental Fegrim, including his indifference to sacrifices, held his peace.

'This I pledge on my life!' the merchant fumed. 'If my daughter carries on the way she's going, I shall never want to speak to her again – nor shall I let her in my house!'

'As you wish, so be it,' said the traveller. From that moment forward the merchant uttered never a word; dumb, he stood by to watch the fine proces-sion in which the girl went to claim her bridegroom, and before she returned home apoplexy killed him, so that the house was no longer his.

But nothing in this was remarkable. Greed, hate, jealousy – these were commonplace, and it was not to be questioned that they should defeat themsclves.

Onward again, therefore, and now at last to Erminvale.

3

In that land of pleasant rolling downs and copses of birch and maple, there stood the village Wantwich, of small white farms parted by tidy hedgerows, radiating out from a central green where of a summer evening the young people would gather with a fiddler and a harpist to dance and court in bright costumes of pheasant-feathers and fantastical jingling bangles. At one side of

this green was a pond of sweet water which the traveller in black had consigned to the charge of the being Horimos, for whom he had conceived a
peculiar affection on discovering that this one alone among all known elementals was too lazy to be harmful, desiring chiefly to be left in peace. While
others older than themselves danced, the village children would splash in the
pond with delighted cries, or paint their bare bodies with streaks of red and
blue clay from the bank, proudly writing each other's names if they knew
how. In winter, moreover, it served for them to skate on, and well wrapped in
the whole hides of goats they slid across it with double wooden runners
strapped to their feet.

Good things were plentiful in Erminvale: creamy milk, fat cheeses, turnips
so firm and sweet you might carve a slice raw and eat it with a dressing of
salt, berries and nuts of every description, and bearded barley for nutritious
bread. Also they brewed fine beer, and on a festival day they would bear onto
the green three vast barrels from which anyone, resident or traveller, might
swig at will, the first mug always being poured of course to Horimos. Content with that small token of esteem, he slumbered at the bottom of his mud.

All this was what the girl named Viola had known since a child, and from
reports she had heard through visitors she felt well satisfied that she'd been
born in Wantwich. Where else offered you a better life? Great cities were
crowded and full of smoke and stinks; moreover, they had more demanding
patrons than Horimos, like Hnua-Threl of Barbizond, black with the dried
blood of those who had duelled by his altar, or that blind Lady Luck who
smiled randomly on the folk of Teq and might tomorrow turn her back for
good on the one she had favoured yesterday.

She had heard about Teq from a finely-clad rider who had come, a while
ago, on a tall roan stallion, twirling long fair mustachios and spilling gold
from his scrip like sand.

He had arrived on the first fine evening of spring, when Viola and her
betrothed man Leluak joined all the other young people in a giddy whirling
dance around the green, and because it behooved one to be courteous to a
stranger – even a stranger who complained about the narrowness of his room
at their only inn, and passed unflattering remarks concerning Wantwich
beer as against the wines of home – and also, she admitted to herself, because
all the other girls would be envious, she had accepted his request to join him
in demonstrating some newly-fashionable dances from Teq. Instruction
took a moment only; she was a skilful dancer, light on slim legs that not even
the bleaching of winter had worn to paleness from last summer's tan. After
dancing, they talked.

She learned that his name was Achoreus, and that he served one of the
great lords of Teq. She learned further that he thought her beautiful, which
she granted, for everyone had always said the same: she had long sleek

tresses, large eyes that shifted colour ceaselessly like opals, and skin of the smoothness of satin. He declared next that such loveliness was wasted in a backwater hamlet and should be displayed to the nobility and gentry of a great city – meaning Teq. She thanked him for his compliments but explained she was already spoken for. Thereupon he proved that for all his elegant airs he lacked common civility, and tried to fondle her inside her bodice, at which she marched away.

Had he acted decently, inviting her to stroll in the woods with him and find a temporary bed of moss, she would naturally have agreed. It was the custom of Wantwich to receive all strangers as one would one's friends. But as things were – so she told Leluak when bidding him good night – he seemed to expect that the mere sight of him would make her forget the boy she had grown up with all her life. What foolishness!

Accordingly, all plans for her marriage went ahead in the ancient manner, until at sunset the day before the ceremony her father, her mother, her two sisters and her aunt equipped her in the prescribed fashion for a night she had to pass alone, during which she must visit each in turn of five high peaks enclosing Erminvale and there plant five seeds: an apple, a sloe, a cob, an acorn and a grain of barley.

With a leather wallet containing bread and cheese, a flask of water, and a torch of sweet-scented juniper, and followed by the cries of well-wishers, she set forth into the gathering dusk.

The tramp was a long one, and tricky in the dark, but she had wandered through Erminvale since she was old enough to be allowed out of sight of her mother, and though she must clamber up rocky slopes and thread her way through thickets where night-birds hooted and chattered, she gained each peak in turn with no worse injury than thorn-scratches on her calves. As dawn began to pale the sky, she set in place the final seed, the barley-grain, and watered it from her body to give it a healthy start in life. Then, singing, she turned back, weary but excited, on the road to her home. By about noon she would be safe in Leluak's embrace, and the feasting and merry-making would begin.

Still a mile off, however, she started to sense that something was amiss. Smoke drifted to her on the breeze, but it lacked the rich scent of baking which she had expected. A little closer, and she wondered why there was no shrill music audible, for no one had ever been able to prevent Fiddler Jarge from striking up directly his instrument was tuned, whether or no the bride had come back from the hills.

Worst of all, at the Meeting Rock that marked the last bend in the road, the huge granite slab by which the groom traditionally took the hand of his bride to lead her into Wantwich, there was no sign of Leluak.

She broke into a run, terrified, and rounded the rock. Instantly she saw the furthest outlying house, that of the Remban family, which she remembered seeing built when she was a toddler, and almost fainted with the shock. Its fine clean walls were smeared with a grime of smoke, its gate was broken, and the Rembans' finest plough-ox lay bellowing in a pool of blood.

And there beyond: the Harring house afire – source of the smoke she'd smelled! Her own home with the shutters ripped off their hinges, the front door battered down with an axe from the kindling-pile! Leluak's, unmarked, but the door ajar, and no one within when she shouted through!

Wildly she raced onward to the village green, and there was Jarge's fiddle broken on the ground. The beer-barrels set out for the wedding had been drained. Near them was a patch of scorched grass she could not account for, and all the water of the pond was fouled with the blood of the ducks which daily had quacked there.

Crouched in her chair, from which for longer than Viola could recall she had watched and grinned at the weddings she had witnessed: the only remaining villager of Wantwich, Granny Anderland, who was in fact a great-great-grandmother, toothless and senile.

'Granny!' shrieked Viola. 'What happened?'

But all that Granny Anderland could do – all that she had ever been able to do since Viola was a baby – was to expose her gums in a silly grin and rock back and forth on her chair.

Helpless, Viola screamed Leluak's name till she was hoarse, but after that she collapsed from weariness and horror, and that was how the traveller found her when he chanced that way.

4

He barely checked his pace as he entered Wantwich, along another road than that which Viola had followed on her return from the five peaks. But his expression grew sterner with every step he took, until when finally he could survey the full measure of the calamity from the canter of the green his brow was dark as a thundercloud.

His footsteps were too soft upon the sward for the weeping girl to hear them through her sobs, and it was plain that the old woman near her either had been so shocked as to have lost her reason, or was far too senile to understand the world. Accordingly he addressed the girl first.

At the sound of his voice she cringed away, her face wet with tears displaying a mask of terror. But there was little in the appearance of this small man leaning on a staff to suggest that he could be connected with the rape of Wantwich. And, for all that he looked angry beyond description, it did not seem that that anger was directed at her.

'Who are you, child?' the traveller inquired.

'My – my name is Viola, sir,' the girl forced out.

'And what has happened here today?'

'I don't know, I don't know!' Wringing her hands, Viola rose. 'Why should anyone want to do this to us? Monsters of some kind must have done it – devils!'

'Well, there are few such creatures left hereabouts,' the traveller murmured. 'More likely it will have been men, if one can dignify them with that name. Were you away from the village?'

'I was to be married today!' Viola choked.

'I see. Therefore you were walking the five peaks and planting seeds.'

'You – you're acquainted with our customs, sir?' Viola was regaining control of herself, able to mop away her blinding tears and look more clearly at the newcomer. 'Yet I don't remember that I saw you here before.'

'This is not the first time I've been to Wantwich,' the traveller said, refraining from any reference to the number or date of his earlier visits. 'But, to pursue the important matter: did this old lady witness what occurred?'

'If she did, she won't be able to describe it,' Viola said dully. 'She has been as you see her for many years. She likes to be talked to, nods and sometimes giggles, but beyond that ...' She gave a hopeless shrug.

'I see. In that case we must resort to other means to determine what went on. Girl, are you capable of being brave?'

She stared at him doubtfully. 'Sir,' she said at length, 'if you can do anything to help get back my man, and right the wrong that's been done to these good people, I'll be as brave as you require of me.' Her fingers curled over to drive her nails cruelly into her palms. 'Oh, that something *could* be done! I've no notion what – but something *must* be possible!'

'As you wish, so be it,' said the traveller, and took her hand. He led her across the green, past the patch of grass scorched black – at which she cast a puzzled glance – and to the very rim of the sweetwater pond.

'Stand firm,' he commanded. 'Do not be afraid of what you see.'

'I – I don't understand!'

'Better for you that you should not,' the traveller muttered, and thrust his staff into the water. He dissolved one of the forces bonding the light of which it was composed, and a shaft of brilliance lanced downward to the bottom.

'Horimos!' he cried. 'Horimos!'

The girl's eyes grew round with wonder, and then her mouth also, with dismay. For the water heaved and bubbled sluggishly as pitch, and from the plopping explosions a thick voice seemed to take form, uttering words.

'Le-e-eave me-e a-a-lo-o-one ...'

'Horimos!' rapped the traveller. 'Stir yourself – you've slumbered eons in that soft bed of mud! Shall I remove you to Kanish-Kulya, make you share the pit of that volcano with Fegrim?'

A noise between a grumble and a scream.

'Yes, he'd be a restless companion for you, wouldn't he?' the traveller rasped. 'Up! Up! I desire speech with you!'

Beside him Viola had fallen to her knees, all colour vanished from her cheeks. Too petrified even to blink, she saw the water in which she had so often bathed rise into tumult – yet absurdly slowly, as though time had been extended to double length. More bubbles burst, and she could watch their surface part; waves and ripples crossed the pond so slowly, one would have thought to push them into new directions without wetting one's palm.

And ultimately ...

'You may prefer to close your eyes now,' the traveller said didactically, and added, 'Horimos! Speak! And be quick – the sooner you tell me what I want to know, the sooner you may sink back into your ooze. What's become of all the people from this village?'

'Been taken away,' Horimos mumbled. It was not exactly a mouth he used to shape the words – but then, like all elementals, his physical form was somewhat arbitrary.

'How and by whom?' The traveller rapped the bank impatiently with his staff.

'Army marched in this morning,' Horimos sighed. 'Went around the village, drove everybody to the green – most of them were there already anyhow. Set up a forge there where the grass is blackened, welded fetters for everyone on a chain. Killed some ducks and hens for their dinner, drank the beer in the barrels, herded the villagers away. Good riddance, say I – never had a moment's peace since you put me here, what with fiddling and dancing and swimming and skating and all the rest of it!'

'Whose was the army? What colours did they fly?'

'Should I know who bears a flag of silver, red and gold?'

The traveller clamped his fingers tighter on his staff.

'And you made no attempt to intervene?'

'Told you – glad to see the back of them.' Horimos made the whole surface of the pond yawn in a colossal expression of weariness. 'And but for you I'd have enjoyed a decent sleep for a while, now I'm alone!'

'For your idleness,' said the traveller softly, 'I decree that until the folk of Wantwich are restored to their homes, you shall itch so much you can enjoy no rest. Begone with you. Hope that the matter is speedily set to rights.'

'But—!'

'You argue with me?'

Horimos declined. When once again he had subsided to the bottom of his pond, the water was no longer pellucid and still as before, but rolled continually without a breeze to stir it.

'Who are you?' Viola whispered. 'I'd always thought Horimos was – was ...'

'Was imaginary?' The traveller chuckled. 'Not exactly. But his worst fault is mere laziness, and compared to what faults one finds elsewhere it's far from the grossest of shortcomings ... As for my own identity: you may call me Mazda, or what you will. I have many names, and only one nature.'

He waited to see whether the information, which he gave only to those who directly demanded it, meant anything to her. Interestingly, he discovered that it did, for on the instant a blend of hope and awe transfigured her pretty face.

But then he took a second look, and his heart sank. For, in along with the rest, he now detected the betraying signs of selfishness.

'Is it true, then,' she cried fiercely, 'that I can require of you my heart's desire?'

'Think well if you do so!' the traveller warned, raising his staff. 'Only you can know what's in your secret mind! Reflect and ponder!'

'I don't have to,' she said with terrible directness. 'I want to be reunited with my man!'

The traveller sighed, but as always was resigned to the inexorable course of events. 'As you wish, so be it,' he replied.

'What shall I do?' Viola whispered, suddenly overcome with a sense of the finality of her request.

'Wait.'

'No more than wait? Wait here?' She turned frantically, surveying the ravished homes, the slaughtered livestock, the smoke that still drifted over the burning house. 'But—'

And when she looked again for the traveller in black, he was gone.

A little after, when the sun was still high in the sky, there were clopping noises on the road by which the army had arrived, and she stirred from her torpor and made to flee. But the horseman easily ran her down, bowing from his saddle to sweep her off her feet and park her on the withers of his steed, laughing at her vain attempts to break away.

'I missed you when they rounded up the rest of them,' said Achoreus of Teq. 'I couldn't forget a lovely face like your's. Even less can I forget an insult like the one you offered me when first I came here. So I dawdled, thinking you'd be back eventually, and here you are. Not for long, though! You're going to rejoin your family and friends, and that country bumpkin you preferred to me!'

5

Laughter rang loud and shrill under the gorgeous canopy that shaded Lord Fellian of Teq from the naked rays of the sun. The canopy was of pleated dragon-hide, bought at the cost of a man's life in a distant land where chaos and reason had once been less evenly matched and strange improbable beasts went about with lion's claws and eagle's beaks and wings of resounding bronze. Report held that there were no more such creatures to be found; even their bones had been rejected by reality.

'But I have my canopy!' Lord Fellian would say.

Its shade fell on a floor of patterned stone: marble was the commonest of the types of tile composing it, outnumbered by chalcedony, jasper, sardonyx, chrysoberyl, and others yet so rare that they had no name save 'one of the tiles in Lord Fellian's gallery'. This was on the very apex of the grand high tower from which Lord Fellian might survey his domain: lands from here to the sky-line and beyond which bled their wealth into his coffers.

But on the houseward side there was a high wall, that when he sat in his throne of state – made of the bones of a beast of which the enchanters declared no more than one could ever have existed, translucent as water but harder than steel – not even an absent glance over his shoulder might reveal to him the sole building in Teq which outreached his tower. Atop that mighty edifice presided the figure of Lady Luck, the goddess blind in one eye and masked over the other, whose smile dictated the fortune of those who ruled in Teq.

It was not the custom to look on her. It was said that those who secretly tried to, in order to discover whither her gaze was bent, would die a fearful death. And indeed the agents of Lords Fellian, Yuckin and Nusk did occasionally deposit in the chief market-square the bodies of men and women who had clearly undergone some repulsive torture, and the common folk interpreted these as an awful caution. More often than not, these corpses belonged to persons who had boasted of their favour with the Lady. It was taken for granted that the others belonged to those who had not even enjoyed the brief pleasure of making that boast.

To look on Lady Luck was the one gamble no Lord of Teq would risk. Why should he? Was not affluence itself proof that the Lady bent her enigmatic smile continually on the man who possessed it?

Lord Fellian on his chair of inexplicable bones cramped with pure gold, robed in cloth dyed with the purple of the veritable murex, shod with sandals of the softest kidskin on which had been stamped, again in gold, a series of runes to guide him in the most prosperous of paths; his foppish locks entwined with green ribbons, his nails painted with ground pearls, his weak eyes aided with lenses not of rock-crystal such as his rivals must make do with but of diamond, his lobes hung with amber, his girdle glittering with sapphires: he, Lord Fellian, the greatest winner among all the past and present Lords of Teq, laughed, and laughed, and laughed.

The noise drowned out the soft rattling from the table on which a trained monkey, tethered by a velvet leash, kept spilling and gathering up a set of ivory dice, their values after each throw being recorded by a slave on sheets of parchment; likewise, the humming of a gaming-wheel turned by an idiot – both these, with bias eliminated, to determine whether after fifty thousand throws or spins there would be some subtle preference revealed, that he might exploit in his ceaseless conflict against Lords Yuckin and Nusk. Furthermore his laughter drowned the chirrup of the gorgeous songbirds in a gilded cage which he had won last week from Nusk in a bout at shen fu, and the drone of musicians playing on a suite of instruments he had won – along with their players – from Yuckin a year or more past. Those instruments were of eggshells, ebony and silver, and their tone was agonizingly sweet.

Facing the chair of bones, Achoreus – who had committed himself to the service of Lord Fellian when he was but seventeen and kept complimenting himself on his far-sightedness – grinned from ear to ear at the brilliant inspiration of his master.

'Before those fools learn that winning from me costs nothing,' Fellian declared, 'I shall have taken the very roofs from over their heads! They will be shamed if they refuse to match my stakes, and I may climb as high as I wish, while they – poor fools! – struggle to clamber after me. Oh, how I look forward to seeing Yuckin's face when tonight I bet him a hundred skilful servants, including girls fit for a royal bed! You've done well, Achoreus, Torquaida, come here!'

From among the gaggle of retainers who by day and night attended Fellian, subservient to his slightest whim, there shuffled forward the elderly treasurer whose mind retained, so he boasted, even such detail of his master's coffers as how many of the copper coins in store had been clipped around the edge, instead of honestly worn, and were therefore reserved to pay off tradesmen.

In no small part, Fellian acknowledged, his victories in the endless betting-matches with his rivals were due to Torquaida instructing him what they could or could not stake to correspond with his own wagers. He had rewarded the treasurer suitably, while those who served his rivals were more often punished for letting go irreplaceable wonders on lost bets, and grew daily bitterer by consequence.

'Young Achoreus here,' the lord declared, 'has performed a signal service.

We have now, thanks to him, one hundred or more extra servants surplus to the needs of the household, and additionally many children who can doubtless be trained up in a useful skill. How, say you, should this service be repaid?'

'This is a difficult estimate,' frowned Torquaida. His ancient voice quavered; Fellian scowled the musicians into silence that he might hear better. 'There are two aspects of the matter to consider. First, that he has brought a hundred servants – that is easy. Let him have dirhans to increase his stake in the wager he has made with Captain Ospilo of Lord Yuckin's train; our privy intelligence states that bet is won on odds of nine to four, whereas Ospilo is yet in ignorance of the result. Thereby the winnings may be much enlarged. I'd say one hundred coins.'

Fellian slapped his thigh and chortled at the ingenuity of the deceit, while Achoreus preened his mustachios and basked in the envy of those around.

'Beyond that, however,' Torquaida continued in his reedy tones, 'it remains to be established what the value of these servants is. As one should not wager on a horse without inspecting both it and its competition, thus too one must begin by looking over the captives.'

'Let them be brought, then!' Fellian cried. 'Clear a space on the gallery large enough for them to parade!'

'Sir,' ventured Achoreus, 'there were not a few among them who resented the – ah – the invitation I extended to enter your lordship's service. It will be best to make space also for the escort I detailed to accompany them.'

'What?' Fellian leaned forward on his chair, scowling. 'Say you that a man on whom Lady Luck smiles so long and so often is to be injured by – by some stupid peasant? Or is it that you neglected to disarm them?'

Seeing his new-found fortune vanishing any second, Achoreus replied placatingly. 'My Lord! There was hardly a weapon in the whole village, save rustic implements whose names I scarely know, not having had truck with country matters – scythes, perhaps, or maybe hatchets … Which, naturally, we deprived them of! But all of those we brought are able-bodied, and hence remain possessed of feet and fists!'

'Hmmm!' Fellian rubbed his chin. 'Yes, I remember well a gladiator whom Lord Yuckin set against a champion of mine, in years gone by, who lost both net and trident and still won the bout, by some such underhand trick as clawing out his opponent's vitals with his nails.' He gave an embarrassed cough; he hated to refer to any wager he had lost. 'Well, then, bring them up, but have a guard around them, as you say.'

Relieved, Achoreus turned to issue the necessary orders. Accordingly, in a little while, to the music of their fetters clanking, a sorry train of captives wended their way out of the grand courtyard of the palace, up the lower slopes of the ramp leading to the gallery – which were of common granite – and stage by stage on to the higher level, where the parapets were of garnets in their natural matrix, and the floor of cat's-eye, peridot and tourmaline.

Refused food on the long trudge from Erminvale to discourage the energy needed for escape, granted barely enough water to moisten their lips, they found the gradual incline almost too much for them, and their escorts had to prod them forward with the butts of spears.

At last, however, they were ranged along the gallery, out of the shade of the dragon-hide awning, blinking against sunlight at their new and unlooked-for master. At one end of the line was Leluak, his left eye swollen shut from a blow and testifying to his vain resistance; as far distant from him as possible, Viola, nearly naked from the struggle that had led to Achoreus ripping her clothes. And between them, every villager from Wantwich bar Granny Anderland, from babes in arms to gray-pated patriarchs.

Accompanied by the proud Achoreus, Torquaida went along the line peering into face after face, occasionally poking to test the hardness of a muscle or the flab of a belly, his forefinger sharp as one of the styli he used to post his accounts on wax tablets. He halted before one bluff middle-aged fellow in a red jerkin, who looked unutterably weary.

'Who are you?' he croaked.

'Uh …' The man licked his lips. 'Well, my name's Harring.'

'Say "so please you"!' Achoreus rasped, and made a threatening gesture towards his sword.

Harring muttered the false civility.

'And what can you do?' Torquaida pursued.

'I'm a brewer.' And, reluctantly after a brief mental debate: 'Sir!'

'You learn swiftly,' Achoreus said with mocking approval, and accompanied Torquaida down the line. 'You?'

'I'm a baker – sir.'

'I? Oh, a sempstress!'

'And I'm a bodger, turner, and mender of ploughs.'

The answers came pat upon the questions, as though by naming their trades the captives could reassure themselves they still retained some dignity by virtue of their skill. At Torquaida's direction a clerk made lists of all the names and crafts, leaving aside the children under twelve, and finally presented the lists with a flourish to Lord Fellian.

Scrutinizing them through his diamond lenses, the lord addressed Achoreus.

'And of what standard are these louts in their professions? Competent, or shoddy?'

'As far as I could judge, sir,' Achoreus answered, 'they might be termed competent. Of course, their criteria fall far short of our own; still, their houses seemed sturdy, they kept their fences well mended, and they had sound byres and folds for their livestock.'

'I see.' Fellian rubbed the tip of his nose on the sharp facets of a gemstone ringed to his left middle finger. 'Then there might be something to be said for keeping them instead of staking them. We have no brewery in the household that I know of. Some scullery drab or turnspit would be less useful than that man – what's his peasant's name? Harring? Therefore do thus, Torquaida: take away their brats and put them to nurse or be apprenticed, then sort the rest and for each one you judge to be worth adding to my staff select one servant we already have who's lazy or sullen or deformed, and set him at my disposal to be staked tonight. Hah! Was this not an inspiration that I had?' He rubbed his hands and gave a gleeful chuckle.

'Oh, how I long to see the faces of those dunderheads when I wager fifty servants against each of them tonight! I simply cannot fail to gain by this affair! If they win, which Lady Luck I trust will prevent, they will merely clutter up their households with extra mouths to feed, while I have acquired new tradesmen, and should I win – which I no doubt shall – I'll have plenty of spare overseers to cope with the servants those two stake! Ho-ho! We must do this again, Achoreus!'

Achoreus bowed low, and once more stroked his mustachios.

'Take them away,' Fellian commanded, and leaned back in his throne, reaching with fat pale fingers for the mouthpiece of a jade huqqah on a lacquered table nearby. An alert slave darted forward and set a piece of glowing charcoal on the pile of scented herbs the bowl contained.

Frightened and angry, but too weak to resist, the folk of Wantwich turned under the goading of the soldiers to wend their way back to the courtyard below. Fellian watched them. As the end of the line drew level with him, he snapped his fingers and all looked expectantly towards him.

'That girl at the tail,' he murmured. 'She's not unattractive in a country way. Set her apart, bath, perfume and dress her, and let her attend me in my chamber.'

'But—!' Achoreus took a pace forward.

'You wish to comment?' Fellian purred dangerously.

'I ...' Achoreus hesitated, and at last shook his head.

'Let it be done, then.' Fellian smiled, and sucked his huqqah with every appearance of contentment.

6

Furious, Achoreus turned to superintend the final clearance of the captives from the gallery, and thought the task was done, but when he glanced around there was one stranger remaining, who certainly was neither a household officer nor a slave: a man in a black cloak leaning on a staff.

'Achoreus!' Fellian rasped. 'Why have you not taken that fellow with the rest?'

Staring, Achoreus confessed, 'I have not seen him before! He was not with the villagers when we assembled them – Ah, but I *have* seen him, not at Wantwich. Now I recall that when we were on the outward leg from Teq he stood beneath a tree to watch our army pass, having that same staff in his hand.'

'And he's come to join the captives of his own accord?' Fellian suggested with a laugh. An answering ripple of amusement at what passed for his brilliant wit echoed from his sycophants. 'Well, then! We shall not deny him the privilege he craves!'

Faces brightened everywhere. Fellian was a capricious master, but when he spoke in this jovial fashion it was probable that he was about to distribute favours and gifts at random, saying it was to impress on his retinue the supreme importance of luck.

'So, old man!' he continued. 'What brings you hither, if it was not the long chain linking those who have been here a moment back?'

'I need to know,' said the traveller in black, and paced forward on the jewelled floor.

'To know what? When the gaming-wheel of life will spin to a halt for you against the dire dark pointer of death? Why, go ask Lady Luck face to face, and she will tell you instanter!'

At that, certain of his attendants blanched. It was not in good taste to joke about Lady Luck.

'To know,' the traveller responded unperturbed, 'why you sent armed raiders to rape the village Wantwich.'

'Ah, yes,' Fellian said ironically. 'I can see how a stranger might put a question of that order, lacking proper comprehension of the priorities in life. Many think that all they need ever do is act reasonably, meet obligations, pay their debts ... and then some random power intrudes on their silly calm existence, perhaps with a leash, perhaps with a sword, and all their reasoning is set at naught! That then is their opportunity to learn the truth. Not sense but luck is what rules the cosmos – do you hear me? *Luck!*'

He leaned forward, uttering the last word with such intensity that a spray of spittle danced down to the floor.

'See you that idiot who turns a gaming-wheel for me? Ho, you! Bring the creature here!'

Retainers rushed to obey. Fellian peeled rings from his fingers, decorated with stones that might bring the price of a small farm or vineyard, and threw them on the soiled skirt of the idiot's robe.

'Turn her free! Luck has smiled her way today!'

'Not so,' contradicted the traveller.

'What? You gainsay me – you gainsay *Fellian!*' The lord was nearly pop-eyed with horror.

'Say rather I see two sides of this good fortune,' the traveller murmured. 'Is it not great luck for an idiot to be fed, housed and clothed by a rich lord? Is this not worth more to her than to be given some pretty baubles and left to fend alone? Where is the benefit if next week she starves?'

Fellian began to redden as the validity of the point sank in, and he glared fiercely at someone to his right whom he suspected of being about to giggle.

'You chop logic, do you?' he rasped. 'You're a schoolman, no doubt, of the kind we take to gaze on Lady Luck, who thereupon die rather horribly!'

'Which event,' the traveller remarked mildly, 'puts a term to the possibility of persuading them to share your views. The dead are not the easiest persons to convert; their attitudes tend to be somewhat fixed.' He shifted his staff from one hand to the other, and continued.

'Let me see if I understand these views of yours. You maintain, I believe, that life is one long gamble?'

'Yes, of course!' Fellian barked.

'If this is so, why should one need to make more wagers? Is not any other, compared to the wager which embraces the whole of life, too trivial to be worth attention? Clearly you do not agree, I grant, inasmuch as you propose to stake human beings against your rival lords tonight, and for this purpose kidnapped the inoffensive folk of Wantwich.'

'Nothing gives spice to life but winning wagers!' Fellian snorted. 'I sit here – is it not plain by that token that I already won a great gamble? I staked my very existence on the right to be a Lord of Teq, and that I am here proves that the lady on the tower smiles my way!'

The traveller cocked his head sardonically. He said, 'Call yourself a great gambler, a great winner, whatever you like. But I can name a bet you'll not accept.'

'What?' Fellian howled, and all around there were cries of shocked dismay. 'Think you can insult a Lord of Teq with impunity? Guards, seize and bind him! He has offered me a mortal affront, and he must pay for it!'

'How have I affronted you – how? To say that I can name a bet you will not accept is not to insult you, unless you can but will not match my stakes!' The traveller fixed Fellian with a sharp stare.

'Am I to bet with a nobody? I bet only against my coevals! It takes uncounted wealth to bet with me!' Fellian snorted. 'Why, were I to treat you seriously, any bumpkin could come to me and say, "I wager my rags and clogs, all I possess, against all that you possess – and that's a match!"'

'But there is one thing any man may bet against any other,' said the traveller. 'For no man can have more than one of it.'

There was silence for the space of several heartbeats. 'My lord,' Torquaida said at last in a rusty voice, 'he means life.'

Fellian went pale and licked his lips. He blustered, 'Even so! A life that may have fifty years to run, like mine? Against one which may snuff out tomorrow, or next week?'

'Regrettably,' Torquaida creaked, 'that is fair stakes. However' – and he gave a tiny dry smile and wheezing chuckle – 'it's over-soon to name the stakes before one knows the bet, is it not?'

Fellian flashed him a grateful grin; this was the outlet he had been unable to spot himself. He said loudly, 'Yes, a crucial point! What bet is this that you wish to make with me, old man?'

'I bet you,' said the traveller into a universal hush, 'that the face of Lady Luck is turned away from your throne.'

There was an instant of appalled shock. But with a great effort Fellian forced a booming laugh.

'Why, that wager's lost already!' he exclaimed. 'Is it not proof of the lady's favour that I sit here among unparalleled riches?'

'They are what you woke to today,' the traveller said 'Tomorrow is yet to eventuate.'

'Why stop at tomorrow?' Fellian said. 'Next week, next month, next year if you like, when I have won still more bets against Yuckin and Nusk, we'll take you and hoist you on a tall pole that you may look on the lady directly and see that she does smile towards me. Meantime, enjoy the hospitality of my dungeon. Hey, guards!'

'Thank you, I am in no need of lodging,' the traveller said. 'Moreover, a week is too long. One day will suffice. I will see you again tomorrow; let's say at dawn. For now, however, farewell.'

'Seize him!' Fellian bellowed, and the soldiers who had remained behind on Achoreus's signal when the party of captives was led away, dashed in the direction of the traveller. But they went crashing against one another, as though they had sought to clutch an armful of empty air.

7

In the great cave-like kitchens of the palace, a cook sweated with ladle and tongs at a cauldron of half a hogshead capacity. The fire roaring beneath scorched his skin, the smoke blinded his eyes with tears.

From the dark corner of the hearth, a voice inquired for whom the savory-smelling broth was being prepared.

'Why, for Lord Fellian,' sighed the cook.

'But no man can engulf such a deal of soup. Will he have guests?'

'Yes, so he will.' The cook grimaced. 'They'll eat two ladlefuls, or maybe three.'

'And you then will enjoy what is left over?'

'I, sir?' The cook gave a rueful chuckle. 'No, on my soul, I wouldn't dare. What my lord leaves in his dish goes to his hounds! Tonight as ever I shall sup off a crust of dry bread and that chunk of mouldy bacon rind. Still, hounds have no taste for wine, so if I'm quick I may claim the dregs from the goblets at the high table, and liquor will soothe my grumbling belly enough to let me sleep.'

Among the fierce ammonia stench of guano, the falconer worked by an unglazed window, tooling with gnarled yet delicate hands a design of rhythmical gold leaf onto the hood and jesses of a peregrine falcon.

'This leather is beautiful,' said a soft voice from over his shoulder. 'But doubtless you put on far finer array when you go forth of an evening to enjoy yourself at a tavern?'

'I, sir?' grunted the falconer, not turning around; the light was wasting, and he was forbidden the extravagance of lamps or candles. 'Why, no, I'm in the service of Lord Fellian, and have no time to amuse myself. And had I time, I'd be constrained to wear what you see upon me now – old canvas breeches, bound around the waist with fraying rope. Besides, with what would I purchase a mug of ale? With a scoop of fewmets?'

In the stables, a groom passed a soft cloth caressingly over the fitments of a stall; they were of jacynth and ivory, and the manger was filled with new sweet hay, fine oats fit to have baked bread, and warm-scented bran.

'Palatial,' said a voice from behind the partition. 'This is merely for a horse?'

'Aye, sir,' muttered the groom, declining to be distracted from his work. 'For Western Wind, Lord Fellian's favourite steed.'

'By comparison, then, I judge you must take your repose on high pillows filled with swan's down, beneath a coverlet of silk, or furs for winter!'

'I sleep on straw, sir – do not jest with me! And if I have time to gather clay to stop the chinks in my hovel against the night's cold, I count myself lucky.'

Beside a marble bath, which ran scented water from a gargoyle's mouth, a slender girl measured out grains of rare restorative spices onto a sponge, a loofah, and the bristles of a brush made from the hide of a wild boar.

'With such precautions,' a voice said from beyond a curl of rising steam, 'beauty must surely be preserved far beyond the normal span.'

'Think you I'd dare to waste one grain of this precious essence on my own skin?' the girl retorted, tossing back a tress of hair within which – though she could be aged at most twenty – there glinted a betraying thread of silver. 'I'd be lucky, when they detected my pilfering, to be thrown over the sill of that window! Beneath it there is at least a kitchen-midden to give me a soft landing. No, my entire fortune is my youth, and it takes the powers of an elemental and the imagination of a genius to spread youth thin enough to satisfy Lord Fellian from spring to autumn.'

'Then why do you endure his service?'

'Because he is a winner in the game of life.'

'And how do you know that?'

'Why,' sighed the girl, 'everyone says so.'

In the high-vaulted banqueting-hall, as the sun went down, the rival lords Yuckin and Nusk came to feast with their respective retinues at the expense of the current greatest winner prior to the onset of the night's gambling. They had come to his palace too often of late; there was no friendly chat between them. Gloomily – though with fair appetite, because their own kitchens did not boast such delicacies – they sat apart, growing angrier and angrier as platters of gold succeeded those of silver, goblets of crystal replaced those of enamelled pottery … and often recognizing items they had formerly owned.

Lord Fellian, who should have been delighted at the discomfiture of his rivals, was downcast, and the talk at his long table was all of the strange intruder in a black cloak who had laid down so threatening a bet.

'It's nonsense!' roundly declared Achoreus, who was seated beside Fellian as a mark of special favour. 'As you rightly said, sir, it's absurd to expect someone of your standing to wager with a penniless nobody – and moreover the bet he named is by definition incapable of settlement!'

But his brow was pearled with sweat, and when he had repeated his assertion for the third time his voice was harsh with a hoarseness no amount of wine could relieve.

'And how say you, Torquaida?' demanded Fellian, hungry for reassurance – though not for food; course after course was being removed from his place untouched.

'There is no need to worry,' the elderly treasurer wheezed. 'Like you or dislike you, Lords Yuckin and Nusk would have to concede the propriety of declining such a wager. One cannot conduct important affairs on an arbitrary basis!'

Even that, however, did not set Fellian's mind at rest. 'Ah, would I knew the outcome of the wager, however foolish!' he grumbled, and at that the black-clad traveller, standing apart in the secrecy of an embrasure, gave a sad smile.

'As you wish,' he murmured, 'so be it. You have won your bet with me, Lord Fellian – and there are and have been few in all eternity who can make that claim. Yet in the same instant when you won, you lost beyond all eternal hope.'

The question settled now, he went away.

Shortly, they cleared the dishes from the hall, bringing in their place the hand-carved dominoes required for the game shen fu, the lacquered plaques destined for match-me-mine and mark-me-well, the tumbling gilded cages full of coloured balls known as The Lady's Knucklebones, the gaming-wheels – those with four, those with nine, and those with thirty-three divisions – blind songbirds trained to pick out one and only one among three disparately dyed grains of corn, jumping beans, silver-harnessed fleas, baby toads steeped in strong liquor, and all the other appurtenances on which the Lords of Teq were accustomed to place their bets. Additionally, from among their respective trains, they marshalled their current champions at wrestling, boxing with cestae, and gladiatorial combat, not to mention tumblers, leapers, imbeciles armed with brushes full of paint, dice-throwing monkeys, and whatever else they had lately stumbled across upon the outcome of whose acts a bet might be laid.

It was the practice for one of the challengers to name a game, and of the challenged to declare the stakes. Thus, in strict accordance with protocol, Lord Yuckin as the last to lose to Lord Fellian cleared his throat and began with a single hand of shen fu, to which Lord Fellian consented, and won a basket of desert-hoppers – a typical low stake for the early hours.

Then Lord Nusk bet on a jumping toad, and won a purse of coins from Barbizond, to which Lord Fellian replied with a spin of the four-part wheel, and won a bag of sapphires. He nudged his companions and whispered that the old fool on the gallery must have been wrong.

Thus too he won the next five bouts, on toads again, on fleas, on two hands of shen fu, and lastly on the pecking birds. After that he lost a spin of the nine-part wheel and had to concede to Yuckin a chased and jewelled sword that Torquaida dismissed as pretty but not practical; its blade was inferior. No special loss.

'Now, I think,' murmured the pleased Lord Fellian, and on Lord Nusk naming shen fu as the next bout, declared his stake: fifty male servants on this single hand.

The impact was all he could have wished. Though they might scornfully disdain involvement with such mundane matters, none knew better than the

Lords of Teq how many were kept employed to ensure their affluence, through what different and carried skills. To bet one servant was occasionally a last-resort gesture after a bad night; to bet fifty at one go was unprecedented.

Captain Achoreus chortled at the dismay which overcame the visiting lords, and nudged Torquaida in the fleshless ribs. 'The greatest winner!' he murmured, and signalled for another mug of wine.

Yet, when the dominoes were dealt, the Star of Eve fell to Lord Nusk, and only the Inmost Planet to Lord Fellian.

Lord Nusk, who was a fat man with a round bald pate fringed with black, grinned from ear to ear and rubbed his enormous paunch. Scowling, Lord Fellian trembled and made challenge to Lord Yuckin at the same game.

Lord Yuckin, thin and gaunt, eyes blank behind lenses of white crystal, named as much gold as a particular man might carry, and won, and challenged back, and Lord Fellian staked the other fifty servants.

Whereupon he displayed the chief prize of shen fu, the Crown of Stars, and mocked Lord Yuckin's petty deal of Planets Comjoined.

A few minutes later, on a hopping toad, he won back from Lord Nusk, the former fifty servants, and again from Lord Yuckin a fresh batch, including three skilled armourers that lord could ill afford to lose, and beyond that a farm in the Dale of Vezby, and a whole year's vintage of sparkling wine, and three trade-galleys with complete crews, and then from Lord Nusk the High Manor of Coper's Tor, with the right to make a celebrated ewe's-milk cheese according to a secret recipe; then lost for five short minutes the Marches of Gowth with all four fortresses and the Shrine of Fire, but won them back on a spin of the four-part wheel and along with them the Estate of Brywood, the Peak of Brend, and the territory from Haggler's Mound to Cape Dismay.

Securely positioned now, he commenced the calculated process of attrition that he had long dreamed of, the process which ultimately would reduce his rivals to penury: a cook who knew how to make sorbets without ice, a kitchen enchanter who could produce strawberries in winter, a charmer who could bring game from barren ground by playing a whistle, an eight-foot-tall swordsman, champion of the last public games …

Torquaida might have grown harried trying to keep track of the winnings and match what was in hand against what remained to the rival lords. By a supreme effort he remained in control, always remembering to send a clerk to inform Lord Fellian when a stake was unworthy, to say for example that this concubine had suffered the smallpox and was scarred, or that guardsman had a palsy and his sword-arm shook, or that coffer of coins bore a geas, and touched by the winner would turn to pebbles.

Lord Fellian awarded him free of feoff the Estate of Brywood as reward for his valuable support, and laughed joyously night-long at the disarray of his opponents.

8

Far down below that ringing laughter, cast back by the high-vaulted roof of the banquet-hall, reached the ears of those miserable deportees from Wantwich who were still awake. Some were asleep – on straw if they were lucky, on hard flags if they were not ... but at least asleep.

One who was wakeful even on a mattress of eider-feathers, draped in a diaphanous gown of finest lawn embroidered with seed-pearls, was the girl Viola, surrounded by other female pleasure-objects destined for Lord Fellian's delight. At a footstep on the floor beside her couch, she startled and peered into dark, seeing only a black form outlined on greater blackness.

'Is someone there?' she whimpered.

'It is I,' said the traveller.

'How – how did you get in?' Viola sat up. 'I tried the doors – and the windows, too. And all are locked!'

The traveller forbore to explain.

After a moment, Viola began to weep. 'Go away!' she commanded. 'I never want to see you again! You did this awful thing to me, and I hate you!'

'On the contrary,' the traveller replied. 'You did this to yourself.'

'I never asked to be locked up here, waiting for some gross—'

'Ah! But you're reunited with your man Leluak, and that's what you said you wanted. You are both under the same roof; when Lord Fellian tires of you, you will be cast forth together to share the same dank alleyway and the same fevers, chills and pestilences. This in essence constitutes reunion.'

'I should have thought longer before choosing,' Viola said after a while for reflection. The traveller nodded. At least, then, this cruel experience had battered some sense into her skull.

'You had, I believe,' he said, 'encountered Achoreus before the rape he supervised on Wantwich.'

'I did so. I companioned him when he joined us for the spring dance.'

'Out of courtesy?'

'Of course.' In the dark, the girl bridled.

'Or was it because he was a stranger, and handsome, and every other girl in the village would have changed places with you?'

'A little of that too,' she admitted meekly.

'Is it not true, my child, that you were more concerned to regain the handsomest, most eligible bachelor in Wantwich, for whom you had competed against all the other girls less attractive than yourself, than you were to right the wrong done to your family and friends upon the day of your projected wedding?'

'I must have been!' Viola moaned. 'Would that hasty wish of mine could be undone!'

'The second time a person calls upon me,' said the traveller, 'I may point out the consequences if I choose. Do you truly wish to find yourself again on the green at Wantwich – alone?'

There was an awful silence, which she eventually broke with a sob.

'However,' the traveller resumed, when he judged she had suffered long enough to imprint the moral permanently on her memory, 'you may rest easy. All is due to come to a satisfactory conclusion. Though if I were to tell you the name of your saviour, you'd not believe it …'

He tapped his staff against the bed she sat on, and concluded, 'Sleep, child. Wake at dawn.'

Dazed with elation, when the returning sun began to gild the turrets of Teq with the promise of a new day, Lord Fellian struggled to the high gallery of his tower in order to witness the departure of his defeated rivals. On their own! No one in the history of this city had won so fantastic a victory in a single night! Stripped even of their closest body-slaves, Lords Yuckin and Nusk were creeping like whipped dogs into the morning twilight. It had been more by grace than necessity that they had been permitted to retain clothing.

Lord Fellian leaned drunkenly over the parapet of the gallery and whooped like a falconer sighting quarry; when the cowed face of Lord Yuckin tilted upward to see what the noise was, he spilled on it the contents of his latest beaker of wine.

'So much for that old fool who bet that Lady Luck's visage has turned away from me!' he bellowed, and laughed until the racket of his boasting was reflected from the nearby rooftops.

'Are you sure?'

On the edge of his politely voiced question the traveller in black appended the faint swish of his cloak as he advanced across the jewelled floor.

'Why, you …!' Lord Fellian gasped and made to draw back, but the parapet was hard against his spine and there was no way to retreat save into insubstantial air. 'Guards! Guards!'

'None of them have followed you up here,' said the traveller gravely. 'They are persuaded that upon a winner like yourself – if there has ever been one – Lady Luck smiles so long and so favourably that no harm can come to you.'

'Ah-hah!' Fellian began to regain his composure. 'I conclude from that statement that you admit you lost your bet with me!'

'Why, no,' said the traveller, and his expression showed regret, for it had always seemed a shame to him that a person of intelligence – and Fellian was far from stupid – should be seduced into a self-defeating course of action. 'I have won.'

'What? You're insane!' Fellian gasped. 'Prove your claim!'

'I shall,' the traveller said, and smote with his staff against the wall that screened this gallery from sight of the tallest tower in Teq. A slice fell away like a wedge cut from a cheese. Beyond, there where Fellian's reflex gaze darted before he could check himself, Lady Luck's pinnacle loomed on the easterly blueness of the dawn.

A scream died still-born in the lord's throat. He stared and stared, and after a while he said, 'But ... But there's only a stump!'

And it was true; against the sky, instead of the celebrated statue, nothing but a jagged pediment.

He began to giggle. 'Why, you've lost after all!' he chuckled. 'You did not make the wager that Lady Luck had ceased to smile on me, which would be a fair victory – you wagered that her face was turned away from my throne!'

'True.'

'Then—'

'Then I have won.' He gestured with his staff. 'Go forward; examine those chunks of stone I have broken from the wall.'

Hesitant, yet ashamed to seem frightened, Lord Fellian obeyed. His finger-tips fumbled across rough plaster while he coughed at the dust he was stirring up, and found smooth chased stones not conformable to the flat slanting over a shoulder-blade ...

'There was a storm,' said the traveller didactically. 'The figure tumbled and landed in the street. It has always been the custom, has it not, that any who looked on Lady Luck should die? Save the breath you'd waste for an answer; I know your agents dump those whom you dislike in the market-square, claiming that it was for that reason they expired.

'Accordingly, none recognised the fragments. When you commanded stonemasons to assemble the necessary material and build this wall atop your handsome tower, they gathered up whatever they could find, and into the wall they set the broken pieces of the statue, in such fashion that the back of the head was behind your throne.'

'But that's not fair!' Fellian shrieked. 'You knew this all the time, didn't you?'

'Who are you to talk of "fair" and "unfair"...?' the traveller snapped. 'Did I not hear you yesterday promising to reward Achoreus by increasing his stake on a wager that your privy intelligence informed you he had won? Be silent! I am not here to argue, but to claim my winnings!'

He pointed at Fellian with his staff, and with one hand clutching a fragment of the statue, the other clawing at air as though he could cram it by fistfuls into his choking lungs, the greatest winner of all the Lords of Teq departed into nowhere.

A while later, when they came upon the corpse, those who had pledged themselves to his service began to quarrel about partitioning what he had left behind, in sum, the total wealth of the city and its environs.

'I will have the treasury!' cried Torquaida. 'It's my due!' But a young and vigorous clerk from the counting-house struck him down with a golden candlestick. His old pate cracked across like the shell of an egg.

'If I can have nothing more, I'll take the booty Lord Fellian cheated me of!' vowed Achoreus, and set off in search of the girl Viola. But he tripped on a slippery marble step at the entrance to the women's quarters, and by the time he recovered from his bang on the head she was awake and away.

By contrast, though: on learning that his lord was a loser in the game of life after all, the groom who tended Western Wind saddled up the stallion, sighing.

'At least this small recompense is due to me,' he muttered, and opened the door of the stable.

Later, in Barbizond, he offered the steed's services to cover some mares in heat, and from the foals which resulted built up a livery-stable of his own.

Likewise the falconer, on being told the news, gathered his prize merlin and went out into the countryside to get what living he could; he lost the merlin by flying it at an eagle which had stolen a child, a match the eagle was foredoomed to win. But that child was the only son of a wealthy landowner, and in gratitude he made the falconer bailiff of his estates.

Also the cook gathered a brand from beneath his cauldron and went forth by a secret passage leading from the back of his ox-roasting hearth. There he turned his ankle on a square object lying in the dust of the passageway, and the light of the brand showed that it was the lost Book of Knightly Vigour, from which – legend claimed – the Count of Hyfel, founder of Teq, had gained the amorous skill to woo and wed his twenty-seven brides. With recipes from it he opened a cook-shop, and defeated lovers from a score of cities trudged over hill and dale to sample his unique concoctions.

Amid all this coming and going, however, the captives from Wantwich were content to find their way to freedom in the warm morning sun.

9

On their first return, the villagers were a trifle puzzled to discover that the pond beside the green, which for as long as anyone could recall had been placid, now rolled unaccountably. However, as their repairs proceeded – new roofs and shutters, new gates and fences, to replace those broken by the troops from Teq – that disturbance ceased. Before the new beer was brewed, before new barrels were coopered, before a new fiddle had been made for Fiddler Jarge, the water had resumed its normal state.

And on the day when – belatedly – Leluak led out his bride to start the dancing proper to a marriage, a person in a black cloak stood with a benign smile in the shelter of a sycamore.

'Was it not clever, Horimos?' he said under his breath to the elemental prisoned beneath the water. 'Was it not ingenious to pervert the thinking of rational men into the random path of a gambler, who lacks even the dangerous knowledge of an enchanter when he tampers with the forces of chaos?'

Unnoticed except by the traveller, the pond gave off a bubble full of foul marshy gas, which might have been intended for an answer.

'*Shu-ut – brr'p – brr'up!*'

'By all means, Horimos,' the traveller murmured, and drained the mug of Brewer Harring's good beer which he, like all passers-by on a festival day, had been offered. He set the vessel on a handy stump, and the music rose to a frantic gay crescendo.

When, a little diffidently, the new bride came to greet him and ask if he would like to take his turn at partnering her in the dance, there was no trace of his presence except the empty mug.

FOUR

Dread Empire

Lo! thy dread empire, Chaos, is restored;
Light dies before thy uncreating word …

– Pope: *The Dunciad*

1

'Good morrow, sir,' the folk said civilly to the person in black who stood leaning on a staff – of unusual substance – watching them fetch and carry water from the Gander's Well. He answered in turn, but absently, preoccupied, and none of them marked him so closely as to recognize him again. It was plain that he was concerned with private thoughts.

Indeed, so absorbed was he that the sun dipped down and the boys and the goodwives whose chore it was to collect water had gone home to their well-earned supper, before he stirred a pace from where he'd wasted the day. Then it was to address a man, well muffled against the evening cool, who came to scrape a few flakes of punk from a rotten tree-stump, not a great distance from the well's mouth, and dropped them as he gathered them into a pottery jar.

Seeing him then apply a fizzling wick of braided withes, the traveller said, 'You go a journey, I take it, sir!'

'Why, yes!' the man said, glancing up. 'I'm called to see my sister, who's in labour with a nephew for me; her man's abroad, and someone responsible must be by to take her other bairns in charge.'

'And this is what you'll use for tinder?' said the traveller, pointing with his staff at the tree-stump.

'None better can be found in this vicinity,' said the man. 'All who must go a trip by night make use of it. It carries fire through the most amazing storms. In fact, it's said' – but here he coughed, as though by way of apology for seeming to give credit to such a superstition – 'there's some bright spirit in it that fosters the sparks against all odds. If you, sir, whom I judge to be a stranger, think of continuing your walk by night, I counsel you should avail yourself of this. More than once friends of mine have been grateful for it, thinking to finish a journey in daylight, and then coming on a washed-out bridge or flooded ford!'

'How far away then can your sister live? As yet, there's light in the sky; there's an hour or two before full dark, at least.'

'Hmph!' said the man, straightening as he capped his tinder-jar and tossed aside his wick of withes, to sputter on ground made wet by water spilled from buckets day-long dipped in the well. ''Tis plain you really are a stranger, sir! Needs must I go by Cleftor Heights, and there the dark falls fast, believe you me! Indeed, if you'll forgive me, I must make haste, even with this to save me in the pitch black.'

'One final question,' said the traveller, and gestured with his staff. 'I've seen these folk tramp weary miles from town to fill yoked pails of water at this well. Is it regarded as especially sweet?'

The man chuckled. 'Why, sir, as to drinking straight, not especially,' he returned. 'But, see you, the season's on us to brew ale and beer, and – for what reason I know not – if you brew with water from the Gander's Well, you remain lively and jolly all evening long, and the morning after your head's clear and your belly calm. Be sure in the taverns of the town they offer you nothing worse; sometimes they'll try and fool a stranger with what they will not drink themselves.'

'Thanks for the counsel,' said the traveller in black.

When he was alone, he shook his head sorrowfully. Once on this site Yorbeth had brooded in his guise of a tree, his longest tap-root fed from a miraculous spring. Then that sad greedy fool of a packman ...

But he was mortal, which the elemental had not been, and what was left? This stump, yielding tinder for overnight travellers, and a well whose chief renown was for the brewing of beer!

Yet it was not entirely to be wondered at. The news was of a piece with all the rest of what he'd learned during this, the latest of so many journeys undertaken in accordance with the obligations which bound him. Latest? Not impossibly, he was beginning to believe, the *last*.

For once it had made small difference that this journey was *this* journey, not the one before or after. In chaos, randomness was so extreme, the very contrasts made for a sense of uniformity. Now there were actual changes: the vanishing of Yorbeth not the greatest.

Back beyond Leppersley, for instance, Farchgrind was a household pet! The people heard him still, but conjured him to entertain their friends, and scoffed when he made his bragging promises. Laprivan of the Yellow Eyes had spent his substance, whatever the nature of it might be, and wearied of his struggle against the past. Footsteps left by those who plodded up his hill endured an hour or more.

And Barbizond had gone with Ryovora, despite Sardhin. The progress or rationality had worn him down – that bright being in his rainbow-gleaming cloud. It was still claimed that a knife from Barbizond would keep its edge forever, but the only man who'd mentioned the notion to the traveller this trip had been a sober farmer in Kanish-Kulya, and he'd employed the same diffident tone as the man just departed, the one who'd been embarrassed at reference to a spirit in the punk which carried fire so well.

That farmer was an earthy man leading a placid life, a little puzzled now and then when one of his fat and happy ploughboys brought some improbable growth to show him: a bunch of grapes that shone like polished metal, a turnip which, split apart, revealed the chambers of a human heart ...

But his wine was plentiful and sweet, and there was never a lack of roasts to grace the spits in his kitchen, so he bothered his head not at all with traces of another age. Even the ancestry of his daughter-in-law was a source of kindly jokes around his table. Time was when any good Kanish family like his would have banished Kulya girls to the goose-run, be they never so beautiful – or perhaps honoured their beauty by gang-rape if there were half a dozen sufficiently drunken men about.

Now, regal in a gown of peach-coloured silk, a Kulya lady nightly shared his dinners, his heir fondly touching her goblet with his own to drink toast after toast to their three handsome boys asleep upstairs. With grandchildren growing apace, who should care when the blade of a harrow caught in the eye-socket of some mouldering skull? That war was over; the armistice continued.

Likewise in Teq they made a mock of Lady Luck: her offering was a gobbet of spittle, launched at the floor when one of the company voiced hopes for an over-bold project.

Yet the rule bound him, and the traveller's nature was not such that he should complain. Forth he went on paths grown unfamiliar, and spoke with many people in many places, as for example in Wocrahin, where once—

Memory! Memory! He had never foreseen that that intangible, binding the fluid nature of eternity into the sequential tidiness of Time, would also hamper the will like age itself! Almost, he began to envy those who could die …

No matter. In Wocrahin a man sat gobbling lamprey-pie in a splendid banquet-hall: gross in a purple doublet smeared with gravy-stains. Words chomped around a full mouth of the fish and crust, he forced out, 'Fonly w'were freah y'muzzhr!'

'Ah, yes!' sighed his wife, accustomed to interpreting such talk: she fat as a prize breeding-sow, though childless, her vast bosom exposed almost to the bulging nipples over a gown crusted with seed-pearls, her head seeming to be depressed into her neck by the weight of the gem-crusted tiara she had put on, though they had no company to dinner apart from the thirty scrag-lean servants ranged around the hall.

'Would we were free of my mother!' she echoed when she had swilled her gullet with a swig of wine. 'Ah, how finely we would live were we rid of her! She eats us out of house and home, the old bag!'

'Sh'yeats zazouter 'ousernome!' concurred the man.

The tall windows of the banquet-hall stood open to the warm summer night. Beyond them, watching the line of beggars who daily came – more from habit than optimism – to beg the cook for scraps, the traveller in black both heard the exchange and also saw the lady's mother, in draggled rags, pleading at the barred grille of the cellar where she was pent for a share of the beggars' crumbs.

He tapped his staff on the wall.

'As you wish, so be it,' he said, and went away. The ceiling of the banquet-hall creaked behind him; it freed the greedy pair within a minute from all burdens, life itself not excluded.

Likewise in Medham, a city noted for its lovely girls, a man sat in a tavern who had tried scores of them and recounted how expert he was at seduction.

'Ah, if I had a quart of ale for every one, I'd hardly be sober again in this life!' he hinted to his listeners, turning over his purse and finding it void of coin. 'Why, did not the lady Fretcha come to me on hands and knees, saying I'd ruined her for life? Haw-haw! Begged me, on my oath – literally *begged* me – to make an "honest woman" of her! Haw-haw-haw! And then there was the lady Brismalet; she did the same – what impudence! And the lady Thespie, and then Padovine ... Ho! As I say, did I but have a quart of ale for each—'

'As you wish, so be it,' said his neighbour, a person in black with an unusual staff, and rose. No one noticed him depart. All were too taken aback at the spectacle of the boastful philanderer, belly distended like a hogs-head, vomiting disgustingly because he could not hold ale amounting to twenty-six quarts.

'You stupid brute!' cried a carter in a hamlet hard by Acromel, and lashed his horse across the hind-quarters with a steel-barbed whip. Violent though was the blow, it barely drew blood – he'd employed the whip so often, the horse's back and legs were cicatrized with impermeable scars. Nonetheless the poor beast whinnied and cringed. Therefore he beat it again, and harder still.

'Ho, that you were blessed with more sense!' he roared. 'Would you could learn how not to spill my load crossing a rut!'

Still grumbling about the horse's lack of wit, he went to the back of the cart to retrieve the ill-stowed sack of grain which had tumbled off.

'As you wish, so be it,' said the traveller, and the horse reared up, tipping the whole ton-weight of bags on the stooping carter. Then it chewed intelligently through the traces and took its leave, to enjoy lush upland grass and roam free.

'By your favour, sir,' said a boy of ten or twelve years, hunting a hedgerow near the village Wyve, 'are such plants poisonous or wholesome?'

Offering for inspection a glabrous brownish fungus.

'Wholesome,' said the traveller. 'They may be fried.'

With a moue, the boy tossed the toadstool aside.

'Are you not glad to have found that it's edible?' asked the traveller. 'I took it you were gathering food.'

'No, sir,' said the boy. His voice and eyes were older than his years. 'I seek poisons to give to my mother; she rules me unkindly and will not let me do whatever I like.'

He sighed enormously, 'Ah, that I might recognise instanter what may be relied on to entrain death!'

'As you wish, so be it,' said the traveller, and went on, leaving the boy weeping because he realized: no matter what diet is chosen, sooner or later death ensues.

Thus, pretty much as might have been expected, the way of the traveller wound on, until that night which overtook him deeper than other nights on the flank of Rotten Tor, in which he discovered why the honest working-man from Gander's Well had carefully sought tinder to bear on a journey a mere hour in length.

And why the tinder had to be of a tree which once had drunk a marvellous spring far underground.

And also one thing far more important: why, when all about him he saw the triumph of the homely commonplace virtues, the prevalance only of the everyday vices such as laziness and greed – earnest, if any were to be had, of the impending conclusion of his task – he first should learn the flavour of that bitter new edge acquired by apprehension, which turns it into something cruder.

Fear.

2

Truly this was not like an ordinary night! Though she was wrapped in a good plaid shawl, and had moreover mittens to her hands, the woman was dismayed by the solidity of the blackness, by the chill that bit from it through garments never so well-woven, to the ultimate marrow. Behind her the child Nelva, whom she had not dared to leave at home, was too weary – or too cold – even to whimper.

At least, though, far ahead there gleamed one spark: the mark of her destination.

Though going back ...

She shivered so violently her teeth chattered. It was something to be faced, the return, and couldn't be helped. Bowing her head, although there was no apparent wind, she clung to her daughter's hand and hurried on.

Lights gleamed fantastical the length of the little shop. Whoever had suffered by the coming of these unseasonable black nights to the Cleftor Fells, it wasn't Master Buldebrime who owned the place. Lamps shone on the adze-shapen counter facing the door that admitted clients from the street, and on all the pale pine planks doing the duty of shelves which lined the room wherever there was solid wall. There was even a lit lamp hung on that other door, of boards nailed to a saltire frame, giving access to the living-quarters of the house.

Certain of these lamps burned candles of good tallow, and more of rank stale fat. Some burned wicks floating in clear sweet oil, but these were few, and fewest of all that were alight this evening were the ones which fed on exotic aromatic distillations and dispersed into the air not only a luminance slightly tinged with sapphire-blue but also a delightful perfume. These last had reservoirs to match their content: fine-wrought in alabaster, amethyst and orichalcum.

Cold on the street it might be, but shutters had boarded in the shop's two streetward windows long before, so well sealed at their edges by strips of wetted leather that the air within was past being only warm. Now it was hot with all those flames entrapped by clear glass chimneys, or tinted crystal globes, or shields of thin-pared horn. The delicate scent of the most costly of them faded into a stench of vaporized fat; on their rich diet, the flames looked almost starved.

Nonetheless, even now, their glimmering colours made the coarse roof of overarching beams look like a mine of dismal coal illumined unexpectedly by an irrupting river that had washed a shaft of sunshine underground and shown that there were also jewels in the rock.

On the counter a tall time-candle, bright red wax crossed at thumb-joint intervals by bands of black, told that the hours of trading for today were nearly done.

Abruptly and in unison the flames bowed, like heads of barley in a field assaulted by a storm, and in from the street dived the woman, her clogs announcing her arrival on the floor-flags. Forgetful on the instant of her weariness and chill, the toddler Nelva at her skirts exclaimed with ooh! and aah! at seeing this wonderland of coloured light. A rush of burnt-wax stink took to the outdoors like a dying man's grasp, and there was a cry from beyond the inner wall: 'I come apace!'

Snuffers in hand ready to douse the time-candle and the rest, the owner of the shop appeared in a tallow-stiff smock. Shaven, his red jowls glistened as though he sweated the very fabric of his wares. He was poised to fawn, expecting one of the gentry who came by ordinary to view his stocks late in the evening, they being readier than the common sort to brave the dark, what with their covered carriages and palankeens.

But that lasted a mere eyeblink. Here was only some nondescript poor woman, likely hoping to trade some useless odds and ends against a lamp instead of purchasing one with honest currency.

'What is it you want?' he demanded.

'What would I come here for but a lamp?' the woman snapped, and added from the corner of her mouth, 'Be silent, Nelva!'

The little girl complied, but her eyes remained enormously round as she gazed from one to another of the shining lights.

'Here!' went on the woman, slapping coins on the counter. 'Three good coppers, as you see – what's more the rims aren't clipped! We need a lamp to eat our supper by. The one we had is broke, and do I set Nelva here close enough by the hearth to see by fire-flame smoke makes her weep and salts her dish with tears. For the bairn's sake, give me the best you can.'

She planted her hands on her hips and stood back. Taking up the coins, Master Buldebrime studied them. As claimed, they were properly round and gave back to the time-candle the proper reddish sheen. He bit one, shrugged, and turned to a shelf of his cheapest lamps.

'This is the best I can do,' he said, selecting one. 'Take it or leave it.'

The woman looked it over cannily. She said, 'But that's a short candle in it, that's been lit!'

'Then take a brand-new candle, and my blessings,' the shopkeeper snorted, catching one up at random from a stack and throwing the shortened one to be remelted later. 'For three coppers that's the most I can spare. And wouldn't part with so much but that yon's a pretty child.' He eyed Nelva, leaning forward on the counter. 'Hmm! Yes! In three-four years you should let me know again. I'll 'prentice her to the candle-making trade. There's men aplenty who'd wed a wife with such a profitable skill."

Wrapping the lamp in her shawl, the woman said harshly, 'Thank you, but no, Master Buldebrime! We hear the tales of apprentices, even out where we live by Rotten Tor. So you like little girls as well as boys?'

The shopkeeper's face darkened below the saddest ruby of any of his lamps.

'Get out!' he rasped, and made as though to hurl his bronze snuffers.

Though the hand which clutched the coins stayed safely resting on the counter.

Once more the flames quavered as, faced with the prospect of returning to that dreadful black and cold, the child objected to the notion of departure; shortly, however, her mother dragged her over the threshold and the door banged shut. Buldebrime remained for a long moment fuming as foully as his cheapest candles, then mastered his rage and went to bar the entrance. He made the rounds with his snuffers, and resorted at last to his cosy living-room, leaving the shop lit only – through a skylight – by the far-off gleam of four crucial conjunct planets wheeling downward from the zenithal line.

3

Not right, the traveller decided – not right at all!

He stood and pondered on the flank of Rotten Tor, a louring crest so friable not even goats might climb it in safety, staring in what long familiarity assured him must be the direction of Cleftor Vale. Granted that the entire valley lay in the daytime shadow of the Heights, should it not now be lit at least by starshine? And, come to that, was not the moon inclining towards its full?

Yet here was such blackness as only a shout might penetrate – or a scream! Like the one which had just re-echoed to him, in two parts: beginning with the cry of a child, continuing in a tone louder, deeper, more heartfelt.

'Ho, that we were safe at home! Help, if there's anyone there!'

The traveller did not need to hide his smile; the blackness performed that function for him. Tapping his way with his staff, he skirted the brink of the rocky torrent which here assured the summertime vegetation of its moisture, and was shortly heard approaching by the woman who had called out.

'Ah! Friend, whoever you may be!' She caught blindly at his arm. 'Save me and my daughter – take us in!'

'*I* have no lodging hereabout,' said the traveller. 'But you do, surely.'

'What?' The woman seemed bewildered; then of a sudden recovered herself. 'Why, what a fool I must be!' She went forward, groping, and shortly was heard to knock her fists on resounding planks. 'Home!' she cried. 'Oh, praise be!'

A door creaked on awkward hinges, and a gleam of firelight showed the outline of a cottage originally built of sturdy four-square logs and boards that now was tilt-roofed and wore a melancholy garb of grey-green lichen. The child ran forward and threw her arms around a man who rose from a truckle-bed, discarding a blanket of threadbare woollen stuff, but could not speak in greeting for a cough which overcame him.

'My dear, you're safe!' he croaked when he recovered. 'Oh, you should not have taken Nelva!'

'You were asleep,' the woman said, embracing him. 'And it's so rarely that you sleep quite sound ... Ah, but I'm forgetting! Yarn, this gentleman who stands at the door: he's my saviour!'

The traveller entered at her beckoning and gave a bow.

'I was almost lost!' the woman babbled. 'It was so dark—'

'But surely,' Yarn began, and coughed a second time, and tried again. 'But surely you went to buy a lamp!'

'Indeed, indeed! To Master Buldebrime's – here, sir,' she added to the stranger, bustling about as she spoke while child and father sat down side by side on the bed, 'do you make yourself comfortable, and welcome too! I'd have fallen in the gorge had you not chanced by, so completely was I lost on my doorstep! Excuse the sparseness of our hospitality, but if you fancy such rude fare we can offer a broth of greens, and maybe some bread, and—'

'But to buy a lamp, and come home in the dark!' Yarn got that out in a single breath, before hacking into coughs anew.

'Hah!' The woman stopped in the middle of the floor, where firelight showed her silhouette, and put her hands on her hips. 'When I get back to town, shall I ever give Buldebrime a tongue-lashing! That lamp! That lamp! Here!'

She produced it from the folds of her shawl. 'Why, did I not light it to see the path by, returning home? And did it not in the same moment smoke over its chimney, blacker than a barn-door?'

She gestured violently at her husband with it.

'Your pardon for my ill-temper, sir,' she added to the traveller. 'But to be without a lamp these nights is more than a body can bear. It's as though the very dark outside comes creeping in at the unstopped chinks of the wall, dulling the fire-glow! And, say all our neighbours, Goodie Blanchett and Goodie Howkle and the rest: go to Master Buldebrime, his lamps are best, we have our own and sit by night in their warm yellow shine …' As she talked, she was rubbing the smoked-over glass on her shawl. Damp logs on the earth sputtered a counterpoint to her speech.

'I'll light it again, to prove my word,' she said, and bent to pick a pine-splinter from the fire.

'What's worst of all,' she added as she carried the flame to the twisted wick, 'he took coin from me for it – not a mere bucket of ewe's milk, or some trifle we could spare! And it does this! Sir!' – rounding on the traveller – 'do you not think it criminal, to take advantage of a poor soul thus?'

But the traveller was not paying attention. Gazing at the lamp-chimney, which as predicted was on the instant blearing over, he was uttering sad words within his head:

'Ah, Wolpec, Wolpec! Has it come to this?'

Once this pallid thing of grimy smoke had been an elemental he – even he – was now and then compelled to consult. There were conditions attached to such inquiry, by which he – even he – was forced to abide. Here, now, on the chimney of a common lamp, there writhed blurred characters such as formerly had expressed transcendent truths … but who alive could certify the meaning of such messages? Those tongues had been forgotten everywhere!

Reacting to the concentration of his gaze, the woman ventured, 'Sir, you're not by any chance skilled in the repair of lamps, are you …?'

Then, registering the fierceness of his expression, she fell into a puzzled silence.

Some of the old laws, it appeared, still stood, but the understructure of them must have cracked, as a building may retain its general shape yet lack huge plates of stucco from its facade and be unsafe to walk the stairways of. For this lamp was showing three truths in the ancient manner, without the ancient and obligatory rites ...

Of three, the first incomprehensible, in a variety of writing that creatures not quite man-like had employed to record dealings in imponderables. It had been hazarded that the records concerned a trade in souls, but that was barely an approximation. In any case, being an invention of chaos, the symbols had any value anyone cared to assign them.

And it was fading, and it was time to ask again.

'How come you to this pass?' the traveller thought.

Now, the one debatable, in a single hieroglyph such as might have been seen on the high pillars of Etnum-Yuzup before that metropolis dissolved into dust with thunderclaps. The Grand Five Weavers had grown self-indulgent, and no longer observed the instructions they had issued to themselves in the days of the foundation of their city. This might be read plainly; the traveller read it.

One would cease.

Now for the final truth, the ineluctable ... but the question must be aptly posed. Indeed, the traveller realized, it had better not be a question but a statement, a truth of comparable import. Within his head he framed it: 'I have many names, but a single nature.'

The weakening elemental understood, and on the glass appeared the characters of a poem by Shen-i-ya Eng-t'an Zwu, who sat for a thousand years beneath an elm while none could tell whether he lived or died, so wholly was he attuned to the world around.

Smoke
fades into the air
is no more seen

The candle-dousing winds of ages seemed to sough in the chimney of the cottage.

'Sir,' the woman said anxiously, 'I wish you'd not bother so much with our trifling problem!'

'Is it not in fact a great matter for you, lacking a lamp?' The traveller didn't raise his head.

The woman sighed. 'Well, I must confess it is, sir. For eating close by the fire, and breathing smoke, is hard on my little one, and my man Yarn above all, what with his chest-trouble … I'd set my heart on having a good bright clear new lamp!'

'As you wish,' said the traveller, not without sorrow, 'so be it.'

He blew out the flame. When he cleaned the glass and lit it anew, it shed a grateful pure yellow light.

Wolpec was little, though wise; candles had sufficed in which to pen him. Fegrim was vast, and underlay a mountain. But he had seen among the snag-toothed peaks of Kanish-Kulya how his volcano slumbered now beneath a cap of white, where once it had spouted smoke a mile high. No ripples stirred the pool of Horimos, and after untold eons the river Metamorphia had changed that nature it once had of changing things. Wives rinsed their laundry in the spring at Geirion, and the eldritch song Jorkas had been used to sing was turned a lullaby with nonsense words to soothe asleep happy babes in wicker cradles. Even the names of the greatest ones: Tuprid and Iaschalanva, Juorril and Lry – were one to speak them, folk would answer, 'Who?'

They had departed, to fret powerless among the stars, and sometimes hurl futile spears of flame across the night … at which sight lovers, hand in hand, would cry merrily, 'Look, there's a star to wish on! Wish for early marriage and long happiness!' And kiss, and forget it in a moment.

Except here, and that was very strange. Disquieting! It was indeed in Cleftor country as had been described to him: as though the black of night could filter through the walls and dull the fire. Flames here were sullen red, and their heat was muted. This was not true of the new lamp, but there were reasons for that.

It would be politic, the traveller reasoned, to behold the dawn.

Therefore, dissolving one of the forces that curdled the light-beams of his staff, he picked his way across the hut's floor silently, abandoning the thick warm fleece he'd been allotted for a coverlet. Outside, the last hour of the night was oppressive with mephitic stench, as though every home in the valley had kept a fire ablaze all night against the mantle of blackness, and all their smokes had come together in a foul miasma. Even the blade of light from his staff was foreshortened a pace or two ahead of his toes.

The trade of lamp-maker hereabouts must indeed be a profitable pursuit.

What this blackness was not was easy to define. It wasn't smoke, although much was now mingled in it. It was not fog, clammy and opaque, yet cleanly, being drops of fine-divided water. It was not cloud, which is of the same substance. It was – well, it was an inverse of brightness.

When dawn came, belatedly by the traveller's calculation, it behaved moreover in a peculiar fashion. Rather than thinning and being dispelled, as night ought to be by the rising sun, it drew in on itself, lying bare yard by yard the countryside, as though one could make thick black tar flow uphill.

And uphill was its direction, out of the vale and towards the ragged pinnacles of Cleftor Heights. There, at some point almost beyond the traveller's range of vision, it gathered itself as it were into a ball, into a spiraling cone, into a wisp … and nothing.

Yet it had left, over every inch of ground where it had lain, a brooding aura of dismal foreboding.

Going by ordinary ways, he later came on some children turned out of the house to play, who were listlessly tossing pebbles at a target scratched on a tree-bole, and seemingly cared little whether they hit it or not; at least, none among them was keeping score.

'Who rules these lands?' the traveller inquired, and one of them answered.

'I think his name is Garch, sir. Would you that I go home and ask my mother? She would know.'

'Thank you; the name's enough,' the traveller said.

4

At the full moon Garch Thegn of Cleftor Heights held certain audiences that differed markedly from the common run of his daily business. One day before the full, he spoke to no one, but locked himself away in private rooms to pore over great tomes and crumbling scrolls; one day after, it was never sure – even to his chief counsellors and stewards – whether he would be fit to resume his normal court, in his great hall tiled with chrysoberyl slabs.

Yet withal his was a domain envied far and wide in this country; by all criteria it was improbable. Though most of it was rocky and its soil was thin, its kine were famed for their fatness and the richness of their milk. Though their roots were shallow, often planted in mere crevices, never a hedge but yielded nuts and fruit to be preserved by boiling down in honey. Though it was unpopulous, with villages few and far between, its folk were tall and strong and raised healthy children; what was more, garments elsewhere reserved to the grandest ladies might here be seen gracing a farmer's wife driving her trap to market, or her daughter on a high-day bound for the wife-taking dance. Velvet and suede, samite and purple plush, were donned as casually as homespun, and only at the very fringes of the Garch estates – as for example hard by Rotten Tor – did families lack for silver spoons and porcelain dishes to entertain company at table.

Paradoxically, with all this the folk of the district were misliked. It was said they were overly cunning; it was said that doing business with them was like trying to stand an eel on its tail. It was further hinted that it was best not to let your daughter marry one, be he never so prosperous, for in a short while her only care for her family would be to take what advantage of them she might, and she'd have become like her neighbours, purse-mouthed, hard-eyed, and fond of coin.

Despite such talk, however, visitors came frequently to Garch's mansion for purposes of trade. Notable among these, and arriving typically in the second quarter of the moon, were persons of a particular sort, who brought not conventional goods, but ideas, and treasurers, and relics – it being at this specific time of the month that the thegn was readiest to receive them.

Few, nonetheless, passed the fierce initial scrutiny of his counsellors; penalties for wasting the thegn's time were severe, and all supplicants for audience must be grilled beforehand by these three. Each morning they assembled in an anteroom beside the great hall, with a scribe and a paymaster carrying a chest of coins, and saw everyone who had come intending to trade. Often the business was quick and simple, concerning only regular goods that might be swiftly bargained for, such as tapestry, or unguents, or fine handicrafts. Similarly, there were those who offered services, skill in carving or tailoring or cobbling, and were desirous to display the shield of warrant of their lord over their place of business; these were invariably permitted to undertake a trial venture for a small fixed fee – or, if they failed a first time, for no fee at all – then engaged on contract if their talents proved adequate. One of this sort had once been Master Buldebrime, and now he supplied the lamps and candles for the mansion, toiling monthly up from the town with a selection of his choicest productions.

Sometimes, however, the proceedings went slowly, and involved interrogation, and it was the hardiest and most venturesome of the visitors who endured this. A few such were on hand today.

Garch's trusted counsellors were three, as aforesaid. In a high-backed chair of horsebones pinned with bronze and padded with bags of chicken-down, the old crone Roiga sat to the left. To the right sat Garch's sister, Lady Scail, on lacquered ivory made soft with whole sheepskins. And in the centre, scorning luxury, presided one-eyed Runch on a common counting-house stool. He wore green; Roiga, brown; the lady Scail, yellow. All else in the room was sterile grey.

'Admit the first,' said Runch in a barking voice, and alert servants ushered in a man who wore the garb of the Shebyas, itinerant traders whose home on the Isle of Sheb had gone back to yellow jungle; no one was certain why, but enchantment was suspected. Doffing his cap, he placed before Runch an object in a small pink sack.

'Your honours, I bring a rare relic, from a city sunken in the depths of Lake Taxhling. Had I but the gold to finance such an expedition, I'd hire divers – of which as you are doubtless aware there are a plenitude in that region where they gather mussel-pearls – and go rake the bottom-mud to produce beyond a peradventure many other potent articles.' He coughed behind his hand and cropped his voice. 'I suspect it would be superfluous to mention that knowledge of an extraordinary kind was available to the inhabitants of that city, which I'm sure you will concede it's better not to name aloud.'

Runch looked over the relic, which was a corroded axe-blade. He said, pushing it aside, 'You cannot name the city because it isn't there. What you have is part of the cargo of a boat capsized by a storm. Go away.'

'But your honour – your grace – your highness …!' the man expostulated. The crone Roiga snapped bony fingers, and an attendant hurried him away.

'Next,' she said in a voice like rustling dried leaves.

A man entered who swept the floor with a blue cloak as he bowed. 'I, sire and ladies,' he announced, 'acquired a book at Pratchelberg. Lacking the skill to read the ancient language in which it's couched, I thought to bring it to your thegn, as being the most renowned, the most expert, the most—'

'Save your breath,' murmured the Lady Scail, having turned a mere half-dozen of the pages. 'This text's corrupt, and anyway my brother has a better copy.'

Protesting quite as loudly as his forerunner, the man in the blue cloak made a forced departure. To the music of his wails, a third supplicant approached, offering a small furry ball.

'This unique article,' he declared, 'speaks when it's gently squeezed, crying out in a small shrill voice. By repute it grew on the ranches of Yorbeth, and I laid out half my life's savings so that it might be brought to Thegn Garch.'

Roiga took it and listened to its cry. She said as she threw it aside again, 'Hah! Yes, indeed, it does speak – by forcing air through twin taut reeds! And do you know what it says? It says, "The man who bought me is a fool!" Get you gone!'

'Will they never learn?' murmured the Lady Scail as this man also was frog-marched out. She had taken a tiny pad of emery and was buffing at her blood-red nails. 'Who remains – anyone?'

And there was a girl.

Suddenly there came an electric tingling in the air, and Scail laid by her emery-pad and Roiga closed her thin old hands on the reassuringly solid nearer edge of the table and Runch confirmed his balance on his stool. She stood before them in a broad hat and fur breeches and a black mail shirt. For a long while there was utter silence.

Then, at length, she moved to place before them a small packet wrapped in parchment and bound with a white ribbon. She said, 'Spices.'

The three counsellors inhaled as one, and it was Roiga who finally said, 'Vantcheen – yes?'

The girl nodded. She was very thin, as though a skeleton had been dressed again in its skin without the underlying fat and muscle, and her eyes burned like a black fire.

'Then name your price!' cried Runch.

'Ah, yes. A price.' The girl tapped a sharp front tooth with a nail even sharper. 'Silver, then. A hammer-head. Three ounces' weight.'

The three counsellors tensed. Lady Scail said, 'As to the shaft …?'

The girl shook her head ever so slightly, and gave ever so slight a smile. She said, 'I thank you for the offer. But the shaft has already been – uh – given to me.'

'Oh, but you're so young!' exclaimed Roiga. 'And yet you're so skilled!'

'Thank you again,' the girl murmured, and turned to go.

'Wait!' cried Lady Scail. 'Do you not wish to speak with my brother the thegn? It's long since one was here who was so adept!'

'If the constellations are proper for the meeting, I shall meet the thegn,' said the girl composedly, and took from the scribe a draft to cover her pay, authorizing the mansion's master smith to forge the silver hammer-head.

There was a deep silence for some while following her departure. The handle of that hammer *had* to be gristly – and some, particularly men, would call it grisly …

Then they were poised, very well pleased, to adjourn for the day, the only other supplicants for audience being of the common run – disputants over boundary fences, or prospective parents-in-law come to determine the proper size of a marriage-portion – when there was a furious stamping and considerable shouting beyond the door, and at the head of a gaggle of stewards, secretaries and waiting-room maids, their master himself came blasting into the room.

The counsellors beheld his expression of blind rage with amazement, rising to their feet.

'I have been cheated and deceived!' roared Garch.

By ordinary he was pretty much a fop, this wealthy lord of improbably rich estates, but now his brown hair and beard were tousled, the laces hung down from his dark red shirt, and his fine worsted stockings slopped over the tops of his boots. To emphasize his outburst, he hammered on the table, and came near to scattering the vantcheen spice.

'Search me this mansion, every nook and cranny!' he shouted. 'Moreover, all the lands about! And if it be not found within the hour, send to the deceiver Buldebrime and bring him here!'

'If *what* be not found?' countered Scail, who as his sister might most freely of the three ask that simple necessary question without inflaming him to further rage.

Garch mastered himself with vast effort, drew close, and whispered in her ear. By watching the change in her face, base attendants from whom he meant to keep the detailed facts deduced at once it was a matter of grave import. Some among the best informed put two and two together and when they received their orders a moment later – to go forth and bring in all the lamps and candles that could be found – decided it would be politic to go in search of service with some other lord.

It was, after all, a mere day and a half short of full moon.

By contrast with the thegn, Master Buldebrime was in a high good humour. Walking through the back rooms of his home, which also served as shop, factory and warehouse, he no more than cuffed any of his apprentices today, not once employing the tawse that hung at his belt for administration of severer punishment.

'Here are eleven candles almost the weight of twelve!' he barked at one child, charged with bearing finished work from the ranked poetry moulds to be checked on the steelyard – but even she and the boy who had filled the moulds escaped with mere open-handed slaps. Satisfied that they were dutifully trimming the surplus wax to be re-melted, he continued.

'Not so lavish with that essence!' he growled at a boy engaged in adding perfumes, drop by drop, to a mix of oils for the most expensive lamps. 'Don't you know it comes from Alpraphand? Hah! I've half a mind to make you walk such a distance on this floor, to brand in your memory knowledge of how far that is! Still, that would take you weeks, and I'll neither feed nor clothe you 'less you're working hard to pay for it!'

Accordingly that apprentice too got off with a smacking.

Persuaded at length that all was well below, as much as affected the making, storing and vending of his wares, he proceeded to the upper floor. This was partitioned into three large chambers. First he came into his own, luxurious, where a couch stood upholstered in deep warm bear-hide and a little girl was industriously polishing a pier-glass.

To her, he said nothing; to himself he murmured that it was a pity she was destined for the eventual requirements of Lord Garch. Otherwise ...

Still, there must be no breath of scandal about this house! If there were, respectable folk would cease to apprentice their brats with him, who kept no wife nor even a serving-maid. For that reason, the two other rooms on this story could be locked at night, and the keys remained always under his hand. One room for girls, the other for boys, they were in most regards identical, each containing heaps of rags soiled by long use and troughs into which at dawn and sunset he poured bucketfuls of gruel for the apprentices to lap. Now and then he also accorded them scraps of bacon and the outer leaves of cabbages, experience having shown that without a morsel of meat and a nibble of greens, the children grew sickly – hence unprofitable. He begrudged the cost, but tolerated it.

One further door remained at this level, and he opened it with the smallest of his many keys. Beyond was a steep flight of steps, hardly more than a slanted ladder, which he climbed. Despite the effort it required to haul his bulk to the top, he was humming a cheery strain when he emerged into the attic that it led to: a large open space lighted by two dusty dormers, lately re-floored with well-planned boards that did not creak.

Below, although they applied themselves to their work, the apprentices found time – as usual – to whisper and make gestures with offensive import. One boy of fourteen, bolder than the rest, and inured to being beaten for his obduracy, filched a more-than-finger-sized piece of wax and began to shape it into a human form. Pausing beside him, a girl who might have been pretty before a pint of Buldebrime's hot tallow seared a puckered scar down her left cheek offered criticism and comment. Others gathered to see what was happening, and suggested improvements. In a little while the likeness to their master was unmistakable, and they chuckled and clutched at one another in delight.

When the doll was perfected, they hid it in a chink between the planks of the wall, to furnish further amusement at some future time.

Above, unaware of this, Buldebrime approached the centre of his attic room. There stood a stool and a table bearing a number of books bound in leather from unconventional sources. Also there was a brazier, and a locked aumbry with carven doors hung from a main-post of the roof. The lamp-maker opened this last, and removed from it a number of small articles: a bundle of feathers, a bag of herbs, and some powders.

Watching from deep shadow, the traveller in black repressed a sigh. He hated these hole-in-the-corner enchanters, not merely because they were victims of the same paradox that had misled their more distinguished predecessors – desiring to control chaos for the sake of the power to be had from it, yet anxious not to destroy it by exerting over-much control – but also because he'd found them ignorant, discourteous and casual. Buldebrime seemed typical of many.

He did not attempt to make himself known. Had Buldebrime been as adept as he presumably liked to think he was, he would not have needed to be told there was a Presence in the room.

He set out what was requisite for the sorcery he intended to undertake, bar one crucial item: a single candle. And then, in the instant before he discovered that the candle was not where he thought it was, there came a thunderous hammering from the entrance to the shop, followed by a loud cry.

'Buldebrime! Buldebrime! Open in the name of Garch Tegn of Cleftor Heights!'

The traveller gave a nod and took his leave.

5

There was a certain spot, a fair sward set with rocks flat-topped as though designed expressly to be sat upon, commanding a fine view of the thegn's mansion and within lazy strolling distance of the villages nearest thereto. In any other community it might safely have been predicted that on fine clear evenings such as this local folk would often congregate here, bring provender and beer and possibly a tabor and some fifes, to enjoy the pleasant outlook and reflect on their luck in serving so notably able a ruler.

Here, however, the safe prediction was that by late afternoon all who did not have utterly unavoidable business would have retreated to their homes, bolting and shuttering them against the onset of that unnatural night which soaked up starlight and bit at the bones with vicious teeth.

So indeed the case proved. The last herds were driven back to their byres, the last flocks were folded, long before the sun had touched the divided peaks of the Cleft Tor. As the shadows lengthened, the air grew thick, and the aura which had infected the whole day curdled into a foretaste of the dark to come.

Seated alongside a curving track, his staff across his knees, the traveller gazed towards the thegn's mansion. It was a handsome, if uninspired, edifice. Girdling it in the place of a curteyn-wall there were low-roofed outbuildings perhaps a hundred paces by two hundred, made of grey stone, interrupted by a gate and speckled with windows. These enclosed a courtyard above ground-level, whose cobbled surface concealed subterranean dungeons and other hidden chambers, and from the centre of this yard upreared a tower, or rather frustrum, its sloping sides approximating the base of a cone. There were the private quarters of the thegn. Terminating its truncated top, there was a winch-house where by shifts a score or so of muscular deaf-mutes waited the signal to save Garch the effort of climbing stairs, by hauling on ropes to lift a kind of palankeen steadied by greased poles and capable of being halted at any floor of the tower.

As the traveller studied this mansion, he saw servants come to set out torches by the gate, though there was still considerable sun-time left in the day.

Eventually there came in sight around the curve of the road a sort of small procession. It began with a striding man-at-arms, suspiciously staring this way and that. It continued with a personage in the garb of a Shebya: blue cap, green coat, black boots and silver spurs. He rode astride a palfrey. Then came a girl attired in pink as a page, but bosomed too heavily for there to be much chance of mistaking her sex, leading the first of a pair of pack-mules whose wooden saddles were half empty, and lastly another man-at-arms leading the second mule. Such was a common spectacle in any well-governed land; the Shebyas were the greatest traders of the age, and even the poorest possessed at least a couple of beasts and an attendant.

The leader of this party, however, was clearly not overjoyed with whatever business he'd most recently conducted. He frowned as he rode, and not infrequently uttered objurgations.

He redoubled them for fluency and loudness when, on spotting the black-clad figure by the track, the leading man-at-arms dropped his spear to an attack position and cried, 'Halt!' The palfrey obeyed with extraordinary promptness, and thereby almost spilled his rider to the road.

'Good morrow,' said the traveller mildly. 'Sir, would you command your man to put up that over-eager point? It's aligned upon a portion of my carcass that I am anxious to preserve intact.'

'Do so,' the Shebya commanded, and pulled a face. 'Forgive him,' he continued, doffing his cap. 'But we're collectively upset, I'd have you know, and very edgy, as it were. We've done so poorly on our errand to this famous thegn – of which we had, I must admit, high hopes.'

'The saddles of your mules seem light enough,' the traveller murmured.

'Oh, ordinary pack-goods one can dispose of anywhere,' the Shebya shrugged. His keen eyes were fixed on the curious staff the traveller held, and one could almost hear the logical, though erroneous, deductions he was making. 'But … Well, sir, might I hazard a guess that you too are bound to call on Garch?'

'That possibility,' the traveller conceded, 'should not be entirely ruled out.'

'I thought so!' the other exclaimed, leaning forward on his palfrey's withers. 'Might I further suggest that you would welcome information concerning the thegn's alleged willingness to purchase – ah – intangibles and other rare items at a respectable price?'

'It would be rash to deny,' the traveller said, 'that I have heard reference to some such habit of his.'

'Then, sir, save your trouble. Turn about, and escape the oncoming night – for, truly, the nights they have hereabouts are not of the common cosy kind. The tales you've likely heard are arrant nonsense.'

'Nonsense, you say?'

'Yes indeed!' The Shebya grew confidential, lowering his tone. 'Why, did I not bring him an object virtually *beyond* price? And did I not in the upshot have to peddle it door to door, for use in some lousy household enchantment instead of in the grand ceremonials of an adept? That it should keep company with polly-wogs and chicken-blood – faugh! I ask you! Would not dragon-spawn have been meeter?'

'And was the article efficacious?' the traveller asked, hiding a smile.

The Shebya spread his hands. 'Sir, that is not for me to determine. Suffice it to say that tomorrow will tell; for the sake of insurance, as it were, against the risk that the purchaser may prove inadequately skilled in conjuration to extract maximum benefit from the acquisition, I suppose to be some distance hence.' His mask of annoyance, willy-nilly, gave place to a grin; it was granted by everyone that, rogues though the Shebyas might be, they were at least engaging rogues.

'Howbeit,' he appended, 'take my advice. Don't go to Garch expecting to sell him remarkable and unique artifacts or data at such price as will ensure comfort to your old age. Apart from all else, the mansion is in a turmoil. Someone, so to speak, would appear to have laden the thegn's codpiece with live ants, and he gibbers like a man distraught, ordering all who displease him to be shortened by the head without appeal. Another excellent reason for departure – which, sir, if you will forgive the briefness of this conversation, inclines me forthwith to resume my journey.'

After he and his companions had gone, the traveller remained. The air thickened still further. It felt almost resistant to the limbs, like milk turned with an admixture of rennet. Lost on a high outcrop, a kid bleated hopelessly for its nanny. Chill that one might have mistaken for agonizing frost laid a tight hold on the land, yet no pools crisped with ice. The traveller frowned and waited longer still.

Over the high tower of the mansion, at last, the coffin-black of night started to appear: solid-seeming blotches on the sky. At roughly the same time, there were noises to be heard along the road again, coming from the direction opposite to that which the Shebya and his troupe had taken. Into sight came a party of hurrying men on horseback, full-armed, glancing apprehensively at the gathering dark. Some had equipped themselves with torches, and kept making motions towards their flint and steel.

In their midst, tied face to tail on a dirty donkey, was Buldebrime moaning and crying out, hands lashed at his back and his grease-stiff smock badly torn.

Some distance behind, unable to keep pace, a furious driver cursed a pair of shaggy-fetlocked horses drawing a cart loaded until the springs sagged with candles, lamps, and articles in bags which could not clearly be discerned.

Of itself, the parade might have been amusing. Given the circumstances which had led to it, the traveller could not find it other than appalling.

The darkness spread, and yet it did not move. Rather, it occurred, moment by moment, at places further from its source.

6

'Be calm!' Lady Scail for the latest of countless times adjured her brother.

'Be calm?' he echoed, mocking her. 'How can I be? Are not they deserting us, the traitors, deserting *me* who gave them prosperity from this lean harsh country and made them the envy of folk in richer lands?'

It was true: news came every few minutes of some trusted serving-man, soldier or steward who had surreptitiously crept away from the household.

'Is it not, moreover,' he pursued, 'the night before full moon? Is it not nearing midnight of that night? Must I not shortly go into the prescribed retreat? And how can we tell as yet how greatly we've been deceived by Buldebrime? Perhaps he miscalibrated our time-candles, so we'll have no means to tell the proper hour!'

Admittedly, it was impossibly to make astronomic observations under nights as black as these.

Nonetheless, she blasted the same injunction at him, saying, 'You fool, you have to keep your head at any cost! How many enchanters have not gone to doom because an elemental took advantage of just that weakness in their character?'

Sweating, gulping draught after draught of wine to lend him courage, he did his best to comply, since reason was on her side. However, self-mastery was hard. The mansion, and not only that but the entire surrounding countryside, was aquiver. The jagged range of Cleftor Heights was thrumming to a soundless vibration of menace, as though one of the beings incarcerated in a restless star had found the means to transmit terror down a shaft of light and struck the bedrock into reasonating the keynote of a symphony of disaster, against the advent of the instrumentalists.

Moreover, it is not good for one who invokes the forces of chaos to pay any attention whatsoever to reason…

'Where's Roiga?' Garch demanded of a sudden.

'Where she should be: making ready in your room.'

'And Runch?'

'They called him to the gate a while ago. They've sighted the party bringing Buldebrime.'

'Then I'll go down to the dungeons,' Garch declared, and drained his goblet. 'I must be first to learn what that traitor's done!'

There was routine in this mansion, as in the household of any great lord, and to outward appearance it was being maintained. At the corner of two echoing corridors the traveller in black saw proof of this. Thump-thump down the passages to the beat of drums came the nightly provisions for the company at dinner: pies stuffed with game so heavy two men staggered under the load, and the whole roasted haunches of oxen and sheep; then serving-girls with jugs of wine and beer, and butlers carrying fine white linen napkins on their arms, and boys with ewers and basins that the diners might wash their hands in scented water, and harpists, and flautists, and a dwarf. This last hobbled awkwardly in an overlong gown, designed to make him trip often on its hem for the amusement of the gathering.

One could not intelligently foresee there being much laughter in the banquet-hall tonight. The stones from which the building was erected shared the incipient convulsions of the landscape, and overmuch dust danced in the light of the torches.

Intermittently, from beneath the floor, issued screams.

Orderly, with professional niceness, the least spoken-of among Garch's retainers – Tradesman Humblenode, the torturer – had set out the varied equipment for his task: here whips and fetters, thumb-screws there; tongs, knives and nooses at another place; and in the centre of all a brazier, at which a little dirty boy worked a blacksmith's bellows in a vain attempt to make the fuel burn as bright as was required. Even here under the courtyard, where the walls oozed continual damp, the pervasive obliterating light-absorption of the strange night made itself known.

At the mere sight of Humblenode's instruments Buldebrime had collapsed into snivelling, and it was long after the thegn's intrusion into his cell that they contrived to make him utter coherent words.

'No, I did not filch any such candle! I have no knowledge of enchantment!'

'Try him with a little red iron,' Garch proposed, and Tradesman Humblenode set a suitable tool to the fire.

'Have pity, have pity!' Buldebrime cried. 'I swear by Orgimos and Phorophos, by Aldegund and Patrapaz and Dencycon—!'

'I thought you had no knowledge of enchantment?' Garch murmured, and gestured for Humblenode's assistants to stretch the lamp-maker on a rack.

But in a short space from the application of the first iron he escaped into unconsciousness, and not all Humblenode's art sufficed to awake him.

'Is Roiga meantime testing the lamps and candles that were brought with him?' Garch remembered to ask, somewhat belatedly. He had given that instruction, and not checked that it was carried out – though Runch and Roiga, of all his retinue, had most to lose by neglecting his requirements.

'I come from her, sir,' a nervous waiting-maid reported, who was trying not to look at the limp body of Buldebrime, or anything else present in the cell. 'She assures me she has tested every one, and whatever you seek – uh – isn't there.'

Garch drew himself up to his full height. 'So the treacherous lamp-man has tricked me,' he muttered. 'Can he not be aroused by midnight?'

'By no art known to me,' said Humblenode apologetically. It was the first time he had failed his master, and he braced himself as though to endure his own style of treatment in consequence.

But Garch swung on his heel and strode away.

He came upon his sister, together with Runch and attendants, at the head of the dank noisome stairway to the dungeons; his private means of vertical transport did not, for logical reasons, extend into this level.

'Have you succeeded?' Scail cried.

'Failed!'

'And midnight nears!' Runch muttered.

'What must be done, must be done,' said Garch. 'Prepare me for my watch alone.'

'But surely tonight it was imperative to conjure Wolpec, and ask his earnest of your ultimate success!' Under her face-mantling layers of rouge and powder, the Lady Scail blanched.

'What's to be done will be done now!' Garch snapped. 'Like it or not! You have tomorrow's daylight to run away by, if that's your plan. For the moment, leave me – time is short.'

Without so much as a brotherly embrace, let alone that other kind which had in the past lent certain crucial potency to his doings, he pushed by them both and was gone.

Under the supervision of the crone Roiga, servants had toiled to bring many articles into the cabinet she was making ready. It lacked windows, naturally; what air there was must seep through tiny crevices, and about each, carefully marked there had been inscribed a line of minuscule writing in an obsolete syllabary. It lacked furniture, too; in place of that it was hung with curtains of goat-hide, woven marsh-grass and the plaited hair of murdered girls. There was a mirror in the centre of its floor, which was as true a circle as the mason's art could contrive, but that mirror was cracked across, and the traveller knew with what hammer the blow would have been struck: silver-headed, hafted with a portion of his anatomy that some man – albeit briefly – would have lived to regret the loss of. He had been aware that enchantments of this calibre were still conducted, but in this case at least one unqualifiedly essential preliminary to them had been totally neglected.

Patience.

Rat's-bane and wolf-hemp; powder of dragon-bone and mullet-roe; candied mallow and murex pigment; vantcheen spice … Yes, all the ancient indispensables were here. Bar one. Bar the one that mattered more than anything.

The traveller withdrew into dismal contemplation.

Then, finally, Garch came, pale and trembling but determined not to let his companions recognize the full depth of his terror, to perform the rites required of him as lord of this land which yielded more than its proper share of good things. He was correctly robed in a chasuble of blood-hue; he correctly wore one shoe of hide and one of cloth; he correctly bore the wand, the orb and the sash; and the proper symbols, though awkwardly, had been inscribed on his palms with henna and indigo.

He entered the door of ashwood clamped with brass, and it was closed at his back with the traditional braided withes: one at the height of his neck, one at the height of his heart, and one at the height of his genitals. That done, Runch and Roiga and Scail perforce withdrew. Unless they chose to run away, indeed, by tomorrow's daylight, the process was in train and they were to be dragged with it.

Even running away might not help.

As for the traveller in black, he had no choice. This was intrinsically a part of that which bound him. From this moment forward, he was compelled to remain. Here was no petty hearthside conjuration, to be laughed at when it failed and probably neglected thereafter; here was no witty tampering with the course of natural events, such as certain happy enchanters had counted a fair reward for the relief of boredom; here was no ritual from which overt profit instantly ensued, such as the merchant enchanters of a bygone age had employed to make their cities prosperous.

No, those trivialities could be ignored. Here, though, was a ceremony so elaborate, so pregnant with possibility and so absolutely devoid of *probability* that its very name, regardless of what language it was uttered in, sent shivers down, the spines of uncomprehending listeners. Here, set on foot in a selfish lordling's mansion, was such a pattern as had not been undertaken since the epoch of the Grand Five Weavers and the Notorious Magisters of Alken Cromlech: the most ancient, the most arcane, the most honourable appellation of the Ones Who—

The traveller froze the progress of his mind. Almost, he had recited the full title to himself. And were *he* to do so, all – all everything would be eternally lost.

If it were not already lost. He feared it was.

7

The Lady Scail slept but ill that night, and when her shoulder was gently touched at last by the waiting-maid who attended her in her chamber, she rolled her face fretfully back into her satin pillows.

'Fool!' she snapped. 'I said to waken me at dawn. I'll have your head for disturbing me when it's still full dark!'

Indeed, across the windows a pall of utter lightlessness remained.

'But, madam,' whispered the poor girl, 'according to our time-candles dawn should have befallen an hour ago. Yet the sky remains like pitch!'

Lady Scail sat up on the instant. Through the opened shutters she saw the truth of the maid's assertion. Rising from her night-couch, she exclaimed in wonder.

'Why – why, that bodes success after all! Here, girl, go rout out Runch and Roiga from their beds, and bid them wait on me at once!'

Unprecedentedly, without waiting to be handed her day-time garments, she threw aside her sleeping-gown and struggled by herself into a creased chemise.

Similarly awakened, Roiga trembled with delight and anticipation. She had spent weary decades pent in a worn-out body, with her knees cracking from the rheumatism and her eyes returning blurred images of the outer world. Now under her shrivelled bosom her heart beat hammer-wise at the impending prospect of re-purchased youth.

It was the same for one-eyed Runch: still a mighty man to outward view, scorning the luxury of his companions and affecting the disciplined, hardy habits of a soldier accustomed to sleeping in fields and marching all day through sleet and hail. Therefore he reposed at night on a simple bed of planks with one blanket.

But over the last few years he had more and more often failed to pleasure the girls he summoned to his couch, until at length he had been unable to endure further humiliation, and took to sleeping alone.

The promise of being able to rectify that …!

These three, however – and perhaps Garch himself, but none could certify what was transpiring in his secret room – were the only persons in the whole of the Cleftor lands who found any semblance of joy to greet the advent of this amazing and unprecedented … day? Well, 'day' it should indeed have been by rights, and everywhere there should have been the normal daily bustle: the younger children playing by the doorway, the older dispatched to their dame-schools with their slates and pencils; the farmers bound to market hauling their travoises laden with cheese and bacon, their wives plucking geese or hunting eggs ...

But over all the country from Deldale to Herman's Wynd, and back again from Contrescarp to the Ten Leagues' Stone, at Poultry Rock and Brown Hamlet and Legge, at Yammerdale and Gallowtree and Chade, at Swansbroom and Swingthrimble and Slowge, it was dark until what should have been high noon.

And when the light eventually came, it was the wrong sort of light. It was the sickly grey glow of chaos, that bleached all colour into the dullness of ash.

Now the mountains showed deformed, like mutant fungi; now the trees, vaguely visible, stood rigid as parodies in a picture, and the random disposition of their branches seemed to summate the entire gestural vocabulary of obscene signs such as might be made with a man's upraised fingers. Watching the changing sky in high delight from the vantage of the tower's solar, Roiga and Scail and Runch shouted in succession for the best wine, the richest mead, the finest delicacies that the stores could offer, by way of pre-celebrating their anticipated triumph. The blackness of night and morning had retreated to the fringes of the Cleftor domain, and now it was as though a tunnel had been opened, vertically to the frontiers of the sky, for the beings from beyond to make a grand re-entry to their former state.

But the servant-maids gawped and gaped and rubbed their ears as they came and went, for there was a dullness to their hearing that occasionally approached an ache, and there was a stale taste in all mouths which twice made Runch accuse a waiting-wench of giving him vinegar, not wine, and a dragging heaviness oppressed all bodies. Yet for the most part those three frenetic counsellors – if no one else – were able to ignore it, and drank toast after toast to the wonderful skills of Garch their thegn.

It was not until they were three parts drunken that they realized there was another in the solar apart from the servants they had bidden to attend them.

'Who's that?' cried Scail, and slopped wine down her dress in turning to look over her shoulder.

'Oh – oh!' Roiga moaned, and would have shrunk into hiding.

'Declare yourself!' shouted Runch, rising and drawing the sword he always wore.

'Here I am,' the intruder said, black cloak swishing as he strode forward to the tap-tap measure of his staff. 'Put up that blade, for it's no protection against the doom that's coming to you.'

Runch hesitated, and the sword-point he had presented to the traveller's chest wavered back and forth. He said, 'Who ...?'

'One who has many names but a single nature.'

They were thunderstruck on the instant. Dropping her mug of wine, Scail whimpered. 'But I thought—'

'Did you?' the traveller sighed. 'Yes, I can believe that you must have regarded my existence as superstition, and your brother likewise. Else you'd have buckled to like sensible folk, and taken what was to hand and made the most of it. Instead of which ... Do you know who awaits admission to this place?'

Uncertain, but feigning bravado out of shame at her spasm of cowardice, Roiga said bluffly, 'Why of course. Have we not agreed to call on Tuprid?'

'Tuprid who takes pleasure only in destruction, whom I saw snuff a star as men would snuff a candle, that he might witness the dying agony of the creatures on its planets as they froze into everlasting ice. And who else?'

'Why, Caschalanva, of course!' Runch exclaimed.

'He who prefers the fire to Tuprid's cold. They're ancient rivals. Each struggles to outdo the other in causing pain. And with them?'

'Quorril!' said Scail, and began to sound a fraction nervous, which though well justified was a belated sign.

'Whose diet is souls,' said the traveller. 'And Lry?'

They all three nodded.

'To whom,' he concluded, 'love is hate – who breeds discord and warfare like the plague. And you believe these to be the only ones your brother has invoked?'

There was a second of silence. 'It was all we agreed he should invoke,' Scail said at length. 'It's with them that we struck our bargain.'

'Bargain!' The traveller gave a sad laugh.

'Why, certainly! Do they not owe us toll, for opening the road back to where they once ruled?' She was on her feet, facing him defiantly. 'Should they not be grateful?'

'Yes! Is it not a trifle, in view of such a grand service, that they should restore my manhood?' Runch demanded. And—

'Will they not give me back my youth?' shouted Roiga.

At the same moment there was a shifting underfoot, as though the land had taken on a colossal weight, and their dialogue with the traveller in black was forgotten. They rushed to the windows and peered out, this way and that, striving to to catch a glimpse of whatever had descended to the earth.

'Oh, my wonderful brother!' Scail cried. 'Had I but the *half* of his skills!'

'Well, well!' the traveller said, and then again: 'Well, *well*! As you wish, so be it.'

None of them heard him. Nor did they hear the later whisper that echoed from the stone walk following his departure, which sounded a little like:

'Now why did I not think of that before?'

8

This, therefore, was the manner of the coming back of the former great ones to the world. And it was not totally to their liking.

Left alone in the stock-depleted house of Buldebrime, the gaggle of apprentices had at first been worried and afraid; then the boy of fourteen who had conceived the notion of making that mocking doll sought to calm the youngest of his companions by producing it again, and they dissolved into laughter as he put it through absurd motions by heating it so the limbs could be deformed. Laughter made them grow bolder, and recalled them to routine. They fed themselves, and then since their master was not present to forbid them they made free of the house, tumbling together in many enjoyable games until sleep overtook them.

On the morrow, however, they were frightened anew by the curious unprecedented length of the darkness enveloping the neighbourhood, and moreover they were hungry, because last night they had eaten their fill from the supplies in the pantry. For some of them it was the first time in months they had had a square meal; so nothing was left but crumbs.

They hunted high and low by the wan light of such candles as they had managed to make for themselves after Buldebrinie's stock had been confiscated by Garch's men, and ultimately found a way to prise off the padlock blocking their access to the attic room. In company of the girl with the scarred face, the leading boy braved the ladder-like steps and looked around the shadowed books and mystic articles with amazement.

'Would that I knew what all these things are for and could employ them!' the girl said.

The traveller spoke soft words, unnoticed, in a corner.

In the increasing chill of their hut by Rotten Tor, little Nelva and her mother listened in agony to the racking coughs the cold afflicted upon Yarn.

'Oh, mother!' the bairn cried, seeing how the fire faded and gave no heat. 'Would I knew what the nice man in black did, to make the lamp burn brightly! Then I'd do it to the logs, and we'd all be warm!'

The traveller again spoke unheard words, and went his way.

Trapped by the incredible darkness in a very bad inn, the Shebya trader scratched his flea-bites and wrangled with the landlord, claiming that anyone who offered such hard beds and such foul beer had no right to the regular score from his clients. At length, losing temper, he shouted at the man.

'Ho, that I knew a way to rid the world of greed like yours, that turns one's stomach sour with fury! Ho, that I dealt here only with honest fellows like myself, having codes and principles that require strict adherence to a bargain!'

He was exaggerating just a little; nonetheless, the Shebyas were frank, as all agreed, though a hint of sleight-of-mind might sometimes give them the better of a deal with anybody less subtle.

Chuckling, the traveller spoke and tapped his staff on the wall.

He wondered how it was faring with Garch Thegn of Cleftor Heights.

And the answer, framed in brief, was – not so well.

Down to him came the powers to which he'd bowed, weary of long con-jurations, but content inasmuch as all had said to him, 'We'll go see first that you have kept your word, and then we'll speak of settling our bargain!'

Which, according to the books in which he reposed his trust, was as fair an answer as they'd ever given anyone.

So, into the nervous night, blear-eyed, he waited on their presence, and ultimately at the moment which – said a well-measured time-candle, and no visible stars – corresponded with the time of full moon, he rose expectantly from his discomfortable posture on the floor in the middle of his cracked mirror.

One came of the four, and only one, and in such rage as made the walls shake and the tower-top tremble. And reached out for Garch, and he was not.

Because …

That elemental, Tuprid, who had snuffed stars, had gone to see first of the places in his allegedly regained domain the nearest to a star, a place of light: to wit, a lamp-maker's shop. And there had found awaiting him a little girl, scar-faced, beside whom a boy clutched her hand to loan her courage, chant-ing at a candle they had brought and making it burn against the fiercest orders of the visitor. Below, the other children cried, and she thought of them, and made her efforts double, and in the upshot melted a maker of great darkness into shapeless wax dribbling across a book bound in human skin.

After that, very suddenly, the stars could be viewed by the skylight.

Also the elemental Caschalanva, who preferred the taste of fire to that of ice, had gone down by the bitter vales under Rotten Tor, and a little girl who wished desperately to make the logs burn more brightly had sensed in an instant of inspiration precisely what was needful to be done …

And in an inn where fleas plagued the customers, the being Lry who fos-tered dissension found a predilection towards greed that was emanating from the spot with such force as gales have, using a mountain-range for organ-pipes. Greed being among the chiefest of his tools, he grasped at it – and when it dissipated fractionally after, he was swept into now-where along with it.

Whereupon, learning of the fate of his companions who were a good deal more than merely companions, Quorril returned to say that they were cheated, and – souls being his diet – seized Garch's with a snatch of an imma-terial claw that laid wide open the wall of his secret room, emitting fumes. The high tower of the mansion tumbled down, its foundations turning to mud and sand.

Among the ruins, with her dying breath, the Lady Scail called down a doom upon him for what he had done to her brother, and – she being now dowered, as she had desired, with the half of Garch's skills, and in particular that half which concerned the binding, rather than the releasing, of elementals – Quorril ceased his flight to the sky, and perforced joined her, and Roiga, and Runch, buried forever beneath that stack of masonry.

'Where let him rest,' the traveller said contentedly; having viewed all this from the vantage of the same sward where he had conversed with the Shebya.

'And Buldebrime, and Tradesman Humblenode,' a quiet voice confirmed alongside him. He had not expected to be alone at a moment like this; he did not look around. 'And many more!'

'And many less guilty, Highness,' he appended. 'Yet none of them entirely innocent. Willing, at least, to serve a lord whose power was drawn from chaos, when it was apparent to any commonsensical mind that no mortal force could make this barren land so wealthy. Equally, prepared to apprentice children to masters who starved and beat them, for the sake of having them learn a profitable trade ...'

He shrugged, both hands clasping his staff. 'No matter, though,' he con-cluded. 'Has it not all come to a very tidy end?'

There was a silence. Also it was dark here. But it was the regular honest dark of a spring night around moonset: nothing worse.

'At end,' the quiet voice said meditatively. 'Yes, perhaps it is an end. It might as well be ... You know, my friend, there's something very curious!'

'Tell me,' the traveller invited, who now knew in any case the most important thing that had guided his existence. Still, there were degrees of importance, and even a triviality might provoke interest.

'Of all the qualities I endowed you with,' the voice said, 'the most potent has proved to be a certain witty elegance. A – a neatness, a sense of practical economy!'

'I've fostered it,' the traveller agreed. 'Having but one nature, I must needs make the most of what I owned.' He gestured with his staff at the barely-seen view. 'Besides, was it not that practical mode of thinging which reduced the opportunities of access for the ancient ones to these few should-be-barren acres?'

'Yes, it was.'

'And was not that the designated purpose of my being?'

There was no answer. After a while the traveller said, 'I'm sorry. You must be feeling grievous loss.'

'I?' Beside him the One Who had assigned him to his task, come to witness this last confrontation in the guise of a tall, pale and extraordinarily thin girl, shook back long locks under a wide-brimmed hat. 'Loss of the other natures that were mine? Why, not at all! Is it not the goal and purpose of the universe that all things shall ultimately have a single nature? I know that to be true, for *I* decreed it.'

This was what they had not realized at Cleftor Heights: that Tuprid and Caschalanva, Quorril and Lry, and moreover Wolpec and Yorbeth and Farchgrind and Fegrim and Laprivan of the Yellow Eyes, and all the countless rest of those elementals, were the fellow-natures of the One Who had conceived an age in which no creature should possess more than one nature – and had created a personage with many names as earnest of that eventual occurrence.

Accordingly, the last remaining nature of that One spoke with the traveller and sounded weary.

'So here I stand, my friend, to link with you like the fingers of a pair of hands, interlocked. What remains to me is what you never had; what remains to you is what I never had. It is a question of complimentarity. But after all these eons you understand that.'

The traveller nodded, and she heaved a sigh.

'Hah, yes, old friend, my page is past – past like that unnatural night which will nevermore be seen in Cleftor's vales! Eternity at last has found its end, because the powers of chaos have been tamed. And with what little fetters! The wish of a child to help her mother; the distaste of apprentices for their master; the annoyance of a pedlar-man; and the love of a sister for her stupid brother!'

'Then my time is past too,' the traveller said, ignoring her recital of his tricks-to-triumph – which was just, because all he had was in her gift. 'And … And I'm not at all sorry. I was almost coming to miss the enemies I matched against in other ages. You could have undermined me by that weakness.'

'I could.' The answer was predictable. She *could* – everything. Now, however, it was a question not of 'could' but 'would', and the time for willing chaos had gone by.

More silence intervened, and then the traveller stretched and yawned.

'I long for rest,' he said. 'But – one more thing. Who is to come after us?'

'Let him decide who he is,' said the pale girl, and took him by the hand which lacked the staff. Turning, they went together into absence.

If you've enjoyed these books and would like to read more, you'll find literally thousands of classic Science Fiction & Fantasy titles through the **SF Gateway**

✴

For the new home of
Science Fiction & Fantasy . . .

✴

For the most comprehensive collection
of classic SF on the internet . . .

✴

Visit the SF Gateway

www.sfgateway.com

John Brunner (1934–1995)

John Brunner was a prolific British SF writer. In 1951, he published his first novel, *Galactic Storm*, at the age of just 17, and went on to write dozens of novels under his own and various house names until his death in 1995 at the Glasgow Worldcon. He won the Hugo Award and the British Science Fiction Award for *Stand on Zanzibar* (a regular contender for the 'best SF novel of all time') and the British Science Fiction Award for *The Jagged Orbit*.